KATHLEEN WOODIWISS

Shanna

Futura

A *Futura* Book

Copyright © 1977 by Kathleen E. Woodiwiss
Published by arrangement with the author

First published in Great Britain in 1977
by Futura Publications Limited

This edition published in 1995
by Futura Publications

ISBN 0 7088 1352 6

Printed in England by Clays Ltd, St Ives plc

Futura Publications
A Division of
Macdonald & Co (Publishers)
Brettenham House
Lancaster Place
London WC2E 7EN

Part One

Is this the horrid dragon beast
Of sinew strong and deep of chest
And never needing rest?
A steed, the best?
Then seize a saddle from the rack
And strap it on the beastie's back,
Of courage never have a lack,
No turning back.

The beast has served and flown the earth arou
You've sought your treasures, forced hi tne
ground.
You loose the reins, your goal is found.
He turns around.

Long of fang, the fiercest eye and talons, not
discounting,
No fault of choice, nor better beast you'd ever take
ahunting.
But now you're caught and find
the peril is
dismounting—

Chapter 1

Midnight, November 18, 1749
London

NIGHT gripped the city with cold, misty darkness. The threat of winter was heavy in the air. Acrid smoke stung the nostrils and throat, for in every home fires were stirred and stoked against the seaborne chill that pierced to the bone. Low-hanging clouds dribbled fine droplets of moisture which mixed with the soot spewed forth from London's towering chimneys before falling as a thin film that covered every surface.

The miserable night masked the passage of a carriage that careened through the narrow streets as if it fled from some terrible disaster. It jolted and tottered precariously over the cobblestones, its high wheels sending mud and water splattering. In the calm that followed the coach's passing, the murky liquid trickled slowly back to mirrored pools pocked with droplets or neatly patterned with ripples. The driver, ominously large and cloaked in black, hauled on the reins, hurling an oath down at the team of dapple-grays, but his voice was lost beneath the heavy thud of pounding hooves and the rattle of churning wheels. The din of the ride echoed in the chilling night until it seemed to come from every direction. The dark shape of the carriage flitted through dim pools of light cast from the flickering door lanterns of the baroque facades it passed. Grinning gargoyles stared down from high above where they squatted on stony eaves, thin runnels of rain dribbling from their carved granite mouths as if they hungered for the prey passing below their perches.

Shanna Trahern pushed back into the plush, red velvet seats of the carriage to brace herself against the breakneck speed. She was little concerned with the murk beyond the leather shades, or, indeed, with anything but her own thoughts. She sat alone and silent. Her face was devoid of expression, yet now and then the lantern would swing with a jolting lurch of the carriage, and its weak light would catch the hard, brittle gleam in the depths of the blue-green eyes. No man gazing into them now would have found a trace of warmth to cheer him or any hint of love to comfort his heart. The face, so stirringly beautiful and young, was dispassionate. Without the usual audience of male admirers in attendance, there was no need to portray a charming or gracious image, though it was rare indeed that Shanna Trahern exerted herself beyond a momentary whim. If it met her mood, she could enchant anyone, but now her eyes showed a stern determination that would have shriveled any but the most heroic spirit.

"I am cursed," the fair lips curled. "Were I heaven blessed, I would not be about this errand. What other woman must venture out upon the streets on a night such as this to ease the torment of her state?" Her mind raced along its well-traveled path. "What cruel twist of fate that I be born beneath the blighting branches of my father's wealth? Would that I were poor and thus could know that a man wanted me for myself."

She sighed in introspection and let her mind probe once again her reasoning as if to find a flaw. Neither her beauty nor her father's riches had aided her. A three-year stint in the best schools in Europe and Britain had bored her to distraction. Those so-called ladies' schools had dealt more with court manners, fashion, and the various tedious forms of needlework than with techniques of writing or dealing with numbers. There she had been pursued for her beauty and exposed to the insincerity of young roués seeking to extend their reputations at her expense. Many had felt the prick of her scorn then, disheartened, sulked away. When it became known that she was the daughter of Orlan Trahern, one of the richest men ever to frequent the marketplace, all those young men in needy circumstances came seeking her hand. She could abide these milksops no better than the rest and heartlessly dashed their dreams with words as painful as a dagger's blade.

Her disenchantment with men led to her father's ultimatum. It had begun simply enough. On her return from Europe he had chided her for not finding a husband.

"With all those eager young studs of the courts posturing about you, girl, you couldn't even get yourself a man with a name to bring recognition to your children."

His words had nipped at Shanna's pride, bringing a rush of tears to her eyes. Heedless of her distress, her father had ranted on, setting the spur deeper.

"Damn me, girl! What have I built my fortune for, if not for my own kin? But seen to your way, 'twill go no further than your grave. Blast it all, I want grandchildren! Are you set to be a spinster who rejects every man that comes courting? Your children could be powers at court if they have a title to aid them. They'll need but two things to be successful in this world and accepted by royalty. I give them one—wealth—more than you can spend in a lifetime. You can gain them the other—a name no one would dare question, a name with a lineage so pure and fine 'twill need a good stock of common blood to strengthen it. Such a name can do as much to open doors as riches. But with no other name than Trahern, they'll be little more than merchants." His voice had sharpened in anger. " 'Tis my hell that I am given a daughter with the looks to choose among the bluest lines, one to make barons, earls, even dukes fawn and drool upon themselves for the want of her. But she dallies like some dreamy twit for a silver knight on a white charger who might match her own untouched purity."

Shanna's folly had been in answering her father rashly and with heated words. They were soon engaged in a stormy exchange which had ended abruptly when he slammed down his brawny fist and dared her to speak further. His angry glare had burned into her.

"You have a year to settle your fancies," he roared. "Your period of grace ceases on your first-and-twentieth year, the day marking your birth. If you have not wed into a family of the aristocracy by then, I'll name the next ready swain still young enough to get you with child as your husband. And if I must drag you to the altar in chains, you will obey!"

Shanna had been stunned into incredulous silence at his crudity, but she knew with a sinking heart it was no jest. Orlan Trahern's word was a promise never broken.

Her father continued in a somewhat subdued tone. "Since we are ever at odds these days, I will give you ease of my presence. Ralston sails for London on my business. You will go with him, and Pitney as well. I know you can bend Pitney around your little finger—you've done it ever since you were a child. But Ralston should be able to keep the two of you out of mischief and honest enough for what I want. You may take your maid Hergus as well. On the second of December next, your year is done, and you will return to Los Camellos with or without a spouse. And if 'tis none you've found, the matter shall be out of your hands."

Orlan Trahern had known a hard life as a youth. At the age of twelve, he saw his father, a Welsh highwayman, hanged from a roadside tree for his crimes. His mother, reduced to working as a scullery maid, died just a few years later of the ague, weakened by years of overwork, meager food, and cold winter drafts. Orlan had buried her and had sworn he would make a better way for himself and his own.

Remembering the gray oak where his father had swung, the lad had worked hard and wisely, careful to be scrupulously honest. His tongue was quick, as was his wit, and his mind was agile. He soon grasped the ways of money, rents, interest, investments, and, most of all, the calculated risk for high return. Young Trahern first borrowed money for his ventures but soon was using his own. Then others began to come to him for money. Anything his talents touched fattened his coffers, and he began to acquire country estates, townhouses, stately manors, and property. In return for notes redeemable by the Crown he had accepted a grant to a small, verdant isle of the Caribbean to which he immediately retreated to enjoy his riches and more leisurely manage the flow of wealth into his accounts.

His successes had earned him the title "Lord" Trahern from dirty-faced vendors and crafty merchants, for he was indeed the lord of the marketplace. Aristocrats used the title out of necessity when they went to him for loans, finding small comfort in having to beg him for moneys but considering him well beneath them they rejected him socially. Orlan yearned to be accepted as their peer, and it was difficult for him to accept that desire in himself. He was not a man to crawl, and he learned to pull the strings well on a man's life. Now he tried to do it with his only child. The slights that he had received during the years spent accumulating his fortune were in a large part responsible for the rift that now made his beautiful daughter withdraw into herself.

But Shanna was of the same temperament as her stubborn and forthright father. While Georgiana Trahern was alive, she had soothed the rifts and softened the arguments between her husband and child, but her passing five years previous had taken from them their mediator. Now there was no one who could gently dissuade the willful, elder Trahern or ply the daughter with her duties.

Still, with Ralston to guarantee that she abided by her father's demand, Shanna had known no opportunity to be anything but compliant to his wishes. It had not taken her long after returning to England to become lost in a multitude of names that accompanied various odd and assorted titles, baron, earl, and the like. Dispassionately she could name the flaw in each suitor; an obtrusive nose on this one, a roving hand on that one, a twitching brow, a wheezing cough, a pompous pride.

The sight of a threadbare blouse beneath a waistcoat or a rumpled and empty purse hanging from a belt abruptly cooled her to offers of marriage. Aware that a handsome dowry would accompany her and that she would eventually inherit a fortune large enough to stagger the wits of the most imaginative, the swains grew zealous and attentive, exceedingly considerate of her smallest desire, except the one she declared most often. They ignored her pleas to remove themselves from her presence and usually had to be assisted by Mister Pitney. Frequently among the courting bachelors quarrels broke out, resulting in blows, then brawls, and what had begun as a quiet social event or a simple outing often dissolved into ruins, with Shanna being safely escorted home by her guardian, Pitney. Some wooers were subtle and devious while others were bold and forceful. But in most she saw the desire for riches exceed desire for her. It seemed none cared for a wife who,

7

with love in her heart, would share simple poverty but rather saw first the gold in her father's hand.

Then there was another sort who actively worked to get her into bed without the ceremony of marriage, usually for the simple reason they were already attached to a wife. A count wanted her as his mistress and passionately vowed his devotion until his children, numbering six, interrupted his proposal. These encounters far outweighed the good and with each, Shanna was left with a little less to endear men to her.

Not the least of her troubles was that her year in London had come near to being totally disastrous for mere existence's sake. The Treaty of Aix-la-Chapelle had let loose soldiers and sailors upon the city and a good lot of them, bolstered with the false courage of gin, had taken to thievery to survive, making the night treacherous for those who innocently wandered the streets. Shanna had, but only once, and that occasion had been enough to dissuade her from further venturings. But for the swift and capable strength of Pitney setting the miscreants to rout, she'd have been divested of her jewels and no doubt her virtue as well. In April she had been nearly trampled to death when escorted to the Temple of Peace to hear a concert of Handel's Music for the Royal Fireworks. In truth, it was the fireworks that had caused the commotion, setting to blaze the rococo edifice, which the King had ordered built to celebrate the Treaty of Aix. In horror Shanna had watched as a young girl's skirt caught aflame. The lass was hastily stripped to her stays and her gown trampled until the fire was put out. A moment later Shanna herself escaped questionable injury when her escort of the evening seized her and dragged her to the ground. She might have believed his protestations that he was only seeking to save her from a wayward rocket if he had not loosened her own laces considerably in the process. The cannon's blast was mild in comparison to Shanna's rage and, heedless of the mob which surged around her, whether to ogle her half-clad bosom or to escape the flames she could not determine, Shanna drew back her hand and sent the viscount to his knees with a stinging slap. She had then stalked through the mass of people, regaining her carriage and some semblance of modesty. Pitney's bulk had prevented the young lord from joining her, and Shanna had made the journey back to the townhouse alone.

But that was all in the past now. What mattered was that her time of grace was almost gone, and she had failed to find an acceptable mate. However, she was a woman with a mind of her own. Like her father, Shanna Trahern could be shrewd and clever. This was one of those times which demanded all of her cunning. And she was desperate enough to try anything to escape the fate the elder Trahern planned for her. Anything, that is, but fleeing altogether. Honesty prevailed when she admitted to herself that, despite their differences, she loved her father deeply.

This very afternoon lagging hope had been rekindled when Pitney, a truly loyal friend, had brought long-awaited word to her. Even the ever-watchful Ralston had been taken care of. It was an exceptional turn of good fortune that he was called away in the early morning hours to investigate the damage to a Trahern merchant ship which had run aground near the Scottish coast. Since Ralston would be gone at least a week or perhaps more, Shanna felt confident she would have this matter behind her before he could return. Then if all went well, he would find the deed done and have no chance to set it awry.

Confiding in Ralston would have been the same as informing Orlan Trahern himself, and Shanna had to take special care to insure that Mister Ralston was convinced of her sincerity and the validity of her actions. If her father ever suspicioned that she had been up to some chicanery, there would be more than his rage to contend with. He would see his word carried out forthwith, and she had no desire to live with the consequence, whoever the fellow might be.

Shanna grew anxious in the sheltered interior of the luxurious Briska, and with the voice of the wheels as protection, she tested the name that was so new on her lips, so full of promise.

"Ruark Beauchamp. Ruark Deverell Beauchamp." No one could deny such a fine distinguished name, nor the aristocracy of the Beauchamps of London.

A slight twinge of conscience invaded the moment as the carriage drew her ever closer to her moment of reckoning, but Shanna summoned her courage in defense of herself.

" 'Tis *not* wrong! 'Tis an arrangement to profit us both. The man will see his final days eased and be laid in an honorable grave in return for his temporary service. In two weeks, my year will be up."

Still, apprehension began to gnaw at the edge of her resolve as questions by the dozen flew at her like bats in the night. Would this Ruark Beauchamp be sufficient for her cause? What if he were some hunchbacked, rotten-toothed beast of a man?

Shanna set her jaw, lovely in any mood, with the willfulness of a Trahern and looked for a diversion to ease the multitude of fears which threatened to envelop her. Drawing aside the leather shade at the window, she peered out into the night. Shreds of fog had begun to seep into the streets, half masking the darkened dram shops and inns they now passed. It was a dreary night, but she could abide fog and dampness. It was storms she feared, lending little comfort and peace to her mind when they raged across the land.

Letting the shade fall into place again, Shanna closed her eyes, finding no release for her tensions. In an effort to still the trembling that possessed her, she pressed her slender hands deep into a fur muff, clenching them tightly together. There was so much depending on this night. She could not expect everything to go well, and doubt thwarted her attempts at calm.

Would this Ruark laugh at her? She had swayed the hearts of many men. Why not his also? Would he deny her plea with a cruel jest?

Shanna shook the qualms from her mind. She primed her weapons, arranging the daring décolletage of the red velvet gown she had chosen. She had never fully exercised her wiles, but she suspected a sane man could hardly refuse a full broadside of tears.

Somewhere a bell tolled in the night.

The wheels of the carriage thumped against the cobblestones, and Shanna's heart seemed to match the rapid pace. Time hung motionless as uncertainty pecked at the outer limits of her mind, and somewhere deep inside she wondered what madness had spurred her to start this thing.

An inward cry surfaced to consciousness. Why must it be like this? Had her father lost the sense and tenderness of love in his greed and desire for court acceptance? Was she only a useful pawn for some greater gambit? He had loved her mother deeply and had given no heed to the fact that Georgiana had been the daughter of a common smithy. Why must he then push his only child into a relationship she would abhor?

It was not as if she had not tried. She had been constantly beset by suitors from the moment she arrived in London, but in all of them she saw flaws. She disliked most those who came courting with a desire for riches exceeding a desire for her. Could her father not understand her longing for a husband of stature she could admire, as well as one she could love and respect?

No voice gave the answers Shanna sought. There was only the steady drum of the horses' hooves bringing her ever closer to her testing.

The carriage eased its relentless pace and swung around a corner. Shanna heard Pitney's voice ring out as they rumbled to a stop before the forbidding facade of Newgate gaol. Her breath seemed caught in her throat, and her heart beat a chaotic rhythm. The sound of Pitney's footsteps falling heavily against the cobblestones reverberated within her head. Like a doomed prisoner, she waited until he opened the door and leaned in.

Mister Pitney was a giant of a man, broad-shouldered, with a full wide face to match his size. A stringy thatch of tan hair was tied at the nape of his thick neck beneath a black tricorn. At the age of fifty, he could best any two men younger or older than himself. His past was a mystery, and Shanna had never inquired into it, but she rather suspected it might rival her grandfather's. Yet she had no concern for her safety with Pitney near. He was like a part of the family, though some might have termed his position one of a hired servant, for her father engaged him as her personal guard to see to her welfare whenever she went abroad. On Los Camellos he was independent of Orlan Trahern's wealth and spent his time there carving and making furniture. The big man served the daughter as well as the father and was not inclined to rush to his employer's ear with tales of her slightest infraction. He admired her on some matters, counseled her on others, and when Shanna felt a need to pour out her troubles, it was Pitney who most often comforted her. He had been her co-conspirator on other occasions that her father would not have approved of.

"Your mind is set?" Pitney asked in a deep, rasping voice. "This is to be the way of it?"

"Aye, Pitney," she murmured quietly and, with more determination, "I will see it through."

In the meager light cast by the carriage lanterns, his gray eyes met hers. His brow wore a worried frown. "Then you'd best make yourself ready."

Shanna set her mind and with cool deliberation pulled a heavy lace veil down over her face and adjusted the deep hood of her black velvet cloak so that it further obscured her identity and held her long, golden-veined tresses from view.

Pitney led the way toward the main portal, and, following, Shanna fought an almost overwhelming urge to flee in the opposite direction. But she checked the impulse, reasoning that if this were madness, then marriage to a man she loathed would be hell.

At their entry the turnkey struggled to his feet with an eagerness born of greed and came forward to greet her. He was a grotesquely fat man whose arms resembled battering rams. His legs were so immense he had to walk with his feet well apart, causing a rolling motion in his gait. Yet for all of his size, he was short, his height barely matching Shanna's, which for a woman was more small than tall. His wheezing breath, quickened with the exertion of rising from the chair, filled the room with an aroma of stale rum, leeks, and fish. Quickly Shanna pressed a perfumed handkerchief beneath her nose to ease the stomach-wrenching scent of the foul fumes.

"Milady, I feared ye 'ad changed yer mind." Mister Hicks chortled as he tried to take her hand to bestow a kiss upon it.

Shanna held back a shiver of revulsion and pulled away before his lips could touch her fingers, pushing her hands safely into the fur muff. She could not decide which was worse, having to stand and abide the fetid stench that hung like an unseen cloud about him or bear the sickening feel of his mouth upon her hand.

"I am here as I said I would be, Mister Hicks," she replied sternly. The obnoxious odor got the better of her, and she again drew the lace kerchief from the muff to wave it in front of her veiled face. "Please—" she choked, "let me see the man, so we might get on with the arrangements."

The gaoler delayed a moment and stroked his chin thoughtfully, wondering if there might be more to gain from this than he was promised. The only other time the lady had been to the prison was nearly two months prior, and she had been heavily disguised then, also. His curiosity was greatly piqued, but she had not elaborated on the reason she wanted to meet with a condemned man. The prospect of a weighty purse urged him on, and he had faithfully supplied the names of prisoners bound for the triple tree, giving them over to the hulking man at her side when he had come to fetch them. On her first visit Hicks had taken careful note of the ring on her finger and the subdued but rich cut of her clothes. It was not hard to surmise this was no pauper's daughter. Aye, she had a fortune all right, and he was not above wheedling a greater portion of it than he had been pledged—if he could. And that was where the difficulty lay. He dared ask nothing of her when she was accompanied by her manservant, and the bloke seemed reluctant to leave her.

Still, it seemed a shame that a woman who smelled as tempting and sweet as she, should waste any moment of her life talking to a doomed man. That fellow Beauchamp was a troublemaker, the worst prisoner he had ever led to a cell. Hicks rubbed his fat cheek reflectively, recalling the man's fist against it. What he wouldn't give to see the damned rogue gelded. It would serve him right. But the knave was to die, and revenge *would* be had, though a slower end would be more to his liking.

Mister Hicks heaved a heavy sigh, and then snorted abruptly. "We'll 'ave to see to him in his cell." The rotund gaoler snatched a ring of keys from a peg on the wall. "Been kept away from others 'e 'as. Likely 'e woulda 'ad the 'ole bloody lot of 'em rising agin us." He lit a lantern as he chattered on. "Why, took a fistful o' redcoats to put 'im down an' chain him when they caught him at the inn. Him bein' a colonial and all, 'e's liken to be 'alf savage, anyway."

If Hicks meant to put a fright into her, Shanna was having no part of it. She was calm now and knew what must be done to ease her own plight. Nothing would stand in her way after she had come this far.

"Lead the way, master gaoler," she directed firmly. "There'll not be a farthing exchanged until I have decided for myself that Mister Beauchamp will meet my needs. My man Pitney will accompany us should there be any trouble."

The smile faded, and Hicks shrugged. Finding no other excuse to delay, he took up the lantern to light the way. With his peculiar rolling gait, he preceded them from the dingy room, through the heavy iron doors leading to the main gaol then down a dimly lit corridor. Their footsteps echoed on the stone steps while the lantern cast eerie, flickering shadows around them. An unearthly silence held the place, for most of the prisoners slept, but now and again a groan or muffled weeping could be heard. Water dripped from some unseen fount, and swift scurrying sounds in dark corners brought chills and a strange foreboding to Shanna. She shivered in apprehension and clutched her cloak tighter about her, feeling the wretchedness of the place.

"How long has the man been kept here?" she inquired, glancing uneasily about her. It seemed impossible for anyone to long retain their sanity in a hole like this.

"Nigh to three months, milady."

"Three months!" Shanna gasped. "But your note said he was only just condemned. How is that?"

Hicks snorted. "The magistrate didn't rightly know what to do with the bloke, milady. Wid a name like Beauchamp, a fellow 'as to be bloody careful just 'oo 'e's 'anging, even Lord 'Arry himself is a mite afeared of the Marquess Beauchamp. Ol' 'Arry was reluctant, ye might say, but him being the magistrate, it were up to himself and no other. Then 'bout a week ago, 'e gave the word—'ang him." Hicks's weighty shoulders lifted then fell as if they were a burden too heavy for him. "I 'spect it's cause the bloke's from the colonies and as far as known, 'e's no close kin to folks 'ere. Ol 'Arry instructed me to have the fellow 'anged quiet like with no fuss so these other Beauchamps and the Marquess wouldn't learn o' the deed. Being the clever man that I am, I figured when they give me to 'andle the matter on the sly that Mister Beauchamp be the one for ye." Hicks paused before an iron door. "Ye said ye wanted a man bound for the gallows, and I couldn't give him over to ye until Ol' 'Arry made up his mind to 'ang him."

"You've done well, Mister Hicks," Shanna replied, a trifle more graciously. It was even better than she had hoped! Now as to the man's appearance and consent. . . .

The gaoler thrust a key into a lock and pulled on a door which, with a loud creak of rusty hinges, yielded. Shanna exchanged a quick glance with Pitney, knowing the moment was at hand when she would either see an end to her plan or a beginning.

Mister Hicks lifted the lantern to let more light into the small cell, and Shanna's gaze settled on the man within. He was huddled on a narrow cot and clasped a ragged, threadbare blanket about his shoulders as meager protection against the chill. As the candle's glow presented him, he stirred and covered his eyes as if they hurt. Where the sleeve was torn from his arm, Shanna saw an ugly bruise. His wrists were chafed raw where manacles had been. Straggly black hair and a dark beard hid most of his features, and staring at him Shanna could not help but think of some fiendish creature which had crawled up from the bowels of the earth. A shudder ran through her as the worst of her fears seemed realized.

The prisoner pushed himself up against the wall until he sat and shaded his eyes.

"Damn it, Hicks," he growled. "Can you not even let me enjoy my sleep?"

"On yer feet, ye bloody cur!"

Hicks reached out to prod him with the hardwood staff he carried, but when the prisoner obeyed, the turnkey hurriedly stepped back several paces.

Shanna's breath caught in her throat, for the lean frame unfolded until the man stood a full head taller than Mister Hicks. She could now see the wide shoulders and, beneath the open shirt, the lightly furred chest which tapered to a flat belly and narrow hips.

" 'Ere's a liedy to see ye." Hicks's voice was noticeably less demanding than before. "And if ye has it to harm her, let me warn ye—"

The prisoner strained to see into the blackness beyond the lantern. "A lady? What madness do you practice, Hicks? Or perhaps some more subtle torture?"

His voice came smooth and deep, pleasant to Shanna's ears and bore no hint of a slur. It was easy flowing and less clipped than what she was accustomed to hearing in England. A man from the colonies, Hicks had said. That was, no doubt, the reason for the subtle qualities in his speech. Yet there was something else as well,

15

an amused mockery that seemed to scorn everything about the gaol.

Shanna held to the shadows for a moment longer as she carefully studied this Ruark Beauchamp. His garments were as ragged as the blanket, and she became acutely aware that they were gathered in places with string in an attempt to cover his slender torso. His breeches were torn nearly to the waist on one side, and the rough mending concealed little of the lithe line of his flank. A linen blouse, perhaps once white, was now mottled with filth and barely recognizable. It hung in tattered shreds from his shoulders and showed thinly fleshed ribs that were still well muscled despite his deprivation. His hair was uneven and wildly tossed, yet his eyes filled with alert awareness as he attempted to make out her form. Failing that, he drew himself up and bowed formally to the blackness that shrouded her. A satirical tone was in his voice.

"I beg your pardon, milady. My quarters have little to recommend them. Had I foreknowledge of your visit, I would have tidied up a bit. Of course," he smiled and indicated his surroundings, "there's not much to tidy up."

"Hold yer bloomin' tongue!" Hicks interrupted officiously. "The liedy's here on business, she is, and ye'll show her all respect—or else." He slapped his open palm suggestively with the club and chuckled at his cleverness.

The convicted man arched a dark brow toward Hicks and stared at him until the fat gaoler began to squirm uneasily.

Having encountered no obstacles to her plan thus far, Shanna was greatly heartened. Everything seemed to be going smoothly, as if she had planned for it all her life when in truth it was not much of her doing at all. Confidence and courage had rekindled within her, and with a graceful, flowing movement, she swept forward into the full light of the lantern.

"No need to bully the man, Mister Hicks," she gently rebuked.

The sound of her voice, low and honey smooth, assured that the prisoner's attention was fully upon her. Shanna walked slowly, completely, deliberately around him, evaluating him as she would a prize animal. His eyes, an unusual amber hue flecked with golden lights, followed her in amused patience. The enveloping black cloak and the wide panniers Shanna wore beneath

16

her gown left much to the imagination, allowing no hint of her age or figure to show forth.

"I have heard the dowagers of court practice strange pleasures," he remarked, folding his arms across his chest. "If there be truly a woman beneath that garb, I see little proof of it. Your pardon, milady, but the hour is late, and my mind is dulled with sleep. For the life of me, I cannot determine your purpose here."

His smile was only slightly mocking, but there was open challenge in his voice.

Purposefully, Shanna moved closer until she was sure the man could detect the fragrance of her perfume.

The first assault was launched.

"Watch h'it, milady," Hicks cautioned. "He's a cagey one, 'at he is. He's killed one filly and her wit' babe. Beat her to a bloody pulp, he did."

Pitney strode to a place in the light behind his mistress, protectively near. His immense size loomed menacingly in the small confines of the cell and dwarfed those about him. Shanna saw only a flicker of surprise in the prisoner's eyes.

"You've come well escorted, milady." His tone was no less audacious. "I'll be careful to make no sudden movements lest I should err and cheat the hangman of his fee."

Ignoring his jibe, Shanna withdrew a silvered flask from the folds of her cloak and held it toward him. "A brandy, sir," she said softly. "If you care for it."

Slowly Ruark Beauchamp stretched out a hand, covering the slender fingers with his own for a brief moment before he drew the decanter away. He smiled leisurely into her veiled face.

"My thanks."

On any other occasion Shanna would have snubbed the man for his boldness, but she remained cautiously silent. She watched him as he removed the cork and raised the flask toward his lips. Then he paused and tried again to make out her features through the black lace cloth of her veil.

"Would you share it with me, milady?"

"Nay, Mister Beauchamp, 'tis yours to enjoy at your leisure."

Ruark sampled a long draught before sighing in appreciation. "My gratitude, milady. I had almost forgotten such luxuries exist."

"Are you accustomed to luxuries, Mister Beauchamp?" Shanna queried softly.

The colonial shrugged in reply, lifting a hand toward his surroundings. "Certainly more than this."

A noncommittal answer, Shanna thought derisively. After three months in the place, the man should have been more welcome for her company. She withdrew her hand from beneath her cloak again, this time offering him a small bundle.

"Though admittedly your days are numbered, Mister Beauchamp, there is much that can be done to ease your circumstance. There is this for your hunger."

He stood without accepting it until Shanna was forced to open the large napkin herself, displaying a small loaf of sweetened bread and a generous share of tangy cheese. He stared at her curiously, making no move to take it.

"Milady," he implored her, "I do desire this gift, but I am wary, for I cannot guess what you wish in return, and I have naught to offer."

A shadow of a smile crept across Shanna's lips. Gazing at her directly, Ruark thought he glimpsed a soft mouth curving beneath the gauzy lace veil. It stirred his imagination no small amount.

"Your ear for a moment and your consideration, sir, for I have a matter to discuss," Shanna replied slowly, placing the food on a rough-hewn table standing near his cot.

Resolutely, Shanna faced Mister Hicks, and her command was quietly spoken but firm.

"Leave us now. I wish a private word with this man."

She was aware of the prisoner's aroused interest. From beneath dark brows, he observed them all with close attention, and with quiet patience he waited, like a cat before a mousehole.

Pitney loomed nearer and worry marked his broad face. "Mistress, are you sure?"

"Of course." Her slender hand indicated the portal. "Escort Mister Hicks from the cell."

The portly gaoler sorely protested. "The bloke'll wring yer neck if'n I allowed h'it!" Who would authorize his purse if some harm befell the wench? He pleaded, "I daren't, milady."

" 'Tis my neck to chance, Mister Hicks." Shanna cut him short and, as if she read his mind, added, "And you'll be paid just the same for your services."

Hicks's bloated cheeks flushed almost purple, and his stuttering lips seemed to flutter in his expelled breath. He threw a wary glance toward the prisoner. Then, with an odorous sigh, he secured the lantern above his head. Taking up a stub of a candle from the rough table, he touched it to the flame in the lantern.

"He's a fast one, liedy," he warned direly. "And ye keep yer distance. If he makes a move towards ye, call out." His glare came close to piercing the colonial. "Try anything, ye ruddy bloke, and I'll see ye swing 'fore the sun is up."

Muttering sourly to himself, Hicks strode out. Pitney remained, standing stock still, indecision etching the deep furrows of his brow.

"Pitney, please." Shanna waited expectantly, and when he still made no move to leave, she raised her hand imploringly toward the iron portal. " 'Tis safe enough. What can he do? Nothing will happen."

The large man spoke finally, but only to Ruark. "If you would see the hour out," he rumbled, "take care that no smallest harm befall her. If it should, you'll well rue the moment. You have my most earnest word on that."

Ruark's gaze weighed the other's broad frame, and respectfully he nodded his acquiescence. Still wearing a discontented scowl, Pitney wheeled about and strode out of the cell. Closing the door behind him, he slid open the small port in it. His back could be seen from within as he placed himself to guard against a possible eavesdropper.

The prisoner stood without moving, awaiting Shanna's pleasure. She walked slowly across the cell, carefully placing herself out of his reach now. Lowering her hood, she faced him and slowly swept away the the lace veil, letting it float to the table beside her.

The second salvo was fired.

It struck home with a crushing weight Shanna little realized. Ruark Beauchamp could not trust himself to speak. Her beauty was such that his knees grew weak. It brought home to him the starvation of his long and forced celibacy. Her pale honey-hued hair, caught in a mass of loose ringlets, cascaded over her shoulders and down her back. It was rich and luxuriant, in studied disarray. Golden strands, lightened by the sun, shimmered among the carefree curls. Ruark felt a great temptation to go to her and caress the bountiful silken mane and gently run his fingers along the delicate cheekbones blooming with color. Her features seemed perfect, the nose straight and finely boned. The soft brown brows arched away from eyes that were clear and sea-green, brilliant against the thick fringe of jet-black lashes. They stared back at him, open, yet as unfathomable as any sea he had ever gazed into. The soft pink lips were tantalizing and gracefully curved, vaguely smiling. Under his warming gaze, the creamy skin flushed slightly. With a will of iron, Ruark clamped a grip upon himself and held his silence.

Shanna murmured coyly, "Am I so ugly, sir, that words are stricken from your tongue?"

"On the contrary," Ruark answered with an apparent ease he little felt. "Your beauty so blinds me, I fear I must be led to the gallows by the hand. My mind can little absorb such splendor after the dreariness of this dungeon. Is it meant that I should know your name, or is that a part of your secret?"

Shanna recognized that she had struck her target and saved the balance of her weapons for a later moment. She had heard similar vows often, indeed much these same words, and they seemed trite to her. That this ragged wretch would use them was almost an affront to her pride. But she played the game on. She shook her head, tossing the curling tresses enticingly, and laughed somewhat ruefully.

"Nay, sir, I give it to you, though I beseech your discretion, for therein lies the weight of my problem. I am Shanna Trahern, daughter of Orlan Trahern."

She paused, waiting his reaction. Ruark's brows lifted, and he could not hide his amazement. "Lord" Trahern was known in all circles, and in that of young men, Shanna Trahern was often the topic of heated debate. She was the ice queen, the unattainable prize, the heartbreak of many a lad, and the professed goal of ten times that number—the dream of unrequited youth.

Satisfied, Shanna continued. "And you see, Ruark,"—she used his given name with casual familiarity—"I have need of your name."

"My name!" he burst out in disbelief. "Ruark Beauchamp? You need the name of a condemned murderer when your own would open any door you wish?"

Shanna moved to stand close before him to lend weight to her words. Her eyes wide and appealing, she stared into his and spoke almost in a whisper.

"Ruark, I am in distress. I must be wed to a man of sterling name, and you must be aware of the importance in England of the Beauchamp family. No one would know except myself, of course, that you are no kin. And since you have little future need of your name, I could use it well."

Ruark's confusion blunted his wits. He could not think of her motive. A lover? A child? Certainly not debts, for she was of money such as no debt could entangle. His puzzled frown met the blue-green eyes.

"Surely, madam, you jest. To propose marriage to a man about to hang? Upon my word, I cannot see the logic in it."

" 'Tis a matter of some delicacy." Shanna presented her back to him as if embarrassed and paused before continuing. She spoke demurely over her shoulder. "My father, Orlan Trahern, gave me one year to find a husband, and failure shall find me betrothed to whom he wills. He sees me a spinster and wants heirs for his fortunes. The man must be of a family privy to King George. I have not yet found the one I would choose as my own, though the year is almost gone. You are my one last hope to avoid a marriage arranged by my father." Now came the hardest part. She had to plead with this filthy, ragged colonial. She kept her face averted to hide her distaste. "I have heard," she said carefully, "that a man may marry a woman to take her debts to the gallows in return for an easing of his final days. I can give you much, Ruark—food, wine, suitable clothing and warm blankets. And surely my cause—"

At his continued silence, Shanna turned toward him and tried to see his features in the gloom, but he had carefully maneuvered their positions until she now was presented full to the light when she faced him. The wily beggar had moved so stealthily that she had not been aware of it.

Ruark's voice was somewhat strained as he finally said, "Milady, you test me sorely. A gentleman my mother tried to teach me to be, with good respect for womanhood." Shanna's breath caught as he stepped nearer. "But my father, a man of considerable wisdom, taught me early in my youth a rule I've long abided."

He walked slowly around her, much as she had done with him a few moments before, then halted when he stood at her back. Scarcely breathing, Shanna waited, feeling his nearness yet not daring to move.

"Never—" Ruark's whisper came close to her ear, stirring awake a tingling of fear in her. "Never buy a mare with a blanket on."

Shanna could not suppress a flinch as his hands came over her shoulders and hovered above the fasteners of her cloak.

"May I?" he asked and his voice, though soft, seemed to fill the very corners of the cell. Ruark accepted her silence as consent, and Shanna braced herself while his lean fingers undid the velvet frogs. He drew the cloak from her, and she knew a moment of regret. Her carefully devised attack was spent in an unplanned rush. But little did she guess the carnage it reaped. Though lacking splendorous trimming and fancy laces, the deep red velvet gown enhanced her beauty divinely. She was the gem, the jewel of rare beauty which made the dress more than a garment but rather a work of art. Above the hooped panniers which expanded her skirt on the sides, the tightly laced bodice showed the narrowness of her waist while it cupped her bosom to a most daring display above the square décolletage. In the golden glow of the tallow lantern, her skin gleamed like rich, warm satin.

Ruark stood close, his breath falling softly against her hair, his head filled with the delicious scent of woman. Time slipped past, flying on silent wings, and still he did not move. Shanna felt suffocated by his nearness. The smell of brandy permeated her senses, and she could feel his eyes slowly roaming over her. Had the cause been less dire, she would have fled in disgust. Indeed, she had to fight the urge to do so now. It nettled her sorely that she had to stand on display for him. But like her father, with a high profit at stake, there was no limit to her patience, determination, or guile.

All his senses completely involved with her, Ruark felt an overwhelming desire to take Shanna in his arms. Her fragrance beckoned him, her soft, ripe curves made him ache with the want of her. Her breathtaking beauty quickened his very soul, stirring his mind with imaginings of what loveliness lay hidden from view. There was a need in him to feel the warmth of her beneath him, to sweep her up in his trembling arms and ease the lust in his loins. But he was painfully aware of his own rags and filth.

And, too, there was a puzzling glimpse just beneath the surface of her beauty of something to which he could not lay a finger, a hint of sarcasm, a brief flash of insincerity, a strange touch of arrogance. Still, he was convinced that had she any other choice she would not have been here. He knew Orlan Trahern was a man of power but found it difficult to imagine that the man would so constrict the life of his only offspring.

Shanna could bear it no longer and whirled to face him. "Do you find it so distasteful, then, this sharing of your name? Do you say me nay?" Why in heaven's name did she have to plead with this cloddish knave?

Ruark drew a ragged breath and by an extreme effort of will replied casually. "There's much to consider here—Shanna?" He peered at her questioningly, arching a dark brow, and at her nod of consent, continued. "My name is all that I have left, and there are those who would be greatly pained at seeing it further dishonored."

"I promise you, Ruark, that I have no intention of misusing it," she hastened to assure him. "I will but borrow it for a time and when I have found the one I can love, then 'twill all be over. If you agree, you'll be buried with all respect in a well-marked grave in a churchyard. Can those for whom you care then long remember your shame?"

"And for my last days you promise me ease, Shanna?" It was as if he had not heard her. "Yet that will take away my one enjoyment—the challenge of Mister Hicks."

As if disturbed, Ruark paced the cell, seemingly deep in thought. He paused before the cot, and again his gaze was inquiring.

"Might I sit, Shanna? I apologize as there is no chair for you. If you wish, you may join me here."

"No—no thank you," she quickly answered. She glanced down at the filthy straw and could not suppress a shudder.

23

Taking a seat in the corner, Ruark leaned back against the damp stone wall, drawing up a knee to let his arm rest upon it, the hand dangling limply. His eyes fastened on her, and Shanna steeled herself for the final act. She must make it good. At least he had not yet openly laughed at her.

"Do you think I lightly consider this, Ruark? My father is a man of iron will, and, though he has been called many things, I have never heard a man question his word. I have no doubt that he will do as he said and force me to marry a man I despise."

Ruark's contemplation was steady, but no words parted his lips. It was her turn to be nervous and pace, and doing so furthered her cause no small amount. Shanna Trahern moved with the natural grace of one who led an active life and bore nothing of the affected daintiness so often displayed by beauties of the courts and salons. There was a sureness in her stride that lent a smooth, fluid grace to her every movement. Ruark admired every side of her, and for the most part her words missed him, for he had already set the price in his mind and only waited the moment.

Shanna stopped, and, resting her hands on the table, leaned toward him. The gown opened enticingly, and she saw his eyes fall where she wanted them.

"Ruark," she said firmly, and his gaze raised reluctantly to meet hers. "Is there something about me which you find distasteful?"

"Nay, Shanna, my love." His voice was hushed but sounded hollow in the cell. "You are beautiful beyond my imagination. And I have enjoyed this repast so much I would not see its end. But please consider this. If your cause is really so dear, I will bargain with you for my name, but the price will be high, Shanna. And I ask you say me yea or nay before you leave, for that suspense I could not bear."

Shanna held her breath in fear of what he was about to say.

"My price is this." His words echoed through her brain. "The marriage will be one in fact as well as vow. I am condemned to hang, and I would elect the chance to leave an heir. The cost is that you spend the night with me and consummate the vows in deed as well as words."

Her breath came out in a rush and her eyes flared with anger. She gasped in stunned rage at his affront. That he should dare!

Shanna was set to shriek her fury in his face, but his laughter rang in the cell and brought quick death to her ire. Swinging both legs onto the cot and clasping his hands behind his head, he was as relaxed as if he were in some inn swigging ale.

"Ah, yes," he chuckled derisively. "I thought that might see the real price of your predicament. You seek my name for a cause so dear, this name which is my last and sole possession and mine alone to give. When I ask the same of you—that the cost be what is yours alone to give—then the price is much too dear. So you reject the price, deny the bargain, and will be seen to that end your father wills."

Ruark seized the flask and raising it high, gave the toast. "To your wedding, Shanna, love."

He drank deeply and then sat staring at her with a wan smile, feeling his loss. Shanna returned his gaze with little warmth in her eyes.

That damned filthy fool! Did he think he could best her?

She came toward him, swinging her hips like a gypsy dancer, hair tumbling and eyes flashing with green fire. She had been stung and felt a need to set his smirk awry. Anger ruled where good sense trembled in fear. She stood before him, feet spread and arms akimbo and slowly reached out a finger to rest it along the straight line of his nose.

"Look," she sneered. "I dare touch you, filthy though you are, swine though you are to mock my need. And if I bed you, what then do I gain? To trade my father's will for your brat?"

Leaning his head back, Ruark laughed into her glare. "Your father's will, my love, seems to be a sure thing that, like death, you will not escape. And, what then, when husband dearly found weds the widow and finds her virgin still? What will he say? That she gave a lie to her father? And my brat, if that be the case—it may or may not take. God wills that. If not, then you are nothing out and have much gained. If so, then a truly widowed wife no father could deny." He sighed deeply. "But 'tis all to naught, for I see that you are not the sort to take the chance. You want my name, and all the bargain in the boot while I have naught to gain, at least not that which I would treasure to my dying breath, a memory that would truly ease my last days. But alas, enough of this. You are indeed most captivating, my Shanna."

He laid a hand upon her arm in a tender caress.

"Do you know that you are mine until I die? 'Tis the price a woman pays to seek out a man and to ask for him in marriage. So the sages say that she must belong to him until his death."

Shanna stared at him in disbelief, aware of the trap that closed slowly around her.

"But my need is great," she whispered and realized some truth in what he said. She would not feel free until he was dead. "I came prepared to plead." Her voice was low and husky. "I did not come to yield, but yield I will. 'Tis a bargain then."

Ruark's bearded jaw dropped for barely an instant. He had not expected this. Suddenly he was elated. It would almost be worth the hanging. He rose to stand before her, though still not daring to touch her, his hands pressed flat against his thighs as he fought the urge. His voice came gentle, almost a whisper.

"A bargain. Yea, a bargain. And be it known that the first to wed you, my lovely Shanna, purchased the right with the dearest price of all."

Staring into those warm amber eyes, Shanna could find no reply or other words to speak for the moment. Taking up her cloak, she numbly accepted his assistance in donning it. She arranged the veil and pulled the hood forward, carefully covering her hair.

At last, ready to leave, she faced him but almost pulled away as his hand rose to touch her. To her surprise he only tucked in a stray curl that had fallen free and slowly fastened the catch that held her hood in place. Shanna gazed into his face. His eyes were soft and yearning and touched her everywhere.

"I must make arrangements," she spoke firmly, bracing up her courage. "Then I will send Pitney for you. It won't be more than a day or two. Good night."

With hard-won poise Shanna turned and left. At that moment Ruark could have shouted for joy. Even Hicks could not dampen his happiness as later, once more in the dark, Ruark stretched himself on the cot and engaged in his pastime of late, chasing fleas.

Chapter 2

HE day dragged out interminably, a matter Ruark Beauchamp would have done something about normally. Within the confines of his narrow cell, he could do nothing but await his end. The remains of his morning meal dried on a trencher, yet he knew a sated hunger not often experienced behind the iron doors of Newgate. The same fare would have eased the lot of any poor soul who had had the misfortune to be locked away in the gaol, whether he was sentenced for a debt unpaid or a worse offense which would lead eventually to a hangman's noose at Tyburn. It was a grim three-hour ride from Newgate to the triple tree at Tyburn, and one could think over a lifetime in that span of time, though usually the way was lined with sightseers and hecklers anxious for the killing.

Ruark had not been trusted with a razor; thus, a full growth of beard still covered much of his face, but with the clean garb Hicks had brought, he presented a neater appearance. A linen shirt, breeches, hose, and a pair of leather shoes could be greatly tolerated after three wretched months in the same filthy rags. In that time his bucket of water, laced with a portion of rum to keep it from souring, had been used both to quench his thirst and for what cleanliness it could provide. But since Shanna's visit,

27

fresh water seemed in good supply, and a bottle of wine accompanied the evening platters.

It was impossible to imagine anything which would turn Hicks's nature for the better or budge his grotesque shape for another's sake other than the promise of a purse, whether small or great. The arrival of clothes and food and the gaoler's good manners were a fine indication that all had not gone astray.

Still, in the dim, lonely cell, Ruark paced restlessly. The shadow of the noose darkened the days that slipped by, and doubt and fear tortured his mind. He had no way of knowing whether Shanna Trahern would hold to her word and send for him. Just to see the world outside again would be a heady draught, but his thoughts were occupied with a vision of that most beautiful maid in his arms. Perhaps she would yet change her mind, deciding she could abide her father's will more than she could a night with him. Or had he imagined it all? Was it a dream that he had conjured from the depths of hopelessness? Did Shanna Trahern, a most delectable figure of a woman and the ethereal goal of every unwed swain here and abroad, actually enter his cell and make such a pact with him? The one vision that totally eluded him was of this proud woman yielding herself to a man branded a murderer.

Pausing before his cell door, Ruark rested his forehead against the cold iron. The haunting image of soft, perfect features, honey and gold tresses swirling around fair shoulders, and ripe, curving breasts swelling almost free of a red velvet gown was branded on his memory with minute detail, stirring an agonizing impatience which could only be relieved when she was truly his—if that moment was to be. He realized that where Hicks's brutality had failed, the illusion of Shanna came close to breaking him. Nevertheless, he held the vision, for when it faded it was replaced by a gruesome one of the triple tree and its fruit.

He paced. He sat. He washed. He waited.

Finally, in increasing frustration he flung himself to his pallet, weary of the agony of uncertainty. He rubbed his hand across his bristly beard and then winced as his own shabby appearance was brought painfully to mind. The best Shanna could have thought him to be was a barbarian.

He flung his arm over his eyes as if to shut out those torturing illusions and dozed fitfully. Even then he found no peace and woke in a cold sweat, a gnawing ache in the pit of his belly.

He was still struggling to contain his emotions when footsteps echoed in the stillness. Ruark came fully awake as the sound halted just outside his cell. A key rattled in the lock, and Ruark swung his long legs over the edge of the cot as the door was thrown open. Two burly guards with drawn pistols came in and motioned him out. Glad for any break in the boredom, Ruark hastened to obey. He stepped out of the portal and found himself face to face with Mister Pitney.

" 'E's come for ye, ye scum." Hicks poked at Ruark's lean ribs with the long cudgel. "I care not for the likes of ye to be nobbin' wit' gentle folk, but the liedy is set to wed. Ye'll be going wit' the man and me own good lads 'ere, John Craddock and Mister Hadley." He leered at Ruark's raised eyebrow. "Just to see, of course, 'at ye do not take to some fancy highjinks."

The corpulent turnkey chortled as heavy irons were fastened on Ruark's wrists. The ends of the chains were handed to Mister Pitney, who grasped them in his hamlike fist. With a gesture to follow, Hicks led the procession through the gaol and halted only when they reached the waiting wagon which was drawn up close before the outer gate. The conveyance much resembled a large, ironbound oaken box on wheels with only a small, barred window mounted in the side door. A third guard was high in the driver's seat with the reins already threaded through his thick fingers. His cloak was pulled close around him against the chill of the drizzling rain, and he gave no heed to them other than the lowering of his tricorn upon his brow.

"Now ye do as Mister Pitney says," Hicks bade his men. "And ye bring this scurvy bloke back 'ere live or dead." His black, beady eyes glared at the prisoner. "Mind ye, if 'e makes one move to escape, blow 'is head off."

"Your kindness is exceeded only by your grace, master gaoler," Ruark told him lightly. Then he squared his shoulders. "Can we be about our affairs, or are there more matters you wish to discuss with these gentlemen?"

Hicks waved him into the wagon. For the deepest cut he knew where to thrust. "Git in, ye bloody rogue. I warrant good Pitney will keep ye from doing in 'is liedy like ye did 'at wench in the inn—an' 'er carrying yer babe."

Ruark's eyes hardened as the gaoler pushed a slobbering grin up to his face and snickered mockingly, but the younger man remained mute even beneath Pitney's frowning perusal. Offering neither nod nor explanation, Ruark stepped past him, reached to the top of the doorway, and swung himself and his chains into the wagon. In the dark, barren interior of the van, he slumped into a corner to seek what comfort could be found. The door was barred, and Hicks rapped his staff against the wooden sides.

"Ye take good care o' this piece now," he admonished them all. "And I would not mind a lump or two if 'e so much as turns a bad eye to ye. I'll be seeing ye after the high gate is closed. Mind ye now, see 'at this comes ter no ill."

With a lurch, the heavy wagon jolted on its way. The hour was close to noon. Ruark could *not* guess how long the ride would be, or where they were bound. Glimpses of leaden sky and rooftops wet with cold drizzle flitted across the narrow scope of the small, high window. They journeyed beyond the outskirts of London, and the horses were urged into a faster pace. Through the iron bars, Ruark caught sight of farm cottages in the distance topped by thatched roofs, and fields, with the remains of fall crops stubbling them, separated by hedges or low stone walls. The winding muddy road swept past hamlets and country manors, but hardly a body was seen, for the rain held the people from work in the fields and kept them off the streets. The wagon sped on with no eyes to mark its passage, save for those of a squealing pig running from the path and of horses leisurely grazing on the damp turf.

It was some time later when the van suddenly swerved from the road and entered a small clearing, narrowly missing trees which grew thick along the way. The wild ride nearly turned Ruark out of his corner, but he managed to brace himself against the jostling. His tensed body relaxed only when the wagon came to a halt beside a green stagnant pool.

"We be well hid now, me hearties," came the booming voice of the driver. "Give 'at bloke a hand out."

Pitney climbed down the opposite side as the two burly guards jumped to the ground and hauled Ruark out by the chains, giving him no opportunity to object or resist. For a brief moment, Ruark was crushed between them and grunted in pain as their elbows found his lean ribs. Then with a hearty shove they sent him sliding into the scummy mire bordering the pond. Guffawing in vindictive glee, they clapped each other on the back with howling good humor.

"Rise yerself, yer lordship," the larger one crowed and kicked at him. "Yer liedy's waitin' fer ye."

Angry amber eyes glared from a begrimed face, and Ruark came to his feet with a snarl, gathering his chains into a long loop and swinging it in open threat. The smaller guard, John Craddock, staggered back in surprise, clawing at the pistol in his belt.

"Now, me hearties," Ruark ground out in a determined warning, "I've already got a rope around by neck, and they'll hang me no longer if I take a few of. you with me. You can use that pistol, but I for one would not be of a mind for explaining to Mister Hicks why he won't be getting his fat purse. You can take your pleasures on someone else, for if you put a hand to me again, I'll lay these links to your heads, then let the devil take the hindmost."

They were simple men and looked on their prisoner with a new respect. He had a nasty way of turning a bit of fun awry and taking the enjoyment out of it. Still, Craddock held his pistol at the ready as Ruark climbed to solid ground and once more assumed the role of proper captive.

Mister Pitney had leaned against the rear of the prison van and taken in the whole of the episode. He chuckled to himself as he recognized that here was a man who just might match Shanna Trahern for spirit. It might prove damn good sport to see his mistress nose to nose with this one. At least, more sport than what was going on. It rankled him to watch a bound man being baited.

Fishing in his waistcoat for the key, Pitney came toward Ruark, but passing close behind Craddock, he appeared to stumble. As a solid shoulder caught him squarely in the back, Craddock gave an explosive squawk and lurched forward, trying to keep his balance as the mud sucked at his feet. Grunting, he fell against his mate, Hadley, and both of them sprawled headlong into the slimy pond. Spluttering and coughing, they came up while Mister Pitney contemplated them calmly.

"Gor! Three of ye lookin' just alike. Now which be the one— Huh, I guess the one with the chains is me man." His mirth drew glares from the two guards, and he gestured to the water. "Blimey, mate, you've dropped Mister Hicks's pistol."

As John Craddock fell to his knees and groped in the mud, Pitney made his way to Ruark. Hadley began to trudge to shore until his companion swiped at his shins.

"Watch yer step!" John Craddock hollered, " 'At thing were cocked, an' h'it'll blow yer blooming foot off!"

Pitney smiled and, having Ruark's attention, threw a thumb over his shoulder.

"There be an inn down the road a piece where ye're to wash and groom yerself for the wedding. These lads will have a time to dry themselves out." His voice rasped as he sternly warned, "Mind ye, hold yer tongue 'bout why ye're here and where ye've come from. And ye're to speak naught of me mistress to any but meself. Do you ken?"

Ruark wiped mud from his bearded chin and peered at the man. "Aye."

"Then I'll set these irons from ye, and we'll be on our way. The day is awastin', and me mistress is awaitin'."

They gained entrance to the inn by a back stairway, and none knew of their coming as they made their way to a small room tucked high beneath the rafters. After spreading their cloaks before the fire to dry, the two guards reluctantly took up posts outside the door, leaving Ruark to the care of Pitney. Pitney gestured to a wooden tub in the corner of the room.

"The chambermaid will fetch water for a bath. There's a mirror for ye to mark yer appearance." He opened a small leather chest and displayed the contents for Ruark. "The mistress sent garments to fit the occasion. She begs ye to groom yerself with care so as not to bring shame upon her."

Ruark glanced askance at the brawny man and laughed without humor. "For one who has gone abegging, your mistress seeks much."

Pitney gave no sign that he heard. He pulled a timepiece from a deep pocket in his waistcoat. "We've no more than two hours to dally here."

Stowing the watch, he cocked his head slightly and regarded Ruark with a rare smile.

"In case ye're ponderin' on what I would be, there's two ways out of here. Through yonder door, with the good men outside just waitin' fer a chance at ye, and this window." He beckoned to Ruark and pushed open the shutters. It was a straight three-story drop to a pile of jagged rocks. "I have only to sound me pistol, and the other guard will bring the wagon around with all good speed."

Ruark shrugged as the man closed the window against the chill drizzle and strode to a spot before the hearth.

"But either way, first ye must get past me." Pitney doffed his heavy cloak and opened his coat to show a pair of over-sized horse pistols tucked in his belt. After only a brief consideration and with complete honesty, Ruark assured him such ideas were far from his mind.

The chambermaid was a small but buxom lass, not quite plain, not quite pretty. If she claimed a score of years, it was a lie by four, and she betrayed her lack of age in her obvious reluctance to approach anywhere near the filthy patron. But having made all the preparations, she could delay only a bit more.

"I'll shave ye in a minute, sir. But me razor's a bit blunt. Let me fetch a strop."

Her pale eyes flickered down Ruark's torn and grimy clothes and warily came to rest on his mud-caked beard. An expression of disgust was all too evident on her face, and her freckled nose wrinkled at the stench of the mire on him. Quickly she skittered out upon her errand.

"Could be the wench doubts I'm human," Ruark remarked wryly.

Pitney grunted as he lounged back on the bed, bracing his shoulders against the headboard and sipping from a mug of ale. "Ye needn't fret none. Ye won't be tarryin' long enough to try her."

Ruark gave him a level stare. " 'Twas never my intent." Considering the manservant, he added, " 'Tis my wedding day, or have you forgot?"

Pitney's scowl darkened as he swung his large feet to the floor, and he strode to the window where he could look out upon the gray day.

"I would not fret much on that, either," he rumbled over his shoulder. Stretching his long arms wide and flexing his fingers in a low squeezing movement, he turned and smiled at Ruark, though there was little humor in his eyes. "I'm here to see out me mistress's bidding, whether I like it or no. Me first task is always to see to her welfare, but that I judge for meself. I would not take it kindly should ye give me cause to doubt that her good is served."

Ruark measured his answer with care. "I know little of this deed of which I am accused. In truth, I do not remember more than accompanying the wench to her room at the inn. With certainty I can avow, 'twas not my babe she carried. I had not been a fortnight in the country and most of that I spent in Scotland. In fact, 'twas my first day in London. Thusly, if I bedded her at all, 'twas on the same night that was her last. But I have no recollection of even that. The next morning when the innkeeper came to rouse the maid to her duties, he found me asleep in her room. So you see, my friend, I cannot deny that I bedded or murdered her, for she was dead, beaten and bloody, and there was I, slumbering peacefully in her bed. Yet I can and do deny that the babe was mine."

Beneath the weight of Pitney's close scrutiny, Ruark stripped off the useless waistcoat and shirt and laid a towel over his shoulders. He settled himself in a chair to await the maid's return and further consider his silent companion's words. It was well possible that the lady, Shanna, had told her man nothing of their agreement. Whether she was bent on treachery or simple caution, Ruark could little guess. But as Pitney himself had made clear, either way it boded ill.

The chambermaid returned, and Ruark submitted to her deft hands as she plied his beard with hot towels to free the dried mud. If this poor girl found him so repulsive, he thought, then the high lady, Shanna, could have seen nothing more than a beast. She must have felt herself in dire straits, indeed, to have submitted to his bargain.

Still, this was a pleasant interlude for Ruark, one he had enjoyed all too rarely in the past months, even if the girl was none too gentle in her haste to be done with him. However, his only injury was a tiny nick dealt on the last stroke of the razor when the girl, surveying her work, took full note of the face whereon she labored.

"Blimey, gov'na!" she gasped and suddenly asmile, wet the towel to press it upon the small cut. Her face reddened now before his amused gaze, and she became more than a trifle flustered. Pitney's attention was drawn when she tipped the pan of water, spilling most of it in Ruark's lap.

Ignoring the man's discomfort, Pitney remarked casually, "You seem to upset the wench. She's as flighty as a nesting sparrow."

The chambermaid bobbed a quick curtsy. "Sorry, gov'na. 'Twas naught 'e did. 'Twas me own doin'."

Snatching the towel from Ruark's shoulders, she began to dab at his lap before he caught her wrists and firmly set her from him.

"Never mind," he bade her dryly. "I'll do that."

The girl could hardly keep her eyes from that wide, lean, muscular expanse of naked chest as she gathered her razor and strap.

"Trim his hair while ye have the shears, girl," Pitney ordered and shrugged away the angry glance Ruark shot him.

The maid grinned widely and bobbed another birdlike curtsy. "Aye, gov'na. Be glad to, sir."

For her strange behavior, Pitney gave the girl a frown of bemusement. Shaking his head, he muttered something to himself and presented his backside to the warmth of the fire while he sipped his ale in a leisurely fashion.

The maid puttered about Ruark's hair with a new zeal as if she would cut every strand the same length, and by no means was it a thin batch. Pausing often to present a small looking glass so that he might approve her efforts, she held the mirror before her, managing to press it between her breasts with amazing results. The girl grew petulant with his lack of interest, and it was with obvious reluctance that she accepted his assurances that he wished no assistance in his bath. Eventually she gathered her shears and tools into her apron and left.

Ruark lost no time in stripping his smelly breeches away and settled himself into the bath, giving a long sigh of appreciation. He scrubbed thoroughly several times with a strong soap to remove the filth and vermin of the gaol, lathering the pungent suds into his hair as well. He was anxious to be on his way and toweled himself briskly before donning the dark stockings and breeches. But he paused long enough to note the close fit of the latter. Perhaps Shanna Trahern had noticed more of him than he realized, he mused with a rueful grin. He had certainly been aware of her.

Discarding the scented powder that had been made available, he combed his black hair into a bagwig at the nape of his neck and brushed it smooth before the looking glass. Standing in front of his image, he donned the cream shirt with its ruffles of lace about the cuffs, attached the lacy jabot, and then slipped into the silk waistcoat that matched the narrow breeches. He put on the brown velvet coat that was lavishly embellished with gold threads twining an ornate way around the wide cuffs and down the front. The leather of the brown shoes was softly buffed and adorned with gold filigree buckles on the high tongues. A tricorn of velvet, embroidered with gold, completed the outfit.

In all, Ruark surmised as he critically surveyed himself in the standing mirror, Shanna had spared no expense to have him garbed as a man of title. Over the shoulder of his reflection, Ruark caught Pitney's eyes as the man regarded him. Pitney reviewed the changed appearance of his charge and managed a bleak smile.

"I think me mistress will be pleasantly surprised." He finished his ale in a gulp and consulted his timepiece. "We'd best be on our way."

It was a small country church, in summer ivy-twined, but with the crisp chill of the approaching winter, the vines clung dark and brittle against the gray stone of its walls. The drizzle had ceased, and bright shafts of sunlight pierced the broken clouds, setting the crystal panes of the rectory windows aglitter with shifting shards of color.

Shanna stood bathed in light coming through an oriel. Her face, as she gazed out upon the rolling fields, held the smile of one confident of her goals in life. She had arrived early at the church, in a hired coach, for her carriage had to carry Pitney to the inn, more than an hour's ride away, and there remain while he journeyed by another hired coach to London and back again with Ruark Beauchamp. But the Reverend and Mrs. Jacobs had been warm and hospitable, and Shanna had managed to endure the wait.

The plump wife of the good clergyman sat nearby, sipping tea while she observed Shanna. It was not often people of wealth tarried in their quiet village, much less within the humble rectory, and such rich garments Mrs. Jacobs had never seen in her whole life. A mauve cloak of silk moire, lined lavishly with soft, gray fox, lay across the arm of a chair, forgotten as if it were discarded. The woman could not even imagine the cost of the matching silk gown with its tiers of pinkish gray lace cascading down the front of the skirt between twin borders of silk ruching. Lace flounces adorned the sleeves where they ended at mid-arm. Pleated lace spread like a fan from a point at the tightly cinched waist upward to the demure display of creamy skin. A narrow mauve ribbon was tied about the slim column of the young woman's throat, and the intricately woven coiffure, left unpowdered, was glorious in its own magnificent color. The effect of the golden strands amid the tawny would have challenged the best efforts of the most artful hairdresser.

Mrs. Jacobs sat much in awe of this beauty, for envy was not in her soul. Deep in her heart she was a romantic and took delight in what was to her the serious art of match-making. The groom, as she envisioned him in her mind's eye, would have to be handsome and charming, for no common sort should have claim upon *this* bride.

Shanna leaned forward to gaze intently out the window, and her movement brought Mrs. Jacobs to her side.

"What is it, my dear?" the kindly woman inquired with eager interest. "Do they return?"

Mrs. Jacobs's blue eyes searched the distant road, and, as she had guessed, a carriage was just topping the crest of the hill and would soon be arriving at the church.

Shanna, a multitude of explanations on the tip of her tongue, thought better of it and bit the words back. If she gave excuses for her husband-to-be, his faults would be all the more apparent. It was better to let the woman think love was blind in her case.

Shanna smoothed her hair, preparing herself mentally to meet the wretch.

"Ye are radiant, my dear." The "r" rolled from Mrs. Jacobs's tongue with a thick Scottish burr. "Daen ye worry none 'bout that. Go greet your betrothed. I'll fetch yer cloak."

Gracefully Shanna obeyed, thankful she could catch Ruark before the clergyman and his wife would meet him, on the chance his appearance could be improved at this late date. As she hurried along the covered pathway from the rectory of the church, a thousand reasons to worry raced through her mind, and she swore to herself, using several of her father's favorite oaths, then gritted her teeth as she thought of the care a gentleman must exercise in dressing.

"That cloddish colonial," she fretted. "At least let him have his breeches on straight!"

The dapple-gray horses tossed their fine, noble heads and pranced to a halt before the church. Pitney carefully tucked his pistol under his coat as Mister Craddock jumped down to the turf and, like any good coachman, swung open the door for them. Accepting Pitney's warning frown, Ruark stepped down from the Briska and paused, pensively gazing out over the moors. He had a great longing to run through the fields for the sheer freedom of it, but he knew he would get no further than the low stone wall. Pitney was strong, but his size hindered his agility, and Mister Craddock and Hadley did not appear too swift of either foot or mind. Even after his confinement, Ruark was convinced that he could outrun them, but Pitney's pistol and its lead could very well outspeed him. Then, too, there was the matter of a bargain he was most eager to see out. This held him in check far better than the threat of death. Of late that dark damsel had been too much his close companion.

Leisurely he strolled toward the steps of the church but found himself the center of a close-knit group. On the first stone, Ruark paused and regarded the three men, all carefully within arms' reach of him.

"Gentlemen." A faint smile twisted the corner of his mouth. "If I should attempt escape, you will no doubt use the weapons you cover so obviously. I do not ask that you be remiss in your duties but do hang back a bit as if you were really hired servants."

At a nod from Pitney, the two guards returned to the Briska and leaned against it, though their attention remained on Ruark, never wavering, for they had grasped enough of the fact to realize their reward would come only with a task well done.

"What now, Pitney?" Ruark inquired. "Shall we enter or await my lady's pleasure here?"

The servant pursed his lips in consideration of the question and then seated himself on the step. In his rasping voice, he stated flatly, "She's heard the carriage. She'll be out when she's ready."

Ruark climbed the several steps to the covered doorway and took a place there to wait. He was seriously pondering striking up a conversation with his stoic escort when the heavy wooden door creaked open, and his intended bride stepped out. Ruark's breath caught in his throat, for in the full light of day Shanna Trahern was the most ravishing beauty he had ever seen. She seemed almost fragile in the subtle mauve gown. There was no hint of the bold wench who had visited the gaol to seek a husband.

Shanna passed the stranger with hardly more than a glance, not even pausing for the sake of politeness as the man swept his hat from his dark head. Instead she lifted her wide skirts to rush down the steps.

Ruark leaned back against the stone and smiled his appreciation as his eyes caressed her trim back. Suddenly Shanna stopped, almost stumbling on the steps as Pitney turned to stare up at her. Then in amazement she whirled to gape at Ruark, her sea-green eyes wide in disbelief. His heavy cloak was thrown back over his wide shoulders, and the sight of the garments she had purchased struck her with the truth. A somber color, brown. She had carefully chosen it at the time. It could cover a multitude of faults and perhaps lend the colonial some slight dignity, she had thought, but now it was marvelously appropriate and so much more pleasing than she had dared to hope.

His face was *handsome*, recklessly so, with magnificent dark brows that curved neatly; a straight, thin nose; a firm but almost sensuous mouth. The lean line of his jaw showed strength and flexed with the movement of the muscles there. Then Shanna's eyes met his, and, if a flicker of doubt remained, it was immediately dispelled as she looked beyond thick, black lashes into deep amber eyes burning with golden lights.

"Ruark?" the question burst from her.

"The same, my love." Now having her full attention, he again swept the tricorn before his chest in a bow of exaggerated politeness. "Ruark Beauchamp at your service."

"Oh, give that damned thing to Pitney," she snapped, feeling the bite of his mockery.

"As you wish, my love," he laughed lightly and sailed the hat to Pitney who all but crushed it as he caught it against his chest. He passed it along to Mister Craddock with such firmness that a breathless "whoof" came from the guard.

"Take this to the carriage," Pitney ordered tersely. "And keep a respectful distance."

Standing with arms akimbo, Shanna tapped her foot irritably. She could not name the cause for her petulance, but Ruark Beauchamp was much more than she had bargained for. There was something insufferable about a condemned man being so cocksure of himself. He was probably the type who would go to the gallows like a swaggering hero, she thought shrewishly.

"Well, since you're here, I see no reason for delay," she said curtly and mentally debated his age. No more than ten or so older than herself, if that, though at their first meeting she had thought him nearly twenty years older. "Let's be about it."

"Your most obedient servant." Ruark smiled, then laughed as she glared at him. He pressed his hand earnestly to his lacy jabot and lightly vowed, "Madam, I am as eager to wed as thee."

Of course he is, she silently jeered. He would, no doubt, brag upon the morrow about the wench he laid. The rutting cad!

Before she could turn her thoughts away, the door opened again, and Mrs. Jacobs appeared with her tall, thin husband. The woman's blue eyes settled merrily upon Ruark and twinkled with obvious delight.

"Oh, my dear, bring your young man in by the fire," she urged Shanna. "We'll have the ceremony when he's warmed himself, and I've a bit of sherry to hasten the chill away."

Shanna mused derisively that he was warm enough. But for the benefit of the older couple, she went to him, resting her hand casually on his chest as she smiled sweetly into that amused and taunting grin. She would have dearly loved to wipe that smirk from his handsome face.

"Ruark, dearest, this is the Reverend and Mrs. Jacobs. I did mention them, didn't I? They've been so kind."

The inane chatter sounded strange from her own lips. She could feel the slow thud of Ruark's heart beneath her fingers while for some odd reason her own pulse raced.

A man to take advantage of all opportunities presented him, Ruark seized upon her cue and slid his hands around her waist, squeezing it slightly as he smiled down into the less than warm depths of her eyes. In his own, there was a kindling fire that touched her like a hot brand.

"I trust the good Pitney remembered to publish the banns. I fear I shall taste death before we be wed, if it not be posthaste."

If Ruark thought he won a victory as Shanna melted against him, pressing soft breasts full upon his chest, he was harshly rebuffed. Shanna herself refused no challenge and rose to this like a cornered feline. Beneath the wide folds of her skirt, she trod not lightly on his instep.

"Cease your worry, my dearest," she crooned and leaned her weight upon his foot. "The banns are published." She feigned worry in her frown. "But you seem somewhat pained. Aren't you feeling well? Or is that old wound plaguing you again?"

Shanna pulled back slightly but not enough to give him ease, and her slender fingers went searchingly to the buttons of his waistcoat.

"How I have pleaded with you, Ruark, to take better care of yourself. You're always so reckless."

Had he been of a mind, Pitney could have warned the colonial this was not the sort of woman to tamper with overly much. From the bottom step, as her hooped skirt swayed slightly upward, he caught a glimpse of the small, slippered foot treading carelessly upon the larger. His laughter softly rumbled in his chest as he folded his massive arms and waited.

The Reverend Jacobs's eyes had widened behind his spectacles as the lady seemed on the verge of undressing her betrothed, and he could only surmise it had not been the first time. Mrs. Jacobs, her plump cheeks a deep hue of scarlet, was suddenly aflutter and didn't seem to know quite what to do with her hands other than to wring them nervously.

Ruark parried the attack in his own fashion, bending his knee and at the same time raising the toe of the foot she trod upon. With most of her weight upon it, Shanna weaved precariously as her balance was suddenly upset. With a gasp she stumbled against him, one arm flying about his neck to stop her fall while her other hand grabbed his sleeve. She heard his chuckling laughter in her ear as he steadied her on her own feet.

"Shanna, love, restrain yourself. We'll be home soon enough," Ruark chided.

His amusement rankled her, and she longed to screech her ire at him but knew all too well the folly of that. She caught Pitney's loud cough as if he were seized with a choking fit and simmered all the more.

"We'd best get this marriage underway," the clergyman suggested with much conviction and peered disapprovingly at them over his square-rimmed glasses.

With a quirk in his brow, Ruark viewed this lovely Shanna who silently glared her rage at him. She might well be the fairest thing he had ever seen, but he glimpsed a bit of a witch there, too.

"Aye," Ruark agreed. " 'Twould appear the proper thing to do before the babe's christening."

Shanna's jaw dropped, and the urge to kill was strong. In another time she would have let fly a stinging slap to the knave, but here she found herself with no recourse but to bear his buffoonery. In a temper she whirled as Pitney's low chuckles broke the stunned silence, and she bestowed upon him a glare of such heat that it should have set the very blood in his veins to boiling. But the man bore the pain with dignity and struggled to control his mirth.

The ceremony was quick and unpretentious. It was obvious the Reverend Jacobs wanted to put right any wrong that the young couple might have engaged in prior to this union. The proper questions were asked and answered. Ruark's deep, rich voice came firm and unfaltering, promising to love, honor, and cherish until death. As she repeated her own vows, Shanna felt an almost stifling sense of doom. It was like a premonition warning her that her ploy would fail. Reluctantly her eyes were drawn to the tiny band of gold on the open face of the Bible, and she could only think, as the minister spoke the words over them, of the years of devotion her own mother had given her father. In contrast this marriage was a farce, and it was a sacrilege to ever pledge her love on an altar of God. It was a lie, and she might well be damned for saying it.

For all of her attempts at composure, Shanna's hands trembled as Ruark slid the ring on her finger, and the final words came.

"By the authority vested in me and in the name of God Almighty, I pronounce you man and wife."

The deed was done. The haughtly Shanna was wed. Vaguely she heard the Reverend Jacobs give his consent for a nuptial kiss, and she was brought abruptly back to reality as Ruark turned her in his arms. That was enough to snap the brittle twig of conscience. Deliberately setting his hands from her, Shanna raised on tiptoes and very primly placed a sisterly kiss upon her husband's cheek.

Ruark drew back and frowned slightly into the exquisite face before him. Her tauntingly sweet smile was not what he relished in the way of passionate response. He was more in a mood for something richer than light pecks of gratitude. Already he had concluded his wife had much to learn of love. He only hoped that his hours were enough to see him through the thaw.

"Come now, my children," Reverend Jacobs urged, his cheerfulness mightily restored. "There are documents to put your names to. And I do fear 'twill be another storm upon us before long. Do you hear the rain?"

Shanna glanced to the windows and experienced a new anxiety. Outside the dark clouds gathered, deepening the dusk almost into night. Her dread of storms had plagued her since she was a child and even now, as a woman, she could not subdue her fear. Hearing a light rumbling of thunder, she cringed inwardly. If only the wost of it would delay until this business was done!

Facing away from the water-speckled crystal panes, Shanna hoped to put the storm from her mind but was much in a panic as she started to follow the minister into the vestry. But a hand on her arm halted her. The touch was gentle but as unrelenting as an iron band, and it gave her cause to wonder what strength lay hidden in the long, thin fingers of Ruark Beauchamp.

"Look at me," he murmured when she refused to acknowledge him. Unwillingly Shanna lifted cool, questioning eyes to his and found a slow, lazy smile that seemed to mock her. Leisurely Ruark passed a knuckle along the fragile bone of her cheek while the golden brands of his eyes plunged recklessly into the perilous depth of ocean green.

"Shanna, my love, I would take it much amiss if you cheat me of this night with you."

Annoyed by his blunt reminder, Shanna tossed her head, lifting her fine nose in the air. "I doubt if these good people have made arrangements for overnight guests. I fear, Mister Beauchamp, that you'll have to restrain your ardor until we have more privacy."

"And will we have privacy, my dear?" he persisted. "Or will you spend the time 'til naught remains?"

"You can hardly expect me to be anxious to fall into bed with you, Mister Beauchamp," she retorted flippantly. "You may be accustomed to easy conquests, but I for one find the thought distasteful."

"That may well be, madam," he replied. "But the bargain is for a full night in my arms, no less."

"You're shameless to take advantage of my situation," she declared. "Were you a gentleman—"

Ruark laughed softly in amusement, and his amber eyes challenged her. "And you did not take advantage of mine? Tell me, my dear, who bared her bosom to that poor soul in the dungeon to seduce him with her wily ways? Aye or nay, madam, tell me truly. Was it not the wench who took advantage of the horny wretch, knowing he was starved for the sight of a woman? And had it met her whim, I've no doubt she'd have drawn the fellow to those fair breasts."

Shanna jumped as if she had been stung, and her mouth flew open to speak her outrage, but she could find no words that would do justice to this callous knave, though she searched her entire vocabulary.

Reaching out a finger, Ruark placed it beneath her lovely chin and gently raised it until her lips closed.

"Do you deny it?" he mocked.

Shanna's eyes narrowed as she gritted, "You vulgar beggar, they should hang you for a molester of women!"

His eyes gleamed like hard brittle amber, and his quip jarred her. "Madam, I believe that's what they intend."

Shanna gulped. She had almost forgotten he was a murderer.

She tried to wrench away as her heart fluttered in her breast, but he held her fast. Fearfully she glanced about for Pitney, but he was talking with the guards. Unless she made a scene, she could not gain his attention.

Her words stumbled out awkwardly. "I—I was foolish to agree."

Ruark's face was inscrutable, but something flickered in those eyes.

"So," he smiled lazily. "Now that you have my name, you say the bargain void."

The prickling of fear became stronger. Something warned her that she dared much with her open disdain. Casually Ruark laughed and stood back, releasing her, and bemused, Shanna glanced up. He raised his hand and called across the empty pews.

"Good sir—"

Seated at a low desk writing the marriage documents, the Reverend Jacobs paused and looked up expectantly. Pitney glanced around, his brows lifted.

"A moment please, sir," Ruark bade. " 'Twould seem my lady—"

Shanna gasped and quickly interrupted. "No need to bother him, my love. Come, let us discuss it further."

As the clergyman went back to his writing, Shanna reached up to snatch Ruark's arm down, clasping it firmly against her bosom. Her eyes dared him to refuse her as she jerked hard at his elbow.

"You are a cad," she said through sweetly curving lips.

The amber flame in his gaze kindled brighter, burning her with its intensity. The muscles in his arm tightened against her breast as he leaned to kiss her cheek, and then his warm mouth hovered much too near hers.

"Tsk, tsk, Shanna. Be kind. My days are few and those with joy even less. Let us at least appear to be lovers, if only for the sake of Mrs. Jacobs. Try to summon more warmth, my dear."

Shanna steeled herself against any outward show of withdrawing while his mouth softly tested hers, playing lightly, teasing, but the stiffness of her body was like that of one waiting for doom.

"You must learn to relax," Ruark admonished, his breath falling softly upon her lips.

His arm slipped about her waist as he straightened, drawing her possessively against his side, and reluctant though she was to have it there, Shanna accepted his attentiveness as he escorted her to the vestry.

While the minister laboriously completed the documents and entered the event in the record book, Mrs. Jacobs went to fetch refreshments. As they waited, Pitney's frowning perusal centered upon the colonial, who he felt displayed a more zealous regard for his bride than necessary. An arm resting lightly on her shoulder, a featherlike caress along her ribs, a single stroke of her arm where it was bare; the long, lean fingers made their claim on her. Pitney could well imagine the trap his young mistress found herself in to stand for this unwelcome pawing.

Pitney's scowl darkened, and, when he caught Ruark's eye, he beckoned the man to him. "We'd best make haste. The storm is building, and we might be caught here."

Ruark paused to listen to the sound of the wind blowing about the corner of the church. It rose forlornly and whistled eerily at a higher pitch. Raindrops splattered against the windows and then ran down them in streams. Candles had been lit to illuminate the gray shroud of the storm.

Ruark studied the other man carefully as he replied. "Aye, I'll tell your mistress."

The square jaw tightened. "Keep yer hands from her, lad. She's not for the likes of ye."

"You are a loyal servant, Pitney," Ruark returned with measured words. "Perhaps too loyal. I am her husband now."

"In name only," the large man retorted. "And that fact will remain true 'til ye've seen yer end."

"Even if you must show me that end before my time?" Ruark queried.

"I've warned ye, lad. Leave her be. She's a good lass and not the sort ye might find in an inn giving a man comforts."

Ruark folded his hands behind his back and looked Pitney squarely in the eye. He spoke with much conviction. "That is my wife, whatever else you may think. Now, I am not a man to start a quarrel with another in such a place as this, but I'll leave you this word of advice. If you intend to stop me from giving Shanna my attention, you'd best draw your pistol now and be done with it. I have naught to lose, and she's worth whatever fight you'd give me."

With that, Ruark turned on his heels and strode to the windows to look out on the rain-swept landscape, leaving Pitney to stare after him with a thoughtful frown. Shanna was observing her new husband as well. There was a quiet alertness in his manner, like that of a cat or a wolf, its strength ready to explode but, for the moment, docile. She was reminded of a large black panther she had seen once in her travels. In repose the animal's muscles were long and supple; yet when the beast moved, the sinews had flexed and stretched and rippled in a fantastic rhythm of life that mesmerized. Ruark was slim yet sturdy and moved with almost sensuous grace. There was a sureness in his stride as if he carefully planned where each foot would fall. At the moment he appeared relaxed and at ease, but Shanna sensed that he was aware of everything that transpired around him.

Turning to her again, he came with that same sure stride, and even in her predicament, Shanna could not help but admire the fine figure he made in the costly garments. She had described him to the tailor as a man lean, muscular, with wide shoulders, narrow hips, trim waist and flat belly. It was rather satisfying to see the results were near, if not, perfection. In fact, the breeches might have been indecent had the tailor taken a tighter seam, for they did fit extremely well—

With the sudden realization of where they roamed, her eyes flew upward to find Ruark's amused gaze warmly upon her. As he came to stand beside her, he murmured just loud enough for her ears alone.

"Wifely curiosity, my love?"

Shanna colored hotly and turned away in sudden confusion. His hand slid about her waist, and she started slightly as his hard chest pressed against her back.

His deep voice seemed to reverberate within her very soul as he announced softly, " 'Twould seem our wedding day will see the best of a good drenching."

In that moment Shanna's thoughts were far from the storm

outside and much centered on the tempest within herself. A white hot bolt of doubt had blasted her confidence, and she was suddenly unsure of her own ability to deal with Ruark Beauchamp.

Chapter 3

THE documents were ready, and the witnesses' marks were made, so the guards could go out and prepare the carriage. Pitney indicated it was Ruark's turn, and Shanna held her breath, for she had forgotten to ask whether he could sign his name. Her concern was wasted. His hand was quick and sure. Then the minister held the quill for the bride. Shanna put her name to the record first and then on a multitude of statements for the shire, county, and the crown. Then came a copy of the vows such as were stated. As she set the quill to the parchment, her eye caught a phrase, "That for thy husband, thou shalt love, honor, and obey." Hushing her screaming conscience, Shanna put her name to the document, and, as she swept the quill in a final elaborate scroll, a bolt of lightning turned the inside of the church ghostly white. Before it dimmed, a growing roll of thunder flared rapidly and ended in an ear-splitting crack. The panes at the windows rattled, and the tiles of the roof seemed to dance. With wide fear-filled eyes Shanna stared at the parchment she had signed, aware of the lie she had put her name to. She rose, throwing the quill aside as if it burned her fingers. The storm was all around her now. Rattling gusts of rain

49

struck the church, and the wind howled like a banshee in the gathering gloom of the dying day.

Seeing her disquiet, the Reverend Jacobs drew her aside. "You seem worried and upset, child. Perhaps 'tis well to have doubts, but I must tell you this. As events have progressed today, I have become convinced that what has been set in motion here today is truly blessed and shall bear a long and enduring witness to the will of God. My prayers shall go with you, my child. Your husband seems a fine young man and will no doubt comport himself well."

His words gave Shanna little ease. Emotions raged through her so turbulently she feared he would see them in her face. But he moved away, heedless of her distress, and began collecting the documents which he had sealed and stamped and were now dry. He folded them in a neat packet, tied it with a ribbon of scarlet, and handed it to Ruark.

"Before you go, my dears," Mrs. Jacobs beamed. She held out a tray bearing dainty stemmed glasses filled with an amber liquid. "A bit of sherry to warm your way."

Numbly Shanna accepted the woman's offering and raised the glass unsteadily to her lips. She paused as Ruark faced her, lifting his own glass in salute.

"To our marriage, my love. May it be long and fruitful."

Shanna stared at him dispassionately over the rim of her glass. Her longing to sneer was almost overwhelming. It was his smug, conceited, self-satisfied expression she hated most, she thought venomously. How she yearned to set him in his place!

Nearby Mrs. Jacobs talked happily to Pitney, chattering about the ceremony as if her husband had performed none finer, while Pitney stood mute, glancing over the small woman's head at the young couple. The set of his mistress's jaw was a good indication of her agitation, and he could only wonder at what next would follow.

Ruark stretched forth a finger and gently urged the glass to his wife's lips as his gaze warmly probed hers. "Drink, my love. We should be going."

After they had drunk the cordial and put aside the glasses, Mrs. Jacobs hastened away to get their cloaks. Ruark took the fur-lined garment and wrapped it about Shanna, flinging his own carelessly about his wide shoulders. He led her to the door as Pitney preceded them. Final farewells were said and the best wishes of the minister spoken. Mighty gusts of wind struck them, billowing their cloaks as the ponderous portal was swung open. Fat droplets of water rushed in to pelt them. Pitney ran ahead to open the carriage door and lower the folding step while Ruark waited with Shanna in the shelter of the portal. The two guards were already perched atop in the driver's seat, hunched in the folds of their cloaks against the pounding rain. Pitney motioned for the newlyweds to come, but as they stepped into the open, a blast of wind, heavy with cold rain, struck them in the face. Shanna gasped breathlessly and whirled away, finding herself fighting for breath against Ruark's chest. He caught her to him, half covering her with his cloak. Then reaching down, he swept her up into strong arms and dashed headlong to the Briska. Handing her into the snug interior, he immediately followed, taking a place beside her. Quickly Pitney folded the step and swung inside, throwing himself into the seat across from them.

"There's an inn down the road a piece in the village," he rasped, "where we can take our sup."

Ruark's attention to the man perked. "Our sup?"

"Aye," Pitney nodded, and in the meager light of dark twilight his gray eyes met Ruark's. "Unless 'tis yer thought to return to the gaol without a full meal to tide ye 'til the morrow."

Ruark's regard moved to Shanna who seemed very small and quiet in her corner.

The carriage swung down the gully-washed road. Lightning flashed, and the thunder echoed across the hills. In the voluminous folds of her cloak Shanna flinched with each shattering explosion of sound. The jagged light streaked across the darkened sky, and only Pitney was aware of her distress.

Ruark broached a question to Pitney. "Will you be journeying back to London tonight?"

A grunt answered him. "Aye."

Ruark thought for a moment about the man's short reply before asking, "Why do you not stay at the inn? 'Twill be a good three hours before you reach London."

"A long enough ride on a night such as this," Shanna flung at him sharply.

Her husband raised a sardonic brow at her tone and contemplated the snapping green eyes that pierced the gloom.

" 'Twould appear you've regained much of your courage now that you're away from the good Reverend Jacobs," he mocked lightly.

Shanna sneered as she had longed to before. "You crowing cock-a-jay, watch your tongue, or I'll set Pitney on your tail."

Pitney lowered his hat upon his broad brow and leaned his head back against the seat as if to snooze. It seemed his young mistress could handle herself once again. Ruark pondered his hulking companion, and then returned his full attention to Shanna who almost cringed as his hand reached toward her. He tugged at one of her hands, which was clenched in her lap, and by greater strength alone won it. Smiling casually, Ruark brought it halfway to his lips while Shanna squirmed nervously on her seat and warily cast glances at her protector to see if he really dozed.

"You are a flower surely, madam, but yonder thorn," Ruark's eyes briefly marked Pitney, "pricks me sorely. Indeed, madam, you are a rose, a soft-textured beauty of the bush, tempting, begging to be plucked, but should a careless hand seek to take you, 'twould only find a multitude of spiney barbs." He laughed softly, adding to Shanna's unease and pressed his lips to a spot above her dainty wrist. "But then there is that one who tends the garden and knows no prodding of the thorns. With careful hands he reaches in to pluck the bloom and gently breaks the stem whereon it grows. Then 'tis his forever more."

Shanna snatched her hand away. "Settle yourself, sir," she admonished crisply. "Your wit is lagging."

Shanna braced herself firmly in her corner as he raised his head and studied her. She did not know exactly what he might do, murderous scoundrel that he was. The thing she could not abide was that slow, jeering grin that came across his face, as if she only amused him. Where was his anger? If he lifted a hand to strike her, Pitney would be there to rescue her. No need, then, to pretend even a mild tolerance for him or bear his presence in her coach. He'd be bound and taken on top to ride with the guards.

A violent lurch of the carriage sent Ruark nearly on top of her, and Shanna quailed in sudden fright, raising an arm to shield herself from his attack. His amused chuckle close to her ear brought her courage back in a flare of scalded pride, and his hand upon her thigh as he braced himself drew an outraged fury. Much in the guise of clumsiness, she thought, the long fingers, whether intentional or not, touched her through her gown where no man had dared before.

"Get off me!" she choked in trembling rage and pushed with all her might against his wide shoulders. "Go fondle your doxies in the gaol."

Pitney peered at them from beneath his tricorn, and Shanna straightened her skirts with a jerk, tossing a glare at both of them.

"And just where is this inn?" she demanded. "Do you suppose we might get there before I'm mauled to death?"

"Calm yourself, lass," Pitney bade with a chuckle. "We'll be there soon enough."

Though only a few short minutes more, the remainder of the ride to the inn was intolerably long for Shanna. Even with Pitney's cautious but relaxed gaze upon them, the nearness, indeed the very presence, of her colonial husband was stifling and made her agonizingly aware of the trickery she practiced.

At last the carriage pulled to a stop before the inn. A sign before the portal swung wildly in the wind, and trees swayed to and fro, barren branches plucking in nervous frenzy toward the sodden earth as if in search of comfort against the gale. The guards, exposed to the full force of wind-driven rain and sleet during the ride, did not linger for their charge but rushed into the place, leaving Pitney to do the duty.

Alighting from the carriage, Ruark pulled his cloak close around his neck and yanked the tricorn low over his brow, and as Shanna stepped to the door he turned and pulled her into his arms though she protested indignantly at this outrage. He bore her across the puddle-laden path. Shanna ground her teeth in displeasure, hating his boldness and the close contact of his hard, muscular chest.

"You take much upon yourself, sir," she rebuked peevishly and then gasped and threw her arms tightly about his neck as he gave a little dip as if he would drop her. Silently Shanna seethed while the muffled sound of his mirth grated on her nerves, but she dared not retort until her feet were safely on solid ground.

As ever, Pitney was close behind them, and when they reached the covered doorway, his vast bulk sheltered them from the force of the storm. A tallow lantern hung beside the portal, and in its flickering light, Shanna's face fairly flamed with resentment.

"I've never been so abused in all my life," she fumed. "Put me down!"

Obligingly Ruark withdrew the arm he had beneath her knees, allowing her feet to slide to the step; but his other arm remained, holding her against his chest. Angrily Shanna pushed at him to set herself free. Astonished, she realized that the lace of her bodice was snared around a button of his waistcoat.

"Oh, now look what you've done!" she wailed.

It was impossible to move back even a step. His feet were braced slightly apart, and she was caught to him and had to stand in the space between or find her gown torn. She could feel his thighs firm and hard against her own, and it was a most compromising and humiliating stance. Having Ruark's arm loosely about her, his head bending near hers, and his warm breath falling against her cheek did not help her attempts at composure. Pitney awkwardly cleared his throat but otherwise was mute. Shanna's fingers shook, and though she tried to work the intruding button free, she was in such a state that she only entangled it more. Her temper riled, she gave a low groan of frustration.

"Here, let me," Ruark said through his laughter, brushing her hands aside.

Shanna choked, and her cheeks burned as his knuckles presssed upon her breast, rubbing casually against its peak as he tried to undo the tangle. She was smothered by his nearness and could not breathe with his hands at her bosom. Finally she could bear no more of his fondling.

"Oh, stop, you bumbling oaf!" she shrieked and losing all patience, thrust hard at his chest with her hands.

At her onslaught Ruark stumbled back, and his movement was accompanied by a sharp rending of cloth and the sound of Shanna's gasp. The lace insert and its silk lining had given way beneath the strain, leaving a small scrap of lace and the button firmly attached to Ruark's waistcoat. In mute horror, Shanna gaped down at her display, for her bosom was now only thinly concealed beneath the delicate batiste of her chemise. Her round breasts pressed wantonly against the filmy fabric, their soft, pink crests seeming eager to burst through. With the candlelight gleaming on her satin skin, it was a most rousing sight for Ruark whose celibate life of late had offered little more relief than his own private imaginings with the four stark walls of a prison cell. His mouth was suddenly dry and his breath a hard knot in his throat. Like a starved man, he stared at the full, ripe delicacies before him, and it nearly sapped his strength to keep his hands from her.

"You dimwitted colonial!" Shanna railed.

At her cry Pitney moved closer in sudden worry, not recognizing the reason for her distress.

"Nay!" Shanna gasped. Clutching the tattered bodice, she presented her back to him.

The panic in her voice sent Pitney whirling on his heels, for he guessed the damage was more than a slight rent. He withdrew several paces lest he cause her greater embarrassment.

Shanna stuffed the end of the torn piece into the top of her shift, weighting the latter down until the repair was almost as revealing as the tear. Ruark choked at this torture, drawing her attention and her accusing glare. His gaze burned upon her bare skin, greedily absorbing the sight of her swelling roundness as if he were afraid it would be taken from his sight. Shanna had been leered at before, but never so completely devoured. Desire flamed in those golden eyes, snatching her breath; and she could only murmur with a bit less rancor:

"If you had any decency, you'd turn your head."

"Shanna, love," Ruark breathed in a tight, strained voice. "I am a man about to die. Would you deny me even the briefest glimpse of such beauty?"

Oddly feeling no grudge against him, Shanna looked at him surreptitiously. His bold gaze stirred something deep within her, and the sensation was not unpleasant. Still, she covered herself with her cloak.

A moment of silence passed as Ruark struggled with his own emotions. Beneath his flowing cloak he tightly folded his hands behind his back.

"Would you prefer to return to the carriage now?" he asked solicitously.

"I've had little enough nourishment this day, fretting over disgrace," Shanna replied in a vein of honesty. "I might as well enjoy what is left of my pride."

Ruark's eyes gleamed with devilish humor, and his lips drew slowly into a delicate smile. "You're the light and love of my life, Shanna. Have mercy on me."

Shanna lifted her fine chin. "Hah! It ever passes through my thoughts that you are much a rake and have had many 'light and loves.' I am hardly your first or only one."

Gallantly Ruark held the door open for her to pass through. "The first I cannot deny, Shanna, for then I did not know of you. But you are my only love and shall remain for as long as I live." His eyes were serious and seemed to probe her being. "I would demand no more of a wife than I am willing to give. I assure you, my love, that no day will pass henceforth but what you will be in my thoughts."

Confused by the gentle warmth of his gaze and the directness of his words, Shanna could find no tongue to reply. It was impossible to determine whether he mocked her or told the truth. He was not like any man she had ever met. When she spoke to hurt him, calling him names or seeking to thrust a deeper insult, he took it in stride or with humor and continued to compliment her. Where was the end of his patience?

Lost in her musings, Shanna moved past him and entered the inn. While he doffed his rain-soaked cloak and tricorn, she waited, for the moment appearing the docile wife. He returned and with a hand riding the narrow curve of her waist, he guided her to the table Pitney indicated. It was tucked securely into a dark corner, leaving no room for an easy escape.

Mister Hadley and John Craddock having preceded them by some moments, were now seated at the long common table that filled the center of the room. The inn was empty save for the keeper and his wife, for the local patrons had fled to their homes with the onset of the storm. A fire crackled cheerfully in the hearth, casting wavering shadows across the rough wooden beams supporting the ceiling and providing warmth for the damp guests. After a long frown of warning to Ruark, Pitney joined the two guards and quickly drained a tankard of ale.

Much relieved to find himself at a table alone with his bride,

Ruark seated her and took a place close beside her. Soon a hearty meal was set before them all, juicy roast meats, bread and vegetables, and a rich wine for the couple. Aware of her husband's unwavering stare upon her, Shanna found her fingers less than steady and her appetite not at all what she had claimed. He was beginning to wear on her nerves. She had never known a man with such persistence and singleness of mind. She could well understand what he was thinking as he leaned back in his chair and regarded her. And not wanting to answer any question he might broach, she asked some of her own.

"Who was the girl you were accused of murdering? Was she your mistress?"

Ruark raised a brow at her. "Shanna, love, must we discuss that on our wedding night?"

"I'm curious," she insisted. "Won't you tell me? Why did you do it? Was she unfaithful to you? Was it jealousy that drove you to kill her?"

Leaning forward to rest his arms on the table, Ruark shook his head and laughed harshly. "Jealous of a chambermaid I spoke but a few words with? My dear Shanna, I never even knew her name, and I've no doubt she had many men before me. I was just there in the common room of the inn where she worked, and she left another man to come to my table. She invited me to her room—"

"Just like that? I mean, wasn't there more between you? You had never met her before?"

Ruark frowned and thoughtfully considered the liquid in his glass as he swished it slowly from side to side. "She recognized the color of the coin in my purse when I paid for my meal. It was enough to make us friends."

The bitter tone in his voice spoke of much Shanna did not understand.

"You are sorry for killing her, aren't you?" Shanna pressed.

"Killing her?" He laughed shortly. "I don't even remember bedding the wench, much less laying a hand to her otherwise. She took my purse and left me with naught but my breeches to meet the redcoats who dragged me from her bed the morning after. They accused me of slaying her, because she carried my child, but God knows that's a lie. 'Twas impossible as I had just journeyed from Scotland and taken a room at the inn that same afternoon. I never laid eyes on the wench before that. But I was brought before the magistrate, Lord Harry, he called himself," Ruark sneered, "and given a moment only to plead my cause before they charged me with lying and cast me in the darkest dungeon 'til Lord Harry himself decided what my guilt was. Murder, he claimed, because I rebelled against marrying the twit. Can you imagine with all the bastards in the world how such a thing could be true? It would have been easier to flee the country. And even simpler yet, if in a maddened state I did kill the girl, to escape from her room before the innkeeper came to rouse her for the day's work. But like a backward oaf, I took my repose upon her sheets until the next day dawned fair and bright. By God, I did not kill her. As I know myself I *did not!*"

Angrily he tossed the wine down and shoved away his plate.

"But how could you not remember?" Shanna asked softly.

Ruark sat back in his chair again and shrugged. "Oh, I've given much thought on that myself, and I have not quite laid it all out yet."

A guilty man always declares he's innocent, Shanna mused derisively. It was not likely he was telling the truth, for only a madman would forget a murder, and she did not believe that Ruark Beauchamp was mad. However, she thought it best to change the subject as she sensed his pensive mood. She accepted his refill of Madeira in her glass and sipped it, letting it ease her tensions. She could almost congratulate herself on the success of the day. Everything this far had worked as she had planned. She began to feel almost cheerful.

"And what of you, my lovely Shanna?" Ruark's regard had turned full upon her again with all the warmth a man could have for his bride.

"Oh," she laughed nervously. In this public place where Ralston, when he returned from his trip and learned of her marriage, could check about the newly wedded couple, she did not dare be anything but pleasant. "What would you care to know?"

"Why you felt you had to marry me when you could have chosen from any man who met your fancy."

"Met my fancy?" Shanna scoffed lightly. "None did. And my father is stubborn to a fault. He would have seen me wed and bedded by the one he chose. Why," she swept her hand in a graceful gesture, "he didn't even ask my mother to wed him."

She giggled suddenly as Ruark peered at her dubiously, a carelessly charming smile spreading across his lips.

"Oh nay, 'tis not what you think. My father is much a commanding person. He told my mother she would marry him and threatened her with ravishment if she refused. I was born quite properly a year after they wed."

The disarming smile remained. "What had your mother to say of it?"

"Oh, she was convinced the sun rose and set just for Orlan Trahern. She loved him deeply. But he still was a rogue. My grandfather was hanged for a highwayman."

"At least we'll have something in common," Ruark remarked dryly. A moment of silence passed. Then, "Do you plan to keep the bargain?"

Shanna fumbled for a reply, shaken by the abrupt question after she had tried so hard to avoid it. "I—I—"

Ruark placed an arm behind her chair, resting his other on the table as he leaned toward her. Kissing her ear, he whispered softly. "Could you just for this night pretend you have a bit of care for me, Shanna?" he cajoled.

His warm breath stirred shivers along her flesh, and a curious excitement tingling in her breast. The wine had certainly had its effect on her, she thought in astonishment, for her senses reeled in drunken pleasure.

"Is it too hard to imagine that we're lovers just wed?" Ruark asked, breathing against her throat. His arm came around her shoulders, and Shanna had to fight to keep her world upright as his mouth, moist and parted, warmly tasted hers. She struggled to push him away and free her lips. Had she drunk so much wine that she was now giddy from it? What was the matter with her? She was neither a tippler nor a woman of easy virtue. For heaven's sake, she was a virgin! And if much was made of it, a tea drinker on nearly all accounts!

"I'll be gentle with you," Ruark sighed as if he read her mind. He pressed his lips to the tempting corner of her mouth. "Let me hold you, Shanna, and love you as I long to do. Let me touch you—have you—"

"Mister Beauchamp!" she gasped breathlessly and avoided his kiss. "I certainly don't intend giving myself to you here in the common room for the amusement of all. Let me go," she begged, and then more sternly, "I'll scream if you don't—"

His embrace relaxed somewhat, and Shanna rose to her feet in a rush, announcing shakily, "We'd best be on our way."

Shanna fled to the door as Ruark paused to fetch his cloak and tricorn; and when he tried to rush after her, Pitney and the guards were there at his elbows. Heedless of the downpour and the puddles that marked the way, Shanna dashed from the inn. Ruark would have followed after her, but there was some delay as the keeper, fearful that the cost of his meals would be lost, began to argue sharply with Pitney, who was more interested in keeping Ruark at his side. A hefty purse tossed to the innkeeper silenced further debate, and at last Pitney allowed Ruark to precede him to the carriage.

The rain was now a steady drumbeat upon the roof of the Briska. Drenched and shaking with the cold and her own emotions, Shanna had slid tightly in a corner of the seat, giving the greater portion of it to whomever would take it. She had managed with trembling fingers to strike the flint and light the small tallow lantern that hung from the inside wall of the carriage.

Ruark stepped in, and Pitney folded the step. He started to swing himself inside but found the way suddenly barred by the younger man's arm.

"Have you no pity, man? Wed only a few hours and bound to hang before a week is out! Ride with the guards."

Before Pitney could protest, Ruark slammed the door in his face. The huge man, however, was hardly the one to do the bidding of a daring swain who rutted after his mistress. In fact, just the opposite was true. The door of the carriage was snatched open with such force it rebounded against the side of the coach with a loud crack, causing Shanna to jump sharply.

Ruark was not about to settle for this intrusion without at least a brief struggle and stretched an arm across the doorway again to prevent the other's entry. Pitney reached up to snatch the ardent bridegroom from the carriage, but Shanna's startled gasp brought her his immediate attention. It was certainly not fear for her husband which prompted this reaction from Shanna, but the noticed presence of the innkeeper and his wife standing in the doorway of their establishment and straining their necks to see what was going on.

" 'Tis all right, Pitney. Ride on top," came her hushed but urgent command.

Glancing back over his shoulder, Pitney saw the reason for her concern. He straightened, stepped back a pace, and jerked his waistcoat down in place.

Ruark smiled benevolently. "That's a good lad. And don't stand there dawdling. Make haste. Let us be on the road."

Pitney's heavy chin jutted out obstinately, and his brows lowered in an ominous fashion. The cold rain trickled down his broad face, but he took no notice. His gray piercing eyes measured Ruark in the light of the carriage lanterns.

"Should ye harm her—" The threat was gritted in a low voice, but it reached Ruark's ears distinctly.

"Come now, man," Ruark laughed scornfully. "I'm not a complete fool. I value what little time on earth I have. I give you my charge that she will be treated as one whom I have the highest affection for, nothing less, and with much respect."

Pitney's frown deepened at Ruark's words. He would have argued the point, but Shanna saw the threat of a public scene in this village where the actions of strangers would be quickly noted. So close to the church where she was wed, the rumors would spread; and Ralston would have no trouble hearing them.

"Let's be gone, Pitney, before you undo the best of my plans."

Finally the man gave in, and though his words were directed to her, he stared hard at Ruark. "I'll bar the doors. He'll have no chance to escape."

"Then be quick about it," Shanna pleaded. "And have a care the keeper and his spouse do not see what you do."

Several moments passed before the richly appointed carriage swung onto the muddy road to London. The rain beat monotonously upon the roof, deadening all other sounds, while the lanterns lent only a weak, flickering light to the ebony darkness through which they passed. Though the luxurious interior was warm and snug and well protected from the miserable night without, Shanna was hardly comfortable. Her dash to the coach had been sheer folly. Her shoes were soaked, her knee-length stockings were damp almost to their full length, and the wet hem of her skirt was cloyingly cold and chilly against her ankles. Gathering the sodden cloak tightly about her, she huddled in its folds and could not suppress a shiver or stop her teeth from chattering.

"Why, Shanna, you're trembling," Ruark said, catching one of her hands and sliding closer.

Angrily she withdrew from him and snapped, "Must you ever state the obvious?" And then, relenting, "My feet are cold."

"Here, love, let me warm them."

There was more than a trace of laughter in his tone, and before she could protest, he reached down and lifted her legs onto his lap. Folding back the dampened hem, he slid the ruined slippers from her feet. A small gasp escaped Shanna as his hands boldly touched her knees, quickly pulling off the lacy garters and wet stockings. Tossing them in a small heap upon the floor with the shoes, he tucked her feet beneath his jacket and drew his cloak over his lap and her legs until she was well wrapped within it. His far arm held her feet close against him, while his near hand slid beneath the cloak to gently massage her slender calves. All thoughts of coldness left Shanna. She had much to consider as she accepted his ministrations and casual familiarity. It had never been her fate to be privately closeted with a man before, and it warmly titillated her imagination. She had entertained many lords and titled men but always properly chaperoned. This had been her choice as much as anyone else's; she had never even met a colonial before Ruark Beauchamp. And here she was alone with him, and he had the grand claim of being her husband, however brief that state would be. It was only natural to wonder what his reaction would be if she tested her womanly wiles. Well enough to let this boorish backwoods clod sample the gift of her beauty, she thought, for soon he would be back on his way to the triple tree. It would do no harm to hone her weapons on his wit.

She sat in the corner facing him, her back against the side of the carriage. The small lantern inside the coach gave off a dim light, and she could see those amber eyes glowing with fervor as he quietly observed her. His fingers softly kneaded her leg from ankle to knee, warming her pleasantly. Shanna's lips curved almost into a smile as she sighed, and as if settling herself like a contented feline, she stirred against the seat. Her cloak sagged open to her waist, but she seemed unaware of it as she gathered her arms beneath her bosom, pressing her breasts upward until she was nearly out of the torn gown and thin chemise. In truth, she did not know how her pale skin gleamed with a satin luster in the light of the single candle, nor could she truly guess the extent of Ruark's passion. She only saw that his eyes roamed downward and felt a tightening of his belly against her leg and the pulse in his thigh quicken beneath her foot.

The softening of her manner enhanced her beauty, and Ruark boldly and appreciatively stared. When he spoke, his voice did not betray the tightness in his throat.

"You are warmer, madam?"

"Aye," Shanna breathed, half closing her eyes as she leaned her head back, letting him view the slender, curving length of her throat. Any moment now he would tell her how he desired her and try to cajole her into giving herself, and she would lead him on until the time they had to part. Through slitted eyelids she watched him and was pricked with disappointment as he appeared to shrug away her spell. Casually he reached into his coat and brought forth the scarlet-bound papers.

"These are the marriage documents," Ruark informed her as he turned them in his hand. "You will need them to prove that we are wed."

Shanna sat up a bit and would have reached to accept them, but he took them beyond her grasp.

"Ah, madam," he laughed, "the price has not yet been paid."

With something akin to horror in her eyes, Shanna stared at him. Would he threaten to destroy them if she did not yield? If they were thrown onto the well-washed road outside, they would be rendered useless.

"Ruark?" she asked wonderingly and withdrew her feet from him, tucking them beneath her. "Would you—"

"Oh nay, madam. That bargain is well made and sealed." His eyes raked her boldly, and Shanna braced herself for the worst.

He smiled slowly. "And I would not question your intent or honor. But this is a new one. I would extract from you—," he paused and tapped the papers against his chin, gazing thoughtfully at the lantern—"a kiss," he said suddenly, decisively. "A loving kiss of a wife as bestowed upon her newly vowed husband. Is the price too steep, madam?"

He raised his brows in mocking question. With some relief Shanna gathered herself, drawing the cloak against his wandering eyes, irritated that her knees kept slipping down to rest against his thigh.

"Very well," she sighed as if most reluctant. "If you insist. I am too frail to battle you for them." She bent forward slightly. "At your pleasure, sir. I am ready."

She closed her eyes to wait, and his low laughter made her fling them open again. He had not moved. In fact, as she stared, he casually doffed his coat and opened his waistcoat before leaning back in his corner of the seat.

"Madam," his smile taunted her, "the bargain was that you should give the kiss. Do you need assistance or instruction?"

Shanna bristled beneath his gibe and glared at him. Did he think her to be some simple serving maid not to see his ploy? She rose upon her knees, determined to set him back upon his heels. She would give him a kiss worthy to be taken to his grave!

Coyly she reached out to place her arms on his shoulders. Again his gaze crept downward where she wanted it. She would make him cringe in utter frustration before this was over. Her fingers lightly caressed the back of his neck as she moved nearer. Then suddenly he raised his head, and his eyes met hers, his brow gathered in concern.

"Try to make it good," he admonished. "I realize your experience may be lacking, but a wife-to-husband kiss should be a thing to warm the pride and not a peck of shame."

For a moment Shanna went rigid with the fury his words stirred in her, and she almost raked both hands across that leering face. Seeing his amused regard, she hissed, "Think you that I have never kissed a man before?"

His eyebrows went upward in a tiny shrug. "In truth, Shanna," he rubbed his neck against her hands, "I was wondering about that. A childish peck upon the cheek could only be from a fatherly tutor."

Deliberately Shanna leaned forward until her breasts rested on his chest; and seizing upon all her imagination, she lowered parted lips and moved them slowly, warmly upon his. Her eyes flew wide as his mouth opened and twisted across hers, his tongue thrusting through as his arms went about her, crushing her in his embrace. Her world careened crazily as he slowly turned until she half lay across his lap, her head pressed back against his shoulder. His mouth was insistent, demanding, relentless, snatching her breath as well as her poise. She was caught up in the heat of a battle she could not hope to win. Her broadside was spiked, her weapons dulled, her wits fled. She should have found his blistering kiss repulsive, but in truth it was wildly exciting. The hard, muscular chest, warm through the cloth of his shirt, tightened against her meagerly clad breasts; and she was aware of the heavy thudding of his heart while her own throbbed a new frantic rhythm.

Slowly Ruark's face retreated. With trembling effort Shanna collected herself, and, as he stared at her, she drew a deep, ragged breath. She struggled to rise from his grasp, succeeded—then found herself seated on his lap.

"Is not the bargain met, m'lord?" she questioned in an unsteady voice.

Without comment Ruark handed her the papers, and she tucked them safely in her muff. She would have slipped quickly from his lap then, but his arm was about her waist and held her firmly in place. With the panniers further restricting her movements, she could not escape him. Her eyes searched the golden flames smoldering in his eyes.

"Was there more to your bargain than you spoke?"

"Nay," Ruark smiled leisurely. "But I would be onto the first one now."

Shanna struggled, but his arms were about her, pressing her close to his body. His voice was a hoarse whisper in her ear.

"Madam, strain your mind and try to realize what it is like to stay in a small, gray room and count the stones for the thousandth time, to know the nearest measure of it, its length and breadth and height; to see again the days that have passed as scratches on an iron door and to know that morning will add another mark and that each moment passing draws you closer to a noose; and to wonder helplessly if the pain will be terrible or quick. Then into that narrow world is thrust a beauty such as yours with its dream and its hope. Aye, Shanna, my wife, I did lust in my dungeon, but mark you this," his eyes gleamed as his face drew near to hers, "before the door opens again you will be a wife in every way."

And Shanna realized his hand was already beneath her skirts and boldly high on her thigh. Her gasp was neither light nor coy, and she grasped his wrist and tugged it away with much determination, only to find that behind her back his fingers were loosening the laces of her gown.

"Ruark!" She twisted and brushed his arm aside.

Suddenly it seemed he had twice the normal number of hands, and her own flew in a flurry to maintain her modesty. Finally she caught both of his and hugged them tight against her midriff in an effort to keep them still. Then a new realization dawned. In the struggle, her skirt had been pulled from beneath her, and her bare buttocks rested full against his loins. His manhood beneath the silk breeches was bold and hard against her. Even now his hands were slipping away from her grasp and creeping up her sides, pulling her closer to him.

"Sir, you are no gentleman!" she gasped in outrage.

"Did you expect to find one in a dungeon?"

"You are a cad!" she panted, trying to pry his hands away.

Ruark laughed softly, and his breath brushed her throat. "Only a husband," he replied, "well warmed and willing."

Shanna fought to reach the small window so she might fling it open and cry out, but her wrist was caught and held to her side. She struggled with renewed energy. Then his hand was hot upon her naked breast, and her free hand snapped forward like a striking falcon but was stopped a bare inch from his laughing face. His grip was iron hard but gave her no pain, and with easy strength he clasped both her wrists behind the small of her back. Shanna drew a breath to shriek in anger, but his mouth smothered her outcry. Her head whirled in an ever quickening eddy, and she struggled against the intoxication of his kiss.

"Ruark! Wait!" she gasped as his lips lifted from hers. His

fingers were at the dainty ribbon on her chemise, freeing her bosom.

"Nay, Shanna. Yield to me now, love," he murmured thickly against her throat. His face lowered. His mouth was scalding upon her breast, and she was devoured in a searing, scorching flame that shot through her like a flaring rocket.

"Oh, Ruark," she panted in a whisper. "Oh, don't—please—" She could not draw a deeper breath. "Oh, Ruark—stop—"

The warmth spread until her skin seemed to glow. Her hands were free now but could only press his head closer. He moved and was hot and hard between her thighs. Her lips were dry, and her tongue flicked out to moisten them. In a last weak effort at modesty she tried to shield herself from the probing staff.

"O, love—love," he rasped, taking her hand and leading it to him, closing his lean fingers over hers. "I'm a man. Flesh and blood. No monster, Shanna."

His mouth was upon hers again, and his tongue was insistent until she met it with her own, first with hesitancy, then with welcome, then with passion. He was pressing her down upon the velvet seat.

Her sanity argued, this is madness! Her passion whispered slyly, let him come!

And he came to her, a first sharp piercing pain that made her gasp followed by a warmth deep inside that made her sob with pleasure. He began to move, and he was kissing her, caressing her, loving her—

Suddenly from without, Pitney's shout roared above the pelting rain, and the pace of the carriage changed. Cursing, Ruark raised his head, realizing they were stopping. Then he heard another voice answer the hail from Pitney; and he recognized it as that of the third guard, the one who had stayed behind with the prison van.

"Ahhh, damn!" Ruark groaned in frustrated agony: "Damn you deceiving little bitch!" He snatched from her roughly and flung her away. "I knew you couldn't hold to our bargain!"

With much urgency Ruark began to secure his garments, his teeth showing in a savage snarl as he cursed her viciously. Shanna cowered in the corner, her hands clutched over her ears as he vented his wrath in searing words. In the dim light his sneering eyes raked her cruelly, marking her pale, quivering breasts and the soft lovely thighs still naked to his gaze.

"Cover yourself," he ground out derisively. And then more harshly, "Or do you wish the guards to take my place?"

Shanna snatched the cloak tightly about her as if to shield herself from his ridiculing jeer and penetrating glare. A second later the door was jerked open, and the wide muzzle of Pitney's oversized pistol gaped its raw threat at Ruark's chest.

"Out!"

Everything in Ruark rebelled. He had been pushed, shoved, beaten, prodded, goaded, tempted, and finally betrayed at a most degrading moment. A ragged growl tore from his throat, and before anyone could react, he kicked the gun aside and launched himself, feet first, against Pitney's chest. The force of his attack sent them both sprawling to the mud. Cries of alarm sprang from the guards.

"Catch the bloke! Hicks'll 'ave our 'eads rolling!"

Shanna cringed as they fell upon him. Muffled oaths and grunts of pain detailed their battle. The guards were bulky, large and heavily muscled; Hicks had chosen them for strength to see the prisoner back to his cell. Each outweighed Ruark by at least two stone, and Pitney was larger than any of them, but Ruark displayed an extensive knowledge of brawling. He fought like a man possessed.

It was several moments before they could subdue him, and even then he was only slightly more battered than his captors, two of whom held him secure now on his knees in the mud with both arms outspread, while the third hurried to fix the manacles to his wrists.

Pitney stood nearby, trying to scrape some of the mucky soil from his cloak. He massaged his shoulder as if it pained him and flexed his arm. Glancing up, he paused as he saw Shanna's face illuminated in the lantern's glow, and, following his gaze, the guards also halted their labors. The third, stepping closer, spoke in humble apology.

"Sorry for the delay, mum. Me wagon got stuck in the mud by the pond, else I'd have met ye sooner, like ye wanted."

Slowly Ruark raised his head and stared into her eyes. His face was bruised, and blood trickled from the corner of his mouth.

Shanna's throat tightened convulsively, and she drew back into the shadows, snatching the deep hood of her cloak around her face so she would not have to meet his gaze. But his voice came, thick with unsuppressed wrath.

"If I fall under the mercy of Almighty God, madam," he grated out, "I shall see our bargain carried through—"

His vow was silenced by the swing of a meaty fist. Shanna flinched, hearing the thud as it met its target. When she could bring herself to look again, Ruark hung limply in the grasp of the guards. They finished chaining him and flung him roughly into the wagon. The bar slammed home behind him, and his bloodied face showed briefly at the small window before the wooden door shut.

Shanna sank back against the cushioned seat and with unsteady fingers began to rearrange her garments. Except for the fact that she had lost her virginity, her plans had gone according to her wishes, but she could summon no smile of satisfaction. Instead, there seemed an overwhelming emptiness about it all now, and her treachery lay like a dead weight upon her mind. Her young body burned with a yearning she had never experienced before; but there was no solace for it now, for beneath the enveloping cloak her arms were achingly empty.

Her carriage door was gently closed, and Pitney's weight on the coach made it rock slightly as he took the driver's seat. The coach lurched into motion, and as they passed the wagon and splashed through the mud into the looming darkness, an almost unhuman, raging howl rose from the wagon accompanied by repeated thuds against the heavy wooden door. Suddenly Shanna could believe that Ruark Beauchamp was a madman.

Clenching her eyes tightly, she covered her ears with her hands. But the image of his battered face was scored into her brain, and nothing could force the image to flee.

Chapter 4

A deathlike stillness hung over the eerie corridors of the gaol. Then a heavy door slammed, its bolt rattled, and the sound of shuffling feet and an ominous dragging broke the quiet. Hicks started from his slumber. Beads of cold sweat dappled on his brow, and he stared with fear-glazed eyes into the shadowed and contorted face bending over him.

"Nay! Nay!" he blubbered pleadingly as he fought the tangled blankets and thrust up fat, pudgy fingers to ward off the ghost of his dreams looming above him.

"Blimey, Hicks, settle yerself!"

The shadow straightened and became more of a man. Hicks blinked as he focused on the group standing before him. Awareness finally penetrated his mind, and his pinched stare turned to one of gaping surprise as he noted their condition. John Craddock gestured to the prisoner.

"The bloody beggar tried to escape, 'e did." He managed to swagger only slightly. " 'E gave us a run 'fore we caught him."

"Run!" Hicks snorted. With a heave of his massive body, he rolled to his feet and surveyed his beefy crew. Craddock nursed a split lip, Hadley displayed a blackening eye, the third guard tested his sore jaw. "Lor' help ye if 'e ever turns to fight!"

A smirk of satisfaction marked his thick lips as he mused on Ruark's sorry state.

"So! Ye thought to cheat the 'angman, did ye?" The gaoler chortled, and there was a gleam of cruelty which brightened his small, beady eyes. "Ye can bet yer old doxy won't care a mite if I lay me stick to yer back now."

Ruark returned mute defiance to the man's challenge. His bruised and bloody face had been beaten, but was as yet undaunted.

Mister Hadley tenderly touched his discolored eye. "Ah, she weren't no old doxie, mate. She were a real beaut, she were, and him hot after 'er. Wouldna mind meself 'aving a piece o' that."

Hicks cocked his eye to Ruark. "She got yer blood up a mite, eh? An' there ye were wedded an' not bedded. Serves ye right, ye ruddy blighter." He lifted his cudgel and poked at the prisoner's shoulder. "Come on, tell us her name. Maybe she'll be wantin' more of a man that what ye are. Come on. Tell us."

Ruark's scornful reply was bitter, harsh. "Madam Beauchamp, I do believe."

The bloated gaoler stared at Ruark a long moment, slapping his stick across the palm of his hand, but the jeering taunt on the other's face did not retreat from the silent threat.

"Put 'is lordship in 'is chambers," Hicks ordered. "And leave 'is braces on. I would na want him ter hurt ye's. 'E'll be taken care of soon enough."

It was two days later, early in the morning, when a loud pounding on the door again caused the snores of the head gaoler to end in a choking gurgle. Hicks rolled himself upright in the bed and after a rumbling belch cleared his throat. He let his ire at being so rudely roused sound in the tone of his bellow.

"Aye, ye blundering lout!" he roared. "Would ye strip the plank from its hinges? I'm up!"

Hicks thrust his short, rotund legs into his breeches and without tucking in the long tail of his nightshirt stumbled across the room to throw aside the bar on the iron door and tug the heavy portal open. As the guard stood aside. Hicks stared with mouth agape as he saw Mister Pitney, his large bulk filling the narrow passageway. In his brawny arms were a bundle of clothing and a basket well laden and with such a delicious aroma it set the gaoler's mouth to watering.

Pitney thrust into the room. "I've come from Madam Beauchamp to see to the welfare of her husband. Will ye allow it?"

Though asked as a question, it was much more of a command, and Hicks knew he had little alternative but to nod and fetch the keys. As he took them from the peg, he gave the man a once-over scrutiny, and his pudgy face compressed into a smirking leer.

"Whate'er it was ye did to the bloke, ye did it good."

The tan brows lifted in question, and Hicks snickered.

"We had to chain the beggar to the wall, else see ourselves done in. He's come on like a raving madman. Ain' even touched a morsel o' the food ye been sending. Just takes 'is bread and water like 'e did afore and just sits 'ere glarin' at us when we brings what ye've sent. If 'e could reach us, 'e'd kill us, or see us kill him which would be the way o' it for sure."

"Take me to him," Pitney rasped.

"Aye," the gaoler shrugged. "That I will."

The scurrying and squeakings of rats, disturbed by the light, intruded upon the silence of the dimly lit cell. Pitney waited for some stir of life from the motionless form sprawled on the ragged cot, and he was quick to observe the chains fastened on the lean ankles and wrists and the length of chain which ran to the wall from the iron collar secured about the prisoner's neck.

Pitney frowned into the shadows. "Are ye well, lad?"

There was no answer or other sign of life, and the brawny man moved forward a step.

"Are ye bad hurt?"

The form lifted itself to a sitting position, and the golden eyes stared through the gloom.

"Me mistress sent fresh garments for ye and bade me to ask if there be aught we can do for ye."

The colonial rose with a wordless snarl and paced the narrow cell, holding the long chain so it did not weight the heavy collar. Raw, red flesh showed on his neck where the skin had been chafed away, and there were marks on his face and body too fresh to have been made the night of the wedding. The torn shirt showed ugly weals upon his back, as if a whip had been used on him. He gave no sign that any of Pitney's words had penetrated to his brain. He was like a caged animal; and for a moment Pitney, for all of his own bulk and strength, felt an unreasoning fear of him.

Pitney shook his head in bemusement. He had seen this Beauchamp as a man and knew him as one. It was an ugly travesty that he had been reduced to this state.

"Here, man! Take the clothes. Eat the food. Wash yerself. Act like ye are a man and not a beast."

The pacing stopped, and Ruark stood half crouched, glaring at him like a cornered cat.

"I'll leave it." Pitney stepped forward and laid the bundle on the table. "Ye need not be—"

An angry growl warned him, and Pitney stumbled back as the chained arms swung. The blow hit the table and swept it clean with a crash.

"Do you think I'd take her charity?" Ruark spat. He gripped the edge of the table with his hands, and the chain to his neck was stretched taut as he leaned forward to its limit.

"Charity?" Pitney asked. "'Twas the bargain ye struck, and me mistress intends to see her part of it well done."

"'Twas her offer!" Ruark roared in maddened rage. "No part of the bargain." He slammed his fist down on the table, opening a split in its top. His voice went low and became sneering, insulting. "Tell your bitchtress she will not ease her conscience with this simple sop you bear."

Pitney would not stand to hear Shanna so abused. He turned to leave.

"And tell your bitchtress," Ruark shouted at his back, "though it be in hell, I *will* see her part of the bargain full met!"

The door closed with a solid clank, and the cell was silent again but for the sounds of the chains dragging as the prisoner paced.

Ruark's message, repeated bluntly, brought a cry of outrage from Shanna. She strode irately across the width of the drawing room while Pitney patiently waited for the stormy tide to stem.

"Then let him be content!" She flung an arm wide. "I've tried to help him all I can. 'Tis out of my hands now. What will it matter in a few days?"

Pitney slowly turned his tricorn in his hands. "The lad seems to think ye owe him something more."

Shanna whirled and the blue-green eyes flared. "That pompous jackanape! What do I care what he thinks! If he's so proud, let him hang and be done with it! He's made his bed—" She stopped abruptly. Flushing deeply, she flounced around so Pitney could not see. "I mean—after all, did he not slay that girl?"

"He's like a man gone mad," Pitney commented with a heavy sigh. "He will not eat the food and takes naught but bread and water."

"Oh, hush!" Shanna cried and began to pace nervously. "Do you think I want to hear? I did not declare his doom. 'Twas done before I knew him. 'Twill be bad enough to face the burial without being constantly reminded of how he went. I wish I were home! I hate it here!"

Suddenly Shanna stopped her agitated prowling and faced Pitney.

"The *Marguerite* sails before the week is out! Go inform Captain Duprey that we desire passage home."

"But yer pa arranged for the *Hampstead* to see you home." Pitney frowned. "The *Marguerite* is only a small merchant—"

"I know what she is!" Shanna snapped. " 'Tis the least of my father's vessels. But 'tis his and homeward bound. And I will not be refused. The *Hampstead* will not be leaving until well into the twelfth month, and I want to go home *now!*"

Tapping her toe against the plush carpet, she smiled with a calculating gleam in her eyes.

"And if he wishes to face my father when I do, Mister Ralston will have to hasten to his business as well. 'Twill give him precious little time to delve into the truth of my marriage. God help us all if he ever finds out!"

With Pitney gone and the servants moving quietly about their labors, Shanna felt strangely alone. Her spirits were far from high, and she sank into the chair at the small secretary, morose of mood and quite ill-tempered. Visions of Ruark as Pitney had described him—ragged, thin, bruised, chained, angry—contrasted oddly with the man she had seen on the steps of the church. What would change a man so, she wondered. And the answer came as she thought of a twisted face pressed against the bars of the van and the wailing cry that had followed her through the night. She knew full well the cause.

Her mind played tricks. She imagined herself beaten, abused, chained, helpless, condemned, hopeless, betrayed—

A small cry escaped her lips, and in the briefest flicker of time she felt a taste of the bitter rage that must now fill him. Angrily she pulled herself away from this morbid bent and did not allow her mind to touch it again lest she feel some further unwelcome remorse.

The bright sun spilled in rare volume through the windows. The day was crisp, cool, unusual for London at this time of year, with a clear blue sky. A fresh sea breeze had risen with the sun and swept away the low clouds and smoke, leaving the air clean and with just a hint of salt in it. Yet Shanna hardly noticed the brilliance of the day. She stared blankly at the top of the secretary, quill in hand and fine parchment nearby. Idly she began to scrawl her new name across the white sheets.

Shanna Beauchamp.

Shanna Trahern Beauchamp.

Shanna Elizabeth Beauchamp.

"Madam Beauchamp!"

"Madam? Madam Beauchamp?"

Slowly it dawned on her that she was being summoned by a voice outside her thoughts. She glanced up to see her maid standing inside the doorway holding several items of clothing, mostly heavy garb for cold weather.

"Hergus?"

"I was wondering, mum, if ye be wantin' me to pack these for the voyage home. 'Ere seems to be enough as 'tis. Or would ye be leaving 'em here for the next time?"

"Nay! If I've anything to say on the matter, I shan't be returning for a good long time. Put them in one of the larger trunks."

The Scotswoman nodded, then paused and gave Shanna a worried look. "Are ye feeling well, lass? Would ye na like to rest yerself now?" Hergus had been unusually concerned about her since the difficult moment when Shanna, with Pitney at her side, had announced her marriage and widowhood to the stunned household staff.

"I'll be all right, Hergus." Shrugging away the older woman's earnest concern, Shanna dipped the point of the long-plumed quill into the inkwell and spoke over her shoulder. "We'll be going back on the *Marguerite* before the week is out. I know 'twill rush you, but I want to go home as soon as possible."

"Aye, and well you should so yer pa can comfort ye."

As the servant's footsteps retreated down the hall, Shanna drew the quill across the parchment again. But her mind did not flow in the direction of the bold strokes she made, straying instead on its own museful venturings. She grew warm and flushed, remembering the fiery wetness against her breast, amber eyes staring down at her almost into her soul, and the last surging impalement that she had welcomed.

With a gritted groan of frustration, Shanna stabbed the quill into the well and came to her feet, sweeping her hand down the front of her wine velvet gown as if to brush aside some imperfection or the memory of a strong, hard body pressing down upon her with heated fervor.

She bent to snatch up the parchment, intending to tear it to shreds; but her eyes saw the work her hands had wrought while her thoughts drifted, the face amid the swirls and flourishes, the sketch of Ruark Beauchamp! The lips, handsome and sensual yet somehow stern, smiled at her in amused mockery while the eyes —Nay, those were not quite right, and she doubted that even a great master of art could capture them with a quill.

Irritated with herself, she rebelled against the strong grasp his memory held upon her mind, and she spat vehemently, "The knave! He's only sorry that I gave him no chance to escape. Truly that was his intention, to get me alone then flee." She flung the parchment down. " 'Twas what he wanted, and I shan't be haunted by what I didn't do."

Almost relieved, Shanna sighed, having defended herself adequately before the high magistrate of her mind, her conscience.

"I will not think of him again!" she firmly decided.

Yet even as she crossed to the window, in the innermost recesses of her thoughts, barricaded against attack, the vague challenge of amber eyes thwarted her victory.

Shanna's confrontation with Ralston was to come sooner than she expected, for it was a few hours later as she again paused in the warm sunlight coming in through the window that a landau rumbled up before the townhouse, and James Ralston alighted. He stood for a moment, rapping the riding crop he always carried against his thin thigh, as he gazed upward toward the higher levels of the mansion where her apartments were.

Shanna wrinkled her nose in distaste, sorely vexed that he had arrived before Ruark's hanging had occurred. Hastening across the room, she rallied herself to a semblance of bereavement, all the while swearing beneath her breath. She composed herself in a large wing chair before the fireplace, smoothing her wide skirts and fluffing the creamy-hued lace flounces at her elbows. She would have given the man a show of tears, but she could not strike such a mood. Then the memory came to her that when Pitney sampled from his snuff box, his eyes watered copiously for some time. If she was not mistaken, he had left it on the tea table.

"Ah, there it is!" Anxiously she flew to it and snatched up the tiny box.

Ralston was instructing the servants as they tossed his bags down from the coach, so she had time enough. As she had watched Pitney do so often, Shanna took a bit of a pinch and held it to her nostril, inhaling deeply.

"My lord!" she gasped. It was as if a searing iron were being thrust down her throat. She sneezed and sneezed and sneezed again.

Thus it was, as had been her intent, that when James Ralston entered the room, Shanna sat in a state of tearful distress, tears flowing down her cheeks and her eyes as red as if she had been weeping for hours. Daintily she dabbed at her nose with a handkerchief and sniffed loudly.

"Madam?" Ralston approached a step, his thin features tense as he tried to control his ire, his hand working on the crop.

Shanna glanced up, wiping her streaming tears with the lace handkerchief. Her chest burned, and she gasped for air.

"Oh, Ralston, 'tis you. I had not expected—"

His reply was curt. "I hastened lest I should find matters awry—"

"Oh, had you come sooner—" Shanna sniffled wistfully.

"Madam." His tone was clipped, short. "I made my way straightforth to the *Marguerite*, escorting some of the precious goods we salvaged from the grounded vessel and there found startling news awaiting me. You have commissioned Captain Duprey to take you aboard for passage home, and in the course of events I found you have been both married and widowed in my absence. Is this correct, or have I been led astray by that erring Frenchman?"

Shanna effectively used her kerchief at the corners of her eyes as a sob lifted her bosom. " 'Tis all true."

"Madam—"

"Madam Beauchamp. Madam Ruark Deverell Beauchamp," Shanna stated.

Ralston cleared his throat tersely. "Madam Beauchamp, am I to understand that in the brevity of a week you have been able to choose a husband for yourself after a full year of failure even to find a man bearable?"

"Do you regard that fact impossible, Mister Ralston?" It was difficult to hide her irritation.

"Madam, with another woman I would not in the least doubt the possibility of such an occurrence."

"And with me, Mister Ralston?" Shanna's brows raised and her eyes were less than warm. "Do you count me incapable of love?"

"Nay, madam," he answered with care, yet he recalled the extensive number of gentlemen he had himself introduced for her consideration, hoping that one of them might marry her, and, afterwards, share with him a percentage of the dowry. "It just seems, madam, that you are more selective than most."

"And so I am," she replied primly. "Otherwise I might have betrayed myself by choosing someone less dear to me than my own beloved Ruark. 'Tis irony that what so late found is so soon lost. The details of his death I care not to dwell upon, for he was taken from me swiftly, a stumble from the carriage, and he was gone. Alas, my loving Ruark."

"And you actually shared a be—"

Shanna's head snapped up in a haughty display of indignation. "Mister Ralston! Do you seek to insult me with crudeness? Or is it unusual to your mind that a husband and wife should lie together on their wedding night?"

"I beg your pardon, madam." Ralston's cheeks darkened as he realized the danger of his question.

"I do not abide this doubting of my word, and it does me ill that you should press me so. But since you have displayed your curiosity so blatantly, let me calm it. I assure you, sir, that I am no longer a maiden, and a child may be forthcoming."

Having issued that statement as any outraged widow might, Shanna turned aside, a slight frown of worry troubling her brow, for she did in truth wonder if she were carrying Ruark's seed. It was such a brief encounter, but still there might be the chance. It was not her desire to raise a child without a father. Mentally she counted the days until she would know the truth. Only time would see an end to her dismay.

Ralston misread her manner. She could well damage his lucrative relationship with her father, and the concern in his voice was real.

"Madam, I did not mean to distress you."

Shanna faced him again and then paused as she looked beyond him to see Hergus in the background. She caught the frown that briefly touched the Scotswoman's face as Mister Ralston turned also. It was with some effort that the maid maintained a semblance of respect toward the man. Having been with the Trahern family for almost twenty years, Hergus was not lacking for confidence and often expressed herself with complete frankness which did not necessarily lend to flattery. She had not approved of the men Mister Ralston had presented to her young mistress, and her dislike of Ralston had grown apace with her disdain for those he brought. It was Shanna she gave her loyalty to, and any who doubted it enough to threaten the mistress would find the fact out to their chagrin.

"What is it, Hergus?" Shanna inquired, grateful for the interruption.

The servant moved nearer. "I did not mean to intrude, but as you told me to hurry I thought I'd better ask. What have ye in mind to do with these?"

Shanna's breath caught sharply in her throat as Hergus held up the cloak and coat Ruark had left behind in the carriage. Ralston frowned slightly as he noted them to be a man's garments and peered at Shanna questioningly. She rose to the test of her wit and, sighing pensively, went to take them from Hergus. Almost tenderly she caressed the soft velvet fabric of the coat.

" 'Twas Ruark's," she murmured sadly. "He was handsome, manly, charming, and with the most persuasive smile. I fear he swept me off my feet."

Holding it carefully over her arms, Shanna presented it back to the woman.

"In one of my trunks, Hergus. I'll keep it for the memories." But already she was thinking how she would get rid of them, for the memories they stirred were anything but consoling.

Ralston's knuckles were white as he gripped the quirt, and his bony jaw grew rigid. "Your father will question me on this matter, Madam Beauchamp. I must give him answers. I must know the place where this marriage was secured and examine the documents. The Beauchamp name is well enough known here in London, but there are things I must be assured of, and I can hardly present myself to that family's door inquiring on their kin, especially in a time of bereavement. But I must acquaint myself with the validity of the marriage for your father's peace of mind."

Shanna experienced a brief moment of temptation to hurl a caustic accusation that he would do anything if it might fatten his purse. However, she managed to appear only slightly injured.

"But of course, sir. I suppose my father would not simply take my word for it." Sweeping across the room to the secretary, she retrieved the packet of documents she had won with a kiss and her virtue. "Here is your proof."

Ralston was already at her side, taking them from her and eagerly untying the scarlet ribbon. But as his eyes fell to the sheet of parchment on the desk, his interest was diverted, and he paused to stare down at it. Shanna followed his gaze and watched helplessly as the man lifted the sketch to more closely inspect it. She could not bear his eyes prying into her secret thoughts, for certainly that was what it was, a rude and callous invasion of her privacy, as surely as if he had witnessed her intimacy with Ruark in the coach.

Her resentment aroused, Shanna made to snatch the paper from him, but Ralston deftly jerked it out of her reach.

"Madam, your talents are many. I was not aware they extended to producing images of people on parchment." He considered her askance. "Your late husband?"

Reluctantly Shanna nodded. "Give it to me."

"Your father would be curious—"

In a quick movement Shanna tore the paper from his hand and ripped it into small pieces.

"Madam, why do you destroy a drawing of your husband? 'Twould appear he had all the qualities you boast. 'Twas certainly done in an amorous vein. Perhaps he won your heart as you declare."

Shanna's mind screamed—poppycock! But her spoken reply came meekly. "Aye, and it tears me so I cannot bear to look upon his likeness."

The same fair, crisp weather graced the morning after. The chill wind whipped around the buildings as Ralston stepped from the landau and clutched his cloak tighter about his long frame. He rapped the handle of his quirt on the portal of the structure until a reply came from within.

"I have business with the gaoler. Open up," he commanded.

After a brief rattle of keys, the iron door swung aside, and he went within. A guard led him through the halls until he was ushered before the turnkey.

"Ah, Mister Hicks," he began heartily. "I find I shall be returning to the island sooner than expected. I've come to see what good merchandise you have for me."

"But, gov'na—" the fat man came to his feet stuttering and wringing his stubby hands, "but, Mister Ralston, I've naught else but what ye've already chosen."

"Oh, come now, my good man." Ralston laughed with little humor as he drew off his leather gloves, wrapped them carefully around the riding crop, then grasped the crop in his slim hand and slapped his leg. "You must have some good young debtors or even a thief or two who would see their paper redeemed for a chance to escape this hole. You know my master pays well with a goodly tithe for the men who serve him." He poked Mister Hick's rolling belly with his whip and smiled coyly. " 'Twould mean some more good coin for your purse."

"But, gov'na—" the gaoler grinned worriedly. "I swear 'ere are none."

"Oh, come now!" Ralston snapped, his irritation showing. "That last bunch will scarce endure a year or two in the cane fields." He slapped his narrow thigh impatiently with the crop. "You must have some new ones. And of course you understand that healthy women and older children are not without their worth in the Caribbean." His thin-featured face frowned ominously. "My master will berate me heavily if I do not show him better than those for his money."

"But—gov'na!" Mister Hicks cried and sweated more, if that were possible. " 'Ere are simply—"

A commotion outside the room interrupted, and the heavy door from the main gaol was pushed open. A guard thrust through, tugging at a long length of chain attached to a man who was weighted with as many iron links and shackles as he could carry. Another guard walked behind, also bearing a lengthy chain attached to the prisoner who showed recent signs of abuse. A swollen eyelid and a thick, bloody lip distorted his face. The short stride of his anklets caused him to stumble, and, for his clumsiness, he received a jabbing blow to the ribs. A grunt of pain issued from the bruised mouth but little else. The two guards were about to lead the prisoner through to the outside yard when Ralston, a fine judge of flesh, put out a hand to stop them.

"Go no further!" His eyes gleamed at Hicks. "You clever swine, you. You've held out on me for a higher price."

Ralston moved closer to better survey the prisoner and after a moment turned sharply to the gaoler.

"Let's not dally, man. I need him. Get straight to the price. What are you asking?"

"But, gov'na!" Poor Hicks was almost apoplectic. "I would na sell—I mean I can't—'E's to the gallows on the morrow and right now bound to the common cell to join the others to be hanged."

Slapping the long, black riding crop Ralston stared at Hicks for a long time. Finally he paused and drew himself up, folding his arms. His shadowed eyes were like a hawk's fixed on a plump rabbit.

"Now, Hicks—"

The fat man jumped with the sound of his voice.

"I know you and some of the—ah—wonders you have worked in the past. A tidy sum for a young one like that, there is."

The gaoler trembled and seemed about to drop to his knees. "But—I can't. The bloke's a murderer, condemned to 'ang, 'e is. Why, I must certify the very—and 'ere's 'is name—" The words stuck in Hicks's throat.

"I care naught for his name. Let him be called by a new one."

At that, a sly look came into the gaoler's eyes, and Ralston did not waste a moment.

"Come, man, buck up." His voice grew wheedling. "Use your head. Who's to know? Why, it could mean as much as—," he shrugged and almost whispered in Hicks's ear, "why, two hundred pounds in your pocket, a tuppence for the guards here, and none the wiser."

Hicks's greed began to gleam in his small eyes. "Aye," he murmured softly, half to himself. " 'Ere's even a body, an ol' man what's been here for years—forgotten—died in his cell las' night. Why, it just might come off. Aye!"

He leered at Ralston, speaking low where none would hear. "Two 'undred pounds? For the likes o' 'im?"

"Aye, man." Ralston nodded. "He's young and strong. 'Twill only be a few days before we sail, but you must keep him hidden. Will there be kin to claim him?" At Hicks's nod Ralston continued. "Then give them the other body tomorrow in a closed coffin with the magistrate's seal upon it so they dare not open it. I'll pick him up with the rest of the men the day before we sail."

Ralston marked Hicks with his penetrating stare.

"I shall expect the man to be carefully handled to let the best of our bargain stand. Do you understand?"

An energetic nod, setting the rolls around Hicks's neck aquiver with an undulating motion, asserted the fact that he well understood.

The business finished, Ralston made his way back to the landau, half smiling as he mentally tallied: two hundred to Hicks, and Trahern would go a good fifteen hundred for a man such as that, thirteen hundred for himself. He smirked in satisfaction and drew on his gloves. He began to hum a tuneless ditty as he leaned back in the seat and enjoyed the ride back to the townhouse.

It was the twenty-fourth of November when Pitney made his way to Tyburn. He had little liking for a hanging, and he felt in dire need of something to fortify his wits. With this in mind he entered a dramshop and loudly called for a pitcher of ale to see him through. The hanging matches always drew a big crowd, and the tavern was alive with those who waited for them to begin. Choosing the only seat available, Pitney settled himself beside a small, wiry, red-haired Scotsman of an age about twoscore. The man was already well sodden with gin and gave him a lame smile. Pitney had not intended to indulge in words, but as the Scotsman was clearly sorrowed by some great tragedy, Pitney sat and mutely nodded while the other spilled out the tale of his life. Some moments later Pitney rose to his feet with a sudden oath and grabbing up his tricorn, left the establishment without further ado and charged off on his way to the gallows. The crowd was thick, and more than once Pitney came close to overturning a whole cluster of people who seemed inclined to bar his way. His elbows sent some flying, and he pushed near to where the guards were unloading the prisoners from the cart. He saw none he recognized as Ruark Beauchamp. One of the gaoler's men passed, and Pitney grabbed the front of his coat, demanding:

"Where is the colonial, Ruark Beauchamp? Was he not to hang today?"

"Let go o' me, ye bloody toad! Be off wit' ye. I got business o' me own."

With one thick, brawny hand, he snatched the guard close until the two men stared nose to nose.

"Where is Ruark Beauchamp?" Pitney roared. "Or would ye be wantin' yer head on backwards?"

The guard's eyes bugged, and he loudly gulped. " 'E's dead, 'e is. They took him out in the van an' 'anged him at dawn, afore the crowds gathered."

Pitney shook the man until his teeth rattled. "*Are you sure?*"

"Aye!" the guard croaked. "Hicks brought him back in a

box. 'E's all sealed up fer 'is kin. Let go!' "

Slowly the heavy hands loosened, and the man slithered to his feet in relief. Incensed, Pitney ground a white-knuckled fist into his beefy palm and snarled a curse. He spun on his heels and returned with the same rapid pace to the dramshop, flinging the door open with a thundering whack. His narrowed gray eyes carefully searched the room, but no sign of the Scotsman remained.

It was a long ride back to Newgate, and Pitney enjoyed it even less than he had earlier surmised. Receiving the same story of Ruark's death from Hicks, he could do naught but accept the closed coffin with the name Ruark Beauchamp burned on its top. John Craddock helped him place the box into a horse-drawn cart, and Pitney journeyed to a small, deserted byre on the outskirts of London. There, securing the doors behind him, he began his work. He dragged a heavier, more ornate casket to the cart and placed it near the one from the prison.

It was much later when Pitney tapped with a chisel, marring the threads of the bolts so the lid of the ornate casket might not be loosened without considerable effort. Its contents were well protected against whatever eyes might pry. As Pitney worked, a strange smile flitted across his face, coming and going like the fleeting flight of a miller moth around a candle.

Taking the casket to a secluded churchyard, Pitney laid it beside an open grave and informed the rector of his delivery and of the burial on the morrow. Then he proceeded in all haste to bear the news to his mistress.

Ralston was at the townhouse, and Shanna seemed impatient. Pitney felt himself growing awkward, not knowing how to tell her without Ralston overhearing.

Finally Pitney stumbled out, "Yer husband—" he twisted his tricorn in his hands as Shanna gasped and stared at him with new attention—"yer husband—Mister Beauchamp—"

Ralston's brows lifted with interest.

" 'Tis been taken care of, and the prior has set the time for two hours after midday on the morrow."

What began as a sigh of relief ended in tearful sobs as Shanna hid her face and fled. Mounting the stairs, she darted into her bedchamber and slammed the door behind her, closing out the world as she leaned against the portal. A dull ache knotted within her chest, and as she stared at her bed she almost wished it could have been different. Now her widow's role was true. Sadly she regarded herself in the tall looking glass, waiting for a feeling of triumph, but strangely it never came.

The *Marguerite*, like the daisy for which she was named, was small and somewhat plainly crafted. She was a Boston-built, two-masted brig, longer, lower, and slimmer than the English ships that shared the slip with her. The cargo that overflowed her hold was lashed down in every available spot. The weight of the cargo lowered the hull in the water until the brig's main deck was only a pike's length above the cobbled surface of the pier. Her captain, Jean Duprey, a short, stocky Frenchman, was as sudden of smile as of frown and flourished a quicksilver wit that made him likable to his crew. His years in service to Trahern numbered six, and if he had a fault it was that he had a great weakness for women. He knew every plank of the ship, every nook and cranny beneath the deck, and he saw every space fully laden with cargo. The *Marguerite* was small; but there was a well-scrubbed and newly painted look about her that spoke of loving care, and her canvas, though mended, was sound.

This was the end of the trading season in the northern climes. Goods for Los Camellos left in the Trahern warehouse were to be divided between the *Marguerite* and a much larger, grander ship, the *Hampstead*, which would set sail in December. Odds and ends of cordage, pitch, and tar went to the smaller vessel, along with other much-needed everyday items. Of special interest were four long, slim barrels carefully crated and treated with much respect by the handlers. Captain Duprey made sure they were securely stowed in the main hold. Trahern had ordered cannons from a German gunsmith, and it was rumored they could shoot twice as far as any gun yet cast. The squire would be put out if harm came to them.

The wan sun had lowered, and the day grew cold, bringing up vapors from the waters of the Thames. Final preparations for the following day's sailing were being rushed, for soon the gray vapors would join and form into a dense hazardous fog that would end the labors. Shanna's trunks were hoisted aboard, the larger ones going to the hold, while the smaller ones, containing those things necessary to meet her needs on the voyage, were placed in her cabin, recently vacated by the first officer and the mate. These accommodations proved scant; the cabin hardly provided room for Shanna and Hergus to move about at the same time. As the only women aboard they would share the tiny compartment. A sturdy iron bolt had been placed on the inside of the door by Pitney, limiting the prospect of unwelcome visitors. Any ideas the men might have had concerning the two women were quickly dispelled, for the servant hung his hammock on the deck near the passageway leading to their cabin. Though Pitney was not in sight now, both Shanna and Hergus had no doubt their safety aboard the vessel was guaranteed, if not by the knowledge of the justice that Trahern himself would mete out upon any who injured or seriously offended his daughter or her maid, then by the sure and certain fact that Pitney's revenge would come far more swiftly.

The fog had slowed much of the activity aboard, and a sense of impatience grew. Standing beside Hergus at the rail, Shanna felt the mood of the crew and captain as well, but laid it to her eagerness to be gone from London and homeward bound. Attending the burial of Ruark had been a highly distasteful task. It had proven difficult explaining to Ralston why the Beauchamp family was not in attendance, and finally she had insisted that it was her own wish for a private service, and, as she had naught but a few days left in England, the Beauchamps had conceded to her desire, granting the new bride that last privilege with her husband.

It was Ralston whom they waited for now, Ralston and the bondsmen he had gone to collect. It had long been the agent's practice to beat the alleyways and inns until the last possible moment for those who would accept bondage for a chance to be free of the squalor of London Common. In these times of relative peace there were hands aplenty to be had, though few of any worth. Some in the past had even been purchased from debtor's prison, but the good workers were those who sought to better themselves. These were the ones the squire valued, and he had often voiced his objection to a man taken into bondage against his will and had sternly instructed Ralston along these lines. Yet there were new cane fields to harvest, and the urgency for more hands was acute.

The last of the cargo had been stowed and hatches closed and secured against the morrow's sailing. As the heavy mist drifted across the deck, the slight creaking of the ship and the slow lap of water against the pier seemed the only touch with reality. Lanterns on the dock below were pale islands in the surrounding blackness. Lights hanging on the bow of the ship ebbed and brightened like twinkling stars. Somewhere in the shreds of the mist, the laughter of a man mingled with a shrill feminine giggle, sounding eerie and strange in the stillness. But as the revelry faded, the silence closed in again like some tangible thing.

Shivering with the chill that penetrated her woolen gown, Shanna snuggled deeper into the green velvet cloak, lifting a stray lock of hair off her neck and tucking it into the smoothly coiled knot at her nape before raising the hood to cover her head against the dampness.

A rattle of wheels on the cobblestones sounded below, and Shanna leaned over the rail as a wagon drew out of the thickening haze and halted near the ship. Ralston's landau was close behind, but the two vehicles were only dark shadows in the fog. Shanna had to strain to recognize the thin, bony frame of her father's agent as he directed the unloading of the bondsmen. Then the clanking of chains stabbed Shanna's awareness, and she drew a sharp breath as she realized that the men were fettered hand and foot and to each other. Therein lay much of the difficulty, for the iron lengths were not long enough to allow just one man to descend alone. There were stumbles and falls as they filed out. Prodding by the several guards did not help the situation, nor did the hearty curses they applied with verve, warming Shanna's ears considerably.

"Why must he chain them?" Shanna snapped as Hergus leaned over the rail to have a look.

"That I wouldna know, mum."

"Well, we'll see if he has a good reason."

In rising temper Shanna descended the gangplank and strode toward Ralston, a growing desire to vent her rage urging her on as she sought his dark shape in the mist.

"Mister Ralston!" Her voice crackled with ire.

The agent swung about quickly and seeing Shanna approach, hurried to intercept her.

"Madam," he called. "Come no further. These are not the usual—"

"What is the meaning of this?" Shanna demanded indignantly and slowed her pace only when he stood before her. "There can be little cause to treat good men like swine, Mister Ralston. Unchain them!"

"But, madam, I cannot."

"Cannot!" Shanna repeated incredulously. She flung her arms akimbo beneath the enveloping cloak. "You forget your place, Mister Ralston! How dare you tell me nay!"

"Madam," he implored. "These men—"

"Do not burden my ear with excuses," she returned sharply. "If these men are to be of any use to my father, they cannot be beaten and bruised and worn raw with chains. The voyage will be hard enough on them."

The thin man half pleaded, half argued. "Madam, I cannot free them here on the dock. I have paid your father's good money, and most would fly if given the chance. At least let me see them—"

"Mister Ralston." Shanna's tone was firm yet bitingly calm. "I said release them. Now!"

"But, Madam Beauchamp!"

Suddenly one of the bondsmen nearby halted in mid-stride, and the others about him staggered as their chains slapped and jerked about their ankles. A loud shout bellowed from a guard who ran toward him.

" 'Ere, ye bloody beggar! Get a move on now. Do ye think ye be takin' a stroll through Covent Garden?"

He raised his cudgel to clout the shackled man, catching Shanna's eye. Angrily she whirled around, flinging the hood back to her shoulders, and the bondsman cowered away, covering his head with his arms as if more afraid of her than any club his tormentor would use.

"You abuse my father's property!" Shanna was aghast at the audacity of the escort. She stepped toward them as if to take action herself upon the stammering guard, but she found her arm seized in Ralston's hand.

"Madam, do not trust these men." His concern was genuine, for he knew the penalty if harm came to Squire Trahern's daughter. "They are desperate and would—"

Seething, Shanna slowly faced the agent. Her tone was low and scathing as she demanded, "Take your hand from me!"

In a helpless gesture the man nodded his head and obeyed. "Madam Beauchamp, your father bound me to your safety—"

"My father would banish you from Los Camellos if he knew of your treatment of these men," Shanna snapped. "Do not tempt me to enlighten him, Mister Ralston."

The muscles in his narrow jaw worked. "Madam has grown spurs since her marriage."

"Aye," Shanna assured him heartily. "And they're sharp. Take heed lest they prick you."

"It bemuses me, madam, why you are ever at odds with me. Do I attend your father's bidding?"

She scoffed caustically. "Only too well."

"Then madam, where is the wrong in that?" His hawkish eyes fixed on her.

"The wrong is what you do in the course of keeping my father's commands," she flung sharply. "If you had any degree of decency—"

Ralston's dark brow raised mockingly. "Like your late husband, madam?"

Shanna's first instinct was to slap his leering face. She was filled with almost uncontrollable loathing for the man, and no mere words could do justice to the way she felt. With jaw set she cast a glare behind her to the guard who stood decidedly less menacing, his gangling arms hanging to his sides. The bondsman was scarcely to be seen, having crowded himself in the midst of his fellow companions, out of harm's way.

A shout from the ship echoed through the misty haze, bringing Shanna's attention to Captain Duprey who leaped down the gangway and rushed to join them.

"Mon Dieu! What iz this?" he insisted.

He saw the bondsmen standing silently and assayed the situation quickly.

"You zere!" He almost danced as he waved his arm at the

guards. "Get these men aboard and take zhem below. Ze mate will direct you. Go now!"

Captain Duprey's swarthy face beamed in a wide smile as he faced Shanna. He swept his plumed tricorn flamboyantly before his stocky frame as he bowed from the waist.

"Madame Beauchamp, you should not be here on the dock," he very tenderly admonished. "And certainment not so near zese filthy wretches."

Shanna coyly implored him with both speech and eye, "Captain Duprey, I cannot tolerate chains, and I would see these poor men treated more reasonably." She delayed a moment in her plea until the last bondslave had passed onto the ship, then entreated, "They're on your ship now, captain. I beg of you, have the chains struck and treat them well."

"Madame!" The thin black mustache twitched upward as he grinned, and his black eyes flashed with warm lights. "I cannot refuse. I shall zee to eet immediatement."

"Sir!" The sharp bark from Ralston halted him. "I warn you! They are my charges, and I will give the orders—"

Captain Duprey held up a hand to stop him as he gazed again into those soft, pleading blue-green eyes. "Madame Beauchamp iz right!" he defended gallantly. "No man should be bound in iron chains. With ze salt, zey rot ze skin and it takes weeks to heal."

Seizing Shanna's small hand impulsively, the Frenchman pressed a kiss to it fervently. "I go at your bidding, madame," he murmured and dashed away like one on a dire errand.

Ralston snorted his disgust but knew he had lost. He spun on his heels and stalked away.

Content with her victory, Shanna watched him go, a self-satisfied smile curving her lovely lips. But realizing she now stood alone on the dock, she lifted her skirts and began to hurry toward the ship. Heavy footsteps followed her and, pausing with pounding heart, she found Pitney close behind her. There was, after all, no cause to fear, but it was the slow, amused grin spreading across the man's lips as he stared after Ralston that gave her cause to puzzle.

Well before dawn Shanna was awakened by the chant of

voices from the main deck. Still drowsy with slumber, she raised her head from the pillow but could see no light of morning through the thick, small windows in the cabin. More shouts from above told her the ship was being winched out on her anchor chain into the main stream of the Thames. With a slight rocking motion, the vessel rode free and then steadied as the sails were spread to catch the early offshore breeze. With the gentle swaying of the ship, Shanna was soon snuggled deep within the downy folds of sleep.

The first night underway Madam Beauchamp was formally invited to share the captain's table with several of his officers and Ralston. Through the following weeks it became the routine and most often the high spot of the day. It broke the monotony of the voyage whenever the group gathered to partake of the evening's repast, share a glass of wine or two from the fine and varied stock, and engage in light repartee. The French cook was a man of considerable talent, and the meals were provided with a pleasant note of decorum, for a young cabin boy, garbed in spotless white, served the table. Having been acquainted with the captain and his officers for several years, Shanna enjoyed the hour and displayed her most gay and charming wit beneath their chivalrous attentions. Ralston, however, was inclined to join these affairs with reluctance. He might not have at all, but his only other options were to dine with the crew or alone on the deck. Sourly he grumbled at the richness of the fare and had the brashness to comment after a full seven courses had been served of especially delectable cuisine, and just when they were enjoying the "issue de la table" of crystallized fruit and sugared almonds, that he would have much preferred a good Welsh kidney stew. His remark was met with carefully blank stares from table mates.

It was the evening of the third Sunday out, after a fine sunny day. The brig heeled slightly alee, a steady breeze filling her sails, and showed a fine beam to the windward. Shanna was light of heart as she made her way to the captain's cabin for the customary evening dinner. With the little vessel pressing ever closer to her home, she tasted a growing anticipation. The sun was gone but had been replaced by a bright new moon as December was well upon them. The night air was balmy and warm, for they were near the southern climes.

From somewhere below deck a voice could be heard singing in a rich baritone. The tune was timed to mark the slow, gentle roll of the *Marguerite* as she skimmed along, treading the miles beneath her keel. The breezes would have snatched the words away, scattering them to the sea, but the haunting strains eluded the airy rushes of wind and drifted stirringly across the deck to Shanna. Wistfully she gazed toward the starlit sky as the melody invaded her mood, and she could almost imagine her own heart's love, faceless and nameless, calling to her as he came over the waters. Some strange quality in the voice held her enthralled with its magic, and she was bound in its spell as the words were crooned:

> Vair me o' rovan o
> Vair me o' rovan ee
> Vair me a-ruo-ho
> Sad am I without thee.

> When I'm lonely, dear white heart
> Black the night or wild the sea
> By love's light my foot finds
> The old pathway to thee.

Warm phantom arms crept about her, and Shanna closed her eyes with the ecstasy of it. A hoarse whisper flitted through her mind, "Yield to me. Yield to me," and her senses reeled in giddy delight. The vision stirred and broadened and became piercing amber eyes and a snarling sneer upon a handsome face. "Damn you deceiving little bitch!"

The illusion scattered, and Shanna's eyes flew open. With a gritted oath, she whirled and entered the passageway to the captain's cabin. At her sharp rap on the door, it was quickly opened, and the swarthy man bowed a flamboyant greeting.

"Ahhh, Madame Beauchamp! You are too radiant for mere words," Captain Duprey exclaimed. "I am your humble servant, madame, now and evermore. Come in. Come in."

Forcing a smile, Shanna swept in. She paused in sharp surprise as she realized they were alone in the cabin but for the young boy who waited patiently to serve them.

"Is there no one else this evening?" she questioned in dismay.

Jean Duprey's eyes gleamed warmly as he fingered his dark mustache. "My officers have found duties to take zem elsewhere, Madame Beauchamp."

"And Mister Ralston?" Shanna raised a quizzical brow in annoyance, wondering what errand the captain could send him on.

"Ah—he—" Jean Duprey chuckled and shrugged. "He found ze crew was taking salt beef and beans and convinced ze cook to have a plate of it sent to him. Thus it is, madame—ah—" He seemed to stumble over her name then continued cajolingly as he tried to take her hand. "May I address you by your given name—Shanna?"

With something of a pained smile, Shanna firmly withdrew from him. She was somewhat curious as to what Madame Duprey thought of her husband's amorous bent and his apparent impartial fondness for women. Inclined to leave the harsh discipline at that woman's door instead of causing an embarrassing scene, Shanna was lenient with the man and spoke with quiet grace.

"Captain Duprey, I knew my husband for only a short time, and he was taken from me not a month ago. I find the use of that familiarity too painful. Pray forgive me. I came here to seek the companionship of many and thus mask my sorrow. I beg you indulge my mourning. His was a stirring manner, and you have awakened memories of fond moments we shared, brief though they were. If you'll excuse me this evening, sir, I must seek solace somewhere else."

Jean made as if to follow, but Shanna put up a soft, white hand to halt him.

"Nay, captain. There is a time even for loneliness." Her voice quivered sadly while the aroma in the room reminded her of her hunger. "But there is one thing—"

Captain Duprey nodded eagerly, anxious to please her.

"Could you send a small plate of whatever fare there is to my cabin later? I will no doubt be able to endure the sight of food by then."

She swept into a delightful curtsy, and when she straightened, the corners of her lovely lips smiled upward mischievously.

"Remember me to your wife when we reach Los Camellos, captain."

Before he could gather his wits, Shanna fled and slammed the door behind her. The sound of her hurrying footsteps echoed in the stillness of the passageway, but she breathed a sigh of relief only when she was again on deck and could see Pitney. He was partaking of a goodly portion of salt beef, sea biscuits and beans. As she came from the companionway, he glanced up from his plate, studied her for a moment, then nodded, needing no explanation to realize her reason for fleeing the captain's cabin. Jean Duprey's infatuation with women was hardly a secret among the men on Los Camellos.

Thoughtfully Shanna strolled across the deck to the leeward side of the vessel. The white clouds took on dark shadows with silver edges as they passed between the high moon and the gently rolling sea. The light breezes touched Shanna. The night was still but for the gurgle of water passing beneath the hull and the creak of rigging and masts. The ship seemed to play a song of its own, a rhythmic whisper of sound that matched the gentle rise and fall of the hull as it took the sea beneath its heels.

Venting a long sigh, Shanna turned away from the rail. For all of her earlier jubilance, she felt pensive and lonely now, as if the night had lost its savor. The voice, wandering up from below decks, had snatched her happiness, and she could only wonder what it would have been like to share a marriage bed for a full, long night.

Chapter 5

IT was as if a tall, billowing cloud had given birth to a spot of emerald green. Several low hills crowded close upon a buff strand of beach which separated the living green from the tumbling surf that licked the naked shore with white-crested tongues of foam. The deep blue of the open sea gave way in the shallows near the island to a brilliant iridescent green that matched the shade of Shanna's eyes.

The *Marguerite* came from beneath her own cloud, and her sun-bleached sails gleamed white in the brightness of the day. A puff of smoke drifted from the peak of the tallest hill on Los Camellos, and some moments later the dull boom of the signal gun reached them. The brig moved closer to her goal. Long verdant arms could be seen encircling a spacious cove, in the nape of which lay the sparkling whitewashed buildings of the village, Georgiana. A darker hue in the waters marked the open channel of approach straight between those arms to the harbor the hamlet served.

There were few on the island who did not drop whatever they were doing at the sound of the cannon and rush to the dock to greet the new arrival. There would be trinkets to exchange, special favors long awaited and, more importantly, the latest news and gossip from the world at large. Orlan Trahern himself was still much the merchant rather than planter, and it was a dire chore indeed that could stay the squire from mounting to his carriage and coming down to see how fortune favored him. If it was a strange vessel, there would be dickering and bargaining which he welcomed for the challenge and played as if it were a game.

Impatiently Shanna waited as the sails were dropped and the *Marguerite* coasted to an easy berth at the pier. Several other ships in the harbor were withdrawn from the dock and anchored aside. Through the winter months the larger ones would be careened and repaired, while smaller ones would ply the islands south and west, trading the goods of the Continent for the raw material of the Caribbean.

The gangplank thudded down as the hawses were winched snug. Shanna's heart nearly soared as high as the sea gulls cavorting overhead, and eagerly her eyes searched the crowd gathering below for the familiar face of her father.

Pitney appeared at her side, two of her lesser trunks tucked beneath his arms, and trailed behind as she descended. As Shanna stepped from the plank, Captain Duprey was there to offer his assistance, having made sure his wife was nowhere in the crowd. His dark eyes begged for some show of warmth in the exquisite oval face, but he was much disappointed, for Shanna hardly noticed him in her haste to be off the ship. As if he were only a servant fit for menial tasks, she thrust a frilly parasol into his hand and glanced anxiously about. Beyond the throng Trahern's open barouche stood empty. But then the crowd separated as the squire came forward, almost hurrying to meet her. A wide grin parted his lips as he saw her, but he quickly squelched that show of pleasure.

Orlan Trahern was slightly shorter than the men around him, but his shoulders were broad, and his body was square. He moved with a deliberate stride, his weight carried easily, for though he was wide of girth there was a great strength in him. Shanna had seen him best Pitney in an arm wrestle for a mug of ale. When stirred to laughter, his whole frame would shake, though the mirth itself would be muted.

With a glad cry Shanna flew to her father and threw her arms about his stout neck. For a brief moment Trahern's arms encircled her slim waist, then he thrust her gently away to lean on his long, gnarled walking stick and give her a sober perusal. With a clear, tinkling laugh Shanna raised her wide skirts of pale blue lawn, danced in a slow circle before him, and then faced him again with a low curtsy.

"Your servant, squire."

"Aye, daughter." He pursed his lips and contemplated her as if seeing her anew. " 'Twould seem you've outdone yourself and grown even more beautiful in the year past."

He half turned, settling onto his head the broad, low-crown hat he affected as his eyes fixed on Captain Duprey.

"And as ever you have men trailing after you to do your favors."

Jean Duprey shifted the parasol in his hands as if he would have liked to find someplace to throw it but then finally handed it back to Shanna. Making the excuse of seeing to his ship, he rapidly retreated before Squire Trahern's amused countenance.

"Have you become more tolerant of hardships, girl? I would not have guessed it in you to lower yourself to travel on such a humble vessel. 'Tis more your wont to enjoy the luxuries of life."

"Now, papa," Shanna beamed. "Be kind. I was anxious to be home. Will you deny that you're happy to see me?"

Orlan Trahern cleared his throat sharply then peered at Pitney who seemed to be having trouble maintaining a sober face. The squire thrust out his hand to the man as the trunks were set to the ground.

"Aye, you're fit," Trahern nodded. "No worse the wear for escorting this lass about for a year. 'Twas oft I questioned my judgment in just sending Ralston to guide you both, but you're here safe, and I suppose that nothing unduly disastrous 'has happened."

Nervously Shanna opened her parasol and, twirling it above her head, managed a brilliant smile for her father.

"Come along, daughter," he half ordered. "The noon hour is at hand, and we shall share a bite together while you give me news."

Orlan clapped Pitney upon the back.

"You'll be wanting to see yourself home I would guess. Cool

your ale, and I'll be along later to best you in a game of chess. Let me get this twit settled properly first."

The squire led his daughter along without fanfare though the people closed around them to shout greetings to Shanna and thrust out hands in welcome. Word had been passed with the first sight of her, and even now stragglers joined the edge of the crowd. In sheer enjoyment Shanna laughed as old friends and favored ones pressed forward. Women from the village jostled close if only to stare at her gown and coiffure, seeing there the latest of fashions, while children fought to touch a finger to the hem of her skirt. Men were present as well, but those not familiar with Trahern's daughter were given to hanging back to stare in awe at her fabled beauty. It was slow passage but filled with excitement and the renewal of fond acquaintances.

Assisted by her father Shanna mounted the carriage at last, and the barouche moved briskly away from the dock. Shanna leaned back, watching the familiar houses and trees roll by. Inwardly she braced herself for that which she knew would come. They were clear of the village and well on the road to the manor when Trahern, without glancing at her, broached the subject. His voice was so abrupt it gave her a small start.

"Have ye had enough of thither and yondering, daughter, or have you set your heart upon a husband?"

His brawny hand lay firm upon his stout knee, and it was there Shanna placed her own so the plain gold band on her finger was ready to the eye.

"You may call me Madam Beauchamp, papa, if not by my given name." Her eyelids fluttered downward, and she ventured a peep at him from their corners. "But alas," she let sadness creep into her voice, "there is also something I must tell you that is most distressing."

Shanna felt strange in her tale, for his eyes, the same shade as her own, turned in silent question to her. Unable to meet them, she averted her face. Tears came, though much in part from shame at her deceit.

"A man I met, most gallant, most handsome—we wed." She swallowed hard as the lie grew more bitter on her tongue. "After one brief night of bliss,"—she dissolved in grief for a moment and then forced herself to continue—"he stepped from our carriage and turned his foot upon a stone. Before the surgeons could do aught, he died."

Orlan Trahern slammed his staff against the floor of the barouche with an unworded curse.

"Oh, papa," Shanna sobbed tearfully. "I was so late a beloved bride and so soon a widow."

With a snort Trahern turned from her and sat quietly staring off into the distance, deep in thought. The well-traveled road passed between thick groves of palms and stretched into the sunlight again. The daughter quieted her weeping and, for the most part holding her peace, gave only an occasional sniffle until they reached the sprawling white mansion. Riotous colors flooded the lawn as poincianas unfolded their scarlet blooms, and clusters of fuchsia frangipani graced the air with sweet scent. The neatly clipped lawn spread as far as the eye could see, broken at regular intervals by the great trunks of towering trees that spread thick foliage high at their tops. Only rare shafts of sunlight pierced the crowns, dappling the wide porticos that stretched endlessly along the front and wings of the mansion. Covered archways of white-washed brick shaded the raised veranda bordering the house on the main floor, while on the second story ornate wooden posts lined the long porch with sections of latticework, lending privacy to the separate chambers. The mansion was weighted down by a steep-pitched roof bedecked with dormers. French doors were an easy access to the porches from most any room in the great house, and the small, square panes of crystal within the doors sparkled with the mottled light, showing the care and attention of many servants.

Trahern sat silent, unmoving as the barouche halted, and Shanna glanced at him with a certain amount of trepidation, not willing to break his mood. She made her own way from the carriage and up the wide steps to the broad veranda, there pausing uncertainly to glance back. Her father sat still, but his head turned and he stared at her, his brow heavily furrowed in thought. Laboriously he rose, stepped down, then slowly climbed the stairs as if his cane were leading him by the hand. Shanna went ahead to the front door and opened it, waiting for him. Several paces away he stopped and peered at her again. The wonderment left his face and slowly was replaced by rage. Suddenly he raised the stick high over his head and threw it flat upon the porch.

"Dammit, girl!"

The door slammed shut as Shanna's hand flew to her throat, and she shrank away from him, eyes wide with fear.

"Do you take so little care of your men?" he roared. "I would have at least seen the lad!" In a slightly lower tone he inquired, "Could you not keep him alive 'til you got with babe?"

In some awe of her father, Shanna replied softly. "There is still that chance, papa. We did spend our wedding night—together. 'Twas only a week before we sailed, and I know not—"

She blushed slightly at the lie, for she was as certain now as a woman could be that she bore no seed of Ruark's in her belly.

"Bah!" Trahern snorted and stomped past her, leaving his cane where it lay and letting the door slam again behind him.

Meekly Shanna retrieved the stick and followed her father into the house. She paused a moment in the entrance hall as all the memories of her years in the manor came flooding back with a rush. She could almost imagine herself a child again, squealing with excitement as she raced down the staircase that seemed to curve around on itself and encircle the long, crystal chandelier suspended from the lofty ceiling. The shimmering prisms that set the hall aglow with myriad dancing rainbows had always been a source of fascination for her. And she could well remember scooting on all fours upon the marble floor as she searched around the large and lavish ever present ferns and greenery that bedecked the room for the small, darting kitten Pitney had given her, or when she stared up in awe at the portrait of her mother which hung near the drawing room door, or squirmed with girlish impatience upon the large carved chest which sat below it while she waited for her father to return from a tour of his fields.

Now as a woman Shanna saw the bleached woodwork of the balustrade and the carved panels of the French doors, which led to other rooms off the entranceway gleaming with touches of gilt. Here and throughout the house, furniture of the French Régence style was in abundance. Rich Aubusson carpets, rugs from Persia, laquers, jade and ivory from the Orient, marbles from Italy, and other treasured pieces from around the world tastefully embellished the rooms.

Long hallways jutted in opposite directions from the spacious foyer, leading into the wings. To the left were her father's large chambers including the library and study where he worked, a sitting room, his bedchamber, and a room in which he bathed and dressed with the assistance of a valet.

Shanna's own chambers were up the curving stairs and to the right, well away from the squire's quarters. There, before gaining the sleeping chamber, one had to pass through her sitting room, where walls of soft cream moire complemented the subtle hues of brown, mauve, and vibrant turquoise of the chairs and settee. A luxurious Aubusson carpet combined all the colors in an ornate pattern. Rich mauve silk covered the walls of her bedroom. On the floor was spread a carpet of brown and mauve. A pale pink silk canopy hung from the large tester bed, while a brown watered silk chaise waited to be reclined upon.

The memories dissipated as her father glared back over his shoulder at her. Grumbling beneath his breath, he turned back and bellowed up the stairs, setting the crystal chandelier gently atremble above the foyer.

"Berta!"

The answer was immediate. "Yah! Yah! I come!"

The housekeeper's light clogs beat a rapid tattoo on the circular stairway, betraying her haste. She came in view, breathless and rosy-cheeked. The Dutch woman barely topped Shanna's shoulder and was plump and round with a fair complexion. She never seemed to move at less than a trot, and her feather duster was always tucked into her long apron's pocket. It was mainly through her efforts and her charge over the servants that the mansion was kept spotlessly clean.

Berta paused a long pace from Shanna, staring at her in awed wonder. After Georgiana's death the housekeeper had taken over in her firm Dutch manner and had on more than one occasion watched tearfully from the door as her protégée departed for Europe. Though it had only been a year, the girl had still been much of a child when she had left home, but now she stood regal, self-assured, poised—a graceful young woman of stunning beauty. Thus is was that the old servant was not quite sure how to approach her. It was Shanna who solved the dilemma. She flung her arms wide, and in the next second the two were clasped together, sharing tears of joy as kisses were exchanged and cheeks were pressed lovingly together. Finally Berta stood away.

"Ah, m'poor babe. Have ya finally come home to stay?" Not waiting for an answer, Berta rushed on. "Yah, dat fool Trahern, he send away his own daughter. Is like cutting da nose from his face. And he leave dat boob Pitney to take care of a young girl. Dat big ox, ha!"

Trahern chafed at her prodding and roared for Milan to fetch him a rum and bitters as he felt himself in need of a strong libation. Berta clucked her tongue at him, and her wide blue eyes danced in merriment as she turned them back to the young woman.

"Let me look at ya now. Yah, I'd lay a guilder ya've done da best of dem all. Ya be lovely, darling, and I missed ye so, I have."

"Oh, Berta!" Shanna exclaimed ecstatically. "I'm so happy to be home!"

Jason, the doorman, came from the back, and at the sight of Shanna his black face lit up with pleasure.

"Why, Mistress Shanna!" He rushed forward and took her extended hands, his clipped, well-schooled voice surprising her as it always did. "Lord, child, you add the sun to the sky with your return. Your father has been most anxious to see you."

A loud clearing of the throat gave evidence that Trahern was still in earshot, but Shanna giggled happily. She was home at last, and nothing could hinder her joy.

The need for warehouses was not critical in the pleasant climate, and the buildings that crowded the dock area were for the most part only roofs standing on wooden piles. It was beneath one of these, in the cool shade it offered, that John Ruark and his companions squatted. Their beards had been shaved away and their hair cropped close. After being issued strong lye soap, they were led to the forecastle and hosed down beneath the ship's pumps. Some of the men had cried out as the caustic soap found raw spots, but John Ruark had enjoyed the bath. Nearly a full month he had lain in his small cubicle with only an occasional exercise on the gun deck to ease and stretch cramped muscles. The fare on the voyage had been ample, but he had begun to despair that there was nothing left in the world to eat but salt beef, beans, and biscuits washed down with warm ale.

John Ruark smiled slowly at his thoughts and rubbed his hand down the nape of his neck, familiarizing himself with the shortness of his black hair. He was garbed like the others in new duck trousers and sandals for his feet. The clothes were all of one size and uniformly large for him and his eight cohorts. Along with the items given him were a broad-brimmed straw hat, a loose white shirt, and a small canvas bag. This last had remained empty until they were taken to the Trahern store and given a razor, mug and brush, a small wooden-handled penknife, two more issues of clothing, and several towels as well as a supply of strong soap and an admonition to use it.

When the fitful breeze waned, the heat was intense beneath the broad roof. A single overseer watched them, and it would have been a simple act to escape. But John Ruark surmised there would be little effort wasted in search or pursuit, for it would only be a matter of time before any man would have to come out of the jungle. There was nowhere else to run.

His eyes took in his surroundings as he plucked idly at the loose knee of his canvas breeches. They waited for Squire Trahern; they had been informed it was his habit to inspect and lecture all new arrivals. Ruark was eager to get a look at the fabled "Lord" Trahern and squatted patiently with the others but kept carefully to the end of the line. He was still alive and in the one place in the world he cared to be, that being the place currently occupied by Shanna Trahern. Or would she more properly call herself Shanna Beauchamp? He chuckled to himself. She had gained his name while he, in the same course of events, had lost it; and that would be another matter to settle.

His musings were interrupted by the arrival of the open barouche that had borne Shanna away from the docks. The tall, thin man called Ralston was the first to dismount and struggling down next came the man Ruark had seen greeting Shanna earlier. He assumed this was the dreaded Squire Trahern.

Ruark watched with interest as the man drew near. The squire's manner was that of authority. He was large and portly, and there was an aura of power about him. Contrasting oddly with the dark woolens of his lean companion, he was dressed in neat white hose and gold-buckled, black leather shoes. His breeches were spotless white linen, serviceable but light and cool. His long waistcoat was of the same cloth and white like the shirt, ruffles and fancy stitchery were noticeably absent. An immense, wide-brimmed, low-crowned, finely woven straw hat shaded his face; he carried in his hands a tall, well-worn black-thorn walking stick as if it were his badge of office.

The two men came toward the shed and after saluting them, the overseer ordered his charges to stand and form a line. The squire took a packet from Ralston and unfolded a paper from it, studying it for a moment before stepping to the man at the beginning of the line.

"Your name?" he asked bluntly.

The bondsman replied in a mumble, and his new master made a check mark on his tablet and proceeded to carefully inspect his purchase. He felt the man's arm, gauging the muscle in it, and studied the hands for signs of toil.

"Open your mouth," Trahern commanded. "Let's see your teeth."

The man obeyed, and the squire shook his head almost sadly and made several notes in his log. Proceeding to the next man, he repeated the ritual. After the third bondsman, he faced Ralston.

"Dammit, man!" Trahern swore. " 'Tis a beggarly lot you've brought me. Were these the best you could find?"

"I'm sorry, sir." Ralston chafed beneath the other's scowl. "These were all I could get for love or money. Perhaps the choice will be better in the spring if the winter is hard enough."

"Bah!" Trahern snorted. "A dear price, indeed, and all from the debtor's block."

Ruark's brows lifted slightly as he took note of the man's reply. So, the squire wasn't aware he had purchased a felon bound for the gallows. Ruark considered this a moment and what effect it might have on him. He glanced up to catch Ralston's frown directed toward him. Aye, 'twas Mister Ralston's doing, Ruark deduced, and if he had no wish to return to London to see his own hanging done, he'd best play the game.

After a close scrutiny of the eighth man, Trahern moved to Ruark, and there he came to an abrupt halt. His eyes narrowed keenly as he surveyed the last of his lot. The bondsman's amber eyes revealed more than an average level of intelligence, and the smile that played about his lips was strangely disquieting. Noticeably different from the rest, this one was lean and muscular with wide shoulders and strong arms, a straight back, and the unbowed legs of a young man. There was no flab on him, and the flat, hard belly bore no hint of a paunch. It was rare that such a fine young buck would be found on the debtor's auction block.

Trahern consulted his list, finding one name left.

"You would be John Ruark," he stated rather than asked and was surprised at the rush of words he stirred from the fellow.

"Aye, sir." Ruark affected a slight brogue to disguise his origin. Too many of the islanders were touchy about the mainland colonies. "And I can read, write, and cipher."

Trahern cocked his head as if listening to every word.

"My back is strong and my teeth are sound." Ruark drew back his lips, displaying the gleaming whiteness for a moment. "I can pull my weight, given a good meal of course, and I hope I shall prove worthy of all your family has invested in me."

"My wife is dead. I have only a daughter," Trahern murmured absently and then silently rebuked himself for chatting with the man. "But you are a colonial, from New York or Boston I would guess. How did you come to be on the sale block?"

Ruark drew a sharp breath and stroked his chin. "A slight misunderstanding with several redcoats. The magistrate was not in the least considerate and believed them over me."

It was not completely untrue. He had not taken kindly to being rudely dragged from a sound sleep, and he had reacted instinctively, breaking the captain's jaw as he found out later.

Trahern nodded slowly and seemed to accept the tale until he spoke. "You are a man of some wisdom, and I think there is much more to your story, but," he shrugged, "that day will out. I care little for what you were, only for what you are."

The bondslave, John Ruark, quietly considered his master, having already realized that he would have to tread lightly when dealing with him, for the man was as sharp-witted as it had been rumored. Still, the truth had a way of coming out, and since he could think of no words worthy of his effort, Ruark held his tongue.

Leaving him, Trahern went to stand before the line of men,

bracing his legs wide and resting his hands on the knob of his walking stick. Slowly he studied them.

"This is Los Camellos," he began. "Named by a Spaniard but deeded to me. I am lord mayor, sheriff, and justice here. You have been bonded to me for debts unpaid. You will be apprised of your debt and its progress upon request to my bookkeeper. You will be paid for Sundays and holidays, but sickness and otherwise are your own account. Your wage will be sixpence a day for each day that you work. On the first of each month you will receive for each day you have worked, tuppence for your needs, tuppence to go against your debt, and tuppence which will be repaid for your keep. If you work hard and advance yourselves, you will receive more and may adjust the payments as you see fit." Pausing, he looked hard at Ruark. "I expect some of you will pay out your debts in as little as five or six years. You may then work for passage back to England or wherever you would go, or you may, if you wish, settle here. You have been given the wherewithal to keep yourselves clothed and clean. Tend your clothes carefully, for whatever else you get you will have to pay for. 'Twill be some time before you have any money and then precious little."

Trahern ceased and held his silence until he had their complete and undivided attention.

"There are two ways to get into serious trouble here. The first is to abuse or steal anything of mine, and most everything here is mine. The second is to upset or annoy any of the people already here. Do you have any questions?"

He waited but there were no volunteers. The squire relaxed his stance and stood more at ease.

"You will be given three days of light chores to recover from the voyage. After that you will be expected to spend the daylight hours in productive labor. You will begin your toil the day after Christmas. Good day to you all."

Without a further glance he mounted to his carriage, leaving Ralston to see to them. The gaunt man stepped before them as the barouche departed. Slapping the palm of his gloved hand with the ever-present quirt, he began to speak.

" 'Tis Squire Trahern's way to be soft with his slaves." His sneer was just barely detectable. "Rest assured it would not be my way, but I must go on to other duties. You will be quartered in an old stable above the town until you go to the fields, and you will be given light work at the dock or plantation. This man,"—he indicated the one who had guarded them—"will be your overseer. He will report to either myself or Trahern. Until you are adjudged worthy of trust, you will stay near the stable at all times that you are not engaged in work. If you have not already noted,"—he swept his whip toward the hills and then the beach—"there is nowhere to hide, at least not for long." Here he seemed almost pained. "You will be given time to rest and will be fed expensively." With the next words he warmed to his topic. "But you will be expected to earn your keep and then some."

Brusquely he gestured to the guard.

"Take them away. All but that one." He indicated Ruark and when the others had left, he drew close and spoke in a low voice. "You seem to display some doubt as to your position here."

Ralston waited but Ruark returned his stare without speaking, and the agent's lips curled back in a snarl. "Unless you wish to return to England and get your neck stretched, I warn you keep a close tongue in your head."

Ruark's eyes did not waver, nor did he make any comment. The man had done him a great favor, though he could little realize its extent.

"Get with them."

Ralston jerked his head toward the disappearing file of men, and Ruark obeyed swiftly, giving him no cause for anger.

Trahern's ships plied the southern waters, staying away from the North Atlantic where great storms raged and icebergs made the voyages hazardous. They took to the islands rich baubles, fancy silks and other produce of the Continent and England, bringing back the raw materials that in the summer would be sent north again. New fields were cleared on the southern slopes of the island, and the timber thus gained was thrown off the cliffs into the sea, there to be gathered onto the smaller ships and taken to greater ports where it could be sawed into much-needed lumber. Gangs of men went from one field to another as the work was needed. Usually their first duties were to rehabilitate or construct quarters for the overseers and then themselves. Simple thatched huts with half walls were the rule, sturdy enough to provide shelter from the rains and constant sun.

John Ruark was first given to one of these overseers. He was diligent in his labors and offered many improvements for the operation. It was under his direction that a brook was diverted into a flume, and the huge logs were no longer laboriously dragged to the cliff's edge, but by their own weight were sent on a rapid ride to the sea, thus saving much toil for both mules and men. The overseer was most thankful for this bright young man, because able hands were short enough, and even the mules tired quickly in the steaming heat. The taskmaster mentioned the bondsman's name in his report to Trahern.

John Ruark was passed to another gang which set about to harvest the winter cane before the dry months came. There, he showed them how to burn the fields which reduced the plant to a charred stalk, still rich in juice, while clearing poisonous spiders and insects that would further reduce the number of bondsmen. He changed the small crushing mill so that a mule could turn the wheel instead of the half-dozen or so men it usually took. Again Ruark's name appeared in the reports.

It was not long before his skills in engineering were known upon the island, and the overseers passed him around so that he might solve their problems. Sometimes the duty was easy, sometimes difficult, and as with the burning of the fields there was much reluctance, and he had to prove his ideas. Still, he progressed. His pay was doubled, then tripled. His possessions increased by one mule rendered him by a village merchant for labors performed in his spare time.

Above all of his other talents, he had a special knack for horses, and the spirited stallion, Attila, was brought to him lame, suffering from a pulled tendon in the foreleg. When it was made known to John Ruark that this was the favored steed of Trahern's daughter, he tended it carefully, rubbing liniment into the injured leg and tightly wrapping it. Patiently he walked it and coddled it until the fine animal would take sugar from his hand, something not even the young mistress could get the horse to do. He taught it to come at his whistle and then, pronouncing it fit, sent it back to the lady.

For Shanna, her return was most welcome. She spent the days

in riding her horse or swimming in the crystal sea, diving beneath its surface and on occasion spearing an edible fish or two to add to the fare at the table. She renewed her friendship with the people of Los Camellos and saw to the welfare of needy families. It was among her larger worries that in the past years they had been unable to find a tutor for the children, and the small school which her father had built stood empty. For the most part, her days formed into a lazy idyllic thread, like pearls on a string. Other ships stopped at Los Camellos for trade, and their officers usually dined at the manor, giving Shanna an excuse to gown herself appropriately and entertain them with her effervescent wit. She was mistress of the island, daughter of Trahern, and it was almost labor to constantly remind everyone that she was now Madam Beauchamp. It was a happy time for her, an interlude of bliss with enough duty entwined with pleasure to keep her from becoming bored with either. The haunting memories that had plagued her were becoming subdued at last.

February was well on its way, and it was on a Friday afternoon that she called for Attila and set out upon a lazy tour. She had taken the middle road up between the hills near the cane fields, much too close to the gangs of men her father had often warned her were dangerous—though few on Los Camellos would ever harm the daughter of Trahern. Yet it was not wise to tempt fate, and here in the cane fields the gangs of bondsmen worked day in and day out. Still, Shanna was one to venture where she would with little thought of the consequences. It was a hot day, and Attila's hooves raised small clouds of dust which floated lazily above the surface of the road. Having passed between the hills, she was headed down the southern slope when she came upon a man leading a mule along the side of the road. He was a bondsman by his garb, though that had been oddly altered. He wore the familiar wide-brimmed hat, and his shirt was thrown over the mule's back, but his breeches were hacked off high above his knees. His back was well bronzed, and the muscles rippling there showed a ready, capable strength.

Attila snorted and shook his head. Shanna would have reined the animal away to give the man wide berth, but as she passed by the bondsman, a tan arm shot out and firmly grasped the bridle of her steed. On any other occasion the stallion would have revolted and jerked away from unfamiliar restraint, but Attila only whinnied as he nudged the outstretched arm. For a moment, stunned by the steed's reaction, Shanna could only stare wide-eyed as the horse nuzzled the fellow. Then gathering her wits, she glared down at this incursion of her freedom. She opened her mouth to demand her release. The man turned, and her ire fled. Her jaw dropped as overwhelming disbelief numbed her brain.

"You!" she choked out.

Mocking amber eyes gazed back at her. "Aye, Shanna. 'Tis the good man, John Ruark, at your service. 'Twould seem you have gained a name, my love, while I have lost one." He grinned confidently. "But then, 'tis not oft a man can cheat both the hangman and his wife."

Some sanity returned to Shanna, but panic was heavily mixed with it.

"Let go!" she snapped and jerked the bridle. She would have fled, but Ruark's weight held the stallion in place. Her voice broke with the fear she felt. "Let go!"

"Easy, my love." The golden eyes glinted like hard metal. "We have a matter to discuss."

"Nay!" She half screeched, half sobbed the word. She lifted the quirt in her hand as if to strike but found it snatched from her fingers and her wrist seized in a merciless grip.

"By God, madam," he growled. "You will listen."

His hands clamped tightly about her narrow waist, and she was seized from the saddle as if she were a child and was set on her feet before him. Frantically Shanna struggled, her small, gloved hands pushing against the dark, furred chest that seemed to fill her whole entire vision. He gave her a rough shake that threatened to snap her head off and did, indeed, send her wide-brimmed hat sailing off into the grass and the neat roll of gilded hair tumbling down her back in a torrent. Shanna stilled, staring helplessly into his scathing eyes.

"That's better," Ruark jeered and loosened his painful grip only slightly. "You are not so haughty when you fear."

Shanna summoned a show of weak bravado and lifted her quivering chin. "Do you think I'm afraid of you?"

The white teeth flashed against his bronze skin as he laughed

111

at her, and Shanna could only mark the resemblance he bore to a swarthy pirate. The pallor of the gaol had faded, and in its stead the brown skin gleamed with the healthy sweat of one who now enjoyed his freedom.

"Aye, my loving wife," he mocked. "And perhaps you have cause. Hicks vowed me mad after you betrayed me, and well I was with a devil's desire to have revenge upon my beauteous spouse."

The color drained from Shanna's cheeks as his words brought back the memory of what Pitney had said. With a choked sob she renewed her efforts to escape, then writhed in silent agony as his fingers clenched again in a cruel vise.

"Be still," Ruark commanded, and Shanna had no choice. She was far from subdued, though she still trembled violently with fright.

"If you don't turn me loose I'll scream until they hang you! And for good this time! Damn it! I'll bring this island down around your ears!"

"Will you, my dear?" he lightly taunted. "And what will your father say of your marriage then?"

Pricked by his scorn, she was reckless and sneered, "Then what do you intend? Rape?"

Ruark laughed caustically. "Do not fear, Shanna. I have no urge to tumble you among the weeds."

She was bemused. What did he want? Could she buy him off?

As if he read her mind, Ruark set the question straight. "And I want none of your father's wealth, so if you think to bribe me, your efforts are wasted."

He raised a dark brow and considered her flushed cheeks and the soft, trembling mouth. His gaze moved even lower and surveyed her heaving bosom, until Shanna wondered wildly if he could see through her riding habit. Beneath his steady regard, her breasts burned, and she could not control her rapid breathing. Feebly she crossed her arms before her as if naked beneath that stare. Ruark smiled evilly and gazed again into her eyes.

"In the gaol my mind was tortured by your beauty, and I could not forget even the smallest detail of you in my arms. That image was seared upon my memory as if you had branded me."

He stared at her for a long time with a half-mad light in his eyes that made her doubt her own sanity at ever having sought him out. Then he smiled and became more gentle.

"I will yet find a way to reach among the thorns and pluck the rose," he vowed.

His hand wandered up her back beneath the silken tresses and fingered them lightly. His smile broadened into a rakish grin, more like the Ruark she had known in the coach. It suddenly penetrated that he was not mad, but instead, was bent on revenge.

" 'Tis not in my mind to let your secret out, Shanna, but I gave to the bargain all that you demanded. The only thing left wanting is your part of the agreement, and my dear, I shan't rest 'til I see it done."

Shanna's mind flew aimlessly in ever-widening circles. "No bargain!" she cried, straining against him. "No bargain! You are not dead!"

"The bargain is met!" he snarled. "You have my name and all you desired. 'Tis no fault of mine that Hicks is greedy. But I seek the full cost of my barter, a whole night with you as my wife, alone, and with no one to snatch open the door to drag me out." He leered down at her. "I think you might enjoy it as well."

"Nay," Shanna whispered, shamed by the memory of her own response. "The marriage was consummated. Be content with that."

Ruark chuckled derisively. "If you're not woman enough to know, my darling innocence, we had barely begun and 'twas not completed by any means. A full night, no less, Shanna. That is my end!"

It was best to humor him, she thought, at least until she was able to escape, and then Pitney. . . .

Ruark's eyes narrowed in warning. "Though your womanhood is sorely lacking, Shanna, I have bested the hangman to find you out. Should you set the hounds or that great oaf Pitney or your father after me, I shall escape them all. And I promise you I will come and claim my due. And now, my loving wife—"

His hands dropped away, and he reached for Attila's bridle, bringing the horse around. Bending, he folded his hands for her to step, and Shanna, eager to be gone, did not hesitate. With a hand upon his sturdy shoulder she sprang upward, lifted by his boost, and settled upon the saddle. A gasp caught in her throat as his hand reached toward her and very boldly led her knee around the horn. Snatching the reins, Shanna jerked Attila around and set her heel to his side until the stallion fairly flew along the road. Ruark's low, mocking laughter rang in her ears long after she had left his sight.

In front of the white sprawling mansion, Shanna pulled the steed to a halt and flung herself from its back, leaving a servant to chase it down the lane in order to catch it. Racing past Berta—who paused to gape in surprise—Shanna plunged up the curving stairway and slammed the door of her sitting room behind her. She locked it quickly against any intrusion and leaned against it, panting for breath.

"He's alive!" she gasped. She threw her riding gloves down upon the tall secretary and stormed toward her bed-chamber. She left her boots and riding habit in a careless heap upon the rich carpet. In the light chemise, she paced angrily.

"He's alive!" she raged. "He's alive!"

There was a dread, sick feeling in the pit of her stomach, yet near her heart, pounding heavily beneath her breast, there bloomed an odd sense of elation, even freedom. Beneath her swirling thoughts, it occurred to her that she had felt bound by the death of a man for her own gain. A recurring dream of that sturdy neck twisted by a rope was cleansed from her mind, and a vision of a rotting corpse in a wooden box disappeared, never to be recalled.

"But how? I saw him buried. How—could—this—be?"

Her fine brow showing a puzzled frown, she walked about her chamber and considered this more deeply.

Bondsman? Ralston was responsible for all bondslaves coming to Los Camellos. But how did Ruark come? The *Hampstead?* Nay, there were no bondsmen sailing on it. Only the *Marguerite!*

Good lord! Right beneath her nose!

Hysterical laughter threatened, and she flung herself back across the bed, throwing an arm over her eyes as if to shut out the vision of those smirking amber eyes.

Chapter 6

SHANNA stayed away from the hills and the plateau on the south side of the island. When bondsmen were brought in from the fields, she made it a point to be elsewhere. Whenever she rode Attila, she was careful to stay close to the village or the grounds of the manor. But as she saw no more of Ruark, her apprehensions eased.

Nearly a fortnight had passed when her father urged her to take a ride with him in his carriage, since he had some business in the high cane fields.

"We'll take a basket of food along," he said, looking at her and almost smiling. "Your mother and I—we would all go on an outing. You used to love to chew on a stick of cane."

Growing uneasy at his own nostalgia, Orlan Trahern cleared his throat sharply.

"Come along, girl. I haven't all day, and the carriage is waiting."

Shanna could not refuse him and smiled at his suddenly brusque manner. In the barouche and upon the road, she considered her father. Since her return he had become more tractable. Or was it herself? When he was wont to rave on some minor point, she no longer challenged him or argued with his idea,

115

but rather let him rave on until he had worn his ire thin; then, smiling and gentle, she would calmly agree, or disagree as might be the case, firmly but without the open antagonism of before. And he would snort and carp a bit if she stood against him or smirk and preen if she were with him. She could almost say he valued her opinion and recognized that often she held more insight than he did.

The air in the hills was cooler, the breezes refreshing. Patiently Shanna waited when the carriage paused here and there while her father talked with overseers or left for a moment to see to some trifling matter. They stopped to eat and then resumed riding. They came onto a large cleared field in the center of which a strange wagon was being drawn at a slow pace by mules. A wide cloth shade spread out on either side of the wagon like the wings of a bird, and beneath it a file of men with bags of seed and long sticks walked along poking holes and dropping the seeds into them, pressing the dirt back over them with their bare feet.

In alert attention, Trahern sat forward in his seat and stared past his daughter at the odd contraption. He waited eagerly for the overseer, who was hurrying to the carriage.

"Aye, sir, he's a smart one that," the overseer answered her father's question. "We cleared the field in record time, just cut out the big trees and burned the rest. He said the ashes'ud sweeten the soil. And then, that thing ye see there. Why, a man would have to take a bag o' seed from the shed, an' 'fore an hour were passed he'd be back for more seed, to take a rest and a drink. That 'ere tarp gives 'em shade, and the wagon has seed and water, so we got the field almost planted. Cleared and planted in a week. That's good, ain' it, squire?"

"Aye," Trahern agreed. He paused for a long time, observing the progress of the planting. Shanna saw that one man stood apart from the rest and did not labor as the others. His back was bare and though it was turned toward them, there was something oddly familiar about him.

Trahern spoke to the overseer. "And you say this fellow, John Ruark, it was all his idea?"

Shanna's breath caught in her throat, and for a moment the

world seemed to stand on end. Of course it was him! Those shortened breeches!

The world was steady again, and she drew air in her lungs and calmed her trembling body, eyeing him surreptitiously. As he walked slowly along inspecting the results, sweat glistened on the firm muscles of his back, and his long, brown legs were straight and strong. . . . She could almost feel again the bold thrust of him between her thighs and blushed profusely at her own musings. Leaning across, she plucked at her father's sleeve.

"Papa," she pleaded. "I've been too long in the sun, and my head aches. Can we go back now?"

"In a moment, Shanna. I want to talk with that man."

Her heart thumped in her throat. She could not bear to meet Ruark face to face. Not here! Not now! Not with her father!

"I'm terribly sorry, papa, but I feel most ill. A trifle dizzy. Can we please go?" she urged in desperation.

Trahern regarded his daughter for a moment in concern and then relented to her request.

"Very well, I can see him later. We'll go."

He spoke to his black driver, Maddock, and the carriage wheeled about, setting off on the route to the manor. Giving a long sigh, Shanna leaned back and closed her eyes as relief flooded over her. But when she opened them again, she found her father staring at her with an odd half smile on his lips. His gaze was steady, and she grew uneasy under it then began to squirm.

"Can it be, Shanna, that you are with child?" he questioned softy.

"Nay!" she blurted out. "I mean, I think not. I mean, the time was so brief. We barely—" She clamped her mouth shut.

"You mean you don't know?" Trahern snorted. " 'Tis been time enough. Surely you know about these things."

"I—think not, papa," Shanna replied and read the disappointment in his eyes. "I'm sorry."

She gazed down at her tightly clenched hands as Trahern stared straight ahead, uttering no further words the entire way home.

Berta met them at the door. Her quizzical glance swept them both briefly and then settled on Shanna. Having had her fill of questions for the day, Shanna brushed by the housekeeper and quickly mounted the stairs to her chambers. This time she had the presence of mind to put away her clothes as was her manner, and, clad only in a light shift, she fell across her bed and stared at the treetops beyond her balcony. The French doors were set ajar to catch the cooling afternoon breezes, and an airy rush stirred the filmy silk tied to the heavy canopy over her bed. The sweet scent of the flowering vine twining over the railing swept across the veranda and filled her room with its heady fragrance and Shanna stared—and she stared—and she stared.

Some time later Berta's knock sounded on the door. She announced the evening meal, and Shanna pleaded illness as an excuse. The sunset faded into darkness, and again Berta gave a gentle rap upon her door. This time Berta would not be put off and insisted that Shanna open the door. Admitted at last, the kindly old woman brought to the bedside a tray with a covered plate of meats and a large glass of cool milk.

"It vill settle your stomach, Shanna," Berta urged. "Is dere something else I can get you?"

Shanna's insistence that it was only a bit too much of the sun left Berta clucking her tongue and mumbling about the carelessness of "dis new cheneration" as she returned to the stairs.

Shanna nibbled at the food and sipped the cool milk. Becoming drowsy, she donned her shortened nightshift and slipped between the silken sheets. She was half asleep when somewhere in her mind came a memory of hands cupping her breasts and a mouth, hot and sweet, caressing the softness of them, kisses bruising her lips and searing downward the length of her throat, strong arms crushing her against a hard body, again that first burning thrust and then—

With a burst of fear Shanna came wide awake and then slowly eased back upon her pillow as she realized she was alone in the room. The familiar shadows stalked across her walls, but there was no help for the hollow ache within her. She drew a pillow close and nestled against it. Was it another trick of her mind when, just before deep sleep took her, she felt the hard muscles of a man's back beneath her fingers?

Morning gave her no answer. The pillow was just a pillow. But the night's sleep had done wonders. She rose, bathed, and donned a gown of pale turquoise, standing still as Hergus laced her narrow waist tightly. With its square décolletage, the garment displayed the higher curves of her rounded breasts. She considered her reflection in the tall looking glass and idly smoothed her hair, which was swept tightly from her brow and caught in a mass of cascading ringlets. A petulant scowl puckered her brow as Ruark's taunting words seared through her brain. Womanhood lacking? How so? Where does he find me lacking? In looks? In stature? In wit? Where? A reply was not to be gained from the mirror, and Shanna left her chambers to join her father in a late breakfast as had become their habit since her return.

It was Orlan Trahern's custom to be up at daybreak, but most often now, unless there was other business pressing, he waited his morning meal upon Shanna's company. It was usually a pleasant time, though few words were spoken. But as she descended the stairs this morning, Shanna heard voices from the dining room. It was certainly not out of the ordinary for the squire to entertain at the morning meal, and business was generally the topic. But somewhat wary of who visited, Shanna made her way more cautiously. It was Berta who forced the issue.

"Goot morgen, Shanna," the housekeeper greeted brightly. "Ya're feeling better today?"

Then her father's voice came through the open door.

"Here she is. My daughter, Shanna."

A chair creaked, and in a moment Trahern's great bulk filled the doorway as he came to greet her. Taking her arm, he led her toward the fresh airy room where white lattice screens allowed breezes to flow through the windows while filtering out the sun and its heat.

"I'm sorry, child, but I wanted to speak with this man," the squire apologized as he escorted her in.

Shanna halted suddenly as she saw the one mentioned, and she snatched her hand from her father's arm. The color fled her cheeks, and her lips parted in surprise. Trahern returned to lift her hand again and consider her with a worried frown. His voice was low, almost a whisper, as he spoke to her.

"Aye, a bondslave." His tone was reproaching. "But I think 'tis not beneath us to share a table with him. If you would be the mistress of this house, be a gracious one and greet all I summon here as my guest."

"Come now, Shanna," he continued more loudly, tucking her hand in his elbow and patting it gently. "Meet Mister Ruark, John Ruark it be, a man of some learning and of a good mind. He has done us well, and I must consider his advice on some matters."

John Ruark rose to his feet and amber eyes smiled at her, touching her everywhere when Trahern turned to have a word with Berta. The blush returned quickly to Shanna's cheeks, mounting high as she experienced again that sensation of being stripped naked by his golden gaze. She mumbled inanely through a greeting while her own regard passed disdainfully over the short breeches. They were clean, but no less objectionable to her state of mind. However, she was thankful for the fact that he had at least donned a shirt. With the straw hat put aside, she noticed for the first time that his hair had been clipped close to the nape. Short heavy wisps curled slightly about his face, accentuating the lean, handsome features. The mocking grin gleamed with startling whiteness against his sun-darkened skin. Grudgingly Shanna admitted to herself that his being a bond-slave didn't appear to have done him ill. Indeed, there was a health and vitality about him that was almost mesmerizing. In all, he was even more handsome than on their wedding day.

"My pleasure, madam," he answered warmly.

Shanna gritted out a menacing smile. "John Ruark, did you say? I knew of some Ruarks in England. Scurvy bunch they were, murderers and cutthroats. Filthy wretches. Are you perchance related, sir?"

The sweetness of her tone did not hide the sneer she intended. He met it with a flicker of amusement showing upon his lips, but Trahern harrumphed sharply and gave her a warning glare.

"You must forgive me, Mister Ruark. 'Tis not oft I find myself entertaining a slave."

"Shanna." Her father's tone was low but challenging.

If only a trifle, Shanna did relent and slipped into her chair. Ignoring Ruark as he settled again in the place across from her, she turned to the small, elderly, gray-haired black who waited to serve her. She bestowed her best smile upon him.

"Good morning, Milan," she said cheerily. "Another bright day we'll be having, don't you agree?"

"Yes ma'am," he beamed. "Bright and shiny, jest like yourself, Miz Shanna.

"And what might you be having this morning? I've a juicy melon saved for you."

"That would be nice," she smiled.

As he set a cup of tea before her and moved away to the sideboard, Shanna dared to meet the amused regard of Ruark across the table.

While the men's conversation drifted across many topics, Shanna sipped her tea, listening quietly as Ruark expressed himself in bold opinions in response to the squire's questions. He quickly took up a quill and made sketches when needed. He acted not as a man who was a slave, but as one who was a valued peer. He leaned with the squire over stacks of drawings which covered their corner of the table and explained in detail the mechanical workings of designs. Shanna was anything but bored as she listened. She realized he was clever, as keen-minded as her father, and he seemed no stranger to the workings of a plantation. In fact, as the conversation progressed, it became evident he could teach his master much.

"Mister Ruark," she interrupted in a pause as Milan refilled their cups. "What was your trade before you became a bondsman? Overseer, mayhap? You are from the colonies, are you not? What were you doing in England?"

"Horses—and other things, madam," he drawled leisurely, a slow smile coming as he gave her his full attention. "I worked with horses quite a bit."

Shanna frowned slightly as she pondered his reply. "Then you must be the one who tended my horse, Attila." No wonder the stallion was not skittish of him. The wily beggar had taken care of him. "You mean you train horses? For what, sir? And why were you in England?"

"Mostly for riding, madam." He shrugged. "And some enjoy the sport of racing their mounts. I went first to Scotland to select breeding stock."

"Then you were trusted by your squire to know good blood stock when you see it?" she persisted.

"Aye, madam, and that I most certainly do." The lights gleamed golden in his eyes as he lightly measured her form. The insinuation was clear. Her father's gaze remained on her, so he missed the slow perusal and the nod that followed it.

Squire Trahern sipped the tea, pursing his lips as he savored the spiced warmth of the brew. "I sent my daughter there on much the same mission, but she only returned as a widow with an empty cradle. I didn't even get to meet her young man and that eats at my heart. Having seen so many swains refused, I was in great suspense to see her final choice."

Shanna spoke to her father, but her eyes were on Ruark, and she smiled behind her cup of tea. "There's little I can tell you of him, papa. But 'twas only fate that decreed I was not to bear his offspring. You see, Mister Ruark," Shanna directed her remarks to him openly, "my father sent me to find a worthy husband who would sire sons for his dynasty. Such was not to be the way of it, despite my efforts. Yet I have no doubt that I shall find another man, perhaps more clever of foot so as to avoid the same end as he."

She raised her eyebrows ever so slightly to emphasize her last words and stared straight into the amber eyes which dipped momentarily to acknowledge her riposte.

"In truth, Madam Beauchamp," Ruark's tone showed concern and he spoke in earnest, "I can only agree that such a fine man could no doubt have made your life far richer. Still, I find that what is called fate oft has the workings of most worldly hands about it. Sometimes a whim or fancy, a base desire, can deny the best-laid plans. My own case for example. Though I was in dire need, my best opportunity was denied by the very one who sought the bargain.

"Aye, I have suffered much because of that one," he continued musingly. "Yet justice, though oft delayed, will usually find its end. I have debts to pay, not the least of them to your father. Still, there are other debts owed me to which I look forward with great anticipation."

Shanna recognized the threat in his statement and with some display of anger retorted, "Sir, I find your reference to justice ill-advised, for you are obviously the victim of it and are where you belong. My father may welcome your advice, but I find the presence of a half-naked savage at my breakfast odious!"

At her vindictive burst, the squire lowered his cup and stared at her, missing Ruark's leer which belied the soft apology in his voice as he replied, "Madam, I can only hope you will change your mind."

Daring no further words, but with turbulent emotions roiling within her and darkening the green of her eyes, Shanna came to her feet and stalked out of the room.

It was only after Ruark left that Shanna dared approach her father, and she did so apprehensively, for she could not name another bondsman who had gained the squire's interest as much as this colonial. Trahern was in his chamber study going over some accounts Ralston had prepared when Shanna strolled into the room, her hands folded behind her back and the look of angelic innocence on her face.

"Do you suppose we'll be having rain before the day is out, papa?" she inquired, staring out through the open French doors toward the dazzling blue sky. If any had taken serious note of her topics of conversation, they might have raised a question over her apparent concern with the weather this day.

Trahern grunted an answer, but his attention remained on the open pages of the account books. Deep in thought, he frowned and scanned the figures before him, hardly aware of his daughter taking the chair beside his desk.

"I wonder if Mrs. Hawkins might have caught some lobsters in her traps today. Perhaps I'll ask Milan if we might have them for dinner. Would you like that, papa?"

The squire cast a glance toward his daughter that barely acknowledged her presence and returned to his task. Shanna was not to be so easily dismissed. She leaned forward and peered over his arm at the work he was attempting to complete.

In a small voice, she inquired, "Am I interrupting anything, papa?"

With a sigh Trahern pushed back his chair and faced her, clasping his hands together over his paunch and nestling his head down between his shoulders like a wary hawk.

"I see I shall have no peace until we have discussed whatever you're here about. Get on with it, girl."

Shanna smoothed her skirt and made a small shrug.

"Ah—this man, Ruark, father," she began hesitantly, unconsciously slipping into more formal address. "Is he really the sort to do any good here on Los Camellos? Can't we get rid of him some way? Trade him? Or sell his papers perhaps? Anything to get him off the island."

Shanna paused and glanced up to see her father staring at her, his lips pursed as if he were lost in thought. Before he could answer, she rushed on.

"I mean, Mister Ruark seems so bold and arrogant for a bondsman. Indeed, it is as if he were more acquainted with being a master than a bondslave. And his clothes! Why, they're simply ghastly! I've never seen a man prance about half naked like that before. And he doesn't even care what people might say. And there's another thing. I've heard it rumored that most of the young girls in the village are simply agog over him. You'll probably be supporting several of his brats before the year is out."

"Huh," Orlan Trahern grunted. "Perhaps we should geld the stud to protect the ladies of our fair paradise."

"Good heavens, father!" Shanna rose to the bait like a half-starved flounder. "He's a man, not a beast! You cannot do that sort of thing."

"Ah, I see." Trahern's voice was slow and ponderous, and he rocked in the chair to emphasize his words. "A man! Not a beast! So fine of you to admit that, dear Shanna. So fine."

Shanna almost relaxed back in her chair until she realized that her father's eyes were hooded, and his tone had been strangely flat, a sure sign of simmering anger in him. Her mind flew as she tried to recall what she had said, and her breath almost stopped as she braced for the approaching storm. She jumped as his hand slammed down onto the desk, quivering the quill in its well.

"By God, daughter. I'm glad you admit that!"

Trahern leaned forward, grasping the arms of the chair as if he would hurl himself from it.

"I own his papers, and he shall serve me as a slave 'til 'tis paid. I know not what his sin was, but I recognize that he has a good mind and indeed a deeper understanding of this plantation than I do. I may know markets and trading, but he knows men and how to get the best out of them. He has proven his worth to me in the short time he's been here, and I respect him more as a man than you ever could. He is not a beast to be broken or trained to some simple task. He is a man to be worked and used where best he fits, and I will wager whatever you choose that he will pay for himself a hundred times over. To that point,"—he shuffled the papers on the desk, throwing one which was covered with sketches and figures into her lap—"he has suggested a large cane mill and a distillery combined which should increase both the syrup and rum production ten times or more. 'Twill take fewer men than now work the fields."

Orlan tossed another sheet of paper at her.

"After that, he has suggested a dam on the river to drive the wheel of a sawmill so that we might cut our own trees into lumber and sell the excess. He has already given a dozen ways to save men and animals. Aye, my high and mighty daughter, I do value him highly and I will not see him put away like some animal because he does not meet your high standards of comportment."

Shanna's pride was raw beneath this rebuke. Drawing herself up, she sniffed haughtily. "If you cannot see my reasoning there, then 'tis certainly within my rights to request that, at least, you do not invite him to my breakfast table where he can gawk and stare or even insult me with his silver words."

Trahern's arm flung out, and his finger pointed stiffly toward the small dining room. "That is my table and my chair, just as this is my house!" he bellowed and continued only a trifle more calmly. "I invite *you* to share *my* breakfast, and 'tis there I begin my working day. If you seek privacy, then find it in your room."

Somewhat stunned by his outburst, Shanna stared at him, but she tried once more. "Father, you would not have denied mother if she had asked you not to bring someone to this house, a person she detested or someone she disliked."

This time Trahern did heave himself out of the chair, and he towered over his daughter. His voice and his manner were harsh.

"Your mother was mistress of this house and all else I owned. Never to my knowledge did she ever turn away one I had asked to come. If you wish to serve as mistress here, you will be a gracious hostess to one and all. You will treat that man Ruark as a guest in my house whenever he is here. You know that I care little for gilt, pomp, and finery. Indeed, I fled it to come here. I cherish honesty, loyalty, and a good day's labor far more. All of those Mister Ruark has given me. And I dare say, daughter, he has given you no less than you deserve. But enough of this foolishness. I must complete these books of Ralston's." His anger eased, and his voice became almost pleading. "Now be kind to a doddering old man, child, and let me finish my work."

"As you will, father," Shanna said stiffly. "I have had my say."

Satisfied, Trahern seated himself and, picking up his quill, was soon deeply engrossed. Shanna made no move to leave as she considered this turn of events. There was no help here, but neither was this the end of her resources. With sudden determination she rose and went to rest a hand on her father's shoulder until he looked up at her.

"I shall be going for a ride now, papa. I have several errands in the village and a few purchases to make. I may be home late so don't worry about me."

She brushed a quick kiss on his forehead then was gone. Orlan watched her leave then slowly shook his head in bemusement.

"Too much damned schooling for a woman," he muttered, then shrugged and returned to the stack of papers on his desk.

It was late in the afternoon when Shanna guided Attila to the hitching post before Pitney's house. It was a quaint cottage set somewhat above the town and reminiscent of those found in western England. Behind it was a small shed where Pitney was usually engaged in making fine furniture from the rare woods the captains of the Trahern ships brought him from wherever their voyages took them. As a child Shanna had spent many hours here watching his skilled hands turn rough boards into handsome, sturdy chairs, tables and chests. Carvings of his own design liberally embellished most of the larger pieces. It was here Shanna found him, drawing a plane carefully across a slim piece of wood, his large feet buried in curled shavings. He saw her approach and rose to greet her, wiping the sweat from his brow with a tattered piece of faded blue cloth.

"Good day, lass," he greeted her amiably. " 'Tis been a goodly time since ye've been up the hill to visit me. But come, we'll sit on the porch. I have some good brew cooling in the well."

Pitney sipped the Trahern wines out of good manners, but his liking for bitter English ale was well known. He slid a cushioned chair around for Shanna as she followed him, and while he turned the crank of his well, she seated herself.

"Just a cup of water for me," she called. "I've no taste for your brew."

The well was an oddity in itself. Pitney had found an ice-cold spring years ago when the Trahern mansion was being laid and the town was but a few sparse dwellings, and he had built his house around it. The stone wall of the well formed the end of his porch. Water could be lifted from the porch or through a window into the cottage.

Pitney brought her a pewter mug filled with chilling cold water that made Shanna's teeth ache as she sampled it. Taking a seat on the rail in front of her, he sipped the foamy dark ale from his own mug, waiting patiently until she was ready to speak. The house faced westward where all the colors of the brilliant sunset could be seen, and from the height Shanna could look down on the roofs of the town spread out below. This was a man's house, sturdy and thick-hewn, with doors a little larger than usual, much like Pitney himself. To Shanna's knowledge only three women had ever set foot here, her mother, herself, and an old woman from the village who cleaned it once a week.

Finally Shanna withdrew from reverie and bent her thoughts to her business here. Facing Pitney, she came abruptly to the point.

"Ruark Beauchamp is alive and here on the island. He is a bondslave to my father and goes by the name of John Ruark."

Pitney nodded and balanced his mug on the rail beside him. "Aye, I know all of that."

His voice was calm, and Shanna stared at him, for once wondering what she would say next.

"I knew that he was not hanged," Pitney labored further, "and that we buried another man, old and wasted in his years. I would've told you at once, but Ralston was there with you. And after that, I could not see the harm in it nor the need to worry ye. I even knew that he was on the *Marguerite*. I followed Ralston to the gaol, for 'twas there I knew he got his men, not from the auction block as he has always said. And I would've told ye that, but there were too many about who would have carried the word back to your pa. If I've done ye harm in this, 'tis no less than the harm I've done for that lad. Ye wouldn't have recognized him when they brought him to the ship, so badly mauled was he. Indeed, lass, he was the one ye saved from a beating the night before we sailed. In God's truth, I do not know how the man bore it all without being maimed for life or at least being scarred. And I've been there myself."

Pitney did not elaborate what his own plight had been, nor did Shanna ask, assuming he would tell her in his own good time. But she felt her own cause failing badly and had to make another try.

"Will you get him away from here?" she asked sternly, already sure of what his answer would be. "Can you not get him off the island, back to his colonies or wherever he wants to go?"

Pitney gazed out across the harbor for a long time before looking squarely into Shanna's eyes.

"Madam Beauchamp." He seemed to try out the title for some whim of his own. His words were studied and slow. "I bounced ye on me knee when ye were no bigger than a spit in the wind, and I've seen ye grow into a lovely young woman. Ye've had trouble with your pa, and I've not always agreed with him. I went with ye on yer journeys under an oath to him to see after ye and to see ye safely home. I'm not so sure I've done the first, giving in to yer pleading about this marriage against Orlan's wishes, but I've seen well to the last. Now there's naught that troubles me but the fact that I've added to a man's woes and abused him for no good reason."

"For no good reason!" Shanna was angered at his excuses. "But the man was accused of murder and condemned to hang. A brutal murder of a woman with child. Why,"—she waved a hand toward the village—"the next could be any down there, or even me!"

"Lass," Pitney slipped back into a more familiar form of address. "Do not take to heart all that comes to your ears. I would say the man could not do such a thing. And as I've heard of him, there are many who would believe the same."

Shanna rose and irritably smoothed her riding habit, unable to meet Pitney's eyes. "Then you will not help me?"

"Nay, lass." His voice was gruff and firm. "I've already hurt the man enough. I will not again lift my hand against him without a deeper cause."

"Then what am I to do?" she whispered almost shyly.

Pitney thought for a moment, and there was an odd half smile in his eyes as he spoke again.

"Go talk to the man, John Ruark, like ye did in the gaol. Before you leave I'll give ye directions to reach him. Perhaps ye can convince him to leave. If he wants to go, I'll help him."

With some anguish in her tone Shanna asked, "You would help him and not me?"

"Aye," Pitney nodded. "Yours is but a whim. His would be a need."

Night descended to cloak Shanna's ride through the village. The people had sought out their homes after the day's work, and the streets were quiet and barren. Leaving Attila at the store where he would not draw undue attention, she made her way through the alleyways, keeping to the dark and shadows. When she came in sight of Ruark's residence, she stopped in amazement. It was little more than a lean-to against the back of an adobe warehouse. A light from a weak lantern leaked from the multitude of cracks between the boards which covered it and from the door which stood half open. Cautiously Shanna drew near and peered within, taking care not to betray her presence. For a moment she thought he stood naked as he sponged his shoulders and arms with water from a small basin, but when he moved further into the light, she realized he still wore those infernal chopped-off pants. Steeling herself for the confrontation, she reached out. Beneath her light knock, the door opened wider, and Ruark swung around instantly, startling a gasp from her.

"Shanna!" His first word came with some surprise, but he quickly recovered, smiled and reached for her hand to draw her in. "Your pardon, my love. I was not expecting a visitor, let alone such a charming one."

Ruefully he rubbed a hand across his bristly chin.

"Had I been warned of your coming, I'd have made some preparations."

In the dim light his eyes shone softly as he gazed down into hers. He stood close beside her, his other hand resting on the small of her back. Nervously Shanna glanced about the cramped room, unable to bear this attention he so freely gave her. The pressure of his touch was light, but to her it felt like a trap of steel. She began to seriously doubt her wisdom in coming here alone.

The smell of the strong lye soap and vinegar which had been used to scrub the bare boards of the place was pungent in her nostrils. Though the fittings were meager, they were almost painfully neat and well repaired. A narrow rope bed with a straw-filled mattress and clean, though threadbare, sheets filled one corner, and a small, rough table bearing a stack of drawings, quill and ink was pushed into another. A single, once-broken chair, bound back into service with small rope, and a high shelf were the only other appointments. The shelf bore several boxes, one with a loaf of bread and a chunk of cheese, a bottle of wine, and a meager collection of unmatched dishes. The light patchwork quilt on the bed was frayed and much mended but was neatly folded back, while the sheets were white with sun-bleached cleanliness.

Seeing where her gaze wandered, Ruark smiled. "Hardly a fit place for a tryst, Shanna, but the best I could manage. It costs me naught of coin, only my services in keeping an eye out for vandals." He laughed lightly and grinned as her eyes turned to meet his. "I had no idea that you would come so soon to fulfill our bargain."

Shanna gasped, stunned at his suggestion. "I did not come here to spend the night with you!"

"Alas," he sighed as if forlorn, brushing a curl from her cheek and bending near as he did so. "I am to be tortured more, then. Ah, Shanna, love, do you not ken that the merest sight of you is enough to bring me pain?"

His voice was low and husky in her ears, and Shanna had to dip deeply into her reservoir of will to dispel the slow numbing of her defenses.

"Do you know how my arms ache to be filled with you? To be so near and never touching is agony for me." His fingers lightly stroked between her shoulder blades. "Are you some dark witch to bring me hell on earth, being that which I desire most and that which I may have the least of? Be soft, Shanna, be woman, be my love."

He bent closer, his lips drawing perilously near.

"Ruark!" Shanna spoke sharply and jerking away from him, commanded, "Behave!"

"I do, my love. I am a man. You're a woman. How else should I behave?" He would have reached out and taken her in his arms.

"Do not press me so!" Shanna eluded his grasp. "Be a gentleman for once!" She held him at arm's length, her riding crop against his chest.

"A gentleman? But how, my love?" He played the simpleton. "I am only a cloddish colonial, unschooled in the postures of court, trained only in honesty and the truth of a bargain fairly met. I cannot bear to see you here, alone with me, and not reach out to touch you."

"I agree." Shanna stepped further away and continued moving as he followed. "We should limit our meetings."

Her glance flitted hesitantly across his hard, brown chest and its light furring of hair before her eyes lifted to meet that steady, predatory stare. Suddenly Shanna felt much like a hen before a wily fox, expecting to be devoured any moment.

"If you will stop seeking favor with my father and agree to stay away from the house, 'twould ease things. Now stop that!"

She brushed away his hand as he reached to caress her hair, but the coil was undone beneath the quickness of his fingers and tumbled in soft curls down her back. She tried without success to gather it again into a sober knot.

"Will you be serious for a moment!" she bridled. "Control your lust. I did not come here to bed you but to appeal to your honor. Let go!" She raised both her voice and the quirt dangerously high. "I'll not be pawed by the likes of you again!"

Ruark stood back and leaned against the wall beside her, "Ah Shanna, love," he said sadly. "Am I really to believe that you will not see out the bargain?"

"Bargain!" Shanna struck the half-open door with her whip in exasperation. "Sir, you are the most—"

"Shhh." His finger lay across his lips. His face was in the shadows, but his eyes seemed to glow, laughing at her, mocking her. "You'll have the village down upon us."

He reached behind him on the shelf and lifted the wine bottle and a cup, pouring a draught into the latter.

"Perhaps a small libation will settle your nerves, Shanna. A bit of sherry?"

"My nerves!" The words were lashed out. "Sir, 'tis your nerve that must be reckoned with." She took the mug he held toward her and sampled a drop, wrinkling her nose then sneering into his warming gaze. "Of that, dear Ruark, you have no short supply."

"You abuse me, madam." His hand reached out toward her tresses but paused as her quirt lifted again. He shrugged. "I but know my wants and seek them out."

"Dear Ruark," Shanna gritted venomously. "When I give myself to a man, 'twill be under the vows of marriage with all the love I can muster."

Ruark chuckled and placed his foot on the bed, leaning an elbow across his knee. "Will you not settle for my everlasting adoration and the bonds of a bargain fairly set? I could add," he gestured casually, "the vows have already—"

"Oh, you crude—!" Shanna was speechless at his brazen disregard of grace. "I have a dream—"

"No dream!" His reply snapped back. "But a barrier set against a flesh-and-blood man."

"Have you so little honor that you would hold me to so vile a bargain?"

"Honor? Aye, I have it." He tossed his head and stared at her, his amber eyes brittle. "And what have you? To offer yourself for a whim and, when once rightly paid, deny the pact?"

Angry tears stung Shanna's eyes. "I was gently born and tenderly reared but then bent to the will of another!"

"Aye." His tone was scornful. "The virgin Shanna, cruelly betrayed."

"I will not be dictated to!" Rigid with fury, turbulent tears streaming down her cheeks, she glared at him.

"Oh?" Ruark feigned surprise. "So now 'tis the Queen Shanna, regal, domineering. Hide behind your thorny throne, my love. Never be a woman!"

"Oh, you filthy clod!"

"Shanna." His voice was flat, hard, and biting. "Grow up."

The quirt lashed out and struck his chest and, coming back, cracked again. She raised it for another blow, but his hand knocked the whip aside, and it sailed from her grasp. Shanna's rage had mounted to violent proportions. The open palm of her empty hand completed the stroke upon his cheek and returned with the back of it against his other while her eyes blazed her hatred. Of a sudden her wrist was seized in a grasp of iron, and her arm was twisted behind her back, crushing her against his naked chest which bore two livid weals across it. Her temper soared the higher at this restraint, and Shanna tried to raise her other hand to claw at that smirking face before her, but his arm encircled her until she could not move. She was caught to him, her breath hissing between clenched teeth and her bosom heaving against his chest.

"Enough, Shanna love," he bade sharply. "You have taken both cheeks 'ere I had a chance to turn the other."

His embrace tightened about her until her toes cleared the floor and Shanna lay against him, gasping for breath. His mouth swooped down upon hers, twisting, bruising, rousing, his tongue thrusting through like a brand, searing her, possessing her. Shanna struggled weakly, trying to summon some logic from the chaos in her mind. Pleasure seeped through the barrier of her own will. The brutal crush of his lips on hers, his strong arms holding her clasped to his work-hardened frame became somehow bearable, and she was answering, not fighting anymore, growing warm. Then his arms were gone, and she stumbled free of him, coming up against the open door. The amber eyes were puzzled as he stared at her for a moment; then filled with anger.

"Arm yourself, Shanna. No young girl's wiles will see you safely away from me. I will have you when and where I bid."

Fear rose up within her, not of him but of herself, for in spite of her words, she wanted to draw him down with her upon the narrow pallet and show him once and for all time that she was more a woman than he could guess.

Shaking, Shanna bit the back of her hand, seeking pain to awaken her will. Whirling, she ran from the hovel, not pausing until she stood gasping against Attila's side. She had to wait for her strength to return before she could heave herself to the saddle. Her face burned where his unshaven chin had rasped against her tender flesh.

Miserably she stared back into the dark alleyway. Had he seen? Did he know the sudden naked desire that must have shone in her eyes?

It was a long ride back to the manor.

Chapter 7

SHANNA rode Attila along the beach until he wheezed, yet she found no pleasure in the exhausting pace. In the afternoons she went swimming, but the water was tepid and filled with weeds; she found no pleasure there, either. In the weeks that passed, she took special care to keep to herself, even avoiding her father unless he was alone. His worried frowns and concerned questions began to wear on her. But she could not bring herself to face the man, John Ruark, and so remained alone.

One sunlit afternoon Shanna sought out the privacy of a small hidden cove beneath the cliffs at the western reach of the island. For the sake of caution, she took Attila the long way around, riding the beach and avoiding the road that cut across inland. Urging the stallion belly-deep into the surf, she made her way around jutting rocks, and then she was there. Cliffs towered on three sides. The only approach was from the sea. Feeling secure, Shanna tethered the animal and left him to graze on the tufts of tender grass growing in the lee of the crag.

On a narrow stretch of sand, she spread a blanket in the shade and removed her clothing down to a shortened chemise. Here at last was privacy no one could break. For a time she lay and involved herself in a book of sonnets, combing her fingers absently

135

through her loosened tresses as she read. With the warmth of the day she grew drowsy and, folding an arm across her eyes, slept.

When she awoke, she did so with a start, unable to determine what had roused her. Her mind was unsettled, but there appeared no reason for alarm. The cliffs were bare as they had been before. No one was there.

Disquieted now, Shanna sought diversion to settle her thoughts and rose and went splashing into the gentle surf. In a clean dive she cleaved the water and with long, flowing strokes swam a good distance out to sea. Playing a childhood game of seeking shells and starfish, she dove to the bottom. For a time she floated on her back, rising and falling with the gentle swells, her hair spreading out in a giant fan, like some shy sea creature displaying its glory to only a few. A huge gray gull on motionless wings came over her and hung there, drifting close to better view this odd sea nymph.

Tiring of the play, Shanna returned to the narrow, hidden beach. She toweled herself dry, wrapped the cloth about her hair, and lay back. She watched a fleecy cloud drifting by. It touched the top of a cliff and—

Smothering a scream, Shanna came to her feet. The figure of a man stood on the brow of the cliff. A wide straw hat shaded his face; his shirt was carelessly carried over his shoulder. Short white breeches covered his loins, and long brown legs showed straight and lean beneath. Shanna knew golden eyes smiled down at her, mocking, challenging, consuming her.

The shriek that rose in her throat was not smothered this time. It was one of pure rage. Was there no place where she could flee from him? Furiously she snatched the towel from her head, flinging it to her feet.

"Begone!" she cried, her voice echoing in the cove. "Go away! Leave me be! I owe you nothing!"

Ruark's laughter floated down to her as he strolled along the edge of the cliff circling the cove. He began to sing in a rich baritone, and the words were inane and silly, put to a tune she had heard before:

> The high Queen Shanna could find no love.
> The high Queen Shanna flirted with a dove.

He watched her as closely as Shanna did him. With a start she realized that her thin chemise was soaked and clinging to her skin like a filmy haze, leaving no detail to be imagined.

Another irate shriek drowned out his song as she pulled her gown over her head, not stopping to lace the back. Tossing her other garments onto the blanket, she gathered it in a roll and threw it over Attila's bare back. Hauling herself astride, she forced the animal again into the water, and around the point then raced full tilt along the beach.

"Good day, my lady."

Ruark's shout made her urge the steed faster, and once more the sound of Ruark's mirth rang in her ears until, home at last, she hid her head beneath the pillow in her room.

The air was heavy, the night was hot. The sheet felt damp and Shanna thrust its clamminess away like the sweaty embrace of some unwelcome suitor. Sleep was not within her grasp, and she lit a candle, setting it aglow before placing it on the night table. Restlessly she paced about the room, seeking out and verifying familiar shadows, but in every one seeing that lone figure standing upon the jutting cliff.

Long ago her mother had instruced her that whatever the heat, she was never to sleep naked. It was a command Shanna had not been able to break, but she had compromised, taking a few of her lightest gowns and cropping them off just below her hips. It was one like this she wore, the briefest wisp of a gown so thin that it could barely be given the name.

Even this heat was better than foggy, wet London, Shanna mused as she pulled at the cloying fabric that stuck to her damp skin. She passed out onto the veranda, where she leaned her hip against the cool, carved wood of the balustrade.

The night was still, but she spread her arms and slowly turned her whole body, trying to catch the cool touch of a stray breeze. Thrusting her arms straight over her head, she stretched, arching her back, feeling the gown tighten over her breasts.

A long sigh slipped from her. She enjoyed swimming in the clear blue waters, racing among the trees, and sitting on the back of a laboring horse as he sped like the wind along the lanes. In

England it was unseemingly for a lady to so exercise, and Shanna reveled in her freedom to do so here. But of late there seemed something lacking, as if some other play might more fulfill the design of her person. She could not name it, but when this feeling came it was usually accompanied by a memory of warm, golden eyes smiling into hers.

Bracing her hands on the balustrade, Shanna leaned outward, staring into the dark night sky. Fleecy clouds flitted by on gusts of wind. A quarter moon, bright and sharply horned, gave light to the grounds below, peeking briefly here and there then hiding coyly, giving silver halos to the fleeing wisps of vapor.

She perched on the rail, placing a slim bare foot upon it and raising her knee. Her gaze leisurely swept the yards beyond. Great patches of blackness gathered under the banyan trees whose tall spreading tops made dense shadows. Spots of light were painted across the lawn by the rapid brush of the flippant moon. One passed beneath a tree. Shanna gasped, for there beside an ancient trunk was a shadow darker and of more manly shape than the rest. Coming to her feet, Shanna leaned against the rail, staring hard at the figure which squatted on its haunches. The shadow unfolded as the man rose, and she could see he was naked but for short, white breeches.

"Ruark!" the whisper rushed between her lips unbidden.

Turning his back, he kicked at the turf with a sandaled foot and then strode casually away, a light and airy whistle trailing a tune behind him. Shanna was certain now. She knew that walk, that graceful half-animal saunter.

"Damned rogue!"

Whirling, Shanna dashed back into the bedchamber, her pride suddenly nipped that he had not come to stand beneath her balcony and ardently entreat for her favors. She blew out the candle and flounced onto her bed and there sat glaring back at her leering windows.

"How can I sleep with him ever about, sneaking beneath my balcony, spying on my every moment?"

In sore aggravation she flopped upon her stomach and propped her chin on folded arms.

What did the knave want of her? Ha! No question there! The bargain! Ah, damned bargain! And he did sorely want the bargain out. And what a price? A night with him, at his every beck and call!

Shanna tried to feel much abused and angered, but the thought of that whole night stirred something more akin to—

"'Tis but curiosity," she vowed. "I have meagerly tasted of the brew and only want to sample it more fully. 'Tis naught but what any woman would want. Aye, and I am a woman and being in a well and hearty condition would seriously test that rogue's ardor. He charges that I am less than woman, not bent to give myself to any man. More fool he, for I do yearn most fervently for that kind and great and noble man who will come and take me in his arms and thus bend my fullest passion to his charms."

Closing her eyes, Shanna tried to form an image of that one of yore who would come to her so readily. He came, this time with raven hair and smiling amber gaze. Her eyes flew open, and anger arched her brows.

"He spies upon my very mind!"

Enraged, Shanna rolled and threw a pillow at the post. What manner of man was this Ruark Beauchamp, who crept into her dreams?

A fortnight passed, and on Sabbath afternoon Shanna straddled Attila's bare back and ran him along the beach some distance beyond the village. She had dressed in a light, casual gown and a wide-brimmed straw hat which protected her skin from the burning rays of the sun. No shoes hindered her slim feet as she urged the powerful steed into deeper water, raising the hem of her skirt well above her knees and tucking it beneath her. The wind snatched her hair free from its mooring until she released the long curling tresses to let the golden-lit mass fly riotously behind her. She clamped her hat tighter upon her head and laughed gaily as she raced faster along the shore, bending low over the stallion's neck.

Suddenly a whistle pierced the air, and the horse slowed. The shrill call came again, and, despite her efforts to direct Attila otherwise, Shanna found herself being carried toward a clump of trees that edged the swamp. Without a bridle she could not enforce her commands upon the steed.

Ruark stepped into the sunlight and whistled again, softly this.

time, offering his hand out to the horse. Attila snorted and came willingly, taking the sugar.

Shanna's lagging jaw snapped shut, her glare boring into Ruark's amused and mocking stare. Casually he caressed Attila's nose while his eyes boldly roamed her bare thighs and the dampened gown that clung to her breasts.

"You've ruined a good steed!" she cried, infuriated that he had gained Attila's trust so readily.

Ruark smiled slowly. " 'Tis a fine stallion and smart. 'Twould have taken me many months with another. I've only taught him to come when I whistle. 'Tis more than you will do."

Shanna seethed, and her bosom heaved with her indignation. "If you think I'll ever come when you beckon, then you are more than addlewitted, sir!"

It was as if he did not hear her stormy words. His smoldering gaze moved caressingly over her meagerly clad body, and his desire quickened. He well remembered the softness of her naked skin.

"Will you stop staring at me like that?" Shanna railed, feeling devoured by those burning eyes.

Without a word Ruark stepped beside her and with a quick movement was up behind her. Shanna gasped in outrage, struggling briefly, but his arms came around her, and his hands took the horse's mane.

"Get down! Are you mad?" she protested, but her mind was invaded with the press of his hard, naked chest against her back and his long thighs showing dark, lean, and muscular beside her own. His loins pressed intimately against her buttocks, and she was suffocated by the manly feel of him against her.

"What are you about?" She tried to twist away from him. "If 'tis rape, I'll have you hunted down. I swear I will."

His voice sounded hoarse in her ear. "Be still, Shanna, and let me ride with you for a space. You're accustomed to a lady's saddle and so is Attila. He needs to be taught obedience by his rider, whoever that may be." Then Ruark added in a jaunty tone. "You'll then be able to restrain him when I whistle. Now watch and I will show you both how a man rides."

Shanna's spine stiffened at the humor in his tone. She snatched her hat from her head as she sneered, "And what if we're seen? What then, Mister Ruark?"

"With the swamp on one side and the coral reefs on the other?" He chuckled lightly. "I doubt it and so do you. Now be at ease. Shanna. Your virtue is safe with me. Who could be more concerned than your husband?"

His low laughter had an edge to it that cut sharply.

"Safe!" Derision rode heavily in her words. "When you are near me, I am constantly pawed, and I feel as if there's but one thought in your mind."

"Because there's but one thought in yours, my love." The whisper came close to her ear as he smoothed her tumbled hair between them. "And you know what the result will be. I'll have the bargain done in my own time, my own way, and fully met."

"You are a rogue to so force a lady!"

"Rogue? Nay!" Ruark shrugged. "I have only the desire to see payment for a service rendered as was promised me. As to force—never! I do not wish to hurt you, Shanna. Rather, I would say, I wish to share a blissful moment and introduce you to the tender touch of passion."

Shanna twisted around to stare at him, a play of wonder and anger fighting for her face.

"Enough!" Ruark settled her in his arms and took a firm grip on the mane. "Today you are safe. 'Tis but a lesson in riding I wish to give you.

"Watch." He grew more purposeful. "Place your knees higher and let the horse feel your heels against him. Then . . ."

He tapped Attila's flanks with his heels, and the steed moved slowly, prancing. Ruark leaned forward, and the stallion quickened his pace. Ruark guided him through a series of maneuvers, and Shanna was amazed. She could feel the movements of the man, and the horse responded as if they were one. Then the knees beneath her tightened, and with a leap Attila stretched out along the beach, and they were racing with the wind.

Ruark whispered in her ear, and Shanna turned a questioning stare at him.

"I asked if your father expects you back soon."

Shanna shook her head, and her hair flew over his shoulder.

Ruark shifted her closer against him. "Good. I'll take you

along a trail I found in the swamp. Not frightened, are you?"

Glancing up into his eyes, Shanna saw the soft, smiling warmth there and could find no fear in herself. Her curiosity was piqued at his apparent ability to turn circumstances to his benefit. Here was the man who had taken her virginity, escaped the hangman, and accepted his bondage with an unusual lightness.

"I am at your mercy, sir." She resigned herself perhaps a bit more cheerfully than she had intended. "I can only hope you are true to your word."

"There is no reason to betray you, Shanna. I shall have my night."

Leaning back, Ruark let his body roll easily with the surge of the powerful beast beneath them. Attila ran harder, his hooves sending up small geysers of wet sand and water when they struck. Shanna had never dared to give the animal his head, yet with the strong arms encircling her she felt oddly secure.

With a cluck of his tongue and a tightening of his knees, Ruark slowed the mount and turned him along a narrow path that appeared to lead nowhere, only deeper into the wilderness. Then they came upon a sunlit glade where a carpet of soft grass was surrounded by a multitude of fragrant fuchsia blossoms, and tall trees bowed their branches humbly to the glen's beauty.

Dismounting, Ruark swept Shanna down beside him.

"You were right," she murmured in admission. "You do have a way with horses."

Ruark rubbed Attila's neck affectionately. "I enjoy working with them. A good steed always recognizes his master once that fact has been established."

Shanna stared at Ruark until he glanced up with a questioning brow.

"Do you know your master?" she asked sharply. "Indeed, do you recognize any man as master?"

"And what man, madam, will master me?" He stood beside her, gazing down, holding her eyes in a willful vise of amber. His voice was soft as he continued, but it held a note of determination which in an odd way both frightened and angered her. "I tell you, Shanna, love, no man will be my master but that I let him."

"Nor any woman either," Shanna snapped. "Will you deny my commands and say nay to my right to give them?"

"Ah love, never that," Ruark grinned. "I am only your humble servant as you are my most fair spouse. Ever do I seek to serve you and gain favor in your eyes."

Unable to bear the heavy weight of his heated regard, Shanna swept around the flowered bower and plucked a fragile blossom, thrusting its stem into her hair and gathering the long fall of tresses at the base of her neck. Much fascinated, Ruark leaned back against a sturdy trunk, folding his arms across his chest, to enjoy more leisurely what had become his favorite pastime since their meeting in the jail, watching Shanna. She could not guess the depth of torture she put him through, for beneath his silken taunts he burned with a consuming desire for her. At night he tossed sleepless upon his narrow cot while visions of her floated teasingly around him: Shanna, soft and yielding in the carriage; Shanna, lovely and haughty across a table; Shanna, beautiful and tempting in a wet, filmy thing that was more stirring than naked flesh. He was ever conscious of her, and whenever her father's barouche whisked through the fields or the village streets, Ruark would turn in hopes of seeing her seated beside the squire. Compared to the portliness of the huge man, she appeared trim and tiny, fragile like a budding rose; but when he was close to her, Ruark was painfully aware that though indeed she was neither very tall nor heavily rounded, she was very much a woman, and he wanted her.

The scent of her lingered in his mind, the fragrance of exotic blossoms crushed on satin skin, and beneath it the sweet smell of woman mingled with a tinge of soap. She was a fire burning in his blood, and he could find no way to quench it, for the thought of other women soured in his mind when he compared them to Shanna. It was like seeing heaven then considering hell for a substitute when he considered someone like Milly Hawkins, the fishmonger's daughter, for the easing of his plight. The girl was willing and not unpretty, but she smelled a bit like fish.

Suddenly Ruark burst into laughter, and Shanna turned to stare with eyebrows lifted in wonder. Casually Ruark gestured to the blossoms she had picked.

"An Indian woman wears a flower thus when she would tell her husband of her desire."

Shanna reddened and snatched the bloom from its place, and then, pouting prettily, thrust it above her other ear.

Ruark grinned. "And that means an unmarried maiden is available."

Shanna took the adornment from her hair and began to idly braid it with other flowers. After a moment she realized that Ruark stood looking at her with a strange and tender smile on his lips.

"My Lady Shanna, your beauty doth dim the very radiance of this haven," he avowed.

"Why, Ruark, do you court me?" Shanna inquired in soft amusement. Her mouth curved into a tantalizing smile as she came toward him with almost sensuous grace, halting a close measure from him and stretching out a finger to lay its tip in the midst of the black fur that darkened his chest. "I've never been courted by a bondslave before. 'Tis the first ever. Not long ago 'twas one who was bound for the gallows. That was the first, also. But mostly 'tis been lords and high gentlemen of the courts."

"Methinks you bait me, my lovely Shanna," he returned without a pause. "Ah love, do you seek to find the end of my patience that you might then have cause to hate me? Would your conscience then be eased at your broken word?" His mouth curved in a devilish grin. "If that be your game, madam, lead on. I will welcome your attention and the challenge."

Irate sparks flared brightly in the blue-green eyes as Shanna snatched her hand away. "You're very arrogant."

In what was meant to be a display of disdain, her eyes skimmed his slender frame barely clothed by the brief breeches, but her gaze faltered as the realization flashed through her mind that there was nothing in all that bareness she could poke fun at. Nothing! He was hard and lean, not thin, but with long, firm muscles beneath sun-darkened skin. Of a sudden she wondered what it would be like to lie against that strong body for one long night.

"I'm going back," Shanna announced abruptly, embarrassed by her own musings. "Help me to mount."

"Your servant, madam."

Gleaming whiteness flashed as he grinned down at her, and Shanna whirled haughtily. Ruark followed along in her wake, appreciatively watching her hips as they swayed with a natural, graceful provocativeness. At Attila's side he bent, folded his hands to receive her bare foot, and boosted her up onto the stallion's back. Quickly straddling Attila's back, Shanna gave the beast a kick to send him in a flying leap from the bower, leaving Ruark staring after her, arms akimbo.

The outer edge of the swamp had been reached when Shanna's mind betrayed her with the memory of a raging howl coming on a stormy, rain-swept night. A frustrated moan escaped her, and with a low, gritted curse Shanna wheeled the steed about and raced along the path leading her back to Ruark. He was running along at a slow, measured pace, but as the horse came thundering down the trail toward him, he glanced up in surprise. He reached out to catch his arm about the animal's neck as Attila jolted to a halt beside him.

"Whoa—easy," Ruark soothed and stroked the velvet nose, peering up at Shanna with a silent question.

"We'll need your skill in the fields on the morrow." She gave the excuse crisply. "If you walk most of the night to return to the village, you'll be little good to us."

"My undying gratitude, madam," he said and Shanna did not miss the inflection in his voice.

"You rogue." A reluctant smile was wrenched from her. "I thought for sure that Mister Hicks would hang you. He seemed eager enough."

"Not as eager for that, madam, as for a coin," Ruark grinned and swung up behind her. "And for that I am most thankful."

His brown arms came around her again, and he tapped his heels lightly against Attila's flanks, urging the animal into a canter. His horsemanship was effortless, and Shanna relaxed against him and allowed him to command the spirited steed, but with the close contact she was ever aware of the hard, masculine feel of him and the tingling warmth that spread through her body.

When they were almost to the place where he had whistled from, he asked against her temple, "Will you meet me here again?"

"I most certainly will not!" She was the proud Shanna again, ignoring the budding excitement that had begun to stir within her. She sat upright and threw off his hand which had come to rest upon her thigh. "Do you honestly think I'd go behind my father's back to meet one of his bondsmen for a tryst in the woods? Sir, you are odious to make such a suggestion."

"Aye, you would hide behind your father's shadow," Ruark retorted glibly. "Like a child, afraid of being a woman."

Shanna's back stiffened, and she twisted away from him in a flare of temper.

"Get down, you—you scoundrel!" she demanded. "Get down and leave me alone! I don't know why I ever rode with you. You —you blackhearted whelp of a scullery maid!"

His low chuckle pricked her anger more, but Ruark drew Attila to a halt and slid from the stallion's back and peered up at her in that deliberate, roguish manner that half mocked, half devoured her. This time Shanna did not turn back as she kicked the steed and set him on a rapid ride down the beach.

Her self-styled solitude having failed, Shanna gave herself over to activity. Without making a plan of it, she became much of a personal scribe to her father. She accompanied him on his trips about the island, making notes of importance as they passed fields and cleared areas. She listened as the overseers and foremen made reports and jotted down their remarks or figures. She kept records of the hours and men required to complete a task and of the crops their efforts produced.

It became apparent that where there were areas of difficulty, she would usually see a mule with a rider wearing shortened pants perched cross-legged on its rump engrossed in the labors of the men or walking about, explaining some innovation with gestures of his hands or a drawing from his ever-ready quill and parchment. It seeped into her mind with a multitude of figures and notes and the frequent mention of his name that where John Ruark was the men were happier and the work moved along apace.

Though Shanna was well occupied with her new duties, it was impossible, despite considerable effort, to ignore the man. As her father commented one afternoon with a chuckle, John Ruark was as well known as himself on the island and apparently better liked. But struggle Shanna did, and she managed to immerse herself in work. When the squire was otherwise occupied and she had no duties at the manor, she made her own tours of his various interests, checking the books, the quality of goods, or just listening to the people and hearing their problems.

It was in this capacity that she found herself in the village store on a late Friday afternoon, reviewing the accounts of the bondsmen. As she leafed through the ledger, the name of John Ruark caught her eye, and curiosity made her scan the columns of his accounts. The figures amazed her.

The column of purchases was quite brief. Aside from writing implements, a pipe, and soap, there was only a rare bottle of wine and an occasional pouch of tobacco. The longest column was that which detailed changes in his pay and there—she traced downward with the tip of her finger—why, it had been increased time and again, tripled, nay, more than ten times the sixpence of a new bondsman. She went further over to the balance of credits and with a swift mental calculation found that by the end of the month he would have nearly a hundred pounds of credit. Then another item caught Shanna's eye. There were moneys other than his wages. At the rate he was building his account, he would probably be free in a year or two.

The back door slammed where Mister MacLaird, the storekeeper, had gone out a few moments before, and the sound of footsteps came across the floor behind her.

"Mister MacLaird," she called over her shoulder. "There's an account here which I would discuss with you. Would you come—"

"Mister MacLaird is busy outside, Shanna. Is there something I might help you with?"

Shanna spun about on the high stool, for there was no mistaking the voice. White teeth showed in the tanned face as Ruark's ready smile spread leisurely across his lips.

"Are you distressed, my love?" He challenged her stunned appraisal. "Have I been away so long you do not recognize me? Some service I can render perhaps or—" he raised a string of shell beads on his fingers—"some bauble for my lady?"

He lowered them and grinned ruefully.

"Your pardon, madam. I forgot myself. You own the store. A pity—and a waste of another of my talents."

Shanna could not contain a smile at his lighthearted banter. "Of those I am sure you have plenty, Ruark. My father reports you have started building the new crushing mill. 'Twould seem you have convinced him 'tis necessary and would be more efficient than what we already have."

Ruark nodded. "Aye, Shanna. I said as much."

"Then why are you here? I would think you hard at work instead of coming and going as you will. Do you oversee yourself of late and set your own hours?"

Ruark's eyebrow raised as he contemplated her. "I do not cheat your father, Shanna. Have no fear." He gestured with his thumb toward the back of the store. "I brought a wagonload of black rum from the brewing house since I had to come in and finish some drawings for your father. Mister MacLaird is testing the kegs now. If 'tis a chaperon you wish, he'll be in shortly."

Shanna flicked her quill to the open ledger. "For a wagon driver you seem highly paid. And there are other amounts here which puzzle me."

"'Tis simple enough," he explained. "In my leisure hours, I work for other people on the island. In return they either do a service for me or repay me with coin. There's a woman in the village who washes my clothes and bedding for—"

"A woman?" Shanna interrupted, her curiosity piqued.

Ruark eyed her with a twisted grin. "Why, Shanna, love, are you jealous?"

"Of course not!" she snapped, but her face was warm with a blush. "I was merely curious. You were saying?"

"'Tis only the fishwoman, Shanna." Ruark did not relent. "No need for dismay."

The sea-green eyes narrowed in a glare. "You're impossibly conceited, Ruark Beauchamp!"

"Shhh, love," he gently admonished, and his eyes sparkled. "Someone might hear you."

"And what do you do for Mrs. Hawkins?" Shanna inquired peevishly, irked with his very presence. She wanted to scream at him! Pound his chest with her fists! Anything to get that smirk from his face.

Ruark took his time in answering; he laid his hat on top of a pile of merchandise and slipped out of the open shirt, tossing it atop his other.

"Mostly what Mister Hawkins could do if he stirred himself—repair her boats and that sort of thing."

"At the rate your money is accumulating, you'll not be with us too long," Shanna commented.

"Money has never been my problem, Shanna. Considering events of late, I would say 'twas women, or more aptly perhaps, woman, as my problem is only one."

Ruark's gaze was now direct, challenging, almost insulting, raking her from her trim and shapely ankles adorned in white silk stockings showing beneath the lifted hem of her skirts, and passing over the narrow waist cinched tightly in the pink-and-white-striped gown, and then more leisurely over her round bosom. The neckline of the bodice was demure with a froth of delicate white lace at her throat. Still, Shanna felt undressed beneath his stare. Self-consciously she plucked at one of the lace inserts in a wide, voluminous sleeve.

"Do you regard me, then, as your problem?"

"Occasionally, Shanna." His countenance grew serious as he met her gaze. "For the greater part, I regard you as the most beautiful woman I've ever seen."

"I cannot for the life of me believe that I am your problem, Ruark," Shanna chided him. "I have scarcely seen you these past weeks. I would say you overstate your case."

His lips spoke no word, but his eyes clearly expressed his wants. The bold stare touched a quickness in her that made her feel as if she were on fire. It flamed in her cheeks and set her fingers to trembling as she stared back at him. He was bathed in a light cast by the setting sun and was aglow with deep golden colors that rippled along his hard, lean frame. He was Apollo cast in gold, and she was no less shaken by the sight of him than by his slow perusal.

"You must have been raised with the savages," she snapped in verbal defense. "You seem to have an aversion for wearing clothes."

Ruark chuckled softly. "At times, Shanna my dearest, clothing can be a hindrance. For instance,"—his eyes again caressed her from toe to top—"a man finds them very troublesome when his wife wears them to bed." His smile grew wicked. "Now that bit of a thing you wear to sleep in, 'tis close to naught. It wouldn't be much of a bother to slip a woman out of it."

The color in her cheeks deepened. "You have your nerve, wandering beneath my balcony like that!"

Abruptly Shanna turned back to the desk as if dismissing him and flipped a page that might as well have been blank for as much as she saw on it.

A soft light shone from a small, high window set in the wall above the desk, outlining her profile in a radiance that made her seem warm, almost angelic. Ruark's eyes touched the hair that tumbled in gold-veined cascades down her back. Just to stand this near to her was a heady wine. He saw the arch of her brow, the delicate line of her nose, the sweet, full curve of her lips which he longed to caress with his own, the firm but gentle thrust of her jaw and the slim, white column of her throat where her hair fell away, baring its ivory softness. His own blood thudded in his ears, and his feet seemed to move of their own volition until he stood close behind her.

Shanna could feel his nearness in every fiber of her being. The manly odors of sweat, leather, and horses invaded her senses. Her pulse raced, and her heart took flight. She wanted to say something, do something to turn away his attention, yet it was as if she were frozen and could only wait for his touch. His hand moved toward her, his fingertips brushed her hair—

Hurrying footsteps came along the wooden planks of the front porch, and a small woman's shape moved across the windows toward the door. Ruark straightened and moved quickly away, and when Milly Hawkins came bursting through the door, he made a show of sorting through a pile of hats. The desk was hidden from view behind a stack of small kegs as one entered from the front, and the girl completely missed Shanna's presence in her hasty glance about the store. She saw Ruark's bronzed back and ran toward him, clutching a bundle of his bondsman's garb against her breast. He had no choice but to face her as she rushed into an explanation.

"I saw ye coming into the village, Mister Ruark, and I thought to save ye from havin' to fetch yer clothes we washed for ye."

"I pass near your house on the way home, Milly. I could have picked them up then." He gave her a lame smile and over her head caught Shanna's brittle regard of them.

"Oh, Mister Ruark, that's all right. I weren't doing anything an' I thought I'd save ye some time." Milly tossed her raven curls coyly, and her wide, black eyes touched him everywhere. Boldly she reached out and ran a hand along the lean ribs.

Shanna's glower was more than piercing as she stared at the young woman's back and watched the slim fingers caress the bronze skin. Absently Ruark brushed aside Milly's hand.

"Are you free this evening, Mister Ruark?"

Ruark chuckled at the girl's tactless approach. "It so happens I have duties which will occupy me most of the night."

"Oh, that old man Trahern!" Milly cried in exasperation, setting her hands on her hips. "He al'ays got sompin' for ye to do!"

"Now look, Milly," Ruark began, not missing the raising of Shanna's brows. He was having trouble keeping his own mirth silent, and it infected his voice. "The squire has demanded nothing more of me than what I have offered." He held up the bundle of clothes. "But thank your mother for these."

It was a known fact in the village that Milly Hawkins was among the laziest wenches about. She and her father were inclined to lie about most of the day complaining of their poor state of finance while Mrs. Hawkins labored hard and long as sole supporter for their family. But the money she earned was much wasted as the father had a taste for rum. Ruark knew it was not the girl who had washed his garments, and he was not of a mind to spread gratitude where it was not due, for the twit would likely be at his shack next with the flimsy excuse of seeing it clean.

"Me ma says ye must be the cleanest man on Los Camellos," Milly reported gayly. "She sees ye cartin' yerself off down to the creek every evening and pretty soon ye come back and give her yer dirty garb. Me pa says bathin' that much ain' good for ye, Mister Ruark. Why, there ain' nobody, 'ceptin' maybe that high and mighty Trahern bitch and her folks there in that big house who waste so much time trying to keep clean."

Ruark's roar of laughter made the girl stop abruptly. Shanna sat stiffly upon her stool, considering Milly with anything but love or affection. The young woman, bemused by Ruark's response, turned to find herself beneath Shanna's glare, which was cold enough to freeze her on the spot. Milly's jaw dropped like a dead weight, and she gaped in wordless astonishment.

" 'Tis Madam Beauchamp now, Milly," Shanna corrected icily. "Madam Ruark Beauchamp, if you please, or, if you don't please, the Beauchamp bitch."

Milly groaned in abject misery and rolled her eyes at Ruark, who had subsided somewhat. Shanna slammed the ledger closed with a bang and, tossing the quill aside, stepped lightly to the floor.

"Is there something else you wanted here, Milly, besides the good man, Mister Ruark?" Shanna raised a challenging brow to the other. "He's not for sale, but everything else here has a price."

Ruark was enjoying himself immensely and moved to the stool Shanna had vacated, there leaning a hip on it while he eyed the two women. Shanna stood majestically proud and haughty, well fired with anger. Sparks flashed in the sea-green pools of her eyes. Milly, on the other hand, slumped and sauntered across the room, hips swaying and bare feet scraping against the wood floor. She was shorter than Shanna, slight of frame with an olive complexion that darkened readily under the sun. She was pretty enough, but it was not difficult to envision her in a few years with a passel of dirty-faced brats hanging to her skirts while one suckled lazily at her breast.

"By yer pa's own law, a bondsman is free to choose any wife who be willing to have him," Milly stated, though the retort was certainly softened. Los Camellos belonged to the Traherns. To anger one of them was truly tempting fate. "Why, Mister Ruark might even choose me. There ain' many others here on the island."

Shanna's surprise displayed itself for a tiny moment. "Oh?" She arched a wondering brow at Ruark. "Has he asked you yet?"

Ruark made no nod or gesture of denial, but grinned lazily into Shanna's regard.

"Why, he ain' had much time, workin' like he does."

" 'Tis what my father bought him for," Shanna quipped

tersely, annoyed with the girl, "not for breeding as you seem to think and most certainly not for siring a string of brats."

Before Shanna could continue with her tirade, the elderly Mister MacLaird entered from the back and announced to Ruark, "Aye, the rum's a good lot. Take it below for me, will ya, laddie?"

He halted abruptly at his spectacled vision fell on Milly.

"Oh, I didna know there be a customer. Shanna, me lovely, see to whatever the lass wants like a good bairn. The tavern keeper will be along after the aged brew, and I'll have to figure his accounts."

Shanna nodded graciously to the man, but for some elusive reason felt a growing sense of resentment toward the younger woman.

"Is there something you wished in the way of goods, Milly?"

"As 'tis I do." The girl could boast later to her friends that she had the haughty Shanna doing her bidding for at least a small space of time. "Mister MacLaird had some scents he said come from far off. I'd like to take me a sniff or two of 'em."

As Milly obviously was encumbered with neither purse nor coin, it was not hard to guess the ruse, but Shanna went anyway to where the fragrances were kept. Milly dallied over the perfume vials until Ruark reentered from the back, carrying a keg on his shoulder with another tucked in the crook of his arm. Under the strain, his muscles and tendons stood out like the cords of a taut rope, while his arms and body gleamed with a film of sweat as if rubbed by a fine oil. Milly gasped, and desire shone in her dark eyes as she whispered in awed observation.

"Gor! Like a bloody Greek statue, he is!"

A line of untanned white showed above his breeches, and the hard, flat belly was displayed with its thin line of dark hair which traced downward from the lightly furred chest. Milly's gaze was so caught upon that stretch of bareness that Shanna wanted to pinch the girl smartly. Sweeping past her, Shanna snatched up the keys and ran to open the cellar door for Ruark. Striking tinder she blew it aflame, then lit the wick of a candle and preceded him down the stairway, lighting the passage. She used the keys to open the lower door. The cellar was cool and dry and, once within, Ruark lowered the kegs to the floor then paused to rest a moment before he lifted one and glanced questioningly at Shanna. She indicated a space at the far end of the rack.

" 'Twill age while the others are used."

Ruark returned for the other he had left, and with a grimace Shanna hooked a slim finger inside the top of his breeches, drawing his somewhat wondering and dubious regard. Snapping the loose waistband against him, she admonished in a true vein of sarcasm.

"Milly is a simple girl and easily excitable. If you show her much more, she may not be able to control herself, and you might find yourself the one ravished."

"I shall take care, madam," Ruark grunted as he hefted the other keg in place. "At least 'tis good to know," his white teeth flashed, "that I am safe with you."

Months of tension and aggravation had built beneath Shanna's supposedly serene exterior. She stood close to Ruark, and her voice was low, almost a whisper, yet burning anger spit through every syllable.

"Sir, I have reached the end of my endurance. You insult me at every meeting and call me less than a woman. You berate my lack of honor, though I but denied your coarse advantage."

"You agreed," he snarled back at her. "You gave your word, and I hold you to it."

"There is no bargain," she hissed in frustrated rage. "You were supposed to die, and I will not he held because you did not."

"What wiles of womanhood would you wield, madam? I gave you the full count. I played your game and trusted you. When I could have fled or at least so tried, it was your part of the bargain which held me." He kept his voice to a hoarse whisper. "I have tasted that most delicious dish, Shanna, the sweet warmth of you, and thereafter have I starved for that which was mine by right of wedlock. And I will have it."

Shanna clenched her fists and slowly thumped them against his hard, bare chest.

"Go away!" she sobbed. "Let me be! What can I say that will convince you that I want no part of you? I hate you! I despise you! I cannot stand the sight of you!"

Shanna fought her tears and gasped for breath, bracing her arms against him. His words were low and harsh in her ear.

"And what am I? Something less than human? Lower than any that have gone before because you found me in a dungeon and I choose to honor a debt to your father I did not earn? More evil than any yet to come? What am I that you can whine and say the fault was mine and deny the bargain was fair? But I tell you this—" He lowered his face until he stared into hers, his eyes bright with his own frustration and anger. "You are my wife."

Shanna's eyes widened and fear began to grow.

"Nay," she whispered.

"You are my wife!" he gritted out slowly and seized her shoulders just as she would have turned away.

"Nay! Never!" she gasped out, her voice rising.

"You are my wife!"

Shanna began to struggle, and he clasped his arms about her, holding her close, smothering her movements in an embrace of steel. Sobbing, Shanna pushed in vain against his chest. Her head tipped backward with her effort, and his mouth crushed down upon hers. In the way of love, rage was transformed into passion. Shanna's arms slipped upward about his neck and were locked in a frantic embrace. Her lips twisted against his, and the full heat of her hunger flooded him until his mind reeled with the frenzy of her answer. He had expected a fight and instead found the fury of a consuming desire sweet on her lips, warm in her mouth, stirring as the quick thrust of her tongue met his own.

They came apart with a gasp, both stunned by the heavy blow of their ardor. Trembling, Shanna leaned against the stacked barrels, helpless, drained of strength. Her eyes were closed, and her bosom heaved with her effort to breathe.

His self-control sorely strained, Ruark almost took her in his arms again, but the thought intruded—Not in a dingy cellar! She was worth so much more than that to him. And they'd only come, and he'd be snatched away again. Patience! Patience, man!

Ruark struck down his ravenous lusts with an iron will and turning, slowly climbed the stairs, letting his body and brain cool as he went. He caught Mister MacLaird's eye as he opened the door and shrugged away his question.

"She's counting the kegs."

When Ruark entered the cellar again, Shanna had also composed herself, but her eyes followed him until he returned to her side, then she whispered, "Thank you."

"Don't thank me yet," he murmured as he gently wiped a smudge from her arm. "There will be a better time and a better place than this."

Ruark went for another load, and as he brought the last kegs into the store, Shanna was being led out the door by Mister Mac-Laird. Milly still gawked, her hunger bold in her eyes; and rather than face her mewling attention, Ruark slammed the cellar doors, snatched up his hat and shirt, and left with what one might have called undue haste.

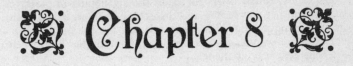

Chapter 8

MORNING blossomed with vibrant hues that glistened upon and changed the color of the waters, touching the tossing surf with the pinks and golds of the breaking dawn. The very air seemed laden with a rosy mist, and the greens of the lawn and trees spread endlessly beneath until they joined the blue of the gently rolling sea.

Shanna stood alone on her balcony, bathed in the pale, soft gold of the rising sun. Her pastel dressing gown was like a cloud swirling about her, rising on the fitful breezes that stirred the fragrance from the flowering vine twining about the balustrade. Her face was cast in a wistful mood, her eyes yearning, and her fair lips parted as if in anticipation of a kiss. Her arms hugged her slender waist as if they sought to replace a lover's embrace which now was but a memory of yesterday.

The glory of the dawn faded into the bright light of day as the sun cleared its bulk from the horizon and began the arching flight across the sky. Sighing, Shanna returned to her bed and tried once more to sleep before the heat reached her room and she would be forced to rise. Closing her eyes, she felt again the almost-pain as her breasts were crushed against Ruark's unyielding chest and the warmth of his breath against her cheek; once more she saw the urgency in his golden gaze as he lowered his lips to hers.

Shanna's eyes flew open, for again the awakening of pleasure deep within her was strong and disturbing. And so it had been the whole night long. When she relaxed, the memory of her own response seared through her brain, flooding her body with a pulsing warm excitement.

What was the cure for this malady? Shanna moaned to herself. Why was she so afflicted? Was she one who would ever yearn for men but find satisfaction with none? She had been mauled before under the attentions of much more lordly men and found no softening of her heart, yet now her mind ever envisioned the face of that one who haunted her, this Ruark, this demon, this dragon of her dreams.

Her eyelids were heavy with the need of sleep, and slowly she succumbed to the weight, her mind sailing uneasily upon a tossing sea of slumber. He was there, with his gleaming, glistening body of oiled bronze, waiting for her just before she could reach her dreams, and she knew if she touched him, he would be hard and real.

Her eyes found his face and were trapped there by some satanic seduction. The eyes raked her like golden talons while he leered and jeered, and the lips moved unceasingly in a low, cracked whisper:

"Come to me. Bend to me. Yield yourself. Give yourself. Come."

She resisted, all on the strength of her fear. Then the face began to change. The nose grew into a long dragonlike snout with smoke curling from the nostrils. His skin became green with warted scales, and the eyes glowed like twin gold-lensed lanterns, snaring her gaze with their hypnotic brightness. The ears stood out like tiny bat-shaped wings. The white toothed leer became a fixed grin, gaping wide and edged with evil fangs. Then with a bellowing roar, he breathed out flames which engulfed her in a searing passion, tingling across her body, sapping her strength, weakening her will, drawing out her every resolve until she groveled in helpless terror, begging the beast to cease, crying for his mercy, fighting for her breath in the airless flame.

Shanna woke with a chill trembling her, yet the heat of the

room brought perspiration. Her gown and the sheets were wet with it. She was fighting for air, gasping to draw a full breath as if some heavy, unseen presence crossed her face. In panic she flung herself from the bed and ran out onto the balcony. There, reason returned, and she calmed. The world was as it had been, the sun but a trifle higher and the day but a trifle warmer.

Listlessly Shanna began to pace her bedchamber, finding any distraction better than surrendering to the fantasies of her mind. Drastic measures would have to be taken to relieve this madness that bound her. She could not sleep. She could not eat. Her life was in a turmoil. Her bedchamber closed around her, and in every corner she heard Ruark's sardonic laughter and saw his dark, leering face. Retreating from this torture, she fled below, seeking out her father.

Orlan Trahern paused with a spoon of melon halfway to his mouth. It took a fair occurrence to halt him in his affair with food, but the sight of his daughter on this morning did it. Her hair was tousled and tangled, her eyes were red and puffy, her cheeks pale, and she was not dressed and ready to meet the day. It was unheard of that she should appear this early or in this state. The squire returned the spoon untouched to his plate and waited her explanation.

Under her father's worried frown, Shanna chafed and knew his distress when he laid down the spoon. She realized she was expected to speak, yet words were dear to her, and she found no ready reply to his unspoken question. She oversweetened the cup of tea that was set before her and then winced as its heat stung her tongue.

"I'm sorry, papa," she began lamely. "I spent an ill night and don't feel too well even yet. Would it be all right if I don't go with you today?"

Orlan Trahern lifted his spoon and chewed as he considered her request. "I have grown accustomed to your company of late, my dear. But I surmise that I should not be overly at a loss if you do not attend a day or two. I've only been about this business a decade or so."

He rose and came to feel her brow, finding it a trifle warm to the touch.

"I would be much amiss if you were ailing," he continued.

"Hie yourself to your room and rest for the day. I shall send Berta to see to your wants. There are matters pressing which I must be about. Now come, child, let me see you up."

"Oh, papa, no!" Shanna could scarce bear the thought of returning. "You need not bother. I'll have a small bite and go."

"Nonsense!" he blustered. "I'll see you abed and tended before I go. Now come."

Wearily Shanna sighed and took his arm, knowing she had erred, for now she was trapped and would see the day out in her chambers.

Trahern saw his daughter carefully tucked in before he bade her farewell and left. Shanna had no time to rise, for in a moment Berta arrived, greatly concerned for her charge. Shanna's forehead was felt again, her tongue was checked, and her pulse taken.

"I do not know for sure, but it may be the fever. You feel a liddle varm. I tink a liddle broth und a tea of bay leaves vill do goot."

Before Shanna could deny any such need, the woman left, bringing back a tray laden with the brew. Shanna shuddered in distaste as she sipped the tea, but the housekeeper would not be put off, and Shanna was ordered to finish it to the last miserable swallow. When finally she was allowed privacy once more, she buried her head beneath her pillow and pounded her fists against the bed in frustration.

"Damned rogue! Damned rogue! Damned rogue!" she whined.

The day aged into evening and still the battle raged. Shanna's mind was exhausted from the struggle and seemed to lie within her skull without movement, while all the arguments trod the same well-worn paths across it. Reason and the undenied logic of her own motives waned under overwhelming fatigue, while the multitude of threats raised by Ruark's failure to be hanged properly bludgeoned her until she grew numb beneath their onslaught. Wearily she sagged in a chair and rolled her head against the high back. She knew with certainty that she would not be free of Ruark Beauchamp. With each day he grew bolder, and each time they met he confronted her more openly. There was so little left for her to be proud of in this circumventure of her father's will. Of all those nearest to her, Pitney was the only one she had not deceived, and the lies did not sit well with her. She had been reared on the truth and taught to face it, and every time she closed her eyes a vision of a dim face behind the barred window of the van tormented her, and her ears rang with the eerie wail in the night. She could no longer bear the struggle. She must free herself from this inner conflict.

With a sob Shanna stumbled to the bed and threw herself upon it. Her groan of despair came muffled against the pillow.

" 'Tis done. 'Tis done. I will see the bargain out. I yield."

Shanna closed her eyes almost fearfully, but only a soft, warm half darkness was there; then sleep drifted like a soundless wave over her, and she was engulfed within its peace.

The Scotswoman, Hergus, was loyal and swift of foot. She led Ruark through the darkness, pausing often to make sure he followed but staying several paces ahead of him, leading him wide around the plantation house then up a narrow path through the trees on the hill behind it. They passed one unused cottage and then another. The lane wandered through a heavy hedge of brush into a small glade. There, in the deep shadows hidden from the moon, was another cottage, larger and more spacious than the others, and here a dim light shone in the windows.

Ruark knew these were the guest houses of the manor. They were hardly used, however, as most preferred the luxury of the big house. But of his summons, Ruark knew nothing. The woman had sought him out of his shack, saying only that she was Hergus and that he was to come with her. He was aware that she was a member of Trahern's household staff, but he could not fathom the squire summoning him in this overly discreet manner.

His curiosity was aroused, and he had followed Hergus, wearing only his sandals and short breeches. She led him across the porch of the cottage, holding the door open until he went inside. It slammed behind him, and he heard her feet pattering off in the night. In some bewilderment, Ruark glanced about him at the small drawing room lit only by a single candle which cast a light barely brighter than the full moon without. The room was comfortably and expensively furnished. The carpet beneath his feet would have easily paid his bondage several times over.

A small sound intruded upon the quiet, and a door swung open. Ruark stared in amazement. It was Shanna, and her name escaped his lips in a whispered question. Like a pale ghost haunting the night, she came forward, clothed in a long, white, clinging robe, her hair wound with a ribbon in a single great fall down her back. Her voice was husky as she spoke.

"Ruark Beauchamp. Knave. Rogue. Murderer. Hung by the neck. Dead. Buried in a grave. You have vexed me much these past months. You prattle of a bargain where I say there is none. But I will honor it and pay my debt so you will have no claim on me. This way I will be free. So, as you say, for this night until the first light of dawn, I will play your wife. Then I will have no more of you."

His abortive laugh ended in a snort, and Ruark stared at her in total disbelief. He wandered around the room and under Shanna's regard checked the anteroom, the dining room, and even behind the silken draperies. He came to stand close beside her, and Shanna returned his stare as boldly as he gave it.

"And your good man, Pitney?" he questioned. "Where is his lair this time?"

"There is no one. We are alone. You have my word on it."

"Your word!" His laugh rang with a sneering undertone. "That, madam, almost frightens me."

Shanna ignored the sting of his comments and waved a slender hand in the direction of the bedchamber. "And would you search beneath the bed? Perhaps your manhood needs some recompense and bolster."

Ruark turned his back upon her beauty. It was in his mind to flee the place before the worst of his fears was recognized. But his feet were leaden, and the thought of her willing in his arms began to cauterize his mind.

"I fear the game is entered once again," he said harshly. "And I have survived so much that I am leery of what deeper fate you have in store for me."

Shanna's laughter softly entwined him as she reached out and caressed his back, tracing the long swell of his lean muscles.

Ruark's knees went suddenly weak as her cool hand touched him and wandered with its soft, silken smoothness, stirring his emotions until they boiled with merry pain in the pit of his belly. He ground his teeth and moaned:

"To hell with thorns!"

He faced her suddenly, and her hand stayed to lightly rub his chest. Ruark's nostrils flared, and his brow lowered angrily. He would see what her resolve would bear.

Purposefully he reached out and loosened the frog at the top of her dressing gown. Shanna met his glare and only smiled softly as his hands worked downward until the garment hung open. She shrugged, and it fell to her feet, revealing a sheer, shimmering white cloth that resembled a gown of ancient Greece. One soft, lovely shoulder was temptingly bare while the other was bound with the same silken fasteners that had adorned her robe. The gown hid nothing from him, and Shanna saw the hard flint of passion strike sparks in the golden eyes as they moved upon her. Her full, ripe breasts swelled against the gossamer web that molded itself to her and to the pale, delicate peaks which thrust forward impudently. Ruark's breath was ragged in his throat, and he could not still the tremor which had seized his body. He had already realized that beneath all her clothes Shanna was what every man dreamed of, a vision of incomparable beauty. Her skin glowed with the soft luster of creamy satin, and through the cloth he saw the inward curve of her waist, amazingly small in its unlaced freedom, the trim and seductive roundness of her hips, and the lithe grace of her limbs.

" 'Tis my one intent," Shanna murmured softly, "to be your wife in every way, whatever your desire."

Ruark's long-starved passions flared high, smothering the anger and leaving only a small suspicion to nibble at the edge of his consciousness. This, too, he discarded. This night was fully worth the risk.

Still, he was frozen in bemusement at her motives, and his eyes reveled in their freedom as they feasted hungrily on her beauty, seeking out every charm once hidden from him. Shanna felt devoured, and it took an effort of her will to remain pliant beneath his probing eyes.

"Come," she urged, and her voice did not sound her own in her ears. She tugged at his arm. "Your bath is ready, Master Beauchamp."

Ruark let himself be led like a dumb animal into the bedchamber where a large, massive tester bed occupied the far wall. A candelabrum sat on a table beside it, its flames flickering in the soft breezes that billowed the draperies at the windows. Beneath it, glasses and crystal decanters of several various brews waited. White, filmy netting was tied to the heavy, ornate posts of the bed, and he saw that the bedding had been folded down invitingly and the pillows fluffed.

Shanna halted beside the tub which faced the room. A taper gleamed beside it, and its light silhouetted her through the gown, betraying the full measure of her beauty. As he stood close before her, her soft, green eyes lifted to meet his, he was almost overwhelmed by the nearness of her, the sweet, exotic fragrance that clung to her. Her breasts pressed wantonly against the gauze of her diaphanous gown, almost touching his chest. It was all Ruark could do to hold in check the urges that flooded him and to keep himself from simple rape.

"I thought you might enjoy a bath," Shanna murmured. "If not...."

Ruark's eyes swept about the room, but he could find no place for assailants to hide and certainly not the broad, hulking Pitney. The draperies and windows were open, and the dense black yard and the jungle beyond lent only the usual night sounds to his ears, the twittering of birds and the occasional croak of frogs or chirp of insects.

He returned his gaze to Shanna, who waited patiently for his answer.

"Such richness might warp my senses." He kicked off his sandals. "But I shall taste its fullness 'ere my final doom descends."

Shanna smiled softly, and her slim fingers plucked at the fastenings of his breeches. "You do not trust me still."

"I remember our last encounter in England," Ruark responded dryly, "and deeply fear that another such interruption might render me useless to any woman."

Shanna ran her hands down his lean ribs but kept her eyes carefully on his face as he tossed the breeches to a chair.

"In the tub, my lustful dragon. Breathe not your fire aimlessly. I am here to see the bargain out. You need have no further fear of me."

Ruark lowered himself into the warm bath and relaxed a moment in the luxury of it. As his wandering gaze moved to her, Shanna gently caressed his shoulder and offered him a large snifter of brandy. Ruark drained the glass in a single breath and welcomed the burning distraction in his throat. Taking the empty glass from him, Shanna poured another draught and returned it to his hand. Her kiss was as soft and quick on his lips as a butterfly's touch upon a rose.

" 'Tis better if you sip it slowly, my love, and taste the fullness of it."

Ruark leaned back against the high rim of the tub and closed his eyes, savoring the feel of the warm water. His baths in the creek had been good enough for cleanliness, but they had lacked much in the way of comfort and relaxation. He opened one eye to peer at Shanna, setting the glass aside.

"Wife in truth you be?"

She nodded. "For this night."

"Then scrub my back, wife."

He tossed a sponge and leaned forward, awaiting her. Shanna came to him, and her hands were gentle, lathering the broad expanse. She was again reminded of a sleek, powerful cat as her hands lightly glided over him, and she could not help but marvel at the rugged strength that lay relaxed beneath her touch. Oddly content at the task, Shanna leisurely lathered his black hair, fluffed it dry, and brushed it into place. She massaged his neck and shoulders, dissolving any fatigue that might have been there. Ruark could remember no other moment in his life when such pure bliss had descended upon him. Then she ran her finger along his chin, rasping her long nail along the short stubble there. Shanna pressed him back until he lay again against the high back of the tub and, taking up a razor and soap, shaved him carefully and then stroked his face gently with a hot towel.

"Is this the way of a wife?" Shanna asked almost hesitantly. "I've had so little practice, I would not know."

Ruark's eyes met hers, shining softly so close above him. He reached out to take her hand and draw her near, but she left him and wandered to the open window where she leaned against the sill and toyed with the tassels on the drapes. Ruark relaxed to finish his bath. He had seen the fleeting frown of bemusement that crossed her face and wondered what dire circumstance had brought the thorn-bound Shanna out of safety and to this end. Certainly no assault of his, for he had not been stirred to risk a flogging or worse in seeking her out.

Shanna tried to quell the trepidation that had arisen, and she fought the flooding tides of coldness that surged within her. When she had met Ruark's eyes, the shock was sharp, for she had suddenly realized the moment rapidly approached for which she had made this tryst. Would he seek his vengeance cruelly or with grace? Would she find pleasure or pain in his arms? It was too late to withdraw from this madness. How could she have believed a bondslave, a colonial who had already proven himself no gentleman, would respect her womanhood? How could she have cast herself in his grasp so recklessly?

A splash sounded behind her, and Shanna glanced around to see him rising from the tub. It was too late! Too late!

Ruark had heaved himself up and seized a towel, catching Shanna's stare and glimpsing the full naked fear within her eyes before she managed to hide it. A betrayal now, he wondered? Would she flee? Or summon a heavy escort? Ruark waited. He was absolutely vulnerable.

Nervous now, Shanna turned her gaze away from the rather frightening sight of the naked man and went to wait beside the bed. Ruark watched her warily, toweling himself dry, then moved toward her. Her eyes wavered beneath his direct stare, and her shaking fingers entwined. She was suddenly like a small girl in a fully bloomed woman's body.

Shanna summoned all her determination to speak, but her voice still came thin and weak.

"Ruark, 'tis my will that this be out. 'Tis my will that the bargain be met. I know you have cause to hate me, but, Ruark,"—her lower lip quivered, and as she stared up at him, tears welled within her eyes—"please don't hurt me."

Ruark lifted a finger and wiped away a tear that traced slowly down her cheek, then murmured wonderingly, "You're trembling."

He turned and hurled the towel in a corner. Shanna flinched

and braced herself for his attack, but instead of being assaulted, she heard a chuckle coming from deep inside his chest.

"Do you really think me a beast, madam, some dragon come to rend you upon your pallet? Ah, poor Shanna, dream-struck girl. This time of love is not a time for taking, but a time of giving and for sharing. You give me this night as I gave you my name, freely, of your own accord. But I warn you now you may find something here that will bind you more eternally than anything else in your life."

Did he mean a child? Shanna frowned and turned her back to him. It was a consideration she had scarce let herself dwell upon. What if—

Ruark's arms slipped with infinite care about her, and she forgot all. His face brushed against her hair, stirring from it the sweet fragrance of the red jasmine, frangipani, until his mind reeled with the heady scent of it. Ruark knew he must be gentle lest her fear destroy the moment, but it took an extreme exercise of will to court her with care. Shanna stilled her doubt and overcame the tension and resistance of her body by reminding herself repeatedly that he was, at least for the night, her husband and that come the dawn it would all be over, and she would be free of him.

Lifting her heavy golden hair aside, she offered him her shoulder, and his long fingers nimbly worked the silken frogs until the gown was free and slid to her feet. Her skin contrasted against the darkness of his like a translucent pearl upon a bed of warm earth. Once more his embrace enfolded her, bringing her back in close contact with his lean frame. Shanna felt the hard, manly boldness of him, and she closed her eyes as his searing lips slowly traced along her throat and shoulder. His hands caressed her, leisurely arousing her, stroking her breasts, and moving downward over her belly. A warm tide of tingling excitement flooded her. She was cold and hot and shaky. Her mind whirled giddily, and she forgot to repeat her reminder. The whisper of a sigh escaped her as she leaned her head back upon his shoulder, spilling her hair over his arm. She lifted her face to meet his, trembling lips slackened and parted as his mouth possessed hers. He turned her to him, and they came together like the forging of irons, their kisses now savage and fierce, devouring as tongues met and their mouths slanted across each other's with hungry impatience. His hand wandered down her back, pressing her hips tighter against him. His passions raged voraciously within him, and the fire in his loins was raging out of control.

Ruark bent a knee upon the bed, pulling her with him, and they were tumbling on the sheets. His open mouth, hot and wet, seared her breasts, and his white teeth lightly nibbled her curving waist and the smooth silken skin of her belly. Shanna closed her eyes, panting and breathless, pliable beneath his caresses. His eyes aflame and lusting, Ruark lowered his weight upon her, parting her thighs, and pressed deep with her. Shanna moved to welcome the hard thrust, her woman's body reacting instinctively to this new, indescribable, budding, splintering feeling that built with pulsing leaps and bounds deep within her. The pleasure mounted so intensely she wondered wildly if she could bear it.

It was magic, a stunning, beautiful, expanding bloom of ravaging rapture that made her arch against him with a fierce ardor matching his. The wild, soaring ecstasy burst upon them, fusing them together in the all-consuming caldron of passion. Clasped tightly to him as if he would draw her into himself, Shanna felt the thunderous beating of his heart against her naked breasts and heard his hoarse, ragged breathing in her ear.

Time seemed to verge on eternity before Ruark raised his head. Shanna lay back upon the pillow, staring up at him with wide, searching eyes, amazement etched in the beauteous visage. The amber eyes held her softly as he whispered:

"Doth the dragon so comport, my love?"

His lips pressed upon hers gently, tenderly, and Shanna gave quick answer, returning warm, fleeting kisses as she breathed, "Aye, my dragon Ruark, my ferocious beastly man, you demanded the bargain met, but the payment was not all yours."

Ruark smoothed her rumpled hair and traced his mouth along the slim column of her throat, tasting the exotic fragrance that seemed so much a part of her, that haunting scent which had plagued him in the gaol every wakeful hour, every moment of his dreams.

"Are you regretful, love?" he questioned huskily.

Shanna shook her head, and oddly it was no lie she gave him. All the qualms she had expected, and the quirks of gnawing guilt she imagined would torment her, were not there. More frightening to her was the strange sense of rightness she felt being in his arms, as if here was where she was meant to be, like the sea on the sand, a tree on the earth. Aye, that feeling of contentment disturbed her more than guilt ever could.

Willfully Shanna set her mind on a different path. It was the fulfilling of her word that satisfied her conscience, naught else. Her arms looped about his neck and were like silk sliding against him. She laughed softly, lightly nibbling at the lobe of his ear, touching it with her tongue.

"Has your sense of justice been appeased, milord?"

Ruark's parted lips played upon hers as he gave reply. "Aye, wench. For the tortured nights I've lain awake thinking of you, for the days I could not rout you from my mind, for the torment I've suffered, knowing you were close and not being able to see you, touch you. Aye, I have tasted of the rose." His brow furrowed. "But like the lotus, deep within this flower is a seed which entraps the mind." His eyes searched her face. "The night is far from over, Shanna."

Gently she rubbed her fingers across the harsh lines of his frown, smoothing it away.

"For this night," she murmured, "I am your wife."

Shanna drew his hand to her lips and slowly kissed the lean, brown knuckles while each gaze warmed and played within the depths of the other's eyes. She showed small perfect teeth in an impish grin before sinking them teasingly into the back of his hand.

"For all the hours you've tormented me, my dragon Ruark, I'll see some gallant knight to my rescue. You have abused this maiden sorely in her distress."

Ruark cocked a dubious brow. "Do you think me, then, to be the terrible dragon of your dreams, madam? Am I to be put away by your silvered knight? And truly, madam, have I abused you so sorely? Or is it that I've dared to treat you as a woman and not some lofty wench on a pedestal, a virgin queen no mortal man can touch?"

Shanna's eyes gleamed as she stared at him from beneath

lowered lids. "Then you at last admit I am a woman, Mister Beauchamp?" she queried.

"Aye, you're a woman, Shanna," Ruark replied hoarsely. "A woman made for love and for a man, not made for dreams of knights and dragons and damsels in distress. If I be your dragon, Shanna, then let it be known your knight in shining armor will have no easy task subduing me."

"Do you threaten me, monstrous dragon?" The sea-green eyes were wide and watched him almost fearfully.

"Nay, Shanna love," he whispered softly. "But then, neither do I believe in fables."

He moved against her, his body rousing, responding to the softness of hers. His open mouth sought her lips, parting them, twisting, burning, devouring, slanting across them as if he could not get enough of the dewy sweetness. Their breaths merged and became one. Shanna lost her last touch on reality. Her world careened crazily beneath the savage urgency of his demanding kisses, and she was swept along in the violent storm of his passion. His hand slipped downward, capturing the soft fullness of a breast before his mouth followed. Shanna caught her breath as the wild flooding pleasure shot through her again. His hot, greedy kisses covered her naked flesh, and in the flickering candlelight, his hair shone with a soft sheen of black satin against her pale skin. Her own hair spread out in shimmering waves across the pillows, and her eyes took on a strange, deep hue of smoky blue. She was his again, and she reveled in the sweetness of bliss.

In a calmer moment Ruark drew away and leaned back against the massive headboard, fluffing his pillow behind him and drawing Shanna up beside him. He poured a glass of Madeira from the bottle on the bedside commode and handed the goblet to her.

"We'll share a glass," he breathed, kissing her throat.

Shanna placed a hand on his chest to stop her reeling world and answered him as his lips found hers and played upon them, his tongue lightly caressing them, his teeth gently tugging.

They sampled the wine as lovers, sipping from the same spot on the rim and then kissing as the taste lingered in their mouths. His eyes devoured her, drinking in her beauty, touching her everywhere. His hand wandered upon her boldly, stroking her thighs, drawing intricate patterns on her stomach. Her ripe breasts, pink-tipped and tantalizing, trembled beneath his soft caress.

Shanna's regard of him was just as inquiring. Her finger followed across his belly where light skin was separated by dark. Ruark held his breath as she traced the thin line of hair that trickled downward from the light furring on his chest, and again the coals of passion were fanned and flamed.

For a time they slumbered, and for both it was a natural untroubled sleep. Shanna had no dreams of what she might have missed, and Ruark had no nightmares of what he was sure he had missed. Feeling the manly warmth beside her, Shanna roused from the depths of sleep and rolled her head to gaze at Ruark. He lay on his back, one arm across his waist and with the other thrown wide, his chest rising and falling with his slow and even breath. She could not resist the temptation and, reaching out, ran her hand through the light hair on his chest. With something akin to wonder, she felt along the lean ribs and was more than mildly amazed at the hardness of the muscles at his waist. Then a finger touched her chin and raised it until she looked full into those soft amber eyes. They were not smiling now; they were intense to such a degree that she was almost startled. She was surprised at her own abandon, for she came to him again, pressing to him, answering his every passion with her own. She sighed as his lips found her breasts and held his head to her, moving so her bosom caressed him softly, stirring him until his lips parted in the agony of it. His hands were beneath her hips, lifting her to him, and again they tasted the full joy of their mutual union.

Much later Shanna lay on his chest, her cheek resting against his neck. The windows of the room opened on the east, and there they both could see the first rosy glow of the predawn light. With a sigh of reluctance, Shanna rose. Ruark watched silently as she slipped into her gown and pulled her robe over it, tucking her feet in a pair of slippers. In the doorway, she leaned against the sill and looked back at him.

"The bargain is fulfilled, then." Her voice was so low Ruark barely heard it.

Quickly Shanna turned and fled. Ruark swung his long legs over the edge of the bed and sat listening to the sound of her footsteps hurrying through the house, then fading as they went onto the porch. His voice, too, softly broke the quiet.

"Aye, Shanna, my love, the bargain is fulfilled. But what, then, of the vows we exchanged?"

Shanna was again her bright and cheerful self, though in the night past the amount of sleep she had gotten had been meager indeed. It was as if a great burden had been lifted from her, and truly she conceded the fulfillment of the bargain and the restoration of her honor had accomplished wonders. Ruark could demand no more of her, no matter how twisted his reasoning. The affair was past. Done! She was free. It had been a delightful interlude, but now it was over. She could set her mind to more important matters.

In the press of the day, Ruark faded from her memory. She was gay, lighthearted, and efficient. In the afternoon, her father sat as judge for some of the squabbles that arose among his people. Shanna was at his elbow, recording and advising. Then there was a tour of the warehouses, and the reports of the various managers were duly noted. The harvest had been rich, and huge kegs of black rum and the lighter tans and whites were stacked high, ready for shipment. Bales of raw hemp brought in from other islands filled several storehouses. There were kegs of indigo, valuable for the rich blue dye it offered, and a wide assortment of tobaccos, native cotton, flax, and other raw material which England needed for its factories.

Shanna and her father had a late, quiet supper together, and she retired, a much-eased conscience bringing her quickly to restful sleep. The next day passed much the same, and her night of surrender was all but forgotten in the rush.

The fifth day dawned as the rest, but became cloudy with fleeting mists and fitful breezes. Shanna and her father, riding in the barouche, ranged high in the hills checking sites. Abruptly Trahern decided to swing by the site of the new cane mill to see the progress there.

A strange sound trembled the air as they neared the spot. A heavy thud came every minute or so, and as they rounded the last bend they saw the source. The smoothed trunks of trees were being driven into the ground by a huge rock raised on pulleys by a span of mules then released to fall on the butts, driving the piles deep.

The carriage halted and Trahern stared, somewhat awestruck. The mechanics of the rig were simple enough. It had only needed a good mind to make it work. Shanna could have named the man before the foreman came to meet them, bringing him along. Ruark approached the barouche on her father's side and at the squire's inquiries began to explain how the piles would bear the weight of huge rollers when the mill was done and how the rollers would be geared to crush the juice from the harvested cane.

" 'Tis only that the smithy is a bit pressed to make the ironware like Mister Ruark told him, squire." The overseer waved his hat toward the works. "If the man's on time, we'll have her ready when the new batch comes in."

Trahern was listening to the taskmaster enlarge upon the explanations when Shanna raised her eyes and found herself staring into those amber ones of Ruark. A slow smile spread across his lips, and it bore a strange note of confident knowledge yet with no threat, no smirk, no leer. Just a simple smile that somehow disturbed her more than it should have. She nodded the briefest of greetings and turned away from him in what she hoped was a pointed rejection. Her father asked a question, but Ruark's answer was lost to her as her mind retreated from this contact.

A few moments later they resumed the ride back to the village, then to the manor house. The incident was submerged in detail, and she was again carefree by the time dinner was served. Pitney joined them, and afterwards he and the squire engaged in a game of chess.

Feeling a good sense of accomplishment for the day, Shanna retired to her chambers and found restful slumber quickly. It was past the hour of midnight when she came fully awake in an instant and lay staring blankly in the dark of her room. A steady drizzle pattered on the leaves outside, and the clouds were low and heavy, giving an unnatural backness to the night. Then she realized what had awakened her. She had known the heat of a body close beside her, warm lips parting hers and arms holding her tightly. There had been the touch of a hand on her breasts and a gentle caress along her thighs and the thrust of a man, hard and hot, between them.

Her confusion came from the haunting sense of pleasure which now ebbed from her body. What spell had Ruark cast upon her that she should desire again that joining with him? She was alone in the room, but was just as sure that had he been there she would have yielded, nay, clung to him and demanded he give again that for which she yearned. She had never felt so fully a woman as when she played his wife. Even now, as she lay on her bed in the dark room, she was amazed that no guilt or shame rose to condemn her for that night or for this one in which she longed for him to come to her. Allowed to age and ferment in the flask of her woman's body, the heady memory of his lovemaking was now all the more intoxicating. She could not shake the exhilarating illusions and grew dizzy with the remembrance of what they had shared.

"He is but a man," she whispered in the dark. "He has no special gift beyond other men. I'll find a husband, and we'll share the same."

Faceless numbers of suitors Shanna had cast away in disgust loomed upward before her consideration. They could strike no spark of fire in her blood, yet when in the midst of those forgotten ones Ruark's tanned visage appeared, her heart thumped with a sweet wildness that stirred her very soul.

"Why must that colonial be the one I should rouse to?" she hissed to the ebony shadows. She was angry with herself for letting him come into her mind again. "Nay, I will deny him! The bargain is done! There will be nothing more between us!"

As much as she forced all her determination behind her vow, it had an empty ring, and the weakness of it echoed through her brain. When sleep came again, it was not the peaceful slumber she had enjoyed before.

Late the next morning, Shanna joined her father in the dining room, and she saw by the remains of dirty dishes that two others had been with him for breakfast. Trahern greeted her and seemed in a hurry to finish his own meal.

"You need not come with me today, Shanna," he informed her as he sipped thick, black coffee.

Shanna said nothing but glanced around the table. She felt an odd presence in the room, and then she noted a small porcelain dish beside one of the plates whereon lay a black ash as from a pipe.

"Mister Ruark was here again," she stated bluntly, sure of the fact.

"Aye," her father snorted. "But no need to trouble yourself, daughter. He's gone. In fact," Orlan wiped his lips on a large napkin, dusted his lap, rose, and took his cane and hat from the hands of Milan, "his shall be the first business of the day. I have given him another increase in pay, and as I deem that I need him closer at hand, I gave him the choice of cottages." Trahern chuckled lightly. "He took the best, the far one under the trees."

Trahern regarded her for a moment, and his voice was only slightly more firm when he continued. "As mistress of my household you will, of course, see that it is presentable."

Shanna could only stare at him, half afraid as he spoke, trying to find some hidden meaning in his words. Seeing none, she nodded and conceded, "I shall send the servants there."

Her father fixed his hat with some show of irritation. "I will expect no further slight of the man. Your dislike of him is apparent, but he is extremely valuable to me, and I hope to persuade him to stay on with us after his debt is paid. I should be home for an early meal this evening."

Trahern paused in the doorway and looked back at her, almost smiling as if to soften his words. "Good day, daughter."

For a long while Shanna sat staring after her father, but in her mind she saw only Ruark's lean, tanned form stretched upon the bed.

He'll be there in the bed we shared! He'll use the bath again! A full rush of visions filled her mind with one brighter than any, that of the tall canopy towering above them as the full measure of pleasure burst within her.

Had Milan turned then from his preparation of her breakfast, he would have seen her face flushed, her eyes distant and dreaming.

The cottage was readied, and Ruark moved his spartan belongings into it that very same night. He made use of the brass tub and enjoyed a steaming bath, lingering in it as illusions of

Shanna in a gossamer veil of white swam about him—Shanna bending to whisper in his ear, standing childlike beside the bed, then naked and writhing in splendorous ecstasy beneath him.

Donning again his brief breeches, Ruark restlessly prowled the rooms, poking in empty chests and armoires, leafing through books, seeking some diversion to settle his mind. He failed abjectly, for there was naught he could put his thoughts to that fascinated him more than Shanna.

Dawn broke clear and bright. Rays of light invaded her bedchamber, waking Shanna from her fitful slumber. As it was her custom to rise at a later hour, Hergus was not in attendance, and pensively Shanna stroked her own tousled curls into some semblance of order. She could not name her mood, but she paused often in her task, the brush threaded through a soft tress while she stared unseeing into the mirror. A wistful sigh escaped her as she donned a dressing gown, belting it loosely about her narrow waist. When she left her chambers, she had no destination in mind and made her way slowly down the curving stairway, pondering the undulating motion of her robe as the opening parted and closed about her long, naked limbs. She had descended halfway when she heard men's voices in the entrance hall and recognized Ruark's deep chuckle in reply to the doorman's jovial greeting. Shanna paused. Her eyes lost their distant look, and attentive now to the world about her, she listened to the rich, confident timbre of Ruark's voice and the precise clip of Jason's articulate speech.

"The squire will be down directly, Mister Ruark. Will you have a chair in the dining room and rest yourself while you wait?"

"Thank you, Jason, but I'll wait here in the hall. I'm early, anyway."

"Master Trahern would want you to make yourself at home, Mister Ruark. He shouldn't be but a moment or two. There is hardly a body who will get up earlier than the squire. He has worked hard all his life and does not appear to be in favor of slowing any. I will be in back, Mister Ruark. Call if you should want me."

Shanna listened to the sound of Jason's retreating footsteps then leaned against the balustrade, peering down toward the hall. Garbed in his usual attire of white shirt and short pants, Ruark stood before the portrait of Georgiana, staring up at it, and Shanna wondered at his thoughts. There had been much similarity between daughter and mother, though Georgiana's hair had been paler and her eyes a soft, smiling gray. Did Ruark see her there within the oil-painted image of her mother, Shanna wondered, or was he just admiring, like so many others before him.

If she made a sound, Shanna was not aware of it, but in the narrow space of time she watched, something passed between them, and Ruark turned, glancing up toward the stairs as if he knew she would be there. Shanna was caught and could not flee in dignity. She waited as he crossed with measured stride to the first step, there resting a sandaled foot on it while he gazed at her, his eyes touching her everywhere. The pale aqua robe flowed in fluid lines about her body, molding itself against her as if reluctant to be parted, showing the womanly roundness of her breasts and the graceful curve of her hips, while openly displaying a long, sleek limb. She looked cool and serene, like a high priestess descending the temple steps.

"Good morning," Ruark murmured, and his voice was like a gentle caress.

"Good day, sir." Her own tone was bright and cheerful, almost laughing. "Will you stay for breakfast?"

"Will you be coming down?" His brow arched questioningly, but it seemed more a plea than inquiry he made.

Shanna glanced down at her attire and indicated it as she replied. "Papa wouldn't approve, not with you here."

"Then change," Ruark urged. "But come. Will you?"

Shanna gave silent assent, and a smile slowly spread across Ruark's face, showing his even, white teeth. He looked rakishly toward the dressing gown, and her breath held while his eyes boldly appraised her.

"Heedless of your father's opinion, madam, I do approve most heartily. I'll be waiting."

Abruptly, without giving her time to reply, he turned and went back to where he had stood before. A moment later her father's voice rang from somewhere in the bowels of the mansion, and Shanna hastily ascended the stairs again.

Once more in her bedchamber, Shanna hurriedly searched

through the armoire for a suitable gown. Happily she snatched a garment out, frowned in displeasure at its wilted folds, and tossed it carelessly on the carpet, completely forgetting her usual neatness. A short time later Hergus entered to find her beneath a billowing skirt as it floated down around her, heaps of discarded gowns at her feet. Shanna thrust her arms through the fluffy sleeves, settled the endless yards of delicate yellow lawn over the hooped panniers, and then urged Hergus to lace her tightly and quickly. The long, gold-veined hair was pulled from her face and left to fall down her back beneath trails of yellow ribbon.

Shanna entered the dining room like a fresh spring breeze sweeping in through the open door. Ruark quickly came to his feet in appreciation of her dazzling beauty and smiled into her radiantly glowing face. Trahern's greeting was more abrupt. He had spent his lifetime toiling for substance and wealth, missing the lightheartedness of youth. He had not known a frivolous moment, and he saw a purpose or an advantage in everything. This caused him some difficulty in understanding his daughter. In his mind, she had no apparent goals for her life, appearing content to be without a husband and, therefore, childless. Indeed, she seemed to find more pleasure riding like the wind upon Attila's back or bobbing effortlessly on a swelling wave.

"I'm about business, daughter. Give me none of your airs. Sit yourself down."

Ruark hastened to assist her with her chair, pulling it out and holding it while she slipped into it. Shanna smiled her gratitude, and when Ruark resumed his place, Trahern muttered grumpily, "Bah! Young men! Heads turned at a moment's notice! Any pretty filly!"

Ruark arched a brow at him and remarked, "Sir, if she were any but your own daughter, I do not doubt your head would also be turned."

Shanna replied sweetly. "You flatter me overmuch, Mister Ruark." She cast her eyes toward her father and raised her lovely nose in the air as if sorely injured. " 'Tis rare indeed I hear words of praise spoken of me here."

"Hah!" Trahern barked. "Should I add coals to that fire, the whole island would be ablaze. Now, with your permission, daughter, may we progress with business?"

"Why, of course, papa." The corners of Shanna's lips lifted upward deliciously as the blue-green eyes twinkled with mischief. "Heaven forbid that I should interfere with business."

"Damn, if you haven't done just that!" Trahern scolded.

Ruark hid a smile behind his cup of tea and after a moment managed to present a serious face to the man. "Your question again, sir? I fear I have lost the thought."

"Huh!" the older man snorted and turned his shoulder in such a way as to shut out his daughter. "I shall repeat it one more time. Now, about the mill. Will it be large enough to take produce from the other islands?"

Ruark nodded, and the talk drifted into minutiae. Accepting a plate from Milan, Shanna dined quietly from a bowl of creamed fruit as she watched Ruark covertly from the corner of her eye. The manner with which he conversed on matters completely foreign to her fascinated Shanna, and she saw the intelligence that so intrigued her father.

It was in the drawing room late that evening when Trahern expressed his hopes for the man, John Ruark.

"As I have been more the merchant than planter in my years, Shanna, 'tis not necessary to tell you I welcome a more knowledgeable mind to advise me upon crops and mills. Since Mister Ruark has been here, he has done much to increase our wealth. When I am gone, you will need someone trustworthy to guide you in such matters. You have been away much of the time, and as an old man I may not live long enough to teach you all you should know. Mister Ruark is capable of advising you, and I am hopeful you will allow him to."

Shanna shrank inwardly. That would be all she needed, for Ruark to be made her advisor, and should he ever be given the right of approval of her suitors, she would most certainly see out her days as a wasted widow.

She sighed mentally, but the sound slipped out.

"You seem distraught at my suggestion, daughter. Why do you dislike the man so much?"

"Papa," Shanna laid a hand on his and gave him a quick, rueful smile, "I only seek to be the mistress of my own fate. I have no intention of going in bondage to that one."

Trahern opened his mouth to enforce his mandate, but she leaned forward and gently placed a finger on his lips. Her eyes smiled into his angry ones, and beneath that steady gaze, the elder Trahern softened. Shanna spoke in not much more than a whisper.

"Papa, I will not argue with you, nor will I ever speak on it again."

She placed a fleeting kiss upon his forehead and with a quick flurry of silk was gone. Trahern sat in his chair, his lips working as he wondered in amazement how it had become possible for him to lose an argument and yet enjoy it.

Chapter 9

HE wind churned up the promise of a storm in small, confused whitecaps as the sun settled on the surface of the water and darkness invaded the day. Night descended with its cloak of black, and cooling breezes settled upon the island, stirring the delicate scents from the flowering vine at Shanna's balcony. She gave herself a last, critical appraisal of her mirrored image, frowning slightly at the thought of having to appear witty and charming for their dinner guests when her mind was in such a turmoil. Everything displeased her, and even the flawlessness of her own beauty, regally gowned in rich ivory satin and costly lace, did not change her mood of discontent. Dispassionately she stared into the looking glass while Hergus affectionately smoothed the elaborately coiled tresses twined with ropes of pearls. Shanna gave a slight adjustment to the square décolletage edged with the same lustrous pearls. The gown was cut deep across her full, swelling curves until it seemed that only some strange sorcery held it from revealing the soft pink crests of her bosom.

"You look grand," Hergus beamed.

Shanna's was that rare beauty which was almost never at a loss. Even early in the morning, with her hair tousled and her eyes blurred with sleep, she wore a sensuality that would have stirred a husband's heart to burgeoning pride if not open lust.

The Scotswoman grunted disapprovingly. "Mister Ruark'll be hard pressed to keep his eyes off ye, and there yer pa will be, betwix ye. Aye, ye'll warm the man's blood a mite." Hergus gave a rather forlorn sigh. "But that, I suppose, is yer aim, choosing that gown when ye know he's to be about."

"Oh, Hergus, don't preach," Shanna begged of the woman. "Ladies attend the French salons wearing much less than this. And I'm certainly not wearing the gown to please Mister Ruark!"

"O' course! Why should ye?" Hergus needled.

Shanna set her hands on her hips and in exasperation faced the woman. "Out with it, Hergus. You've beaten about the bush ever since I bade you fetch Mister Ruark to the cottage. You might as well speak your peace."

Hergus nodded firmly. "Aye, and that I will. I've been with ye since ye were a babe, and I tended ye then though I weren't any more than a babe meself. I watched ye grow into the loveliest thing a man can imagine. I've been with ye through the thick and thin of it. I've taken yer side when yer pa would have ye marry a name rather than a man. But I canna understand ye sneaking off like a little trollop, meeting Mister Ruark on the sly. Ye've had the best schooling, ye've had the best care. We've all wished the best for ye, even yer pa, stubborn man that he is. Can ye na see that ye need to marry and have wee ones? Oh, I can understand love. There was me own Jamie when I was a girl, and we pledged our troth, but he was impressed onto one of his majesty's warships. Me folks died, and I had to find work to feed meself, and I never saw me Jamie again though it be a score of years since. And I can see why ye're taken with Mister Ruark, handsome he is, and more of a man than any oo' dared to court ye. But 'tis wrong what ye're doing. Ye know it. Give him up 'fore yet pa finds out and marries ye off to some driveling lord."

Shanna groaned her frustration and strode across the room. She could not confide in the woman lest her father find out and have them all sent away for the conspiracy. But Hergus's chastening pricked her.

"I'll speak no more of Mister Ruark," she declared over her shoulder.

The maid followed her, determined to talk some sense into the lovely head. "And what if ye're carrying his wee one? Pray tell what would yer pa say to that? He'll have yer Mister Ruark gelded, and ye willna have a word to say on the matter. Aye, ye'll be the mother of his babe, but ye have na thought of that, have ye? Why?" Hergus persisted. "Ye're hoping ye willna get caught with his seed. Ah lass, ye're fooling yerself. He's a bold man. He'll plant his best in ye, and there ye'll be plump as any melon and with no husband."

Shanna chewed her lip, fighting to stem the flow of words that threatened. It was rare she remained mute beneath a rebuke, for she could well wield a tongue-lashing whenever she chose to anyone, the only exception being her father.

"If he hasn't done the deed already, 'twill only be a matter o' time before he gets ye with his babe. Will ye stop this foolishness afore 'tis too late? If ye canna help yerself, then I'll go for ye and ask him to leave ye be. Though I doubt that he will, stricken that he is with ye, him risking his life and not carin'. Nay, 'tis best ye stop it now. He'll be the one to suffer the most should yer pa find out."

Hergus pressed the heels of both hands to her temples and laying her head back, moaned to the heavens.

"Ah, the shame of it all. And ye so newly widowed. Yer own poor husband barely cold in the ground, an' ye've taken to foolin' with a common bondsman! Oh, the shame of it."

" 'Tis done with!" Shanna cried and flung out her hand sharply. Was there no peace from this woman? "I won't be seeing him anymore."

Hergus contemplated her mistress narrowly. "Ye say that, but do ye mean it?"

Shanna nodded her head passionately. "Aye, 'tis the truth. I won't lie with him again. 'Tis done with."

Hergus straightened, satisfied. " 'Tis best for the both of ye. Ye'll find a man yer pa will let ye marry and have his wee ones. Ye'll forget about Mister Ruark."

Shanna stared after the woman long after the door had closed behind her, wondering if this thing with Ruark were truly done with. Aye, that fire-breathing Ruark, so confident in his own abilities. He had known the secrets of her woman's body better than she. How many unsuspecting maidens had he bedded to make him so knowledgeable? The vulgar cad! Was this the sugar she was meant to nibble from his hand? Did he think she would fly to nuzzle him gently when he whistled?

Her mind rebelled. She was not some dumb beast to hold herself at any man's beck and call.

"Does he think to have some handy hold upon me," she hissed to herself, "that I will come begging his favors like one of those simple doxies he found so willing in bawdy inns?" Suddenly she thought of Milly, who drooled with mouth agape, seeking any tiny tidbit of his attention. How many other wenches of the island had he entrapped?

"Aye, bronze dragon, if you think to lead me on a leash, you'll see the set of my own fangs upon your scaly hide." Her eyes narrowed with venomous thought. "Come hither, my dragon Ruark, and I will show you what entrapments the thorny rose can twine. I will have you groveling at my feet before this night is out, begging some morsel of my kindness."

Her determination set, her goal in mind, Shanna readjusted the neckline of her gown again and dabbed a touch of fragrance in the deep hollow between her breasts and behind each earlobe.

"Perhaps I will let him touch me," she mused shrewishly, and, at the thought, a hot, searing excitement shot through her breasts. "Aye, I will wander on the porch alone and knowing the lusty wretch, he will join me on some flimsy excuse." She savored the imagined scene, and a slow smile curved her lips while her eyes sparkled like those of an impish elf. "I shall appear willing—for a time, then grow annoyed and reject him. Then he'll plead for some kinder consideration."

But first, she would shame him to the core for his savage garb before the officers of the Spanish frigate that was in port so he would never wear those disgraceful breeches again without remembering the shame he had to bear. Cloddish colonial. She would teach him a stern lesson on the simple grace of the genteel!

At her father's breakfast table, he had comported himself well enough, but this would be the first time he would attend a dinner, a formal occasion. Ahhh, no doubt the young ladies would find him attractive. There would be women enough to admire him, for most of the ship captains of Los Camellos had sailed, and their wives and older daughters would be attending. But the matrons were generally older than he and their daughters somewhat giggly. But then, there was no accounting for tastes, and he had gone after that wench at the inn quickly enough. He might enjoy another virginal conquest or two.

Shanna passed through the formal dining room, gazing over the table arrangements. The room was aglow with the dazzling, dancing lights of myriad candles, setting asparkle the crystal prisms in the chandeliers, as well as the goblets and china on the long table beneath them. Bouquets of flowers gave off a delicate fragrance that seemed to be magnified in the soft breezes lightly laden with the promised scent of rain sweeping in through the open windows. It had long been the squire's custom to treat the people of his island, when they dined at the manor, with all the decorum of lordly peers. Sometimes it was just overseers and their wives, but they would have a feast set before them worthy of royalty. Tonight there would be an assorted group; though Ruark was to be the only bondsman in attendance, a few of the senior overseers had been invited. When dining at the Trahern table, one never knew just who their seating companions might be, and it could just as easily be a slave as a duke.

Shanna paused outside the drawing room and her eyes swept the guests within. The French doors were set wide to catch the coolness of the night. A small group of musicians played chamber music, the strains of which floated above the low buzz of voices. The guests were dressed in their finery, the Spanish officers resplendent in their uniforms, the ladies beautiful in silks and satins and wide voluminous skirts. There was a well-dressed stranger with his back to her who reminded her briefly of Ruark, but Ruark was nowhere to be seen. Perhaps he had had the common sense to excuse himself from this gathering.

Trahern approached his daughter and smiled with pride. "Well, my dear, I had almost begun to despair of your joining us, but as usual you have saved the best for last."

Shanna laughed brightly at his compliment. Then as he led her into the room, she spread her fan before her face and spoke behind it.

"Papa, you did not tell me there would be other people here."

185

She gestured over her shoulder toward the stranger. He would be the first she would taunt Ruark with, she thought cleverly. "Would you introduce him?"

Trahern stared at her with an odd look in his eye, and Shanna realized the room had slowly grown quiet as they entered. Glancing around, she saw that all eyes were upon her. The men stared with great appreciation, while the women gazed at her with a bit of envy. A few of the matrons cast worrisome glances toward their own suddenly plain, flat-bosomed daughters and greatly wished that Shanna Beauchamp would find herself another spouse and leave the rest of the men to be duly snared by the lesser-endowed maidens.

Shanna nodded graciously and smiled a greeting and then, in the manner of a hostess, turned to welcome the new—

"Ruark!" The name burst from her lips, and surprise showed on her face for the briefest moment before she could contain herself, fluttering her fan nervously as she felt his eyes wander down her in that slow regard, unclothing her. He wore a deep hue of blue which accentuated his tall, lean, broad-shouldered frame. A bit of lace fell over his brown hands from the cuffs of a snowy white shirt, and the dark silk stockings and finely tailored breeches showed the narrowness of his hips and the long, firmly muscled legs.

"I was certain you had met," her father's voice came from her side, and from the sound of the underlying mirth Shanna guessed he was enjoying himself.

At my expense, she mused, but Ruark would not escape that easily.

Renewing her smile, Shanna swept forward gracefully, presenting her hand as Ruark stepped to her.

"Mister Ruark." Her tone was as bright and shiny as a new coin, and she ignored the slight tremor of pleasure that went through her as he caught her fingers. "I did not recognize you in your finery. I had grown so used to your breeches."

Ruark's smile was dazzling and his manner debonair. He showed a fine leg before her in a courtly bow and pressed his lips to the back of her hand, touching his tongue upon it lightly. Shanna gasped and snatched her hand away. She reddened as she realized they had the attention of the entire room. Ruark straightened and gave a lopsided grin to her congealed smile. With an effort Shanna composed herself as the squire, giving her a frown of warning, joined them.

" 'Twas a gift from your father, Madam Beauchamp," Ruark commented as if asked. His voice caressed the name like a treasured possession, and his eyes dipped momentarily to her breasts. In that brief glance, Shanna felt herself almost branded. Demurely she spread the lace fan across the low cut of her gown, now wishing she had worn something that would have given her more protection from him.

"On such short notice," he continued, eyeing her, "I suppose 'twas the best that could be done with a bit of thread and a bolt of cloth."

"Bah!" Trahern burst in. "If that be so, then my tailor has cheated me." He spoke as if pained as he continued, explaining to Shanna. "This man pleaded poverty until I offered to pay for a brace of suits; then I checked his account. With his miserly ways 'twill not be long before he owns the island."

Ruark chuckled at the chiding. " 'Tis easier to save a coin than to earn another to replace it."

"And 'tis my art to know a bargain, Mister Ruark," Trahern replied. "Rare enough that I am bested in that game. You may count yourself one of few."

"Your pardon, sir." Ruark's tone was soft in answer, but as he looked at Shanna his words seemed only for her. "But I am one of one."

It was as if he clearly announced his intention of being the only man in her life. Beneath his stare Shanna bridled and laid her hand upon her father's arm.

"With your leave, papa, I shall see to our other guests."

Both men watched her go, and each was troubled in his own way.

"I cannot fathom this young generation," Trahern fussed. "I fear they do not have common sense."

He halted a passing servant and bade the man fetch rum and bitters for both himself and Ruark.

Shanna had placed herself as far as possible away from Ruark and smiled her thanks as Milan brought her a cup of tea. As she sipped it, she mentally regathered her scattered forces. She had lost the first encounter but was far from ready to yield the battle. She espied Madame Duprey with her husband, animatedly chatting with several of the Spanish officers. Aye, Shanna thought, she would launch her campaign here. Let the fool Wyvern know that she was not chattel he could claim exclusively.

Shanna took another sip of her tea then set it aside, spreading her fan before her as she approached the group.

"Dear Fayme," Shanna smiled. "How lovely you look." And indeed, Madame Duprey was beautiful. Shanna could not understand Jean's infatuation with other women when such a rare jewel waited at home for him. Shanna thought Jean looked a trifle nervous, and well he should, the cad.

"Shanna!" Fayme greeted her brightly with that intriguing accent of hers. "And how perfectly wicked you look!"

"Why, thank you," Shanna laughed and nodded to the Spanish men who were all smiles and teeth and roaming eyes. "Won't you share the company, Fayme?"

Fayme tossed her head back with careless grace. "Ah, Shanna, we will talk of ze less fortunate. Ho-ho, but you are not one of zem. But seriousment, I was so sorry to hear of your misfortune." She sighed heavily. "Ah, so soon a widow! But come, let me present you to zese men. Zey do very eager to catch your eye."

The officers and their captain responded with zealous enthusiasm and long-winded compliments as to the beauty of the women on Los Camellos.

"Shanna," Fayme spoke in a pause. "Oo' eez zat man over zere? Ze 'andsome one oo' kiss your hand?"

Shanna knew well the one. "Mister Ruark, my father's bondsman."

"Such a man!" Fayme exclaimed, causing her husband's eyebrows to raise. "And a bondslave you say?"

"Oui, cherie," Jean broke in. "We brought him back on the December voyage last year. Purchased from the debtor's block, I believe."

"But Jean, the clothes! Certainment he eez not still—"

"Oui, ma petite," the Frenchman responded, annoyed that his wife should find another man fascinating. He could not know the ploy she used to spur his jealousy; she was a loving wife but she had had enough of his philandering. Jean straightened his scarlet coat and testily brushed the cuff. "The bondsman has gained the squire's favor and some say he's earned it, though rumors have a way of being wrong. Why, some would even go so far as to claim he eez a man of letters and a skilled engineer. Do not believe everything you hear, ma cherie."

"Ah, but strange, Shanna," Fayme mused aloud. "How a man of much talent eez being a bondslave. He eez magnifique!"

Jean Duprey chafed and grew a bit red-faced. Shanna watched him with satisfaction and freely joined the conspiracy. Perhaps he would be a little less free-footed if aware that his wife might also be tempted. For revenge's sake and because she had been so lenient with the man before, Shanna felt a desire to heighten Jean's qualms.

"Aye, Fayme," she whispered behind her fan, just loud enough for Jean to hear. "And I've heard it rumored he has a habit of sleeping without any clothes."

Fayme sucked her breath in through her teeth. "Such a man!"

Jean blustered and cleared his throat. He beckoned a servant near and took a fresh glass of champagne, eyeing his wife carefully as he sipped it. Suddenly he saw her in a new light and realized that the title "wife," had not detracted from her beauty.

"Capitán Morel," Shanna said, smiling graciously at the tall Spaniard, "tell me of Spain. It has long been my desire to go there, but, alas, I have found so little time to bring that dream into reality."

The man, thin and swarthy but not overly handsome, turned his full and appreciative regard upon her. "Señora, I would take you there myself. If you but speak the word, I shall go to prepare my ship. But," he spoke aside to his young lieutenant, "we must cover every man's eyes lest the beauty of this princess blind them or distract them from their duties."

Shanna laughed behind her fan. "You are enchanting, Capitán, but you flatter me overmuch I fear."

"Flattery, señora? Never in my life more serious have I been," the man assured her warmly. Lifting a glass of champagne from the tray the servant held for him, Captain Morel presented it to her with a slight bow. "Señora, you make the glory of the heavens dim in comparison to your beauty."

And so Shanna played. Her laughter rose with a sweet, seductive softness that entrapped men's minds. She was gay and charming, but she limited much of her flirtations to the Spaniards, for they would soon be gone, and she would not be encumbered with unwanted attentions overly long. The dinner was served, and Ruark was placed beside her father at the far end of the table and well away from her. In a quiet moment after they returned to the drawing room, Shanna stood alone, and her gaze slowly swept the room. Pitney and her father had settled into chairs in a corner and were arguing over the chessboard they had left the night before. She saw Ralston nearby, alone as seemed his preference. The agent nodded in greeting as their gazes met, and Shanna coolly returned a smile. She paused to sip from her glass of Madeira. Then, with a suddenness that was startling, her eyes met Ruark's. He stared across the shoulders of two men who were discussing some matter in front of him, and she realized he had been watching her for a long time. Now there was almost a naked hunger in his eyes as they burned into her. Though he voiced no words, she heard his thoughts as if he had shouted them across the room.

Lord! Shanna turned her back to him and drained her glass in a single breath. Her hand shook as she set the goblet on a nearby table. Suddenly the room was warm and stuffy, and she began to feel lightheaded. There were too many bodies pressing in too close to her. The mood of gaiety slipped away, and Shanna felt an urgent need to be alone for a moment, if only to compose her thoughts. The shock of that golden gaze across the room and the unguarded message it conveyed had stunned her to a point where her mind reeled in confusion. Her breasts tingled and her loins ached, yet her mind withdrew in horror from the bold, unmistakable urging of her body.

It was as if she viewed herself from a distance. The beautiful woman, pale but calm, passed through the crowd, acknowledging greetings, and somehow made her way to a deserted corner of the veranda.

"Damn the bastard," she raged silently. Her fists clenched tightly as she swayed against the railing and gasped for air. "He comes at me from a thousand directions at once. I crush him here, and he is thrice there! He is only a man! A man! A man!" Her fist thumped the balustrade with each repetition.

Trying to regain serenity, Shanna drew a deep breath and then another. Some measure of quiet returned to her, and she renewed her resolve to go back and enjoy herself in spite of him. Let him stand and gawk if he would.

She turned, once more reassured, took a step—then almost screamed.

He was there! Leaning calmly against a post and smiling at her. Every bit of the courage she had strived so hard to erect was shattered in an instant.

"Get away from me!" Shanna sobbed. "Let me alone!"

She pressed a hand across her lips to still their trembling and fled. She brushed past Jason at the door and flew up the stairs, never pausing or caring until she was safe behind her locked door.

Her bedchamber was hot, though she stripped and donned a light gown. She wiped beaded perspiration from her trembling upper lip and sat on the edge of her bed, trying to stem the shaking that had seized her body. An awareness persisted she could not thrust away. She knew what he wanted, and her own loins throbbed with her answering need.

The night grew strangely still. The sounds of the guests died away as the last of them took their leave. Shanna's bedchamber was stifling and seemed to close in on her. Fretfully she rose from the bed, blowing out the candle beside it, and began to pace the dark, determined to think of anything but Ruark.

Attila! On his back! Riding as swift as the wind! Attila! A sharp piercing whistle! Ruark! Angrily Shanna shook her head and tried again.

The sea! Floating on its swells! Diving to watch the fish! Coming out on the beach! Soft, warm sand beneath her feet. A shadow on the cliffs! Ruark!

A ride with her father in the carriage! Ruark!

Her own breakfast table! A dinner! Ruark! Ruark! Ruark!

Shanna stood with her eyes clenched tightly, her fists pressed against her temples. Everywhere she turned it was Ruark!

But not here, not now. She was safe.

Shanna relaxed, heaving a sigh, and opened her eyes. She walked out onto the terrace outside her room. The wind had freshened, and heavy clouds flitted across the face of the moon.

A wide halo shone about the silver disk, a sure sign of approaching rain. Leaning against the balustrade, she stared at the yard beneath, one tree at a time, watching until the fickle moon gave meager light to each. But alas, they were all barren. None bore the shape of a man crouched at its base.

Suddenly Shanna stiffened as it came to her that she was looking for Ruark! The name blazed across her mind. Anger stirred because she had so little control of her own thoughts.

Petulantly Shanna returned to her bed and threw herself upon it, flinging her arm across her brow and closing her eyes tightly, determined to sleep. But she had tasted the sweetest of nectars; she knew now the long, sleek hardness of his thighs, the rippling muscles of his back, the flat, hard belly, the strength of him pressed against her. Her eyes flew open and Shanna realized she lay sprawled tense upon the bed.

With a muted groan she rose again and dressed in a long skirt and loose blouse, the usual garb for women on the island. She bound her hair in a brightly flowered kerchief. Her bedroom had ceased to be a haven, and Shanna fled from it, climbing from her balcony and dropping to the ground. The cool, damp grass beneath her bare feet brought memories to mind of her childhood when she had run across the lawns with carefree abandon. Slowly she strolled away from the manor and sighed as she stared up toward the moon. The clouds had gathered in density and the wind had quickened, whipping her peasant's skirt about her. Aimlessly she meandered through the trees and reveled in the privacy the darkness gave her. When as a child she wished to pass unnoticed, she often dressed as a peasant. Few gave a young, commonly garbed girl more than a second glance, and although she could not bear close scrutiny, she could with casual caution pass unhindered. Now she wandered the grounds of the mansion as she pleased, pausing as a memory marked a tree or a path. It was not until she stood before a porch and saw the light of a single lamp burning in a dining room, that full awareness penetrated, and she realized she had come the way her mind had so often led her of late.

A great weariness had come over Ruark in the quiet of the cottage. The battle for Shanna's attention suddenly seemed inane and pointless. She ever welcomed the considerations of other men and ever rejected his. The labors in the heat of the day as well as the party had sapped his strength, and his mood plunged into the blackest depths of despair. He lay naked across his bed in the unlit room and stared upward into the darkness. His mind was numb, and the very air he breathed seemed heavy and oppressive. His eyes closed, and wispy, foglike tendrils of slumber drifted about him. It was as if he stood in a dense mist while colored lanterns moved about beyond his sight; then a single bright beacon flamed alight, and he hastened toward it until he came into a stone-walled garden, sunlit and barren but for a single stem which bore a rose of such beauty as to make him halt for breath. As he stared the stem dissolved, and the rose floated free amid glittering mists that obscured all else. The deep red bloom filled his mind. Then it seemed to drift away, shrinking, lightening, changing shape. It was a pair of lips, moist, gently parted; then above them pale green emeralds became a pair of eyes, sea-green and haunting, with a depth that beckoned to him. The swirling mists became a face of fragile beauty formed with the skill of an artist expending all his talent in one effort. The eyes held him entranced. The lips formed voiceless words that enthralled his soul.

"Reach out thy hand. Pluck me. Take the bloom. 'Tis yours for the holding."

When he stretched forth his hand, a long, black tipped thorn thrust into his flesh, and in searing pain, he withdrew. The face laughed and tossed brilliant tresses which flowed about it in a wild disarray of dark honey streaked with gold.

It retreated from him until it floated in the midst of a leafless, thorn-twined jungle. The siren song increased and became intense, blinding his will to all but the beauty that beckoned, calling, crying out for his touch. He lunged forward carelessly. His fingers almost seemed to brush the blood red petals before the vines caught him, held him, and with evil eagerness the thorns plunged deep into his limbs and body until he sobbed in agony and the burning whiteness of the pain wiped away his vision. He tried to withdraw, but each movement freshened the ecstatic torture. Then he was falling, plunging through a green, flower-bedecked forest—

Ruark's eyes flew open, and he stared into the darkness again as his senses returned. Cursing he rose, lighting a candle beside the bed, and donned his short breeches. He would turn to work for ease of mind, and he'd be damned before he would let Shanna's little games torture him.

He strode into the dining room where he had been working and sat on the table's edge. An oil lamp hung on a chain overhead, and in its light he stared blankly at the parchments and the sketches scattered across the table's surface. Even here, Shanna was too much on his mind to allow him freedom.

Slowly Ruark felt a presence in the room and raised his gaze to see the shadow of an island woman. She leaned silently against the door. With fluid movements she came forward into the light, and Ruark rose quickly to his feet, recognizing Shanna. He tossed the quill to the table and then went without a word to the sideboard, there pouring a glass of Madeira. Returning to her, he offered her the goblet, standing close before her, desiring yet not daring to touch her. Was this another dream which would fade if he reached out to take her?

Shanna took the glass with both hands and sipped from it while her green eyes softly searched his face. The goblet was lowered, and Shanna's gaze followed as confusion filled her mind. She could find no word to break the spell. Ruark's hand came up and gently swept the kerchief from her head, loosening the long, thick tresses, spilling them downward over her soft, white shoulders. He set the glass on the corner of the table then blew out the oil lamp. Shanna's lips parted in a low, wordless moan as his arms went about her, folding her into his embrace and bringing her against his hard muscled chest. His mouth touched hers and tested the softness of her lips, playing, warming, rousing until her arms crept about his neck. He bent slightly, and his arm went behind her knees, lifting her from the floor. A soft sigh escaped Shanna as she laid her head upon his shoulder. Ruark strode swiftly through the rooms until he gained the softly illuminated bedchamber where without pause he turned and fell on his back across the bed, still holding her clasped in his arms. Shanna gasped at the fall then braced up on an elbow to stare down in wonder at his face. Folding an arm about her, Ruark pressed a kiss upon her lips and traced a molten path downward to her neck and finally to her bare shoulder. In her mind, Shanna wanted to pull away from his touch, but her mind stumbled and fell before his persistent caresses. Shanna rose above him slightly, shaking her head until her hair formed a shimmering canopy about their faces. Staring into those hungry golden eyes, she lowered again to kiss him long and ardently, moving slowly, the hot peaks of her breasts teasing his chest. His hands moved to her waist, and the skirt fell loose. A tug at the tie of her blouse and it was off her shoulders. Like a savage cat Shanna crouched on her knees above him, tempting him with a kiss, an intimate touch, until Ruark rolled, pulling her beneath him. Then with fierce, naked abandon he possessed her, sweeping her with him to breathless, spiraling heights.

Climbing up from the depths of sleep, Ruark woke as if from a trance, for a brief haunting moment fearing that he had dreamed it all. But then he felt the soft, warm body entwined with his, and he relaxed upon the pillow. The memory of Shanna's passion fanned the fires in his mind. She had teased him like a vixen, tempted him with her softness, made love with him as openly as if she were a cherished wife. Her effect on him was total and complete—devastating when wanting her only led him to frustration and agony of mind and body, beautiful when they joined in love and she was his, for a time, for a space. The fragrance of her perfume filled his brain, and her lovely curving form nestled close against him, a warm, soft thigh resting casually between his, her arm flung out across his chest. She moved against him, and her breath was a warm tickling at the base of his neck. Her lips touched there, and as he looked down, she drew back, her eyes smiling into his. Their lips met and met again as if each kiss were sweeter than the one before. His arm beneath her curled about her shoulders, and his other hand caressed downward along her spine to press her hips close to his. They moved apart then came together with a heat that melted them into one, each oblivious of everything but the other. All that had gone before was dimmed in the brilliance of the union.

Jagged lightning cracked the ebony sky, and raindrops pattered on the leaves of the poinciana trees close outside the window. Errant breezes brought the fresh smell of the storm to fill the room. Both of them were awake, but they were silent and somewhat awed by the bliss they had found together. Shanna lay nestled in his arms. Her finger traced the outline of his ear, and she brushed the tousled hair back from it.

"I am to bid you go before my father learns of us," she said quietly. "Hergus fears what will happen."

Ruark chuckled softly. "And I am to go, just like that? Upon my word, the woman is blind, else she would see how you have bewitched me."

Shanna rolled her head to watch the play of flashing bolts across the broad expanse of velvet blackness. It was strange the strong sense of security she felt here with Ruark as the storm enveloped the world beyond the windows. She had always slept alone, and as a child she had been frightened of the thunderous winds and the blinding flashes that lent an eeriness to her bedroom long after the storms passed. On more than one occasion she had fled in terror to the safety of her parents' chamber, only a few doors away from her own. Now with the raging winds outside, the comforting arms within, she could not find it in her to leave them.

Ruark's fingers brushed the softly tangled curls from her soft nape, and his kisses ventured unhindered along the creamy whiteness. Shanna closed her eyes, bathing in the peace of her contentment.

A long sigh escaped her. "I suppose I should go back before the storm worsens."

Ruark's lips brushed her temple and pressed a kiss to her cheek. "Stay 'til dawn," he breathed against her ear. " 'Twill be past by then. Let me hold you for a few hours more."

Shanna turned her face so her lips might meet his, and their mouths played with increasing warmth as she whispered, "But you'll need your rest. What of the morrow? You have to work."

"I'll manage." His mouth became insistent. "Stay. Will you?"

Shanna nodded slightly, and her voice was muffled beneath his kisses. "Aye, 'til dawn."

The storm rattled against the window, and together they watched while the heavens played out their fiery dances and tiny twinkling stars appeared between the racing clouds.

The chimes of the clock in the hall sounded the hour of four, and Ruark came sharply awake, aware that Shanna lay curled against him, sound asleep. Gently he kissed her, urging her to wake as he spoke her name. She moaned sleepily, slipping a silken arm about his neck. His mouth lightly caressed the softly parted lips as he murmured huskily:

"Come, love, there's no help for it. I'll take you back."

Searching in the dark, Ruark struck a flint to flame, then lit a candle which blazed and illuminated the room. He rose and went around the bed, collecting her clothes from the floor. Shanna carefully pulled the sheet around her, sitting up on the edge of the bed, and her eyes avoided him as he handed her the garments.

"Will you put your breeches on?" she requested softly as she stared down at her hands folded primly in her lap. She threw him a quick, furtive look and shrugged at his questioning gaze. "You seem so naked standing there."

Her gaze flicked down him then fled completely. She felt awkward, conscious of him watching her while he waited for her to continue. Pointedly keeping her eyes toward the window, she spoke in a rush.

"I don't think you are very modest. You—you seem so casual about it all."

Ruark's brow twisted dubiously as he studied the heightened color of her cheeks. Would he ever understand her moods? But he relented to her request and donned his breeches.

"Madam, as you should remember," he said as he fastened them, " 'tis most difficult making love fully clothed, and I for one prefer it more intimate. I fear you'll have to get used to seeing me in the altogether. A bride can only claim shyness for so long."

The green eyes were wide as they turned on him. "You don't believe this can continue?"

Ruark frowned at her. "And why, madam, should I believe otherwise?"

Shanna came abruptly to her feet, dropping the sheet to the floor, and began dressing herself, oblivious to her own nakedness and its warming effect on Ruark.

"This thing—last night—it just happened," Shanna hotly insisted. "It must not continue, for your sake as well as mine. Can you not be satisfied that the bargain is done? Must you be a rutting knave who's always lusting and never appeased? If you were a gentleman—"

Ruark's burst of laughter halted the flow of words abruptly, and Shanna spun around, her eyes flashing with indignant sparks.

"How quickly you chasten me, as if you're sorely set upon. You can hardly blame me for the whole of what happened last night, madam. And there you stand, all soft and tempting and naked. Then you rebuke me for staring. Fickle woman," he teased. "You would taunt me and reject me like all those other men you've led about with your silken looks."

"Ooohh!" Shanna fumed and hurriedly snatched her garments on. "You're despicable!"

"Do you think so, madam?" Ruark took her in his arms, kissing her hair, her cheek, and caressing her lips with his own. He pressed her back upon the bed, and his mouth traveled downward to where her blouse left the higher curves of her breasts bare, then went lower still to venture the crest. Shanna held her breath, and the fires of passion again began to flare within her. A touch, a kiss, a look, and he could rouse her. What madness was this?

"Your heart beats much too swiftly for you to claim disinterest, my love."

Her lips trembled as he claimed them fiercely with his own.

"Promise to meet me later," he breathed.

"I cannot. Do not ask."

"I ask."

"Nay, I cannot. I must get home, Ruark. Let me go." Shanna's head swam dizzily beneath the assault of his kisses, and her voice became weaker. "Please—Ruark—"

"You've set your mind to torment me," he sighed.

For a long moment his hungering mouth searched the sweetness of hers. Then quite suddenly he released her, bouncing off the bed with a quick display of rugged muscles. Her soft lips still throbbing from the demand of his, Shanna came almost reluctantly off the bed, having somewhere lost much of her desire to leave. Slowly she walked before him as they left the cottage, feeling his hand now and then brush a tumbled lock or lightly stroke her bare arm.

They went through the darkness toward the manor. The birds were already awakening with the freshening breezes of the coming dawn and were testing their voices for their overture, sounding much like the first hesitant notes of flutes, oboes, and other woodwinds. Silent and introspective, Shanna strode beside Ruark. The damp grass was cool beneath her bare feet, and the trees sprinkled the two of them with raindrops as the breezes rustled the lush foliage. Staying to the deepest shadows, they quickly crossed the clearing to the house and were soon beneath Shanna's balcony.

"You'd best go back now," she murmured. "I'll go around to the stairs."

Ruark gazed upward toward the veranda. " 'Twould not be a difficult task getting you up if you'd care to venture this way."

Shanna peered at him doubtfully. "I'd likely break my neck."

"Trust me, love," Ruark laughed. "You're not very big. I can have you up in a moment." He bent his knee slightly. "Turn your back to me, give me your hands, and put your foot here on my thigh. You can sit on my shoulder and you're halfway there."

Hesitantly Shanna did as bade and was amazed at how effortlessly the maneuver was performed. When she paused on his shoulder, she glanced down, and the sound of her gaiety bubbled in the stillness of morn. She remarked rather risquély, "For a bondslave you always seem to give me a lift in my hour of need. I think I shall keep you around for your service."

Playfully Ruark nipped her buttock, drawing a muffled protest from Shanna and hastening her journey upward. With his hand under her backside and the other steadying her leg, he raised her up until she could grasp hold of the lower part of the balustrade; then he lifted her higher until she could put her foot on the vine and pull herself up the rest of the way. When she found firm footing on the balcony, Shanna gave a soft, pleased laugh at her accomplishment and bent over the railing to wave him off.

"My thanks, sir dragon," she called softly.

Ruark chuckled lightly as he swept his arm before his chest

and bowed. "Anything to be of service, madam."

He strode off with that slow, deliberate saunter that reminded her so much of a hunting animal. Fascinated, Shanna watched until she could see him no more. She turned languidly, lifting her hair high off her neck as she smiled to herself, her eyes dreamy and bright with a glowing radiance. She moved into the bedroom, tugging at the ties of her blouse, and froze as a figure stepped from behind the draperies.

"Sir dragon, indeed!" The voice was heavy with displeasure.

"Hergus!" Shanna gasped and tried to quiet the frightened pounding in her breast. "You scared me nigh free of my wit! Why are you about at this hour? And in my room?"

"I was worried 'bout ye. I know how ye fear the storms so, and I come to sit with ye 'til it passed. When I found ye gone, I waited, fearing yer pa might come, too. I was set to put meself in yer bed and make him think it were you there safely asleep, as ye should've been, had ye any sense."

Anxious to be alone with her own thoughts and memories of the hours passed, Shanna was not in the mood to argue with the woman.

"I'm going to bed," she firmly stated. "Stay if you will or go. It makes no difference. But whatever, hold your tongue. I won't listen to you at this hour of the morning."

Brushing quickly past Hergus, Shanna crossed to the bed where she had left her nightgown. Dawn was beginning to break over the horizon, but she doffed her peasant garb, turning her back to Hergus who stood in a much aggravated stance, arms akimbo, and wore a much-perturbed scowl. For the first time in her life, Shanna felt awkward, even embarrassed by her own nudity with the servant present, though the Scotswoman had helped her to dress almost from her first breath. Was it just the magenta hue of the wakening sun that painted the rosy glow on her breasts and thighs, or was it a brand from Ruark's body joining hers? At the flooding memory of the hours gone by, Shanna flushed with hot color and hastened to slip on the short gown.

"I'll go," Hergus sighed unhappily. "But I will na be content 'til ye cease yer foolery. Shameful 'tis, sleeping with a man, letting him do what he wants with ye without the least of vows atwixt ye. Aaiiee, I knew 'twould bode ill when ye were widowed so soon after ye wed, lovely thing that ye be and hot-blooded—that I can see for myself. You and Mister Ruark, both of ye the same. Too many fires to cool."

Showing a small pout, Shanna plopped herself down in the middle of the bed and watched Hergus from beneath lowered brows as the woman picked up the discarded clothes, folded them and carefully put them away in the armoire. When the maid had gone, Shanna threw a last glare at the door. Then, presenting her back to it, she slid down between the silken sheets and drifted contentedly to sleep with the memory of strong arms about her and persistent lips against hers blending into her dreams.

Chapter 10

THE Sabbath came; one chapel on the island served those who felt inclined to meet together in worship. It was the custom of the Trahern family to attend services, and this day was no different in that respect. The exception this morning was that Ruark was there. Passing into the church, he brushed against Shanna and by some strange instinct she knew who it was even before she turned. Her gaze moved, as if compelled, to the back of the trim, tall man clothed in forest green silk.

"Ho, Mister Ruark," the squire called jovially, and Ruark faced them as if surprised to find himself so near the Trahern family. Shanna marveled at his coolness. He was so casual about it all that no one, except perhaps Hergus who stood beyond them several paces looking back, could have guessed he had maneuvered himself so with deliberation.

Ruark returned the elder's greeting before his regard passed to Shanna, feasting for a brief moment on her beauty as she stood in a shaft of sunlight, gowned in pale green lawn. She was as tempting as any confection he had ever set his eyes upon. She smiled at him coolly from beneath the wide brim of her hat.

"Why, Mister Ruark, I do believe you're becoming civilized.

Wearing clothes and coming to church? I can hardly believe my eyes."

A roguish grin twisted his mouth. "I didn't want to shock the minister unduly with my meager garb."

"Oh?" Shanna responded. "I didn't think anything bothered you, Mister Ruark. You've certainly shown no hesitancy wearing those dreadful breeches in the village where all the girls gawk at you. If you were modest, 'twould seem that the village is the place to begin so you'd not abuse innocent minds overly much."

Trahern leaned on his cane, eyeing the two, and wondered if their discussion would dissolve into more biting barbs. He could not understand his daughter's irritation with the man.

"Madam," Ruark said, spreading a brown hand over his lacy white jabot and seeming to make mockery of a humble apology, "I do not mean to abuse the innocent mind." His eyes met hers squarely. "Nor do I wish to overly confuse the simple mind. But I have always respected a man of the cloth and give due credence to words and vows spoken in a church."

Shanna's eyes narrowed slightly. So, the rogue! Now that the bargain was done, he would claim her by right of wedlock. Well, so he might think, but she had other things in mind, and she would not play wife to any bondsman.

"Sit with us, Mister Ruark," Trahern invited, trying to avoid a public scene, and caught his offspring's glare for his effort.

"I'm sure Mister Ruark will much prefer sitting with Milly Hawkins," Shanna replied tersely. She waved her fan in the direction of the young woman, who craned her neck to watch Ruark over her mother's shoulder. "She seems to be agog over your new clothes, Mister Ruark."

Briefly Ruark glanced in the girl's direction, and Milly was suddenly aglow, a wide smile of pleasure beaming on her face.

"Why, thank you, squire." He directed his words to Trahern, ignoring Shanna. "I would enjoy that very much."

The squire preceded them, a low, muted chuckle setting his belly to shaking. His hands folded behind his back, Ruark walked along beside him and nodded as Trahern spoke. In the family box, Shanna quietly took a place beside her father and mostly ignored Ruark as she found herself again the object of Hergus's shaming frown.

The chairs in the Trahern box were massive, with tall backs, and were spaced close together so all the carved wooden arms touched, except for the one belonging to Orlan Trahern himself. He sat slightly apart in order to give his bulk adequate room. The remaining chairs and those smaller ones placed before them, obviously made for children, were reserved for Shanna and her anticipated husband and offspring. Shanna would have choked before she would have revealed to Ruark that the chair he chose was the one intended for her spouse. He had already claimed too many of his husbandly rights for her peace of mind. Watching him askance, Shanna saw Ruark's eyes take in the smaller seats and sweep the three large chairs that were occupied by them. Since there was a second row of chairs behind them for guests and she sat between her father and him, there was only one conclusion to be drawn. Shanna saw in his knowing grin that he well accounted for the chairs.

Dropping her gaze, Shanna surreptitiously studied the hand resting near her own. It was dark against the dazzling white of his ruffled cuff but clean, with nails neatly trimmed and given some care, out of character for an ordinary bondsman. Yes, John Ruark was a man totally different from any she had ever come across. Though known as a bondslave, he could pass as a peer in any circle of nobles and lords.

"How is it that you never found a wife in the colonies, Mister Ruark?" Shanna asked deliberately. "Is there a shortage of women there?"

"No shortage, milady. Indeed, there are many beautiful women there." He grinned as his eyes met hers with warm communication. "Though none to equal yourself, madam. 'Twas only that work held me much in hand and permitted little leisure time for me to pursue a lady's company. It sorely plagued my father as he believed I was too dedicated to a single life of toil. But then in England, a sweet young thing quite firmly caught my fancy. Someday I hope to convince her that I would be a fit husband."

"There's room enough for a large family here," Trahern commented, gesturing about to the chairs. "But alas, I have yet to see the pew sufficiently filled. Should she ever find a fit husband, 'twill be a miracle."

Shanna gave little heed to her father's gibe and pointed glance and refused to acknowledge even hearing Ruark's comments.

"I am still young," she said primly. "And I will no doubt mother many children for your old age, papa."

"Huh," Trahern snorted. "I am already old. Find yourself a hearty man, and hurry, daughter, I pray thee, hurry."

"Papa!" Shanna gave a quick smile to her father which he accepted more as a grimace of irritation. "I'm sure we are boring Mister Ruark. Indeed, he seems to be lacking sorely of rest."

The squire peered past his daughter at his bondsman, who was hiding his mirth behind what appeared to be a pained yawn.

Saved from further aggravation by the call to worship, Shanna gave a special prayer of gratitude for the promptness of the minister. Throughout the service, however, she was ever aware of the presence at her side. As the harpsichord played and the congregation sang, the deep richness of Ruark's baritone roused a tingling within her, and she could do little more than mouth the words to the song herself.

It was only after they had left the small church that Shanna finally drew an easy breath and relaxed a bit. The strain of having to guard each glance and of trying to appear unaffected by Ruark's nearness while at the same time displaying a polite, albeit somewhat strained, facade for the benefit of her father had proved much unsettling. In the barouche on the ride home, she could only question her own sanity at ever taking Ruark Beauchamp as husband. He was like a beast of the wilds, caught and tamed to all appearances but dangerous to the unwary. Her once firm belief that she could control him was rapidly being replaced by a nagging fear that she had made an awesome error.

Shortly after lunch, feeling in need of strenuous exercise to tire her mind as well as her body, Shanna ordered Attila saddled. She sought out her father in his study to invite him on the outing.

"There is naught about a piece of leather strapped to the back of a horse," he snorted derisively, "that appeals to my sense of ease. I have not the least desire to have my backside pounded around this island whenever you are wont to venture out." But to soften his words, he added, "Go and enjoy yourself, girl. Pitney will soon be here to see me to another game of chess."

Thus Shanna rode alone up the hill toward the site of the crushing mill. On one of the narrow streets of the village she passed Ralston, but as he paused and tipped his hat in greeting, Shanna pressed her steed into a faster pace, ignoring the man and spurring on the stallion along the road to the hill.

The day was pleasant, almost cool, with gusts of wind that billowed out the skirt of her dove gray riding habit and loosened tendrils of hair about her face. As she drew near the construction site, Attila began to prance a bit beneath her, tossing his fine head and lifting his legs smartly as he sidled along the road. Shanna was an experienced equestrienne, yet this afternoon she gave little heed to the animal whose nervousness on any other day might have been a warning to her. A tinkling of a bell and a rustling in the bushes alongside the path proved to be a goat loose from its tether. It darted onto the road in front of them and shot away, making Attila rear in fright. Pawing the air with his forefeet, the horse jerked his head against the bite of the bit. Caught off guard, Shanna felt the reins snatched from her hand. She had to struggle to keep from falling. The stallion came down free of restraint and was set to run. He had taken only a single lunge when a sharp, clear whistle split the air. Attila halted with a bounce that brought Shanna's teeth together with a click, then, as sedately as a weaning colt, the horse began to trot along the path toward the mill.

The horse responded in that manner for only one person. Ruark! Clinging to Attila's mane, Shanna glanced about in search of him and saw him waiting beside a partially raised wall of the structure. Once again he was clad in the brief breeches, his lean, brown torso contrasting sharply against the bleached whiteness of the garment. At the sight of those pants, Shanna could have screamed her ire at him.

Ruark gathered the reins to tie them to a hitching rail. His own anger sounded in his voice. "If you must ride this damned beast, madam, you might do so with more care for your safety. If you ride out to dawdle and daydream, then find yourself a gentle gelding."

The rebuke did not sit well with Shanna and was even more rankling because she knew he spoke the truth. Attila was not what most young ladies would have chosen for a genteel mount. The animal was spirited and eager and needed a firm, attentive hand on the reins.

"Is my father such a harsh taskmaster that he must set you to laboring on the Sabbath?" Shanna snapped. "What are you doing here?"

"I wanted to look over a few things without the workmen here." Ruark took hold of her, his long fingers slipping about her narrow waist, and as he stood close beside the horse, he let her slide down against his nearly naked frame until his eyes gleamed devilishly into hers. "Until you appeared, my love, I was certain my day was lost."

He set her feet to the ground and bent to kiss her. But casually, as if oblivious to his nearness, Shanna swept off her hat, placing it between them.

"And pray, sir, how have I saved it for you?" There was a coolness in her voice that she struggled hard to maintain. She stepped away from him, tossing her hat on the horn of the saddle. Where his body had touched, her own burned, and she could still feel the pressure of his fingers on her waist. "I came only to see the progress of the mill. Had I known you were about, I would have sought a different pleasure."

Ruark grinned and stretched out a hand to smooth her hair. "Ah, love, do you still fear me?"

Shanna straightened indignantly and pushed his hand away. " 'Tis only that I prefer not to be mauled and ogled as you seem to have a penchant for doing. The completion of the bargain has hardly cooled your lusts."

"Aye, love, not very," Ruark confided lightly as he drew her to him. "Indeed, it has done much to stir them."

Shanna placed her riding crop pointedly between them, but Ruark's strong, possessive fingers clasped her tightly, and she could not still the tremor that passed through her body.

"Try to restrain yourself, Ruark," she cautioned. "I did not come to lie with you, only to view the mill. Now I wonder if 'tis safe to stay. You seem never appeased."

Ruark's eyes burned like golden embers behind his dark lashes "Aye, you tempt me sorely, Shanna."

His gaze touched a quickness within her, and Shanna quickly averted her eyes. No one before Ruark had ever set her to trembling for any reason, much less with a look or mere words. What was there about this colonial that aroused her so? There had been other handsome men, some most dashing and daring who had gallantly begged for her hand. They had bored her. There had been those whom she considered intelligent, but she had admired their minds and little else. There were young men she had thought much in need of maturing, yet the idea of having an old man as her husband and bedding him repulsed her immensely. Ruark had both youth and an agile mind, and just the memory of his lovemaking filled her with a delicious excitement, leaving her breasts almost aching for his caresses and her loins hungering for the consuming heat of his passion.

Greatly disturbed by the path of her mind, Shanna drew away. Was she some hussy that she must crave his amorous attentions all the time?

"Will you show me the mill?" She glanced away then peered up at him. "And will you behave?"

"I'll show you the mill," Ruark lightly replied but made no vow to the latter question.

Slowly they strolled along as he pointed out and explained the construction. Shanna was familiar with the operation wherein the cane was fed into the wheels of a small mill mounted on the bed of a wagon and then taken to the fields where it was needed. But she stared with some awe and amazement at the structure that was being raised in the sheltered vale.

The three huge rollers had been set in place to await whole wagonloads of cane, and there was a mammoth vat to catch the juices. Two wings extended outward from the crushing mill, one being fitted with large copper boilers to cook the thin syrup into treacle, while the other was to house fermentation vats and a brass distillery which would turn out various rums—the black to replenish His Majesty's ships with grog and the light brews which would grace any table.

Part of Shanna's mind followed Ruark's words while the rest of her attention centered on the man. Here, she thought, he was in his element. His voice bore an edge of authority, and his manner was sure and confident. He stood out on a beam barely wide enough for his foot and strode casually to the middle of it as he explained and pointed out the workings of the mill. From every angle, Shanna saw him: from behind as he preceded her along a narrow walk, from above as he reached up to lift her down an unfinished flight of stairs, from the side as he swept his arm outward to show her the easy simplicity of his plan, from below as he climbed up a ladder to a lofty platform high above the works.

Silently Shanna followed him, sensing the pride he took in his labors. It came to her that he was a man who did not know how to do less than his best. He committed himself to every goal and pursued it to an exacting end. Her wonder grew as she studied him, and her curiosity grew apace.

Surely there is more to him, she mused, than a simple bondslave. The answer came of its own accord in her mind. Of course, she had always known that. He never was a slave to any man, nor, for that matter, to any woman.

Shanna's mien grew thoughtful. She tried to imagine what kind of home gave birth to a man such as he and what sort of a hand had nurtured him.

Ruark's soft chuckle shattered her imaginings, and Shanna looked at him questioningly. His eyes were on her, and they twinkled with tiny golden lights of amusement.

"I fear I've been too detailed in my tour." His smile was only slightly apologetic. "But at least you will be able to answer any questions one might ask of the mill."

"I've seen parts of the mill before and listened to others describe it. 'Tis truly a marvel."

Shanna leaned back against a timber as much to steady herself, for the height was dizzying, as to brace her mind, because the door she was about to open with her words might hide many sorts of spectres.

"And what do I answer when people ask me of you, John Ruark?" She plunged on, though his brow raised at her change of topic. "I know so little of you. What of your family? You spoke of your father this morn. Does he know of that affair in London?"

"I hope not. Nay, I pray not." Ruark stared into the distance, his countenance troubled. "His strength would be sorely tested if those rumors reached his ears and he thought me dead. Would that I could spare him that."

"What of your mother?" Shanna persisted. "Do you have brothers? Sisters? You have made no mention of them."

Ruark faced her with a smile threatening at the corners of his lips. "How can I boast of them, Shanna, when the lot of us are only cloddish colonials?"

Shanna took the chide in stride and despaired of gaining more knowledge of him. Wistfully she moved her gaze outward to the green-swathed hills that shouldered around, closing in the mill site. A blue haze hung on them as a cloud thrust deliberate billows upward as if drawing in its breath repeatedly and expanding itself until it could exhale all in a sudden storm. A pair of sea eagles wheeled in wide circles beneath the clouds, riding upward on the currents of air until they entered the white mists. A few moments later they plunged out with folded wings on the other side of the hill. They seemed to play the game of riding the cyclone currents of the storm until they were hurled free of it.

With a gay laugh Shanna turned to bring Ruark's notice to the strange antics of the birds but found his attention boldly measuring her softer parts. When she had relaxed against the timber, she had presented him a daring profile of her round bosom straining against the cloth of her bodice. And Ruark was a man to enjoy all sights, though of late he was bent to limit his observations to Shanna whenever she was around.

Immediately Shanna straightened herself and faced him squarely, waiting until his gaze rose to meet hers. Even in church that morning, she had felt herself the prey of that hawkish stare.

"Your eyes betray the path of your mind," Shanna accused him brusquely. " 'Tis rude to stare so openly, and most slanderous to do so in church."

"I was but admiring you." The amber eyes glowed, and his grin was almost taunting. "You were the most beautiful woman I saw there, and like most of the other men I was but admiring beauty."

"You are more bold than others," she scolded. "I feel ravished every time you look at me."

Ruark's grin grew almost into a leer. "You read my thoughts too well, madam. Frequently I have fantasies of you naked in my arms."

"You're a rogue! A lewd, evil-minded rogue!" Shanna cried, her cheeks flushed and hot. "I despair of what will come from all this. And what if I'm with child? 'Twould be disastrous!"

"Only if you make it to be, love," Ruark replied smoothly.

"Oh, you!" Shanna raged. "What care you of my dilemma? I'd have to face my father, while you no doubt would find some safe haven to protect your precious back from a flogging!"

Ruark peered at her closely. "Have you some indication you're with child, Shanna? Perhaps the month has been overlong with you?"

Shanna shook her head with a small, irritated jerk and turned away from his searching eyes, somewhat embarrassed. "Nay, not yet."

Ruark reached out to touch her shoulder. "Then soon, mayhaps, love, and you'll be more at ease."

Shanna pulled away from his soft caress. "Must you pry into my very life?" She bristled more than a mite. "Am I to have no secrets from you?"

Beneath his fingers, the smooth coil of hair at her nape tumbled to freedom. Ruark lifted a copious lock of her hair and inhaled the delicious fragrance that wafted from it. He murmured close to her ear, stroking the silken locks.

"From your husband, nay, my love. If the seed has already taken, we can only accept the fact."

With true anger Shanna whirled to face him, and Ruark knew he had pressed too far. "Oh? And what would you do if I were with babe, my bumptious knight, my gracious lord and master?" She sneered. "Will you take the child from my loins and name it yours?"

"Of a certainty, madam," Ruark assured her. "But therein lies the problem." He stroked his chin thoughtfully. "Should we name him after John Ruark, admit ourselves lovers, and then be wed? Again? Or should we name him after Ruark Beauchamp, as is his right, and then confess the lot—that we were married from the first—and throw ourselves upon your father's mercy?"

In outrage Shanna stamped her foot. He was making a jest of it all and laughing at her. Oooh, how she loathed him! Vehemently she longed to set him back upon his heels.

"You are crude," she railed, magnificent in a high rage, her eyes flashing hot sparks. "You're a barbarian of the lowest sort! You banter with my pride and toss about my honor lightly. You would spirit from me the very thing I have thus far labored to have, my right to take the husband of my choice." She threw up a hand to emphasize her words then jerked it down to glare at him. "Am I, then, to bear your bastards meekly?"

The stony silence finally penetrated through her consciousness, and Shanna's heart leapt almost fearfully as Ruark's thin, hard fingers slipped through her hair to the nape of her neck, curling in the soft mass until her head was pulled back and she stared up into his face. The muscles in his jaw flexed tensely while the amber eyes, cold with rage, bored into hers.

"They'll not be bastards, madam. You are my wife."

Shanna started and shook her head in denial, trying to struggle free. She closed her eyes tightly and clenched her fists as if by sheer dint of will she could deny his words.

"The bargain's done with!" she gasped breathlessly. "You agreed!"

"Then what of the vows?" he snarled. "Do you think they were lightly spoken to be discarded at your will?" In the face of her stubborn refusal, Ruark pressed on jeeringly. "Do you honor that which was sworn on an altar less than that in a lowly cell? How do you explain that you're a widow when I'm much alive and in a good state of health, to which you can well attest?" His words became cruel, insulting. "Have you found my vigor wanting, madam, that you must take another husband, spreading yourself beneath him to sample the delights he might give you?"

Shanna stared at him aghast, and Ruark laughed caustically.

"Might, madam. I said might. Mayhap 'twould be your lot to wed some well-named but poorly able lord and spend the rest of your nights yearning for a real man. Or would you beckon me then to please you when your fine lord cannot?"

The bright hue of Shanna's cheeks and the flashing of her eyes gave mute evidence to the effect of his savage, cutting words.

"You beast!" She snarled the words slowly, raising her quirt as if she would lay it across his face. "You would set me to your ends and deny my say in the matter. You are frivolous when there is little to be lost by you. You could as well flee and leave me fat-bellied with child!" She tossed her head away from his hand. "As men are, you are free to your every whim."

"Free!" Ruark gave a derisive snort. "Nay, madam, I am a bondslave, and if my master should choose to sell me away, I would have little choice in the matter." He leaned close before

212

her now, and his voice rose as he chafed under the lash of her words. "And flee? Be a renegade all my life? Madam, let me assure you *I will not!*"

"Aye, a renegade you truly are," Shanna stormed, throwing her arms akimbo. "But I have all to lose."

"All to lose! Ha!" he snorted then bellowed into her face as he bent nearer. "And what more can I lose but my neck? Do you think I value it so little that I lightly regard your state? Do you think I seek the hangman for a godfather?"

Shanna's voice shrilled. "I think you're a pompous ass!"

"And you're a much-coddled brat!" Ruark roared. "Methinks I shall do what your father didn't and turn you across my knee for a good backsiding."

The green eyes glared at him threateningly. "You touch me, Master Ruark Beauchamp, and I'll flay the hide from your naked carcass!"

They stood high above the half-constructed mill, nose to nose on a narrow platform which trembled beneath their rage, but neither took notice. The small storm cloud broke free of its mooring on the hill and sailed straight across the valley, leading a whole flock of its kin toward them.

"You jackanape!" Shanna choked beneath those smirking amber eyes. "You senseless clod! You brutish dolt—"

There was a blinding flash of lightning close above their heads. In the next instant the deafening, crackling sizzle of thunder encased them in a volley of sound. Shanna started violently, and in sudden panic she fell against Ruark, half turning, her hands clutched at his bare arm, her fingers biting deep, and her eyes wide with fear. Close on the heels of the fading roar, another charge of lightning seared the air, and Shanna, pale and shaking, could only cringe like a frightened child. Ruark had thought there was little in the world that could stir her to such a fright. She had shown such courage in the face of diverse difficulties. His anger dissolved rapidly, and he placed an arm about her shoulders, holding her trembling form close as he led her to the ladder. The first chilling drops of rain were already pelting them, and the wind rattled the loose boards beneath their feet.

"Have a care, Shanna," Ruark warned above the gusts. "The place is high and the way steep."

The wind swept any reply from her lips, and Shanna had to gasp for breath itself. She eagerly began the descent after Ruark. By the time they reach the landing, he had to shout close by her ear.

"The overseer's hut. That shack over by the road. Run!" He pushed her ahead of him, and, lifting her skirts, Shanna dashed across the platform, down the steps, and across the cleared yard to the simple shanty he had indicated. Gasping for breath, Shanna fell back against the door. Ruark was a step behind her, and he bent close above her to give her some shelter from the now brutal force of the rain as he fumbled with the latchstring on the door.

A jagged flash crossed the sky, and a rolling crash of thunder boomed in their ears. Shanna shuddered fearfully, hiding her face against Ruark's chest and huddling close to him, her long fingernails digging into his naked back. The awesome peal faded, and after a long moment Shanna drew back and gazed up at Ruark, not caring that streams of water ran down her face. There was an odd look in his eyes as he stared down at her. Slowly his head lowered, and his lips parted as they met hers. The rain drummed his back unheeded while his mouth leisurely savored hers. His hand on the latch moved, and the stubborn door opened easily now as if welcoming them into the sheltered dark interior. Sweeping her into his arms, Ruark strode within, pushing the door shut with his shoulder.

The wind howled, the thunder roared, the lightning flashed and the hut shook—whether from the storm within or the storm without the two of them gave it no mind. In the aftermath they lay close together on the narrow cot which served as an occasional bed. Shanna's clothes were draped over a chair before a fire that crackled and spit on the small cooking hearth, while outside a light rain still fell. Beneath the patter on the roof, they were silent in each other's arms, much subdued, their emotions for the moment spent.

Her cheek against his sturdy brown shoulder, Shanna lightly stroked the furry expanse of Ruark's chest and the bare skin of his arm and ribs. The languid contentment of the moment refused to be disturbed. She had not meant to tumble into bed with him so willingly, but now that she was here she could gather no urge to leave.

Shanna propped on Ruark's chest to stare down into his face, meeting his warm regard. Her soft breasts were like velvet against him, and it was sweet, delicious torture to have his skin seared by the pale peaks.

"Have you ever been in love?" Shanna inquired softly, tracing the tips of her fingers across his lips.

Ruark cocked a wondering brow at her. "Why, Shanna," a lazy smile tugged at a corner of his mouth, "I've told you before that you are my only love."

"Be serious," she gently rebuked. "I know you've had other women. Were you ever in love with any of them?"

He shrugged slightly and lifted her hair from her shoulder, smoothing it down her back. "Only a small infatuation when I was a lad, 'tis all."

"A lad?" Shanna queried. "Nine? Ten?"

"Not so young," Ruark grinned. "I was eighteen, and she was a young widow with flaming red hair. She taught me much about women."

Shanna's curiosity would not be satisfied with only bits and parts. "What happened? Did you make love to her?"

"Shanna, Shanna, my inquisitive little mouse. Why would you want to know that? 'Twas long ago and best forgot."

"I'll leave if you don't tell me," she threatened. "And you can lie here and rot."

"Vicious wench," he teased. "Jealous, too, I think."

"Of the widow? Ha!" Shanna scoffed. "You are conceited." A moment of silence passed and then, "I suppose you were terribly in love with her. Was she pretty?"

"Pretty," Ruark conceded. "Tall, slender. Twenty-and-four she was. She bought a stallion and I did but deliver—"

"Then you became her stallion," Shanna broke in and could not fathom the rising irritation within her. "Is that not right, milord? Was she like your little trollop in the inn?"

Ruark recognized the sneer in her words and sought to divert her interest, hooking his arm behind her head and drawing her down. But Shanna gave a small, muffled shriek and flung his arm away, sitting up on her heels.

"Tell me, damn you," she cried. "Was she like your little trollop in the inn?"

"Oh, hell!" Ruark growled and knelt before her, frowning into her eyes as he leaned toward her, forcing her back against the wall. "I don't even remember anymore what either of them looked like."

He softened as his eyes lowered to caress her nakedness and, giving a ragged sigh, he tried to carefully explain.

"I was but a lad, Shanna. The widow was worldly. If you can believe this in that beautiful, stubborn head of yours, she seduced me. For a time I thought she was everything to me. Then I grew up. Much of the splendor faded. She began to demand too much of my time. I was training horses and working other places besides. She married an old but wealthy lord, and when I refused to continue as her lover, she became angry and ended the affair. I was actually relieved. 'Tis simple enough. I was glad to be rid of her. And if you can believe another thing, Shanna, there have not been too many entanglements since. What I said this morning was mostly true. My father thought me married to my work, and perhaps I was—until you."

Shanna chuckled wickedly, and her eyes gleamed with gleeful mischief as Ruark braced an arm on the wall beside her, contemplating her impish smile.

"What devilment are you up to now, wench?" he inquired. " 'Tis naught of good, I swear."

Shanna ran her fingers through the light matting of dark hair on his chest as she spoke in a teasing tone.

"I suppose if I'm to be free of you I must bore you first with constant demands."

Ruark smiled with an easy assurance. "Try, lady. Send for me whenever you're free, and we'll find out if you can bore me. 'Twould be interesting to see if you have the strength, if you can stay in bed that long working your heart out to weary me. I find the idea most intriguing. But there is some danger, of course, and we're both susceptible. What happens should hearts grow fonder? What would you do if you fell in love with me?"

Shanna dropped her eyes from his, wondering what she would do if she found herself in love with him. Silence dragged out, growing pained, yet Shanna's mind still struggled in a turmoil. No answer came to the surface. She was almost afraid to plunge into the turbulent depths because of what she might find there.

She had never been in love with anyone but the ideal man of her imagination and, in fact, had never even been attracted to a man before Ruark. The whole idea was simply beyond her experience, although she could little admit it, even to herself.

The rain had stopped. Its soft patter was gone from the roof. The birds were still, the wind had died, the quiet was thick—almost as if one could rend it with a blade—and still Ruark waited for an answer.

Then from a distance, a thud of horse's hooves rapidly nearing the shanty broke the silence. With a curse Ruark leaped from the cot and snatching up his damp breeches, hurriedly slipped them on. It appeared very likely that the door would be flung open momentarily, revealing the tryst, and Shanna could do naught but draw herself into a small shape as she huddled beneath the linen quilt in a corner of the bed. The hooves rattled on the boardwalk and halted just outside the door. A pause intervened, in the midst of which Shanna exchanged a somewhat pained grimace with Ruark. Then an odd scraping sound intruded, and a slow smile spread across Ruark's face as he looked at Shanna. It became a chuckle and grew into a laugh. At Shanna's bemused stare, he stepped to the door and threw it wide despite her gasp of protest.

"Nay! Wait!"

Shanna slowly dropped her extended hand and stared in amazement. There, filling the sun-bright portal, stood Attila. He had broken loose from his tether. The horse shook his head, snorted, and pawed the ground again. Reaching for his shirt, Ruark searched through it until he found the pocket.

" 'Tis the way I trained him," he explained, holding out his hand for her to see two lumps of brown sugar candy. "He's become overly fond of it, and I forgot to give him his ration."

"Oh," Shanna sighed weakly and sagged back against the wall limply. "That beast has frightened me into an early graying."

The steed daintily nibbled the sweets from Ruark's hand, crunching the sugar loudly and tossing his head in obvious pleasure. Ruark closed the door and leaned back against it, gazing across the room at Shanna. The quilt had dropped away from her, and Ruark devoured his treat as greedily as Attila had the candy. Her breasts glowed like amber melons in the muted light, and her slender limbs were laid bare to his heated gaze. Seeing where his interests wandered, Shanna reached for her chemise, giving him an accusing glance before she slipped the garment over her head.

"If you seek food with the same lust you do me," her voice was light with humor, "you shall soon exceed my father's girth."

Ruark caught his arm around her waist as she rose to turn her gown and see to its drying.

"Would that my wasting body could feed upon such nourishment as I have found from you," he murmured huskily, holding her close to him and smoothing her hair away from her shoulder. "But should my food come with the regularity of your love, I would be long dead of wanting. Like food, my need of you is a daily thing, and these lengthy fasts do not appease my hunger."

"Daily! Ha!" Shanna leaned back against the circle of his arms and absently traced a finger in a pattern on his chest. "Your lust is a slavering dragon devouring all I can offer on the moment. I fear you would never get beyond the bedchamber door should we live as man and wife."

Shanna's brow suddenly furrowed as she stared at what her finger had drawn. Against his darker tan the white marks faded even as her eyes touched them, but they were burned like a brand into her brain. The words, "I love," were unfinished, but still they dismayed her with their betrayal. She cringed as if pained, quickly pulled away from his embrace, and began to dress in fevered haste.

Confused by her abrupt change, Ruark watched her closely as he rolled one of his drawings and played with the cylinder of parchment.

"I had intended to spend the night here," he began almost hesitantly. "Mister MacLaird gave me a lift up here when he brought supplies for the morrow's work, but I left several sketches I shall need on the morrow. Will you give me a ride back?"

Shanna paused in drawing her gown over her head.

"You are welcome to the ride," she murmured, sliding her arms into her dress and settling it on her hips. Once within the barrier of clothes, she calmed and presented her back to him, holding her hair aside.

"Will you lace me up?"

Ruark leisurely complied, taking his own good time as he settled one hip on the edge of the wooden planks of the table. He was reluctant to see the afternoon gone.

For the most part Shanna held still for his lengthy administering, though she reached across him once, bracing her hand on his thigh, to turn several sketches spread across the table. She studied them recognizing Ruark's handwriting scrawled boldly across the bottom. As he gave a last tug on the strings, she turned.

"You've been working," she commented, rubbing away a smudge of ink from the brown skin over his ribs.

Ruark smiled into the depths of twin aqua pools. "As I had no hopes of seeing you again today, Shanna, I put my mind to something less tormenting."

Shanna scoffed playfully. "Pray tell, sir, how do I torment you? Do you see me as some witch who pricks you sorely for the sake of amusement? How can I, a mere woman as you see me now, trouble you so?"

Grinning lazily, Ruark folded his arms about her, drawing her between his legs, and brushed his lips against her temple.

"Aye, you're a witch, Shanna. You have cast some strange spell over me that makes me yearn for you every moment of my waking." His breath stirred the light curls that lay against her ear. "But you're an angel, too, when you lie beside me soft and warm, letting me love you as I will."

Shanna placed a trembling hand across his lips, recognizing the quickening of her own pulse. The effect of those burning amber eyes was total and devastating.

"Say no more, devil dragon."

Ruark kissed her soft palm, her slender fingers, the narrow wedding band she wore. His gentleness touched a quickness in Shanna's breast, and she gazed at him in soft bewilderment, unable to fathom the tenderness that she suddenly felt for him. Abruptly he frowned and caught her hand, staring at the ring.

"What is the matter?" Shanna asked, seeing nothing about her hand that was odd.

His frown deepened. "I wore a ring on a chain about my neck, and it was there when I visited the wench at the inn. I haven't had it since. With everything that has happened, I completely forgot about it until now. The band you wear reminded me. The ring was to be yours."

"Mine?" Shanna's own brow showed bemusement. "But you didn't even know me then."

"It was meant for my wife, whenever I married. It once belonged to my grandmother."

"But, Ruark, who took it? The girl at the inn? Or the redcoats when they laid hold of you?"

"Nay, I came awake the minute they touched me. The girl must have taken it. But if she did, then I had to have been asleep."

"Ruark?" Shanna asked quietly. "What does all this mean?"

"I don't know as yet, but I'd swear the little bitch meant to rob me all along. Perhaps she gave me some drug in the wine." Ruark shook his head. "But she drank from it, too." Then he tilted his head as if remembering. "Or did she? Damn fool me for not being more wary!"

After a long moment he gave up trying to recall the events and, sighing, gathered Shanna's stockings and frilly garters and handed them to her.

"We'd best go before your father comes out in search of you. The next time we might not be so lucky to find Attila at the door."

Shanna seated herself again on the cot and, beneath Ruark's admiring regard, lifted her skirts and smoothed the silk carefully over her shapely calves. Finished, she dropped her gown and smiled at him with her question.

"Ready?"

"Aye, love," Ruark grinned, scooping up his shirt.

His hand rode on the small of her back as he escorted her through the door. Closing it behind them, he stepped around Attila and lifted Shanna up onto the animal's back, guiding her knee around the horn of the sidesaddle. Placing his foot in the stirrup, he swung up behind her, taking the reins from her hands. Smiling, Shanna leaned back against him and enjoyed the ride up along the hill, well away from the village and prying eyes. A quiet peace descended upon them as they shared the brilliant panorama spread out before them, seeing the blue-green of the sea through the tall trees.

They were, for that moment, aware only of each other and knew naught of the lone figure that stood some distance off, watching them. Ralston held the reins of his horse firm lest the animal betray his presence, and his brow lifted thoughtfully as the couple exchanged a long kiss. His surprise mounted as the bondslave, John Ruark, made bold with his hand upon Shanna's breast. Instead of the stinging slap the agent expected, the intimacy was accepted most casually without an attempt even to brush away the hand.

" 'Twould seem Mister Ruark has caught the lady's eye and dallies where he should not," Ralston muttered to himself. "I'll have to keep an eye on the man."

✦ Chapter 11 ✦

THE clouds raced over the face of the island, seeming to herald in the billowing sails of a mighty vessel which glided effortlessly through the tossing sea, curling the blue crystal water beneath her lofty prow. The azure sky was vivid beyond the fluffs of white, and, against the indistinct horizon, the ship was like an eagle in flight, soaring gracefully on outspread but motionless wings.

"That's a big one, 'tis," Mister MacLaird stated as Ruark lifted an eyeglass to peer through it. "Can you make out her name, laddie? Is she English?"

"Colonial. She flies the Virginia Company's flag," Ruark replied, squinting through the glass as he focused on the banner waving below the other. "She's the *Sea Hawk*."

"Aye, she moves in like one," MacLaird rejoined. "A beauty she be. As fine a ship as any of Trahern's."

Ruark lowered the glass, and even as they watched, the ship dropped some of her sail and entered a trim tack to the harbor entrance. Almost anxiously Ruark turned to the older man, who stared out the window over the top of his small, square spectacles.

"That wagon you have loaded with rum out there." Ruark

gestured with his thumb toward the front of the store. "Is it to be taken aboard one of the ships?"

Mister MacLaird moved his attention to Ruark, lifting his nose and staring at him through the metal-rimmed glasses. "Aye, lad, to the *Avalon* it be going. The schooner's making the rounds of the islands this week. Why do you ask?"

"I was wondering if I might take the load down for you. 'Tis been nigh to a year since I left the colonies, and I want to see if that ship might have news of home."

The aged storekeeper waved a gnarled thumb toward the door as a merry twinkle lit his blue eyes. "Then get yourself down there, laddie, before the rum spoils from sitting in the sun."

A grin spreading wide on his face, Ruark nodded and eagerly set about his task. Jamming his hat on his dark head, he leapt to the seat of the wagon and clucked to the team of mules, slapping the reins against their broad backs and sending them down the lane toward the pier. As he went, an odd smile played about his lips, and he began to whistle.

Late afternoon brought a cooling breeze, and Shanna escaped the tedium of book work for a ride on Attila's back. She urged him along the beach where once she had met Ruark, following the same path they had taken through the wooded copse and eventually halting in the clearing to enjoy the serenity of the peaceful glade. Birds called high overhead and fluttered through the trees; frogs croaked from the marshes. Gay-colored flowers bedecked the lush green carpet, while butterflies flitted on vibrant-hued wings, touching a blossom, perching on a leaf, weaving a riotous path on a light and fragrant breeze.

Shanna sighed, content with the day. All fears had been set aside with the affirmation that she was not with child and that those pleasant interludes with Ruark had not left her carrying his seed within her belly. In time, she thought, there would be another man to give her as much pleasure as that cocky colonial, and she would bear his child, but until then she would take no more chances. No matter what, she would hold Ruark at arm's length and say him nay on every turn. She could not let all she had planned for be swept away in a moment of passion and weakness. Aye, 'twas weakness which made her forget her resolve and like any common lustful wench fall into bed with Ruark. She had not seen him since that stormy Sabbath nearly a full week before and had purposefully kept to herself and out of his way. If she had learned anything in her dealings with Ruark, it was that she could not handle him or the situation. In any confrontation with him, her plans always went awry, and she could not chance another quirk of nature sending her flying into his arms with no thought of the consequences. However stubbornly she declared her intentions, it was still best not to tempt fate.

In the leafy bower the flowers were the same, the riot of color, the heady perfume, the dark coolness. Beneath her, Attila pawed restlessly at the soft turf, anxious to be at a fast run, but Shanna's thoughts were elsewhere. Amber eyes invaded her unwilling mind, and a warmth slowly spread through her. They stared down to the depths of her being, stirring unwelcome longings as parted lips bent closer—closer—

"Get out of my mind!" Shanna shrieked to the treetops, setting to flight a flock of birds resting there. Then she slammed her gloved fist into the skirt of the saddle with frustrated rage. Clenching her jaw in determination, she gritted out, "Get from my mind, dragon beast! The bargain is complete as agreed! I have not betrayed you!"

Angrily snatching the reins, Shanna whirled the stallion about and fled from the place, no longer at peace there. She wasted no mercy on the horse as she pushed him to his fastest gait. His hooves churned up the wet sand along the beach, sending heavy clumps of it out behind them. The wind whipped tendrils of hair from the coiled knot at the nape of her neck. She raced as if the whole forest behind her were ablaze and she would be consumed if she but eased her reckless pace. Indeed, there was a plea haunting those amber eyes that burned her even now.

Soon Attila began to labor, and Shanna knew his endurance was near an end. She slowed him to a calmer pace and meandered along the beach until they came to a spot where a small rivulet of water trickled its way across the beach. Turning the mount, Shanna sent him splashing to the source of the brook. The dense foliage opened to reveal a cliff which reached above her head, and from its brink the small stream plunged, giggling like a virgin maid as it tumbled down from rock to rock until it fell to an emerald pool at the bottom.

Shanna flung herself down, and Attila waded fetlock-deep in the water, plunging full half his head beneath its cool surface while he quenched his thirst and rested. Shanna gathered her hair into some semblance of order and laved her neck with a handkerchief she dampened in the chilled spray. As her warmth and excitement waned, she wet the kerchief again and drew it slowly over her face until the flush subsided and she began to regain her composure.

Once more the unruffled daughter of Trahern, Shanna mounted and reined the horse about, continuing on toward the village. Attila had enjoyed the run, and his blood still raced hot in his veins. He fought against Shanna's hand and would have thrown himself into a wild dash again had she relented but a bit.

This was the apparition that entered the town and rattled across the cobbles to the dock, the mottled gray steed with his darker muzzle and stockings, prancing, flinging his legs wide and high, chafing against the control of the bit, his tail arched high and his full mane flowing with every movement. And on his back a vision of beauty such as few men see in a lifetime, cool and relaxed, controlling the beast with a practiced hand. A low-crowned, wide-brimmed hat sat squarely on her head, and the full riding skirt covered both herself and the side of the horse like the draped mantelet of some gallant knight.

Small wonder that the colonial seamen dropped what they were doing and paused in their labors to watch with gaping stares. Finding their gentle attention not unpleasing, Shanna gave them a brief nod in greeting and headed for the slip where the newcomer lay. There Shanna espied her father's barouche and drew up beside to ask Maddock where the squire might be.

" 'Board the ship, ma'am," the black man drawled and threw a careless thumb toward the tall barque. "Palaverin' wit' the cap'n, I 'spect."

When Shanna tossed the reins to the man and began to dismount, there was an immediate scuffle. A small crowd of tars had congregated and now jostled for the honor of helping her down. Patiently she waited until a young giant, who would have dwarfed Pitney, elbowed his way through the others and with a blushing grin offered his hand for her assistance. Swinging down, Shanna gave the lad a gracious smile of thanks then proceeded to the gangplank, trailing behind a chorus of half-muffled groans and sighs. Her dainty boots had not yet touched the deck of the ship when another young man stumbled to a halt before her. He stood ramrod stiff and clutched a brightly polished telescope beneath his arm; a brand new tricorn crushed his tousled hair. Recalling his manners, he snatched the hat from his head, almost dropping the glass, and greeted her loudly, overeager to be of service.

"Good afternoon, ma'am. May I be of service, ma'am?"

"If you will." Shanna smiled while the poor youth seemed to swallow his tongue. "Might you carry a message to my father, that if he is to be shortly finished with his business here, I would enjoy a ride home with him."

The young man began a salute but remembered himself. Instead, he did a smart quarter turn and flung out his arm to point.

"Is that your father, ma'am, with the captain by the—"

He snatched his hat as it threatened to blow overboard and caught the glass again from certain disaster. Holding the two clutched to his chest, he jerked his head toward the men.

"That be him, ma'am, with the captain?" he mumbled, a bit red-faced.

Shanna nodded as her eyes settled on the stocky shape of her father. The other man's back was presented to her, displaying only a dark, thick thatch of auburn hair tied in a queue above his tall, blue-garbed frame.

The youth brightened. "Whom shall I say is aboard, ma'am?"

Shanna laughed at his spirit. "Madam Beauchamp, sir."

"Madam Beau—" The young officer's voice trailed off in unmasked surprise, and the tall man with her father turned abruptly and fixed her with a piercing gaze from beneath a glowering, frowning brow, as if he half expected some leering witch to be aboard his ship. Beneath that condemning stare, Shanna stood transfixed, unable to move or speak.

Ever so slowly the scowl faded. The eyes roamed over her briefly then returned to her face. Now a smile played just behind his features, and he gave a slow nod of what appeared to be approval.

Shanna let out a sigh and realized she had been holding her breath since he faced her. Had her life depended upon it, she could not explain why the approval of this man, whom she had never seen in her life, should please her.

As the captain strode across the deck, Shanna noticed that he was thin, almost to a fault, yet he moved with the easy rolling stride of a seasoned seaman. His face was long and squarish, somewhat angular. Though a hint of fine humor showed about his brown eyes, there was a trace of sternness about the lips, or rather the firm decisiveness of a man accustomed to command. Pausing before her, he locked his oversize hands behind him as he rocked back on the heels in the briefest of cordial bows.

"Madam Beauchamp?" The words rolled from his lips in a drawl, yet they were spoken as a question.

Like the bow wave of a ship rolling forward, Orlan Trahern came to join them. Placing both hands on the gnarled end of his staff, he leaned heavily on it.

"Aye, captain, I would have you meet my daughter, Shanna Beauchamp." Something odd twinkled behind the elder Trahern's eye and, thus warned, Shanna braced herself. Still, the shock was no less stunning. "My dear, this is Captain Nathanial Beauchamp."

The words were slow and deliberate, and he waited as, with crushing slowness, the full weight of the name dawned on the daughter. Shanna's mouth opened as if she would speak, but no words came. Her eyes turned their burning question upward to the tall captain.

"Aye, madam." His rich voice rumbled again. "We shall have to discuss this at length, ere my own good wife disowns me for a knave."

"Later perhaps, captain." Orlan Trahern cut short any further conversation "I must be on my way. If you will excuse us, sir. And will you join me, Shanna, my dear, for a ride back to the house?"

Numbly Shanna nodded her assent, unable to shape a comment. Trahern gently guided her to the rail, there pausing as he called back over his shoulder.

"Captain Beauchamp."

Shanna flinched at the name.

"I shall send a carriage for you and your men later."

Without waiting for a reply, the squire departed from the ship, leading his mute and confused daughter on his arm. The captain strode to the rail, leaning against it as he watched the barouche swing about and disappear around the corner of a warehouse.

Shanna paused outside the drawing room door as she recognized Captain Beauchamp's voice replying to Pitney. Ralston interrupted, cutting him short, but that deep, confident voice was unmistakable. Shanna clenched trembling hands together, trying to calm herself, and cast a glance toward the front door where Jason stood tall and silent.

"Jason," she asked softly. "Has Mister Ruark arrived yet?"

"No, madam. He sent a note by a boy from the mill. There has been some difficulty, and he will need to remain there."

"The wily knave!" Shanna thought. "He's left me to flounder about for the explanations! I don't even know if he's really a Beauchamp. For all I know, he might have borrowed the name. So what then is that bloody beggar's name? And *my* name? Madam John Ruark?" Shanna groaned inwardly. "Heaven forbid!"

Panic almost made her flee like a coward to the safety of her chambers, but she struck down the corrosive feelings which ate her composure away.

Soothing her raging emotions with the single thought, *"I am Madam Beauchamp,"* Shanna smoothed the multiple yards of pale-pink satin cast with the iridescent luster of pearls. Delicate pink lace, dainty as the tiny satin rosebuds which caught the billowing skirt into little tufts, cascaded to the floor between twin borders of ruching. At mid-arm the same rich lace was gathered in flounces, and a narrow satin ribbon was tied about her slim, graceful throat where the lace had been stiffened to frame the expanse of flawless skin.

Shanna was just touching a hand to her elaborately woven coiffure when the young third mate who had ushered her aboard the *Sea Hawk* strode near the door to set his empty glass on a small table there. When his eyes discovered her, he came to a halt and almost gaped.

"Madam Beauchamp!" he beamed, recovering himself. "What

a lovely—" His eyes dipped to the high curves of her bosom displayed above her gown, and he stammered, blushed, and collected himself once more. "Ah—home you have here."

Conversation in the room ceased and thus having been announced, Shanna could no longer hesitate. Forcing a smile, she swept gracefully into the room, lightly resting her hands on the wide panniered skirt to keep it from swaying too much. She was a vision men struggled to grasp as reality, and it was all too obvious the junior officer of the *Sea Hawk* was smitten. He stumbled in a parody of a bow when she paused before him, then flushed with pleasure as she bestowed the brilliance of her smile on him, ignoring his clumsiness. A long sigh escaped him as she turned to her father who had come across the room to greet her. Brushing aside the gawking young men who had come with their captain, Orlan Trahern was obviously filled with pride as he presented his daughter to them. Throughout the introductions, Shanna was aware of Nathanial watching her with a slow, steady regard and was puzzled at his frown as his junior officer slipped through the press of admirers to stand beside her. She was also conscious that Ralston's attention seemed more acute than usual, but she gave him little thought, not really caring what the man had on his mind.

The duties over, and secure on her father's arm, Shanna paused before the colonial captain.

"Sir, it quite bemuses me how we've come to have the same name. Have you kin in England, mayhap?"

Nathanial Beauchamp smiled, and the brown eyes twinkled their humor as he looked down at her. "Madam, I came by the name quite honestly as my parents gave it to me. What we shall really have to discuss is how *you* came by it. Of course, all Beauchamps are kin in one way or another. Though we've had our rogues, pirates, and a blackguard or two, the name seems to recur with amazing regularity."

The corners of Shanna's mouth lifted impishly. "Your pardon, sir. I did not mean to pry. But should I not call you uncle, cousin, or some such?"

"Whatever suits your whim, madam," Nathanial grinned. "But welcome to the family."

Shanna nodded and laughed but dared press the matter no

more, for her father was giving undue notice to the exchange and appeared to treasure and enjoy each morsel of it.

The dinner passed with relative ease as Captain Beauchamp and his officers conversed with Trahern on the possibilities of trade between Los Camellos and the colonies. Ralston was not in favor of this exchange, and spoke boldly.

"What can you get there, sir, that England and Europe cannot give you better? The crown will not be too pleased with you taking your business elsewhere."

The purser of the *Sea Hawk* snorted. "We pay good taxes to the crown, but hold it our right to trade where we choose. As long as the duty is met, who is to complain?"

Ralston's contempt was held to a sneer, but his tone was carefully polite as he spoke to Trahern. "Surely, sir, you cannot hope to gain much from trading with backwoods colonies."

Edward Bailey, the first mate, sat forward in his chair. He was a short man, barely taller than Shanna, but broad and with brawny arms and shoulders. His short, stocky neck supported a face that was ruddy and almost cherubic behind an ever-present grin. His round, rosy cheeks never lost their vibrant hue, and when his ire was pricked, as it was now, they darkened even more.

" 'Tis apparent ye've missed the colonies in yer travels, Mister Ralston, else ye'd be aware of the riches to be had. Why, in the northern climes they produce woolens and other goods, the likes of which would rival the best of England. We make a long rifle what can take the eye from a squirrel at a hundred paces. There be cordage and lumber mills along the southern coasts which provide quality cable, planks, and spars. The very ship we sail was made in Boston, and the likes of her has never touched the sea from another land."

Trahern slid his chair back. "Your tales fascinate me, sir. I will have to look into this."

With the signal that the dinner hour was at an end, the junior officer hastened to stand behind Shanna's chair, almost kicking his own over in his rush. As she leaned forward to rise, Shanna caught a brief glimpse of Captain Beauchamp's face and the heavy, pointed frown he directed to his third mate. But when her eyes returned to scan the visage, it bore once more its gentle half smile. Had it only been vexation at the youth's clumsiness, Shanna wondered, or had the captain warned the lad away? At any rate, the young man limited further attentions to those of common courtesy and seemed much chastened.

The evening nearing an end, Shanna retired to her chambers, a sense of dissatisfaction wearing her mind raw. Finding no ease from her discontent, she sat silent before the dressing table while Hergus brushed out her hair. The maidservant sensed the pensive mood of her young mistress and held her tongue, realizing the effort Shanna had taken to avoid Ruark in the days past.

Dressed in a gown and heavy silk wrapper, Shanna paced the length of her rooms, empty now of Hergus and lit only by a candle. Her mind raced and settled on no single point. Names pressed in upon her from every side, plaguing her with their questions.

Shanna Beauchamp? Madam Beauchamp? Captain Beauchamp? Nathanial Beauchamp? Ruark Beauchamp? John Ruark? Mistress Ruark Beauchamp? Beauchamp! Beauchamp! Beauchamp!

On and on the name rasped through her mind until, with a stifled cry of frustration, Shanna shook her head, wildly tossing the radiant mane about her. In search of clearer air, she stepped out onto the wide veranda and tried to walk away the goading doubts.

The night was gentle, warm, with a soft quality known only on the Caribbean Islands. High above the trees the moon flirted with white billowy clouds, kissing them until they glowed with its silvery light, then hiding its face behind their fleeting shoulders. Shanna wandered along the veranda, past the latticework that separated her balcony from those belonging to the other chambers. A face began to form in her mind's eye, and an amber gaze penetrated the night. Shanna groaned within herself.

Ruark Beauchamp, dragon of her dreams, nightmare of her waking hours, why did he haunt her so? Before she had sought him out in the dungeon, she was frivolous and witty, even gay, but now she wandered listless and dreamy like a moonstruck maiden.

Shanna stared out across the shadow-mottled lawns.

"Ruark Beauchamp," her whisper fell as soft as a wispy breeze, "are you there in the dark? What spell have you cast upon me? I feel your presence near me, and it touches me boldly. Must my passions hunger so when my mind tells me nay?"

Shanna leaned over the rail and tried to control her suddenly vivid imagination. "What spell has this man cast upon me?" she wondered. "Why can't I break free and see my own ends out? I feel entrapped, as if I were his slave. Even now, he's sitting in the cottage, mumbling some enchantment to bring me to his side. Is he warlock or wizard that I am bound to his demands? Nay, I shall not be! I cannot be!"

Drawing away from the balustrade, Shanna continued with her stroll, her eyes downcast, her mind occupied with musings.

Suddenly a dark shadow beside her moved, and she was engulfed in a cloud of fragrant smoke. Her heart fluttered into her throat.

Ruark! The name almost burst from her lips, but she choked it back.

"Your pardon, madam." The deep, rich voice of Nathanial Beauchamp wore its concern heavily. "I did not mean to startle you. I was only taking a pipe in the open air."

Shanna stared, trying to penetrate the dark shadow that hid his face. Her father had invited the captain to stay the night, but she thought little of him in her musings of Ruark.

"That smell—tobacco," she spoke hesitantly. "My husband—used to—"

"A common enough habit, I suppose. They grow the stuff near my home. The Indians taught us to smoke it."

"The Indians? Oh, you mean the savages."

Nathanial chuckled, his voice rumbling easily. "Not all savages, madam."

Shanna wondered how she would dare broach the subject that burned so in her mind. Deep in concentration, she started as his voice broke the lengthening silence.

"Your island is most beautiful, madam." His hand with the pipe cradled in it came out in a brief span of moonlight, and the long stem swept to encompass the rolling hills beyond the trees then dipped to point toward the town. "Your father seems to have made the most of it"

"Los Camellos," Shanna murmured absently. "The camels, so the Spaniards called it."

She turned to look directly into the shadows that surrounded him.

"Sir? There is a question I must ask you."

"Your servant, madam." He thrust the pipe into his mouth and puffed it alight, illuminating his features slightly.

Though her desire to know was strong, Shanna was at a loss as to how to frame her request. "I—I met my husband on a somewhat frivolous affair in London, and we were married only a few days later. We were together only a short while before he was—taken from me. I know naught of his family, or if he even had one. I would most dearly like to know if he has—I mean—left any—"

Her voice trailed off, and the pause grew strained as she struggled to find adequate words. It was he who answered her unspoken question.

"Madam Beauchamp, I can account for all my immediate family, and to my knowledge I have no cousins or distant kin by the name of Ruark Beauchamp."

"Oh." Her voice was small with her disappointment. "I had hoped—" She could not finish that statement either, for she did not know what she had hoped for.

" 'Tis a widespread name, and though we Beauchamps can usually trace back to a common origin, I do not claim to know everyone by his given name. Perhaps there are some I am not acquainted with."

"No matter, captain." Shanna shrugged it all away with a sigh. "I am sorry to have troubled you with my impertinence."

"No trouble, madam, and indeed, no impertinence."

With his thumb, he tamped the coals into the bowl of his pipe. His hands were huge, and though they appeared to have the strength to squeeze a cannonball in two, they were amazingly gentle, and the slim clay pipe seemed like a fragile bird between them.

" 'Tis my pleasure, madam, and be assured—to discourse with a woman on a moonlit night on a tropic isle can never be a trouble. And with you, Madam Beauchamp," his tall shadow bowed briefly, "it has been a pleasure beyond compare."

Shanna laughed and waved a hand toward her loose hair and dressing robe. "You are gallant, sir, to so grace my blighted appearance, but you have made my evening. I shall bid you goodnight, Captain Beauchamp."

Nathanial paused for a moment before he answered. "Whatever the beginning or the end of it, I consider at this moment that you honor the name. Goodnight, Madam Beauchamp."

Shanna was still musing upon his words when she realized the shadows surrounding her were empty. Without a sound or a stir of air, he was gone.

The early morning breezes swept through the intricate latticework, stirring the potted greenery in the informal dining room. The sea-freshened air brought with it the fragrance of jasmine which bloomed alongside the veranda, mingled with the tantalizing aroma of hot, glazed meats, bread, brewed coffee, and tangy fresh fruits that graced the table for the morning meal and presented to Captain Beauchamp as he paused in the doorway a most heavenly scent after long months of sea fare.

"Good morning, Squire Trahern," Nathanial greeted.

Trahern turned from a copy of the *Whitehall Evening Post*, which he received in small bales from his ships. It was his only remaining link with London after years of separation.

"And a good morning to you, sir," the older man returned jovially. "Sit and join me in a bite to eat." He beckoned Nathanial to take a chair beside him. "A poor thing to start the day on an empty belly, and I speak from experience, if you please."

"Aye," Nathanial chuckled, accepting a cup of steaming coffee from Milan. "Or a slab of salt meat ripe with age."

Orlan Trahern gestured to the newspaper propped before him. "Peacetime quickly separates the real merchants from the warmongers." At the captain's raised brow, he continued. "Almost anyone can turn a tidy profit during a war, but only the good merchants manage to stay afloat when the country is at peace. Those who made their money skimming the king's barrels and shorting the navy's powder with sand cannot compete on an honest market."

"I shall yield to your wisdom on the matter." Nathanial leaned back in his chair. "Treachery is dealt with harshly in the colonies, and, although a certain amount of caution is due, one rarely meets with a cheat."

Now it was Trahern who leaned back in his chair to watch the other. "Tell me more of this place, your colonies. The idea of going there fascinates me."

The captain toyed with his cup for a moment before he spoke. "Our land is in the foothills of Virginia. Not so much settled as Williamsburg or Jamestown, but there is much to be said about it. Green rolling hills, forests for miles on end. The land is rich with opportunity for poor men and wealthy alike. My parents raised a family of three boys and twin girls in what most people would term as uncivilized land. In turn, each of us but the youngest lad, who is coming to a full seven-and-ten years next month, and one of the girls who is a score of summers old, have married and, God willing, will raise up their families with as much success. We have been called hearty, because we survived. Perhaps we are. But 'tis love and pride in our land that has made us so. If you could but see it, sir, I'm sure you'd understand."

Trahern nodded thoughtfully. "I will come." He thumped the table and laughed with his decision. "By damn, I will come and see it all."

"I am glad, sir, but I doubt you will see it all." Nathanial Beauchamp, too, was elated. "There is land beyond us as far as man can walk in a year. I have been told of prairies like the sea where if a man does not mark his way he will become lost, for he can see naught but grass. There is a river to the west so wide it is a strain to see across and beasts the like of which have not been seen in any other part of the world. There is a strange deer, taller than a horse and with antlers like huge shovels. I tell you, sir, there are wonders in the land that I cannot describe."

"Your enthusiasm is amazing, captain," Trahern chuckled. "I had expected most colonials to be a tired, carping lot."

"I know of no other land as beautiful, sir, nor one that promises as much," Nathanial replied, subdued, a trifle embarrassed at his own outburst.

Both men paused as the front door of the mansion closed. Footsteps could be heard coming across the marble floor toward the dining room. The sound stopped in the dining room doorway, and Trahern twisted around in his chair. Ruark stood with one hand on the jamb, surprised to find the older man occupied. Mumbling an apology, he half turned to leave.

"Nay, John Ruark. Come in, lad," Trahern bellowed and faced Captain Beauchamp. "Here is a man whom you should meet. A colonial like yourself, he is. He has made himself most valuable here."

As Ruark approached the table, Trahern introduced the two. They shook hands briefly. The captain, with a twisted grin, looked pointedly toward the short breeches Ruark was wearing.

"You have adapted yourself to the climate here very well, sir. On occasion I have coddled the idea myself, but I fear my wife would be much distressed at the sight of me gallivanting around like a half-dressed savage."

Trahern's belly shook with muted mirth as Ruark seated himself, casting a dubious glance toward the captain.

" 'Tis a fact Mister Ruark has turned a few of the ladies' heads with his garb. Whether from shock or approval remains to be seen. When I see which of the young maidens grows fat-bellied with child, perhaps I'll have the answer."

Under Nathanial's amused scrutiny, Ruark shifted uncomfortably in his chair. He readily accepted a cup of the steaming brew from Milan and paid close attention to the servant filling his plate. While the black man fetched him a bowl of fruit, Ruark changed the subject and spoke to Trahern.

"I came for the sketches of the lumber mill if you have finished looking them over, sir. We want to start laying the first stones this afternoon. The brewing house will be finished before the end of this month, and I see no reason for delaying."

"Good enough," Trahern declared. "I'll have a boy fetch them from my study while you eat."

The conversation drifted to a myriad of topics, and the subject of the colonies arose again. To the squire's inquiries, Ruark replied in much the same fashion as the captain. As the breakfast was concluded, Nathanial wiped his mouth on a napkin before laying the cloth aside, and turned to Trahern.

"While you are in the colonies, squire, it might be convenient for you to have someone along who knows the country, like this man here. My wife and I have a house in Richmond, but my parent's home—and I'm sure they'll want to meet you—is about a two-days' journey from there. If you are serious in coming, I could take my wife on ahead to my folks and send the carriages back to meet you. The drivers know the way of course, but you might want one of your own men along."

Ruark frowned slightly. His one thought was of Shanna and being separated from her. With him in the colonies and her left behind, he would not see it as a very pleasurable voyage.

"Of course! Of course!" Trahern agreed enthusiastically. "'Tis a good thought. No doubt Mister Ruark would enjoy a visit to his homeland."

Ruark fought the sense of pervading gloom that began to grow in him and was not completely successful in hiding his consternation.

Nathanial Beauchamp gave Ruark no notice as his laughter rumbled. "And you must bring your lovely daughter. She is sure to catch the eye of every swain there, including several of the married ones. My parents would count it a pleasure to have you both as guests in their home and anyone else you choose to bring with you. Indeed, I urge you to invite whom you will and stay long enough to settle your curiosity about the place."

"October, perhaps," Trahern mused aloud. "Or thereabouts. 'Twould be after the harvests in the colonies, and I could see, then, what produce you have available." He rose from his chair and met Nathanial's hand across it as he, too, came to his feet. "Agreed. We'll be there."

As Trahern and the captain crossed the foyer and left the house, Shanna stepped back out of sight on the stairway and waited until Jason had closed the door behind them and returned to the back of the house. Then she flew down the steps, hoping to catch Ruark before he was gone. Her concern was as much modesty as secrecy, for she had come awake at the sound of her father calling back a question to John Ruark from the entrance hall, and in her haste, she had snatched only the thinnest dressing gown to cover her brief sleeping attire. She sought this chance to speak with Ruark and found him with his back to her, whistling softly as he gathered parchments into a stack on the table.

Ruark rolled his sketches into a neat bundle and tucked them beneath his arm then turned to leave. He stopped abruptly, his whistle hanging in mid-phrase and tapering away on a reedy discord. Shanna was just closing the door behind her, a determined set to her jaw as she fixed him with her gaze.

"Blimey!" Ruark mimed in a cockney accent. "A veritable nymph springin' from the blank walls to force me attentions in the dining room. And a bloomin' near-naked one at that."

Momentarily Shanna's eyes flickered downward, and a light blush warmed her cheeks as she realized the boldness of her garb. Hurrying to catch Ruark, she had left her dressing gown hanging open, and the transparency of the batiste nightshift left nothing from his regard. Still, he had viewed more than this, indeed had more than viewed what she displayed, and she felt no more than a fleeting embarrassment at his close appraisal.

"Well, Mister Ruark, you certainly have made yourself scarce. I missed you at dinner last night."

As she spoke Shanna left the door and came toward him warily, like a hungry cat might approach a large gander, seeing the meal it desired but deeply aware of the danger of drawing too near.

Ruark smiled lazily, his eyes glowing as he took in her abundant beauty and admired the full swell of her pale breasts beneath the filmy garment.

"Only the demands of my duty, Shanna. The mill is nearing completion. As much as I longed to be near you, my presence was required."

"Of course." Shanna stared at him with open suspicion. "I saw your note to my father. A most convenient occurrence, if there is anything between you and this other Beauchamp."

"Madam?" Ruark's brows raised to mirror his spoken question.

"Or perhaps there is too little between you." Shanna cocked her head slightly aside, contemplating him. "Am I in truth Madam Beauchamp? Or was that only a convenient choice for you?"

Ruark shrugged casually. "I've no way of proving that to you, Shanna, but would not the magistrate have verified such a name? And of course you asked the good Mister Hicks for my name before you ever saw me, so I had no choice in the matter of names then. Call yourself Madam Beauchamp, but if you cannot accept that as truth, then call yourself Madam Ruark, or whatever you will. But I swear—"

"Enough!" Shanna held up her hand. "Do not swear. Make no more oaths or bargains to me. The last we made together has already cost me dearly."

Ruark studied her closely. "You've been quite distant of late, Shanna. Perhaps there is something you wish to tell me?"

He let the question hang but lowered his gaze pointedly to the smooth, flat belly little concealed by her light garment.

Shanna caught his meaning. "Have no concern, my lord dragon." Her voice mocked him lightly. "I do not bear your child. But to my other question. You have met this Captain Beauchamp?"

"Aye, love." Ruark flashed a grin. "We dined together this very morn."

"And you say that you be no kin of his?" She almost held her breath, waiting for his reply.

Ruark stared at her as boldly as she at him. "Madam, if he were, can you say me one reason why I would still be here?"

Shanna's curiosity changed slowly to perplexity. Finally she dropped her eyes and turned away from him.

"Nay." Her voice was low. "That bemuses me. And of course you would most certainly leave here and be free—if you could."

Ruark moved close and slipped an arm around her below her breasts, raising it beneath them so the gown gapped away from her, revealing their creamy roundness to his downward gaze. Shanna did not resist or pull away, but she sighed shakily.

"Do not handle me so, Ruark. I will not take the risk again, for 'twould all be for naught."

His lips touched her ear as he murmured, "Then I will leave you, maiden nymph, and be on my way—for a price."

Shanna turned in his arms until she faced him.

"Only a kiss, my love," Ruark teased. "A tuppence or two of your time. A tiny bribe as it is. A sweet, small candy to taste the whole day long."

Shanna saw the price as a small one and an easy way to be rid of him. Raising on tiptoe, she touched her lips briefly to his then would have stood away, but his arm held her close. Ruark sighed as if disappointed.

"Madam, by no miser's warped imagination would that be called a kiss." He smiled into her eyes as he chided lightly. "I see you have returned to your old ways."

Shanna had played the game of coquette on many occasions and chafed that he should again accuse her of being cold or naive.

Lifting her arms, she laid them around Ruark's neck and half pulling him down, moved her body slowly in a seductive way, her thighs bare against his and her meagerly clad breasts caressing his chest. She had learned much from him, and now she used that knowledge in a most provocative manner, giving him a kiss that could have set the whole Black Forest ablaze. It was enough to sap the very strength from Ruark's limbs. Yet it was not all one-sided as Shanna had intended, for she was as much a victim of the scalding kiss as he. It was a strong, intoxicating nectar; once sipped it only begged the more to be consumed. When she finally drew her lips away, she did not pull back but tried to steady her trembling limbs. They stood thus, each enjoying the nearness of the other.

"Ah, Shanna," Ruark breathed softly. "A taste of such rare, fine fare is more a torture than delight."

Shanna sighed against his throat as her fingers threaded through the short, curling hair at his nape. "Then for torture did you beg and another bargain fairly struck." Her eyes shone into his. "But as has been my wont, I will give you thrice the price that you need not sore belabor my honesty."

She reached parted lips up to his, moving them slowly and touching his with her tongue. Beneath the flowing robe, Ruark's arms tightened around her, and the kiss intensified as he slanted his mouth across hers, feeding greedily of the honey sweetness.

"Harrumph!" The throaty sound shattered their moment asunder.

Shanna snatched away from Ruark, her first reaction anger at being so rudely interrupted. In the next moment it congealed into a lump of cold fear in her belly. The very thing she had been afraid of had finally happened. They were discovered. As she stared at Captain Beauchamp, the cold knot grew, filling her until she trembled. Wishing for something more substantial to cover herself, she clutched the dressing gown before her in tight fists, acutely aware of its thinness. Her mind raced on in blurred confusion as she fumbled lamely for any excuse.

The briefest of moments had passed before Nathanial spoke. "I beg your pardon, Mister Ruark—Madam Beauchamp." He stressed the names oddly. "I forgot my pipe and pouch."

Without waiting for their assent, he crossed the room to his chair and retrieved the articles from the table and then paused again at the door. His smile had a strange quality as his eyes touched them each in turn. His fingertips brushed his brow in the briefest of salutes.

"Good day, Mister Ruark." And with a quick nod to her, "Madam Beauchamp."

Without another word he turned and closed the door gently behind him. It was some moments before Shanna could find her voice, and when she spoke it was as if she were certain of her words.

"He'll tell my father. I know he will." She stared at Ruark, despair written on her pale face. " 'Tis over—all my plans for naught."

A flicker of a frown crossed Ruark's face, but he sought to ease her worry. "He seemed a good enough chap to me, Shanna, not the kind to run and tell. But I have cause to be on the docks today. I'll stay close and should the chance present itself, I'll talk to him and try to explain—something." He shrugged. "I don't know what."

"Would you? Would you really, Ruark?" Shanna brightened a small shade. "Perhaps he'd understand if you'd put it right to him."

"I'll try, Shanna." He took her trembling hands in his and kissed her fingers. "If all goes awry, I shall at least try to send you a warning."

"Thank you, Ruark," she whispered gratefully. "I'll be waiting."

Then he was gone from her, and Shanna slowly made her way back to her rooms. The rest of her day was spent in nervous waiting. From moment to moment she expected her father to arrive, breaking down the doors as he sought her out; or a messenger from Ruark with word that she should flee; or Ruark himself to state all was well; or the whole lot of them, including the captain, to accuse her and have the whole thing out. All sorts of imaginings flew through her mind, and she could not sit still long enough even for her hair to be combed. With unusual patience, Hergus waited three times for her mistress to be seated before the task was done.

Late in the day Ruark returned with her father, but his only indication was a noncommittal shrug as he passed her at the front door. It was only as he was leaving for the evening that she managed to catch him alone for a moment and to her frantic, "Well?" Ruark smiled wickedly and whispered, "The captain assured me that no gentleman would carry such tales."

In her absolute relief, Shanna was in her rooms and dressed for bed before she realized that Ruark had deliberately let her stew until the last moment.

Chapter 12

THE late August day whimpered under the cruel heat of the sun. The sand on the beach was too hot to walk upon; even the playing children had withdrawn into the cool shelter of their homes. The island grew quiet as its inhabitants sank into the torpor of a long siesta. Heat waves rose from the rooftops and shimmered on the distant horizon like a thousand shards of rippling aqua. A languid lapping of the sea on the shore was the only movement that could be seen; no breeze stirred the smallest leaf. The sky was devoid of clouds and seemed bleached of its normal blue by the sheer heat of the day.

Sighing, Shanna turned from her balcony and entered into the coolness of her room, shedding the light robe which in the warmth was almost unbearable. Her firm, young body glistened with a light film of perspiration beneath the short shift, and her long, heavy mass of hair was damp against her nape. For a time she plucked idly at a tapestry, but she gave that up to sprawl on the cool silken sheets of her bed. The sewing had only been brought out to keep her mind and hands busy. This piece was one she had begun years ago but never had had the patience to finish. It was a labor for her, and thus a thing she hated. In the days of her schooling it had been even more loathsome, being a required skill each girl had to master. Her mentors taught it with diligence, not understanding her sighs and groans of frustration. In a fit of temper she had torn many a piece to shreds, detesting her errors and having no patience to correct them. The chastening frowns of her tutors would have turned to openmouthed gapes if they could have known of her desire to train under the artist, Hogarth, at St. Martin's Lane Academy.

"How crude!" They would have trembled. "Why, 'tis said the young men sketch from live models there. Naked ones!"

Shanna laughed to herself and wiggled on the bed. They little guessed that some of their own "innocent children" volunteered for the task, or if they guessed they carefully averted their thoughts.

"But at least the stitchery has served its purpose," Shanna thought. "It diverts me from thinking on that dragon Ruark when he's about."

Rolling onto her stomach, she propped her chin on crossed forearms, closing her eyes in the bliss of memory. Ruark had become almost a fixture in the manor. He was present at most every meal and accompanied her father on many of his trips. Shanna could hardly descend the staircase without the prospect of meeting him, and whenever they met his eyes devoured her with a boldness that in itself roused her. Even that she could bear. In fact, she rather enjoyed his warm perusals. It was during the quiet moments when no one else was looking that those golden orbs turned toward her with a hunger in them that nearly tore her heart, a longing so intense she had to avert her own gaze. Then, if her mind were free to roam, she would remember the exciting touch of his hands, the warmth of his lips on hers, the whisperings—a memory of the times they had shared love. She could hear again his murmurs, coaxing her, gently directing her in the ways of love, and recalled the pleasure of his mouth at the crest of her breast, teasing, rousing, hot, devouring—

Shanna's eyes flew open. "My lord!" she whispered. "My own mind betrays me!"

Her breasts tingled against the thin fabric of her shift, and there was an empty ache in her loins. She rose and flew to the tapestry frame but a moment later sucked her finger where the needle had teased a drop of blood to the skin. Slowly clenching her hands into fists, Shanna stood staring at her chamber door, knowing that if Ruark walked in now she would welcome him with all the willingness of her ripe woman's body. Tears flooded her eyes, in part tears of anger. She wanted him and hated herself for that weakness. In the depths of her was a passion only Ruark could ease, and it was a desperate struggle to keep even a small anger alive.

Suddenly she was tired, tired of having to avoid even the briefest moment alone with him. Yet she was afraid. Captain Beauchamp had surprised them once. The next time it could be someone of less sympathy or manners, perhaps even Orlan Trahern himself. Shanna's mind soared on in endless circles as she tried to resolve her plight. Again she lay upon the bed, and as sleep overcame her she had solved no more of her problems than the sun in its brief passage across the sky had eased of its heat.

Night drew down upon the island, and the heat of the day was quenched to a point that clothes could be borne. Light, gusty breezes further abated discomfort as the meal was served. Just the day before, an English frigate on its way to the colonies had put into port, and the dinner guests this evening included persons from the ship—her captain, a major of the Royal Marines, and a knight, Sir Gaylord Billingsham, who traveled as a minor emissary. Several of the overseers had brought their wives, and Ralston, Pitney, and Ruark filled out the table.

The group adjourned to the drawing room where the women gathered at one end while the men congregated at the other, there to fill their pipes or light cigars. After the ladies exchanged amenities, several produced items of sewing and began a low-voiced exchange of recipes and gossip. Except when questions were directed to her, Shanna remained silent, and under the guise of her needlework watched Ruark as he leisurely drew on his pipe and conversed with the other men. He wore a brown coat over tan breeches and waistcoat, a white shirt with a ruffled jabot. His fortune had continued to grow, and shortly after Nathanial Beauchamp had left, Ruark had spent a part of it for clothes, plainer and not as formal as the ones with which Trahern had gifted him, but no less flattering to his own fine good looks.

Shanna bent her attention back to her work as one of the women leaned closer.

"I say, Shanna, isn't that young Mister Ruark a handsome man?" the woman whispered over her embroidery.

"Yes," Shanna murmured. "Handsome, indeed."

She smiled, warming with pleasure. For all her avowed dislike of him, she felt an unusual pride when someone boasted of Ruark.

With half an ear to the gossip, Shanna learned that Sir Gaylord Billingsham was single, unattached, available. He was traveling to the colonies to seek financial backing for a small shipyard in Plymouth that his family had acquired.

He's a strange one, Shanna mused, lightly considering him. He was taller than Ruark, a trifle large-boned, and moved with an odd disjointed grace that bordered on the awkward yet seemed somehow appropriate for his lanky frame. Light tannish hair curled about his long face, hinting of some attention to direct it thus, and was tied in a bagwig at the base of his neck. His eyes were pale grayish blue, his wide mouth full-lipped for a man and expressive. His manner ranged from stilted inanity to haughty arrogance, yet he was quick to smile at a quip and seemed to enjoy the sometimes coarse humor of the overseers. His quick temper displayed itself briefly when he had been informed that he shared a table with a bondsman. Though he recovered quickly, he made a point of avoiding Ruark from that time on. Shanna found it strangely upsetting.

Even as she studied him, he decried the "filthy habit" of smoking tobacco and instead, taking a small, silver-chased box from his waistcoat pocket, he laid a pinch of the finely powdered leaf on the back of his hand and delicately sniffed it into one nostril then the other. A moment later he sneezed lightly into his lace handkerchief then leaning his head back, sighed, "Ahh, truly the man's way." And at the stares he received, further explained, "One must bear the bite before the pleasure."

Snuffing loudly, he directed his next remark to the frigate's captain. "But for all of it, sir, I must admit I could never be a proper seaman. I abhor the narrow space of a cabin when it is well tossed upon the seas and cannot stand the confines of it in a safe harbor."

With a flourish of his hand, he bent his regard to Trahern. "Good squire." His nose was at an arrogant height. "It hardly seems possible that there is not some good inn or tavern where I might find proper lodging for the days I am here. Or perhaps some gentlefolk have space in their home?"

He raised his brow and let the question hang.

Trahern smiled. "There is no need, Sir Gaylord," he assured the man. "We have more than ample space here, and it shall be my pleasure that you reside with us."

"You are most kind, Squire Trahern." The knight almost simpered with the success of his own ploy. "I shall send a man for a few of my belongings."

Trahern raised a hand and shook his head. "We can see to your immediate needs, sir, and should you desire something more, we can have it fetched on the morrow. You shall be our guest for as long as you wish."

And though Trahern knew he had been maneuvered, he was still pleased at the prospect of playing host to a titled gentleman.

Having heard the exchange, Shanna gestured for a servant and in a low voice bade him prepare the guest chambers in the squire's wing. As the servant left she caught her father's eye and nodded slightly. Trahern returned to his conversation, assured that the preparations were made and glowing at his daughter's efficiency.

Shanna concentrated on her tapestry, frowning briefly over a difficult stitch. Then, feeling eyes upon her, she raised her own to seek Ruark out among the men. To her surprise he was not watching her but stared across the room, a frown creasing his brow. Following his gaze, she found herself looking into the eyes of Sir Gaylord Billingsham. They were filled with more than light interest as he obviously admired her beauty. The wide lips twitched then spread into a slow smile which somehow was more like a leer. It was enough to make Shanna glad she had set him a room far from her own. Quickly she averted her gaze. Her eyes swept the room and halted on Ralston. With an enigmatic smile, the man was slyly perusing Sir Gaylord.

Before the evening drew to a close, Orlan Trahern invited all those present and the entire ship's complement to take part in celebrating the opening of the mill. Since all the townsfolk would be there, he explained, there was little else for them to do but join the festivities on the morrow.

Shanna's nap in the afternoon delayed her sleep, and for a

long, hectic hour she tossed and turned, fighting a vision of Ruark in the bed beside her and struggling to quell the insistence of her own mind which threatened to send her dashing down the lane toward the cottage. Still, she prevailed and finally found victory in sleep, though that, too, was riddled with dreams which left her trembling between sweat-dampened sheets.

Early the next morning Ruark arrived at the mill long before anyone else and took care to tether his mule, Old Blue, well away from the stock barn. The cantankerous mule had a penchant for teasing the simpler and much more handsome horses by nipping them about the rump or ears. This play usually degenerated into a fight at which the venerable old street brawler excelled. Many a fine horse limped off, quite ragged from the encounter. So to preserve peace with the drivers and overseers, Ruark was forced to seclude his steed.

Ruark gave a glance over his shoulder as Old Blue laid back his ears and with a rasping, seesawing voice brayed his challenge to the animals. Ruark jammed his hat down lower over his brow, not overly willing to be a party to any row that might be forthcoming. Pushing open the small door beneath the hopper, he retreated from the mule's sight. He stood for a moment in the collecting room, letting his eyes adjust to the dark, while he savored the pungent scent of the new woods which formed the greater part of the structure. The rich, warm tones of the unweathered surfaces still bore the marks of ax and adz and reflected the sun to lend the interior a hue of mysterious golden brown. There was an atmosphere of expectancy; everything was new, ready, waiting.

Here, where the juices were collected, were the huge rollers that would crush the cane. Six oversize tubs stood on a circular platform which could be rotated when each became full. Allowing his imagination to wander, Ruark could almost see the tubs as giant gnomes squatting on their table, awaiting the first stir of life in the mill to fill their gullets with the sweet nectar of the cane. Ruark rapped his knuckles against the bellied side of the nearest tub to dispel the thought and listened to the echo of the hollow sound within the room.

A frown lightly crossed his brow. Would Shanna view this

building of the mill as an attempt to woo her father's favor?

He moved on to the cooking room, strolling along between the two rows of great iron kettles, idly swinging a stick against the sides of each. They, too, seemed to wait like elephantine elves resting their distended paunches over the brick hearths wherein fires would be stoked to render the thin juices into thick, brown molasses.

And what on this day would Shanna's mood betray, Ruark wondered idly. Was she to be the fiery-tongued vixen whose words of denial were sharp enough to cut or the docile sweet maid who of late he had seen much of?

Reaching the end of the room, Ruark paused and looked back, listening to the hollow notes of his passage die like the bronzed chorus of the church bells on a Sabbath morn. A slow smile touched his lips as a memory came to mind of one evening, several nights back, when he and Trahern had withdrawn to the drawing room after the evening meal, and Shanna had taken a place beside the French doors to catch the last of the fading light as she bent to her tapestry. It had been a most idyllic time, a gentle time with the peace of a good pipe, easy conversation and her presence there, the soft beauty at hand whenever his eye should wander to it, lighted by the rosy glow of the waning sun. He had found himself envisioning her in a similar scene, but with a babe in her arms and her face tender with love. It was a gracious thing to relax and enjoy a meal with Shanna, beautiful and demure across the table, yet the agony had been there as well, for though she seemed much mollified and serenely pleasant, he had not had the briefest moment alone with her.

He sighed, slapping the stick against his fawn-clad thigh and continued his tour into the brewing wing. Nearly half the room was filled wall to wall with great barrels where the younger green sap could be fed into them and, with careful additions, would be fermented into the new rum. Here above the stills, red serpentine pipes writhed in a frenzied Stygian dance, frozen for all eternity, then plunged down to dribble the cooled spirits into kilderkins for aging and sale. This was the master brewer's place, his realm where his talent and skill would wring the best from the cane.

The site of the mill had been chosen carefully. It was far

enough from the settlement so that the stench of the fermenting mash would not offend the noses of the villagers, but centrally located near the high plateau where the cane fields thrived. Beneath its foundation were caves where the barrels of rum could be stored for aging. Water was carried in shafts from freshwater springs running close by, and wood was in plentiful supply from the forest around it. Not inconsequential to all of these was the fact that it nestled in a small, protected valley and was safe from the late summer storms that often raged through the islands.

A slight quickening of Ruark's pulse came as he felt the thrill of success followed by a deeper quickening still, as he realized his doubts and thought of the hundreds of things which could go wrong.

"No need to ponder on it," he reasoned. "This day will see the test of it all."

A narrow stairway led into the loft, and he climbed to where a small cupola had been added at the highest point on the mill roof so that a man could view the approach and departure of wagons during the rush of the harvest peak and with a set of signals could direct the drivers to avoid the inevitable road jams. At this vantage point Ruark would await the arrival of the Trahern carriage.

Already a long file of wagons, carriages, and carts were coming up the village road. Several wagons had been provided for the crew of the frigate, and he could see the colorful uniforms of the officers riding in the carriage. From one of the fields Ruark noted the approach of five wagons heavily laden with cane, and closer about the mill, piling out of the back of a cart, were the score of bondsmen who would see the mill into its first operation. At a shout of greeting from the overseer, Ruark waved his hand then lifted his gaze again to the lower road. No hint of Trahern's barouche could be seen, least of all that bright bit of color for which his eye hungered.

It seemed that every soul on the island was turning out to see the first operation of the mill and the actual workings for themselves, for the once empty yards were now becoming a jumble of people. Still, there was no sight of Shanna.

"I should have better tied my fate to the tail of a whirlwind," Ruark mused wryly, "than be so committed to that whimsical bit of woman." That sweet Circean witch had cast her spell on him from the first moments in the gaol. Perhaps he did, in fact, commit the crime on that other wench in the inn and this was his punishment—to ever know Shanna as his bride, but never to know the joys of marriage. If that were truth, then he should accept his state and the rare monthly wedded bliss and, for the other days, his slavery. What a dreadful twist of fate. As a man unattached, he had threaded his way among the wiles of tender, fetching maids and lightheartedly plucked that which they offered, but now, wedded to that one who in all honesty he would have chosen in any circumstance—he was denied the state of matrimony and must creep into each tryst, enjoying only the hidden hours between the dark of midnight and the break of dawn. Even then, the chance footstep, the mistaken door, might see them snatched apart and, like wayward children, brought before her father for whatever punishment the man would dictate.

A shout from below interrupted his musings, and Ruark glanced up to see Trahern's barouche coming through the trees lining the narrow, low road. Leaving the cupola, he hurried down and quickly crossed the empty storeroom to the door where he had entered. As he caught sight of Shanna beside her father, Ruark's spirits soared, but they were dashed quickly when he identified Sir Gaylord in the seat opposite her. It had been in his mind to greet them, but now, angry and silent, Ruark retreated into a shadow and watched the lanky popinjay hand his wife down from the carriage. Ruark's displeasure deepened as Gaylord's hand lingered at Shanna's elbow. It was doubly hard for him to bear when he could not even touch her himself in public. Ruark clamped the white, straight-brimmed hat tighter on his head and leaned against the wall of the mill in frustration.

A goodly crowd had gathered around the Trahern carriage, and soon the squire was happily introducing his titled guest to the various shopkeepers and other personages of importance on the island. Sir Gaylord was forced to turn away from Shanna and left her side to acknowledge the compliments and salutations. Smoothing her gown, Shanna scanned the press of people for Ruark's face. She saw him in the shade of the building, arms folded across his chest as he braced a shoulder against the wall.

His hat was cocked forward, obscuring his face, but she knew that tall, lithe form. He was dressed casually, and, in the heat of the day it appeared the most sensible fashion. A white shirt, opened at the throat and ruffled at the cuffs, contrasted sharply with his bronze skin. He was as dark as any Spaniard and his lean, muscular build was accentuated by the close-fitting breeches and white stockings.

Shanna smiled in thought. The tailor must have waxed gleeful at the opportunity to garb such a handsome figure. Most of the men on the island who had money for the richer fabrics and latest styles were well past the prime of life. But Ruark had the good looks and the trim frame to complement the lowest garb, even those boldly shortened breeches. Still, Shanna felt a twinge of disapproval that these breeches should be so narrow in their cut and that Ruark should carelessly flaunt his manliness for the goggling stares of love-smitten girls. Yet she knew he was not one to be overly conscious of his appearance as the dandies of court were, or even this Sir Gaylord who was garbed in laces and velvets and seemed hot enough to burst.

Seeing Shanna momentarily alone, Ruark seized upon his chance and began to make his way toward her through the crowd. His haste and his singleness of mind, however, were his downfall, for suddenly his arms were full of the soft body of a girl, and he was abruptly knocked off balance. A sharp feminine squeal pierced his ears, and Ruark spun half about, grasping the young woman close to keep them both from sprawling headlong.

"'Od's blood, Mister Ruark," Milly's shrill voice giggled. "Ye're a mite too sudden for a bit of a girl like meself."

The apology stumbled lamely from Ruark's tongue. "Uh, your pardon, Milly. I was in a hurry."

Ruark would have extricated himself, but the girl held onto his arm, clasping it firmly against her small bosom.

"Aye, 'at I can see, John." Her familiar use of his name grated against his ears. Suddenly her voice sounded loud enough to carry across the island. "'Twould seem of late ye're always in a hurry." Milly's chuckle struck an uneven chord. "But no need to cart yerself away, John Ruark. 'Ooever she be, she can wait."

Ruark tried to hide his irritation. Twisting his arm in an effort to be free of her grasp, he glanced over her dark head toward

Shanna who watched them rather tensely. Milly's hand reached up to caress his chest, and her black eyes smiled into his invitingly.

"Oooh, John," she sighed. "Ye're so strong. Just looking at ye can make a tiny girl like meself feel weak and helpless."

Ruark bit back a harsh speculation as to where her weakness might lie and attempted to pry her fingers loose from his shirt. "Come now, Milly, I'm in a hurry," he half growled.

Milly was insistent. "I packed a good basket of vittles with a leg of mutton, John. Why don't ye come and have a bite to eat with us?"

"My regrets," Ruark hastened to deny her plea. "The squire has bade me join them at his table."

He almost freed his arm, but Milly had still another ploy to work.

"Oh," she whined and leaned heavily against him. "I think I've bruised me foot a bit. Will ye 'elp me to our cart, lovey?"

A broad shadow joined them, and they both glanced up to find Mrs. Hawkins standing before them, arms akimbo and a frown clefting her brow like the blade of an ax.

"Huh!" the woman snorted before either of them could speak. "Bruised foot, indeed! I'll help ye to the cart. Come along, ye shameless twit. Throwing yerself at Mister Ruark like that. Ye ought to be ashamed."

Mrs. Hawkins took her daughter by the fat of the arm and, with a quick glance of apology to Ruark, led the girl away. Milly limped until her mother's hand swung low with a loud whack, startling a yelp from the girl. The bruised foot forgotten, Milly did an amazingly spritely scamper all the way back to their cart.

Ruark chuckled in amusement as he witnessed the haste of Milly's flight, but he sobered as he turned back to Shanna. She stared at him with a quizzical quirk playing about her lips and a wondering dip to her brow. Ruark knew her well enough to read the storm warnings and hurried forward to allay her wrath. Alas! Such was not to be his luck, for with a shout of greeting Trahern rushed to intercept him, and Ruark was swept aside by Trahern's bulk just as he reached Shanna. Again Ruark found his arm clasped in another's grip and, much to his chagrin, he was steered by Trahern back toward the mill. Casting a glance over his shoulder, he saw Sir Gaylord return to Shanna's side. The knight took her elbow and bent low over her shoulder to whisper some witty comment in her ear.

"Now, Mister Ruark," Trahern was saying, "let's get this mill opened and allow these good people to get their feasting. My daughter will cut the bunting, but I'd like for you to share in this moment."

Ruark lost the rest of what the squire said as Shanna's laughter rippled behind him. The sound of it bit at his heart like vinegar in a thirsty man's throat.

In a salute to King George, tankards of ale and rum and various other brews were raised while the women chose a mild wine to sip. Dedicating the mill led to a series of other toasts, and by the time Shanna was led to the wide doors fronting the place, spirits were high. She was not unaffected by the gaiety, but her elation stemmed from an entirely different source. A few tiny sips of wine could hardly make her so heady with joy. She could not fathom the reason for her own buoyant emotions as she moved to where the bunting was secured, but the realization abruptly dawned when she gazed at Ruark standing with her father. This mill was Ruark's achievement, and it was ecstatic pride she felt at his accomplishment. Tears suddenly brightened her eyes, and she smiled until the unbidden moisture subsided. Laughing happily, she yanked hard on the hidden rope that held up the mass of bunting. The knots slipped, and the many yards of colorful cloth fell with a multitude of flutters to the platform.

Ruark's hand joined hers to push aside the heavy bolt, and before this vast audience they both sought hard to ignore the contact. Their eyes met briefly before Ruark stepped away to open the doors, and Shanna was the only one who knew her blush was not completely from the excitement of the moment.

When the doors were flung wide, the people stared into the gaping storeroom which in its emptiness gave more the impression of a cathedral. The noise of the crowd died to a low murmur of amazement; then their attention was drawn away by a shout from the milling gates. Two of the wagons were already being backed into place above the hopper that guided the cane downward. Another shout rent the air, and a team of oxen were prodded into movement in a circular path, setting into motion a great cog above them. It meshed with a large spoked wheel which rotated a shaft that in turn ran into the building. The man who drove the oxen waved to another beside the bin who bent his back to lay a huge lever forward. A loud thump was followed by another, and then the rollers began to turn with slow, ponderous majesty. A heavy rumbling seemed to tremble the very ground, and it caused a feeling of exhilaration in Shanna's breast. Her heart swelled almost to bursting, and she felt like laughing and crying at the same time. A buzz of voices rose from the people as they watched the first cane taken into the rollers. Restlessly they waited until the lever was moved again, this time ceasing the motion. The rumbling stopped, the oxen were halted. The sudden silence lasted for what seemed to Shanna a very long eternity—then a rattling came from inside the mill. Slowly, one at a time, four great hogsheads of juices were wheeled out onto the platform to be viewed and sampled by all who cared to do so.

It was a crowning achievement. That which would have taken a score of men most of the afternoon had been done in the time it might take one to sip a cup of tea. A loud, boisterous shout of approval rang from the onlookers. Even Ruark smiled, until Sir Gaylord crossed the platform, stepping between him and Shanna, and took her outstretched hand.

Since the mill was something entirely new to the island, the villagers were allowed to view the interior for themselves now that the actual crushing of the harvested cane had been demonstrated. For many weeks the townsfolk had wondered at this thing being constructed in the hills above their hamlet and now, at long last, their curiosity was to be appeased. They were filled with awe at the ingenuity which had brought it into being, and more than a few were somewhat contrite, because they had once slapped their thighs in uproarious disbelief when informed that the production of the mill was limited only by the speed with which the cane could be dumped into the hopper and that what had been a long tedious month of backbreaking labor could now be handled between Sabbaths.

"May I escort you within, Madam Beauchamp?" Sir Gaylord requested. "I've a bit of curiosity about the thing myself. Must have been an Englishman who brought the idea into being."

Shanna smiled in amusement, recognizing the typical English mind. If it was good, it had to be English.

"I've already been given a most splendid tour of the place by our bondsman, Sir Gaylord. I'm sure Mister Ruark will be interested in your deduction, but he's from the colonies, not England as you surmised."

"Egad! You don't say he was the one—" Gaylord was clearly astonished. With arrogant poise he sniffed lightly against his handkerchief. "Ah, well, for a simple brew I suppose one might rely upon some basic common knowledge in the building of a brewing house. Myself, I cannot abide the stuff. I prefer a good wine to that beastly concoction. No gentleman's brew."

Shanna smiled like a cat that had just ensnared a rat. "I must inform my father of your findings, sir. Actually, he finds the drink quite tasty."

Sir Gaylord folded his large hands behind his back and appeared to grow museful. "Perhaps your father would be interested in a more sound investment, Madam Beauchamp. My family has acquired a shipyard in Plymouth, very promising 'tis, and with your father's wealth—"

Again the knight blundered like so many others before him, but Sir Gaylord hardly realized what lay behind Shanna's sidelong glance. Instead, he had suddenly become fascinated with the advantage his height gave him. Standing head and shoulders above Shanna, he had a very pleasurable view of what lay beneath her demure bodice whenever he chanced to look that way, which now was rather often. The higher swell of her creamy breasts was a tantalizing sight for any man, and Sir Gaylord most certainly enjoyed this treat.

Seeing where the knight's perusal wandered, Ruark was anything but jovial. He hid his churning anger behind a brimming tankard of ale, tipping the mug and drinking the fluid down until the last drop was tasted. After witnessing this feat, Shanna peered at him questioningly, but Sir Gaylord moved between them again, taking her arm. Bending low over her with some inane comment, he casually led her away from Ruark's presence.

Ruark had no time to react, for his own arm was seized in Trahern's huge paw. As he was tugged along, he heard a flow of eager words begin with:

"Now as to the sawmill. When do you think—"

Ruark was unaware of what he replied, for in his memory the

rest of the conversation was covered by an angry haze through which he saw only the back of the swaggering Sir Gaylord.

Trahern left him as a train of wagons arrived from the manor. The squire's flock of servants spilled out of the conveyances and began to set up a long row of tables which were quickly covered with hogsheads of ales and beers and smaller kegs of selected wines, sweet and dry, red and white. A last cart was opened and still-steaming sides of lamb, roast pig, fowl of all sorts, and seafood were all laid out with a vast assortment of delicate sauces to complement the meats and to tease the palate. The ladies of the island brought forth their own preparations to add to the feast. As Shanna led Sir Gaylord to inspect the dishes, he spread his hands in surrender and chortled lightly.

"Gracious, I am overwhelmed by this abundance on such a tiny island. Why, surely this must rival the outings in England of my own good kinfolk."

He missed the glare of several ladies and took Shanna's amused smile as encouragement. Trahern had come upon them in time to catch his last statement and hastened to offset the error of his remark.

"Ah, Sir Gaylord, 'tis only that you have not tasted this magnificent fare the ladies have contributed, else you would agree that in all the world no simple outing would rival this one."

Ruark had followed slowly along, halfheartedly selecting another ale to sip as he regarded the posturing Sir Gaylord. The knight dabbed repeatedly at his forehead with a lace handkerchief and seemed generally to be suffering from the heat. Ruark was not above hoping the man would collapse from it. But at least with Trahern's close presence, Sir Gaylord held his gaze to something less appealing than Shanna's bodice.

"I say there, John Ruark."

Ralston hailed him with his riding crop and came toward him, glacing briefly over his darkly clad shoulder toward the Trahern party. Ruark paused to wait for the man, though his eyes, beneath lowered brows, never left that bit of pink almost hidden by the tall, lanky form of the knight. Ruark was not aware that Shanna returned his perusal, gazing past the Englishman's arm as she smiled and nodded at the man's senseless chatter. Ruark only saw Sir Gaylord again lead her away to the end of a separate table where the servants were placing their plates.

"John Ruark." Ralston demanded his attention in a curt tone and grew red-faced with anger as Ruark responded slowly, finally turning to meet the cold, penetrating glare. "I suggest, Mister Ruark, that you try to keep your yearnings under control, though I well understand the cause." Ralston gestured casually in the direction of Shanna. "Remember that you are a bondsman and do not think you can exceed your status while I'm about. 'Tis long been my duty to turn riffraff away from the Trahern door. Indeed, you seem to lack for duties. I suggest you see the pressings to their proper disposal. 'Twill be a shame for the juices to be lost, for this first should become a selected brew."

"With due respect, sir," Ruark's tone was measured and tightly controlled, "the master brewer approved the laying of every stone and has established his skill. 'Tis unseemly that I, with less experience in the matter, should oversee his work."

" 'Tis more than apparent to me, *Mister* Ruark,"—the title was a sneer—"that of late you presume too much. Do as you are told and do not return until the labor is done."

A long moment passed as haughty glower met carefully blank stare. Then Ruark nodded and strode away to do what he was bidden.

When all the guests were seated at their plates, Shanna found Sir Gaylord at her side and; gazing around the table in wonderment, she noted that Ruark's plate had been pushed to the foot of the table, far away from his usual place near her father, and that his trencher was as yet unattended. She was quick to note Ralston's arrival, and the smug smile playing about his normally taciturn lips.

Seating himself at the middle of the table, Ralston gazed with obvious satisfaction at Ruark's empty place. "For once," he thought, "that rogue is where he belongs, doing what he should, laboring that his betters might take their ease."

Lifting his eyes, the agent found Shanna staring at him with a frown gathering on her brow. Hastily Ralston bent his attention to his food, neither marking nor caring that it was not the simple English fare he favored.

Ruark's day had reached its zenith with the success of the mill. Thereafter, it began to sink with a series of rapid plunges to its nadir. However, that point was not reached until later in the evening, when, returning from his errand, he overheard Madam Hawkins and Mister MacLaird discussing the advantages of the squire's daughter marrying a lord. He listened for a while and then turned away in disgust, only to find himself again an unwilling eavesdropper as Trahern expounded upon the touted virtues that a knight might present as a son-in-law. The low ebb was truly found when Ruark overheard the captain of the frigate and the marine major discussing Sir Gaylord's decision to journey to the colonies with the Traherns. He had even made arrangements for part of his baggage to be taken to the manor, while the greater portion would be carried on the frigate to Richmond to await his arrival there with the Traherns. It was their premise that the knight was looking for a worthy wife and had settled his sights on the squire's lovely offspring.

The handwriting was not on the wall, but it blazed furiously in Ruark's mind. The scene was set for that mincing, foppish knave to be proposed to Shanna for a husband. As Ruark drained his cup for the twelfth time, he growled to himself that even *she* had not seemed too displeased with the gentleman, indeed had been most gracious the entire afternoon.

Ruark made no excuses as he withdrew from the gaieties. Snatching up a large, full flask from the table, he sought out his old mule, mounted its back, and sent it plodding down the hill.

As usual Shanna was the center of much attention. The officers of the frigate came to pay their compliments and lingered long, enjoying the fresh draught of feminine pulchritude after long weeks at sea. Musicians mounted the platform and played for the pleasure of the crowd. A young marine captain led Shanna through a rigadoon, encouraging the other officers to ask for the same favor. The evening should have made her gay, as Shanna had always enjoyed dancing and the lighthearted company of men. However, this evening there was a strange note of discord in her pleasure, and when the rare moments occurred in which she could be alone, Shanna puzzled at her own mood. Events began to drag out interminably, and she became wearied with the tedium of them. She postured and smiled graciously through it all, but her relief was immense when her father finally suggested that the townsfolk be left to enjoy themselves and formed his entourage for departure. For Shanna, it seemed the ride back would never end, and even the breathtaking view of the moonlit surf failed to stir her. Upon their arrival at the manor, she quickly excused herself from Sir Gaylord, drawing a frown of disappointment from the man, and sought the peace of her own chambers.

Ruark came awake with a start. One moment he was asleep, the next wide awake. He could find no reason for it. He was alert and seemed in the best of health, though he had dozed off in the chair where he had been sampling from a jug. Pulling the cork, Ruark sniffed then grimaced at the bitter pungency of the oily black rum. He had never acquired a taste for it and much preferred the lighter, gentler brews.

The tall clock behind him in the hall gave a single chime, and, turning, Ruark verified the hour as the first of the morning. A frown drew his dark brows together. Rising from the chair, he went to stand beside the window. Old Blue was in his own small yard, though the gate stood wide, dozing beneath the open shelter Ruark had built.

Loosening his linen shirt and slipping it over his head, Ruark went to the washstand in the bedchamber and, having naught else to do, shaved and washed the sweat of the day from his body. He rinsed the bitter taste from his mouth and then donned a pair of shortened breeches before going out onto the small porch to catch the coolness of the night. Though slightly light-headed, as if some of the effects of the rum were still with him, he had a sense of well-being and clarity of mind.

The moon was low and skimmed the treetops. Where it penetrated the high canopies it lit the cool but oddly tense night with an eerie gray cast. There was an urging in him that made Ruark uneasy. The night seemed to call, the shadows to beckon. Stepping from the porch, he felt the dampness of dew beneath his bare feet. He passed the shrubbery and wandered beneath the tall trees. The manor house drew him. Its great dark hulk squatted in the midst of slimmer trees. All the lights were gone now, and he knew that the revelers had returned and were abed.

A familiar bulk loomed beside him, and reaching out his hand Ruark felt the bole, identifying the tree that stood before

Shanna's balcony. He leaned a shoulder against the comfortable bulwark of sturdy wood and stared upward toward the open doors that marked her room. His mind wandered until it touched on a scene of Shanna sleeping beside that hulking English knight. The vision was most distasteful, and Ruark banished it quickly from his mind. Thus freed, his thoughts trod gently backward to a night when he had watched her in slumber, her honey- and gold-streaked hair spreading in careless cascades across the pillow, framing her perfect face. Her lips parted slightly with her breathing as she slept in innocent trust upon his bed. Then there was a time in the cottage when she had knelt above him naked and leaned across to kiss him, her breasts in silken tresses caressing his chest until he nearly dissolved in bliss. And once she had curled close beside him, cuddling her body against his, her warmth touching a warmth deep within him, stirring his passions to a soaring flight like a covey of quail from an upland lea. The burning inside him grew hotter until it became an exotic torture, and he found himself beneath her balcony, stretching upward to grasp the vine.

Shanna floated in a deep well of dream stuff, a limbo, an endless void. She was swimming in a gently rolling sea, bright turquoise water shattering with the easy strokes of her arms. A small panic began to build as she realized there was no land in sight, not even the green-hued clouds that reflected its presence, but then the fear fled. Beside her, a man's golden, bronzed arms matched the movements of her own, stroke for stroke. The man turned, and the visage was Ruark's, his white teeth flashing in a tantalizing grin. His lips moved in a voiceless plea, then he rose and arched his muscled back to dive beneath the waves. With a playful laugh she followed, going deep where the light faded into dark green and endless tendrils of seaweed twined about them as they came together in a timeless kiss. She felt no need to breathe. They were like two nymphs drifting in an oceanic nirvana, deeper, deeper. Then suddenly she was alone—

Ruark's face returned in gigantic proportions drifting above her. It came ever closer, yet she could not touch it. She blinked her eyes and moved her head, trying to banish the vision. Suddenly she realized she was awake, and he was there. His arms, braced on either side of her, trembled beneath his weight. His lips hovered over hers, and his voice was soft as he spoke, like a small boy pleading for a favor.

"Shanna—love me, Shanna—love me."

With a small, welcoming cry, she reached silken arms to draw him down to her, her heart flooding her body with warm gladness. It was like a time for things meant to be, like the trees, the sand, the sea, the sun, and the stars. It was a thousand twinkling stars blending to a single sun, the naked hunger that caught them both into a sweet, violent whirlwind. Shanna arched against him, opening her thighs and meeting his deep thrusts with all the vigor in her trembling body, holding no reserve. They were one, belonging and possessing, giving and taking.

Sated, they lay entwined, Shanna warm and secure in his arms, knowing the strange peace she had found nowhere else. There was no shame, no sense of having strayed, not the smallest tinge of regret that she had yielded once again. In the record of her mind, the words of the clergyman long ago in a small country church came drifting back. A long and enduring marriage, he had said. For some reason those words no longer frightened her.

Shanna sighed contentedly and kissed the side of Ruark's neck where she nestled close. The slow drum of his heartbeat lulled even the peaceful thoughts, and she drifted to sleep, cradled in his arms.

In the still, ebony darkness that precedes early dawn, Shanna came abruptly awake, realizing Ruark was easing from her side.

"Wait, I'll light a candle," she murmured drowsily. Her hand searched the dark for him, touching his hard, muscular thigh, and she rose, slipping an arm about his neck as he leaned to her.

"I thought you were asleep," he whispered, his lips playing upon hers.

"I was, until you moved," she replied softly. Wistfully she released a sigh. "Dawn comes so quickly."

"Aye, love. Much too quickly." She was like a fragile bird resting against him, and Ruark almost feared to move lest she fly away. The soft, delicate peaks of her bosom touched their warmth to him, and, aware that he must soon leave her, he was like a man on the rack.

Shanna drew away to light a candle on the bedside commode.

Then she knelt back upon her heels to smile at him, her hair cascading in a wild torrent over her naked body.

Ruark half groaned, half sighed in longing at the sight of her. "Lord, you're a witch. A beautiful, sweet witch."

His hand brushed aside the thick curls from her rosy breasts so his gaze could roam unhindered. Shanna laughed as she raised on her knees, her eyes sparkling with bright, happy, glittering lights. Throwing her arms about his neck, she fell against him in playful abandon.

"A witch, am I? Fie upon thee, sir, for taking the best I have to offer and then calling insults. Is this how you've kept your coins, plying your manhood through wicked brothels then claiming you've been cheated?"

Small, white teeth nipped at his ear before she rolled him on his back and raised her fist as if she would lay him lower still. Chuckling, Ruark cringed in mock terror.

"Please, mistress, have pity. I've been sore misused this night."

"Sore misused!" Shanna gasped. "Indeed, knave, you will soon know what misuse is. I'll tear your fickle heart from your bold chest," she tweaked a few hairs of his chest, drawing a quick grimace from him, "and feed it to the crabs. How dare you call me a witch when little Milly is so simpering, sweet, and willing. I vow 'twill be more than your heart go missing."

A strange note of sincerity in Shanna's teasing made Ruark give her a questioning look, but Shanna chuckled wickedly, raking him with a mischievous stare that nearly drew his breath from him and rekindled the fires in his loins. Satisfied with the rapidity of his response, Shanna sat back upon her heels again.

"A mere glance? Can Milly boast of such? That skinny, flat-bosomed twit tempting the dragon Ruark? Ha! I've seen better matches in my day."

Ruark relaxed upon the bed, folding his arm beneath his head. He looked much like the sleek panther her mind had often compared him with. He gave her that slow, careful scrutiny that made her feel devoured.

"You're a bold wench, Shanna Beauchamp. Bold enough to tame a dragon."

Ruark stretched out a finger and leisurely traced an imaginary line over the full, swelling curve of her breast, studying her eyes as he traveled the peak, seeing them grow dark and limpid like two bottomless pools staring at him from behind lowered lids. Her soft mouth parted with yearning, and Shanna leaned down to him and kissed his waiting lips, touching her tongue to his. His arms came around her, pulling her lithe body over his, and, once again, time ceased to be, though on the eastern horizon the sky lightened to a dark blue.

Humming a light and airy tune, Shanna almost skipped with glee as she descended the stairs for breakfast. She shocked Berta by greeting the housekeeper with an exuberant hug, and the old woman almost gaped as she stared after her young mistress. It was a rare thing, indeed, when Shanna appeared before the elder Trahern came from his chambers, and never so cheerfully. Laughter mingled with her words as Shanna dismissed Jason to admit the bondsman, John Ruark, into the manor. Her face glowed as radiantly as the very sun that shone in the eastern sky. Much bemused, Berta took herself to the back of the house, shaking her head in wonderment as she went. Shanna hardly noticed the woman's confused retreat as she gave Ruark a sprightly curtsy and accepted his warm appraisal as a silent compliment.

"You seem to have suffered no ill in your witch hunt, Mister Ruark." Shanna's eyes scanned him. "No scars? No festering wounds from the witch's fangs?"

A rakish grin spread lazily across his mouth. Taking her slender fingers into his, he made a show of examining her long, carefully tended nails while Shanna watched in amusement.

"Nay, none to be seen, milady. 'Twas only a bit of skin she came away with when she clawed at me."

Shanna tossed her head in a playful scoff and disentangled her hand from his grasp. "You are speaking nonsense, sir. I remember nothing—"

"Shall I tell you what you whispered in the dark?" Ruark interrupted, speaking in a hushed tone as he bent slightly to her. His smile was tantalizing as he gazed down into her wondering, searching eyes.

"I said nothing—" Shanna began defensively, but she was

curious. Had her thoughts betrayed her? Had she spoken some unbidden words?

"You sighed in your sleep, 'Ruark—Ruark.' "

A light blush touched her cheeks, and Shanna quickly turned away not wanting to meet this close perusal.

"Come in, Mister Ruark. I believe I hear papa coming down the hall. And Mister Ralston should be here any moment. You'll not have long to wait."

Thus dismissing his words, Shanna led him to the dining room and there some moments later greeted her father, brushing a light kiss upon his cheek as Ruark looked on, still as much unable as ever to fathom her moods.

Sir Gaylord was a late riser. The conversation at the morning table had been leisurely and well marked with varied opinions of the lumber mill, but he did not make an appearance until well after Ruark and the squire had left to inspect the sawmill being built. So it was that Mister Ralston, after being coolly bid good day by Shanna, remained the only one to greet the swaggering Englishman as he came into the dining room.

"I say there, 'tis a bit of a balmy day without," Gaylord remarked, taking a pinch of snuff and sneezing into his lace handkerchief. "Mayhaps I should invite the Widow Beauchamp on an outing this morn. No doubt she will be anxious for some gentlemanly companionship after these months of widowhood. Such a lovely, young woman. I am endeared to that sweet face."

Ralston folded his accounting books and studied the man. A calculating gleam brightened his dark eyes.

"If I might suggest a bit of caution there, sir—I have known Madam Beauchamp for a considerable part of her life, and she seems to have a natural aversion to most men who come courting her. I can tell you much of her, though I am considered in the ranks of those she detests."

Gaylord dabbed at his sweat-moistened upper lip. "Then how, my good man, do you propose to help me if you cannot help yourself?"

Ralston's thin mouth almost smiled. "If you should succeed in wedding the widow with my advice, would you be willing to divide the dowry in return?"

Ralston had guessed rightly. Gaylord was eager to strike up

any agreement that would lead toward his gaining riches and reestablishing his family's depleted wealth. The knight was not ill-advised on the Trahern fortune, and he was determined to make the most of it, through marriage to the lovely widow or through dealings with the squire. His inherited shipyard was badly impoverished and needed a goodly amount of coins to set the whole of it right. With Trahern providing the purse, he could share a simple dowry with this man.

"As gentlemen," Gaylord stretched forth his hand, and the bargain was made.

"First of all I would suggest impressing the squire with your importance at court and your good name," Ralston said. "But you must be warned. If Madam Beauchamp suspects you have taken me as your counsel, all is lost. Even convincing the squire of your merits will not mend that error. So take care, my friend. Take special care in courting the Widow Beauchamp."

Chapter 13

A pair of sea eagles nested on the bluff along the east shore of the island. Shanna had often watched them hang on motionless wings as they rode the currents of air high above the crashing surf. Her spirit soared with them. Even with the renewed assurance that motherhood was not forthcoming, she gave little thought to the consequences of letting Ruark invade her chambers again. Her mind was filled with the pleasurable remembrances of when he had come to her in the deep ebony of night and tomorrow had ceased to be. She was content to live moment by moment, surrounded by an airy castle of bliss. She was in tune with her world, and she felt an overriding sense of peace and a strange aura of confidence that all was as it should be. The realization that this state was due to Ruark's daily presence in the manor did not seem to disturb her as it had in the past. She was like a flower, a rose, unfolding under the warm rays of the sun as she bathed in the glow of Ruark's eyes.

Nearly a week had passed since his visit to her room. The day had dawned with heavy black clouds threatening to engulf the verdant island in a storm. Standing on her balcony, Shanna contemplated the ominously dark sky which seemed to press down upon the hills with evil portent.

A loud, angry whinny rent the air, and Shanna whirled to find several men in the lane before the manor, struggling to subdue a horse that reared up before them, pawing the air with its forelegs. Even from where she stood, Shanna could see the bloody slashes that marred the glistening reddish brown coat. Her rage soared at the thought that such a magnificent beast had suffered abuse.

"Here there, be careful with the nag. The beastie is already sore."

The voice that bellowed was one Shanna had never heard before, but she recognized the garb of the men as being that of seamen—the largest boasted a braided coat, while the other three wore the dress of common tars.

"You there!" Shanna called down as she hurried along the veranda. "What is the meaning of this? Have you no ken to the value of that animal? Were you all born on the wooden planks of a deck?"

Like a whirlwind she descended the wide steps, gilded curls bouncing riotously, and approached the four, glaring at them before she turned to the task of calming the mare. Speaking soothingly she reached out a hand to caress the silken nose of the steed and stroke its shivering sides. Gradually the animal quieted beneath her gentle touch and condescended to stand still as the men gaped their amazement. They had battled the mare all the way from the village as she had refused to be led either by wagon or themselves.

The large, bewhiskered man took a step forward and spoke apologetically. "We had a bit of a tiff with the weather after we left the colonies, and the ship was tossed to such a degree that the mare was bruised against the stall we built for her. 'Twas not from ill use, I assure you, mum."

Shanna contemplated the man and decided he spoke the truth. "What is your name, sir, and for what purpose have you brought the animal here?"

He gave a quick bob of his head. "Captain Roberts at your service, mum, of the Virginia Company. Captain Beauchamp bade me see the mare safely to Squire Trahern or his daughter in return for their generous hospitality while he was here. Might you be the Widow Beauchamp?"

Shanna nodded. "I am."

The captain fished in his coat, withdrawing a sealed letter which he handed to her. "This be for you, mum, from Captain Beauchamp."

Accepting the packet, Shanna gazed a moment at the wax seal bearing an elaborate "B." She was overwhelmed by Captain Beauchamp's generosity, for this was no pauper's gift he had sent. She had long ago learned of horses and their value. The broad but tapering head of the mare, the large, expressive eyes, and the gracefully arched neck bespoke Arabian blood, and as she read the letter, Shanna was assured of this, for Nathanial had detailed the blood line. The mare was as worthy a steed as Attila, and no doubt would produce good foals it bred to the stallion.

The note went on to reassure her that the Beauchamps were happily anticipating their visit, and Nathanial expressed his hopes that nothing would delay their journey, for he predicted it to be a colorful autumn this year.

"We had no one to tend the beastie's wounds, mum," Captain Roberts explained, mistaking her slight frown of bemusement.

"Oh, no matter," Shanna replied slowly. "There is a man here on the island who has a knack for that sort of thing."

A young lad, perhaps ten, stepped forward from where he had been staying out of harm's way and juggled a large bundle around in his arms so that he could yank at the captain's coattail.

"Where am I to take this, sir?" he questioned, holding forth the hide-wrapped bundle.

"Mum?" The captain looked to Shanna again. "Do you know where the lad might find a Mister John Ruark?"

Shanna responded in surprise. "I'm not sure. He might be working at the sawmill, but he has a cottage behind the manor. Can I help you?"

"This here thing," the man gestured to the package, "be for him. Can we leave it at his house?"

"Aye." Shanna pointed toward the back. "There's a path through the trees after you pass the manor. Follow it around. 'Tis the large cottage beyond the others."

As the men left, Shanna affectionately rubbed her cheek

against the mare's muzzle, pleased with the gift.

"Jezebel, the Beauchamps have named you. Aye, and you shall surely tempt my Attila, for nowhere on this isle is there so fine a filly. But I must fetch Ruark to care for you, for I'd not trust another to tend you. My dragon has a way with ladies," she whispered, smiling wistfully. "I know you will like him."

Inquiring at the village store on Ruark's whereabouts, Shanna drew a shrug from Mister MacLaird.

"Doan know, lass. He was here early this morn to order some supplies, but I have na laid me eyes upon him since. Have ye checked the sawmill?"

At the building site, Shanna received the same unknowing answer.

"Seems 'ere was something doing at the brewing house, and he was needed."

Yet even there, none could say where Mister Ruark had gone after leaving. Finally, late that afternoon, Shanna gave up the fruitless chase and returned to the manor. Her father had returned, and Sir Gaylord had engaged him in a discussion of shipyards. Hearing the man's voice, Shanna cautiously made her way across the entrance hall, but the squeaking of the front door had alerted Gaylord and he hailed for her to wait. He was insistent that she join them in the drawing room and would not accept her excuse of wanting to change for dinner, firmly declaring she was ravishing enough. Silently Shanna cursed her luck but nodded and smiled lamely, letting the man lead her across the hall. It was the most boring evening she ever spent in her life, for the man seemed incapable of discussing anything but his family's aristocracy and even had the nerve to point out to her father the advantages his good name would lend to the Trahern fortune. It was some time after the meal was concluded before Shanna managed to escape to her chambers where she immediately ordered a bath and slipped out of her riding habit, dismissing Hergus for the night after the bedcovers were turned down and her sleeping gown laid out.

Sinking into the steaming water, Shanna leaned back in the ornate porcelain tub and languidly sponged her creamy shoulder. Curling tendrils of hair dangled coyly from the luxuriant mass secured with combs on top of her head. The heat of the bath caused her cheeks to bloom with a rosy color, brightening the sea-green eyes beneath their ebony lashes. But in the midst of this comfort, the softly curving mouth showed a petulant pout, and as she caught her reflection in the tall mirror which stood behind a chair, Shanna made a face at herself, wrinkling the slim, lovely nose in aggravation. First her failure to find Ruark, then his absence from dinner had left her in a fitful mood. His mere presence at the table put monotony to flight, and she had felt somehow deserted. Of late there was little enough left of her privacy outside her chambers to have even a word with him, for Gaylord seemed to scent her out like a hound after a bitch in heat. The knight was forever taking her arm, and she was becoming increasingly aware of Ruark's displeasure over this event. Seeing his growing scowl, she would disdainfully set Gaylord's hands from her, but the knight was persistent and would not be put off easily.

Shanna closed her eyes and rested her head back against the tub's tall rim, letting the warm bath ease her tensions. It was rare now to go a full day without even glimpsing Ruark, though he was usually in demand wherever a problem was to be solved or an easier way to be found. Somehow her day did not seem complete.

The silken draperies behind her rustled with the stir of evening breezes. It was a warm, gentle night with the heady fragrance of frangipani scenting the air. The threat of the storm had subsided after only a light sprinkling, just enough to season the night air with a heightened aroma of freshness mingled with the smell of flowers. From afar, the shrill, repetitious song of a tree frog mixed with the sounds of night. The clock in her room daintily chimed in the tenth hour, and at its last note, a new melody began, one Shanna had never heard before in her chambers. Her eyes flew open with a start and immediately saw the source, a rather large music box which had been placed on a table near her. And in the chaise beside it, Ruark reclined comfortably, a gracious smile on his handsome lips, his long legs stretched out before him and casually crossed at the ankles.

Shanna sat upright in the tub, staring at him in amazement. A quick glance about the room indicated that he had made himself at home. His hat was tossed upon the bed with his shirt beside it, leaving only the brief breeches to clothe his brown torso. A nod accompanied his greeting.

"Good evening, love, and thank you." His eyes dipped briefly to her wet, glistening breasts.

"You have no propriety," Shanna railed above the tinkling melody. But beneath his calm regard she settled herself to continue less harshly, as if only mildly injured, "You invade a lady's private bath and advantage yourself with unsuspected peepery."

Ruark grinned in exceptional humor. "I do but exercise my spousely rights, Shanna. 'Tis an occurrence that happens so rarely that I am indeed much disadvantaged. While other husbands nightly view their treasures, I, for the greater part, must rely on recall, even then harshly reining my desire to my will, for I cannot oft seek relief from that which pains me."

"You rant of nonsense, Ruark." Shanna rinsed herself slowly with the sponge, noting that his eyes followed closely where her hands led. "Have I not been more than kind to your whimsy?"

She taunted him subtly, lolling back in the tub and raising her arms so that trickles of water traced down their long, slim length then raced in runnels across her round breasts. His eyes devoured her every movement, the heat of them scorching her wherever they touched. Wickedly, Shanna reached for a towel to shut off his view, knowing full well that she tested his starved appetite.

"It strikes me, Mister Beauchamp, that you must surely have some reason to risk my chambers at this hour," she said offhandedly as she patted at her arm with the end of the towel.

His hand swept toward the music box. "I brought you a gift."

Shanna smiled coyly. "Thank you, Ruark." Then a thought struck her. "Is that from the colonies?"

"I begged a favor of Captain Beauchamp to see it purchased and sent," Ruark replied. "Do you like it?"

Shanna listened for a space before she recognized the tune as the same one she had heard on the *Marguerite*.

"Mmm, I like it very much." She watched his fingers close the lid, shutting off the melody, and raised her gaze innocently. "Could there be another reason you came to my chambers, Mister Beauchamp?"

A slow, tantalizing smile spread across his lips, and his eyes raked her. "I was informed you asked about me across the island,

and I could find no cause for such urgency save one." His white teeth gleamed in a quick grin. "Thus it was, though the hour was late, I hastened here at the first opportunity to assure you that I had not fled in the face of fatherhood."

For a brief moment, Shanna dried herself, letting this sink in. Then she understood what he had said.

"Cad! Viper!" she snapped. "Pompous fool!" Her hand searched in the water. "Do you think I would banter that about the island?"

The dripping sponge was raised to throw.

"Ah—ah!" Ruark grinned evilly and wagged a finger at her. "Have a care, Shanna. Hergus would not approve of the mess."

"Ooooh," Shanna moaned, her teeth clenched in frustration. The sponge was thrust deep beneath the surface and held as if she were choking it.

The towel began to move away from her, and Shanna looked up to find Ruark pulling slowly at the other end. She clutched at the cloth, trying to hold it to her, but it was relentlessly drawn away, leaving her nothing but her hands with which to cover her bosom. Her best attempt at that only aggravated the situation, pressing the delicious fullness to even more enticing display.

Ruark raised himself from his chair and came toward her, his eyes like two glowing coals as they burned into her, locking and holding her gaze. He stood above her, towering tall like some bronze, half-naked savage. The room was silent but for the slow ticking of the clock. The play of shadows in bold relief upon his torso fascinated her, and her eyes wandered slowly down the long, corded veins that stood out in his arms. Ruark leaned down until his elbow rested on the edge of the tub. His finger trailed in the water, and the passion in his gaze was as naked as his chest. It fanned the sleeping fires in her own blood. His forefinger entered the deep harbor between her breasts and traced lazily across the beaches they formed and then moved inland along her shoulder and around the base of her slim, white throat. His voice came soft, husky, almost a whisper.

"Must I ever woo you, Shanna, as if you were some untainted virgin child, destroying your fortress stone by stone, tearing down your walls of resistance until you yield to that which is inevitable? You plead widowhood so dearly and then surrender to me with a passion that rends the roots of my very sanity."

Beneath his touch Shanna nearly quaked. His fingers traveled across her, searing the ends of her nerves until she ached to be drawn to him. Her lips were parted with her rapid breathing, her eyes half-closed as his face drew near. She waited in anticipation of his kiss. Then his finger dipped again into the water and touched her nose, leaving a large drop trembling at its tip.

Ruark straightened and stood back a pace, chuckling at the bemusement in her face. Shanna struggled to raise herself in the tub and thrusting out her bottom lip, huffed the droplet from the end of her nose. When finally she sat upright, she glared at him and spoke half chiding, half ruefully.

"You're a beast, Ruark Beauchamp."

"Aye, love, a beast."

"A dragon! One of the most irksome sort."

"Aye, love, a dragon."

Shanna stared at him, then a delicious grin broke upon her lips. "And I am a witch."

"Aye, love, a witch." His smile was slightly broader.

"And I will someday take your heart from you."

"That, love, you already have."

Shanna lowered her eyes, at once confused and embarrassed.

"Come, witch." Ruark's voice was soft but rich with laughter. "Out of your kettle and dry yourself."

Handing her the towel, Ruark waited close beside the tub. Beneath his warm regard, Shanna rose and wrapped the linen securely about her, tucking the end down between her breasts. Casually he offered his hand to assist her in stepping from the bath. He followed her to the dressing table, warmly admiring the gentle swing of her hips beneath the linen cloth.

"Why were you looking for me, my love?" Ruark inquired, meeting her eyes in the mirror as she brushed out her long hair.

Remembering Jezebel, Shanna turned excitedly and caught his thin fingers. "Oh, Ruark, Captain Beauchamp has given me the most marvelous gift. A beautiful mare, but she's been abused and needs attention."

Ruark's eyebrows lifted in surprise. "Abused?"

"Captain Roberts said there was a storm at sea and she was tossed about dreadfully. I instructed the stable boy to do what he could until you came." The blue-green eyes begged him. "Oh, Ruark, you will see her made better, won't you—for me—please."

Ruark stretched out his free hand to stroke the gilded locks, and his eyes were soft and caressing. "Do you like her so much, Shanna?"

"Aye, Ruark, I do. Very much."

"I will do what I can for her," he smiled. "You know that I am your most ardent slave."

Shanna tossed away his hand in rebuff of his tender gibe and faced the mirror again. "What if you were free?" she questioned under his perusal. "Would you say me yea or nay? Would you be gone from here, seeking your fortune somewhere else?"

"What great treasures can tear me from your side, my love?" he spoke in a teasing vein as he played with a captured curl. "Would I ever leave you? What madness would see me to that end? Ah love, do you not ken?" His eyes glowed into hers. "You are my treasure, the rare jewel of my desires."

Shanna pouted, throwing the brush aside. "You jest, Ruark, and I would know the truth."

"The truth, milady?" Ruark swept a bow before her mirrored image then grinned. "Milady should herself remember the vows spoken before the altar. I am pledged to you until my dying breath."

Flinging her lustrous mane with a flick of her arm, Shanna flounced off the velvet bench and strode across the room beneath his regard. She was not unaware of the effect her nearly naked state had on him. The linen towel was very accommodating, meagerly covering her breasts and displaying the full length of her long, shapely legs for his pleasure. Her movements were slow and languid, graceful and flowing, as she punished him severely for his impertinence in reminding her of her vows.

"How you love to taunt me about that. You smirk and posture in my chambers as if you owned more in this world than that foolish garb you use to cover your loins."

"If I be a pauper, madam, then you are indeed a pauper's wife," Ruark pointed out with a chuckle.

"You're a rutting rake who uses any flimsy pretext to invade my rooms," Shanna retorted. "And to silence you I must submit lest I find my secret prated about like common knowledge.

There is a name for you, sir—a blackguard. One who would use a lady so is not worthy to be hanged."

Ruark paced forward with measured tread, a slow, hypnotic grin stretching across his lips. Shanna backed away, aware of his stalking her, and tried to keep the distance between them open.

"Madam, I must admit I would seek you out on any excuse. But a rutting rake? Surely my life of late should be compared to something more monkish."

"Ha!" Shanna scoffed. She gasped and twisted away as he lunged forward. Ruark's sweeping arm caught nothing more than the air, though the fragrance of her warm body and the scent of her dampened hair filled his nostrils and clouded his mind. He was undaunted and came after her. Attempting to evade him, Shanna darted behind the long chaise, trailing behind a fluid sound of musical laughter not unlike the chuckling burble of a swift mountain brook. Safe for the moment with the lounge between them, Shanna made a comic face at him, but her eyes spoke volumes as they sparkled in coquettish witchery, half challenging, half beckoning him.

His eyes flared in answer as he stepped onto the chaise, showing her that it formed no barrier between them. Giggling, Shanna retreated behind a small, marble-topped table, seeking whatever shelter it might offer her.

"Ruark, control yourself," she admonished and tried to sound stern. "I would have this out once and for all."

"Oh, we will have it out, madam," he assured her and grasped the edge of the table, moving it aside and proving it no obstacle to his advance.

The wall halted Shanna's retreat, and she glanced around frantically. To her left was the bed. Certainly no haven there. To her right, screened by the silken draperies, were the open doors to her balcony.

Ruark was as quick, and his hand caught the top of the towel, then the curtains were flung into his face. When the drapes stilled, he found himself holding what he had caught, the empty towel. He almost gloated as he mused on Shanna's consternation at being trapped naked on the open balcony. A small, furtive movement at the far end of the draperies caught his eye, and he cautiously took a place there to capture her should she try to re-enter. He had no more than settled in his stance when the silk billowed heavily where he had stood only a moment before. With a quick flash of bare skin Shanna ran in, raced to the bed, threw herself upon it, rolled, and came to her feet on the far side with the gown in her hand. She thrust her arms high, letting the garment fall down over her head and with a quick wiggle slipped her arms free again. The shortened gown caught on her bosom, and she snatched it down, letting it fall. But its flight downward was halted, for Ruark's hands already rested on her waist. He pressed her naked hips against him, letting her feel the rising fullness of his manhood against her.

Of a sudden their playfulness was gone. Their eyes were locked together, and their pulses quickened. Ruark's head lowered as her arms came around his neck, and their lips joined their bodies in a mutual, crushing embrace that forged them together and plucked them as one into a private world of consuming passion. Time stood still, and the moment seemed to drag blissfully on— until it shattered like a crystal goblet with a sudden knocking at her chamber door.

"Shanna?" Orlan Trahern's question came softly. "Are you awake, child?"

Her voice was thick and husky with what might have been sleep as she replied, snatching away from Ruark, "One moment please, papa."

Shanna cast her eyes wildly about the room as if seeking some escape from this predicament. Ruark rested his hand upon her shoulder and with a finger to his lips, bid her to silence. He pointed to the bed, and with his hand to her rump pushed her toward it. When Shanna turned to stare at him again, he was gone. Like a soundless rush of wind he had left the room. The drapes stilled after his passing, and Shanna settled herself upon the bed, pulling the covers high up under her chin.

"Come in, papa," she called.

Shanna waited, listening to the click of the latch and her father's steps in the outer sitting room. Then in horror she realized Ruark's hat and shirt were still on the foot of her bed. Quickly she snatched them beneath the sheets and when the squire entered the bedchamber, Shanna had retrieved the covers under her chin.

"Good evening, child." He tried to soften his usually gruff

voice. "I trust I have not disturbed you unduly."

"No, papa." She gave a trembling yawn and stated truthfully. "I was not really asleep."

The elder Trahern patted the edge of the bed then lowered his bulk upon it as Shanna moved over, making room for him to sit. The squire plucked a grape from a bedside dish and chewed on it for a thoughtful moment.

"You seem to enjoy being home again," he half questioned almost hesitantly.

"Most surely, papa," Shanna reassured him with a wide smile. For the present she seemed on safe ground. "I'm afraid that, like you, I was never meant to prance and posture in the courts, and I value the gentler ways and freedom of this island much more than pomp and splendor."

Orlan's chest rumbled with his version of a chuckle, and he reached out a huge paw to cover her dainty hand. "I never could stand those milk-white maids with their mincing ways, and like your mother you are more beautiful with the color of the sun on your cheek and in your hair. Indeed, in my eyes you grow more lovely with each passing day. And I have found to my surprise that you have a mind and a will of your own. But there is that which I cannot explain. There is almost a wifely manner about you lately."

Shanna blushed and lowered her eyes, suddenly afraid that he might guess the truth. What had Ruark done to her that even her father could see the difference? To herself she was the same as she had always been, and it came as something of a shock that anyone would see her changed.

"Do not worry, papa." Shanna wondered if Ruark had left the balcony or still lingered there. " 'Tis quite unlikely that my husband could have affected me much in our brief days together."

Her father fixed her with a baleful eye. "Do you know that you have affected Sir Gaylord sorely?"

Shanna froze.

"He has been mewling about all afternoon, and finally after you left the table, he made so bold as to petition me for your hand." Orlan read the sudden startled look in Shanna's eyes and hurried to allay her fears. "I told him the first condition he must meet was to win your approval. So do not fret, daughter. I

278

promised your mother that I would find you a worthy husband, and I shall not yield on that account."

Then it was Trahern's time to lower his eyes, and he rubbed his palm awkwardly on a buckled shoe.

"There is something that troubles you, papa?" Shanna asked in awe, for she had never seen her father so much at odds before.

"Aye, much that has troubled me for some time."

Shanna's heart went out to this large man whose words came with painful slowness.

"I have for my own ends brought upon you some pain and sorrow. This was never my intent." He looked straight at her, and his shoulders seemed to hunch about his thick neck. "I am old, Shanna, child, and getting older." He raised a hand to still her protest. "I have a strong need to see my dynasty continued with a flock of bouncing babes." The chuckle rumbled again. "A dozen or so if you would meet my mark. But I am moved to believe that whatever wisdom guides our fates will see to that in all good time. I defer to your choice, as I have found no man worthy of your hand. I will press the matter no further, and I bid you seek out your husband wherever you would find him."

"I understand, papa." Shanna spoke with love heavy in her heart. "And I thank you very much for your understanding."

For a long moment Trahern stared at his daughter and then gave a single, loud sniff before he rose to stand where his face would be hidden in the dark shadow.

"Enough of this chatter," he said gruffly. "I've kept you awake beyond your hour."

The minute dragged out until Shanna spoke, her voice tiny like a small child's.

"Goodnight, papa." And as Trahern turned to leave, he barely heard her continue. "I love you."

There was no answer, only another loud snort before his footsteps hastened through the sitting room and the door closed gently behind him.

Shanna stared in the shadows, her eyes unusually moist, her mind lost within itself. It was a long time before she lifted her gaze and found Ruark standing at the foot of her bed, gazing down at her, an odd half smile twisting his lips.

"You heard?" Her inquiry was barely audible.

"Aye, love."

Shanna sat up in bed and hugged her knees, resting her head upon them. Wistfully she sighed, "I never realized he was so lonely."

It was a giant step from self-centered youth into caring adulthood and awareness of others. The transition was great and painful, and Ruark remained silent, letting her take it at her own speed. Shanna weltered in the depths of her new-found maturity. It was a new experience and not all unpleasant. She was assured her father loved her, and that knowledge warmed her heart, yet beneath it burned the memories of harsh arguments and the sting of his angered words spurring on her own stubborn willfulness. Her vision of a handsome lord kneeling to beg her hand was suddenly trite and childish. Beneath the attack of reality, it faded slowly from her mind. A blur of faces flew before her mind, hauntingly vague and nondescript. They all faded before the memory of her father sitting at her bedside, lonely and apologetic. His tirades had only stirred her determination the more, but this almost humble declaration bound her more firmly to his desires.

He wanted her married and with babes. And who would she choose? Sir Gaylord, a foppish caricature of her envisioned knight? In the shadows behind him another figure stood, dark and mysterious. There her peace dissolved like snow beneath spring's pelting rains, and her mind struggled to grasp the significance of her unrest.

Slowly Shanna lifted her gaze to Ruark. Her dragon. Had he snatched away the quiet spirit of her soul?

Ruark had wandered aimlessly about her chamber, pausing to run a finger along the edge of her dressing table whereupon lay her brushes and combs, her powders and perfumes.

The outward substance of a woman, he mused silently. Soft hair, beauty, tantalizing scents. But how much more fascinating was the underlying person? The quicksilver moods, responsive to her world; the whimsical wit, quick to humor and as quick to anger; the softness of her body and the unsuspected strength when the demand was made; the incredible warmth of her caresses and the bliss of her lips on his.

He turned, and his eyes went to Shanna where she sat huddled on the bed lost in thought. She seemed so small and defenseless, yet he knew if challenged she could rise with determination and stand forth with a fury that would dim the rage of a wounded tiger. At the moment she was soft beauty in repose, and he longed to give her some bit of wisdom that would calm the turmoil of her mind.

"He said I'm free to choose my own husband when I will," Shanna murmured, and Ruark realized she watched him, too. "What am I to do with you?"

Ruark came to stand at the food of her bed. "I have no wish to seek the hangman out, Shanna, but I find little to fear of the truth."

"Well enough for you to say." Shanna was irked that he should take the matter so lightly. "But I might yet find myself the bride of some popinjay if my father is angered again."

Ruark laughed caustically. "Madam, if the truth is out, you will find yourself well wed and most assuredly with husband. Me! Thus until my neck is stretched, you need have no fear of other men. Indeed, if my services are of value to your father, he might extend my debt to the cost of barristers and a defense." Ruark leaned forward and grinned wickedly. "Consider this, my love. It could well be my game to get you with child, that your father might not be disposed to see his heirs the offspring of a hanged man."

"How can you suggest such a thing?" Shanna gasped in astonishment. Her rage flared as bright as a bolt of lightning across a darkened sky. "You're a vile rogue! A cad! A thrice-damned, bloody, half-witted guttersnipe!"

"Ah love, your endearments bestir me," Ruark taunted. "I can only note your pleas in the dungeon were more gentle and you saw your cause so dire that you would yield your maidenhood to see a better end."

"Vulgar unsired son of a fishmonger!" Shanna railed, her face crimson as she pounded the sheets with her fists. Her burgeoning tirade dwindled to a spluttering search for further epithets. This was unusual in itself, for Shanna had in her youth been exposed to the coarse language of seamen and other laborers and could upon proper incentive tinge the air with a shower of phrases the like of which the meanest urchin would envy.

Ruark leaned closer, and his own rage and frustration began to show. "And now would you have me as your pocket paramour, Shanna?" he sneered. "To be hidden in your chambers from the world and denied the right to stand beside you in the light of day? You decry your fate should all be known and bemoan some fancied punishment, but I, madam, have more to lose. Even so, were it my choice to face your father as your husband or hide in the dark corners of your boudoir, madam, I can assure you that I would rather be your spouse, honored, loved, cherished for all the world to see." Ruark turned aside, and his voice was bitter. "Were there more to gain other than my death and your undying hatred, I would seek out your father this moment and claim my rights, putting an end to this mockery."

"Mockery!" Shanna's voice was ragged with emotion. "Is it mockery, then, that I sought to avoid a life with some doddering count or baron? A mockery that I want to share a life with a man of my own choosing? Is it mockery that I want more than that in life?" Her tone took on an accusing snarl. "Yea, you mock me when I only seek to live out my days with some hope of happiness."

"And you are certain that life with me would bear no happiness?" Ruark stared at her, waiting for her answer.

"The wife of a bondslave?" Shanna was incredulous. "You could not afford one of my gowns."

His scowl was dark, brooding. " 'Twould not be so for long."

Shanna scoffed. "Aye, your neck would soon be lengthened beyond your endurance. Then I would truly be a widow."

"If I believe you, then I must abandon all hope." Ruark gave her a wry smile. "Your pardon, madam, if I continue, as you did, to seek a better end than fate would indicate."

"You test me with your inane bravado." Shanna's tone was hard, but she could not meet his eyes. "And you tire me with your theories." She lay back on the pillows with a sigh, turning her face away from him.

"Of course, my lady." Ruark spoke with exaggerated concern. "If you would be so kind, my shirt and hat. I value my meager garb since 'tis all that belongs to John Ruark."

Petulantly Shanna reached beneath the sheets and flung the shirt to him without a word. She had more difficulty locating the hat. Then, as a look of dawning flooded her countenance, she raised her hips from the bed and drew the hat from beneath her. She sailed it toward him and, with a flounce, presented her back.

Ruark caught his hat and surveyed its flattened form for a long moment before he swept it across his chest in a stiff bow.

"Your leave, my lady," he jeered. "I shall not bore you further with my woes."

Shanna lay still, listening for the sound of his departure. Finally she rolled onto her back to see what delayed him and was amazed that she was alone.

Dismally Shanna stared into the empty shadows. An ache began to grow within her chest, seeming to erode her very soul. Suddenly she wanted to call Ruark back. Even their battles held more joy than the painful void she now was lost in. There was no happiness in the world; it was cruel and cold, holding no warmth to ease the chill in her heart.

Her lips trembled, and tears blurred her vision. With an agonized cry, she buried her face into the pillow and like a child sobbed and beat the bed with clenched fists to shut out the loneliness that sucked her down into a blackened pit of despair.

"Oh God," she moaned in abject misery and whispered plaintively, "please—"

But even as she prayed, Shanna could not name for what she asked. She shook her head, struggling against the sudden overwhelming depression. Groaning, she threw herself from the bed and snatched a long, white robe from the armoire. Her chambers had ceased to be a haven, and like a displaced wraith she prowled the furthermost corners of the manor, seeking some ease for her troubled spirit, but nowhere in the darkened rooms did she find what she wanted. Listlessly she wandered down the stairs and paused beside the drawing room door, standing uncertainly as her father glanced up from his papers.

"Shanna?" His tone held a note of surprise. "What be you about, child? I was about to retire."

"I thought to take a stroll through the gardens, papa," she replied softly, finally meeting his concerned frown. "I'll return shortly. No need for you to wait up."

Orlan Trahern watched his daughter move away from the door and then waited in the silence of the house as her bare feet padded across the marble floor. The front portal opened, then closed, and stillness returned. Sighing heavily, Orlan heaved his large bulk up from the chair and slowly made his way to his chambers.

Shanna stood on the lawn, enshrouded in the night. Stars peeked through the drifting shreds of clouds, and the moon made a brief appearance before hiding its silvered face behind a lacy fan of vapors.

Shanna meandered through the trees, a deep voice, husky with passion, and amber eyes haunting each path she took. She had come a distance from the mansion and was passing near the stables when she heard a neigh from within the stables and moved in the darkness toward the sound, scuffing her small feet against the dew-dampened grass.

A light shone from the stables. Drawing near the door, she heard Ruark's voice, low and gentle, soothing the mare. Shanna's mood lifted. Pausing in the open portal, she saw his profile etched in the glow of the lantern. His dark brows were drawn downward in a heavy scowl, blunting the straight, thin nose; and in the sharp line of his jaw a muscle twitched angrily. Still, his long, agile fingers tended the mare's bruises and scrapes with the same gentle touch that Shanna herself had often responded to. The horse snorted and nudged her muzzle against his shoulder familiarly, and in a distracted manner Ruark reached up to caress her silken nose.

"Not now, Jezebel," he admonished.

Shanna's whole awareness perked at his use of the steed's name. She had not mentioned it to him.

"How came you to know her name?"

Ruark straightened, his eyes searching the ebony blackness behind the lanterns. He stood wiping his hands as Shanna came forward, his gaze casually caressing her as if the robe did not exist.

"Her name?" He waited for Shanna's nod before he shrugged. "The boy, Elot."

"Oh." Her voice had lost its challenge. Shanna glanced around, wondering where the stableboy had gone.

Ruark threw his thumb over his shoulder toward the tack room. "His usefulness lies in cleaning and grooming, not in healing. I sent him to bed."

Shanna folded her hands behind her back, letting her eyes roam about the stables, unable to meet Ruark's open stare.

"What is that?" She nodded toward a small wooden bowl that held a rather noxious concoction.

Ruark briefly followed her gaze then returned his regard to her. His reply was clipped and curt. "Herbs and rum in warm tallow. Cleans the sores and seals them."

"Oh." Again he barely heard her.

After a moment of continued silence, Ruark returned to his labors, dipping his fingers in the odious mixture. Behind his back, lying on a tall stool, Shanna espied the crushed circle of straw that had of late represented his hat. Lifting it, she took its place, drawing up her bare feet to rest them on the top rung. She slowly turned the ruined headpiece around in her hands.

"I'm sorry about your hat, Ruark. I didn't mean to destroy it," she ventured, fighting the heavy quietness that had descended upon the stables.

Ruark grunted his reply without pausing in his ministrations to the mare. "'Twas a company gift. I have another."

Shanna was a trifle piqued at his rude manner and retorted tersely, "On the morrow I shall leave a shilling for its costs by your plate."

Ruark's laughter was quick and stung as much. "A turnabout indeed, madam, that you should pay me for damage done in your bed."

"Blast it, Ruark," Shanna began angrily, and her tone brought his gaze around to fix on her. Her flaring rage quelled under the calm golden stare, and lowering her eyes, Shanna continued on a softer note. "I am sorry, Ruark, about everything. It has never been my intent to hurt you."

Ruark stood beside the mare and stirred absently in the bowl with his finger. "In your good intentions, madam, you have never failed to strike me where it hurts the most." He smiled wryly. "If you will, my love, ask any of your suitors, and they no doubt will agree. The slightest blow from you bloodies the spirit."

Shanna protested. "And were your own words so tender, mi-lord? You do berate me sorely, though I have given much more to the bargain than was ever agreed upon."

"Damn the bargain!" Ruark growled. In exasperation he went

back to the mare and began to smear his poultice along a welt below the beast's neck. "Do you think that contents me now?" he questioned brusquely over his shoulder. "I was a man condemned, the hours left to me few. The agreement brought sweet respite, and I could ease my mind anticipating the consummation of it." He laughed shortly. "What more did I dare hope for?"

The stilted silence that followed made Shanna crane her neck in an effort to see him, but, with the deep shadows in the stall, she could not. Fetching herself one of the lighted lanterns and climbing up the boards beside him in the next stall, she draped her arms over the top board, holding the light for him. Ruark accepted her service and issued no comment or notice until he finished where he was and moved to dress a wound on the steed's rear leg. He hunkered on his heels, almost between the hooves, then gestured with the bowl.

"Over that way a bit," he said over his shoulder. As Shanna shifted the lamp, he said, "There, that's right."

At the first touch of the unctuous stuff, Jezebel snorted and began to prance, startling Shanna, and she gasped.

"Ruark, be careful."

He only reached up a hand and patted the mare's flank, speaking in a soft, soothing tone.

"Easy, girl. Easy now, Jezebel."

The horse stilled, but when Ruark again touched the poultice to the gash, the mare snorted and half reared, her hooves swinging perilously close to Ruark's head.

"Will you get back!" Shanna commanded sharply, angry with his recklessness.

Ruark glanced up over his shoulder. "She'll be all right, Shanna. 'Tis only a deeper cut than the rest. It smarts at first, but 'twill soon ease the pain of it much."

Shanna nearly groaned. "Oh, you dolt." She gnashed her teeth at him. "Get out from beneath her hooves."

Ruark slapped a last handful of the mixture on the mare's leg and then ducked hastily to avoid her thrashing hooves. He set the bowl high on a timber and left the stall, closing the gate behind him. Leaning against a post, he stared back at Shanna, a grin spreading across his handsome face.

"Blimey, love," he mimicked. "Have ye come to be so fond o' me then?"

"Aye, as I care for all fools and children," Shanna snapped testily, stepping down from the boards. " 'Tis a wonder your guardian angel has not collapsed from overwork for all the care you give."

"Of course, my lady." Ruark switched to a stilted schooled speech akin to Sir Gaylord's. "But what a perfectly marvelous job the good chap's done 'til now, eh what."

Shanna could not repress a smile at his foolery. In passing him, she gave him the lantern and returned to the stool, propping her feet high again. Ruark set the lamp on a shelf and began to wash his hands in a bucket beneath, using large amounts of soft soap from a crock. In some fascination, Shanna studied the play of muscles across his naked back until he turned to regard her, accepting his perusal but hastily shifting her own away lest he mistake it for a deeper passion.

"Am I a fool to hope you no longer wish my death, Shanna?" he smiled.

Shanna gaped back at him with widened eyes. "I never longed for such," she defended tartly. "How can you think it?"

"The bargain—" he began, but Shanna's reply came swiftly in echo of his.

"Damn the bargain!"

Ruark chuckled softly and stepped toward her "Have you not said you loathed me, love?" he taunted gently, eyeing her closely.

"And when have you ever said you loved me?" Shanna retorted. "What manna have you bestowed upon my heart?" She flung out a hand, and the violence of the gesture warned Ruark to keep his distance. "I have had lords aplenty, princes by the score, and feverish rakes all pleading for my hand, or at the very least a most singular favor. They plied me with tender words meant to stir my heart or make me know that I was wanted, even admired. But what of you? Where are those words that would nourish my woman's vanity? Have you once just held my hand and told me that I was"—she shrugged and spread her hands in a questioning gesture—"pretty? Graceful? Warm or gracious?

Soft or lovely? Nay, you ply me ever with arguments like a nagging child seeking a bite of sweets."

Ruark laughed, tossed the towel to a peg, then paused to ponder for a moment. When he continued, he addressed her like an orator before parliament, striding back and forth, arguing his case and accenting his statements with flourishes of his hands like a learned barrister.

"Madam, you most surely speak the truth. But I for one"—he softened his voice and tapped his chest with a finger—"have never been wont to question the method of success. Where are those mincing fops and drooling lads? Name me one who has not fled holding the halves of his heart together by dint of will." He leaned forward and his voice was almost a whisper. "The favor you extended was mine alone to sample, Shanna, my love." He straightened and considered the back of his hand for a moment. "Of course, since then I cannot vouch—"

Shanna was outraged at his suggestion. "You know no other has been where you have."

Ruark met her stare with anger in his own. "There is one of late who seems to attract you overmuch."

Shanna shook her head.

"And fondles you—"

"He but took my arm," she denied, wondering at Ruark's sudden venom.

"And ogles you as if he possessed you beyond the common lot."

"Sir Gaylord?" Shanna giggled at the sheer ludicrousness of his charges. "But he's just a—" She paused and her gaze became incredulous. "Why, Ruark! You're jealous!"

"Jealous?" His look of surprise ebbed to one of pained realization. He dropped his eyes and scuffed the straw beneath his feet. "Jealous? Aye." His voice was so low that she barely understood his words. "Of any man who stands beside you openly in public and touches so much as one soft curl and looks at you when I may not. While I must strangle dead the slightest show of yearning for you." He whirled suddenly with fierce determination. "You speak of tender words." His lips were strained and tight. "My tongue has formed them by the thousands while I lie alone in my bed at night, half feeling the warmth of you beside me. There, unspoken, they writhe and twist beneath my flesh until good anger smothers them. Still, the arguments were there and always between us, burning to be spoken. And speak I did, trading away the softer terms of love for that which was ignored though obvious. I found no time to speak them, though they were ever in my mind."

"Then speak them now," Shanna bubbled gaily. "Come on," she urged against his reluctance. "Pretend that I am a high-born lady." She straightened. Raising her nose appropriately, she brought her arms beneath her heavy mass of hair, lifted it to a momentary towering edifice, then let it fall to an even more glorious splendor. "And you," she pointed a finger imperiously, "will be my lordly suitor come to pledge your troth. Let me hear a sampling of your treasured rhymes."

Ruark laughed and found his crushed hat, raised its splintered crown and set it jauntily upon his head. Shanna choked back a giggle at his appearance.

"Milady, you look more like a great white stork with four wooden spindly legs," Ruark accused as he eyed her with a roguish grin.

Shanna's eyes were animated and full of gaiety as she gathered the bulk of her robe around her and tucked its folds between her knees, unconsciously bringing to his full view dainty ankles, long, slim calves, and a good measure of thigh. With a quick jerk, Ruark doffed the hat and held it in both hands before him like a bondslave suddenly confronted by his master.

"As my lady wishes," he murmured. When his voice came again, it was warm and rich, with a texture one could almost feel and a strength that belied his humble stance. "Oft have I wandered witless in the dark, bemused by a vision of such beauty that my simple mind refused to leave it. 'Tis thee, my love. 'Tis thee whose fair face is ever before me. I have set my feet on many foreign lands and ventured boldly forth to sample the womanhood thereof. But had I in my strongest moment drawn a likeness of that one who could bring me senseless to her feet and set me mumbling in rapturous pleas for the slightest touch of her soft hand, a kind smile, a brief caress, I would most surely have drawn this silken glory that rests upon your head."

Ruark raised a hand as if lifting her hair and let it fall.

"And would I add a visage that would haunt me in my loneliness like a nightmare in my dreams, most certainly it would be yours. If beneath my trembling quill a woman's form takes shape, it is that one I have known once warm and living in my arms and that one which brings me chilled and shaking from the deepest sleep."

Shanna's breast ached, and her eyes were soft and moist as she heard words that set themselves like tiny, swift barbed arrows into her flesh.

"You are the one whom I fear to meet each day, and yet I cannot wait until I do. I know the pain will come. I know the choking in my throat of the words that are never spoken. I know your beauty and seek it out, though the slightest taste will leave me weak and mindless. I have no other world but you. Your smile is my sun. Your eyes, my stars. Your face, my moon. Your touch and warm caress, my earth and food. Yea, this is Shanna," he whispered, "as I have never said before to anyone." Shanna sat mesmerized, enthralled by the stirring warmth of his words. As if she came from a daze, she realized he stood close before her. The stool was tall and gave her added height, but still she had to raise her eyes to meet his, which gazed down at her gently. Confused, Shanna could only stare back at him. There was a part of her that yearned to take him to her and return like tender words of love. There was within her, too, that part which reeled beneath the shock of their near discovery a few hours past and was not yet prepared for surrender and, indeed, feared the slightest touch from him. And his manner set her at odds with herself, for she had no way of knowing if he spoke from the heart, or merely recited some memorized verse he had used oft before. Shielding herself, she took refuge in light-hearted banter.

"Good sir, your tongue is smooth and doth plead your cause worthily. But I am reminded of one who seized the bridle of my mount and threatened me with anger in his eyes and of another who plagued me sorely until I yielded myself to his pleasure. Your pardon, milord, but he does not seem the same as the one who vows me his ideal of womanhood. The words ring falsely when taken in the light of what has passed. I fear this to be but another ploy designed to please my ear but somewhat departed from the truth."

Ruark's grin was devilish. "I beg milady to hasten in her decision. Your father has spoken of a dozen offspring to please him, and even so young a maid as yourself needs time to accomplish the task." He rested his hands casually alongside her thighs and leaned close to leer into her face. "Do you not think we should be about it?"

Shanna carefully lifted his hands and placed them aside. " 'Twould no doubt please you should my belly grow with child each winter and then in spring find me laboring to add another to your house until your proof of potency exceeds the most prolific of the princely heads at court." She turned away and then back again to confront him with a further reproof. "But tell me, sir, should I bear you a score or more, by what name shall they be called?"

"The choice be yours, my love. And upon your choice will rest the comfort of your conscience."

"You are impossible," Shanna chided. "You offer little in the way of solution and much in the way of confusion."

"Then let the problem lie." Ruark was little put aside by her reasoning. "In time and by the grace of God, all will be solved."

"You simply refuse to comprehend." Shanna thumped her knees with her fists in frustration. "Why can't you see my plight?"

"I understand perhaps more fully than you realize," he said tenderly. " 'Tis the same problem every woman faces: when to give up the dreams of childhood and face the realities of life." He lifted a shining lock of her hair from her shoulder and devoured its luxuriance before he let it fall again. His golden gaze found the sea-hued depth of hers and held it in a gentle bond which roused again the warmth Shanna had felt with his speech of avid admiration. It was like some strange spell he wove around her, and it was a struggle to free herself.

"Stand clear of me." Her command was sudden, but it lacked in firm conviction. "Keep your distance, knave. I see through this simple assault. Once again you contrive to toss me on my back and mount me like some horny stag."

His lips were close to hers, but Shanna was not yet ready for a quick surrender. She ducked beneath his arm and flew her perch, finding another on a saddle rack near the door but remaining ready for further flight.

Ruark seemed to discard his intent, and, lifting a long-handled wood-tined fork, he began to clean wisps of straw and hay from the stable floor.

"Do you really like the mare?" he asked innocently.

"Aye, I do," Shanna replied, keeping a wary eye on his progress. " 'Tis a shame she suffered so from the voyage."

" 'Tis, but she should heal well," Ruark commented. "She is of good stock, that Jezebel."

The mare stomped and snorted at the mention of her name. Ruark peered into the mare's stall as if concerned. "She seems to chafe against her pain." He straightened. "What's that?"

Unwarily Shanna turned her head, and as soon as her gaze left him, the fork sailed into the corner. As it clattered down, Shanna found herself swept up in Ruark's arms. She cried out, but not too loudly lest she wake the stable boy. For the most part her struggle took place in silence.

"Ruark, put me down." She managed to twist herself around until her toes were touching the cobbled floor, but his arm was wrapped around her beneath her robe, and she felt his hand against her bare buttocks. "Behave! This is no place—"

He laughed against her ear. "For fools and children you said. If that should mean you love me, I care not for which it be."

Shanna wedged her arm between them and clutched the robe at her throat, well aware of her near-nakedness and the familiarity of his hand wandering up her back.

"Ruark, you can't. Oh, stop that."

He nibbled at her ear, sending a flood of shivers up and down her spine.

"Ruark, I tell you we just can't—not here! Now stop that!"

Shanna managed to get his hand away and almost escaped as his grasp loosened for a moment. But Ruark trapped her again as she made to flee. With a sudden heave, Shanna pushed with all her strength. Ruark's heel caught on a loose flagstone, and he sprawled full length backward onto a pile of hay. It was his good fortune that his hand caught her gown, and Shanna found herself pulled down on top of him. Their bare limbs were entangled, her hair wildly tossed about them. For a moment Shanna struggled to rise as she recognized the fires in her own loins kindling with the hard flint of his, but with a low chuckle Ruark rolled with her, imprisoning her beneath him. Her robe had parted, the light nightshift strayed upward over her belly. Braced on his elbows above her, Ruark smiled down into her eyes.

"So, temptress, I've caught you. Will you change into another form and fly away? Or will you play your siren song until my poor befuddled head shall lose its wit and I am tossed mindless onto the rocks of this barren shore? My gaze does see a vixen bold with enchanted form, mermaid eyes and seafoam breasts, who doth ever lure me on, stirring me beyond my ends; then crying nay, nay, nay, she flies and leaves me mewling like a hungering child for her."

Shanna's voice was soft as she gazed into those golden eyes that hypnotized her and slowly sapped her will to resist. "When have I ever tempted you so sorely then denied your manly lust?"

"You are, my love, the Circe of my dreams who, when I close my eyes, does make me a rutting swine to slaver at your feet for the merest tidbit of your favor."

"If I pain you so, good sir,"—Shanna laughed with a warm twinkle in her eyes and plucked a straw from his hair—"why don't *you* leave? Perhaps when the sawmill is done, I can ply my father for your freedom and your fare to the colonies. Would you then leave me?"

She was suddenly serious and watched him closely, waiting his answer. Ruark was as serious and gently smoothed a curl from her brow.

"Nay, madam," he whispered. "Though you send me ten thousand miles away and build a wall against my chance return, I would ever, like a moth, come fluttering to your fires to seek my passion and my pain."

Though Shanna had thought to feel provoked with his sure denial, instead there came a warming deep within her and a strange softness began to grow toward him.

"And then, kind sir,"—it was indeed a devilish serpent who bade Shanna to pluck the apple from the tree and take this bite—"would you too decry your affection for the girl, Milly, and pledge to me alone?"

293

Ruark drew back from her in surprise, astonished that the girl's name should even be mentioned.

"Milly!" The word burst from him unbidden. "Why, that little twit—"

A trickle of chaff fell upon them from above, then a breathless squeal pierced the air, and a full shower of hay nearly covered them. Ruark rose to his knees and spitting chaff, brushed the stuff away as Shanna scrambled to her feet, snatching her robe together. There was a thrashing beside them. The form stilled and sat up. Again the name burst from Ruark's lips, louder still.

"Milly! What the hell—!" He could find no further words.

The girl smiled gingerly. "I heard ye call me name, and I stepped closer to see what fer."

Beneath Shanna's wild-eyed stare, Milly gathered her gaping blouse and began to secure the front of it to cover her small, naked breasts.

"Besides," Milly pouted petulantly, casting an angry eye toward Shanna, "I was getting tired o' waiting fer ye up there, and I ain't one to like second best."

"*Whaaat!*" The word exploded forth from Shanna's lips. A sudden cold, violent rage flooding all reason whitened Shanna's cheeks and struck green fire from her eyes as she understood the implication of Milly's presence.

"Shanna!" Ruark began to struggle to his feet, already seeing the disaster ahead.

Blindly Shanna reached out a hand for a weapon. Any weapon! Her fingers brushed several harnesses hanging from pegs. An infuriated moan escaped her gnashing teeth as she flung the entire mass of leather straps across the two in the straw. The heavy draft collar caught Ruark in the back and flung him again into the stack. He rolled and saw Shanna standing above him, feet spread, arms raised, hair flying and full, white robe flowing about her like a rampant whirlwind. She was like some ancient avenging druid roused from the past. He had never seen her more beautiful, nor more enraged.

"Have your little toss in the hay!" she railed in a voice that could have frozen a flooding tide. "Enjoy yourselves *first hand!*"

She whirled toward the stall and, as Ruark struggled against the tangle of straps, threw open the gate. Milly began to fight the willful web of harnesses and only engulfed them both all the more. Shanna seized the rope bridle of Jezebel and dragged the animal from the stall. Then grasping a handful of mane, she flung herself astride. With thumping heels she drove the mare through the open stable door.

"Dammit, Shanna, stop!" Ruark bellowed.

Horse and rider cleared the pasture gate as if the steed had wings, and they were gone in the dark.

Ruark struggled to fling the harnesses from him, but Milly's writhing defeated him. He snarled through gritted teeth.

"Hold still, damn you."

Milly froze. "I was only funning," she wailed, suddenly afraid of his wrath.

Ruark's only reply was an inarticulate growl. Finally he freed himself and running full tilt for the door collided with the stableboy Elot who, rubbing his eyes, had chosen that moment to emerge from the tack room.

The stunned lad struggled to a sitting position from the floor of the stable where he had been knocked and managed, "Wha—"

"Go back to bed!" The words fairly lashed him with their force, and Ruark fled, leaving Elot to stare with amazement at the young girl who seemed to be trying to wear several harnesses at the same time. Mumbling something about nightmares, Elot stumbled back to his cot where he would rise with the morning and wonder at the soreness and bruises that mysteriously afflicted him.

Milly gave an exasperated groan as she tried to free herself from the tangle of straps. She froze as a dark shadow towered over her. Fearfully she raised her gaze.

"Lor', gov'na," she sighed in relief. "Ye gave me a start, ye did. I thought it mighta been Mister Ruark returning."

A black-gloved hand reached down and lifted the harnesses from her, hanging them on the pegs from which they had been hurled. The black cape swirled, displaying a tall, thin figure as the man knelt to help Milly to her feet. She leaned against him, her ebony eyes smiling coyly into his, and rubbed his shirted chest familiarly with her hand.

"I said what ye told me," she murmured, peering up into his

narrow face. She could see his smile broaden, though his features were shadowed by his tricorn. "But why'd ye push me? I nearly broke me bloomin' arse, tumblin' like that." She paused and grinned knowingly. "Would've ruined yer fun if I had. Aye, that's the truth."

The man only nodded then assisted her to the ladder, helping her up into the loft again, there to continue with whatever had occupied them before Ruark's coming.

Chapter 14

SHANNA flung herself down from the mare's back and raced up the front steps of the manor. If Ruark came after her, no locked door would bar his entry. Indeed, she wouldn't put it past him to create a scene right beneath the nose of her father, possibly even demanding to have it all out in the open if she refused him. She must fly before he could catch her. But first to clothe herself. The stable was some distance from the mansion, and Jezebel had crossed the grounds quickly, but Shanna knew she must hurry, for Ruark seemed part savage in some of the feats he accomplished. He was equally swift of mind and foot and had the uncanny ability of appearing almost out of nowhere.

Shanna's bare feet scarcely touched the curving stairs as she raced up them, at the same time tearing off her robe. She wasted no time in locking her sitting room door behind her, but ran through to her bedchamber to snatch open the armoire, pulling from it the peasant garb. Tucking her slender feet into a pair of soft hide slippers, she stepped into the skirt and yanked it to her waist under the short shift which she quickly drew over her head, donning in its place the peasant blouse and a shawl for modesty. She belted the garments about her narrow waist with a sash and

297

snatched a dark cloak from her wardrobe before she fled across the balcony, from there dropping to the ground.

Jezebel stood waiting. Shanna heaved herself again onto the horse's back and wheeled the animal about to send her flying across the lawn where the thud of hooves would be deadened against the sod.

Ruark came on a run around the end of the manor just in time to see the two racing off through the trees, too far now to be caught or called to. In deep frustration he ground a curse beneath gnashing teeth and with a much slower pace continued around the mansion, past Shanna's wing, through the shrubberies surrounding his cottage, and made his way across the wooden planks of the porch. Once within, he poured himself a hearty draught of strong brew and stood staring at the clock in the hall, wondering how long it would be before Shanna ran out her anger and returned.

Milly's words had struck a violent note in Shanna, like the high pitch that shatters a crystal piece. The explosion in Shanna's mind could have fair resembled the eruption of a volcano, and it was not to be quickly cooled, though the first bright burst had dwindled to a constant flow of red molten rage that pressed her onward with no particular destination in mind.

The vapors began to rise, and the moon, stark and silvery as it shone through a halo of whitened drifts, lent a ghostly eeriness to the island. Shanna rode in the meager light, and where she went she could not say for sure. Her mind was numb. She gave the mare her head, and although not knowing the island, the beast wandered the paths and roads with abandon. Jezebel had been confined to a stall on the deck of a ship for the sea voyage, and at this freedom she stretched her legs out in an exhilarating run. Finding herself at last in a succulent field, she paused to graze a bit. The silent figure on her back sat motionless, sick with an ache that gnawed at her heart.

Shanna would have denied aloud that her pain should be the result of anything more than a casual regard for Ruark.

" 'Tis just that I almost gave myself to him in the hay like any little strumpet, she gritted. "And there all along he had that tart Milly waiting in case I should refuse." Though she was alone, Shanna's face burned with the scalding memory. "And for all my caution, he would have had his fun with an audience to witness all."

Outrage at his duplicity began to sear her, and the ache was forgotten. She sobbed. She cried. She cursed the night and the bastard rake it hid from her sight. The mare echoed the mistress's unquiet and began to snort and prance. The flare of fury burned out and left the woman hardminded, her wrath unrequited.

Shanna thumped Jezebel with her heels and obediently the horse began to move. They descended a shallow slope and came out upon the beach, pale of sand and wide with the lowness of the tide. Beyond curled the fluorescent line of breakers that marked the water's edge. Jezebel waded into the sea and dipped her head for a drink, then snorted at the brackish brine, and danced away in disgust. Shanna crooned a soft word and laid her hand upon the silky neck, rubbing gently. The mare calmed and cantered along, sending jets of spray up with her hooves. Jezebel reveled in the freedom of it all and stretched out again in a run, not pressing but racing easily along the beach, her passing making little sound on the wet sand.

A late fisherman pulled his dory up from the surf. He quailed in sudden fear, for, from nowhere, a vision appeared and flew at him—a great dark horse making no noise as it came down the white beach, and upon its back a fury out of hell, face death gray in the moonlight and beautiful beyond earthly flesh, pale hair streaming out behind from a black hood. He would swear she rode with no reins to guide the mount or saddle to hold her on its back. Though he mouthed a rosary of "Aves" and fell on his knees, the rider took no notice of him. Instead, sitting erect and proud, she flew silently by as if bound on a dire mission. For months afterwards he would blame all ills that befell him on the visit of this night-born spectre, and in his cups he would bore his companions with endless recountings of his vision.

The pale lights of the sleeping village ahead stirred Shanna's mind, and she felt in desperate need of companionship and conversation on her woes. There was but one person whom she could trust, and she made her decision to seek him out. Entering the village and slowing the horse's pace, she passed the quiet, dark houses like a wraith. If some unwelcome eye had seen this shadowy apparition pass, he would have been loath to mention it for fear of being thought mad.

Horse and rider climbed the hill to where Pitney's whitewashed house perched on the bluff like a lookout scanning the horizon. Here was a haven for Shanna and someone to listen as she gave vent to her troubles. No lights illuminated the windows, but at her urgent rapping a flickering glow of a candle appeared, and a mumbled voice bade her wait a moment. Several lamps were touched with flame before the panel swung wide and Pitney's huge bulk filled the door. A stocking cap sat askew atop his thinning pate, and breeches had been hastily hitched up over his nightshirt. Stepping aside and rubbing the sleep from his eyes, he called for her to enter.

"Aye, come in, lass," he rumbled. "What brings you out at this hour?"

Shanna avoided his gaze as she moved past him. "I had a need to talk, and there was no one else—"

Her own mind confused, Shanna was hard put to find the beginning of her plight. Restlessly she paced the room and twisted her hands; she opened her mouth to speak but found the ready words empty. Pitney sat on a bench before the cold hearth as he checked his pocket watch against the clock on the wall. It was well past the mid of night and into the wee hours. Stifling a yawn, he rubbed the heel of his hand across bleary eyes and arched his large feet away from the cool stone of the hearth, waiting for her to broach the subject. His attention perked to amazement as Shanna seized the rope at his well and raised his cooling ale jug up. She took the tin cup that hung on the trestle and poured a hearty drink. In alarm Pitney half rose as she slammed the cork back into the jug and pushed it carelessly back into the well. The rope twanged, but no sound of shattering crockery came from the shaft. Much relieved, Pitney sank down again, letting out his breath in a long sigh.

Watching her closely now, he waited as she sipped daintily from the mug, wrinkling her nose at the bitter brew. The inevitable shudder of revulsion followed. No surprise to Pitney. For her to even taste the stuff was highly out of character, and he surmised her distress was more than a trifling irritation. Grimacing, Shanna thrust the cup out toward him, and Pitney calmly accepted her offering as he continued to contemplate her in some bemusement.

" 'Tis your father again?" he ventured carefully.

Shanna shook her head and grew more upset with the thought. " 'Tis not him. In fact,"—she laughed faintly—"he has released me from any further demands of marriage until I find a husband I would have." Her brow gathered like a dark storm, and Pitney saw in her frown no good for the one who had provoked her. " 'Tis that rogue we dragged from Newgate who haunts me."

"Oh," Pitney shrugged. "Mister Ruark. Or Beauchamp. Whatever. Your husband."

"*Husband!*" Shanna snapped and threw a glare at him. "Do not use that title for that blackguard! I am a widow." She stressed the word. "You prepared the coffin yourself and witnessed the burial." Her voice sharpened as she added, "Perhaps if you had taken more care, you might have saved me much suffering."

Pitney grew a bit piqued himself. "I explained it all before. I see no need in going through it again."

Shanna released a wavering sigh, realizing she would get nowhere blaming him. Her problem as it stood stemmed solely from Ruark.

She groaned inwardly. Damn him! Damn the strutting peacock! Playing with all the wenches on the island behind her back and then coming and mewling about his monkish life.

She could not let him remain on Los Camellos, sharing her table, frequenting the manor house where she would be forced to meet that mocking jeer. He had used her; like a bauble on a string he had added her to his collection. How many others on the island were there? An isle of lonely sea captains' wives and young girls seeking husbands. He must have thought it paradise to find so many willing women, and herself among them. Surely he was rolling with mirth by now, the proud daughter of Orlan Trahern, toppled and tossed by a common slave. She cringed painfully at the thought. The roving stud deserved no more than the fate of a shipwrecked tar on a deserted island. 'Twould do him good to truly realize the celibate life.

But how could she implore Pitney to do her bidding? He had denied her once and might well again if she could not convince him that her need was dire.

"Pitney." Her tone was soft and plaintively appealing. "You have done much to aid me where I had no right to ask. I did not mean to sound ungrateful. 'Tis only that I am sorely plagued by that man. He has begun to pester me—"

Pitney's brow raised in question, and Shanna managed a blush.

"He claims to be my husband truly wed and wants me to admit to being his wife."

The strapping man was silent, but his countenance had grown thoughtful. He started a small fire and set a kettle on for tea.

"I have often wondered." He spoke over his shoulder. "That night after the wedding when we took him from your carriage, he fought unseemingly fierce for a man who had seen a simple bargain met, and in the gaol his words indicated that he had been cheated, that there was something more due him. His reference to you was not the kindest."

He faced her, waiting for her answer, and Shanna knew no out. Her face was hot, and she was aware that Pitney's perusal had grown more pointed.

"He—he would not agree"—her voice was small and the words came haltingly—"unless I promised"—the last came in a rush as she squeezed her eyes shut in agonized shame—"unless I promised to spend the night with him."

Pitney rocked back on the small bench and roared. "And you wonder why the lad pursues you?"

He trembled the room with another gust of humor. Shanna stared at him a bit confused, seeing no reason for amusement. Finally Pitney quieted and in a more sober vein stated, "Such a good bargain would torture any man, and I cannot fault him for that." His eyes fell, and he stared at the floor, at once serious and pensive. "And I have been much his villain. Aye, I have brought much pain to him. Yet he has never been less than courteous to me. Of course, a slave has little choice."

"You take his side against me?" Shanna asked incredulously.

Pitney's tone was flat and expressionless. "I do not know what you plan, but I'll have no part of it."

Shanna's eyes filled with tears. She sniffed daintily and brought all her wiles into play for the argument. "He has come to me several times and tried to claim his marriage rights."

"I cannot fault the man there. He has a need to be a man,

and I am not so old that I cannot appreciate his fine choice.

Shanna sensed the futility of pleas and grew desperate. "I want him off this island! Tonight! I don't care how, but if you don't help me I will find those who will."

"Damned and be dogged!" Pitney roared. "I'll not! And I won't see you with that sort of deed on your conscience. I'll go to your father first."

"Ruark tried to take me in the stables!" Shanna railed, angry tears brightening the stormy, sea-green depths.

In open surprise Pitney looked at her sharply.

"He did!" Shanna cried and then choked on threatening tears. Her lips trembled in shame as she remembered her own responsive passion. "He snatched me down on the hay—"

Wringing her hands, Shanna turned away, unable to continue. She had given voice to no lie, but she knew the absence of the full truth had twisted the meaning of the part she gave.

Unknowingly Shanna presented to Pitney confirmation of her claim, for wisps of straw still clung to the tumbled locks that cascaded over her shoulders. Pitney could well understand Ruark's infatuation with the girl, but his own rage stirred at the thought of Shanna being mauled—by anyone.

Shanna managed to choke out, "I hate him. I cannot abide the man. I cannot face him again—ever." She drew away and spoke in deadly earnest. "I want him gone, off this island, tonight."

Pitney gave no outward sign that he heard her. He sprinkled tea leaves from a tin into the boiling water and set the pot aside as he pondered what he must do. There had been a ship come into port from the colonies that very morn. He had been down at the docks when the captain and some of his men led away a horse for the Traherns. Appearing nearly on the brig's heels, another colonial vessel had come in sight, flying the Georgia Company flag. Apparently it was a sister ship to the other, for it anchored some distance out, and only a small dinghy was put ashore with but a hand's count of men who had retreated to the dramshop to pass the hours. Trahern might search the colonial ship in port for his most valued bondsman, Pitney mused, but if there were enough coins, perhaps the captain of the other

303

vessel might be persuaded to sail his ship off aways where it could not be seen.

"I will get him away for you," Pitney finally muttered. He doffed his nightcap and replaced it with a tricorn then slipped his long feet into a pair of brass-buckled shoes. "I'll not see you abused."

He closed the door behind him, and Shanna was left staring at the portal, knowing the victory of winning her way yet feeling no joy in it. Aware that she must stay away from the manor until Pitney concluded his business, she poured herself a cup of tea and sat down at the trestle table to sip the brew, there watching the last of the embers die into blackness. In the empty house, the chiming of the clock seemed to echo Pitney's words.

"Abused!"

Shanna was suddenly struck by the absurdity of it, the sheer ludicrous fallacy of the word. Hysterical laughter spilled from her, and if anyone had heard, they might have doubted her sanity.

Ruark was sprawled carelessly across his bed, staring at the canopy above him when hoofbeats sounded on the path outside the cottage. He was halfway to the door when a light rap came against the wood. His mind roared with relief. 'Twas Shanna, of course. But on flinging open the portal Ruark saw only Pitney's broad, angry face. Then the night exploded in a billion twinkling lights before darkness descended with the thud of his body against the carpet.

The surging pain in Ruark's head made him aware of the slow rolling motion of the floor beneath him. It seemed to rock him in a cradle, and through his muddled senses he heard only an odd creaking. His world expanded, and he realized he was gagged and bound tightly with a musty sack pulled down over his head and shoulders. The rough flooring beneath him became a small boat. He recognized the squeaking of oarlocks and the slow lap of water against the wooden sides. There was only this and heavy breathing from close-by, and he realized he was being rowed out to sea, for what mischief yet he could not perceive, but he had a fair guess it stemmed from Shanna. He jeered bitterly in the dark void of his confinement. She could not even hear him out before she passed judgment.

"I guess ye've done it this time," Pitney's voice rasped, and Ruark became aware that the man was muttering to himself. He lay still, feigning unconsciousness, and listened at the rumbling words that threaded through his aching brain. "I cannot drop ye to the fish, and mayhap this here will be worse for ye, but she said to get ye gone, one way or the other, and I'd better do it ere she find some other way to be rid of ye." A long pause of silence mingled with the creaking of oars, then a heaving sigh. "If ye'd only had the good sense, lad, to leave the filly be. I warned ye once, but I guess ye forgot. I've been too long seeing the lass safe to let her be taken against her will, even by you."

Ruark cursed in his mind and tried to loosen the ropes about his wrists, but they were tied hard and fast. There was only futility in struggling anyway. He could not imagine Pitney taking away his gag to listen to him, not when Shanna had convinced the man of her plight.

The rowing slowed, and a voice hailed the boat. Pitney called back, and several moments later Ruark was thrown over the huge man's shoulder and carted onto the deck of the ship where he was unceremoniously dumped. Ruark held back a groan and remained motionless, though it seemed his whole body throbbed with the pain in his head. He could not catch the words in the exchange of voices, but he heard the clink of coins as a fair sum was counted out. A heavy thud of feet crossed the deck, and Ruark knew Pitney was making his departure. Not long afterwards, the sack was jerked off Ruark's head, and the gag snatched from his mouth. To his displeasure a bucket of sea water was tossed upon him, and he was roughly hauled to his feet as he sputtered beneath this assault. Still bound, he was tied to a mast. A lantern was thrust near, and an ugly face leered in its light.

"Well, laddie, so ye're comin' round," a hoarse voice snarled. "Ye'll do nicely here 'til we can tend to ye."

The lantern went away. Amid soft commands the sails were unfurled, the anchor raised. Soon a freshening dawn breeze was licking at Ruark's face, and the schooner was skipping along over the waves. Ruark bent his neck around and watched as the lights of Los Camellos faded from view. At last Shanna had seen him off her island.

Sighing, Ruark resigned himself and leaned his head back

against the mast. Somehow he would find a way to return and renew his claims. This changed nothing. She was still his wife. But first he must make the best of his situation and survive.

Ruark spent his first night aboard ship lashed to the pinrail at the base of the main mast. The schooner had little more than left sight of the island when the anchor was dropped again, and, with sails flapping loose, the ship swung about and rested on her chains. With the exception of the watch on the quarterdeck, the vessel remained devoid of life. It was not until the sun was a good two hours up that a crewman wandered close enough to be halted by Ruark's request. The man shrugged his shoulders and made his way aft where a few moments later a heavyset Englishman ventured forth and, after leaning against the rail for a space, noticed Ruark and came to stand before him.

" 'Twould seem to me, sir," Ruark opened the conversation, "that there is little reason for me to be so bound and secured, as I have done you no harm and most certainly intend none. Is it not possible that I could be released to see to my needs?"

"Well now, laddie," the Englishman drawled. "We ain' got no reason to see ye uncomfortable, but I ain' got no reason to trust ye, neither." He squinted one eye down at Ruark. "Why, I don't know ye none at all."

" 'Tis a simple enough problem to cure," Ruark returned. "Ruark's the name. John Ruark, of late a trusted bondsman to his majesty Lord Trahern." It was inspiration alone that let a trace of a sneer creep into his voice. "I'm aware that you received a goodly sum to take me aboard, and I would think as a paid passenger I could at least have freedom of the ship." He gave a nod of his head toward the unbroken horizon. "As you might have guessed, I have no plans to travel from the deck."

"I sees no 'arm in that." The man spat downwind, clearing the rail easily. Taking out a knife, he tested its edge with his thumb. " 'Arripen's the name. Captain of me own ship when I'm aboard 'er. An' 'Arry to me friends." He leaned forward and with quick movements slashed the ropes that bound Ruark to the mast.

"My gratitude, Captain Harripen." Ruark chose the more respectable title as he rubbed his wrists vigorously to restore circulation. "I am forever in your debt."

" 'At's good," his benefactor grunted. " 'Cause I don't owe no man nothing." Again Ruark was fixed with that squinted one-eyed stare. "Ye talks mighty fancy fer a bondsman." Though a statement, it was also a question.

Ruark chuckled. "A temporary state I assure you, captain, and in truth I do not know yet whether to condemn those who turned against me or thank them." He jerked his head toward the forecastle. "If you'll excuse me, captain, I have needs that have gone long awanting. I would be further indebted if you might arrange for me to speak to the captain of this vessel later."

"Ye can be sure o' that, laddie." The man spat again and with the back of his hand wiped brown spittle from his stubbled chin.

Ruark eased his condition and then found food and a mug of ale. The latter seemed the most plentiful commodity aboard the ship. His breakfast taken, he sought out a coil of rope in a spot of shade and lay down, quickly regaining the slumber he had lost during the night.

It was near dusk when he was roused and taken to the captain's cabin and there subjected to a long, silent scrutiny from those men who sat around the trestle table. Ruark had never seen a scurvier bunch. A mulatto sat forward in his chair, leaning heavy arms upon the tabletop, and fixed Ruark with a dark glare.

"A bondslave, ya say? How come ya to be one?"

Ruark debated the question a brief moment, staring at the scarred and brooding faces across from him. If these were the gentry of any society, he was a wee, innocent babe.

"Murder it was." His eyes swept them all, and no flicker of surprise brightened those black stares. "They bought me from the gaol and made me work to pay the debt."

" 'Oo got ye off the island?" Harripen inquired, picking his teeth with his fingernails.

Ruark lazily scratched his chest and smiled ruefully. "A lady who didn't like the little filly who was waiting for me in the hayloft."

The Englishman roared his mirth. "Now that, laddie, I can believe. Must o' been a rich one, the coins she paid to see ye gone."

Ruark shrugged, noncommittal.

"What does the squire keep in his warehouses?" The scar-

307

faced captain of the schooner sat forward. "Riches? Silks? spices?"

Ruark met the man's eyes with a lazy grin and rubbed his belly. "Been a long time atwixt meals, mate." He jerked a thumb at the platters that still filled one end of the table. "Might I have a bite?"

A half-eaten leg of some smallish animal was pushed toward him along with a mug of warm ale. Ruark found himself a chair and settled to dine.

" 'Bout those warehouses?" the swarthy, scarred man reminded him.

"Pass the bread will you, mate?" Ruark wiped his mouth on the back of his hands and washed the meat down with a draught of ale. Tearing a chunk from the loaf tossed to him, he mopped at the gravy on the platter then seized a shirt that hung on the back of his chair and cleaned his hands on it.

"Ya've had yer fill now," the mulatto growled. "What's in them sheds?"

"Everything." Ruark shrugged and laughed jeeringly. "But 'tis of no value to you." He grinned back as the men stared at him with heavy frowns. "You'll never get into the harbor." He dipped his finger in the ale and drew a partial circle on the table, leaving the ends unjoined. His finger widened the bottom of the circle into a puddle as he commended, "This is the town—where the warehouses are," he added for the mulatto's benefit. "Here" —he drew an "X" on one end of the arc—"and here"—he drew another "X" across from the first—"are batteries of cannons. To enter the harbor, you sail right between them." He traced a line through the opening.

Ruark sat back, surveyed the faces watching him, then gave a soft chuckle.

"You'd be blown from the water before you got close to the sheds."

Ruark had only guessed they might be pirates, but now the disappointment on their faces proved it. The Englishman, Harripen, leaned back and again picked his teeth with a fingernail.

"Ye seem light'earted, me lad," he rumbled. "Could it be ye've somethin' up yer sleeve?"

Ruark folded his bare arms and let the question go unanswered for a long moment as he appeared to ponder a problem.

"Well, mates," he gave them a lopsided grin, "had I a sleeve, that might well be said, but as you can see I have naught but a sorry pair of breeches hardly worthy of the name. Thus in my poverty, everything I have is most dear and commands a price." He laughed at the suddenly angry expressions. "Like yourselves, I do nothing for nothing. I have long looked upon the weaknesses of Trahern's island and know a way to come off with little loss and the probability of much gain." Ruark leaned forward and spread his elbows wide on the table, motioning them near as if in confidence. "I can tell you of a way in, and I can tell you where the moneys of the store and of Trahern's own accounts are kept." The pirates would gain enough coin from these coffers to make it seem like a haul, but Ruark knew that Trahern removed most of the money to the manor and held it in his own strongbox.

"Of course,"—Ruark reclined back in his chair and seemed to dismiss the pirates' now eager looks—"if you want the raw oakum and the bales of hemp in the warehouses, you can as well go there." He waited a space then shrugged, spreading his hands. "I have little else to trade, gentlemen. What say you?"

The French half-breed captain thrust forward a wide-bladed knife and fingered the well-honed edge of it.

"You have your life, bondsman," he sneered.

"Aye, that I have." And Ruark reminded him, "I returned the favor by warning you of the guns. I will advance my cause further and tell you that the *Hampstead*, with twenty-odd fine cannon, is at anchor in the harbor. Should you gain the inner port you would have to face her, and how long would you stay with that one breathing fire and shot down your neck?"

"And you'll no doubt demand a captain's share for your plan," the half-breed snorted with rich sarcasm, "while we risk our necks for it."

"A captain's share will do nicely, thank you," Ruark accepted with a chuckle, ignoring the jeer. "I am not overly greedy. As to the necks, I will lead you and thus risk my own from both sides."

"Done then! A captain's share it be if we take a haul," Captain Harripen chortled, enjoying the turnabout on his French cohort.

"Now, laddie, out with it. What be yer scheme?"

Though no movement was detectable, the air of expectancy grew to great proportions. They were all ears to hear the details of his plan.

"Near the east end of the island," Ruark improvised as he spoke, "the water is deep, and you could lay the ship less than a cable's length from shore."

"An' to the west?" the mulatto asked suspiciously.

"Shallow!" Ruark replied. "Two or three fathoms at most, with a reef well offshore. Closest you'll get there would be a mile or two." He did not want them landing near the manor house, but his words were for the most part truth, although he made no mention of the men who patrolled the shorelines at night.

"Let the lad say his piece!" Harripen railed impatiently, and the mulatto reluctantly subsided.

"There's a signal gun on the hill," Ruark started again.

"Yah, we know dat. We hear it when we come in," the Dutchman said.

"One shot is just a ship sighted, but if you hear two 'tis a warning," Ruark continued. "Now, you can put ashore a light force, and I will show them where to get the best of the loot in the quietest way without rousing the whole island."

The heads drew nearer, and Ruark spun his spurious plan out for them. He knew the gun would sound, and at night one shot was as much a warning as two. Where he would have the pirates land would give the town a good hour to prepare, and none of the small boats he had seen on deck would carry more than a score of raiders. Even if two boats were lowered, no more than thirty could be embarked, and several of those would stay to guard the boats. Trahern should have no difficulty dispatching the landing party and, with the schooner's crew shorthanded, the *Hampstead* would have no trouble overhauling the privateer.

It would be no mean feat for him to escape once ashore, and Trahern would surely give him a hearing before any punishment. He felt no further commitment to protect Shanna's secret and would speak whatever portion of the truth became necessary.

The pirate captains seemed satisfied with his plan and let Ruark return to his bed of rope. It was in the darkest hour of night that the crew was turned out to weigh anchor and set sail. The ship had barely begun to move when Ruark found the Englishman and the half-breed, Pellier, standing over him with drawn pistols.

"We make two changes in the plan," the Frenchman laughed. "You stay on board as hostage to your good information, and we pick our own spot to land."

Ruark stared at them, and a deep-seated fear began to gnaw at his belly.

It had almost been dawn before Shanna returned to her chambers from Pitney's house, sinking almost immediately into an exhausted sleep, but this lasted only a few hours before she was jarred abruptly to awareness by her father bellowing a command that echoed through the whole manor.

"Well, dammit, find him for me!"

Leaping from bed, Shanna scrambled to dress herself and hurried down, carefully slowing her pace before she entered the dining room where a vast assortment of men were gathered. Overseers, several bondsmen, Elot holding Ruark's flattened hat, Ralston, and even Pitney made up the number who stood around the table facing the squire, who was anything but happy.

"Papa, what is it?" Shanna feigned innocence as she approached her father's chair. Trahern quickly tossed her a glance that showed a black, thunderous scowl.

" 'Tis the lad! He's gone—missing!"

Shanna shrugged sweetly. "Papa, of what lad do you speak? There are at least a score or more—"

Trahern interrupted with a bellow. " 'Tis the good lad, John Ruark, I speak of! He's nowhere to be found!"

"Oh, papa." Shanna laughed lightly. Her acting was brilliant. "Mister Ruark is no lad. A man, surely. Have we not discussed such some months ago?"

Trahern roared. "I've no ear for simpering wit when there's work to be done! And there's naught that can be done without Mister Ruark!"

"But surely, papa," Shanna laid a soft hand upon her father's arm, "these men here are as worthy of the task. Can they not continue with Mister Ruark's work until he can be found?"

"He's gone!" Ralston's firm statement came quickly on the heels of her question. "He's fled from bondage. He'll not be caught lest a fleet be sent out to search for that colonial ship anchored off the way yester morn." Ralston was quick to cast blame elsewhere before any remembered it was he who brought John Ruark to Los Camellos.

Pitney slowly sipped a morning toddy of rum and remained coldly remote as he watched father and daughter.

"Elot found his hat in the stables," one of the overseers rejoined. "He was tending the mare which was brought."

"Aye," Ralston sneered. "A mare for a bondslave. Is this what these treacherous colonials think is a fair trade? They've taken Mister Ruark under their wing and spirited him off, right beneath our noses."

"Be at ease, Mister Ralston." The squire fixed the thin man with an introspective eye. "I do not blame you for his presence or this trouble. Indeed, we have all benefited from Mister Ruark's talents. 'Tis more that we have a project under way and cannot complete it without him."

Ralston was no more willing to accept this approach, for it seemed Mister Ruark might return without harm and that went strongly against his grain. He could think of no retort and sputtered into confused silence.

It was in the midst of this discussion that Sir Gaylord sauntered in, looking well rested, his pinkened cheeks boasting of his health.

"I say, there seems to be much ado." He glimpsed Shanna's momentary frown. "Can I be of assistance?"

Shanna nearly growled in his face but knew the folly of that with her father near. Instead, quite primly she took a cup of tea to sip as she answered. "It seems, sir, that Mister Ruark has been misplaced. Perchance have you knowledge of his whereabouts?"

Gaylord's brows lifted in surprise. "Mister Ruark? The bondslave? Egad! Gone missing, you say? Why, I haven't laid sight on him since—ah, let me see—'twas night before last, at this very table. My gracious, has he been gone that long?"

Trahern gave a heavy sigh of impatience. It took considerable effort on his part to gentle his words. "He was to be here at my table early this morn. I have never known him to be late."

"Mayhap he's taken ill," Gaylord offered. "Have you sent to his quarters—"

"The lad's not there," Trahern interrupted tersely. "I have sent about this island and none have seen him."

Gaylord appeared perplexed. "My word, I've no thought as to where a man might disappear to, especially on an island like this. Is he inclined to—wander a bit?" At Trahern's raised brow and Shanna's questioning stare, he cleared his throat and made his apologies to the latter. "Pardon me, dear lady, for being so bold in your presence. But being a widow yourself, you must be aware that some men enjoy the company of a—ah—lady on occasion. Mayhaps he's been—ahem—detained."

Shanna's cup rattled on the saucer, and she almost spilled the hot liquid over her lap before she managed to reclaim her poise. It was Gaylord's misfortune that Berta stepped to the door in time to hear this last exchange. She quickly bustled in to give the man a hot retort.

"She be liddle more den a babe, ya lanky galoot, a mere child, and I tank ya to hold dose wile tings ta yaself."

Casually Pitney sipped his toddy and peered at Shanna from under his brow while Gaylord hastened to make humble apologies to both women.

Trahern snorted and ignored Gaylord's plight. "I give the lad credit for knowing the difference between work and pleasure. I fear some disaster might have befallen him, else he would be here."

"Aye," Ralston agreed derisively. "He found himself a tidy hole on that ship that sailed in the night. Why else would it go, leaving like some slinking hound who's been up to no good? Ye'll not see Mister Ruark again lest ye set a purse for his return. Then I swear if caught, he should be hanged for an example, or you'll be having the lot of them trying the same."

Trahern heaved a heavy sigh. "If he cannot be found, then I must assume he's gone of his own will. If that be so, I'll set a purse of fifty pounds for his capture."

Ralston smirked with his renewed importance and cast a glance toward Shanna. "What do you think, madam? Do you not agree that a treacherous renegade should be hanged for a villain?"

Shanna was stunned, unable to answer. Her thoughts clanged

together in confusion. Even in her wildest imagination she had not thought they'd hunt Ruark down like a mad beast. Her eyes caught Pitney's scowl upon her, ominous and accusing, and she knew not what to reply.

The search for Ruark continued through the afternoon. Shanna retreated to her bedchamber and tried to dismiss the gnawing fears that had begun to plague her. Giving Hergus the excuse of not feeling up to dressing, she sought the comfort of her bed again and attempted to retrieve some hours of the sleep she had missed during the night. Exhaustion finally overcame her racing mind, and she drifted into sweet oblivion. Then dreams began to invade the peace of sleep. She was happy, surrounded by children of varying ages, while she cuddled an infant to her breast. Laughter squealed from the playing youngsters, and a toddler ran between his father's legs to be swept up into strong arms. Their dark heads came together, and the father became Ruark, laughing as he came to her and bent near to kiss her lips—

Shanna woke with a start, her body clammy with perspiration. It was a lie! She recoiled in sudden sadness. The dream could never be! An oppressive, aching, down-trodden feeling of loneliness assailed her, and she cringed beneath its crushing weight, burying her face in her pillows. Because of her actions she would never see Ruark again, no more know the sweet, caressing warmth of his lips upon hers, nor again be comforted in his protective arms.

It was dark when Hergus came with a tray of food. Shanna hid her swollen eyes and tear-blotched face behind the pages of a book and lamely directed the woman to leave the platter on a table, not even caring to inquire why she had brought it up. The maid, however, offered the information as she peered suspiciously at her young mistress.

"Yer pa said for me to tell ye. Sir Gaylord thought he sighted someone who looked like Mister Ruark in the village, and the squire's gone to search the town, taking all the men from the island with him to see if Mister Ruark might be found. Why, there ain' even one single soul of a man in the house left. Yer pa is mighty determined to catch Mister Ruark if he's to be caught. I wonder meself where he's got to."

Shanna was mute, and the woman finally left, gaining no more information than she had entered with.

For Shanna, time slowed to an agonizing eternity. She could not force herself to take even a small morsel of the food on the tray. She donned a fresh nightshift and belted a light robe over its thin batiste and then sat staring at a book of poetry in her lap. She could not concentrate—in every verse she saw the hero, slender and dark, a half-naked, savage-looking man with amber eyes. With a moan she threw the volume aside and flung herself across the bed to stare moodily across the space of her chamber. Her dainty clock heralded the eleventh hour. Sometime later she heard a noise below and could only reason it was her father returning, in defeat of course. Then her ears caught the sound of shattering glass. Her father in a rage? She could understand that. He had been fond of Ruark. Now, he must imagine that he had been betrayed.

A slam of a door drew a frown from her, and she rose and, taking up a candle, passed through her sitting room to the hall. Hergus had stated that her father had taken all the men. If he had returned, then the servants would have come with him. But the house was dark and, for the first time in her life, seemed strangely menacing to her.

"Who's there?" Shanna called down from the top of the stairs and tried to see into the shadows below.

No answer came, only a hushed and oppressive silence. Bravely she set her feet on the steps and began to descend slowly, listening, waiting for some familiar sound to ease her tensions. A muffled shuffle of feet broke the eerie quiet, making the skin on the back of Shanna's neck crawl. Much the stranger to fear, she plucked up her courage and hastened her steps downward, shielding the candle with her hand.

"Who is it, I say? I know you're there."

She had only taken two steps from the stairs when a hairy hand reached out of the darkness and snatched the candle. Shanna gasped and whirled. The light was lifted until it revealed a pockmarked face; a scar running the length of it pulled down the corner of one eye in a curious pinch of skin. A leering grin displayed uneven, blackened teeth. In that moment of nightmarish terror, it seemed the devil had taken human form.

Part Two

🕸 Chapter 15 🕸

WHEN gunshots sounded from the island, Ruark suffered an uneasy moment, expecting Harripen and the waiting crew to turn on him. They were clustered on the quarterdeck gazing off toward the island, and they seemed for the moment to have forgotten him. As no threatening moves were made toward him, he continued worrying at his bonds in an attempt to loosen the ropes looped tightly about his wrists. It was sometime later that he was again interrupted by Harripen, who called several of the men to join him and pointed to land. Ruark could see nothing of what transpired ashore but was relieved that no further attention was directed toward him. He redoubled his efforts, but the knots were stubborn and well tied.

Harripen resumed his pacing across the deck of the schooner, and Ruark made little progress with his bonds. The night grew still, the only sounds being the creaking of the ship, the slip-slap of waves against the hull, and an occasional muffled voice. There was no further activity from Trahern's island.

Almost two full hourglasses had run when there was a shout from the masthead and word was passed that the landing party returned. Though it was far from his expectations, Ruark sighed

319

his relief at the news. By the grace of God he might survive it all yet.

That thought, however, was short-lived, and he braced himself for the worst as Harripen dashed down from the quarterdeck, drawing his cutlass as he came. Ruark eased considerably when he realized the man's blow was not for him but was, rather, a quick slash that severed his bonds and set him free. Quickly Ruark disentangled himself from the now limp strands as the pirate captain hurried back to the rail, throwing a comment over his shoulder.

" 'Twould seem ye've served us true, laddie. Our men come now."

The schooner was hailed by a whistle in the night, and soon the pirates were swarming aboard, hoisting with them bags and chests heavy with loot. Ruark seized upon the distraction and eased back into the shadows at the far side of the deck, waiting for a chance to dive overboard and swim ashore. He was slipping off his sandals to be free of them when a large, carved chest with an unusually ornate brass lock was sweated aboard. Apprehension raised its worrisome head as Ruark recognized it as the one which had sat below Georgiana's portrait in the manor house. It took six of the deck hands to sway the ponderous piece over the rail, and it settled to the deck with a thud that bespoke its weight. Ruark stepped nearer, cold dread beginning to build within him.

From the boats below, a muffled screech suddenly pierced the air, raising the hackles on the back of Ruark's neck. He waited tensely as the French half-breed, Pellier, climbed over the side of the ship and reached back to lift aboard a struggling form covered from top to knees by a heavy burlap sack that was firmly bound with cordage. Trim ankles and small, bare feet protruded from the bottom, with the trailings of a white garment twisting about shapely calves.

Ruark swore viciously under his breath and strode forward into the lantern's light as the bonds were loosened and the sack was snatched away. Then he found himself staring into the most enraged green eyes he had ever seen.

"You!" Shanna gasped. "You—blackguard!"

She seized a short oar from the railing and, before anyone

could move, swung it with all her strength at Ruark's head. He ducked easily, and the weapon splintered against the mast behind him. Shanna yelped, and the shaft fell from her numb hands. Fighting tears of pain, she could only glare her hatred.

"You damned witless fools!" Ruark roared, stopping Pellier's loud guffaws. "Do you not ken what you've done? This is Trahern's brat, and he'll be after you with a sail full of vengeance!"

"Aye, and I'll see he hangs you first!" Shanna railed. "Then I'll laugh when he feeds your foul carcass to the sharks!"

Before her blazing glower, Ruark bowed in mockery. He well knew the depth of their precarious situation. With only himself to worry about, escape would have been relatively simple, but to get them both away to safety would take careful planning.

Three other prisoners were pulled aboard, and Ruark recognized them as bondsmen. They were thrown roughly to the deck against the rail and lashed together there. They would continue to know slavery, Ruark surmised, but now beneath the ready whip of less than humane masters.

Ruark made a turn about Shanna, a careless swagger in his walk. He gave her a lusty perusal as if his mind held lewd thoughts. At the moment Pellier and Harripen were more interested in the material treasures which were being hauled aboard from the small boats and had left their lovely captive to be guarded by several of the men.

"You traitor," Shanna hissed as her eyes followed Ruark.

"No traitor, milady." His voice was low and reached her ears alone. "But a simple victim of fate and a woman's whimsy. I bend with the winds of chance and make the best of what they offer."

Shanna was furious. That she had even felt a tiny inkling of remorse for her actions was now bitter gall to swallow.

"You beggarly wretch of a knavish whoreson!" she sneered. "You bastardly rakish cur!"

Beneath the onslaught of her insults, Ruark laughed sardonically. Her robe hung open, forgotten in her plight, and the shortened batiste nightshift she wore underneath little impaired his wandering gaze. Ruark coud see that she was causing a stir among the crew, for they were beginning to come forth from different parts of the ship to better view this dazzling beauty whose hair tumbled in magnificent disarray around her shoulders and shimmered like gold in the lantern's glow. His task was laid out for him, to be sure.

Suddenly, Shanna felt Ruark's hand bold upon her breast, seizing her in a rough caress, and in choked outrage she flung it from her, snatching the dressing gown tightly about her narrow waist and belting it securely. She saw the challenge in his eyes and rose to it in a vengeful fury.

"This time you've betrayed my father," she gritted through clenched teeth. "And he'll hunt you down like the dog you are."

"Betrayed!" Ruark laughed caustically and continued in derision, "Nay, madam. I pray you consider. I but sought the favors of my own wife. 'Twas she who callously betrayed my trust—"

"You filthy guttersnipe! You gallivanting cock!" Livid with rage, Shanna flew at him and sought to claw the smirk from his handsome face, hating him with every fiber of her being. Snarling, Ruark caught her wrists and jerked her close, crushing her brutally against him. Shanna gasped in pain, feeling the terrifying strength of his lean, hard body and her own helplessness. Her ribs creaked beneath the strain, and breathing seemed futile. Though she mustered every bit of her energy, she could not escape and finally collapsed limply against him. Her tears trickled through thick lashes, and Ruark heard her mutter in bitter defiance:

"Hicks should have hanged you, and I wish he had!"

Cupping her lovely chin in his hand, Ruark forced it up until Shanna stared into those savage amber eyes. His dark face was rigid, and his words snapped into her like bolts from a crossbow.

"Little thanks to you, I have thus far survived this last bit of your treachery." His tongue gave his words added venom. "But if my luck holds, I'll see this matter to my advantage as well."

He pushed her into the bony hands of Gaitlier, Captain Pellier's wizened manservant.

"Hold the wench and keep her from mischief," Ruark commanded. He stepped to the rail and climbed onto the ratlines to peer toward the village.

"Pellier, give me your glass," he called after a moment. He received the instrument without delay and through it scanned the port. In the bright moonlight he could see the dark masts of a ship and barely discerned movement on it. He tossed the glass to the Frenchman. "They're already warping the *Hampstead* out. You will soon be feeling the cast of her guns."

Ruark had seen the carnage a broadside could wreak aboard a ship and knew it played no favorites. He could guess that Trahern's rage at this attack would be at its fullest, and he wondered yet how it had come to be. If the squire were aware that they had kidnapped his daughter, he would proceed with caution, but Ruark could not take the chance. The *Good Hound* bore two bow chasers and two stern chasers with several small falconettes on swivels along the rail. The small guns would be no match for the armed brig setting to the chase, but the schooner was trim and with her blackened sails could easily slip away.

Ruark stepped down from the rigging and faced the silent group. "Unless you fancy a long night's swim, my hearties, I suggest you get underway."

Harripen was more a man of decision than the others and bellowed, " 'E's bloody well right."

The Englishman set the seamen to action with a flurry of commands. "Get those boats aboard. Ahoy there, Pinch," he called to an elder seaman who mounted watch on the forecastle. "Hoist the bloody anchor. And, Barrow, set every inch of dark sail you can find."

Then he turned in a calmer manner to Pellier and grinned into the scowling, scarred face.

"Excuse me, Robby. 'Tis your ship. If ye'd care to set the course for Mare's Head, we'd be only too 'appy to be on our way."

The Frenchman took a mean swipe at one of the men who had gone ashore with him. "We could have gone unnoticed had you not let that other bitch escape the manor."

His victim squawked, stumbling backwards under the man's assault. " 'Tweren't me 'oo let that tongue-lashin' Scottish biddie go. It were Tully! She kicked him in his jewels and struck out fo' the village."

"I'll see him gelded," Pellier threatened, going aft.

Tully, a sparse man, peered after his captain doubtfully.

"Why, cap'n, if it weren't fer her," he called after Pellier, "we wouldna caught ye these three who come running at her call."

His words were ignored as the pirate captain set his crew into motion. Soon the dark schooner had a bone in her teeth and was racing away in the night. It was not until the square, white sail of the brig was lost on the horizon that the picaroons turned again to counting the booty. A weighty iron box was opened and was found to contain gold coins. This was hastily transferred to the captain's cabin, where it was stowed in a larger chest for division later. There were several huge bags of silver and gold plate to be valued and shared and a barrel of fragile porcelain carefully packed. The latter, of no value to the pirates, was marked for the mayor of Mare's Head for his tithe, as were some crates of finer wines and food. Then only the one large chest remained, and all held their breath, for this promised to be the greatest treasure.

Pellier leered and boasted loud. "The Trahern wench says this has a wealth no man can count."

Shanna stepped closer, a wry and twisted smile curving her soft lips. Ruark read her face and knew full well that mischief was brewing in her beautiful head. For the sake of caution he waited nearby, watching the proceedings but taking no part. A blow of an ax crushed the lock and freed the pawl. Pellier shouted and threw open the lid. His dark eyes gleamed at the tray filled with small leather pouches.

"Jewels!" he proclaimed. "We'll all be rich!"

Greedily he snatched a sample, pulled open the cord, spilled the contents in his hand, then stared in mute amazement, for he held no greater wealth than the trigger, lock assembly, and the butt plate of a musket. Frantically he rummaged through the bags and found only the hard clink of iron. He and Harripen lifted the heavy tray and pulled aside an oil skin to reveal beneath it tier upon tier of long, slim musket barrels stacked neatly in place upon notched wooden strips.

Harripen lifted one in bemusement and turned it in his hands. " 'Pon me saints," he remarked as he hefted one of the pouches. " 'Tis not but muskets—without butts even. Useless bloody muskets!"

Shanna could contain herself no longer and laughed in derisive glee. "Of course, you fools. What else?"

The sound of her mockery rose above their murmurs to ring against their pride, reducing it to shattered shards.

"And should you have the butts," she jeered, "you'd find them useless still, for you see the chest was dropped on the dock, and all the barrels are bent. My father kept them as a reminder of his one failure at profit. It always pricked him, but now I'm sure he'll find the memory of it tickles his wit."

Ruark groaned inwardly at her foolishness, recognizing that her words might well draw real blood before the hour was gone.

Pellier whirled on her with a curse. "But you swore it held a wealth no one could count."

"Of course," Shanna answered sweetly. "And does it not?" She tossed her head, sending her hair flying over her shoulder.

In a rage Pellier snatched Shanna's arm, cruelly twisting it until she cried out in pain and fell to her knees before him. Drawing a dagger from his boot, the Frenchman held it close in front of her eyes, which now betrayed a first hint of fear.

"Then I'll carve the price from your precious skin, bitch."

Suddenly Pellier found his wrist seized in a grip of iron. Slowly, against his will, the blade was raised away from Shanna until he stared into Ruark's softly smiling face.

"I know you are rash, my friend, but I think not foolishly so."

Pellier let Shanna sprawl to the deck. His free hand dipped quickly toward the pistol in his belt, but Ruark caught that arm as well. The half-breed struggled against Ruark, but his arms were held between them where none of the crew or captains could see the battle. The more Pellier tried to free himself the tighter the vise became until he could feel his hands growing numb. His eyes sought his captor's face and saw in it a strength and will he had until now doubted existed. It was born in the back of his muddled mind that he could not rest until this one who held him like a child was made to feed the fishes. Having no other choice, he ceased the useless fight, but the grip held where it was.

"Now I, for one, have great love for my neck and would not see it stretched upon the *Hampstead*'s spar," Ruark continued easily. "You have already tweaked Trahern's nose, but would you draw the full wrath of his vengeance on us all? There is also this to consider. The wealth you draw from her flesh will be meager indeed and done with all too soon, but her father treasures the wench as his only kin and will no doubt pay handsomely for her safe return."

Seeing some logic in this, Pellier relaxed in the tenacious grasp, and Ruark released him.

"Oui, you speak true," the half-breed grunted reluctantly, his hawkish eyes lowered to Shanna who, though bruised and shaken, let her gaze show contempt as it roamed his filthy person. With a sly leer he chuckled, "But 'twas Pellier who brought her here, eh? She will be mine 'til the ransom is full paid."

Shanna's breath caught sharply in her throat, as much in outrage as in shock, and she scrambled up, staring at him in horrified disgust. His lustful perusal pierced her meager garments, taking a path downward over her round bosom and gracefully curving hips. Shanna could not hold back a shudder of revulsion and clutched the thin robe higher about her neck. When she had seen Ruark aboard the ship, she had thought he had somehow planned her capture, whether for revenge or desire she could only guess. The idea, though it had angered her mightily, was at least remotely acceptable as her fate, and she reasoned it could be dealt with. Now a cold, sickening dread of what really lay in store for her began to make itself known. This swaggering brute, Pellier, could hardly have made himself more sickening to her eyes. He was a rank, filthy man with not the shallowest knowledge of decency. Given her choice between throwing herself overboard and submitting to him, she could only surmise she'd seek the former end without hesitation. Indeed, in the matter of choices, Ruark was her only refuge. But if he had betrayed her before, he might well again.

Ruark's manner was almost calm as he watched Pellier's eyes covetously survey and obviously savor that which he named his. A more observant man than the half-breed might have noticed the distinct hardening of Ruark's lean features, the tightening of his jaw, the coldness in his gaze—and taken a warning.

Deliberately Ruark caught Shanna's wrist and in spite of her resistance and attempts to snatch free, he pulled her before the pirate captain. He ignored the flashing green daggers that fair riddled him and with a finger under her chin, raised it beneath the lantern until Pellier could clearly see her fine and delicate beauty.

"This further caution I would give you, Captain Pellier. If you've eyes in your head, you might see this is a rare piece of considerable cost." Ruark's fingers softly stroked the fragile column of her pale throat. Beneath his light touch Shanna trembled, and he wondered what emotion betrayed her. "But the piece bruises easily with abuse and once returned, her vengeance might well be more costly than Trahern's own. This is his valued pet, and he'll see her will carried out. To be the treasure you seek, she must be tended carefully and kept against the day you've gotten her worth."

Ruark dropped his hand away from her, but not before he frowned a warning into Shanna's eyes. Then, with a casual salute to Pellier, he strode past her and made his way to the forecastle where he leaned upon the rail and watched the iridescent sea curling beneath the prow.

A puzzled frown troubling her brow, Shanna studied him covertly and wondered if this man who seemed to ever mark her life would be her champion or her end.

"Bind the wench!" Pellier bellowed.

Gaitlier scurried across the deck, catching Shanna's wrist, and dragged her along in his wake as she cast repeated glances over her shoulder at the lone figure by the rail.

Dawn had brushed the heavens in deep magenta before the sun, rising golden on the horizon, bleached it to a softer pink and sharply etched the detail of the craft in its gilded light. The morning bloomed into full day. The sky faded to a subdued blue, and the translucent aquamarine that rose and fell in a languid, heaving motion became the sea beneath it. Triangular sails billowed with the full breath of a brisk wind, and the schooner skimmed the waters like a gull in effortless flight.

Tied with the other prisoners to the pinrail at the base of the main mast, Shanna found little comfort. She dozed fitfully, rousing whenever footsteps paced near. Usually it was Pellier who came to stand above her, his legs braced apart and arms set akimbo. His dark face twisted in a malevolent grin as his black eyes bored into her. Shanna shivered in apprehension as she sensed in him a twisted, vengeful desire to see her writhing in agony while he had her in some perverted way.

Noon cast Shanna in the shade of the sails, protected at last from the glaring sun, but it had already brightened the pale, slim nose and brought a deeper flush to her cheeks. Her long, curling hair, lifting on the freshening zephyrs, swirled about her face and bosom, the ends entangling in their abandon.

Pellier's men paused often to stare at her with more than a longing glance, but they knew their captain and held a deep fear of him. His temper could rise without warning, and his skill with weapons had earned a healthy respect bordering on fear from them. Long ago they had learned to stay well away from the half-breed and that which belonged to him. It was only Gaitlier who brought her an ocassional bit of cheese or bread or a drink of water, and even these minor ministrations were wont to draw Pellier's disapproval.

Ruark kept his own vigil at a more distant spot, viewing Shanna through slitted eyelids while he appeared to slumber peacefully, his back braced against the rail, and his legs stretched out before him.

In the lengthening shadows of late afternoon, the schooner trimmed her sails and slipped cautiously along a string of small, swampy islands, little more than reefs choked with sand and crowded with cypress and occasional groups of palms. A dark, blood-red flag slashed with a black bar sinister was hoisted, and the ship passed a slightly larger island where, on a placid white beach, a single hut could be seen beneath an overhanging thatch of palms. A shiny surface reflected the light of the waning sun, and the signal was answered with waves from the pirates on the schooner. Shanna and the other hostages were loosed from their tethers and grouped together near the gangport. Ruark roused from where he catnapped near the prow and set his gaze toward the lay of the lands and reefs, carefully noting details.

When the *Good Hound* had cleared the end of the point, she was faced with an open stretch of shallow water spotted with breakers which signaled reefs and sandbars. Ahead of them lay a much larger island that sprouted a low hill overlooking a shallow, half-protected cove. A scattering of ramshackle huts could be seen on the shoulders of the higher ground. In the center and on the brow of the dune squatted a large, once whitewashed structure surrounded by a low stone wall which enclosed a barren courtyard. Behind the port and for several miles on either side, a mangrove swamp extended, which combined with the reefs and bars beyond the shoreline to provide a good half mile of protection from attack.

Harripen joined Ruark by the rail and leaned beside him. The whole side of the Englishman's face seemed to compress in a weird smirk as he squinted his eye at the younger man.

"Well, me lad, ye see our haven. Mare's 'Ead she be. What do ye think of 'er?"

He observed Ruark closely, but he only shrugged noncommittally. "Appears safe enough."

"Aye, 'at ye can say." Harripen's arm stretched out toward a spot where the broken ribs of a ship rose amid the shoals. "Ye see 'at 'ere wreck? 'Twas part of a Spanish fleet what tried to warp a galleon through the shallows near enough to bombard our town, but the currents at 'igh tide are strong and treacherous." He chuckled heartily and grated a hand across the heavy, coarse bristles darkening his scarred chin. "After the ship hung up 'ere, we floated a raft with a single gun into range and chewed 'er to bits."

Ruark noted the man's obvious relish of the event but pointed out, "If a determined man covered his ship with another and went carefully, he could succeed, and other ships could stand off and intercept anyone trying to escape. You'd be trapped in there."

"Aye, lad." Harripen laughed briefly. "And so 'twould seem. But 'tis only fair to say, the wisest rat sees to 'is hole 'fore 'e builds the nest."

Ruark peered at the pirate with a cocked brow.

Harripen gave a secretive chuckle. "Just in case the dogs try to dig 'im out."

Ruark led him on. " 'Twould be a crafty rat to get from here unscathed."

The Englishman was eager to explain. "As long as ere's a ship to sail, we've a way out, lad. 'Ere's a channel through the swamp and no reefs on the other side. The Spaniards cut it through." He stared at Ruark for a moment as the younger man accepted this silently. Then he warned, "But a man must know the way, and Mother keeps it well hidden."

With that, the hoary buccaneer turned away and busied himself with preparations to debark, leaving Ruark to stare after him, his curiosity much aroused.

A crowd had gathered on the white sand beach, outcasts from the world trapped in this backwater way of life with little hope beyond the meanest existence. Indeed, the town could not sustain itself and survived only by servicing the corsair fleet. Vendors came with their baskets, hawking their wares, hoping the warriors would feel largess with their victory and share some of the spoils for a new bauble or a trinket. Gaudy, unwashed harlots sought any favorable glance, the bolder ones calling invitations to the crew while they revealed plump bosoms and round thighs or sauntered with cocked hips and arms akimbo. The children, few that they were, bore the vacant stares of hopelessness or the savage leers of minds already twisted into the mold of malice and greed. Running sores and scars marked the beggars and bespoke the merciless deprivation suffered on the island. They were the fortunate ones. The unfortunate were those who had been dealt a deep wound in battle or had an arm or leg severed and were dying slow and agonizing deaths in this hellish hole. These poor wretches, whose maimed, misshapen bodies wore a grimace of pain permanently on their faces, and women who were worn and abused until they looked like hags of some horrific tale stood back in mute surrender while their counterparts who still sustained a meager vigor crowded close in hopes of catching some coin, some treasure, some rejected morsel, some sharing of whatever was to be shared. Crewmen tossed coppers from the ship and guffawed as scrawny youngsters and grown men splashed into the shallows for such wealth.

Shanna's stomach tightened and wrenched with the cruelty of it all. She had always considered herself worldly, well traveled and educated, but nothing she had seen or read had prepared her for this. A twinkling began to dawn of just why her father had so desperately desired to secure his loved ones from poverty. In the tormented faces of the children, she glimpsed her father's despair as a youth, and something stirred deep within her consciousness, trying to surface into realization, but Shanna was too tired, too exhausted to think.

A questioning murmur rose from the bondsmen who stood near her. This place frightened them as much as it did her, and they cursed their luck to have been captured. They could expect no more than slavery here and were quick to recognize their own plight would scarce be better than that of Trahern's daughter. As Shanna raised her gaze to them, uncertainty written heavily on her face, they quieted their grumbles. One man swore and faced away while another remarked hoarsely:

"Bloody savages they be. The devil's own. God save us all."

Shanna sagged wearily, setting her back to them. She knew they voiced her own apprehension. Awkwardly she brushed a wayward tress from her cheek with her bound hands. She was numb to every emotion save a gnawing fear that feasted heartily upon what courage she tried to muster. She set her mind not to appear frightened, yet her knees had a strange tendency to shake beneath her, and an uncontrollable shivering made tatters of her resolve. Just when she had won some semblance of composure, her chin quivered and the sting of tears smarted in her eyes. Despite her show of self-control, however strained, she was terribly afraid, not knowing what lay in store for her, but convinced now that the miscreants planned some hideous fate for the daughter of Trahern. The constant stares of the pirates and their bold leers when they caught her eye unnerved her considerably. Bruised and hungry, exhausted from lack of sleep, she was listless and dazed. Her head ached from the merciless sun which beat down upon her.

Disconcertedly, Shanna moved her gaze to Ruark. He stood near the fore of the ship watching as the vessel worked her way toward the crude jetty that formed a landing dock. His dark hair was stirred by the light breeze, and his broad, tanned shoulders gleamed with a fine mist of sweat. He seemed like a stranger, a man she had never known, distant, frowning as if his cares weighed upon him sorely. She felt a rising bitterness that he had trifled with her so casually, yet she also recognized the folly of the anger that had caused her to have him cast away. Had she only cooled her need for immediate revenge, she could have made him pay a thousandfold for his indiscretion. Now she had only herself to blame and must admit that he had ample cause to seek redress upon her person.

Fear pricked her consciousness that Ruark would be willing to see her demeaned and abused at every hand, and the surety of such was beginning to loom monstrously large in her future. Her already depleted strength would little deter Pellier's assault when he chose to launch it. But it was best not to dwell on the degradations that would precede the final one, and Shanna fought the despair that threatened to reduce her to a whimpering, sobbing wretch.

As his entire fortune was on his person, there was little to occupy Ruark. He was glad he had not doffed the breeches before Pitney's visit or he might well have been more exposed to the air. Though the pirate captains had promised him a share of the loot for his assistance, he was not bent to believe that Pellier had accepted his interference with Shanna kindly. Considering the halfbreed's possessive attention, she would need much in the way of protection. Still, Ruark thought, if he appeared anxious to defend her, it would arouse suspicions against him. He must gain some degree of trust, or at least some sort of respect, from the picaroons, or escape would be doubly difficult. On the other hand, he could not abide anyone mauling his wife, and he knew if they pricked Shanna's defense, she could well flay anyone's pride with her tongue and might bring odious penalties upon herself.

"It may well be that I shall have to fight the whole lot of them," he mused wryly. "And for that selfsame wench who will not accept my protection, thinking I took my ease with another. But I am set in any event to choose the course that will take us both clear of this hellish place, whether she will have aught of me or not."

For a space Ruark stared down into the sparkling blue-green sea and thought how much it resembled those eyes that had led him to this corner of the universe and still beckoned with the promise of a reward beyond his ken.

The schooner slid against the dock, and when the ropes were secured to the quay, Harripen strode across the deck, clapping his hands as he loudly called, "A wager for the first wench tossed on 'er back, me 'earties. Which do ye say? A sovereign on Carmelita."

A sharp grunt came from the stern. "Have ye no eyes in yer bloomin' head, mate? The Trahern wench I'll put me wager on. 'Twould take me not but a thrice count to roll her on her arse and give 'er me all."

"Aye," a derisive snort answered. "And should ye beat Robby for a turn on her, ye'll find his sticker in yer back."

Shanna remained motionless, giving no outward sign that she was affected by their crudity, but inwardly she quailed, and her mind recoiled. Her night had been unpleasant enough, but she realized it was only her potential value as a hostage that had kept her from an even more unpleasant one in the captain's cabin or the crew's quarters, if not both. For that small respite, at least, she had Ruark to thank.

Ruark gave little attention to the banter. He accepted the men's talk as just that, at least for the time being. As long as Pellier was alive, Ruark was well aware from where the real threat came. Warily he watched the Frenchman approach Shanna and began to saunter forward as the man placed a long leather thong about the slim column of her throat. Then suddenly, without warning, Ruark found his own way blocked by the broad, hairy chest of Pellier's apelike mate and three of the hands he had seen warping the ship in. Ruark elbowed one aside to force his way, but with a wide grin drawn back from uneven, gapping teeth, the mate moved to stand before him, and over his brawny shoulder Ruark caught Pellier's evil smile directed briefly toward him.

"Well, man," the huge mate leered. "If ya're to be one of us, let's see how ya fare at tidying up a ship."

The gangplank touched the dock, and the corsair captain began to move toward the open way. In that moment a cold, chilling fear washed through Shanna, and her eyes turned a last desperate plea toward her only hope, Ruark. She saw him standing with several crewmen, and he made no move to come to her. His frown deepened even as she looked, but he seemed willing to surrender her to this pig of a pirate.

"So much for his high ideals and wedding vows," Shanna thought bitterly.

His lack of action stung her to the quick. Their eyes met, and, threatened with a rush of moisture in her own, Shanna lifted her chin with a defiant gesture of dismissal. Then the leash tightened about her neck, and she was jerked stumbling along in Pellier's wake.

Shanna was paraded behind the pirate captains as part of the booty which was carted after her, the only exception being the large chest; it was left where it sat on the deck of the schooner. Her wrists were bound before her, and her long hair tumbled in wild disarray about her shoulders, half masking her face from the curious eyes of the waiting townspeople. The sting of ire she felt at being so crudely displayed was sharp, though it gave her cause to remember Ruark being hauled aboard the *Marguerite* in chains.

Some of the strumpets poked grimy fingers at her and tugged cruelly at her golden hair. Shanna bristled angrily and snatched away, but this show of temper only aggravated their pestering. Viciously they began to pinch her limbs and buttocks, calling coarse insults, many of which Shanna could only just grasp the meaning of.

By the time she emerged from the press of bodies and snatching hands, Shanna was much the worse for wear. Her appearance no longer bore any resemblance to a highborn lady. Her dressing gown was torn, the remains of a sleeve hung in shreds from her shoulder, and her bare feet were bruised by the pebbles and blistered by the hot sand. Still, she walked with the unbowed dignity of a Trahern and allowed wrath to mask her pain and trepidation.

A sigh of relief almost escaped her when she was urged on no more. Wearily she lifted her gaze to the large, whitewashed structure before her. A broad veranda stretched across the front, and a gaudy figurehead carved in the likeness of a heavy-bosomed mermaid hung from a post above their heads. The place was badly worn and shabby, in desperate need of repair, but Shanna had already guessed that most who lived here were hardly more than parasites doing as little as possible in the way of work and honest labor.

Beneath the coyly smiling nymph, a monstrously huge man, every bit as tall as Pitney and half again as wide, called a greeting to the victors. His bald pate glistened with sweat above long sideburns which were braided into queues with bright ribbons adorning the ends of each.

"So, ye scurvy swine!" his oddly tenor voice rang. "Ye've gone

to Trahern's isle like ye said ye would, and I see ye return whole."
He giggled in glee as he surveyed the crates and chests they unloaded onto the veranda. "And ye've even brought back some
baggage."

A quick pull on her tether, and Shanna was yanked before the
enormous man and there made to stand while he rudely evaluated
her. She shivered in disgust as the man cupped her chin in a hamlike hand then turned her head from side to side, inspecting her
much as one might a steed.

"A pretty filly, to be sure, though Trahern left me little enough
to appreciate her with. But why bring her here?" he questioned
his cohorts.

Pellier grinned slyly. "This is the plum of Trahern's orchard,
Mother, his own daughter. She'll bring us all a fine lot of coins."

"Aye, if we live long enough to enjoy them," Harripen
snorted.

" 'Tis impossible for him to get a big enough ship through the
reefs without going aground. We're safe enough here," Pellier
argued.

The giant pursed his lips and let his gaze scan the horizon, seeming to grow nervous.

"H'it'll set Trahern on edge, to be sure," he half mused in a
worried tone. Then he gestured toward the prisoners who huddled behind Shanna and mumbled, "We may need extra hands if
Trahern decides to make himself felt. Bring the wench inside,
hearties, and we'll have us a mug."

The sun rested on the horizon, and night would soon spread its
velvet cloak of darkness over the island. As she was led inside
Shanna threw a glance behind her, but she saw no sign of Ruark.
Resentfully she wondered if he had already found some wench
on the dock to fill his time.

A short stairway led down to a tavern room where lanterns
were lit to ward off the coming shroud of night. The large, flat
stones beneath her feet were cool and a welcome relief from the
burning sand. Pellier crossed the long, dark room, yanking her
along with him, and he joined Mother at a long table. A fist crashing down on the wooden planks startled Shanna as their host
bellowed for ale. Immediately two women appeared and from
barrels lining the wall filled immense tankards. Harripen caressed

the bovine breast of one and grinned into her face.

"Carmelita, ye're as pretty as ever, me lovely. Care for a toss?"

A voice chortled loudly from the rear of the common room. "He bet on ya, Carmelita. And he's trying to win the wager."

With a fling of her dark head and a wanton smile, Carmelita roughly pushed a mug into the Englishman's groping hand, sloshing a share of the contents over his breeches.

"That should cool yer loins 'til me work is done, ye lusting rogue. I'll bed whom I please, and 'tis not likely to be you, you scrawny gander."

Loud guffaws sounded around the table until Harripen glared his fellows down. Eager to demonstrate his own prowess with women, Pellier threw an arm about Shanna's waist and sought to snatch her to him for a quick kiss and a long-awaited fondle. In violent reflex Shanna swung out with her round hands clenched into fists, intending only to hold the stinking, sweaty body away from her. The blow struck him just beneath the ribs. Startled and gasping for breath, the half-breed stumbled back. As he fought for balance, one foot waving precariously, Shanna saw her chance. She caught her toe behind his heel and kicked hard. Pellier spun about then dusted a full six feet of the floor as he slammed down upon it.

The smaller of the serving women, a plain, drab thing with a listless manner, who had stepped near to fill Pellier's tankard, gaped in horror. Shanna began to realize the danger of what she had done. The mirth of the corsairs shook the rafters, and it dawned upon her that she had embarrassed Pellier before all the others—to her a well-deserved deed but one quite likely to bring her end.

Harripen snickered. "Hey, Robby, get up. Ye'll do no good down there alone. Ye forgot the wench."

The Frenchman's dignity was sorely bruised, not to mention his backside where he had struck the floor. His eyes were shot with blood, his face scarlet with rage as he came to his feet, glowering at Shanna. The words sounded choked in his throat.

"You high-flown bitch, I'll teach you to be a proper doxy who'll come when she's called."

Savagely he snatched the leather thong, nearly jerking Shanna off her feet and raising a welt where the rawhide strip sawed at her throat. Half dragging her after him, he strode across the room until they reached a large, open hole in the floor. Pellier drew a blade from the top of his boot and to her amazement slashed her bonds, setting her free of both her collar and wristlets. Shanna frowned at him inquiringly, but smirking, he kicked a ladder into the hole and gestured for her to descend.

"Unless of course you wish my assistance," he sneered and reached for her, but Shanna avoided his grasp and obeyed. She climbed down into the dark, rank pit and then raised her gaze in wonder at what was expected of her. The ladder was pulled away, and she saw Pellier reach over into the shadows near the wall. A heavy, iron-barred grating crashed down to cover the hole. In some bewilderment Shanna glanced around her. A checkered pattern of light from above filtered down, and she realized she stood on the top of a pile of rubble beneath the opening. Did Pellier intend to frighten her with isolation and darkness? The idea was ludicrous, of course, when she was more terrified of his loathsome attentions.

A skittering in the dark chilled Shanna's confidence like a flood of icy water. A squeak near her pierced the quiet, and she glanced down as a large rat ran across her feet. Her shriek brought guffaws of glee from Pellier. Anxiously Shanna strained upward to reach the grating, but the pirate wheeled a weighty barrel onto the grill to preclude her moving it. A scurrying came behind her, and Shanna whirled to see several of the gray furry beasts crouching on the edge of the light. Their eyes gleamed oddly red and evilly bright as if they contemplated her end. Gasping, Shanna scrambled away from them further down the slope of the debris—anywhere to be away from them.

The odious stench of the pit choked her and brought her close to retching. Shanna could only guess what the pirates used it for. The small, red-eyed furries grew bolder. A half dozen or more now sat watching her, creeping nearer whenever she glanced away. Shanna retreated another step, and her foot went ankle deep in the slime. A rat scurried toward her, and stifling a scream, Shanna kicked at it, sending it squeaking back to the pack. More rodents slithered from the darkness until their number had doubled. They began to move forward in a body. A shuddering sob escaped Shanna as she splashed backwards until she stood knee deep in the foul water. A sardonic laugh came from above, and a crust of bread and pieces of meat fell through the grating.

"Here, milady," Pellier's voice mocked. "Here's your supper!" He snickered wickedly. "That is, if you can save any from your greedy little friends. And here's something to quench your thirst, milady." His humor was high as he poured ale through the cover, drizzling it over the squeaking, fighting rats now tearing at the food he had tossed. "Don't be lonesome for me. Your friends will keep you company 'til I'm ready for you."

His footsteps faded from her small world, and Shanna, conscious of her own ravenous hunger, stared mutely at the greedy rodents. The droplets of moisture glittering as they fell made her throat dry. The fetid stink of offal caused her to cough. The rats, now searching eagerly for any last morsel, turned as one to stare at her. Something bumped her leg, and Shanna reached down, closing her hand over a piece of wood. It was firm and real, which little else around her seemed to be. Her hunger gnawed at her belly, her thirst burned in her throat, her fatigue eroded her will, her fear undermined her resolve.

She was afraid she might dissolve to tears at any moment and plead to be taken from this pit of hell. Even as she faced the scurrying animals, she imagined she felt small, wiggling things between her toes or something slither now and then against her leg.

The rats tested the edge of the water but were reluctant to enter. Then one bolder than the rest leaped in and began to swim toward her. Shanna stilled her quaking and waited tensely, raising the board. A moment more! With a sob she brought the wood down edgewise upon the furry thing, and after a brief, frenzied splashing, Shanna saw no more of it. Warily, the others backed away to a safer distance to consider her, their red eyes twinkling as if they whispered among themselves and plotted against her.

A violent shaking possessed Shanna, and even her defeat of the rat could not buoy her spirit. If only there were a spot, dry and safe, to which she could escape. The board sagged in her hands. The rats grew still and watched her with a malevolent alertness. She wanted to sob but knew what greater disaster awaited her if she weakened. She was so tired! So hungry! So thirsty! So faint!

Evil eyes stared at her from the darkness, creeping closer.

"Someone help me!" her mind screamed. "Anyone! Ruark!"

Chapter 16

OVER the mate's shoulder Ruark had watched Pellier lead Shanna across the gangplank and down into the milling throng until she disappeared from his sight. Then he returned his attention to the four who crowded before him.

"I have more important things to occupy me than sweeping any deck," he stated bluntly.

"Gor, love the likes of him," the mate guffawed. " 'E wants to start at the top, 'e does. Well, man," the beady eyes narrowed, "to be a captain ya 'as to 'ave a ship and then ya 'as to be the best man o' the crew. Oi've little enough to recommend of ya. Ya've done naught but eat our food and drink our ale."

Slowly Ruark backed away until he felt the rail behind him. His foot struck a bucket of sand kept handy for small fires. His hand found a pinrail where the long, oaken belaying pins were stored. The pirates wore no pistols but, with obvious relish, fingered the hilts of the cutlasses thrust into their belts. Ruark could only surmise that Pellier had left orders that would negate the share of the loot which was promised him. A quick end, the halfbreed no doubt expected, but this colonial had other plans.

His eyes fell on the half-open door to the captain's cabin, and Ruark remembered a stack of arms he had seen there when they had questioned him. Casually he leaned against the rail and stared back at the men. He had played much the part of a yearling calf with these men, hoping they might relax their vigil of him. He should have considered they were jackals and would readily devour the helpless.

Ruark almost smiled. "Let's see what the jackals will do when they face a man instead."

Seeing naught to be gained by waiting any longer, Ruark bent and with a swift movement hurled the bucket of sand into their faces, sharing it liberally with the four of them. As the men stumbled back, cursing and rubbing sand from their eyes, he quickly snatched a pin from the rack and laid it alongside the head of the nearest. He bent another over with a hard jab beneath the ribs and parried the wild swing of the mate who had freed his cutlass. Coming to blows with the sword, the belaying pin was nearly sheared in two. Its continuing service as a weapon was badly in doubt, and Ruark hurled it into the face of the fourth man, who ducked to avoid it and collided with the mate. His respite won, Ruark ran for the cabin and slammed the door behind him as several bodies thudded against it on the opposite side. He threw the bolt and spent the few moments he had gained in search of a weapon. He cast aside an ornate dress sword and laid his hand upon the worn hilt of a long, curved sabre. He drew the piece from its sheath, and the naked blade winked blue in the dim light as if sharing a pun with him. Though sturdy, its balance was such that it scarcely weighed anything in his grip.

Stepping back to the door, Ruark timed the heavy blows that bowed its panels. Then, in the pause between, loosed the latch and waited. The door crashed open, and the weight of the men carried them forward headlong into the cabin. Ruark kicked the rear of the last one through, and the hapless man sailed heels over head into the sprawling cluster. The mate gained his feet and with a bellow of rage charged, lashing out with his cutlass. The heavy blade turned on the sabre's edge and smashed into an iron-bound trunk. The long, curved sabre returned with the speed of a cobra to lay open the mate's shoulder and the front of his jacket as he stumbled back.

His arm hung useless, and the mate gaped down at his chest where a thin, red line began to ooze droplets of blood. The other men gathered behind their helpless leader as if his body would shield them from the weaving, threatening blade. One of them hesitantly raised his cutlass, and Ruark smashed it aside, running the sharp edge of his blade along the man's forearm where it left a trail of red, welling from its path. The poor chap screamed as if his heart had been torn from him. This was no unarmed clod who would plead for mercy, as they had been told, but a live, fighting man determined not to yield his person without a struggle.

The smallest of the four men decided bravery had had its day; running across the cabin, he hurled himself against the stern windows. Alas, the thick glass and heavy frames had been made to withstand the force of towering seas, and he recoiled onto the floor where he rolled moaning, bleeding from the head and holding his shoulder. Another had the foresight to free the latch and swing the panes outward before he took his leave. His success led his companions in his wake. The mate cleared the transom with an agility amazing for one of his years, and as Ruark neared him, the man on the floor saw the wisdom of a hasty retreat. He, too, cleared the transom and took to the water, striking out for shore with one arm thrashing the surface.

Ruark leaned out the windows to assure their hasty departure and saw a long, dark shape pass under the stern of the ship. A tall fin cleaved the surface a moment later, and the bellow of the mate announced that he had also sighted the shark. As was befitting, he passed his men to lead them ashore, and soon they had all disappeared into the swamp, leaving only four wet trails across the beach to mark their passing.

Ruark now surveyed the cabin with less urgency, though the need to follow after Shanna made him hasten his selections. He found a pair of fine pistols on the captain's desk and checked the load and priming. He marveled at the snug way they tucked into his waistband. A broad brim, low-crowned hat of woven straw was made with a skill of workmanship that rivaled Trahern's headgear. Its fit justified his confiscating it. He added a sleeveless leather jerkin and borrowed a clay pipe and pouch of tobacco from a shelf. The sheath from the sabre was hung on a sash over his shoulder, and, thus equipped, Ruark went out onto the deck and made his way along the jetty to the shore. He had not seen which way the captains and their party had passed but guessed the white structure, being the largest one about, would be their quarters.

Along the path, through a jumble of lesser dwellings, Ruark found himself the object of many stares, though none moved to stop him. The looks were bolder from some of the women, who paused where they stood and watched him pass, posturing for his benefit and then frowning as he gave them no heed. He cleared the town, and at last paused before the inn and gazed up toward the figurehead swinging gently from its bracket. From within came the noise of boisterous merrymaking. Pellier's loud bellow called for more ale, and Ruark stepped within, keeping to the shadows.

The bedlam assailed him. The odors of sweaty, filthy bodies crowded together in the common room mingled with the aromas of strong ale and a pig roasting on the open hearth. It was Mother who set down an empty mug and waited in silence while the din continued around him. When the giant spoke, directing his gaze toward a dark corner, angry murmurings rose around him, and many hands reached for weapons.

"Come have a draught with us," Mother beckoned. "And tell me why you lurk in the gloom."

Pellier slammed his cup down and stared in surprise as Ruark strode from the shadows and accepted the proffered mug of ale. Leisurely Ruark quenched his thirst, letting them await his pleasure, then sighed as he lowered the tankard. His gaze passed about the room, touching on the waiting faces. Then he grinned casually and shrugged.

" 'Tis no fault of mine that I'm here, but 'tis still somewhat by choice. It seems there is a matter of a small debt which these gentlemen owe me." He swept his hand to indicate the captains, "I would not be so pressing on the subject, sirs," he apologized with mockery, "but as you know I am penniless, and it seems that even here there is little that is free."

Ruark noted that many eyes went to the sabre and the pistols whose butts were close to his hands.

"Bah!" Pellier sneered. "Give him a copper or two and throw him out."

"A copper is it?" Ruark snorted. "You must have promised that much to your mate. He did you a copper's worth or less." His own sneer was evident. "I have never seen a man so born to water as that one." He directed his statements to the others. "I was promised a full captain's share, if you remember, and I can forgive the attempt to gain even that. Still, had I not warned you, you would have sailed directly into the muzzles of Trahern's cannon," Ruark reminded them boldly. "They could have sunk you with the sheer weight of lead long before you neared the village."

"He's right," one of the lesser captains grudgingly admitted. "He did tell us the truth of it."

"And had you landed out of sight as I suggested," Ruark continued easily, "you might have reached the village and returned with something of real worth."

This last was not the complete truth, for he had been to the lookout hill himself and knew the entire coastline was visible from there.

"Ah lads!" Harripen broke in. "I 'aven't the stomach for this bickering." He snatched a small bag of coins from his sash and tossed it to Ruark. " 'Ere, bondsman, find a wench to amuse yerself. When the gold is weighed, ye'll 'ave a full share."

Hefting the pouch, Ruark guessed it not an untidy sum. He nodded his thanks, but Pellier snorted in disgust and returned to his cup.

At the word bondsman, Mother had turned a more attentive perusal to the newcomer and now leaned forward. "Bondsman, you say?" His eyes gleamed in the dim lantern's light. "Were you in bondage to Trahern?"

"Aye," Ruark replied. " 'Twas a choice of a hangman's noose or bondage, so I was shipped from England to Los Camellos." He braced a shoulder against a solid, rough-hewn post and openly studied the men seated around the table. "There is also another score I'd like to settle, but time enough for that."

Mother chortled and saluted him with his mug. "We've a tie between us then. I was a bondsman of Trahern's many years ago. The lass were but a tot at her father's knee." He swilled more of the ale then mused aloud, "I fought a man in a fair fight, I did, and killed him. Trahern said I 'ad to do his work as well as me own 'til the man's debt was paid." He sank back in his chair and beneath bushy brows, glowered darkly. "I tried to escape, and they caught me. Spread me on a hatch cover for the whip as an example. The field master was happy at his work, and when he had bloodied me back well enough, he bloodied my chest and struck lower."

Mother emptied the mug and threw it across the tavern, shattering it against the wall.

"He made me a bloody eunuch!" His fist crashed down to emphasize the last word. Then he slid low in his chair and his neck disappeared in folds of fat. His eyes glowed, tiny and feral, deep in their sockets. He chortled, almost as if to himself. "But he won't get hold of me again. No he won't."

Harripen rose to stretch his legs and nudged Ruark with his elbow in passing, nodding toward the enormous man.

"That's our dear Mother," he grinned. "He takes care o' the town 'ere, sort of lord mayor as it be."

Ruark contemplated the eunuch who was blubbering in a fresh cup. Mother was not what he had expected, but he made no comment as to that. He had seen many men in his travels, but these brigands would have made the poor wretches in Newgate seem like mild-mannered children. Mother and Harripen acted friendly enough for the thieves they were, but he had no doubt that if their way of life were threatened, they would turn on an enemy with the ferocity of wolves.

Ruark's eyes roamed further. No sign of Shanna and the other captives. But with Pellier present she could not be in too great a danger. Still, it would have eased his mind considerably to know her whereabouts.

Pellier snorted and came to his feet. "Bah! This ale sours my gut." He caught the arm of the shy young woman who served his fellow captains, making her crouch away in sudden fear. "You doltish slut, fetch us meat and better wines."

The girl nodded quickly and skittered off to do his bidding. Pellier leered after her, taking his seat again, and rubbed his hands together in anticipation. Heaping trenchers of pork and fowl were brought, and Carmelita delivered him a flagon of wine, placing several others around the table. As she offered one to Ruark, she leaned against him and smiled seductively into his carefully blank face. She pranced off and returned with a tray of fine crystal goblets. Giving him one, she brushed hard against him, and for a moment her hand dipped brazenly beneath his belt to fondle him.

"Gor, she's after ye, lad!" Harripen roared and watched her swinging hips as she paraded off to distribute the glasses. "But mind yer ways, lad. She has a temper, that one."

Ruark declined comment but decided she was one person to avoid in Shanna's presence. The woman could have almost made two of Shanna. A full skirt was hitched up to show her bare feet, and a loose blouse clung precariously to one shoulder, the other sleeve drooping down her arm. As he had already observed, she wore nothing beneath it, and her dark-nippled breasts swayed ponderously with each movement. Her hair was raven black, her skin dark. There was a Spanish look about her, though her speech was flavored more like Harripen's. She was comely enough for a man who wanted an easy toss.

A scowl had blackened Pellier's face as he witnessed Carmelita's provocative invitation to the bondsman. It was an affront to the half-breed's pride that she had never displayed such eagerness for him—and another reason to hate the bondsman. Carmelita set the glasses down beside him, and Pellier lowered his plate abruptly to seize her, snatching her onto his lap and roughly caressing her heavy breasts.

"Come, Carmelita," he crooned. "Share a bit of that with an old friend."

Driving her heel into his instep, she whirled away from him. A ringing slap cracked through the room. In stunned surprise, Pellier gaped at her.

"Old friend, hah!" she jeered. "You come to my door and beat it with your fist. Boom! Boom! Boom!" She stood with feet spread, shaking a fist as she raged at him. "You tell me of all the duels you've fought and all the men you've killed, and then you fall asleep drunk." She laughed at his reddened face and deep scowl then dangled a hand limply toward the others. "He is like the little octopus who catches a big fish and doesn't know what to do with it. Huh!"

She hurled this last insult to the Frenchman over her shoulder then came to take an open bottle from Ruark's hand and pour the wine for him before placing a choice piece of meat in his mouth.

An odd noise came from Pellier, and Ruark turned to stare in amazement. The half-breed had seized an entire joint of pork and was ravenously ripping the meat from it, stuffing the pieces into his mouth with his fingers until his eyes seemed almost to bulge. He chewed open-mouthed until he could wash it clear with a gulp of wine and then repeated the procedure. Disbelief crept into Ruark's expression as the man shoved three ripe plantains into his mouth and swallowed without chewing.

Harripen sneered. " 'E's a bastard from St. Domingue, 'alf French, 'alf Indian. 'E tried to pass 'imself off as gentry 'ere, but as ye can guess 'is table manners gave 'im away." After a moment Harripen continued in derision. "As bloody crude as Robby is with 'is food, 'e's a bit o' a wizard with 'at fancy shiv 'e wears. 'Tis a fact we're all aware of. 'At's why 'e's here. 'E speared too many o' the young Frenchmen in St. Domingue with it. The frogs would stretch 'is neck on a dozen counts. And if the truth were known, three times the dozen is more like it." The Englishman sipped an ale and eyed Ruark. " 'E also dislikes anyone 'andsome and young enough to challenge 'is rights with the women." Then Harripen chuckled. "Aye, we've some odd ones 'ere, and this is the cream of our little colony. Wait 'til ye see the rest."

Ruark decided he had the patience to wait a lifetime for that. Right now all in the world he wanted was to know where these scum had put Shanna. He sampled the wine, a heavy Italian red, and briefly wondered from what cargo ship it had been taken. Without turning, he directed a question to Harripen.

"How do you settle differences here? If there is an argument over a piece that two claim, how is it decided which one gets it?"

Harripen laughed with a grunt. "A duel, me friend. And if h'it's to the death, winner takes all. 'At's why Pellier is the richest among us. 'E's killed the most."

Ruark nodded. That was all he wanted to know. He stretched lazily, like an unhurried cat, then hung a leg over the back of a chair, bracing his arm across it as he peered at the pirates one at a time until they became uneasy beneath his expectant scrutiny. When the tension had blossomed to an accepetable level, he broke the silence.

"Well, hearties, you dawdle over your cups while good time slips away."

347

Even Pellier stopped and stared questioningly at him.

"How long will you give Trahern to hunt you down?"

There were puzzled mumbles and much shifting of eyes, for they found his inquiry rankling and confusing.

"I mean," Ruark explained slowly, casually waving a hand, "would it not seem wise to send word that you have Trahern's daughter and that she is safe? Perhaps even the ransom should be made known. Let's see." He rubbed his arm with a fist thoughtfully. "She should be worth perhaps—fifty thousand pounds." He had caught their imaginations, and eyes brightened all around the table. "That would be enough to see any one of you to a good life of ease—after, of course, say a tithe is paid for Mother's haven and mayhap a thousand or so for myself." These men could understand greed, in fact would be suspicious of a man who did not expect his share. Still he hastened to add, "My own part would be small as I only showed you the way in, and it was your own boldness and bravery that caught her." He paused and watched them while he seemed to ponder.

"I know Trahern though," he stated cautiously. "He will be after you with all sails set, and he will be difficult to bargain with when you're looking down his guns."

Though Pellier had turned his shoulder and pretended not to hear, the others listened carefully.

"If some of your prisoners wish to return, why not send them back with the word." There was a general murmur of approval, and Ruark continued innocently. "Where are the men? Let me question them."

Before the others could say nay, the large mulatto captain crossed to the back of the room, threw a bar from a thick oak door, and pulled it open.

"Out here, ya gutless swine," he snarled within and stood aside.

There was a scrambling, and the three men who had been taken with Shanna came out to stand blinking at the light. They crouched together, fearful of their fates. Ruark gave no pause but strode boldly across to them and inspected each.

Then he turned and braced his feet wide, put hands on his hips and demanded, "And where's the wench?"

Pellier snorted. " 'Od's blood! Now you'll see! He wants to

see the little tart's body again. 'Twas his game all along."

Angry growls came from the group, but Ruark's voice snapped like a whip.

"Aye, fool."

Pellier drew taut in his chair at the insult.

"Will you send these to Trahern to tell him they know not if she is alive. Where's the wench?"

"Where the bitch'll learn to be a proper slave," Pellier roared. "And 'tis no concern of yours."

"My need is my concern." Ruark's tone was acid. "When Trahern learns we have her and that she's alive and unharmed, we're safe but not until then. If he has a doubt, he'll level this place and take the chance."

The half-breed threw a foot onto the table and leaned back to sneer at Ruark. "You're the fool if you think I'll let you run this island."

Ruark's eyes narrowed dangerously. He was about to challenge the man openly when there came a splash and a muffled shriek. In that same moment Ruark saw his opponent's glance flicker to the grating whereon sat a huge barrel. Ruark cursed as he ran across the room.

"You twice-damned maniac!"

His face contorted by a snarl, his lips drawn back from gnashing teeth, Ruark kicked the barrel, sending it crashing to the floor where it rolled crazily until it reached the wall.

"You'll see us all hang for your want of a night's play!" he flung viciously.

His pistol was out and quieted any thoughts of interference as it wandered over the group. No one appeared anxious to stop him. Indeed, Harripen eyed Pellier and appeared to gloat in anticipation of some bloodletting. As if it was a gaming table, Ruark snatched the grating up and flung it aside. At his intrusion a scurrying and chittering came from below, then silence. Keeping a wary eye on the pirates, Ruark called down.

"Milady?"

A splash in the water and Shanna sprawled across the pile of rubble. A muffled groan of pain escaped her as she rolled over, and he could see her pale face in the dim light, pinched and drawn, twisted with fear. Her eyes sprang wide as she recognized him, and she scrambled to her feet, sobbing his name. A violent curse came from Ruark, and his angry gaze scornfully raked those at the table, most promisingly Pellier. There would be some payment for this, he vowed.

Dropping to a knee and resting the pistol against the edge of the hole, Ruark reached down a hand to hers which were raised in silent supplication. Shanna seized his wrist with both hands in a panicked grip of desperation, and Ruark knew it would have taken a bar of steel to pry her fingers loose. Lifting her as if she were of thistledown, he set her to her feet on the stone floor. Trembling she clung to him, sobbing softly against his chest. Then she saw the leering faces of the pirates as they watched her, and she resolutely pushed herself away from Ruark to stand on her own feet. However, the effort was too much for her quaking limbs, and, like a puppet whose strings had been suddenly severed, she crumpled weakly to the floor. Her muffled weeping burned through Ruark's mind. He would not be satisfied until he tasted revenge.

"You see?" Pellier laughed jeeringly. "She has already lost much of her Trahern ways."

The pistol in Ruark's hand came around quickly, its single black eye settling on the corsair captain where it stared unblinkingly for a long, long moment. Beneath the cyclopean threat, even that brave fellow froze, and the gloating grin faded from his scarred face.

The cold fire in Ruark's eyes bespoke the fury churning within him. He held himself in tight rein until the rage cooled. What was left was a gnawing wish to see Pellier at the end of his sabre. This was no man, but a rabid beast with a warped mind who had abused the wife of a Beauchamp!

"I see the simplest of plans escapes you," Ruark taunted. "Is your reasoning, then, so shallow that you cannot see a valuable piece must be guarded with care?"

Pellier scorned the words and would heed no argument. "Step aside, knave. I would see how the Trahern bitch has fared."

Shanna raised her head and favored the pirate with a glare of hatred that would have shriveled the swamp to dry sand.

Moving away a mere step, Ruark permitted the man a glimpse of the disheveled beauty but directed an appeal to the rest of them. " 'Tis sure Trahern will pay the ransom, but when he sees his daughter thus, do you doubt he will find a way to see you all hunted to the ground?"

The picaroons stared at him but carefully gave no hint of agreement. The danger of drawing Pellier's wrath to them was a surety of the present. All else was in the future and thus doubtful.

Pellier rose and hitched up his breeches. "Methinks the lady needs more of the pit."

"Ruark!" Shanna's whimper came choked with fright, and she clutched his leg frantically, pressing close against him.

"Why, milady," Pellier mocked. "Did your quarters disagree with you?" He stepped a few paces nearer but then paused as if to muse. "Mayhap the linens were not as fresh as you like." His voice deepened to a rasping snarl. "Or mayhap your little friends are more a comfort to you than the likes of us." Then he roared, "Back to your dungeon, slut!"

With his command he charged forward to seize Shanna, but she flung herself behind Ruark and several spaces beyond. It may have been that Pellier simply did not believe that another man would dare interfere with him. Whatever the cause, he ignored Ruark, and that was his downfall. He never saw the foot that was thrust out in front of him as he passed Ruark. Nevertheless, he again tested the sturdiness of the stone floor, this time with his face.

An almost deathly silence gripped the room; those who watched held their breaths in anticipation of what they knew would come. Pellier rolled over, spitting dirt from his mouth, and his dark, glaring eyes settled on Ruark. Casually the colonial caught the back of a chair and spun it about to place his foot on the seat. Leaning forward and resting an elbow on his knee, he shook his head and chided lightly.

"You learn so very slowly, my friend. I have more claim to the wench than you. 'Twas I who watched her strut about while I sweated for her father. 'Twas I who guided you onto the island. And were it not for me, you'd be feeding the fish at the bottom of Trahern's harbor."

Pellier's glower shifted to Shanna, who sidled back to Ruark's side, taking refuge there. Deliberately Pellier rose and dusted himself off. He was oddly calm now and there was an air of deadliness about him.

"You've touched me twice, bondsman," he commented arrogantly.

"The more to instruct you with, my good man." Ruark's words lashed Pellier's pride raw in spite of their softness. "In good time I might teach you to respect your betters."

"You have hindered me from the first," Pellier sneered, struggling to keep his temper in check. "You're a swine! A colonial swine! And I never have had any use for colonials."

Ruark shrugged the insult off and stated simply, "The wench is mine."

"*The Trahern bitch is mine!*" Pellier bellowed, losing all restraint. This was too much! He could allow no further erosion of his position if he were to maintain dominance over the other pirates.

He lunged forward, hoping to catch his tormentor off guard, but the chair slammed painfully into his shins. Then he found his shirtfront gathered in Ruark's fist, and his toes brushed the floor as he was nearly lifted clear of it. An open hand struck the side of his face and returned to slap the other side.

Ruark shook the dazed pirate until the man's eyes stopped dancing. "I believe the slap is a challenge," he informed Pellier, loud enough for all to hear. "The choice of weapons is yours."

Ruark shoved and let go. Pellier staggered backward to crash into the table, sprawling helplessly across it before rolling into his own chair. Red-faced, he drew himself to his feet, straightening his jacket with a jerk. A calculating gleam grew in his eyes as he considered the weapons at hand, and he began to relish the thought of the bondsman sprawled lifeless in a heap. The pistols hung on the back of his chair, ready and tempting, but he had heard much of the marksmanship of the colonials.

"You have a blade, pig," he growled. "Do you know how to use it?" He had killed too many with the sword to doubt his own skill.

Ruark nodded and, setting the chair against the wall, guided Shanna to it. He drew his pistols and, cocking them both, laid them atop a keg, well within her reach. For a moment he gazed down at her. Shanna ached to say some gentle word at what might be her last chance, but there was still a bitterness towards him that sealed her lips. She could not meet his eyes.

Carmelita leaned against the door to the back room, her eyes eager for the bloodletting. Behind her huddled the thin girl, no emotion on her face, carefully keeping her place. The other pirates settled themselves for the show as the table was pushed back and a large space cleared for the duel. Money changed hands as wagers were made. Only Mother abstained. He studied the young man closely.

Ruark took the sheath from the sash and held it in his hand. A loose, swinging scabbard had been the death of many a good man and it was, itself, a weapon of sorts. As he drew the sabre, its long length gleamed pale blue, and he was glad he had taken the time to select a fine weapon. He swished the blade through the air; its balance was superb; the edge was keen.

Ruark's eyes caught Harripen's as the man exchanged gold pieces with the Dutchman.

"Sorry, me lad," the Englishman laughed with a shrug. "But I must recoup me losses. The purse you have goes to the winner as does all the loser's possessions."

The grizzled man completed his wager with gusto. It was only Shanna who was dismayed by the forthcoming event. Her gaze followed Ruark's every movement. Within her wearied mind a thousand thoughts clashed in riotous confusion. This man who made ready to defend her was the same one she had lain with in passion and cast away in anger. Her ire seemed only a memory of another day, unreal and irrational now with her anxieties for him.

Pellier's own light épée was no match for the sabre, so he snatched up a cutlass that hung with his pistols on the back of his chair. It was a broad, heavy piece, shorter by inches than the sabre Ruark held.

"A man's weapon!" he sneered. "One made for killing. To the death, bondsman!"

Leaping away from the table, he plunged into immediate attack. His rush was vicious and intense, but Ruark fell into a comfortable stance and parried each thrust easily. For too long he had been forced to depend on the decisions of others for his survival, but now he could rely on his own skill. Come what may, at least once more in his life he was nobody's man but his own. He cut and thrust and now began to swing the blade into attack. Feeling out his opponent, he was aware that he faced no neophyte. Pellier was determined and adept, but as their blades met again and again, Ruark began to sense the lack of finesse in the other man's arm. He gave a quick quartet of attacks, and a small gap appeared in Pellier's jacket as if by magic. The man fell back in surprise.

The cutlass was a weapon for killing, but it was also weighty and cheaply made. The edge nicked, caught, and hung again and again on the fine steel of the sabre. The victory was not going to be as swift as Pellier had expected. This was no farm-reared colonial he fought! The effort of swinging the unbalanced cutlass began to tell, and when it caught, he had to jerk it free to parry the continual ripostes.

Seeing an opening, Ruark reached deep and low on the outside, drawing blood from Pellier's shoulder. A shallow cut, but he drew back, prepared to give quarter. Pellier's challenge was not an idle threat. He followed, swinging the heavy cutlass with both hands. Shanna cringed in trembling fear, expecting to see Ruark sliced through, but he braced the back of the sabre with the scabbard and took the blow full, edge to edge. The fine steel held. For a moment the two men stood nose to nose, the swords crossed above their heads as every muscle strained. Pellier quickly retreated, and Ruark jumped back to escape a wicked slash to his belly. He riposted, and Pellier barely recovered in time to parry.

Now the battle became wearying. The swords met repeatedly in heavy-handed blows. Pellier thrust and as Ruark parried, a wide nick in the cutlass blade caught on the curved back of the sabre. The thick, soft blade was turned sideways, and, already weakened, it snapped as Pellier fought to free it. In surprise he stumbled back several paces and stared at the empty hilt. Dropping the useless thing, he spread his hands as if in defeat. It would have been murder to charge him through, and Ruark nodded and began to sheath his sabre.

Shanna's scream alerted him. His head snapped up as Pellier's hand came clear of his boot top, clutching a long stiletto. Pellier raised his arm to hurl it. Ruark was too far away to strike, but he swung the sabre, sending the scabbard sailing to strike full across the pirate's face. Pellier cursed and stumbled again, and his knife clattered to the floor. The Frenchman caught himself, faced Ruark, and read his gaze.

A slim rapier was quickly handed to him, and Pellier defended himself with all the skill he could muster. Ruark no longer smiled or enjoyed the game. He understood the rules. To the death! His attack was relentless. Ruark could smash through the light defense, but he would then leave himself open, unable to match the speed of recovery with the heavier sabre. His sword flashed blue fire, ever touching Pellier's. Ruark could give no room to allow Pellier a thrusting attack. He pressed his own. His visage was stern, and he began to feel the effort in his arm, but still he gave no relief. Now a slash opened the front of Pellier's shirt. Another thrust caught his thigh and dark red blood stained his trousers. Ruark's riposte took him under the arm. For the barest moment the point of the rapier dipped, and the sabre hummed with the force of the blow. Pellier fell backwards, taking Ruark's weapon with him. His body arched once against the floor, then lay still.

Ruark's face was dark as he glanced around to meet the astonished and gaping stares of the brigands. None challenged him further. After a moment he retrieved the sabre and wiped it clean on Pellier's short jacket. Sheathing it, he rested its end on the floor and then leaned on the hilt as he faced the others again. He looked to Mother who still sat in his strange hunched posture.

"A fine weapon," Ruark stated. "It has served me well."

Mother nodded. "I wonder if you realize the rest of it."

Ruark shrugged, noncommittal, and hung the scabbard again on his sash. Harripen rose and came around the table to clasp Ruark's shoulder.

"A foin fight, lad! And ye've gained a bit for it. The *Good Hound* be yours, of course, and all of Robby's goods, his share of the booty and"—he turned and surveyed his companions—"What do ye say, me buckoes? Do ye think 'e's earned it?"

Ribald laughter and a hearty chorus of "Ayes" answered the Englishman.

"A fittin' justice!" shouted Mother. Bracing his meaty fists on the table before him, he rose to his feet. "Trahern's slave shall have his daughter!"

" 'Tis done then!" Harripen announced. "Ye'll 'ave the girl 'til the ransom is settled."

New tankards of ale were brought, and Ruark laughed, his own tension easing. A toast was shouted for his victory while Pellier's body was unceremoniously hauled out. No one seemed sorry at his going, least of all Shanna, who sat with her hands covering her face, quietly sobbing out of her absolute relief. She could not disguise her gratitude, and, when Ruark returned to her side to fetch his pistols, she managed a brief, trembling smile before tears came flooding back.

Boldly Ruark strode across to the other three captives and demanded, "Which of you has a mind to stay?"

None answered him as they glanced sheepishly at each other, no one willing to take the fore and declare his desire.

"So! You prefer slavery to freedom here," Ruark loudly surmised then demanded, "Should we let you go, will you witness to the squire that his daughter is safe and shall be held as hostage to his payment of ransom?"

The three bobbed their heads in eager agreement, drawing a derisive snort from Mother.

"Fools they be to trade this for Trahern's yoke."

"We'll send them out on the sloop come the morrow's dawn," Harripen offered. " 'Til then, let the poor lads 'ave a bit to fill their bellies. And by me saints, the wench, too! She'll need it if she's to ride beneath this bucko."

Shanna favored the man with a glare, but she gratefully accepted a plate when the thin girl brought it. In the midst of the revelry, she was intent upon satisfying her hunger. She mostly ignored the coarse scurrility that she and Ruark had become the subject of. Harripen found a bolt of bright red silk and with his dirk sliced off a long length of it. With much fanfare and ceremony he and the Dutchman formed a loop in one end of the silk and placed it about Shanna's neck. With suggestive leers they led her to Ruark and bestowed the other end in his hand, declaring her bondage to him. Playing the game, Ruark held it high that all might see. Then with a fiendish, wild laugh he crushed her against his chest and forced a savage kiss upon her lips. His hand boldly stroked her buttock, wandering upward, while Shanna squirmed in mute protest of this public fondling. Her face burned in outrage as he held her in a steellike hold until he snatched her up and tossed her over his shoulder, jolting the breath from her. His hearty slap on her rump brought a shriek of rage from Shanna and loud guffaws from the men.

Following Harripen's directions, Ruark carried her up the stairs and to the quarters Pellier had of late relinquished. The Dutchman held open the door, and Ruark swung Shanna from his shoulder, setting her to her feet. His hand upon her backside, he thrust her into the room. His companions made as if to follow, but Ruark stopped between the sills, blocking the way and daring them with mocking gaze until each in turn lowered his eyes and turned away with a mutter of disappointment. When they had gone, Ruark closed the portal, dropped the heavy bar in place, and leaned against it in great relief.

In the dark void of the chamber, Shanna stood where she had stopped, reluctant to go further lest she come upon some nightmare worse than her dungeon below. Her nostrils were assailed by the fetid stench that pervaded the place, an unwelcome reminder of the pit. Half in panic she groped for Ruark, needing the reassurance of his strength to carry her through a bit longer, just until she could see what she faced. His hard fingers folded securely around hers, squeezing gently as his other arm came around her shoulders. The monstrous fears, which crowded close in about her, reluctantly retreated to a bearable distance, leaving her drained, her limbs heavy with exhaustion. She sagged weakly in the protective circle of Ruark's arms.

"Pellier's sty," he commented in disdain, choking on a deep breath. "Let me find a candle. Perhaps 'tis not half so bad to the eyes as the odor indicates." He felt her sway against him. "Will you sit?"

Shanna shuddered. "I dare not until I know what's here."

"Aye," Ruark agreed ruefully. "I fear there is something dead on Mare's Head and we've found it."

After locating a stub of candle, Ruark emptied the priming from one of his pistols and, placing a bit of lint in its place, snapped the lock until a weak spark glowed in the pan. Blowing it aflame, he touched it to the wick. A soft, dim glow spread over the chamber as the candle flickered then blazed.

The room was a shambles of discarded clothes, empty bottles, and assorted sea chests and wooden barrels, looted no doubt from unwary merchants. A massive, ornately carved, four-poster bed seemed to float on a sea of trash. Several layers of fat feather ticks were stacked beneath a covering of stained linens, while ragged and filthy netting hung askew from the canopy frame. The foot of the bed was hidden by heaps of cast-off clothing. A tall armoire gaped open with garments of various silks and satins, rich coats and gowns, carelessly draped over its sagging doors. No chair was empty; all were piled with assorted debris. Heavy red velvet drapes, dusty and worn with age, covered the windows. A huge porcelain bathtub bore the remains of empty flasks, bottles, and flagons which had been tossed in that general direction. Shanna's bare feet had narrowly missed treading upon a jagged piece of glass. Several mirrors stood about the room, all facing the bed. A chamber pot appeared much the villain in the way of odors.

Shanna gagged and whirled away from the sight of it while Ruark took more positive action. He snatched back the drapes, flung open the shutters to let the ocean breezes sweep the room, and tossed the menace out the window to the courtyard below. Crusted blankets and linens from the bed followed its descent, and soon a tall pile of Pellier's clothing—distinguishable mainly by the sour smell—began to form beneath the window. Bottles from the tub shattered against the stones below; anything else that would threaten their comfort left the room. Ruark swept his arm across the wooden planks of the table, sending the dried scraps of many meals flying into a sheet which he had yanked from the bed. He bundled it with other filth and sailed it through the window. Though the air still offended the senses, it was at last rendered fit to breathe. Ruark blew into the depths of a pitcher which sat on the washstand and was greeted by choking dust.

" 'Twould seem Pellier had an aversion to bathing," he remarked with a snort of derision.

Shanna gave a repulsive shudder as she picked the cloying, stained folds of her own garb from her body. She yearned for a bath and the soft comfort of a clean bed for her tired and drooping body. Ruark contemplated her and was sympathetic to her plight, but there seemed to be an almost waiting silence in the common room below. He came to stand close before her, and, as she lifted her gaze, he made his request.

"Scream."

Shanna's eyes searched his face without understanding.

"Scream. And loudly," he commanded firmly.

But with a mute frown Shanna only stared at him.

Almost leisurely Ruark reached out his hands and locked them in the soft fabrics covering her bosom and with an easy twist, split the robe and flimsy gown full length, flinging them wide so that she stood openly displayed to his rapidly warming perusal.

Now, giving vent to all the pent-up rage, fears and frustrations, Shanna complied with a piercing shriek that trembled the mirrors. She paused only to draw breath and then raised her voice again. This time Ruark stepped close and cut it short with his hand across her mouth. In the quiet that followed, they heard the gale of loud laughter that filtered up from the common room below.

Ruark folded her in his arms, crushing her naked breasts against his leather jerkin, and Shanna felt the chuckle deep in his chest.

"That should give them something to think about for a while."

But some of Shanna's spirit had revived. Angrily she snatched away from him.

"Take your hands off me!" she sneered. She moved to put the bed between them and struggled to close the shreds of the dressing gown around her in a late burst of modesty. "Find some simple little tramp if you want to play, but I'll not be the waiting wife in your game."

The muscles in Ruark's jaw worked tensely, but he held to a stubborn silence, not giving credence to her accusations by arguing his innocence.

"You play the stud so well," she raved, warming to her subject. She gave him a slow, contemptuous perusal and trembled with her rage and fatigue. "So strong, so virile, so very talented in bed. Do you think I will twiddle my thumbs while you lay every bed-minded trollop who'll take a tumble with you?"

Ruark gave voice to his own frustration. "What in the sweet, loving hell do you prattle about?" He aired his injured pride. "I sit and watch you with your audience of men and bite my tongue to keep from shouting that you're mine!"

"*Yours!*" Shanna stared incredulously and took a step toward him. "Do you think me your slave?" She snatched the red silk from her throat and trod upon it in a high temper. "So much for your slave's collar, Mister Beauchamp. You do not own me."

"Must I abide the sight of lecherous hands upon you and say naught?" he retorted, shrugging the vest from his shoulders and throwing it across the room. "By damn, woman! You *are* mine! My *wife!*"

His statement seemed to inflame Shanna. "*I am not your wife! I am a widow!* And I no longer wish to be encumbered by your wandering lust!"

"My wandering lust!" Ruark laughed caustically. "Madam, I have watched you swing your hips through a knot of men and lead them amincing after you, frothing in anticipation. Aye, you must feel a need to stand amid your stable of rutting consorts and find it too difficult to limit your attention to your husband."

Shanna's jaw dropped, but she quickly recovered with a low shriek. "You accuse *me* when you roam the hills like a horny goat and bed each willing wench?"

Her eyes raked him again, and the torment came to her, knowing he had welcomed other women into his arms while he used her like any common wench he could find in a brothel. She had been humiliated, and she wanted to hurt him. She struck out in defense and blurted, half in hysteria, "Why can't I be free of you? Is there no end to your persistence?"

The amber eyes snapped. "You tried well enough! But good Pitney's simple soul has no mind for murder. So here I am to play your game once more. I killed a man in your behalf, but do you thank me? Hell and gone! You'd see me run through as well if not for your fear that the others would take you."

"You're a devil!" she half sobbed. "A spawn of Satan sent to torture me!"

"Nay, Shanna!" His tone cracked sharp. His own ire brought penetrating golden lights to his eyes as he caught her by the shoulders, none too gently. She stared full into his face, seeing the rage there, and her own abated in the face of it. Ruark shook her angrily.

"Nay, Shanna, 'tis only I, that one who has twice felt the bite of your betrayal! Your husband, well and rightly vowed, whom you would diligently set away—not kindly by the law, but with my blood upon your hands!"

Shanna's exhausted mind could not bear this attack from Ruark, and it brought her trembling to the brink of collapse. Her eyes grew wild, and she gave a mewling moan as she struggled against his grip. Mouthing a curse, Ruark shook her hard until her teeth clicked and her eyes regained some sign of sanity.

"You will be my slave," he gritted with deliberation.

Shanna opened her mouth, but he shook the denial from her. "You will be my slave when there are others about. You will obey me. You will be meek and loving for the benefit of those oafish knaves." He tossed his head toward the door before continuing more harshly. "And if you disobey me, I will treat you like a disobedient slave. Do you understand?" He shook her again but more gently. "You will be my slave as long as we're here."

Shanna stared at him blankly as he waited for an answer, and in the silence of the room, the timid knock on the door echoed loudly. Ruark threw a glare over his shoulder at the offending portal, angry with the interruption, then turned and faced Shanna again. Her head rolled listlessly against her shoulder, and she had not the strength to stand but sagged in his restraining hands, oblivious to her open gown. Some of Ruark's rage fled and with gentle care he placed her in a chair, where she sat unmoving, her hands folded, like one stricken of mind. Ruark covered her nakedness with a light quilt before he strode to the door.

Snatching the sabre from its sheath, he lifted the bolt and threw the portal wide. The man Gaitlier stood before it, straining beneath the weight of two wooden buckets filled with water. Under Ruark's glare, the man shrank away and was quick to offer explanation, staring at him over a pair of square, wire-rimmed glasses.

"Sir—ah—I was Captain Pellier's man, and now they tell me you are my master. Ah, captain, I brought water. Maybe you'll be liking a bath?" he asked gingerly, his gaze flitting toward Shanna, now asleep in the chair. Brusquely Ruark gestured him in, and the man hastened to comply. Ruark watched him narrowly, lowering his sabre and leaning on it.

"How come you to be a pirate's man?" he inquired. "You speak like an educated man."

Gaitlier paused and cast him a glance, somewhat hesitant to answer. "I was a schoolmaster in St. Domingue. I taught Captain Pellier in his youth, though I warrant not very much. Several years ago I was on my way to England in a small ship when it was taken by him." He stopped and rubbed his hands in a nervous gesture. "It was his pleasure, Captain Ruark, to make me his slave." He nodded toward Shanna. "There are others like her, brought against their will and forced to stay." Gaitlier heaved a sigh. "Will there be something more you wish tonight, sir?"

Ruark gestured about the room. "Perhaps on the morrow you can find time to clean this chamber. The place is hardly fit for a man, and the lady most certainly is not conditioned to live in a sty."

"Very well, sir. I'll see it freshened and scrubbed for you. And if you need some woman's chores done, sir, for a copper or two the lass Dora will be glad to oblige." At Ruark's questioning look, he explained. "The wee lass in the common room, sir."

Once Gaitlier was gone, Ruark turned his attention to the bed. Pellier had indulged his creature comforts well enough. He threw two more of the filthy ticks out the window before he found one that seemed clean enough. He took fresh linens from a chest and spread them across the bed, smoothing them out as best he could. His early training had not extended to the proper laying of a bed.

Finally he brought a bucket to sit at Shanna's feet and carefully removed the quilt and sodden garments, tossing the latter out the window. Dipping a cloth in the tepid water, he lifted Shanna's face and wiped it clean, taking tender care not to unduly chafe the sun-pinkened cheeks. As he washed her hands and arms, his jaw tightened at the red welts around her wrists and the bruises that bespoke cruel pinches and blows from her captors. At least he had sent one of those to a well-earned end.

Placing her slender feet into the bucket, he washed the caked mire from the slender calves and thighs then patted them dry. For a brief moment he let his gaze wander over her in a longing caress. Though she had been roughly used, her beauty still held a piquancy that stirred his heart. As he considered her tangled hair, he frowned slightly, but there was little he could do for that now. Gathering her up in his arms, he carried her to the bed and covered her with a sheet. Then, for a long space, he stood staring down at her, a scowl furrowing his brow.

" 'Tis a sad thing, my love, that you choose to take a lie as truth without question. Believe me, I have not betrayed you."

It was almost as if she heard him, for her face softened and she rolled to her side, cuddling beneath the sheet, and in her slumber seemed more restfully content.

Placing a large chair in front of the door, Ruark set his pistols on a table beside it and slid around a small stool to rest his feet on. Taking a seat, he rested the sabre on his knees, relaxed, and sought his own rest.

✥ Chapter 17 ✥

WAKING came with a brightness that seemed almost painful. Shanna's mind became slowly aware of the disturbing glare. Light filled the entire room, and though she lay with her back to the windows, it still intruded, shining through her closed eyelids, penetrating into her brain. She retreated beneath the pillow, hugging it close over her head, to sink again in the outer fringes of slumber. She stirred sleepily as a hand began to caress the small of her back, kneading away the stiffness that she sensed more than actually felt. Lazily she stretched like a sleek, contented feline and rolled onto her stomach to let the strong fingers better do their work. A throaty moan came from her as she arched her back against the gentle massaging, letting it soothe her aches and pains. The hand plied her back and the soft muscles across her shoulders, sending waves of weakening pleasure up and down her spine. Languidly she rolled toward the source of her enjoyment until her back pressed against a hard, furry chest. Her head lolled upon the strong-muscled shoulder, and she rubbed her cheek against the smooth, warm skin. Then her mind tripped into full awareness. Only one person in her whole lifetime had ever shared a bed with her, and no one, not even Hergus, had rubbed her back. Her eyes came open, and all memory flooded back as she stared into Ruark's smiling golden eyes.

"Oooohh!" The groan escaped her as she fell forward on her stomach and snatched the pillow over her head again, pressing it tightly to her ears. Still, she heard the gentle voice with a hint of laughter behind it.

"Good morning, madam. I trust your sleep has agreed with you."

"Never before," she railed with muffled disappointment, "has heaven turned so quickly to hell!"

"Reality, madam," Ruark mocked lightly. "And a poor reality at that. 'Twould seem we've adopted the local ways, as I note the sun is high and the noon hour is near. I fear we've slept the morning away, and as much as my poor, bereaved body cries out for yours close beside it, I must bid you rise lest our dastardly antagonist steal a march on us and set the whole day awry."

Shanna snatched the covers from her head and gasped, realizing that she lay completely exposed to his gaze. Even more humiliating was the fact that he had apparently undressed her and put her to bed. Giving a moan of despair, she caught the sheet beneath her and rolled to bring its protective cover over her, but she came to an abrupt halt, once more against Ruark's chest. He reclined on his side, head propped casually on his hand, pinning beneath his body the greater portion of the sheet. As his eyes played with hers, glowing devilishly, his arm curled warmly about her, and his hand stroked her bare back.

"Why, Shanna, love," he crooned. " 'Tis a dread late hour of the morn for wifely passion, yet I would not dare turn you away."

His lips began to lower to hers. A soft breast was crushed against his lean, hard chest, their thighs were caught together, and Shanna became abruptly aware that he was more than willing, and most certainly ready, to make the hour later still.

She scrambled away from him, surrendering the sheet to whatever purpose he might make of it. It was easier to contend with her own nakedness than with his amorousness. She rose from the bed and sought cover, aware that she must garb herself or face the prospect of rape. Ruark indulged himself in a leisured observation of her flight across the room.

Hastily Shanna snatched up and donned Ruark's leather jerkin, which offered at least some protection—it reached to her knees. Generally large, there were no fastenings above the slim, belted waist of the garment or any below.

Slowly Ruark grinned as his look ranged over her, halting momentarily upon the full, ripe curves showing between the lapels. He rose from the bed, strode naked across to the chair beside her to fetch his short breeches, causing Shanna to glare at him in suspicion.

"I truly admire the garment on you, madam," he commented. "And I really don't mind sharing my possessions with you, but I suggest more discretion among the pirates. Without warning, you might find yourself tossed upon your lovely backside by some horny knave."

Shanna's eyes flickered down him and carried the implication.

"Excluding myself, of course, madam."

Shanna rolled her eyes disbelievingly. "Are you sure that day will ever come, sir, when you will resist the urge to tumble me?"

"Not even when I'm fourscore and six, madam," he reassured her lightly. "With you near me I would need the frigid north seas to cool my blood."

"True," she nodded. "And so 'tis with every wench you meet."

Ruark straightened and peered at her in open question of her insult. "Every? Lord, woman, allow me some discrimination."

Shanna's small chin raised a notch. "You could have had more, but it doesn't matter now. 'Tis over between us."

"So, 'tis torture you have planned for me." He stood beside her, hands resting low on his hips, his breeches trailing in a casual grasp on his fingers. "Madam, the sight of you naked in my bed makes my loins ache. The sight of you in my clothes makes my loins ache. Just thinking of you makes my loins ache. Madam, if you do not relent soon, I shall spend the rest of my days in a stoop like an old man bent with age. Do you have no mercy? You're a wench, Shanna Beauchamp, a hussy to so parade yourself"—he stalked about her and slapped the rounded tail of his jerkin heartily—"when you have forsworn that very thing you strut about."

He seized his breeches in both hands and slipped them on while Shanna laughed at him.

" 'Tis a simple mind, my lord and master, that bends the meekest movement to a strut. Indeed, of strutting I have much to learn from you." She clamped the straw hat on her head and struck a posture, one knee forward and a hand braced upon her hip. "The Pirate Captain Ruark, conqueror of all he sees, be it maiden, budding child-girl or heavy-breasted harlot. Pray tell me, sir, have your conquests so burned your brain that you ignore the twist of words which brings our fate to this? You prattle of oaths and pledges, bargains fully made. And what of you, good sir? Have you a special standard where you hold yourself to no single pledge?"

"Shanna, love." Ruark checked the priming in both pistols and laid them down again. "You have oft declared that I am no husband and that you are widowed full and true."

"If that be the case," he leaned close and spoke into her face with almost a snarl on his lips, "then, my love, what claim do you have on me? Why do you defame me loudly for this supposed taking of another? You gave me naught to say, no simple chance of denial, but set your hound on me. All that goes beyond that day, my love, must rest upon your pretty head, for had I not been cast asea by your anger, none of this would have come to pass. A crew of men would have been at your house thus to protect it, and close at hand another score or more to raise arms and set these curs upon their heels. Now what say you, my lovely? Am I your husband? Or am I free? And if the last it be, then why should you at every turn set upon me like a jealous vixen on her mate? Do I stray from you? Or am I some toy pulled along on a string meant to perform when milady would turn and play, but ever on the string?"

Shanna's anger subsided, and she tried vainly to replace it with reason. " 'Tis not the wedding vows I claim. 'Tis the other that any woman hates, to be trifled with, to be taken to bed and there warmly plied with love and devotion then brought to listen as another woman lays honors to that selfsame love and warmth. How can I lie with you, tender and loving in your arms, when I know that others have of late been there like me and that others in times coming will usurp my place and with their pleasures make a common thing of that which I would treasure?"

"Now there's a word." Ruark strode the full length of the

room and returned to stand before her. " 'Tis my first sight of something worth the keeping. A treasure? Aye, so 'tis, my love. A thing of value, but cheapened if not valued. And now I have it from your lips. A treasure." He nodded. "Aye, I have a need to hear that word from you."

He went to the window, there to stand staring thoughtfully out across the island. In confusion Shanna frowned at his back. She had meant to prick his pride but somehow had given him a weapon to use against her.

She made use of his averted attention and crossed to the armoire, shrugging out of the jerkin and kicking it free as it fell to her ankles. She snatched a black velvet gown from the door, slipped it over her head and with a quick wiggle, settled it in place upon her body. The deep front gaped open to her navel with a crisscrossing of laces across her bare skin. The fabric barely held the rosier hue of her breasts in its confines. Shanna worked the laces tight as she moved to stand before the nearest mirror, and there she stopped, her breath catching in a gasp as she viewed herself. The gown did more to destroy her modesty than protect it.

She saw of her image a somewhat disheveled maid with wildly tossed hair tumbling over her back and shoulder and, with breasts pressed together, forming such a vale as to entice the sternest miser. The velvet gown would not close, coyly showing the white of her belly. Shanna glanced back to the armoire, wondering what she had overlooked in her haste to don the dress. There had to be something more to the garment. A blouse? A shift?

Wrinkling her nose in aggravation, she turned slowly before the mirror and over her shoulder caught sight of Ruark. He no longer watched the breezes, but, instead, yielded her his full attention. A wicked grin lifted a corner of his handsome mouth as he sat on the edge of the window, arms folded across his naked chest, silent but deeply appreciative.

"This cannot be all there is to the thing," she said in some perplexity. "There must be more."

Leaving his perch, Ruark came to stride behind her musingly, rubbing his chin thoughtfully as he contemplated her reflection. In a casual tone he finally commented as he looked pointedly toward the overflowing bosom, "There doesn't seem to be much room for anything else."

"There should be at least a shift," Shanna argued.

Ruark went to stand beside the mirror to ponder the matter, gazing at her directly. He nodded. "Harripen should like it. The Dutchman too, I think."

"Ruark!" She stared at him in horror that he might make her wear this below, but suddenly she saw the laughter twinkling in his eyes. In impatient exasperation she stamped her foot, setting her hands on her hips, letting go the ends of the lacing. Ruark choked on his breath as her splendorous beauty nearly burst forth. As he stepped forward, Shanna cast him a challenging glare, struggling with the strings in an effort to cover herself.

"Madam." Ruark's voice was strained, strangely tight. "I have never cast my coin for a lady's bed nor exerted my will beyond a tender lass's power to resist." His stare was fastened on the swelling curves, which seemed so eager to be out. He heaved a slightly tremulous sigh. "But on occasion there comes a point in a man's life when he is greatly beset and tempted beyond his will." At her raised and questioning brows, he stated himself more bluntly. "Madam, rape does have its rewards, even if they be one-sided. And if I'm brought to this brink, do you think yon pirates will hold themselves in check? I suggest you find a gown that would not entice them overmuch and in the course of such, spare me as well from thoughts of violence."

Petulantly Shanna went to search through the sea chests, discarding garment after garment; none would suffice. It seemed when the size was right, the cut was overbold, and when the style was right, the size was large enough to boggle the mind with the immensity of its wearer.

It was a treasure near the bottom of a large trunk which caught her eye, and she could barely suppress her glee as she examined it. How a Puritan garment found its way into a pirate's possession, she could not guess, but she was as happy with it as if she had received a precious gift. It was black wool, high at the neck, with sleeves to the wrists. A wide, stiff collar and cuffs were folded in the long skirt, and beneath it lay a bonnet, as drab as the gown.

Tossing a glance over her shoulder, Shanna assured herself that

Ruark was paying no heed. He stood with his back turned, stropping a razor at the washstand as he prepared to shave. Gathering everything into a bundle, she slipped behind a mirror where she would be screened from his wandering gaze. She doffed the black velvet, donning in its stead the heavy woolen. No chemise had been found, not even the simplest shift, and the prickly gown was, at the least, a monstrous torture for her tender body, causing second thoughts to gather quickly in her mind. Still she had a need to disturb that confounded complacency of his, and with puckish anticipation she carefully settled the straight-cut garment in place over her narrow waist and round bosom. Moving to stand behind Ruark, she made a small request.

"Will you lace me?"

"Aye, love," he readily replied, setting the razor down, before facing her. He suddenly appeared pained. His eyes slowly descended and his tone reflected his lack of appreciation. "Where did you manage to find that?"

Innocently Shanna shrugged and waved a hand toward the chests. "Over there." She smoothed the gown where it was loose around her waist. "Am I covered well enough?"

For a reply Ruark only snorted derisively.

Shanna pouted defensively. "'Twas all I could find."

She lifted the long, heavy tresses from her neck and presented her back where the unfastened garment revealed the smooth, creamy nakedness of it. A long, quiet moment slipped past as Ruark performed this service for her, time enough for Shanna to reflect upon the advantages of having a husband. There was almost a domestic tranquility, or more rightly a truce, between them in this moment when her need dictated his attention.

"Have you found a brush for your hair?" he asked over her shoulder.

Shanna shook her head, all too aware of its unsightly state. She felt his hand against it, smoothing the snarled mass, and stepped away, not wishing him to be repulsed by the feel of the wind-ravaged locks.

Sweeping the dampened tresses into a large knot on top of her head, she went to the bed and perched on its edge. The heat of the day had increased, and it was distressingly warm. The prickling of wool against her soft skin as she secured her hair was a forewarning of what was to come. She could not help squirming beneath it and glanced at Ruark to see if he noticed. He had returned to his shaving, and her eyes found his tall, slender back. She looked away and caught sight of herself in the mirrors. A Puritan's wife, she mused in disdain. But then, that end would be infinitely more acceptable than what the pirates intended for her. She tried to imagine the kind of life a woman would have in Puritan clothes, living by Puritan maners. She envisioned a small plot of land, a cabin in the wilds, Ruark behind a plow while she, large with child, trod the furrows behind him, spreading a handful of seed. Shanna had meant to make mock of the idea, but strangely the illusion was not so distasteful as she had guessed, and she was baffled. Much in justification of her own lifestyle on Los Camellos, she stubbornly concluded that she would soon pine away for luxuries.

Ruark finished shaving, and Shanna watched him make preparations for his role of pirate. Her red silk tether was thrown over his shoulder and across his chest. Tied in a knot over his left hip, it became a sash from which to hang the heavy scabbard. He selected a handful of medals from the armoire to adorn his jerkin, and in his hat he stuck a long, red plume. He spread his hands, presenting Shanna a clear view of his outlandish creation, and she groaned. He portrayed a truly roguish pirate.

"But, madam, I must be a pirate." He glanced down at his array of arms. "Is there something lacking?"

"Nay, Captain Pirate," she sighed. "I vow no strutting cock could outshine your display."

"Why, thank you, Shanna." His teeth flashed in a bright smile. "Shall we be about our business?"

Striding to the door, he laid his hand on the latch, looked back at her, and gestured imperiously with his finger.

"Come along, madam. A step or two behind, as a good slave should."

Before Shanna could grit a reply, he was in the hall, leading the way with a jaunty confidence in his step. Shanna struggled to her feet and followed humbly down the stairs, having lost the heart for argument beneath the discomfort of the wool dress.

The group was already swilling ale in the common room and

for several moments Ruark and Shanna were the center of amusement. Ruark played his charade to the hilt. With open arms and great gusto, he greeted them. He flipped the medals and related impossible, lurid tales of how he had earned them. His entertainment was supreme, and the other picaroons soon held their sides in pain, while Shanna stood quietly and quailed at their overly vivid retorts. When the greeting had worn thin, Ruark bellowed for food and banged the table loudly until Dora scurried in fear to do his bidding. He tore a joint of roast goat from the carcass that was brought to him, took up a loaf of bread, and tossed a bit of both to Shanna. With a hearty whack on her rump, he sent her to a corner where she crouched and halfheartedly chewed on the noisome fare, observing Ruark with a jaundiced eye. He did not settle himself to a seat but strode around the table and exchanged banter with the men between bites and swills of ale. Pausing, he set a foot on a bench and gestured for them to gather about. Shanna could not hear his words, but she knew the tale was lusty, for the pirates leaned forward eagerly as it progressed and doubled over with gales of laughter at its finish. Ruark smiled at them, then waved an arm in farewell. He snapped his fingers loudly as he passed Shanna's corner, and she quickly rose and fell into place behind him.

Once out of the cool, dark shadow of the inn, Shanna met the full weight of her folly. The black cloth drew the heat until it scorched her nearly as much as the hot sand beneath her feet. The gown had been cut for chaste modesty and allowed no room for the swell of her breasts. From there down it fell in a straight, loose mass that widened into a full, heavy skirt, which swung as she tried to match Ruark's gait. His legs were long and the pace faster than she would have walked. In desperation, she seized the skirt and fought to keep it still lest her bosom and hips be scoured raw.

Ruark strode along as if he were enjoying an afternoon stroll. He seized a small branch and with a knife trimmed it until it made a neat walking stick, and as he went along, he aimlessly swatted tufts of grass and hanging twigs. A tuneless whistle wandered from his lips. Apparently he gave no notice to the girl who struggled along in his tracks.

The wide collar chafed her throat, and Shanna started to remove it but found the coarse wool more painful. The starched cuffs slid down against her wrists, and she had to constantly raise an arm to shake them back into place. They entered the village, and the worn pebbles that marked the paths between the squalid shacks were hotter than the sand. She almost moaned with pain, but seeing the careless swing of Ruark's shoulders, she bit back the urge and vowed to ask no favor of him that might ease her distress.

"He wants me to crawl and beg of him," Shanna fumed silently, "I will not! I shall not! Though I am worn to bleeding flesh, I will not give him the pleasure of knowing it."

The sun beat down with a merciless glare from straight overhead. There was no shade, and most of the inhabitants had slunk into their dens to take a siesta in the heat of the day. Beneath a small thatched shelter, a withered, ragged old crone dozed amid stacks of vegetables and fruits. When Ruark roused her to ask for a sample of her wares, she was sorely aggravated, but her temper moderated greatly when she saw the color of his coin. While he and the old woman dickered, Shanna sat on a bale of hemp to ease her burning feet and testily refused Ruark's offer of a tidbit or two to lunch upon. When they resumed the march, she rose and gritted her teeth with the effort it cost her. Ruark's pace had slowed as he nibbled on small, ripe plantains and chunks of dry coconut meat, and Shanna had no difficulty staying with him, but she was already much the worse for wear. Sweat began to tickle maddeningly as it traced a slow path down the middle of her back. She wanted desperately to scratch, but her hands were occupied with the skirt and floppy cuffs. When they passed a small tangle of brush, she tore the wristlets off and threw them behind it, careful lest Ruark should see her. It was little comfort, for now the sleeves grew moist with perspiration and clung to her arms with a cloying prickliness.

They marked the end of the beach in one direction and saw the beginning of the swamp on that side. The sun moved in the sky as they retraced their steps to the dock and followed the beach in the opposite direction. It was here that Shanna strayed to wade where the gently lapping water touched the sand. She grimaced at the brief sting of the salt in the myriad tiny cuts and scrapes on her feet. She longed to tear the stupid garment from her body and race out into the lazy sea and stretch her muscles and cleanse her body in its tepid waves. Having slowed, she now found Ruark some distance ahead of her. Reluctantly she raised the damp skirts and ran after him.

Ruark paused upon a small knoll and stood thoughtfully surveying this end of the beach and the steaming mangrove swamp that stretched as far as the eye could see. He heard Shanna approach and turned, a question on his lips, but it died as he found her limping toward him, the heavy skirts flopping about her legs and hobbling her stride. Her face was flushed, and her breath rasped in her throat. Her hair had half fallen from its knot. As she flung herself down upon a small tussock of grass, Shanna glared her anger at him and painfully raised a slim foot to touch the heel from which a thorn protruded.

"Here, let me, Shanna," he offered, true concern in his tone. He had taken out his knife and would have knelt at her foot.

"Keep away from me." Her snarl halted him. "You drag me on a tour of this Godforsaken sand pile without proper shoes for my feet or as much as a shade to protect me. Ouch!"

The last came as she pulled the stub of thorn from her heel. Ruark stepped to a low bush and pulled several of its small, narrow leaves, twisting them together until they formed a wet mass.

"Press these to the spot," he directed. " 'Twill sting for a moment, but it draws away the soreness and any poison."

Shanna did as she was told and nearly shrieked as the searing juices penetrated. Almost immediately, however, the pain began to ebb. In a few moments her heel was numb. Ruark never ceased to amaze her. His resources were completely beyond her ken, and his knowledge seemed full of these small tidbits.

Facing the swamp again, Ruark spoke over his shoulder as his eyes ranged far, his voice gentle. "You've called our outing pointless, Shanna. And so it must seem to all of them. But 'tis out there that we might find our escape." He bent earnest eyes upon her. "The Spaniards cut a channel through the swamp, but Mother hid the entrance and will not yield its secret." He nodded with his head toward the tangle growth. "You hear the birds?" he asked. There was a constant murmur of sound from the swamp. "There are birds, my love, but then there are other things. Caimans, lizards, all sorts of snakes. Tis impossible to cross on foot, and if we could, there is open sea beyond. We shall need a boat, a fairly large one, though the *Good Hound* is too much for the two of us to handle." Then Ruark shrugged. "But 'tis useless to prattle on. We'll find what we need if we must. Perhaps your father will pay your ransom and see you safe before too many days are passed. The bondsmen the pirates sent back will reach him tonight or early on the morrow. He will surely come apace."

Ruark gazed down at her, knowing well that if he managed to get her back to Los Camellos, it might very well mean a severe punishing for himself. Trahern would take his leaving amiss, as he no doubt already did, and Ruark wondered if Shanna would see him thrashed rather than offer the truth to her father. Whether she did or not, his only concern at present was getting her out of this hellhole.

He took out his knife and knelt beside her.

"Poor Shanna." He smiled softly, though she turned a still heated glower upon him. He lifted his broad shoulders in a shrug. "I only meant to spy out the lay of the land should I need to know." He reached toward her and as she drew away his tone became brusque. "Hold still."

His command brooked no refusal. The knife bit into the sleeve of the gown, cutting it off at the elbow. Then he split the seam on the underside so that a small capelet hung from her shoulder, demure but loose and cool. He repeated the operation on the other sleeve and then sat back on his heels, considering her tightly pressed bosom for a short time before leaning forward again. The starched yoke sailed off into the brush, startling a flock of birds with its flight. Lopping the loose end from his sash, he rolled the soft silk beneath the neck of her gown, frowning as he saw the raw skin there.

"I'll not have you abuse my property, madam. I command you to take better care."

Shanna sniffed at his attempted humor, but, somewhat ashamed of her own foolishness, she held her tongue and submitted herself further to his ministrations. As he plied his blade to the outer stitches of the seams, she could feel the binding bodice loosen in stages across her breasts. His hushed voice came to her ear.

"I've sought to find an alliance with you, Shanna, and in my search I have tried to conduct myself with wisdom and make the best of whatever is offered. 'Tis my aim to see you safely back to your father, and to that end I beg you cease this self-abuse and lend yourself to seeking out whatever will serve our welfare. That same is common to us both, my love. At least for a time. There!"

He rose to his feet and stepped back a pace, staring down as Shanna took the first deep breath she had been able to draw since donning the garment.

"What is left of the seams," he remarked, indicating the bodice, "should hold until we are in our room again. Are you comfortable now?"

"As much as can be expected," she replied, much sharper than she had intended.

Ruark presented his back, and his own voice was gruff as he spoke again. "If you are able, we can return now."

Shanna tested her heel, amazed to find it without pain. She was more surprised to find Ruark's arm waiting to assist her. Taking it, she leaned against him until they came in sight of the village and then dropped back in her usual place. He whistled and swung his stick again, appearing for anyone who cared to take note as if he were out for a lighthearted stroll. But now his stride was shortened and his pace more considerate; his gaze wandered around now and again to take notice of Shanna's progress.

They had passed through the village and were approaching the inn when Ruark left the well-traveled path, exploring along a narrow trail which wove a way through grass-tufted dunes and low, scrawny brush leading them eventually to a small, clear pond. A herd of goats scattered at their approach and fled into the scrubby bushes that hid the oasis. It was a vale well hidden from the casual eye. A small, seeping spring fed the pool which in turn gave its moisture, through a shallow rift, to the sea. The air hung motionless in the hollow, and the sun beat down mercilessly, lending it the warmth of a kiln.

With a quiet word to her, Ruark stepped away a short distance while Shanna stood in some dismay, wondering where she might find privacy for *her* own needs, at least more seclusion than Ruark appeared worried about. Such intimacy she had never had to contend with before and was not willing to indulge in it now.

Determinedly she strode along the edge of the pool toward a thick cluster of brush near the far end but stopped abruptly as Ruark called a warning.

"Not too far."

Shanna's back stiffened, and she stood with clenched fists, silently fuming. Without turning, she asked tersely, "Am I not allowed some privacy, milord and *master?*"

Ruark's chuckle was soft in reply, "Stray too far, my love, and you might have more company than you wish. We are too close to the inn for you to be wandering off alone."

Shanna was unappreciative of his reminder and gritted between gnashing teeth. "Then permit me to see your back turned, sir. At least that much privacy, I beg you."

"Done."

Cautiously she looked over her shoulder to see if he had really complied with her request. He had, and she fled into the protection of the trees. Shortly she returned to find Ruark wading in the pool. He had removed his weapons and vest and left his sandals and hat beside them.

"Would you share a bath, my love?" he inquired as he gave her a laconic grin.

Shanna's sunburned nose snubbed him. However, the pool offered the only relief in sight, and the temptation to join him was almost overwhelming. She trailed a toe in the water and watched surreptitiously as Ruark sought out the deeper part. In a slow, leisurely motion he swam across the pool, returned again to the shallows near her, and peered up at her expectantly.

"Well?" He came to his feet and stood beside her. "Are you coming in?"

He slapped the sodden breeches that covered his lean hips then plucked the clinging cloth away while Shanna twitched under her woolens. Droplets of water clung to his bronzed skin and tinier beads sparkled in the dark furring on his chest.

Shanna shrugged, noncommittal. Taking her reply as affirmation, Ruark waded out into the deeper part again until the water played in widening circles about his chest. Shanna made her decision. She reached behind her to the laces of her gown, but paused as she heard the clanking of a bell coming closer. A pair of big-uddered nanny goats appeared with their bleating kids trailing at their heels, and not far behind them, humming a tune-less air, strolled Carmelita. Espying the group that had preceded her, she gave a cry of greeting.

"Eh, gov'na, I sees ye got me spot. Well, move it over then, laddie, cause 'ere I come."

Her clothes seemed to take flight of their own and landed on a nearby bush. Then with open abandon, a total lack of modesty, her ponderous foreparts naked to the breeze, she cleaved the air in a joyous dive and landed upon the formerly glass-smooth surface of the pond, raising a geyser that left Ruark's hair dripping across his face and ears and dampening the still-shocked Shanna no small amount.

Ruark waded to the shallows and stood gasping and wiping wet hair from his eyes. He looked up in time to see the last twitch of Shanna's shirts before she disappeared up the trail. He called after her and heard what he thought might have been a wild goat snort in anger for a reply. Hastily he bent to pull the sandals onto his feet.

"Damn little fool," he muttered. "She'll find trouble yet."

He snatched the rest of his gear into his arms and was trying to thrust an arm into the jerkin as he ran after his charge. Behind him a disappointed Carmelita, great dark-peaked bosoms floating before her like twin short-fused bombs, leaned back and stroked the water.

"Bloody rude beggars," she mused. "Couldn't stay for a little fun. Huh! Had his britches on anyways."

Ruark had caught up with Shanna as she stalked along. Shrugging his sash over his shoulder, he settled the sword to his hip and patted his hat in place, restoring himself to his jaunty image. Her pace was now the one that made him hustle and he had to stretch out to gain his position in front of her. Shanna strode along in silence, her gaze fixed straight ahead, her lips clenched tightly in vexation. Ruark made it through the door of the inn in front of her, but as he paused inside she pushed by and without a break in her gait took to the stairs and fled into their room. Luckily the place was empty save for Mother, who dozed in his chair. The huge man started and roused and stared at Ruark for a moment then, just as quickly, returned to his slumbers.

Shanna still stood just inside the door as Ruark closed it behind him, surveying the chamber in surprise. It had been scrubbed clean and smelled of strong lye soap. The wooden floor showed damp spots from a recent mopping, and every piece of furniture gleamed with a sheen of light oil rubbed on it. The stained feather ticks from the night before were gone, and fresh new ones replaced them; clean linens were neatly tucked in at the corners. Large, soft pillows in clean casings were propped at the head of the bed, and every piece of clothing had been put in its place. Even the tub had been scoured and glowed softly like a fine jewel at the end of the room. One small table was stacked high with linens and towels and close beside it another bore a rich assortment of scented oils, attars, sundry perfumes, and salts. A clean chamber pot was in the bottom of the washstand, and the pitcher on top brimmed with clear cool water beside a basin that had miraculously lost its coating of scum.

Shanna gave a small start as if returning to reality and reached behind her neck to tug loose the bow of the lacing. A forward movement of her shoulders spread the back of the dress, and she shrugged, letting it fall to the floor. Oblivious to Ruark, she stepped out of its folds, giving the hated garment a disgruntled kick. She strolled leisurely to the washstand where she poured water into the basin, thrust her hands into the refreshing liquid, then drew one after another up her arms, letting the cool water trickle down. She sighed deeply and taking a soft cloth and a sliver of soap, began to wash herself with undisguised pleasure. She stretched her chin upward, displaying the long, shapely column of her neck and gently laved the reddened area where the collar had chafed. After a moment, she opened her eyes and in the mirror caught Ruark's eyes on her. Half turning, she tossed him a withering glare.

"Fill your eyes, you gawking ass. Perhaps your Carmelita still waits in the pool."

Ruark snatched his hat from his head and with an irritated flip of his hand sailed it onto the bed. His voice came curt and bitter. " 'Tis plain you've lost none of your talent for teasing, my love."

He lifted the sash from his shoulder and paused beside the woolen gown, raising it up on the point of the scabbard.

"Shall I air your gown, milady?" he mocked. "Perhaps for a stroll on the morrow?"

"Aye, milord," she sneered, her tone every bit as loving and gentle as it had been before. "Air it out the window"—she pointed her chin in that direction—"with the rest of the trash."

Obligingly the garment was banished. When it had sailed from sight, there was a sudden flurry of voices beneath the window. Ruark braced his hands on the iron rail and, leaning out, saw below a pair of urchins, no more than a half-score years to either of them. They argued spiritedly, playing a tug of war with the dress. At his appearance they halted their squabble, looking up; then, perhaps fearful that he might recall the treasure, they skittered across the low wall and into the brush, each keeping a desperate hand locked on the coarse black cloth. Ruark's amazement knew no end, for there below, where a high pile of cast-off garments, ticks and blankets and other assorted rubble had been, was nothing but a thin scattering of broken glass. Even the maligned chamber pot was gone. Ruark drew back inside. Little had he realized that such offal would be so valued in the hovels of the village.

A trickle of water ran down his neck from his hair, and tossing the sword and jerkin into a chair, he snatched a towel from beside the tub and began to dry his hair. Shanna still washed herself, and from beneath the folds of the towel, he could view her unnoticed. Her ripe, young bosom caught his eye and so enticing was that soft peak where a small lather of soap collected that he could not resist the urge and reached out, wiping it from her with his finger, then cupping the whole of her breast in his eager palm. A sharp pain caught him in the ribs, and Shanna drew back her elbow for another blow. This one brought a grunt from him, and he pulled back his wandering hand to rub his own bruised flesh.

Shanna faced him, a snarl on her lips. "Get your hands from me. You do not own me."

"Have I, then, your permission, milady, to seek from another that which you would not yield?" he jeered.

"I'll yield you nothing"—she snapped and, jaw thrust out, put a finger to his chest and slowly twisted it about a lock of hair—"but a fist in your belly if you touch me again. Get off."

She jerked her hand away from him, wringing a flinch of pain as the hair went with it and turned away, dismissing him as if he had never existed. Still, she casually fetched a sheet and wrapped it about her, bringing it up snug beneath her arms and tucking it carefully over that tempting fruit he had been wont to test.

Shanna returned to washing her face, and with a rueful snort Ruark finished drying his hair. He threw the towel down, picked up a carved shell comb that lay atop the linens, then flicked his dampened locks into a general semblance of order. Admiring the careful workmanship that had shaped it, he turned the comb over in his hand, but suddenly it was snatched from him, and Shanna stood beside him, staring at it, her vengeance forgotten.

"Where did you find this?" she asked in wonder.

"There." He pointed casually. " 'Twas right beside the brush."

With a cry of joy Shanna flew and caught up the brush, also. She clutched them to her breast as if they were a highly valued gift.

"Oooh," she crooned softly. "Thank you, Gaitlier. You do have a way with women."

Ruark stared at her with injured pride. " 'Tis nothing but a brush and comb," he observed gruffly.

"Nothing but!" Shanna threw him a glance of some surprise then smiled softly at her treasures. "You simple oaf, you would do far better in your fickle meanderings with half that man's understanding."

Happily Shanna scrambled to the middle of the bed. Gathering her legs beneath her and sitting back upon her heels, she laid the articles before her gently as if they might shatter at the slightest abuse. Lifting the comb and ignoring Ruark's scowl, she began to work the tangles from her wildly cascading tresses, framed in reflections from her audience of mirrors.

Day ended, bringing Carmelita and Dora with oil lamps to hang above the long table in the common room as darkness invaded the inn. Boisterous joviality grew louder with each cup that was passed among Harripen and the other captains. Ruark sat in the shadows away from the mainstream of coarse banter and watched as these outcasts bolstered their spirits on the plentiful rum and ale. He sampled the brew in his own mug more than a small bit and cast many a glance toward the shadows at the head of the stairs, waiting for Shanna to make an appearance.

Her toilette had proved too much for him, and he had retreated here to the safety of numbers, before lust overcame him and he attacked her.

Harripen drew away from the loud group which had gathered near his seat and approached Ruark. "Ah, man, ye're just the one I would see," he ventured in a slurred voice. "Ye see, I've been wondering now as to the wench."

Ruark raised a brow questioningly. In the meager light his eyes were like stone, staring into the man without a trace of warmth.

"Be it true, lad? One of Trahern's bondsmen said the liedy were no virgin at all, but a widow."

Ruark shrugged. "She was made a widow some months past. Some fellow by the name of Beauchamp."

"Oooii," Harripen breathed, lust showing in his eyes. "And a new widow'd be most grateful for a good man on her belly."

He lay back on the table and bellowed his mirth at the timbers on the ceiling. His companions clustered around, and Ruark could feel the muscles in his own gut tighten. Shanna, as the topic of their conversation, would only brew trouble.

Hawks sat on the table and leaned over his captain, gathering the others to him as if to share a secret with them, but his voice rang loud enough for Ruark to hear the words clearly.

"If one man should please the liedy," he leered, "is it not sure that a dozen would please her more? I say we should each take turns, being fair-minded like we are, that no man"—he hooked a thumb toward Ruark—"should have a giant's portion of the loot. Share and share alike, I sez. And he already has had his own and poor ol' Robby's."

A general nodding of agreement followed, and lecherous grins gaped about the table, showing the readiness of the rogues to enter into a common arrangement. Harripen pushed himself up through them and slid back into his chair. Still chuckling, he peered at Ruark, but his eyes glinted as he connived to be first in any such arrangement.

Ruark leaned back, his tension becoming a relaxed readiness to do instant battle. He returned Harripen's stare over his mug as he sipped calmly at his ale.

"Where is the wench?" Harripen asked. "She's usually hanging onto yer coattails."

Ruark waved his mug toward the stairs. "In the room, but I would warn you—"

"Ah, warn us not, ya Yankee swaggy," the mulatto captain made bold to speak. The black rum had given him an unusual measure of courage. Swinging a meaty fist, he stood away from the table. "I'll bring the Madam Beauchamp down to greet her peers."

Guffawing loudly, he plowed an uneven path to the stairway. "Don't call if it takes me a while," he roared over his shoulder and set his foot on the first step.

The explosion in the confines of the room numbed the ears of all, and the mulatto froze as plaster flew where the huge ball struck the wall a bare hand's breadth in front of his nose. In anger, he whirled and saw Ruark lowering the still smoking pistol. Snarling a curse, the man snatched the cutlass from his side and leapt down to seek vengeance upon his assailant. His feet barely hit the floor before he stopped abruptly. The bore of the second pistol seemed twice as large as the other, and it gaped hungrily at his chest. He did not miss that the hammer was at full cock, and his rage vanished as rapidly as he sobered. He stared into the golden eyes of death, which gleamed behind the flintlock like twin orbs of hardened amber, and his swarthy face paled. Slowly, carefully, he replaced the cutlass in his sash and straightened, while he tried to twist suddenly thick lips into a smile.

"I—," he stammered, "I meant no harm, cap'n. I was only funning, you see?"

The pistol dipped away from his chest, and Ruark nodded stiffly. "Your apology is accepted."

Ruark's gaze went beyond the man and found Shanna at the top of the stairs. She had donned a modest gown of proportions approaching Carmelita's. It hung almost straight from her shoulders, but its previous owner had not the height to allow the garment to cover Shanna's trim ankles and bare feet.

There was a glimmer in the shadows beside her skirt, and he took note of the small, silver dagger she held, no doubt found among Pellier's effects in her search for appropriate apparel. It was a pitifully tiny thing, but, knowing her, Ruark could guess she stood prepared to fight the world.

The mulatto took a place at the far end of the table, keeping carefully away from Ruark even though he had tucked the loaded pistol back into his belt.

"Join us, Madam Beauchamp. Please do." Ruark called, striding forward a pace or two. He beckoned to her and indicated a place at his side. "Come, stand here."

Before she came down into the full light, Shanna tucked the knife away in a shadowed fold of the skirt. As she appeared, Ruark faced the pirates and made a slow, deliberate show of reloading the fired piece. He rammed the shot home, tapping it gently against the powder, then rested the ramrod on Shanna's shoulder when she moved beside him. She seemed very pale, very small, and very obedient.

"This is mine," he barked, and even Shanna started at the sound of his voice cracking loud in the silence of the room. He stepped to the table and put the butt of the pistol on it while, with a solid click, he slid the rod into its place beneath the barrel. Opening the pan of the flintlock, he primed it carefully, then placed his foot on the bench and rested his elbow on a knee, letting the pistol dangle loosely in his hand. Calmly he scanned the faces before him.

"You speak of shares," he sneered, his tone dangerously soft. "I could have claimed yours." He pointed to the mulatto captain with his weapon. "And yours." He stared directly at Hawks and ran his thumb almost longingly over the hammer. "Or even yours." He smiled at Harripen. Then he laughed sardonically and spoke over his shoulder. " 'Twould appear that Mother is the only one who will not challenge my rights to you, Madam Beauchamp."

Replacing the pistol with its companion, he drew the long sabre, resting its point on the table in front of the men.

"If anyone would challenge my right to anything, let him speak, and we'll have it out now."

His eyes mauled the pride of each of them until each man either turned away or shook his head, refusing the glove. Ruark slammed the blade back into its sheath.

"I thought not."

He went back to stand beside Shanna and began to speak in a stilted tone as if lecturing a group of small boys.

"You may consider Madam Beauchamp a piece of merchandise which has by your own rules and consent been given over into my care. She is a treasure of great wealth, the bounty of which could send many of you to the colonies as wealthy country gentlemen." He lifted a lock of her hair and displayed it for them. "A tapestry or a painting is a thing of great beauty and a thing of great value, but if abused and torn it becomes of no more worth than a rag, of little use to anyone. Do you think to trade a ravished daughter to her doting father for a rich reward? Have you heard of Trahern?" He grunted. "I have! Mother has! He will bear me out. If Trahern's daughter is one whit less than she was, the man will hunt you all, each and every one to the ends of the earth if need be, and he will make you dance from the yardarm for his vengeance."

The room was silent as they considered his warning. Mother rose from his chair, and the table creaked as he leaned his weight upon pilelike arms.

"Listen to him, lads," his tenor voice commanded. His bald pate gleamed beneath the lamps, and his braided queues swung as he moved his head to look at each of them. "The man speaks well, and I fear that even should you take him, there would not be half of you left fit to pace a deck. We need every good hand, his with the rest."

Reluctant murmurs rose in assent, and after a moment Harripen slammed his mug down.

"Carmelita! Dora! Fetch some vittles," he bellowed. "Me belly aches with hunger, both for food and a good toss."

The tension was broken, and the corsairs turned to their cups. Ruark gave a nod of his head toward a bench in the shadows behind his chair, and Shanna quickly crossed to it, her knees still weak and trembling beneath her. She glanced up into Ruark's face as he took his seat beside her, but even now it was hard for her to show gratitude. Not wanting to meet his eyes, she looked away.

The men bantered and exchanged jibes as before, but every now and then Ruark caught a glare tossed in his direction. Orlan Trahern had best come apace to fetch his daughter to safety,

Ruark mused, for he could not himself say how long he would be able to hold the pirates at bay. They were, for the most part, criminals fleeing the law—outcasts, rejects. With careless abandon they faced death, for it meant only an end to a meaningless existence. Maiming was what they feared most of all, for like wolves they must be healthy and strong to roam. Once crippled, they would have to beg scraps from the cruel and ruthless pack.

Appearing to the others relaxed and confident, Ruark stretched his long legs before him and rested his arm on the edge of the table. Only Shanna knew there was that in him which was like a beast in the wilds. One could never be sure of his mood and must always treat him with the respect due a dangerous animal.

"God help the world should he ever become a real pirate," she thought. "He'd make a hellishly good one. He has a flair for leading men"—her eyes narrowed as Carmelita sauntered near him with a platter laden with roast meats—"as well as a way for leading women."

Dora kept as far from the men as she could, loading the trenchers at the hearth and filling the pitchers of ale and wine from the huge casks, setting both on a low table there and letting Carmelita serve, a task that she accomplished most heartily. She could skillfully balance a large tray of meats on one hand, seize a brace of brimming mugs with the other, and still walk with a full swaying motion of her hips. Laughing gaily, she spun away from encircling arms and avoided the rougher grasping hands which seemed eager to seize portions of her body. Still, she pranced and displayed the deep cleavage of her ample bosom with amazing impartiality, though beside Ruark she lingered overlong and rubbed her thigh unnecessarily against his. She bent low so he could not miss the full display of her endowments and leaned well over his arm to refill his mug with ale. As she drew back, her bosom caressed the full length of his arm in an open, deliberate way.

Shanna bristled, incensed that Ruark did not remove himself from the woman's attention. She could not see the disturbed frown he fixed upon Carmelita, and she dearly longed to lay the sole of her foot smartly against those broad buttocks.

Carmelita drew away to a safer distance, fetching another armful of food and drink and allowing Shanna to cool her rising temper, if only a small bit. As Ruark turned in his chair to Shanna, offering his plate for her to select a morsel, he could not miss the import of her squared jaw and the fine, tilted nose that somehow snubbed him while she chose what she wanted from his trencher.

Suddenly Mother slammed down his tankard and glared at them all accusingly. "There's a stench in this room," he snarled, "of the rich and haughty." He silenced them all with a vicious swipe of his hand across the table. " 'Tis an odor of whips and blood and sweat. 'Tis a stench of wealth and twisted justice. It smells like—"

His gaze flitted about the room again until it settled on Shanna. She stared into his mad eyes and had she been alone, without Ruark beside her, she would have hidden herself in terror. With a sudden movement Mother flung out a thick arm and pointed an accusing finger at her.

" 'Tis the smell of a *Trahern*," he screamed, and Shanna quaked convincingly as all turned to stare. Ruark stiffened imperceptibly and lowered his glass. Mother's high laughter rang in the room. "Rest yerself, Mister Ruark. No one here disputes yer rights to the vixen. Ye know full well I cannot hinder yer claim. But 'tis my end that she serve us as we served her father—like a *slave*."

Bellowing agreements came from every side, and Carmelita smirked as the noise died and added her verdict, "Aye, let the little twit earn her keep."

Mother waved his arm toward Shanna and commanded, "Let her be about her labor like any good slave."

At Shanna's questioning glance, Ruark ever so slightly nodded his consent. In some confusion she rose to her feet, not quite aware of what was expected of her. Her gaze flickered across the leering faces until it came to rest on Mother. The giant smiled slowly.

"If ye please, Madam Beauchamp—a goblet of wine will tide me for a spell."

A flagon was thrust into Shanna's hand by Carmelita, who regarded her with dark, lazy eyes and a self-satisfied smile. With shaking fingers, Shanna clutched the pitcher to her, feeling the full weight of many stares and Mother's sly eyes upon her. She refilled the eunuch's cup. Then as others beckoned her with raised glasses and gaping grins, she moved hesitantly about the table, carefully filling the goblets with the thick, heady brew.

Harripen leaned back in his chair, watching her every movement, his eyes testing the soft curves hidden beneath her oversize gown. With a flip of her wrist Shanna brushed a curl off her cheek, and his heated gaze turned to the loose bodice which lay against her round breasts. Reflectively he let his perusal leave her to pass over the robust Carmelita, who sliced meat with an energetic motion, setting her heavy breasts swinging. He sipped his wine and began to eat again, having decided that at the proper time he would ease his needs—but not with the slut.

The mulatto showed no such patience. As Shanna came near him, he grasped her wrist, causing her to slosh wine over his knee. Fearfully Shanna tried to snatch free, but he pulled her ever closer until he chanced a glance toward Ruark. Then he froze, seeing those golden eyes hardening with that same piercing coldness he had seen glowing behind the flintlocks. With a pained smile he set her from him, and Shanna made haste to step beyond his reach.

Ruark waited until all had been served then motioned to Shanna, who came quickly. She leaned over to pour wine into his goblet, and in a careless moment her breast lightly brushed against his shoulder where the sleeveless jerkin left it bare. The contact caught them both unawares, startling each with a quick excitement that rippled through their bodies. Their eyes met with a suddenness that made a blush suffuse Shanna's cheeks. Unsteadily she straightened, clutching the pitcher against her bosom in painful confusion.

Having witnessed the whole of the encounter, Harripen burst out into loud guffaws, grasping the shirt of the Dutchman, who joined his glee when the Englishman pointed to them, drawing everyone's attention.

" 'Ey there, Mister Ruark, ye've trained her well."

Ruark slipped an arm about Shanna's hips, placing his hand with bold familiarity upon her buttock, and returned a grin to the leering men. "Aye, but she has a mite to learn yet. 'Tis like breaking a good mare. I can't leave her alone too long."

He felt Shanna stiffen and could guess how his words must rankle.

"Aye," the Englishman bellowed. " 'At's the way of it. But here, lass, let Carmelita show you a thing or two."

Carmelita came forth eagerly, swinging her broad hips, and leaned against Ruark's chair, oblivious of Shanna, who slowly burned while brown fingers curled in Ruark's dark hair. In the face of the smaller woman's glare, Carmelita laughed.

"Take it easy, lovey. He looks like he's got enough to please the both of us. The mores the merrier, I al'ays say."

Shanna's eyes narrowed as the woman fell giggling into Ruark's lap, causing his breath to leave with a "whoof." He struggled to sit up beneath the weight and seemed somewhat pained as Carmelita spread eager kisses over his face and chest. Twisting upon his lap and crooning in his ear, she pulled his hand to her breast and settled her own hand intimately upon the bulge of his manhood.

Something within Shanna snapped, like a dry twig beneath a heavy foot. With a low, rising shriek of rage, she reached out and gave Carmelita a heave that sent the woman sprawling to the floor. There Carmelita sat, somewhat dazed by the attack of this supposed lady. The roaring laughter of the pirates, however, would not let this affront go unpunished, and a long, slim blade suddenly appeared in Carmelita's hand.

Ruark rose to his feet as it again looked as if he would have to intervene, but a shattering of glass brought his attention around to Shanna. His brow raised in mild wonder as he saw that she faced the larger woman with a cloth slung through the handle of a broken pitcher. He removed his chair and himself from Shanna's way, though not far. She stood her ground, swinging the sharp-edged shard on the length of towel. It made an excellent mace. The graceful line of her jaw was set with the same stubbornness he had often witnessed before. He could not but admire the savage beauty her wrath brought forth as her sun-streaked hair swirled in glorious disarray around her.

Carmelita retreated a step, her uncertainty written plainly in her face. Even if she managed to cut Shanna, the jagged edges of the shattered pitcher could mar her for life, and in this place, having to make her living from men, she could ill afford the loss of any part of her meager beauty. She saw the determination in Shanna's eyes, the fire in the bluish-green depths. She had not been bested before, but she thought it wiser, for the moment at least, to retreat.

She tucked away the knife, and relaxing, Shanna set her own weapon down. Harripen chuckled as he reached out to pat Shanna's rump in approval, then almost swallowed his tongue in surprise as the open palm of her hand struck him smartly across his face. Ruark held his breath, awaiting the Englishman's reaction; but Harripen, after the first shock, gave a hearty roar of laughter.

"Damn and be damned, me hearties, she's as mean as Trahern himself."

The Dutchman was feeling high of spirit, mostly the strong black rum he preferred. He stepped close to Shanna and, before she could react, locked her in a sweaty bear hug while he roared his merry chortles painfully in her ear.

"Dat Harripen don't have goot luck wit' women. Now, lil' gal, ol' Fritz Schwindel vill keep ya from des hahnhunders."

Shanna's knee found a likely spot, and the Dutchman reeled away with a shout of pain while his meaty hand swung around to deliver a cuff to her head. Shanna was faster than the obese Netherlander and ducked beneath his paw, but his huge fingers caught in the nape of her dress, splitting it down the back seam to her waist. She gave his booted toes the best of her heel and spun away from him, grasping the front of her gown in sudden distress. She whirled to Ruark, and in a split second a rush of fleeting emotions held her rooted to the spot: her desire to fling herself into his arms and beg him to take her from this flared; her anger that he would expose her to such debauchery raged; her humiliation roweled; and her fear of that yet to come reduced all to a confused jumble of feelings. Tears came, ready to spill from her eyes, but all was solved for her in a twinkling. With crystal clarity she saw it all, though much was lost to the others.

A snarl twisted Ruark's face. He crouched low then uncoiled like a striking snake. He flew across the space, stretched out like a leaping tiger on the attack. Herr Schwindel was still hopping about, trying to hold his twisted toes and soothe his ruffled groin at the same time, when Ruark struck him full on the chest. The assault carried the Dutchman backwards to slam against the wall, and as they rebounded Ruark set his feet and heaved. The fat man rode across Ruark's shoulder to sail his length and more, before crashing onto the floor and, still spinning on his back, sliding beneath the table.

The sabre hummed its bittersweet song as it sprang from its sheath, and the Dutchman scrambled onto the other side of the table, spilling chairs and men from his path in his eagerness to escape.

"Nein! Nein!" he blubbered. "Der recht ich nicht haben!" Seeing his words had no effect on Ruark, he struggled with the English. "I have no right! I give! I yield!"

The sight of the coward groveling behind the table brought Ruark to his senses, and he slowly relaxed and put away the sword. He glanced at the faces of the pirates and saw no challenge. He need speak no further. They understood at last the tooth of his claim to the wench and that he would tolerate no encroachment of it. He presented his back to them and, though his muscles twitched, he felt no prick of steel. A motion of his hand sent Shanna ahead of him, and he followed with slow, measured tread until the door to their chamber was closed and bolted behind him.

Ruark leaned against the portal and breathed deeply to ease the tension in his back. It had built with every step he had taken away from the table, and he was sure that, with the possible exception of Mother, there was not one below who did not yearn for the courage to sink a blade between his ribs. He watched Shanna cross the room to the window and there she stood, silently staring out into the darkness beyond the shutters. He could guess she was still riled about Carmelita and would have nothing to do with him.

He sighed, as much in frustration as in any relief he might have felt for even being alive. He'd be damned before he'd crawl to her begging forgiveness for what he was innocent of; yet he wanted the tenderness his explanations could bring from her. He craved an understanding look, her lips against his, her silken body within his arms, but knew it would somehow be lacking if trust were not mutually shared.

A candle had been lit beside the bed. Gaitlier, he guessed. And the bed was turned down invitingly. He couldn't remember seeing the small man below or on the stairs. Must have come and gone the back way, Ruark mused, the stairs outside.

Aimlessly Ruark wandered about the room, shucking his weapons and jerkin, leaving them lay where they would be handy at morning's first rising. No hint of a glance came from Shanna, only brooding silence. He paused beside the tub, realizing it had been filled, and smiled to himself. Gaitlier really did know a lady's heart, especially Shanna's.

Ruark went to stand close behind his wife and gently lifted a curl from off her shoulder. "Shanna?"

She jerked around, red-rimmed eyes wide with anger and a challenge on her lips.

"Hush," he breathed before she could speak and laid a finger upon her mouth. Taking her hand, he led her to the tub. Here, the room was dark, and she could not understand his purpose until he lit a candle. Her gasp of surprise warmed him, and she gave no pause, but pushed him away and quickly made a make-shift drapery between two mirrors with a sheet. A moment later Ruark smiled as he heard a splash followed by a long sigh of pleasure. Moving to the window, he lifted a leg onto the sill and sat gazing out across the low, forbidding blackness of the island.

It was sometime later when Ruark turned and noticed that Shanna's candle cast her shadow on the sheet. His perusal of the darkness was forgotten as his attention shifted to her performance. Once she rose and reached into the armoire, and her silhouette showed in full detail upon the cloth. His blood warmed, flooding his body with desire. He remembered a night gone by when she had come to him and laid herself in his arms with a passion such as he had never known in a woman. There was a great longing in him for it to be that way again. With a slow but purposeful stride, he went to the drapery and lifted it aside, giving her a start. His eyes caressed all that they touched. Her swelling breasts gleamed with wet droplets, which seemed to sparkle in the candlelight. The shallow water held nothing from his regard, and his passion fed upon the stirring sight. Her own gaze was soft, and her breathing shallow as she stared up at him. Then her eyes moved downward and something less than desire kindled within them.

She pulled a cloth over her bosom. "My Lord Captain, you intrude. Am I to have no privacy?"

Ruark scowled. "Shanna love, you are indeed ravishing beyond words, but I feel the bitter bite of ire much too sharply and too often of late. Am I to endure this outrage when you have no cause?"

"No cause indeed!" Shanna snapped. "You flaunt yourself with cutoff breeches and shirtless back, roam the lower streets of town, then prance yourself across my balcony to beseech me greet you as some long-lost lover. Am I a fool? Am I simple? For them," she jerked her head toward the door, "I will play the mopish slave, but do not mistake yourself, my Captain Rogue. In this chamber you will lie alone. Or if you be in truth the pirate bold, then you may ease yourself by force and nothing less."

"Shanna," Ruark was set to argue the point. "Why do you do this? I—"

"Will you straighten the panel please"—she cut him short—"and let me find some comfort for a moment?"

So dismissing him, Shanna leaned back in the tub and, raising a shapely limb, began to leisurely wash her leg. Ruark fought the urge to snatch the towel away and set an end to the indifference she portrayed. His passion demanded it, but his mind knew the folly of such. He was well aware that Shanna, confronted with force, would rally to meet it with all the energies of an outraged feline and would not yield short of exhaustion. Where would the pleasure be in taking her then? He had known the joy of her willing response. He could settle for nothing less.

Angrily he jerked the barrier over the mirrors again and stretched out on the bed to watch her shadow for his enjoyment. Her silhouette fled as she left the tub. Long moments passed. Ruark doffed his breeches and slipped beneath the sheet. With something less than patience he waited, aware that Shanna could not so easily dismiss his presence once in bed. He had already noted the tendency of the feather ticks to gather in about them, drawing them to one another. Even with her sternest efforts, she would be hard put to stay away. He folded her side of the sheet down further so she would find no hindrance there. The candle by the bed lit the room with its dim glow. Still he waited. Finally her light was doused and the sheet taken away. Shanna was fully dressed, but *how* she was dressed. A long, black silk skirt garishly embroidered with colorful flowers was tucked up upon itself as Carmelita's had been, showing a trim and shapely thigh. A loose, thin blouse, several sizes too large, barely held its place across one shoulder and the high, full curve of her bosom. Her hair, highlighted with its own gold, was drawn back with a scrap of ribbon and cascaded down her back to its long, glorious length. Her sea-green eyes sparkled with mischief as she cocked her hip and ran her hand along its curve.

"Does this fashion suit my Lord Captain Pirate? Is it common enough for your taste?"

She came slowly across the room toward the bed, rolling her hips like a ship aground in a heavy sea. Her breasts swung wantonly as she moved, threatening the security of her modesty as the oversize blouse slipped ever lower.

"Does my Lord Captain Pirate wish a warm bedmate for the night?" she simpered sweetly.

Pausing at the foot of the bed, she swayed her hips invitingly, and her look was teasingly seductive, her lips wet and parted with a hint of a mysterious smile. Ruark closed his mouth when he realized it had sagged open. Then suddenly Shanna's eyes flashed with rage, and she whirled in majestic fury, strode to a sea chest and snatched out a heavy woolen blanket, folding it into a long, tight roll as she returned. She placed it carefully in the middle of the bed beneath the top sheet, dividing the area neatly in half. Bracing her hands on the bed, she leaned forward with no modesty at all. The blouse gaped away from her body completely, and Ruark could see to her waist. The very fruit he desired to caress hung ripe, ready to be tasted. In rapt attention, he stared at her display before finally raising his eyes to hers. A withering sneer spread slowly over her face as she looked closely into his.

"Then my Lord Captain Pirate," she gritted, "can find himself another bed and another bitch!"

Primly she presented her back, slipped out of the skirt, the blouse, and loosed her hair. Fluffing the pillow, she slid beneath the sheet and laid her head back upon the feather-filled rest. Casting her gaze beyond the foot of the bed, she saw the face of her Ruark smiling back at her, the lazy grin spreading across his lips. The roguish face haunted her, but lo, each mirror has a weakness and no less the likes of these. She raised her head, and whatever occurred upon it. A full dozen Ruarks stared back at her, as if the one were not beyond endurance. The roguish face haunted her, but lo, each mirror has a weakness and no less the likes of these. She gave a derisive grunt and, wetting her finger on her tongue, snuffed the candle.

Mouthing a low curse, Ruark punched his pillow heartily with his fist, yanked up the sheet to cover himself, and felt the rough coarseness of the blanket against his back. Sometime later his voice was heard in the dark.

"Woman," he muttered. "I yield that you are certainly mad."

✦ Chapter 18 ✦

THE night held no comforts for Ruark in sleep or blissful pleasures. He tossed restlessly and could find no solace for his mind. Though the rough blanket separated them, he was ever aware of Shanna's presence beside him. The silvery glow of the moon shining in through the open shutters cast shadows with its brightness, and in its light Ruark rose to fetch himself a strong bracer of rum. He prowled the room, liberally sampling the brew and casting more than occasional glances toward the softly curving form in the bed.

In abject frustration he slipped into the shortened breeches, filled a pipe from a small cask of tobacco, lifted the bolt and eased open the door, taking care not to wake his peacefully slumbering wife. He went below to the common room. It was empty save for Mother. No sound came from the eunuch to give him clue whether he slept or was fully awake. Ruark stepped quietly to the fireplace and lifted a small charred stick, blew the coal at its end into life, and touched it to his pipe. He puffed until the tobacco caught too, then seated himself at the table to enjoy his smoke.

" 'Tis a warm night, Mister Ruark."

Ruark stared in surprise at Mother and saw the small, alert

eyes watching him in the dim light of the subdued lantern.

"Aye," Ruark finally nodded and gave the excuse. "I'll never be accustomed to this heat."

A snicker of amusement set Mother's rolls of flesh quavering. "The Trahern wench warmed ye a mite, eh? She were a spirited one, even as a tot. She'll lead some man a merry chase for the want of her favors. Beware 'tis not you, me hearty."

Ruark grunted and averted his face. He drew on the pipe then leisurely blew a slim column of smoke into the air, leaning his head back to watch it curl down upon itself.

"I was not always a buccaneer." Mother interrupted his thoughts, and Ruark contemplated the man in the meager light, amazed because his voice no longer bore any hint of the guttural tones or crude speech which he had used earlier.

"I was a young man at the peak of my profession," Mother continued. "A tutor at Portsmouth. The cream of the blue bloods came to hear my lectures, but alas, one of the hypocrites twisted my reasoning, and I was accused of preaching treason. They gave me a quick trial and threw me in the gaol. Then I was placed on the lists and impressed into the service as a common seaman."

He paused, staring into the low-burning embers in the hearth. Ruark waited, his interest aroused, until the eunuch snorted and resumed his tale.

"Would you see the stripes on my back, Mister Ruark? I was a slow learner and did not take to the sea as well as the mate thought I should." He sipped from a mug of strong rum to wet his tongue before he sighed heavily. "The captain deemed me useless and sold me to Trahern as a bondsman. 'Tis Trahern's justice that finds me here amid this scurvy lot. Be careful you do not fall victim to his revenge. His daughter is his pride, and he'll see you gelded for having used her. You can never go back to Los Camellos without losing some portion of your life, if not all of it. I give this advice freely. Do not let the wench get in your blood, lad, else you might be tempted to test the fates to have her again."

"Bah," Ruark returned gruffly and played his part well. "What's one skirt from another? I'll tire of her before her father pays the ransom."

"Then 'tis wise you be." Mother nodded at his own wisdom as he murmured, "I know that you are no common thief. And I know, too, that you will not long stay with us."

Ruark would have denied the statement, but Mother held up a hand to delay him.

"The others had decided to do away with you at a convenient moment. That is why Harripen freely gave you the purse. He expected to regain it soon. But you killed Pellier, which all of them desired to do, and became one of them, thus gaining some measure of respect and freedom. 'Tis fully expected that you will leave. We find that young, energetic men who find their way here are soon gone. We only hope your going will not cost us dearly, and most will be glad to see you go, for you are a constant reminder of the youth and vigor we have lost. Go your way, my young hearty, but trust no one, not even me, and do not press us beyond what we can bear. As you may have guessed, even our own lives are less than desirable in this hole and are held rather cheaply. I, myself, only mark time and hold my freedom until the day death releases me from this shallow existence. Perhaps that is why we dare danger and challenge death for the very luxuries we crave."

Ruark could make no denial or comment on Mother's insight and felt a small measure of respect for the mind trapped within the hulking body. Thoughtfully he stared at the pipe he held in his hand. There was no further word from Mother, and, for all Ruark knew, he had lapsed into slumber, having exhausted his moment of sanity. Ruark got to his feet, counting himself far luckier than any man on the island, despite what they might have termed poor luck in being imprisoned for murder and sold into bondage. In truth, if he hadn't been in the gaol, he never would have married Shanna, and he counted all the abuse he had suffered there well worth the gain of such a wife. There were matters to be settled yet, but by God's grace they would be settled and be all the sweeter for the trials.

In a thoughtful mood, he climbed the stairs and bolted the door securely behind him. He stripped, careful not to wake Shanna, and sat on his side of the woolen barrier, his back braced against the baroque, carved headboard, an arm slung across a drawn-up knee. For a long time he contemplated his sleeping wife, taking solace in the fact he didn't have to leave her with the coming of dawn. Her gilded tresses spread like a wide fan over the downy pillow, touching her pale shoulders. Her slender hand lay in the midst, and in the gentle glow of moonlight the single band of gold upon her finger gleamed with its own luster.

"You are my wife, Shanna Beauchamp," he whispered. "And I will have you as that. There will come a day when you'll proudly declare our marriage to the world. God help me, you will."

The warmth that came with the dawn was an insidious omen of what the later hours would bring. Shanna lay asleep with the sheet covering all but her head, and Ruark again slipped from the bed. Donning his breeches, he went below to the common room to see what he might find in the way of food for them. He knew Shanna hadn't been able to eat much before Mother's harsh command. He would assure this time that a modicum of peace accompanied their meal.

The night of merrymaking by the pirates had reduced the place pretty much to shambles, a situation Dora, the young serving woman, was trying to remedy. Mother, dozing heavily under a series of loud snores in the chair, was the only other one present. It seemed the eunuch had given up the use of a bed long ago, so Harripen had explained. Mother found only acute discomfort with his great weight pressing down upon him and feared that he might be somehow trapped in those muffling confines. A living nightmare, Ruark mused.

He bent his attention to the girl, a thin, bony thing with straggly brown hair and a plain face that betrayed the smallest hint of charm when she smiled, but that was rare indeed. Gaitlier had said she would do chores for a copper or two, and Ruark wondered if she preferred that method of earning her keep to Carmelita's.

Pausing beside her, Ruark asked for a tray of food, and at his first words the snoring halted abruptly in mid-snort. From beneath the shadow of his beetled brow, Mother fixed his small eyes on them. Then with a grunt he heaved his large shape from the chair and padded out of the room.

The door slammed behind the obese man, and Dora scurried to fetch what Ruark had requested, setting out fruits, bread, and meats, while she brewed a pot of strong tea. His show of patience on this morning quite bemused her, for he had nearly scared the wits out of her the previous day with his bellowing. He was handsome and moved like a dream, yet she had seen him kill a man and threaten others just last night—although that was not an uncommon occurrence on this island, nor the first she had witnessed. Still, she was fearful of him and went to great pains to avoid raising his ire. But because of his awesome presence, she was awkward and more inept than usual, and in her haste she dropped the hot kettle, nearly scalding herself as the steaming water flew upward like a geyser.

Dora's heart thumped wildly as Ruark rose and stepped close, but to her amazement he only inquired of her welfare and returned the kettle to her trembling hands. Assuring him that she was not injured, she flew to refill the copper kettle and hung it again on a hook above the fire. While she sliced meat, her large eyes moved to where he sat smoking his pipe, and she frowned in confusion. The other pirates would have descended upon her in rage at her clumsiness. They were always eager to rebuke her with a hamlike fist or booted foot on her buttocks. Ever since they had taken her captive some nine years before, at the age of twelve, she had suffered much humiliation and abuse from them all, not the least from Carmelita and that evil one, Pellier.

Only Gaitlier and some of the village folk had been kind to her, but her days were passed in servitude to these beasts and marred by the hardships the pirates heaped upon her. They had killed her parents and raped her before she was even a woman. They delighted in everything perverse and cruel, and long ago she had made it her purpose in life to escape this brigade of thieves. She could envy the young woman taken captive from Los Camellos while, at the same time, pitying her for having to submit to this man's lust. At least Trahern was rich and could ransom his daughter from this hell. There was no one in the world who knew or cared that she, Dora Livingston, was alive, let alone slave to madmen.

Ruark shifted his gaze to her, and she wilted into shy retreat as he indicated her blouse, pointing at it with his pipe. Numbly she half expected him to order her to disrobe.

"Is there a place where I might find a waistshirt like that for the Trahern wench?"

Dora's fear became suspicion, but she nodded and answered haltingly. "There's an old woman who makes 'em for 'er keep."

Ruark fished into the purse hanging from his belt. "Fetch me several for the maid and some of whatever is worn beneath. And a pair of sandals, if you will." He glanced down at Dora's own and indicated with his pipe. "Not too big. About your size or less. You can have what coin is left."

He flipped her several, and she caught the pieces between her palms then looked at them, somewhat puzzled. She did not know how to respond to kindness, for any small show of it from her captors had only been followed by some further depravity. She eyed him now in bewildered apprehension.

"But, sir, 'ere are rich gowns in Pellier's chests. In the room they are, sir."

A sneer crept into Ruark's voice as he replied. "My tastes differ from Pellier's brothel garb, and I must keep the Trahern brat alive for her father. 'Twould only brew trouble to parade her around half naked."

Dora hung her head shamefacedly. "Whenever some of the women would go with him up there, Captain Pellier would make 'em wear those. He fetched the old hag what sells fruit in the village to put on the best of them and strut about for him while he laughed at her." Dora's face flushed crimson, and her eyes fell to her twisting hands. "And even meself."

The shame she felt was apparent, and Ruark would have said some consoling word, but his role of pirate did not permit displays of kindness.

"I'll wait while you run to fetch the things for the wench. But hurry. She may grow restless if I'm gone too long."

When Ruark returned to the chamber above with the clothes Dora brought, he secured the door behind him. Then he set the food tray down on the table next to the bed with a deliberate clatter, startling Shanna from sleep. She sat up in alarm, snatching the sheet high under her chin.

"Easy, love. 'Tis only your master bringing the morning fare to his beautiful slave," he mocked lightly and flashed her a devilish grin as his warm gaze caressed her.

"Oh, Ruark!" Shanna's voice cracked with fear, and she rubbed a hand across her brow as if to clear her mind. She regained her composure and remembered the state of her relationship with him as she ran her fingers through her tangled mane of hair. "I dreamt you had left me here with them and fled to the colonies to be free." The sheet was draped carefully over her bosom and held under her arms, but she was oblivious to the fact that she salved Ruark's gaze with the reflection of her naked back in several of the mirrors. "Do dreams come true, bondsman?" Her bright sea-hued eyes caught his and held them.

Ruark shrugged. "Sometimes, Shanna, but mostly because you want them to and work at it." He prepared her a plate of food and placed it before her, sitting beside her on the bed. Reaching out a hand, he smoothed her sleep-tossed curls, grinning in that one-sided, roguish way. "You know I'll never leave you, Shanna. Never!"

She tried to read his eyes, wondering whether he teased or gave a statement of fact.

"I brought a gift for you," he said suddenly, rising from the bed and retrieving the bundled garments from the chair beside the door. He presented them with a decorous bow. "These should suit the occasion better than what the good gentleman, Pellier, left behind."

"Pellier was no gentleman," Shanna assured him as she sipped her tea.

"Well spoken, my love," Ruark agreed. His handsome brow knitted as if he considered some deep subject, then he pointed out, "You can never declare a gentleman by his collection of riches or lack of them, by a name or lack of one. Now take your father, for instance. He is basically a good man, a gentleman by any twist, yet his father was hanged. What great harm has your father suffered? He is an honest man, rich, powerful. Do you hold him beneath lords and dukes, Shanna?"

"Of course not!"

"And what of yourself, my love? The granddaughter of a highwayman, you have the airs of a grand duchess. Yet if I bore the title or the blood of a noble, I would not think you beneath me. Perhaps if we had children, 'twould go well for them rather than bad." He paused at her gasp of indignation and then leaned forward and stared at her as he continued slowly. "Suppose, my love, that I had wealth and came from a family with more than a fine name, could you then love me and be content to bear the fruit of my devotion, giving life to our children as beautiful and honorable offsprings of our love?"

Shanna shrugged, not wanting to answer. "If—if you had been true—I suppose—Oh!" She flared. " 'Tis foolishness to speak of these things when we both know they are not so. You can be nothing more than what you are."

"And what am I, madam?" he persisted.

"You ask me?" she snapped irritably, turning away from those amber eyes which seemed to bore into her. "Of all people, you should be the one to know."

"Then the reply is, madam, that you could easily accept me as your husband if I were rich and titled? You would find no argument with me if I had these qualities and none of those I have now?"

Shanna squirmed uncomfortably. "You put it crudely, Ruark, but, aye, I suppose I could abide marriage with you, if all you say were true."

"Then, my dear, Shanna, you're a prudish snob."

He said it so kindly, with a sparkling flash of white teeth, that it was not until he uttered the last word that Shanna felt the prick of his sarcasm. She choked on a mouthful of tea then stared at him in speechless outrage.

"Please put your clothes on, madam," he suggested and turned away to sample his portion of the morning fare.

In a petulant mood, she rose, snatched the garments he had provided and donned them. She retrieved the embroidered black skirt she had worn the night before, though this time she did not hitch it up. She laced the wide waistband tightly over the white gypsy blouse then braided her hair into one long, heavy plait which hung down her back. Lastly she slipped the leather sandals on and crisscrossed the narrow thongs about her ankles.

Her appearance was so stirring it momentarily numbed the

wits of Harripen and a goodly number of men who had gathered in the common room. There was no dallying with the pirates this morning, for Ruark felt the need to hasten her from beneath their heavy perusals.

Catching her wrist, Ruark pulled her along after him, feigning annoyance at her slowness. "Get a move on, wench. Do you think I have nothing else to do but wait on you?"

" 'At a lad," Harripen roared with mirth. "Keep that twit 'opping, in bed and out!"

Loud guffaws rang in the room as Ruark and Shanna quickly fled the inn.

"Don't they ever think of anything but—making love?" she questioned with a derisive glance over her shoulder.

Ruark peered down at her and hastened to correct. " 'Tis not love they do in bed, Shanna. They have not learned that gentle art. They release an urge on the one they've chosen for the night, like an animal. They call themselves lovers because of the great number who've passed beneath them. A bull can do the same. Love is that wherein two people share themselves because of some deep and abiding emotion between them. They cast away all others and seek out the one they have chosen to go through life with, and be it thick or thin, they'll stand by each other until death."

"Strange you should be the one to say that, Ruark," Shanna said coolly and turned her face seaward as they meandered across the dock area. The breezes whipped strands of hair around her face into a frame of soft, feathery curls.

His scowl darkened on her. " 'Tis not I, my love, but you who cannot settle on one."

Shanna lifted her nose disdainfully. " 'Tis only that I have yet to find my proper mate."

Ruark snarled. "Madam, may I remind you once again that I am your mate, proper or otherwise."

She ignored him deliberately. "My father will expect me to choose a husband soon. He wants grandchildren, and I cannot disappoint him."

Ruark's insides wrenched with the coldness of her tone. "Dammit, Shanna! Do you think if I had been the chooser, that I would have chosen you?"

Struck dumb by his statement, Shanna stared at him.

Ruark flung an arm wide, encompassing the sea that stretched endlessly into the horizon and sneered, "What were you? The Goddess Shanna from Mount Olympus, raised upon that pedestal of your own construction, that all men must approach you from beneath your level. The haughty Shanna, beautiful, untouched, pure, who strolls this earth for but a pressing whim and sighs for that great knight upon a charger, that perfect man who will snatch her from this squalor and take her to some hidden Eden and there with dovelike tones of adoration meekly serve her every wish. Hah!" Ruark snorted. "Beware, my love. That perfect man might also seek a perfect woman."

He turned away, his brow black with rage while Shanna stared at him, confused and not knowing the reason for this attack.

"What do you say?" she demanded, much stirred by his accusations. "I but held myself for the man of my own choosing, and, God willing, I will yet find that man."

Ruark whirled and looked at her in wide amazement. Then his scowl darkened thunderously. "You held yourself too high, Shanna. Of course each man has some flaw and once you found it, you rejected him. What did you make of yourself, pray tell? A prime wife? Hardly! A gentle mate to share a man's life? Nay! Rather the regal Shanna." He answered his own question. "A challenge to any man, a goal for a night's toss, and a mark well worthy of the game. That man who could shatter your wall of ice would be an instant hero to every bachelor. You were the high fortress to be assailed but once taken, worthless. You were a fortune to be gained, but of what value as a wife? A worthy man would seek that gentle dame who with calm and sweet repose would thus enrich his life. Have you then so greatly enriched mine? I was given as a slave to pirates at your command. Now your father thinks me not only a flown bondsman but a pirate, and he has in all likelihood placed a high reward upon my head. If taken by his men, I might yet find a rope my final unearned reward. And that because of you, my loving wife."

Shanna met his words with a stiff back, standing straight and unbowed. "You say that truth will out. But do you say you love me?"

Spreading his arms, Ruark faced into the breeze and spoke as if to the open sea. "Madam, at this moment you are the last one to whom I would admit my love."

It was a twisted truth, for love her he most certainly did. But there was much to pass before he would place that weapon in her hands.

He glanced over his shoulder to see her reaction but found her walking slowly away from him, her head high, the wind whipping her skirt, her shoulders erect, her pace carefully measured. He wanted to run to her, to take her into his arms or grovel at her feet and tell her of this all-consuming desire that gnawed at the roots of his being, but he let her go, hoping the challenge of his denial might spur her to some new consideration of herself and him.

Shanna walked along the beach toward the edge of the water, away from the village and the inn. From where he stood on the jetty, Ruark observed her solemnly, feeling more than a trifle unsure. He could not help but wonder what her mood might bring. Would his words find his intent or would she turn away from him in injured pride and reject even his attempts to help? Briefly she glanced back at him, then, facing forward again, went further away. Reaching down, she caught the rear hem of her skirt and brought it forward between her legs, tucking it in the wide waistband like a fishwife. She removed her sandals and slung them over her shoulder. Wading in the shallows, she kicked idly at wave tops and rolled shellfish and rocks with her toe while Ruark continued to watch, unable to ease the ache in his chest.

It was some time later when a shout came from behind him, and Ruark turned to find Harripen and several of the crewmen rowing out to the *Good Hound*. The pirate waved, and Ruark returned the gesture, wondering what they were about. Harripen and another man boarded the schooner, and the longboat was positioned beneath her stern. The crew caught the end of the cable Harripen tossed to them and made it secure to their own boat, then, rowing heartily, began to swing the slim, dark ship so that her stern was to the dock. Harripen barked an order forward, and the other man struck loose the latch on the anchor capstan. Now the dozen men in the longboat strained, bending their oars, and slowly the *Good Hound* began to move inward toward the slip, playing out her anchor cable as she came. As the ship neared her berth, the longboat swung away, putting slack in the tow and letting the *Good Hound*'s own momentum carry her until she bumped gently against the pilings. She scrubbed her side against them, and Harripen tossed down a looped cable, which Ruark made fast to the cleat. Then he ran along the pier to catch another from the man on the forecastle. Harripen called for him to come on deck, and Ruark glanced to see what had become of Shanna. She stood with her hands shading her eyes, having watched the ship drawn in, but as his gaze found her she resumed her stroll in the shallows. Confident that she was well in sight and not so far away that he could not be quickly at her side, Ruark climbed up the tumble home. Somehow he felt Shanna needed this time alone to straighten her own thoughts. He swung his legs across the rail and found Harripen waiting, leaning on his elbows while he stared at the lone figure on the beach.

"Hell, man, I envy you that bit of fluff," the Englishman moaned huskily. "Even from there she warms me loins."

Ruark scowled, but his tone was light as he replied with a great deal of truth. "Aye, she's hard to walk away from. But enough of her, Harripen. What are you about with my ship?"

"Yer—ah—well, that she be of course, laddie, what with Robby gone and all." The man scratched his scarred and stubbled chin reflectively. "We—uh—took a vote. Aye, 'at we did, she being the biggest and all." He gestured to the smaller vessels swinging at their tethers in the bay. "We thought we would put a few things 'board her, supplies and what not, just in case his lordship, Trahern, comes along with his bloody little fleet. We expect the sloop to return sometime tonight, and we're not anxious to 'ave our tails blown out of the water."

Ruark nodded toward the wreck on the reef. "But surely, if the Spanish fleet could not—"

"Ha!" Harripen interrupted. "Them dons were a bunch of clucks, with a lot of brass and flags and show. But Trahern, now, is another tale, and if there's one to do us ill, 'tis him, if'n he sets his mind to it."

Ruark agreed silently. The Englishman leaned over the rail and as Ruark followed his gaze he saw a pair of heavy carts, each laboriously dragged along by a pair of mules, moving down from the edge of town toward the dock. When they drew alongside, Ruark noted that the first bore several kegs of water and twice the number of hogsheads of rum and ale. The second was half-filled with casks of salted meats and meal, and the rest of it was crammed with crates filled to overflowing with silver, gold plate, and other loot. Beside Hawks on the driver's seat rode the small, black chest of gold coin. It was the first item to come aboard. The treasure was quickly hauled into the captain's cabin, while all the other stuff was swung down on the gun deck, there to be lashed down, carefully out of the way so they would not interfere with the operation of the small cannons. Ruark saw with amusement that the great chest of musket barrels still sat on the deck where it had been left.

When all was secure, Harripen returned to him. "Well, lad, if ye'll be good enough to cast us off, we'll winch her out to her hook again."

Ruark paused as the grizzled fellow stared at him, an odd look in his squinting gaze.

"I'm leaving a pair o' me own men aboard 'er to see what's all 'ere is kept safe. And if ye've noted, the wee box is locked, and 'tis more than one man can hoist." He gave a sly chuckle. "And Mother 'as the keys. 'Tis his way of protecting 'is share. But then, with the possible exception of me an' thee, he's the most honest one 'mongst us."

The man leaned back, guffawing heartily at his own abused humor, then sobered, wiping his nose on his arm.

"Well, I see yer liedyship is waiting for ye, laddie."

Thus dismissed, Ruark had no choice and climbed down to the crudely cobbled jetty, there to cast off as Harripen had indicated. The crew was ordered to the capstan and with a singsong chant, began to march around it. The clank of its pawl counted time, and the anchor cable grew taut, water dripping from its length as the *Good Hound* slowly slipped out into deeper water.

The sun was scarcely more than its own width above the horizon when Ruark strode the length of the pier and passed where Shanna waited for him. She was still stiff and proud, though she kept her eyes from meeting his. Several paces behind she fell in, dropping her skirt into place and walking barefoot across the sand.

Back in the common room, Ruark stopped for an ale, but Shanna went quickly past him and fled up the stairs to their chamber. Listlessly she leaned against the door, closing it, and moved to sit upon the windowsill, pushing out the shutters. Dark clouds had begun to roll overhead and, with the sticky heat, she recognized the ominous signs of a storm. Releasing a ragged sigh, she began to loosen the heavy braid, raking her fingers through the long tresses as she gazed down upon the courtyard below where a young child played chase with a small piglet. His black hair gleamed beneath the waning rays of the sun, much the same way Ruark's did under a candle's soft glow. Wistfully she watched the dark head bob along until, with angry squeals giving evidence of his success, the youngster scooped the animal up into his chubby arms and merrily trotted off toward the village. As he disappeared in the distance behind thin, scrubby trees, Shanna smiled ruefully, and in the silence of the room, the memory of Ruark's words whispered in her brain.

"Beautiful and honorable offsprings of our love."

"But he doesn't love me!" she cried aloud and flung her sandals across the room. Petulantly she began to pluck at the lacings of her skirt while she paced aimlessly about.

"Haughty Shanna! Queen Shanna! Unloved Shanna!"

Hot tears scalded her cheeks. She dropped the skirt and she snatched away the shift. A cool breeze, the first of the day, stirred the draperies at the windows as she lit a candle on a small table beside the tub. She lowered herself into the tepid bath Gaitlier had prepared and lifted a decanter, trickling drams of scented salts through her fingers. They sank into the liquid, dissolving like the fading stars of dawn.

"A strange man you are, Mister Beauchamp," she mused aloud. "You ply me as a lover then berate me as if I were a child and set your cause much awry when you say that I am the last of your choices for a wife."

Relaxing back against the rim, she lost herself in thought. Those words bit deep and rankled hard, but there was a gritty truth in them. Those who had seemed most eager to wed her were those most in need of her father's fortune.

Her gaze settled on a mirror which stood nearby and she stretched out a trim, well-curved leg to turn it until she could see herself. Calmly she considered what she saw, noting the deepening golden color of her oval face. Blue-green eyes rimmed with thick, sooty lashes shone startingly bright in contrast. They were her best asset and usually effective in most any situation when she wanted to gain her way or charm a man. Wheaten streaks, newly bleached by the sun, swirled amid the mass piled high on her head. In the main, she was pleased with her image. Her breasts were high and full, softly hued in creamy white and delicate pink. Without being thin, she knew her waist was smaller than most women could claim, and her legs were long and well-shaped.

She smiled at herself: White, even teeth flashed back at her from the glass.

"Well, my Captain Pirate Ruark, if I have set you to these dire straits wherein your neck is forfeit, you must realize I am also the key to my father's pardon. You would do well to see me safely back to his care. So on that score, my beloved, we shall be even."

The room had darkened when Ruark finally entered. Shanna returned her makeshift draperies to the mirrors and engaged in a leisurely toilette. She heard him rummaging through the sea chests, and some moments later the quietness which had descended pricked her curiosity. When she peeked around the curtain, she found him at the table with a large sheet of parchment spread out before him. He was intent upon the sheet and made notes here and there with a quill. Restoring her shelter, Shanna stood thoughtfully chewing on a knuckle; then with sudden decision she went to the armoire and drew out a red silk gown of daring cut which she donned. It hinted of a Spanish owner, for the bodice was long, and the dress fitted well over her hips, spreading from there to a full hem which gathered up to show tiers of multicolored underskirts. The bare expanse from shoulder to gown was startling and most inviting. The back of the gown dipped low as well, revealing much of the soft, alluring curve of her body. Shanna ran her hand from bosom to hip, smoothing the soft silk.

"This should show that wandering stud the difference between a lady and a common street wench," she mused shrewishly. She did not pause to consider there was little of a ladylike appearance about her. Still, there was nothing of a common wench either.

Tossing aside the screen. Shanna moved toward Ruark, hips swaying provocatively, hair flowing about her shoulders in a manner that belied the care she had given it. It was what Ruark had expected, another assault upon his senses. It took an effort to return his gaze to the parchment, giving no hint of the success of her ploy.

Shanna wandered about the room, doing small, inconsequential chores in an effort to draw his attention but, much to her disappointment, he appeared completely engrossed in his study and gave her no apparent notice.

There was a light knock on the door, and Gaitlier's hesitant voice called for entry. At Ruark's nod, Shanna unlatched the door for the man and was delighted to see him carrying a large platter which bore an assortment of fruits, breads, roasted fowl, and boiled vegetables. There was even a bottle of good French burgundy. Shanna's mouth watered at the enticing aroma, and she could hardly contain her eagerness to taste the fare.

"Oh, Gaitlier!" she exclaimed, "You're a dear man!" She smiled brightly for his blushing pleasure and missed the dark scowl Ruark threw at them over his shoulder.

"Dora prepared it," Gaitlier remarked timidly, casting a cautious glance toward Ruark. He hastened to set his burdens down seeing that Ruark pulled his papers aside for the tray to be placed, then stood sheepishly, rubbing his feet together and looking hesitantly toward the rolled map. Ruark thought the man might speak, but as he leaned back in his chair to wait the servant's pleasure, Gaitlier appeared to lose his nerve. With a quick nod to Shanna and Ruark, he left.

Setting the bolt in place behind him. Shanna seated herself across from Ruark and began to nibble tidbits from the platter while he opened the wine and poured it into the goblets.

"What are you doing?" she finally asked as he took up the map again and began to study it as he ate.

"Trying to find some hint of the channel through the swamp," he replied without looking up.

The meal continued, though both of them took no great relish in the tasty fare. Ruark sipped his wine and sampled the food without so much as a glance in Shanna's direction. After a while he pushed his half-filled plate from him, having lost his appetite under the stoical manner he forced upon himself.

It was with a good measure of dejection that Shanna rose, releasing a sigh. Taking a small slice of melon, she went to the window. A distant rumble of thunder echoed her mood. An errant gust of wind swept into the room, setting the heavy drapes astir and rustling Ruark's charts as he held them down against its teasing. Worried, Shanna pushed the hinged shutters wide and leaned against the sill, watching the evening squall race toward the island. The aging dusk was turned white briefly by a flash of lightning that drew a gasp from Shanna and made her pull back with a start. The storm clouds drew overhead, and the first drops splashed on the thirsty sand. Soon more distant detail was lost in the haze of pounding rain.

His arms spread wide across the charts to keep them from going astray, Ruark raised his eyes to the window. His breath caught in his throat at the stirring sight there. Shanna half sat, half leaned, upon the sill, her thigh raised upon its edge, her face presented in profile as she gazed out at the darkening clouds. The diffused late light made her seem some classic statue in gold and robed in brilliant carmine. Her hair appeared almost transparent, tumbling like an amber waterfall of dark rich honey to her waist. The gown clung to her breasts, conforming to the natural swell that dared the touch of man. As he stared, a flash of lightning crossed the sky, and in its pure light she became a carving in fresh white ivory, her garment mellowing to a gentle pink. The dark clouds sapped the brightness from the sky, and, with its fading, her skin became the oiled oak of a ship's bold figurehead, her hair knotty swirls of ebony. Her face was pensive, her smile sad. Her eyes alone took on a lighter hue, that of a brilliant green sea stirred and swirled by the storm.

"My God," Ruark groaned inwardly, frozen at the table by this innocent panorama. "Does she know how beautiful she is? Does she know how she tortures me?"

His mind whirled. "How can she tease and taunt like a shrewish vixen and refuse me that which I crave? What hellish task has she conjured for me now? She cannot believe that I can long ignore her. Perhaps here again she seeks from me some violence so she can have reason to hate me."

The rain pattered down, and she became a cameo, a work of art, but no artist ever touched a brush who could portray this beauty. Darkness descended with its cloak of black, and she was etched in the candles' glow. Again she became the mysterious beauty with gown of deep red crimson which showed her every movement. Ruark forced his eyes away and stared at paper suddenly bare, void of any marking. His mind wandered, and he considered what plea might bring an end to her unreasoning anger.

Should he ply her as some loving swain? Nay, not that. She'd only throw it back at him. But what did she expect of him? He was lost. He sat bemused. If she knew his mind, would she have pity on him? A simple touch, one finger laid onto his arm. "A gaze," his mind screamed in agony. "Anything!"

Nothing came. No touch. No kiss. No gaze. He looked away in despair.

Shanna's eyes turned slowly to Ruark, who was, it appeared, still poring over his maps. Her throat ached slightly with the effort of suppressed tears, and she had a sudden, intense desire to be held in someone's arms. Forlornly she crossed the room and stretched out across the bed, staring at his bronze, naked back, while a thousand ideas flitted through her mind only to be rejected one by one. A desperate longing welled within her, the need to run her fingers over that expanse and feel his muscles flex beneath her hands.

There were numbers on a sheet before Ruark, notes in his own hand, but his mind no longer made sense of them, though he tried for a long time. Finally he began to fold them away. Shanna saw his movement, and her thoughts flew:

"He's coming to bed! What shall I do now? Perhaps I shall yield to him if he only presses me a bit."

"Nay, damn him!" Her ire rekindled. "He takes a common trollop beneath my nose and so shortly after begging truth and love from me. I'll tutor him rightly on truth and love. I'll see him straining at the bit before I'm through with him."

Ruark rose and stretched, his arms flung high above his head to ease the cramp in his back caused by sitting so long. Fleeing from the bed, Shanna strode haughtily to her makeshift alcove. Frowning, Ruark viewed the sway of her hips until she stepped from his sight. Muttering a low curse, Ruark finished the wine in his glass in a single gulp. He dropped his breeches over the back of a chair and reluctantly slid between the sheets to await her return. He knew he would then enter the battle of knowing she was so close and yet untouchable.

After a moment Shanna came back with a wide linen cloth wrapped around her. Retrieving the blanket, she avoided his gaze as she rolled it again into a barrier and came to place it in the middle of the bed.

It was too much! With a roar of rage Ruark snatched the thing and came to his feet. In a single bound he was to the window and sailed it to the courtyard below. His wrath flared high as he turned, and his nakedness made it all the more magnificent. Shanna stared in rising fear and much admiration.

"Madam, I will have this out!" He approached the bed again and stared at her, a full measure of determination showing in his gaze.

"Oh, you will have this out," Shanna sneered, recovering herself. "You are bold enough to claim that I should be your wife and bold enough to make it understood that this should never hinder you in any way."

"Once on a time in my dungeon, I passed the hours and marked the days unto my end," Ruark began to state his case. "The gaoler made life for me a challenge, and I met it." He flung up his hand dramatically. "Indeed, I threw it in his face."

"What arrogance!" Shanna threw up her hand in a mocking gesture and watched him wrap a discarded towel around his hips.

Ruark gave her words no mind, but continued with his own. "And then into my dark, damp world, there came a light and warmth of a like I had forgotten long past. The bargain she made was beyond my wildest dream, and once again my world was more than the four stone walls with roof and floor and a narrow iron door to check my flight."

It was as if she had not heard him. "And when I came to you, confused and beset, you gave no slightest pause, but tossed me on the bed and once more took advantage of me."

Ruark paused his pacing to point a finger accusingly. " 'Twas on my honor that I acted out my part and waited on your pleasure. Alas, I saw my last hope dashed and was snatched from the lap of its fulfillment to be cast into my hole again."

"And you crept into my chambers in the dark of night and took advantage of the slumber still clinging to my eyes." Shanna whirled away from him and paced the room angrily.

"Once again, madam, fate did favor me." Ruark became avid in his oration and rubbed a fist into his palm. "The hangman was cheated, and I found myself thrust into my fair one's life through purest chance. My rage was great. My need for revenge trembled my knees."

"Indeed, you lost no chance to see that I might be set with child and thus your own ends won. I can guess"—Shanna tossed her head and glared at him—"the fault of the maid in London-town was that she held your seed in her belly."

Ruark stroked his chin, pondering. "But still, I was led a gentler way. I saw the tender breast before me bared and the promise of a righted wrong was made and the bargain done. I despaired, for I could make no further claim and the fairness of that one haunted me at every turn. I had no smallest chance of escape from my own word. But then she came again and overdid the bargain, then I was the one indebted. Still, she welcomed me when I most needed welcome. But fate closed her hand against me, and the vilest of rumors did me out. Another's name was linked to my own by wagging tongues."

"Poor Milly," Shanna sighed heavily. "She fell to you as easily as I did, though she has not yet found the brutish bend of your nature."

"One whose simpleness I could ill abide was said to have enamoured me and taken me to pallet. A clumsy incident was made to mar what little happiness I had."

" 'Twas only her simpleminded clumsiness that made her full aware of your wandering lust. Poor wench that she should have no wealth to lure you. She will certainly end as the one in England."

"I would have sought the lady out to plead my cause, but

therein lies the woe of it." He began to warm with anger. "I was betrayed again and met with no more than good Pitney's boney fist."

"But still you ply me with all the boldness of a rogue, a pirate." Shanna stamped her foot and accused. "You make the cruelty of those below seem lambishly gentle."

"You deny our vows. You deny my rights. You abuse my pride and leave me nothing of yourself. You send me from you on some lackey's strength. You betray me at every turn."

Shanna met his glare and hurled a fierce reply. "You took my heart and set your fingers firm around it, then, no doubt delighted at your success, you rent it with unfaithfulness."

"Unfaithfulness is only from a husband. You play the same to me and yet do say I am no spouse."

"You plead you are my husband true and spite the suitors come to woo me."

"Yea!" Ruark raged. "Your suitors flock about your skirts in heated lust, and you yield them more than me."

Shanna paused before him, rage etched upon her face. "You're a churlish cad!"

"They fondle you boldly and you set not their hands away from you."

"A knavish blackguard!"

"You are a married woman!"

"I am a widow!"

"You are my wife!" Ruark shouted to be heard over the rising wind outside.

"I am not your wife!"

"You are!"

"Not!"

There they stood with but a yard's length between them yet an ocean's breadth apart, each firmly set in conviction, neither bent to yield, and anger writhing on each face until each seemed the visage of some twisted evil sprite. They gave no heed to the mounting fury that closed its grip upon the island; instead a thousand words rushed to their lips. Of epithets, a score or more were ready. For each it was a cause too righteous to be surrendered. But the raging night without had heard enough of petty threats and pleas.

A bolt of lightning flashed, bringing the room to a stark white and black for the sizzling space of a full breath. Long before the lightning died, the chamber was filled with a stunning crash of thunder that held its pealing voice until the stones of the walls seemed to tremble. It was still echoing when another bolt rent the air outside, and, in its deathly light, Shanna's face showed suddenly stark with fear, her mouth frozen in a soundless scream of terror. The thunder came again and seemed to fling her toward Ruark, and suddenly her arms were choking tightly about his neck, her face buried against his throat. A pitiful, keening cry threaded thinly from her lips as she mindlessly sought whatever shelter he would offer. His ire forgotten, Ruark wrapped her in his arms and tried to still the quaking of her body as she clung to him. A gust of wind struck the inn and flung the inner shutters wide, sending gusts of rain and wind to lash the room and touch the candles out.

Ruark stood the shaking Shanna near the bed and closed and bolted the shutters against the violent blasts. The night was assaulted with an endless flash of lightning that seemed to touch the low island everywhere. The thunder followed in bellowing rolls and nerve-shattering crashes. The whole island was whipped and stirred into a hellish brew by the winds, which shrieked around the eaves and cornices to pelt any unwary fool who might venture in its paths. Rain rattled like leaden shot against the shutters, now bowed and strained with the unrelenting fury of a hurricane.

Shanna cowered in the dark. The flickers of light showed Ruark her face, and his heart was wrenched by what he saw. Her eyes were wide, and tears streamed down her cheeks. She crouched as if she sought some den or lair away from the storm. As he took her into his arms, she clawed at his chest and mewled:

"Love me, Ruark."

"I do, my love, I do," he whispered softly in relenting pity.

The room flashed white, and he saw Shanna's head roll from side to side. Her eyes were tightly closed, though tears still crept between the lids, and her face was twisted in a grimace of fright. She pressed her fists against her ears to shut out the beat of thunder that washed over them like a crashing breaker on the beach.

"No! No!" she shrieked against the din and caught his arm. "Take me! Take me now!" Anything to shut out and release her from this flood of fear that assaulted her from every side, even, it seemed, from within.

Shanna fell back upon the bed, pulling Ruark down with her. In another flash he saw the intent eagerness of her face as she pressed against him. His blood warmed, and he forgot all else of the moment.

The storm could have been contained in the room and they would have given it no heed. There was between them that storm of passion that blinded as surely as the greatest stroke of lightning and deafened their ears as completely as a crashing roll of thunder close about. Each touch was fire, each word was bliss, each movement in their union a rhapsody of passion that rose and built until it seemed that every instrument in all the world combined to bring the music of their souls into a consuming crescendo that left them still and quiet, warm like the softly glowing after-coals of a universal holocaust. Shanna lay limp and drowsy on his arm, her cheeks still flushed with the gentle blush of pleasure, her breath softly stirring the furriness on his chest. Had the world beat at their door, Ruark doubted that he could have lifted a finger for their defense: With stupendous effort he turned his head and buried his face in her hair, savoring the fragrance of it.

Some moments later Shanna's voice came, small and quiet, hesitant. "Am I so lacking that you must seek out others?"

"There's been no one else, Shanna," he stated simply.

Shanna leaned her head back against his arm and tried to see his features in the dark. "Milly?"

A streak of lightning illuminated his face, and he met her inquiring gaze. "That little vixen brewed a mischief in her mind, love, and used it to prick you. There was never anything between us. I swear."

Shanna rolled onto her back, struck by her own folly and what it had wrought. In shame she covered her face with her arm. "Why didn't you tell me?"

Ruark raised himself on an elbow and leaned over her, resting his hand upon her flat belly. "You never gave me a chance, Shanna."

A miserable moan escaped her, and tears began to trace down the side of her face. Gently Ruark lifted her arm and kissed her trembling mouth, hushing the sobs which shook her. Her worried whisper came against his lips.

"Do you hate me overmuch, my Lord Captain Pirate Ruark?"

"Aye," he muttered hoarsely. "I hate you when you hold yourself from me. But it never lasts beyond your first, soft kiss."

Fiercely Shanna locked her arms about his neck and began to spread eager kisses mingled with salty tears upon his face and lips, half crying, half laughing until her fears, much subdued, vanished completely. Trusting now as she had never done before, Shanna nestled snugly in the comfort of his encircling arms. Thus, even with the threatening peril below and nature gone mad without, they drifted like tender babes into the nether world of slumber.

Howling winds still beat the gables, and torrents of rain battered against the rattling shutters as the sky lightened to a dark, leaden gray. Shanna paid no heed to the storm as she stirred from sleep, for as long as it continued they need not hasten from the bed, and Ruark would remain in her arms. Her eyes, soft and caressing, traced the sleeping face pressed upon her breast, and she smiled warmly with kind recall of the hours past, as sweet in her mind as any treasured nectar upon the tongue. Releasing a sigh of contentment, she sank again into blissful sleep.

At the noon hour Gaitlier brought them food but hastened away after depositing the tray on the table, seeing that Shanna frowned at him over a highly clutched sheet, while Ruark, hair tousled and shortened breeches hurriedly donned, waited beside the door, seeming impatient for him to leave.

When the man retreated from the chamber, Ruark leaned back against the door, closing it, while his eyes turned to Shanna. At her soft, welcoming smile, he crossed to the bed and fell upon it to take her into his arms and nuzzle her throat while his hand slipped beneath the sheet to explore softer places. She giggled, nibbling at his ear, and answered his caress by curving her body seductively against him.

"Madam, you have the wiles of a vixen," he lightly teased. "Now say the truth, are you seducer or seduced, ravisher or ravished, witch or bewitched?"

"Why, all of course," Shanna rolled away from him, laughing. "What would you have me be, sir? The seduced?" Lazily she stretched, arching her back.

Ruark watched her soft, curving body, shimmery pale in the glower of enraged day. She was lovely beyond words. Becoming aroused, he reached for her, but with a throaty chuckle, Shanna averted his outstretched hand and came to her knees.

"Or perhaps today the seducer?" She pushed him down upon his back then boldly leaned low until her breasts touched against his hard, brown chest and kissed him with such passion that Ruark trembled with his eagerness.

"Or do you prefer a witch?" Shanna tossed her head, flinging her hair wildly, and made a claw of her hand, raking her nails lightly across his naked ribs.

With a low growl Ruark rose, and in a sudden moment it was she who lay beneath him. There was a merry twinkle in her eyes, but he had lost all the mood of playing and was most serious as his lips met hers.

In the hall outside their chamber, a loud clump of boots thudded, and Harripen's booming voice roared, "Ruark! Ruark! Ahoy there, Captain Ruark!"

With a curse Ruark flung himself across the bed and snatched his pistol and sabre. Shanna made frantic haste to place herself beneath the sheet and jerk it high about her neck. The door swung open and with a crash rebounded against the wall. In that moment Harripen found himself staring at an enraged man who held a full-cocked pistol centered squarely on his forehead. The empty scabbard still slid across the floor and clattered against the table legs. More than a trifle worried, Harripen flung his arms wide.

"Avast there, laddie!" he bellowed. "Belay that now!"

"Dammit, man!" Ruark growled. "What brings you here?"

"I've come unarmed and only meant to talk."

Harripen stood carefully motionless until Ruark lowered the pistol and placed it, still cocked, on the bedside table.

"Unarmed?" Ruark snorted and pointed with his blade to the top of Harripen's boot where the hilt of a small dirk showed. The Englishman shrugged as he lowered his arms.

"Were I that honest, me bucko, I would not be a pirate."

The man's eyes went to Shanna and stayed a bit longer and burned a bit brighter than Ruark cared for. At the open lust she saw in those gray eyes, Shanna shivered and clutched the sheet tighter to her.

"Didn't know ye were engaged, laddie," Harripen leered. " 'Tis sorry I am that I disturbed ye."

"Get the blasted hell out of here!" Ruark snapped. "I'll be down in good time."

The Englishman gestured with his hands. "Now simmer down, laddie. I meant ye no ill. I thought ye'd be eating now, 'tis all."

With a shrug that seemed to excuse his intrusion, he strode across the room to the platter of food and hefting half a fowl with grimy hands, began to consume it as he talked.

" 'Tis only that I wanted to have out a matter of importance wit' ye, lad."

"There is nothing I can think of that we need discuss," Ruark replied tersely.

Harripen chortled and came around to Shanna's side of the bed. His small, watery gray eyes never left her. He ignored Ruark's deepened scowl and flopped down upon the bed, giving Shanna a greasy smile as he tore a chunk of bird and stuffed it into his mouth with his fingers. Shanna backed away from him in disgust, jerking the tail of the sheet from beneath his sandy boots. She came quickly into the welcome shelter of Ruark's arms. Ruark half sat, half knelt, with one knee on the edge of the bed directly across from Harripen. The sabre blade completed the circle about her, the sharp edge presented outward toward the other captain. Beneath the Englishman's leer, Shanna's skin crawled, and she clutched the sheet higher as she pressed back against Ruark's chest. He was as rigid as a rock, and beneath her head she could feel the tick of a muscle in his shoulder.

Harripen pointed with the hen and picked a piece of its meat from his bristly chin. "Aye, but she's a lusty one. A mite 'ot and eager for ye, too, 'twould appear, the way she snapped Carmelita off yer lap. What will ye take for her? She's hardly worth the trouble she's caused ye, lad." The aging buccaneer leaned forward eagerly, and his red-rimmed eyes gleamed, belying his bickering. Tilting his head, he grinned with one eye half closed in an unfinished wink. "Bend your ear, bucko. I'll give ye another pouch for a thrice of nights with her."

"It may be your time will come," Ruark replied slowly, "but for now, at least, she's mine."

"Aye, ye made 'at clear already, ye 'ave," the older man sighed. "Still—"

Harripen could not resist reaching out a greasy hand to caress the shining rich tumble of locks Shanna displayed, but he halted suddenly as he realized if he moved his hand but one small degree further he would have less than a whole finger left, for the razor edge of the blue blade abruptly barred his way. His eyes shifted to Ruark's and widened slightly. He was met with a smile that was at once calm yet filled with such a strange, deadly patience that the skin on the back of Harripen's neck crawled. He was immediately sure that he could feel the cold breath of death upon his nape.

Harripen jerked his hand back as if he had touched fire and rose quickly from the bed, putting a goodly space between himself and the other.

"Hell and damnation, you're touchy!" he growled. "But I came not to speak of her."

He tossed the half-eaten bird at the table and missed by a wide margin. He caught Ruark's reflection in the mirror, and those amber eyes marked him like those of a wary hawk. Facing about, Harripen clasped his hands behind his back and rocked on his heels for a moment before he began almost delicately:

"Me own ship is a bit smaller than Robby's, but I've had me eye on the *Good Hound* for a long time. I do not wish to test the edge of your sword for her, but perhaps a bit of a bargain. Ye're new here and know little of our ways. I could make us all a good fortune with a ship like the *Good Hound* and would not waste her sail or worthy men puttering about the likes of Trahern. I have in mind that my share of the gold and my own ship would be a fair trade for the one you have."

He paused, seeming to run out of words.

Ruark rose from the bed and moved to stand at the end, bracing a shoulder against the massive post. He rested the point of the sabre on the floor, now turning the edge of the blade away from

Harripen, acknowledging the truce. It was a long moment before he answered.

"This is a thing which I will have to think on for a time. I am not in doubt as to my skill, but much of what you say is true. And though I have my own share and Pellier's, I still have need for wealth. I will think on it and give you an answer soon."

He strode forward and took Harripen's arm, leading him slowly to the door.

"There is but one thing now which I would ask of you. This portal is solid." He tapped the door with the hilt of his sword. "And a fist upon it makes a good sound. You know," he stared thoughtfully through Harripen, "I almost stilled your bargain before you spoke it. I would suggest that hereafter you pause a bit and not startle me again."

Almost eagerly Harripen nodded and was ushered out. The door closed behind him, and he heard the bolt slam firmly in place. The pirate wiped a drop of sweat from the end of his nose and released his breath. Ruark seemed almost too gentle, but his eyes savaged a man's very soul when he was angry. Harripen walked away and felt lucky that he had not taken a nick or two.

Ruark pressed his ear against the door and listened to Harripen's boots clump down the stairs, while Shanna hurriedly donned her clothing. Ruark had barely stepped away from the portal when a soft tapping came on the panel. Cautiously he opened it a crack and found Gaitlier crouched outside. The small man straightened and met Ruark's gaze over the top of the glasses he wore.

"Might I come in for a moment, sir?" His voice was almost a whisper.

Nonplussed at the servant's presence and manner, Ruark opened the portal wider and beckoned him in. Gaitlier fussed over the table for several moments and retrieved the fowl from the floor. In the nervous gesture Ruark had noted before, he rubbed his feet one against the other, appearing at a loss. Ruark considered him from the foot of the bed where he half sat upon the end rail, waiting for Gaitlier to speak, and finally he sought to bring the problem out.

"Well, man!" he urged. "Let's have it."

Shanna knelt behind Ruark and rested her chin on his shoulder, as puzzled as he and twice as curious. The small man shuffled his feet and swept his eyes across the ceiling as if he sought divine aid. Now he faced them and, drawing a deep breath, began as if stepping into a chilling sea.

"I know you are man and wife!"

His statement was blunt and brought a gasp from Shanna and a low growl from Ruark. Gaitlier plunged on.

"I know, too, sir, that there is something in your past to be afraid of and that you are, in fact, Trahern's bondslave." He gestured to a small grill high on the wall where it had not been noticed and explained. "A listening port and a servant's room beyond." At their bemused stares he continued. "A way for a serving man to know before he enters what is amiss that he should not interrupt. A necessary thing with Captain Pellier."

Shanna blushed in painful embarrassment and hoped fervently that the storm had shielded their passion.

Gaitlier caught Ruark's frown cast toward the door and eased his worry. "Those fools know nothing of the port and would never guess its existence. An idea from the Far East, I believe. At any rate, quite handy." He drew a ragged breath. "I have a bargain for you, and I would hope a more honest one than Captain Harripen's. I know the way through the swamp." He paused to let the significance sink in, and the only hint that it had was a new attention paid him by Ruark. "I would be shot if any of them"— he jerked his head toward the door—"as much as suspected that I knew."

For a long moment there was no sound but the shriek of the wind and the pelting of the rain on the tiles of the roof. Gaitlier removed his eyeglasses and polished the lenses with his shirt.

"There is a price, of course," he ventured timidly. "When you escape, I will go with you, and the girl, Dora, as well."

He replaced the spectacles on his nose and stared at the two of them with a hint of sternness playing about his lips.

"I will aid you in every way possible and go with you to point out the entrance to the channel."

Ruark gave the small servant his closest regard. He had never guessed the courage the man contained and was a little amazed.

His frown showed for a moment, and Gaitlier misread it.

"You cannot force the secret from me," he warned with enough determination to make his point.

Ruark smiled and caressed the butt of the pistol with his palm, meeting Gaitlier's eyes squarely before he asked, "And what makes you think we plan to escape?"

"You should, if you don't." Gaitlier's gaze did not waver, and he explained further. "The sloop came back from Los Camellos last night just before the storm broke. The *Jolly Bitch* was nearly caught by a frigate standing off the shore as she was cutting the bondsmen adrift in a whale boat. She was given no chance and took several hits before she could fly for safety."

"A brigantine." Ruark laughed.

"The *Hampstead!*" Shanna joined from behind him. "No frigate, surely."

"Whatever!" Gaitlier waved away the correction. "These brigands have become doubtful of your wisdom and chafe at the loss of several good men. They only wait on the proper moment to do you in, and the lady will suffer a far worse fate if half of what they plan comes to an end."

Ruark considered the information, and Shanna held her silence to give him the space to think. He stared at the floor for a long time and then began to nod his head. His gaze lifted and fixed on Gaitlier.

"You are right, of course. We must see to our opportunities and make the best of them." He turned to look at Shanna, and the set of his jaw tightened. "We shall flee the place at the first chance."

Eagerly Gaitlier pulled a chair close and sat in it, leaning forward. "The channel is difficult at best with the westerlies blowing, but after a big storm passes, the winds bend northerly and blow light for a day or so. 'Twould be the best time for a short crew to sail a ship through."

"There are things to see about." Ruark grew restless, but his eyes sparkled with excitement. "Can you return after dark? We must venture out in the storm, but none can know."

Gaitlier had one last question. "You will take the girl, Dora, too?"

"Aye!" Ruark assured him. "To leave an innocent here is unthinkable."

"I will be here, then. Of a late hour, or if the storm slackens any, before. I will tell Dora to gather what we will need."

" 'Tis done then!"

Chapter 19

THE room became a world unto itself, a haven against the raging hurricane that swept across the seas and hurled its winds against the impudent structures made by puny man. It was the swamp that took the force from the waves and left the humble dune of sand unwashed. The inn huddled beneath the crest of the hill and with its solid walls and heavy tiled roof gave shelter to the ones within.

The oaken door protected Ruark and Shanna further against the drunken, gluttonous beasts below. Several times during the afternoon the pirates mounted the stairs and pounded their fists upon the chamber's portal, begging Ruark to bring his charge before them for a dance or something better to while away the hours. It was only his threat of leaden ball and well-honed blade that held them at bay. They were made to slink away, muttering curses and dire threats, but go they did as none of them felt brave enough to test Ruark's skill, and a quick accounting of the odds left all too few standing.

The hour aged, and darkness fell. Still the shutters groaned and rattled against the unabated onslaught of the storm. Shanna welcomed the noise and fury of the tempest. It brought to her a respite, for, as it raged without, it sealed them in, and it seemed

427

that Ruark's presence was the factor she had sought her lifetime through. He was ever near. If she turned suddenly, he would raise his eyes to her and smile. If she dozed a space and woke, she could lie still and listen to the sounds he made as he moved about or shuffled his charts. Even though the storm threatened to sweep them into the sea, she feared its strength no longer, and there was a thought in her mind that she would never again be terrified by lightning or thunder.

Still, it was a relief when Gaitlier knocked on the door. The mild man kicked in a large bag with his foot, and when he had placed the supper tray on the table and carefully closed the portal, he opened the bag with covert pride, to display a rope ladder. It would serve them well for their escape. As he was about to leave he paused at the door and shook his head with some worry.

"Dora has had to hide in the pantry to escape the attentions of Harripen and the others. Carmelita has served them food and drink and much more, but they grow weary of her and seek new entertainment."

The hours took on the elderly hue of night. The din outside had become wearisome, and the drunken revelry below dwindled until only an occasional sound was heard. The night wore on, and Ruark waxed restless. He paced the room; fondled his brace of pistols and repeatedly checked the priming; and drew his sword to test its edge.

A slow and subtle shift came in the roar of the storm. The wind no longer howled as loudly around the eaves, and the rain dwindled to a fine spurting mist. No sooner had they both become aware of this than a light tap came at the door, and Ruark ushered in a grinning Gaitlier.

"We'll set these fellows on their heels," he chortled, rubbing his hands together gleefully. "A blow or two for vengeance, eh?"

Ruark remained aloof from the man's eagerness, and his brow knitted. "I fear I shall have to forego our journey, at least for tonight," he stated solemnly, and the servant's face fell. "The pirates seem restless, and I am wary of some treachery afoot." He halted near the door and listened for a moment. "They are all too quiet to please me."

Gaitlier grinned in renewed elation, and his eyes twinkled beyond the tiny panes. " 'Tis only that they are all besot," he chuckled. "Carmelita grew tired with their play and served them only strong black rum. 'Twill be some hours before they recover."

Ruark contemplated the man for a moment. He opened the door and crept to the head of the stairs to see for himself. The common room was dark with only a few short stubs of candles burning for light, yet he could make out a full dozen dark shapes scattered about in ludicrous positions of slumber. Mother was sprawled upon his belly, full length on the table, and snored loudly with a deep grumble and high-pitched whistle.

Satisfied, Ruark returned, bolted the door, and then slid a heavy iron-bound chest before it. At his nod, Gaitlier began to secure the ladder to the iron grillwork outside the window. Ruark doffed all but his breeches. After checking his pistols again, he laid them at full cock on the table where they would be handy to Shanna's need. Gaitlier, too, stripped to his pants and hung a heavy cutlass from his rope belt. Ruark ducked beneath his sabre's sash, and the two of them rubbed lamp soot over their bodies and limbs. As Shanna stood brushing her hair, Ruark peered over her shoulder into the mirror and smeared the black, greasy stuff over his face. A gay laugh of amusement escaped her as she faced him and, with rich enthusiasm, helped him spread the soot on his chest and arms.

"I always thought there was something of the blackguard in you. 'Tis at last beginning to show."

Ruark drew a blackened finger along the slim, delicate line of her nose in revenge and chuckled as she gasped in feigned outrage and scrubbed heartily at the sooty streak.

The candles were doused except for the one in a ship's lantern, which they set upon the table. Brushing Shanna's lips with a kiss, Ruark closed the door on the lantern, bringing the room to blackness. Shanna felt a last squeeze on her hand, then heard the ladder rattle down. She waited until she was sure they were gone and then retrieved the ladder as Ruark had instructed her, tucked it inside the rail, and closed the shutters before she opened the lantern.

Now it was only a matter of waiting. Ruark had tried to tell her what they planned, but she had been anxious to be assured of his safety and missed much of what he said, remembering only that it had something to do with the pirate's powder magazine and gathering brush in the gulley. Without thinking Shanna mimicked Ruark's actions as she checked the pistols, saw to their priming, then laid them down again; she tested the edge of the small dagger and then slipped it into her waistband; restlessly she paced the room and the only difference was that, in a woman's way, she tidied here and there.

Ruark's jerkin lay across the arm of a chair and lifting it, she smoothed its soft leather over her arm. It was odd how the garment already seemed a part of him, like the short breeches. It even bore his scent. She rubbed her cheek against it, savoring the manly smell of leather.

"What have I become?" Shanna murmured in some wonder. "A wife waiting for her man? Is it always thus with wives? Do they seize upon some manly garment and relive past moments of bliss while they bide the time?"

She glanced about the room and was bemused by her mood. "Strange, I feel him gone. There is that which is missing now. I never felt his presence as much as I feel his absence."

It suddenly rankled Shanna that she should find life incomplete unless she could reach out her hand and touch him.

"I will not be trapped," she assured herself and hung the jerkin neatly on a chair back. She had set a glass to mark the time since no clock graced the room, and she now noticed it was only half run through. She gave a deep sigh to ease the lonely ache that sprang up within her bosom and began to pace again.

A gust rattled the shutters and made her jump. Large drops of rain began to fall again, and the wind curling around a cornice gave a low moan. The inn creaked as the storm renewed its attack upon the island. Her eyes fell to the hourglass, and her spirit showed its shallow depth as she saw only a small amount of sand remained in the top. "Nearly an hour gone! Has aught come amiss?" Nervously Shanna began to nibble at a fingernail. "Have they been found out? Or perhaps fallen upon some evil fate?"

The grains of sand raced in eager frolic for the bottom of the glass. "Does he lie dead somewhere with this storm beating down upon him?" She shuddered at the thought. "Oh, I must be calm. He will come soon."

Deliberately Shanna placed her hands to her sides where they made small fists, but they opened only to clench again—and again—and again. For the thousandth time she paced the chamber but returned to watch the last grains trickle to the bottom. She reached out to turn the piece over then froze as a small sound intruded over the noise of the wind-driven rain; as she listened, another pebble struck the shutters.

Smothering a cry of joy, Shanna whirled and flew to the shutter latch then suddenly remembered that she had forgotten to close the lantern. Rushing back, she did so quickly then ran to the window and threw the ladder over the railing. She could not see below and for the sake of caution stood back in the shadows, training a pistol on the top of the rail until she recognized the dark head and broad shoulders of Ruark. He came through the window with a bound and turned to boost Gaitlier over the railing. Shanna only intended to touch Ruark's arm and ask him of his success, but somehow as he faced around, her arms went about him, and she held herself to him with all the strength she was capable of. Ruark felt the trembling of her body against him and tightened his embrace securely about her, lifting her chin to kiss her, oblivious to Gaitlier, who busied himself retrieving the ladder, closing the shutters, and cautiously opening the lantern.

The two finally parted, and Gaitlier handed a towel to Ruark and began to dry himself. It was as if their entry signaled the storm to return in all its furiousness, but Shanna no longer cared about the tempest. She curled herself in a chair as the men huddled over the charts and talked in hushed tones. Her cheek rested against the leather jerkin, and its smell filled her head. The barest hint of a smile played across her lips, and her eyes glowed with a warmth no one could explain, least of all Shanna.

When their discussion ended, Gaitlier clothed himself, mumbled a last good night, then let himself out. Ruark barred the door after him as Shanna rose and went to stand beside the bed. Her fingers tugged at the lacing of her waistband; suddenly there were willing hands to help. When the skirt and blouse had been joined on the floor by her shift, Shanna turned in Ruark's embrace and slid her arms about his neck, seeking his lips with feverish abandon.

Morning came, and Shanna felt Ruark leave the bed. She listened to him move about as he dressed. There was something wrong, but she could not quite put a finger on it. Opening her eyes, she stared at the peeling walls where his shadow played with odd distortion in the bright sunlight streaming in the windows.

That was it! Bright sunlight! The room was silent as it had not been for several days. No wind whistled. No storm thundered. She rolled onto her back and saw only the blue sky beyond the open shutters. An occasional fluff of cloud spoiled an otherwise unblemished sky and lent a counterpoint of dirty white to the crystal blue.

Ruark came to the bedside, fully arrayed in his pirate attire. He placed two weapons on the table, a small flintlock and a huge horse pistol.

"Gaitlier scavenged these from the pirates while they slept. They're loaded, primed, and ready," he admonished carefully. "I must go and lay the fuses so all will be in readiness for tonight." His brow furrowed with worry. He did not like the idea of leaving her, but Gaitlier was unfamiliar with the workings of gunpowder. During the storm he and Gaitlier had prepared a contraption which would hopefully divert the pirates' attention and allow them to escape. All that remained to do was to place the oiled fuse and gunpowder beneath the brush in the gully on the hillside above the blockhouse, which was used as a magazine. The brush was held in place by slim poles. Hopefully the lot of it, put on fire by the gunpowder and aided by heavy logs above, would roll down against the wall of the magazine when the charge was set off and cause a general alarm to be raised. He could make no test, but only trust in his design. It was as ready as it could be, and fate would see the whole thing out.

"Gaitlier is watching the door, and the pirates are still asleep below. I'll only be gone for a short time, and I must leave while the moment is ripe."

He bent over her, and his mouth took hers in a fervent kiss.

His hand passed along her arm and squeezed it reassuringly before he straightened. With a last glance over his shoulder, he slipped from the window, dropped to the ground. His eyes searched the quay. The schooner was still out in the bay though she had dragged her anchor a bit, but if anything the *Good Hound* was better aligned for their purposes than before. Ruark made his way quickly around the structure to the back. In his haste, he did not see the lone figure leaning in the shadows of the rear doorway. A long moment passed, and Ruark was gone, and the silhouette staggered into bright sunlight to become a man. The red, watery eyes squinted down the path and blinked painfully.

"Be damned!" the swarthy pirate slurred. "The hawk has fled his nest and left the little bird ripe for the plucking."

Shanna huddled in the corner of the bed as she listened to the muffled voices in the hall. Only a few moments before, Gaitlier had whispered through the door that he had overheard the pirates plotting to invade the room to seize her. One of them had seen Ruark slip away. She had bade the servant hurry to seek out Ruark since Gaitlier's slight frame would delay the miscreants only a small while. Testing the heavy bar on the door and the weight of the large chest Ruark had placed to further block the entrance, she had found them both sturdy bulwarks for her protection. Still, she had prepared for attack. The smaller of the two pistols, along with her dagger, went beneath the pillow; the oversize flintlock she held in both hands, its long muzzle resting on the bed before her. She braced herself for the worst the pillagers could deliver.

A stealthy testing of the portal, followed by a creak of the wood as someone leaned a shoulder against it, soon brought a meaty fist pounding on the planks as the man outside found the door both bolted and barred.

Making her voice sound as though she had just roused from slumber, Shanna called out. "Who is it?"

A gruff clearing of the throat came before the answer. "Captain 'Arripen, milady. I bid ye open the door. I have a bit o' news to discuss with ye."

Shanna gave no credence to the crude ruse. "On a cold day

in hell," she replied. "But you're welcome to test this bit of lead I hold."

Her voice had barely stilled before a loud crash resounded from the door, trembling the planks. The bolts, bar, and hinges groaned in protest. Then another jarring of the thick planks followed and still another, which was heavier than those before. Another deafening crunch, and the wood began to splinter away from the hasps and bolts.

The bar jumped and began to crack as it took the full weight of the assault. With trembling hands Shanna raised the horse pistol until it centered on the door. Closing her eyes tightly, she squeezed. The flintlock went off with a roar that numbed her ears. The shot seemed to shatter the door asunder, and it caved inward with a mighty crash. Though one of the picaroons was flung backward against the far wall, the others charged through with a rush, the mulatto, Harripen, and the Dutchman squeezing through before the last two followed.

Shanna threw the useless weapon at them and fumbled with her numbed fingers, but before she could find the other pistol they were upon her. She snarled, shrieked in rage and fought like a demon in a frenzy, kicking, scratching, biting, but desperate as it was, her strength was not such to prevail against the five who had fallen upon her.

The Dutchman seized his fingers in her long hair, and she was cruelly jerked back upon the bed. Hands clawed at her thrashing limbs, stretching them on the bed. Harripen twisted a towel across her mouth to stifle her cries and bent low until his ale-soured breath smothered her.

"We've come for our share, wench. We cast lots for ye to see what one of us will go first on ye. And there's no Mister Ruark saving ye this time. We've seen to that."

Shanna's eyes were wide with outrage and horror. Her mind raged on in fear. Had they killed Ruark? Is that what he meant? She lunged beneath their pawing hands and writhed frantically to escape their rough caresses.

"Hold her!" a younger man snarled when Shanna's knee struck his groin. He retreated from the side of the bed where he had tried to mount her and glared at his companions. "She ain't but a little thing, and you can't even hold her still."

" 'Ell's bells, boy! Move aside and let a real man show you what to do," chortled Harripen.

"Like hell I will!" the youth railed. "Now hold her!"

The meaty hands bruised Shanna's wrists and ankles, spreading her out on the bed. The pirates leered down at her, and the fetid stench that clung to them nearly made Shanna retch in revulsion. The dark-skinned mulatto withdrew from the fray and lounged beside the door, while the young one, having boasted much of his prowess with women throughout the night, began to unfasten his garments while he laughingly bragged.

"No need to trouble yerself with any more show of struggles, milady. I'll make you forget that bastard bondsman."

"Get on with it!" Harripen sneered. "Or I'll see ye made last. I've 'ad it hot for the wench long enough."

The Dutchman chortled. "Just yer luck, Harripen, to draw the last lot."

Shanna squealed beneath the towel as the youth reached out his hand toward her blouse. Though she tried to twist away, the other three held her, and she could not move. The sound of rending cloth went through her very soul, and she was filled with a sickening horror. Again she tried to scream as the young man's grasping fingers began tearing at her shift and pulling up her skirts. Suddenly he was lifted as if by a giant hand and thrown from the bed. Before he touched the floor, the room reverberated with the deafening crash of a shot, and all eyes flew to Ruark as he charged through the door, raising the other pistol as he flung the empty one aside to reach for his sword. It was obvious that Gaitlier had found him just in time. But now the mulatto stepped from behind the door and swung a heavy belaying pin across Ruark's shoulders, sending him sprawling forward; the pistol flew from his grasp. The sword was pinned beneath him, and half dazed, Ruark tried to roll and free his blade, but all four of the captains fell upon him. It was a wild melee as Ruark fought to regain his feet, but he was lifted up and pinned against the wall. Harripen stood free, snatching out his cutlass. He raised it for the blow.

A weird moan escaped Harripen's lips, and the blade fell from his fingers. In horror he looked over his shoulder where the hilt of a small silver dagger stood out boldly. His gaze lifted, and he stared into the wicked bore of the small flintlock Shanna held. She faced them all in magnificent rage.

"Back off!"

Her snarl held a ragged warning, and Harripen stumbled back to seat himself unexpectedly on a large chest. The pistol was now trained on the huge mulatto. Seeing the sureness of her vengeance, he backed away carefully. Ruark sank a fist into the soft belly of the Dutchman and scooped up the loaded pistol before he drew the long, thirsty sabre. He went to stand beside Shanna, and his cold gaze swept the pirates slowly.

"It seems your own laws fail you, but if you have a taste for it, I'll be glad to oblige."

He raised his brow in a question and the blade in a threat toward Harripen. The Englishman shrugged and, having worked the small blade from his shoulder, now tossed it to Ruark's feet.

"I am wounded," he grunted and remained seated.

The blade moved on to the Dutchman who still held both arms across his gut. He shook his head with such vigor that his heavy sagging jowls seemed to flap. The mulatto frowned and might have accepted the bait, but he stared at the small pistol Shanna still held on him and backed slowly through the door. The others made haste to follow, but once out the door there was a dead silence in the inn.

Ruark stepped to one side of the door and unloaded the pistol through it, hearing the shot whine viciously as it ricocheted down the corridor. He laughed in satisfaction as the sound of running boots now filled the hall.

"You have lost more over this maid," he shouted after them, "than over any other treasure you ever sought. Run, my good friends. Flee from her."

Muffled curses drifted back as at least one of the brigands stumbled in his haste on the stairs. Ruark turned back toward Shanna. When she saw the concern in his eyes, she shook her head and stuffed the tattered corners of her blouse into the top of her shift.

"I have endured much better than they," she assured him. "But what now, my Captain Pirate Ruark?"

Ruark sheathed his sword and surveyed the damage while he

reloaded his pistols. The young pirate lay sprawled on his back, his eyes rolled upward; the door was a shambles and would offer no further protection. Another pirate was a shapeless heap in the hall.

"We must go," he stated bluntly, "before they gather their wits and drink up their courage."

Preparations had already been made. Ruark snatched the rope ladder from the chest and threw it over the narrow balcony outside the windows, tying the upper end in place with a knot that could be pulled loose from below; Shanna snatched the bundles of clothing Gaitlier had brought from the bottom of the armoire.

Ruark checked the courtyard below before he tossed the bundles to the ground. He gestured Shanna to the window and lifted her over the railing. As she climbed down, he slipped over the sill and closed the shutters behind him. It was a small misdirection, but it would compel the pirates to search the rest of the inn before setting out in pursuit. Shanna grabbed up the bundles and as Ruark directed, headed for the back of the inn and the edge of the swamp. Ruark tugged on the cord, and the ladder fell down to him. He let it trail in the sand behind him, erasing their footprints as he backed along, following Shanna's path. Once well into the dense undergrowth with its stunted, wind-twisted trees, he hid the cumbersome ladder in a crevice beneath a bush and joined Shanna, taking the bundles from her. Taking her hand in his, he led her at a breakneck pace across the brow of the hill and downward until they waded up to their knees in slime-covered water. The swamp was dark at this level, for, though the sun was high, little light filtered through the dense foliage above them. A fetid stench rose from the water, recently roiled by the storm, and Shanna, pulled along by Ruark, gagged on the suffocating odor of it.

There were strange splashings and slitherings, an occasional rapid fluttering punctuated by startled squawks or grunts as the creatures of this dark morass fled from these intruders who entered their domain. Shanna was gasping for breath, and her chest ached when Ruark finally stopped and lifted her out of the water onto the twisted bole of a huge cypress. He pulled himself up beside her, and they both rested, lying back against the trunk that rose behind them like a towering bulwark. It was a long time before they could breathe easily again. Shouts sounded on the hill high above them, and they waited in silence, brushing leeches and biting insects from each other. The noise of pursuit gradually faded as the pirates realized that an attempt to search for them in the swamp was hopeless.

Ruark opened one of the bundles, lifted a gourd filled with water, and broke the wax seal, handing it to Shanna. She took a large draught then choked as she discovered it was heavily laced with rum. She sipped more slowly and savored the bite of it. The grog soothed her parched throat and helped to relax her. He handed her a small strip of dried meat, tough and chewy but, in this moment, as savory as any they had tasted. Shanna gnawed another piece of it, and Ruark filled his own mouth, sated his own thirst, and, as he chewed, looked upward to mark the passage of the sun.

"Gaitlier and the girl will be waiting for us." He spoke past his food and chewed for another few minutes before swallowing heavily. He washed his throat clear with another long pull on the gourd.

"Our fine friends are not of long patience and they know we must eventually come out of the swamp, but they will expect it on the morrow or later. They will go now to lick their wounds and drink away their soreness. We'll change clothes on dry ground." He hefted the other bundle. "They'll not be alert to two common seamen. Are you rested enough to travel now?"

Shanna nodded and struggled to swallow a mouthful of the meat, finally washing it down as Ruark had done. Ruark lowered himself into the water and, slinging the bundles over his shoulder, reached up to lift Shanna down. She had to steel herself as her feet again broke the scummy surface and sank into the ooze beneath. Now they proceeded more slowly, for any sound might give them away. On higher ground they found a small glade in a tangle of brush where they shucked their garments. The clothes Gaitlier had found were striped seamen's shirts, knee breeches, floppy hats, and sandals. Shanna's problem immediately became apparent, for even in the loose duck shirt and the knee breeches of her costume, she was obviously a woman to anyone's eye.

Ruark grinned and bade her doff the shirt again. He tore the cloth that had wrapped the bundle into wide strips and wound the fabric over her bosom until she was pressed as flat as she could be. With more cloth stuffed into her breeches to disrupt the curve of her hips, she now appeared more like a seaman, albeit a slightly lumpy one. Tucking her long hair into the hat, Shanna pulled the brim low over her face. Ruark added a bright scarf about her neck to cover the slim, soft lines of it then stood back to survey their efforts.

"Hunch your shoulders a bit," he directed. "Now walk around." He grunted. "Huh, no seaman ever walked like that."

Shanna faced him, dropped a shoulder askew, hung her jaw slackly aside, and swung her foot as if it were clubbed.

Ruark grinned. "Aye, Pirate Beauchamp. No one would now guess your true virtue."

Shanna giggled and stumbled as she neared, grasping at his arm to steady herself. Her eyes danced as she turned her face upward and sought his approval. Ruark could not resist the impish visage incongruously framed by floppy hat and vivid kerchief. Pulling her into his arms, he lowered his mouth to hers. Her response was warm and eager, and it was a long, long moment before Ruark raised his head.

"Gaitlier will be waiting," Shanna reminded him and handed him the jerkin from the bush where he had thrown it.

Ruark spread the jerkin, placing within it the food that was left, her silver dirk, and the small pistol. He shoved the rest of the garments beneath a bush before tucking the bundle he had made into Shanna's breeches. He pushed the pistols into his own waistband, not an unusual sight on this island. Making a small puddle of mud with some of the water, Ruark rubbed smears of it on Shanna's arms and legs to further mask the feminine grace of them. He considered the sword for a long moment, loath to discard the fine piece. Finally he chose a stick of wood the same length, wrapped the two of them together with strips of cloth, then rubbed the whole with mud. It made an odd-looking staff, but with the pistols once fired it would prove to be worth more than the risk.

Thus it was that a small, begrimed and oddly shaped seaman with a clubbed foot strolled with another who was tall and handsome to a fault, but who limped and leaned on a crooked staff. Slowly the odd pair passed along the hillside, nodded to a bespectacled older man, and finally passed to lounge in a spot strangely near the schooner. Lying in the shade of the fronds of a leaning palm tree, they seemed to doze.

The island lay quietly beneath the full heat of the late afternoon sun.

On the quay, a man with glasses stood near a young woman who was seated, and if one watched closely, it seemed that the man gazed frequently and nervously up the hill where an alert eye could pick up a thin trail of smoke rising. Then a dull thump was heard, and the smoke thickened. The whole hillside seemed to burst into flame. Sparks scattered, and the black smoke billowed.

Voices from the village rose into shouts as a huge ball of fire separated from the rest and ponderously rolled down the hill until it stopped, showering flames full against the side of the powder-filled blockhouse. Loud cries of alarm rose as the entire citizenry of the island ran to quench the blaze. Bucket brigades from the nearby stream were formed and smoking blankets were used to flog the smoldering brush.

No one noticed the man who helped the girl into a dory by the pier. Casting off they began to row out toward the schooner. As the guards aboard the *Good Hound* went to the other side of the ship where the pair approached, the two slumbering beneath the tree leapt to their feet, sailed hats in the brush, kicked sandals after them, and began to run down the beach.

Ruark had freed the sabre and had made a sling of the unsound cloth so that it now rode between his shoulder blades with the hilt close behind his neck. Realizing he was alone, he halted and turned back in exasperation to find Shanna frantically pulling a long piece of cloth from beneath her skirt. He would have taken her arm to pull her along but she jerked away.

"I can't breathe," she gasped, "let alone swim like this."

With a last hearty tug, the cloth came loose, and Shanna took two deep breaths while Ruark stamped the rag into the wet sand at their feet. Clasping hands, they ran into the water, dove, and cleaved the surface as one. They swam rapidly until they neared the ship. Then they slowed and took care to make as little noise as possible. Beside the hull, Ruark reached up, dragging himself slowly and carefully, with sheer strength, into the chains. Then he crouched down until Shanna's hands caught his wrist. The muscles in his shoulders and arm bulged as he raised her gradually, easing her from the water so no splash would alert the guards. Her toes found a chine, and she leaned safely against the tumblehome.

Ruark climbed upward until he could look over the edge of the railing. Two guards were leaning over the edge on the opposite side, refusing the argument of Gaitlier and his repeated pleas that they were needed ashore to fight the blaze. Ever so cautiously Ruark lifted himself over the rail and set his feet quietly on the deck. With the silent tread of a woodsman, he closed the space between them. Without warning one man suddenly felt a shoulder at his back. He shrieked as he spilled headlong over the side. The other spun around in surprise, met a crashing fist, and in a moment joined his companion. He came up sputtering and gasping, and the two of them struck out with hearty strokes toward shore.

Catching the rope attached to the bow of the dory, Ruark pulled the small boat to the side of the ship. He secured the line and kicked the rope ladder over the side. Shanna shrieked his name and he whirled about. He followed her gaze to the quarter-deck. The huge mulatto, naked but for a pistol and a cutlass in his hands, was running from the captain's cabin. He raised the pistol, and Ruark drew his sabre, realizing his own guns were wet and useless. The pirate aimed to fire just as a form tried to jostle past him in the doorway.

Carmelita's voice rang out. "Eh, what the bloody hell is going—"

The shot exploded, but the ball whistled harmlessly through the rigging. The dark man roared his rage and swung his arm, knocking Carmelita back into the cabin. The mulatto shouted again and charged with his cutlass.

Ruark knew the shot would draw attention of all ashore, so there was no time to engage in a duel. He drew a sodden pistol with his left hand and hurled it into the mulatto's face, stunning him. Ruark raised the sabre high and swung with all his might. The pirate barely met his blow and stumbled back, dropping the cutlass from a numbed hand. With hardly a pause, the man turned, hurled himself over the rail and splashed into the water below.

Ruark leaned against the railing as the mulatto also struck out for shore. He gazed beyond—the shouts of the two seamen had drawn many others to the edge of the water. Some ran toward a shed on the pier where Ruark knew four old cannons sat, well protected and always loaded.

A sound behind him made Ruark whirl, ready to do battle again, but this time it was only Carmelita, a linen sheet half wrapped over her body and trailing behind. She saw the cutlass on the deck and the threatening sabre and imagined only the worst. She began to back toward the other rail with her hand raised before her pleadingly.

"I've done ye no harm. Spare me!" she begged. Then, with a flash of broad, pink posterior she whirled. The sheet flapped from the rail as she departed like the rest.

Gaitlier had helped Dora on deck and hastened to obey Ruark's shouted order:

"Cut the forward cable! Set her free!"

Ruark himself raced to the quarter deck. Seizing an ax, he took a mighty swing at the aft anchor cable. Raising the ax, Ruark swung twice again before the heavy hawse parted. The ship began to swing and then rode free as, with a final blow, Gaitlier also accomplished his task.

Ruark threw a quick look toward the village. The ports were open in the heavily timbered shed, and with menacing slowness the muzzle of a cannon appeared. A flash flared, and a cloud of smoke billowed to obscure the shed. A few seconds later a geyser of water spewed as a ball skipped past, well off the stern. A ranging shot. The others would be closer. The ebb tide was taking the *Good Hound* out, but far too slowly. Ruark bellowed forward.

"Get a sail up! Any sail! One of the foresheets!"

Gaitlier found the appropriate line and loosed it; Shanna and Dora joined him to lend their weight to the task. They strained heartily, and slowly the foresail began to rise. The breeze took a tenous grip on the canvas, and the head of the ship began to swing. A ripple formed as the schooner moved forward, ever so slowly.

Ruark spun the wheel, waiting for the bite of water against the rudder so he could set her heel into the sea and head her out away from the harbor. Another gun flashed, and this time a single geyser spewed up close under the stern, wetting Ruark with its spray. The guns were set to cover the channel through the reef where an attack might be expected. There they could blast any ship out of the water, but inside the barrier of shoals one could reach the edge of the swamp then, pressing through a thin cover of brush, could enter the channel—if one knew the spot. And Gaitlier did.

The first sail was up and Gaitlier belayed the line while Shanna undid the next. With this one they could reach the deck capstan and were soon marching up its shroud.

Another boom bellowed from the cannon, and this time Ruark ducked as the rail on the quarterdeck splintered and the huge shot careened off the mizzenmast into the sea. Ruark felt a blow against his thigh but stumbled back to the spinning wheel, caught it, and leaning against the binnacle head, brought the schooner back on course.

The second sail was set, and a third was slowly spread as the small crew worked their hearts out on the main deck. A curl of foam formed beneath the prow. A cannon fired again from the shore; immediately another came, but both shots whizzed by astern. Now they were crossing the line of fire, and the heavy guns could not be handspiked around fast enough to track the schooner. A final flash and the ball spewed water far astern.

Ruark checked the course and brought the vessel around a point to the starboard. He glanced back toward the pier and saw that the pirates had left the guns. Several boats were rowing out toward the other schooners and ketches. With three sails firmly set on the *Good Hound*, Ruark waved to his crew, and they ceased their labors. With Dora beside him, Gaitlier stumbled forward so that he could guide their path through the channel, and Shanna worked her way aft to join Ruark.

The schooner left the bay, and Ruark warily watched the shoals speeding by on his right as he brought the ship about parallel to the shore. A too-narrow width of dark blue water stretched out ahead, and Ruark knew he must keep the ship in the middle of it until Gaitlier signaled him to turn.

As she climbed to the quarterdeck, Shanna suddenly halted, and Ruark cast a quick glance to her. Jaw agape and horror in her eyes, she stared at his leg.

Following her gaze, Ruark looked down and could not suppress a shudder, for thrust through his thigh, standing out from both sides, was a splinter of oak from the railing. It was a foot long and, though thin, over an inch across.

Shanna gasped and flew to his side, reaching to pull the splinter out. He brushed her hand away.

"Not now," he barked. "There's little blood and no pain. I'm all right. I must get us free before you tend it." Even now, Gaitlier had raised his left arm and was beckoning for a slow turn in that direction. Ruark eased the wheel over, and the schooner responded lightly. They neared the shore, and Ruark could not help bracing himself as it seemed they would drive the vessel hard aground on the swamp.

Gaitlier dropped his arm and pointed hard left. Ruark spun the wheel, and the ship came about. With a loud clap the sails flapped and then billowed as the schooner caught the following breeze across her other shoulder.

No sickening lurch hindered their progress, only a gentle rasping scrape against the hull as tangled masses of dead wood and trees, covered with vines until they appeared living, parted before the prow of the *Good Hound* and swung slowly aside. The ship passed through and eased into a narrow canal that barely cleared her sides.

A shot from astern whizzed through the mastheads, and Ruark peered aft to see the sails of the mulatto's sloop coming rapidly upon them, a full stand of sail filling their masts to the last inch. The *Good Hound* was not free yet. With a full crew to man her, the sloop could quickly overtake them. Though the two stern chasers in the captain's cabin would hold them abaft for a while, Ruark doubted Gaitlier's skill with the guns. It seemed only a matter of time before they would be taken.

They were now several hundred yards in from the entrance of the channel, and when he glanced around, Ruark stared in amazement. The sloop's captain had tried to make the entrance under full sail. In making the turn, the small ship had careened heavily with the press of the wind. Her bowsprit had swung past the course and was locked fast in the tangle of wood. Now she heeled slowly broadside in the channel entrance, firmly jammed in the floating gate while her stunsail and mizzen rigging became entangled in the tall mangrove that marked the far side. Nothing larger than a dory could make passage into the channel, and it would be hours before they could chop the ship loose and pull her free.

The small cannonade sounded again, but it was hastily aimed, and the ball shattered the trees well off the port beam. The schooner rounded a shallow bend, and the other ship was hidden from sight.

Ruark concentrated on threading the ship through the narrow channel. The swamp was several miles deep, and it would be well over an hour before they were into open water. And until they were clear of the swamp, one mistake could leave them aground like the other ship. It would be impossible for them to drag it free. If the pirates didn't catch them, they would die the lingering death of the swamp.

Shanna scrounged food from the captain's cabin, gave a share to Gaitlier and Dora, and brought a plate of dark bread, meat, and a large slab of cheese to Ruark at the wheel. She balanced it on the binnacle and, as he concentrated on guiding the ship, fed him mouthfuls.

"They were having a feast below." She tried to laugh lightly, but her brow knitted with worry. "We shan't starve at least." Her eyes wandered to his leg, where the splinter still protruded boldly.

"What's that you have in the bottle?" Ruark asked.

"Rum, I think," she murmured. " 'Twas with the rest."

Taking the flask, Ruark poured a healthy draught down his throat. Instant fire was his reward, burning its way downward as he choked. It was issue rum, uncut, black as sin, and just as potent.

"Water," he gasped when his breath came back to him, and Shanna hastily handed him a gourd from the bundles Gaitlier had brought. Ruark drew on it to his pleasure, and the fire waned to a warm glow in his belly. The rum served to numb the ache that had begun to seep upward from his pierced thigh.

Shanna set the tray aside and took a packet from her waistband. She unfolded it to reveal a small tin of salve and strips of cloth bandages. Laying them out on the deck, she spoke over her shoulder.

"This was all I could find in the cabin." She rose and stared up at him, concern etching a frown upon her brow. "Will you let me tend your leg now?"

Ruark glanced down at his wound. A small ring of dried blood showed on his pants with a thin streak going downward. He shook his head in reply. As long as he was standing and alert he would press on.

"Nay, love, not now. Not until we're clear of this swamp." He smiled at her to gentle his words. "You may have your turn at barbering when we've a good sail set on open sea."

Shanna hid her frown and tried to mask her anxiety; the thought of him in pain distressed her sorely.

The sun grew lower in the sky, but the heat did not abate. A myriad host of insects descended to bite, sting, gnaw, and otherwise torture them. The breezes eased until the ship barely crawled along. Sweat trickled down their bodies, soaking their clothes and making the garments stick clammily to the skin.

The air pressed in around them, and the rank smell of the swamp clogged the very nostrils. Indeed, the sky held a greenish cast as if it reflected the slime that covered the waters through which they sailed.

Then suddenly the sky seemed bluer. Ruark glanced around. The trees were fewer, the channel wider, the slime was gone, and wavelets lapped along the hull. There was a whiteness in the water as they passed over a shallow sandbar. Ruark held his breath. A slight scrape on the hull, a jerk on the rudder, and they were free, sailing into the deep blue of the Caribbean. The course was maintained until the swamp was only a vague blur on the horizon.

Then he turned the ship easterly to sail along the southern side of the string of islands. On leaving them, a northeasterly course would bring them to Los Camellos in a day or two.

Gaitlier came aft, and for once there were wide grins on all faces.

"Do you think you can raise the mainsail?" Ruark questioned. "We'll make better time, but 'tis the most this crew can handle."

Gaitlier was eager and took Shanna below on the main deck. In a moment they were marching the capstan round as the huge sail on the mainmast creaked slowly upward.

Going aloft to rig the topsail was out of the question, so Ruark trimmed the ship on course and had Gaitlier lash the wheel in place. Ruark rejected the idea of going to the captain's cabin, for he was not sure of his ability to return, so Shanna and Dora fetched blankets to make a pallet and prepared a space for him against the rail, while Ruark carefully directed Gaitlier on the course, pointing it out on the map, and gave instructions on reaching Trahern's island.

This was the best Ruark could do. The sun was low in the sky, and the light would be gone in an hour. He must now see to himself. Relenting to Shanna's pleas at last, Ruark accepted her assistance and stretched out on the pallet. Heedless of what the ship might do, the three knelt around him in concern. Ruark took the bottle of rum and splashed it liberally over his leg, then took a long draught, his eyes watering as he choked it down. Tucking a wad of shirt into his mouth, he clenched his teeth against it, then reached above his head to grasp the rail posts. He gave a quick nod to Gaitlier. The man's hands were gentle as he laid them upon the splinter, but sharp daggers awoke in Ruark's leg as he braced himself.

"Now!" Gaitlier half shouted and pulled hard.

Ruark heard Shanna gasp. An explosion of white pain seared inside his head, and, when it cooled, there was only merciful darkness.

It seemed he awoke only a short time later. The red and golden hues were gone from the sky above. The sun was still low, yet they seemed to be staring into it. Ruark became aware of a warmth against his right arm and rolled his head to see Shanna snuggled beneath the blanket that covered them both. Her eyes were closed in sleep, and her breath touched him gently, like a small child's. Carefully he moved his arm until it was around her, and sighing softly, she nestled closer to his side.

Ruark lifted his gaze to the tall masts swaying against the blue sky. Then he realized, " 'Tis morning!"

He had slept the night through. His hand went down and felt the heavy bandage that wrapped his thigh. For his own peace of mind, he wiggled his toes and then his foot. All seemed well but for a persistent dull ache from the wound.

Shanna stirred against him, and lifting her face upward, he kissed her lips softly and nuzzled her hair, breathing in the sweet fragrance of it. Her hand caressed his chest beneath his shirt, and she settled her head comfortably against his shoulder, her eyes searching his with brimming warmth.

"I would stay here forever if you were with me," Ruark sighed in her ear.

He kissed her again, his parted lips savoring hers for a long, blissful moment as his hand slipped under her shirt to capture a round breast. Shanna's arm went about his neck, bringing the cover over his shoulder to protect his caress from the witness of others. Her cheeks grew warm and flushed with the pleasure he aroused in her as his thumb teased the soft nipple into an excited peak.

"Your leg?" she whispered eagerly. "How does it feel?"

Ruark glanced toward the forecastle deck where Gaitlier and Dora had spent the night. They were just now beginning to stir, and he gave a nod in their direction.

"If we didn't have guests aboard, I would be eager to demonstrate my health."

Shanna's soft chuckle held a hint of a challenge as she snuggled closer. She murmured low in his ear. "Would you care to go below, milord? I know a private place in the captain's cabin."

"You tempt me sorely," Ruark moaned. His hand slid down, inside her loose breeches, and found the womanly softness of her. Her eyelids lowered and her breath trembled from parted lips.

It was only Gaitlier coming aft that cooled their play. In nervous embarrassment Shanna drew away and sat on her heels, facing Ruark. She tightened the rope belt around her waist. Ruark watched her, unable to resist a last stroke of his hand along her thigh. Warily Shanna glanced back over her shoulder to see what had become of Gaitlier and saw him walking back to Dora in response to a timid-voiced question. Shanna turned back and placing her hand over Ruark's, smiled in soft, intimate communication. She leaned down to him, bracing her elbows on the pallet beside his head, heedless of the loose shirt that gapped away, presenting every detail of her ripe, tempting bosom. As Ruark boldly eyed her display, a lazy grin spread across his lips.

"You're an evil temptress, Shanna Beauchamp."

Her finger twirled in his hair as she admitted, "Aye, but only with you, my Captain Pirate Ruark."

"Good enough then, my love." Reluctantly he raised on his elbows, and his voice was firm as he stated, "I must see to the ship lest she race on and plunge herself against the Africa shore."

"Oh, Ruark, don't get up!" Shanna pleaded. "I'll do whatever needs be done. Sit still."

"I can't, Shanna. I must be about. My leg will be better after I've walked on it a bit."

Shanna saw that he was determined, though he winced as he moved his leg and would get up by himself if she refused to help him. His leg was stiff and sore, but with some difficulty Ruark soon stood beside the wheel. Shanna was reluctant to leave him even then and remained beside him as he checked the course in the binnacle. Lifting his head, he scanned the sails. The wind had shifted slightly, and he would soon have to correct for it. But how far had they come, he wondered. If the wind had blown hard, they would be long past the islands and would have to turn back into them. In this breeze it would be a difficult task, which Ruark doubted his crew of three could handle. But where—

His eyes searched the horizon to port, and Ruark lifted himself as high as he could.

Ah, there! Low clouds with a dark shadow beneath. That heralded an island. He felt Shanna's hand upon his ribs and glanced down to see her watching him, a worried look on her face.

"We'll soon be there," he assured her, mistaking her distress. "No need to fret."

Shanna opened her mouth to deny his thoughts but silenced the words before they were spoken. How could she explain her own feelings when they were a mystery even to her?

Ruark looked pointedly toward her bosom. "That garb has served you well, but it does not seem right for you. A bit too mannish would be my opinion."

Shanna smoothed the rumpled shirt and straightened the loose breeches over her hips.

"If my memory serves me right, Carmelita left without her clothes. Perhaps they might be taken in here and there—"

"Bah!" Shanna cut him short. "I threw them overboard last night. Do you think I would wear anything of hers?"

Shanna set her back to him, raising an impertinent nose to scan the sea. Ruark reached out to tug a tress until she faced him again. White teeth gleamed against the darkness of his skin as he teased her with a smile.

"You're a devil, Ruark Beauchamp!" Shanna declared but softened and rubbed her cheek against his knuckles. She raised on tiptoes and brushed a kiss upon his lips. "You must be hungry. I'll go see what's left in the cabin."

As she strode from him, Ruark stared after her with warm attention, observing the graceful swing of her hips.

It came to his mind there was no possible way a sane man could mistake those curves for anything but woman. That only left two possibilities. The citizens of Mare's Head were either blind—or terribly mad.

Chuckling at his thoughts, Ruark slipped the lashing from a spoke then leaned against the chest-high wheel, whirling it around and trimming the schooner against the wind. The ship plunged along the gently rolling sea, and as he replaced the lashings to hold the vessel on the new course, Gaitlier left Dora and ambled aft.

"Captain?" The man appeared bemused. "Is Trahern as bad as Mother complained? Will I be taken as bondslave, too? Which master will I serve, you or him, sir?"

"You'll have no master, Mister Gaitlier," Ruark returned boldly. He was unable to say what his own fate would be, but he could assure this man a return to dignity. "Mayhap you might find the island to your liking and wish to remain. If not, I am sure that Trahern will give you passage to any port of your choosing. He will be grateful for your help in rescuing his daughter, and a tidy sum might be forthcoming."

"And what of you, sir?" Gaitlier laid the question to him, but Ruark chose to misunderstand his meaning.

"I have no need for money." He looked at the man. "However, there is one thing I would ask of you, Mister Gaitlier."

He nodded. "Anything, sir. Anything at all."

Ruark rubbed a thumb against his unshaven cheek. "Trahern knows me only as bondslave. Unless Madam Beauchamp tells him differently, I would ask your silence in this matter of our marriage. I am, to those on Los Camellos, John Ruark, and the lady is Madam Ruark Beauchamp, a widow."

"Rest your fears, sir. Dora and I will say naught of you and the madam. I give my word to that."

The four of them shared a leisurely repast around Ruark's pallet. Shanna was quick to see to his comfort, gently propping his leg on a pillow, filling his plate and taking his cup of pale wine as he reached to place it on the deck. His hand rested possessively upon her thigh as she sat cross-legged beside him, while he explained to Gaitlier about handling the ship. It was a quiet time, a restful time, and when it was over, Ruark limped again to the wheel. Raising the brass-bound telescope, he studied the still distant island off the port bow. It was the last of the chain; high bluffs dropped sharply into the sea at its eastern end. Once past it, they would turn toward Los Camellos.

Returning to his pallet, he stretched out full length again. His leg ached, and the muscle began to jump in his thigh, sending white-edged shards of pain through his body. He rubbed his hip and thigh to ease the throbbing and found his hand brushed away by Shanna's as she took up the chore. Beneath the tender care, he dozed and dreamed of soft pink lips bending near and caressing his.

The island was low on the horizon behind them, and the sun hung high overhead when Ruark set the course for Los Camellos then stumbled back to his pallet. Gaitlier had rigged a shade for him, and Shanna now shared that small spot of coolness with him. His leg ached agonizingly, and each time he rose, the effort was greater. He sampled the rum again, but this time its fire did little to ease his discomfort.

He laid his head back on Shanna's lap, and with her cool hand she gently stroked his eyes and forehead until he began to relax and the pain ebbed. As she sat holding his head, Shanna hummed a few lines from a tune that flitted through her mind and softly Ruark's rich baritone began to fill in the words. Shanna's humming stopped, and she listened quietly. Suddenly she knew the voice that had drifted up to her from below decks on the *Marguerite* one starry, moonlit night as she sailed homeward from England.

"Oh, Ruark," she whispered softly and kissed the brow that was hot beneath her hand.

A shout came across the deck and both of them rose. Ruark lurched and leaned against the rail to steady himself, staring forward to see Gaitlier prancing along the deck waving his arms, Dora following close behind.

"Ships! Ships up ahead!" the man shouted as he ran toward them. "Two of them! Big ones!"

Unable to calm himself, Gaitlier jumped up and down, gesturing with his arm. Ruark laughed almost wildly as he scrambled for the wheel and the long spyglass. He braced the instrument on a spoke, centering it on the sails that gleamed white in the sun and drew closer with each breath. He moved the glass to the fluff of color that floated on the masthead. It was blurred for a moment. They all waited. Finally it cleared.

"English!" he shouted. "They're English! But there's another flag." He put his eye to the glass again. After a moment he turned and grinned at Shanna. " 'Tis your father! The *Hampstead* and *Mary Christian*."

A cry of joy escaped her, and Ruark fought for balance as she flung her arms about his neck. Holding her close, he called past her to Gaitlier.

"Drop the sails! Get them down! We'll come about and wait for them!"

The man needed no urging. He leapt to the rail, snatched the ax, and with a single blow severed the riser to the mainsail. The yard came crashing down to bounce and lie still, spilling canvas onto the deck. Gaitlier scrambled over the billowing sail to the foredeck where with like energy he brought the spritsails rattling down.

Ruark threw the lashings off the wheel and spun it hard aport. The schooner groaned and creaked and dug her nose into the waves as she slowed and came about until she was stern on to the approaching vessels. The *Hampstead* drew near, and soon there was no doubt. Beside the thin stick in black that could only be Ralston was the white bulk which could only be Trahern. Shanna gave a glad cry and ran down to the main deck where she joined Gaitlier and Dora by the rail. Ruark would have joined them, but his leg would not bear his weight. As the huge bulk of the *Hampstead* drew alongside, he held fast to the wheel. The ports were opened and the guns run out. Behind the gaping black muzzles he could see the eager, white faces of the gun crew, alert for any sign of hostility.

Grappling hooks were thrown fore and aft as the two ships bumped together. Then at a shout from the mate a detachment of men swarmed up from behind the *Hampstead*'s rail and leapt onto the deck of the *Good Hound*, pistols and cutlasses at the ready as if they expected to do battle. The *Mary Christian* stood off the port side, and all the while her four small guns were run out, ready for a fight.

When any possible resistance had been quelled, Ralston cautiously joined the men on the schooner then more boldly began to order them about before stalking aft with his angry, jerky, storklike stride.

One of the seamen, seeing no threat from the small crew, put aside his cutlass and gave a hand to Shanna as she stepped over to the *Hampstead*.

She had barely set her feet down onto the deck before she ran across it and up the gangway to the lofty quarterdeck. When her eyes fell on her father, she dashed to him and threw her arms about his neck, sobbing her joy and relief. Trahern fought to keep his balance. His arm came around her tightly for a moment, and his breathing was curiously hoarse and somewhat ragged. Then with a quick pat on her shoulders he thrust her away to arm's length to survey her.

"You are indeed my daughter," the squire chuckled, half questioning. "And not some ragamuffin thrusting himself on my good nature."

Shanna laughed brightly and opened her mouth to reply, but her gaze went astray, and she jerked away, her intended words ending in a choked gasp of dismay as she stared at the deck of the schooner below them.

Ruark had been willing to greet even Ralston as his deliverer and reached out a hand to grasp the other's as the thin man neared him, but Ralston ignored the gesture, instead striking out viciously with the heavy butt of his riding crop. It caught Ruark full across the face, and the force of the blow was such that he spun away from the wheel, careened off the binnacle, and crashed heavily to the deck. As Ruark struggled groggily to rise, Ralston placed a foot roughly in the middle of his back, forcing him down against the splintered planks. The thin man gestured imperiously to two burly seamen he had commandeered. Without ceremony the pair heaved Ruark to his feet, bound his wrists tightly behind him, and, as he regained his senses, stuffed a rag into his mouth to still his curses. Ralston walked stiltedly to the head of the stairs and stood glaring back as he waited for his prisoner to be brought forward. The men thrust Ruark before them. He could not walk on his own, and he crashed down, twisting to protect the injured leg. When he was dragged to his feet again, an ugly bruise had swelled on his forehead and a small trickle of blood coursed down from it. They dragged him along between them, with Ralston leading the procession in the full glory of his victory.

Aghast, Shanna whirled to her father, but he was not of a mind to hear her pleas and set his back to her, stating firmly over his shoulder, "He'll be hanged for piracy as soon as we return to Los Camellos. The three bondsmen set free by the brigands told me well enough of our Mister Ruark."

With that Orlan proceeded to climb carefully down from the quarterdeck and went to greet the party from the schooner.

"Nnnnooo!" Shanna moaned as she struggled past the captain and the helmsman to race after her father. As she reached the main deck, she saw Pitney leaning back against the rail, his arms folded across his chest, huge horse pistols in his belt, and a sour frown on his face. He stared at Shanna for a long moment then with a cluck of his tongue turned his back, as if unable to bear the sight of her. A muffled groan was heard as Ralston's henchmen threw Ruark onto the deck while the thin man himself raged about, gloating in the power he had seized.

"This slave is guilty of a dozen crimes," he bellowed. "Hoist him up on the yardarm." He gestured wildly to those who had gathered about. The pair tossed a rope over a yard and, stretching Ruark's arms upward, bound them again over his head. Then, doing as they were told, they lifted him up until his toes barely brushed the deck.

Again Shanna turned a frantic appeal to her father and again he ignored her as Ralston halted before him. Instead of its usual gray color, the agent's face was flushed. He coughed in his glove to clear his throat and argued boldly.

"If an English seaman can be flogged for disobeying an officer, then surely this man deserves a thousand stripes or so. Let us see now that he pays for at least a few of his heinous sins, one of which being his abduction of your daughter. Justice must be swift to be of any good.

"Quartermaster," he shouted, bent upon showing no mercy at all, "fetch your cat-o'-nine and let's make the bloody beggar whimper."

Trahern remained silent, for to his mind the once trusted man deserved what he was getting. Arrogantly Ralston strode to Ruark and lifted his sagging head with a gloved hand.

"So now, my good man," he sneered, "you shall find the full folly of your adventure at escape. You shall feel your justice on your back and also serve as a good example for the other slaves."

He snapped his hand away, and Ruark's head lolled loosely between his arms. Ralston snatched the gag away, and, his dry metallic breath close in Ruark's face, he mocked, "Have you no comment, milord? No defense? No plea for mercy?"

Ruark's tongue was thick in his mouth, and he could not ease the searing pain that seaped upward from his thigh; it seemed to fill his entire body. A brighter red began to mark the left leg of his knee breeches. The effort of the past days had sapped his strength. He could not fight this farce now set upon him.

Almost wildly Shanna glanced about her. Was there no one to help her?

The quartermaster emerged from below deck, shaking out the

nine knotted cords of the implement. The small lead balls woven into the end of each rattled on the deck as he flexed the handle. Pitney stood away from the rail and hitched up his britches. He had viewed enough of this travesty and was not about to let it go further. But before he moved, he glanced down at Shanna and paused. Her face wore a grimace of outrage he had never seen before.

Ralston saw the quartermaster approach, and his sadistic penchants forced him on to new heights. Bravely he posed, staring at Ruark, and reached back his arm. "I shall mete out the punishment myself," he boasted, "to assure that there be no light strokes to cheat justice. Give me the whip."

A moment later Ralston gave a frightened shriek of pain as the wicked strands shredded his sleeves and bit deep into his arm. In stunned surprise he whirled to stare directly into Shanna's enraged face. Snarling, she drew the whip back and shook it out, ready for another stroke. She stood her ground like some wild animal, her hair spread back over her shoulders like a lion's flying mane.

"I'll give you the whip, milord bastard, if you touch that man again!"

The quartermaster stumbled forward apologetically and reached out to take the cat from Shanna's hand but suddenly halted and gaped with sagging jaw. Pitney had pulled a pistol from his belt, and now its muzzle was less than an inch from the seaman's nose. Ralston himself would have stepped forward in indignant rage, but he held his heroism in check for Pitney drew his other piece and with a slow, casual grin spreading his mouth, cocked it.

"Cut him down!" Shanna's wicked snarl broke the silence, and the whip waved toward the two men who had hoisted Ruark up.

They hastened to slash the rope, and Ruark crumpled to the deck. Shanna yearned to rush to his side but held fast lest he be taken again. She stood rigid before her father, while Pitney held at bay any who would have interfered. One of the pistols stayed centered on Ralston's chest, and he stared agog at the menacing black bore.

"You have made a dreadful mistake, father," Shanna declared, using the more stilted form of address. " 'Twas this Mister Ruark who saved us all from the pirates' hands as these good people will attest." She nodded to Gaitlier and Dora, who had followed it all with widened eyes, fearful lest this be their reward also. "Indeed," Shanna murmured, " 'twas Mister Ruark who saw that"—she paused, uncertain, but for a reason none of them guessed, and continued more cautiously—"he saw me safe from those bloodthirsty villains at the risk of his own life. I am as I was, untouched by them because of him."

Ralston sneered and cold, sea-green eyes turned on him, but Shanna went on with her defense though she faced away from her father's gaze and could not bear to meet Pitney's, either.

"Mister Ruark was taken to Mare's Head from Los Camellos much against his will and 'twas by his wits he managed to get the rest of us away. If you insist upon taking him, you must do so over me. I swear you will."

At a groan from Ruark she dropped the whip and flew to kneel beside him.

"Fetch the surgeon!" Trahern's voice rang out in command. "Then make sail for Mare's Head."

Shanna gathered Ruark's head into her lap and brushed his tumbled hair from his forehead. As Pitney bent to straighten Ruark out more comfortably on the deck, he heard Shanna croon very low.

"It's all right now, my darling. It's all right."

Ruark closed his eyes and sank into merciful oblivion.

By midmorning of the next day, Ruark was able to stand with Trahern on the quarterdeck of the *Hampstead*. He leaned on the merchant's grotesque black thorn quarterstaff which had been loaned to him—somewhat reluctantly—in lieu of a crutch. Shanna stood between them, clutching her father's arm while she kept a careful eye on her man. The surgeon had removed several small splinters and threads of cloth from his leg, dressed the ugly wound with pungent salves and herbs, then wrapped it with fresh bandages. Though slightly feverish and a trifle lightheaded, Ruark refused to lie abed. He welcomed the refreshing breeze that swept the quarterdeck and savored the anticipation of sighting Mare's Head. On the main deck, the crewmen had already checked the long steel sackers, and when the *Hampstead* dropped anchor just outside the reef of the pirates' island, the dull silvery gray barrels were loaded and primed.

When all was in readiness, the *Hampstead* entered the cove beyond the reef.

The scene that greeted them was one of chaos. Boats began setting out to the ships in the harbor. The mulatto had retrieved his ship from the tangle of the swamp, and it now lay close beside the dock. There was feverish activity aboard the sloop and at the shed which hid the guns. Even before the *Hampstead* was in range, a flash and a cloud of smoke appeared from the sloop, and a column of water rose abruptly a good two hundred yards short of the bow. It was a poor warning shot, for it marked the maximum range of the pirates' aged guns.

The sound of the cannon was hidden beneath a sharp bark of one of the *Hampstead*'s sackers, and, a split second later, the other. Thus the battle was begun. A geyser showed short of the sloop, and a huge roll of dust formed on the hill above the town.

In the village there was an abrupt halt to all activity as the guns sounded, for all suddenly realized that the island was not safe, as they had supposed. Suddenly there was a frantic rush of people running to and fro between the houses as they snatched their most precious belongings and tried to carry them to safety.

The sackers barked their staccato duet again, and this time plumes of timber and debris rose above the town. Ruark had an unpleasant vision of the innocents cowering beneath the barrage that descended with merciless indiscrimination upon them. The *Hampstead*'s gun crews were not skilled in the use of fine pieces; they knew, instead, the haphazard ranging of the older iron and brass cannon. Ruark mouthed a single silent curse and painfully began to make his way to where the gun crews labored. The sackers barked again, and again pointless showers of dust and splintered timbers rose to scatter down on the people. Meanwhile, the mulatto's sloop was being winched out on her anchor cable, and sails were rising along her mast.

Ruark used Trahern's staff to brush aside the captains of the gun crews and, seizing a handspike from one of them, aimed the guns himself. Standing back, he raised his arm, and two men stood ready at the touchholes. Ruark dropped his hand, and the deck jumped beneath him as both guns fired in unison. The deck of the sloop became a shambles as the twin shot crashed upon it and brought down masses of rigging and the foremast. Ruark urged the gun crews to reload with all due haste and aimed the pieces again. At his signal they spoke together. This time the pirate's ship's mainmast fell, and she heeled heavily as a long gash opened in her starboard side at the waterline. Men dived overboard as she swung astern against the pier and began to settle in the shallow harbor.

Ruark shifted the direction, and two of the smaller ships bucked in the water as the shots smashed through their sides. Smoke began to pour from one, and the other rammed hard ashore, her crew fleeing into the swamp. More shots were fired until the small fleet was a smoking mass of floating wreckage. Now Ruark set the aim more carefully, but it still took three rounds before the blockhouse dissolved in an explosion. Again the direction shifted, and Mother's Inn took the brunt of the attack. Nearly twenty rounds had been fired before the facade slowly began to crumble, leaving the interior agape.

Once more Ruark bade the crews reload, and, sighting carefully, he adjusted the barrels. His hand dropped and Shanna stared as the eastern wall and the room wherein they had resided dissolved in a cloud of dust.

From the main deck Ruark called to Trahern, "Unless you wish to slay innocents, the most damage is done. It will be months before a ship sets sail from here. Those responsible for your daughter's capture are either dead or fled. I await your decision, sir."

Trahern waved an arm and turned to Captain Dundas. "Secure the guns. Set sail for Los Camellos. We have seen enough of this place. God willing, we'll see no more."

The exertion had cost Ruark his strength. He hung his head and sagged weakly against the handspike. One of the gun captains handed him the squire's staff, and, taking it, he moved a step aft toward the quarterdeck, toward Shanna. His mouth was strangely parched, and his face and arms felt hot while the sun began to make dizzying loops around the masts above him. He saw Shanna running toward him, then the rough deck was beneath his cheek, and the smell of gunpowder was strong in his nostrils. The day grew dark and faded further still. Cool hands were under his neck, and a strange wetness fell on his face. He thought he heard his name called from afar, but he was so tired, so tired. The blackest of nights closed in around him.

Chapter 20

THE surgeon muttered and swore as he tried to steady
the wounded man's legs against the lurch of the barouche.
"Have patience, Herr Schauman." Shanna Beauchamp's
voice was soft and sure. " 'Tis only a bit further."

She held Ruark's head upon her lap and placed a cool, wet cloth
against his brow. Trahern sat on the other side of her and studied
his daughter in some bemusement. He noticed a new self-con-
fidence and quiet reserve that he was sure had not been there
before. She had made much of keeping a silver dirk. It and a
pistol so small as to be almost useless were wrapped carefully in
the leather jerkin at her feet. With a single-minded purpose and
a tenderness she had shown no other man, she tended this bondslave whom she had once hated.

"The leg festers." The surgeon's voice broke into his musings.

Trahern brought himself to awareness and listened to the
doctor.

"It should be removed. Now! Before he awakens. The longer
we wait, the more difficult the task will be."

Shanna gazed silently at the doctor and her mind was filled
with the terrible vision of Ruark struggling to mount a horse
with his left leg gone at the hip.

461

."Will it save him?" she asked quietly.

"Only time will tell that," Herr Schauman answered brusquely. "There is every chance he will survive."

For a long moment Shanna looked down at Ruark. His face held a deathly pallor, and she could find no courage in herself; yet, when she spoke, her voice was both soft and firm.

"Nay, I think our Mister Ruark will fight for his leg as well. Perhaps between the two of us we'll save it for him."

Both men recognized her statement as final and said nothing more.

The carriage rattled to a halt in front of the manor and before the horses had stopped their prancing, Pitney, who had ridden ahead, was reaching to take Ruark carefully in his huge arms. Immediately Shanna stood beside him.

"To the chambers next to mine, Pitney, if you will."

Her father's eyebrows rose sharply. She had been anxious to see Sir Gaylord quartered completely across the house from her, and now she took the bondslave into her own wing.

Sir Gaylord meekly held the door ajar for the returning party. As Trahern passed through, last in the procession, he paused to consider the knight's bandaged foot.

"Well, Sir Gaylord," the squire grunted. "I see your ankle is much the better."

"Of course," the man replied heartily. "Dreadfully sorry I couldn't go with you, but the bloody animal stepped away just as I— Well, he banged me up, you see, then trod all over it. But it's mending rapidly." Gaylord lifted his cane and then winced as he bravely tried the foot.

With a snort Trahern brushed by, struggling with the sneer that threatened to conquer his face.

"The fate of the courageous, I suppose," Trahern said over his shoulder as he brushed by.

"Aye," the reply came quickly. "Rightly so. Would have come anyway if it hadn't happened in the last moment there, but didn't know how bad it was, or what good I'd be in a fight. There *was* one, I see." He gave a nod toward the wounded man being carried up the stairs. "I see you've captured that chap, Ruark. Dastardly thing he did, running off like that and kidnapping your daughter. A foul man, to be sure. Get him well enough to stand a hanging."

It was Gaylord's good fortune that Shanna was arguing her point with the doctor and completely missed his words. Trahern's answering grunt was noncommittal; he rather savored the idea of letting his daughter set good Gaylord right in his thinking. He had no doubt that the event would occur soon enough without any urging on his part.

"Join me in a rum while they get Mister Ruark to bed," Trahern invited and mounted the stairs after the group. " 'Twill be interesting to see what they must do to keep him alive for the hanging."

The knight hobbled up after his portly host as best he could, since no one paused to give assistance. When at the head of the stairs Pitney bore the bondslave off in the direction of Shanna's chambers, Gaylord managed to disguise some degree of his concern. Still, he hurried to catch up with the squire to bring the matter to the elder's attention.

"Do you think it wise to have that renegade so close to your daughter's rooms? I mean, if the chap hasn't done his worst by now, he's likely to, eh? The sly one that he is, a lady should take precautions or be reminded of the dangers when she cannot see them for herself."

Trahern replied with a touch of humor. "I think it wise of me not to deny my daughter anything at the present moment."

"Still, sir!" Gaylord became adamant. "A gentleman's future wife can hardly be quartered in the same wing with a knave without some wagging tongue claiming that the good man's being cuckolded."

Squire Trahern halted abruptly in his tracks and faced the man, and as the humor faded, a glint of anger shone piercingly in his green eyes.

"I do not question my daughter's virtue, nor would I believe rumors put to the fore by some rejected suitor or mewling bitch. My daughter has a mind and will of her own and a good sense of what is decent. Do not strain my hospitality by indicating differently."

A shout from Pitney had sent Berta and Hergus running ahead to the chambers Shanna had indicated, and by the time he came through the door with his burden, they had folded back the linens and placed a double layer as a rest for Ruark's wounded leg.

The room became a place of activity. Pitney was followed closely by the surgeon who stepped aside to allow Shanna to enter before him. Trahern joined them with Gaylord directly behind him, and the two of them observed the proceedings from just inside the door. Shanna urged their care as Ruark was stretched on the bed. The linen shirt and his stockings were stripped from him. The surgeon directed that a small table be set near for his knives and instruments. Hergus hied to slide one close, glancing anxiously toward Shanna, who had dipped a cloth into a basin of water and had begun to lightly bathe Ruark's face and chest. The breeches had been split up the one leg to the hip, and as Herr Schauman yanked away the sticky bandage, the maid caught a glimpse of the blood-caked, oozing wound. Unaccustomed to the sight of gaping flesh, Hergus whirled and fled the room, her hand clutched tightly over her mouth. Shanna stared after the woman in amazement. Hergus had always seemed so stalwart and unruffled, not at all inclined to be squeamish.

"Females!" the doctor muttered. He gestured irritably to Ruark's stained breeches, which were blackened with gunpowder and bore the same acrid scent. "Unless you find your delicate nature abused, girl, I suggest you rid him of those."

A gasp of astonishment came from the shocked Berta at such a bidding, but Shanna did not hesitate. With her small dirk she reached out to rip the seam of the breeches and had made only a frayed spot at the knee when Pitney brushed her hands away and took out his huge, broad-bladed knife. He separated the garment to the waist with a single stroke and then finished parting the other leg of the garment.

Shanna turned in exasperation as Berta plucked for the third time at her sleeve. Pitney was easing the breeches from Ruark's slim hips, and the housekeeper raised a trembling hand to carefully shield her eyes from the bed. Her cherubic face was crimson as she cautiously held her gaze upon Shanna's face.

"Come, child," she whispered urgently. "Ay tank dis is no place for you. Ve leave dis to the menfolk."

"Aye, Madam Beauchamp," Gaylord agreed, stepping forward, then wincing and leaning heavily on his cane. "Let me escort you away. 'Tis certainly no place for a lady."

"Oh, don't be an ass!" Shanna snapped. "I am needed here, and I can help."

Gaylord's jaw slackened, and he beat a hasty retreat, colliding with Trahern, who had possessed the good sense to leave his daughter alone. But Berta tried again, though her comment dwindled into a confused stutter as, from the corner of her eye, she caught Pitney flinging the breeches to the floor. Seeing the woman's distress, Shanna laid a comforting hand on the plump shoulder and spoke gently.

"Berta, I'm—I have been married." Shanna paled slightly as she realized what she had almost blurted out and continued more carefully. "I am not ignorant of men. Now, please, stay out of my way."

Berta felt herself dismissed and fled to soothe her abused modesty in the fresh air outside the chamber. Shanna leaned across the bed and held the oil lamp high for the doctor who was again probing into the wound.

The leg was propped on a pillow so the doctor could better do his work. He drew out more splinters and, carefully, a coin-sized piece of cloth. Ruark groaned and twisted. He was still deep in his unconscious state, but not immune to the stabbing reality of pain. Shanna cringed; she could almost feel the agony he suffered. She helped swab the fresh flow of blood, aware that her father studied her intently, puzzled over her concern. She could not hide it, nor did she even try. If he guessed there was more to her anxiety than seemed proper, she'd answer to that later. Right now, all that mattered was Ruark and getting him well.

Some of the poisons were washed away with the blood, and Herr Schauman cleaned the ragged flesh and spread his unguents and balms liberally. Then he bandaged the leg with wide strips until it was held almost immobile.

" 'Tis the best I can do," he sighed. "But if the rot should set in, we'll have to remove the leg. There will be no question then. 'Tis infected enough already. You can tell by the purplish color and the red which spreads away from the wound. I shall have to bleed the man, of course." He laid Ruark's arm so that it projected over the side of the bed and began to set out his knives and bowls.

"Nay!" The word burst sharp from Pitney's lips. "He has bled enough, and I have seen too many die with their life in a barber's bowl."

The German drew back in righteous anger but held his tongue as Trahern spoke in agreement with Pitney. "There will be no bleeding here. I, too, have watched a loved one die beneath a knife, and I do not think it wise to further weaken an ailing soul."

The surgeon's lips were white and tightly pressed as he threw his scalpels back into the bag and snapped it shut. "Then I can do nothing more here," he retorted sharply. "I shall be in the village if you need me."

Shanna stretched a cool linen sheet over Ruark and touched her hand to his fevered brow. His lips were moving, and his head rolled slowly from side to side. A sudden fear nipped at her. What if he should become delirious and begin to talk or call her name or speak things better left unsaid? Quickly she whirled and began to sweep everyone toward the door.

"Leave now," she commanded. "Let him sleep. He will need every ounce of strength. I will sit with him for a spell."

As Pitney and Trahern went off down the hall, Gaylord paused in the doorway. Though Shanna tried to close the portal, he was not daunted by her eagerness to be rid of him. Taking out a lace handkerchief and daintily touching a pinch of snuff to each nostril, he stepped back into the room and glanced about him imperiously.

"Terribly decent thing you're doing here, madam, after all this fellow, Ruark, put you through."

Shanna shrugged in annoyance and tried again to usher him to the door.

"I know you must have suffered hideous atrocities at the hands of the pirates." Another bit of snuff, a sneeze, and the handkerchief delicately dabbed against his nose. "But I wish to assure you, madam, that my proposal of marriage still stands. And in fact, I would advise the nuptials be spoken with all due haste to quiet the rumors that will no doubt spread of your ravishment and shame. Perhaps you even know of a woman on the island who can be of benefit to us should you carry the proof of your ill use."

Shanna was aghast and for a moment accepted the affront in stunned disbelief.

"Yet I would not speak of your—ah—adventure to my family. 'Twill be difficult enough to convince them of your rather questionable heritage."

Shanna became stiff with fury.

" 'Tis charitable of you, sir, but whatever seeds I might have gathered in my—ah—adventure,"—her smile was grittingly sweet —"I will carry through to their fruition!"

Sir Gaylord dusted his cuff as he continued to demonstrate his magnanimity. Surely this common wench would be impressed. "Still, my dear, we should get into marriage before you are disgraced. Should you be found with child, we will deny all rumors, and I shall stand forth as its father."

He glanced toward her to see the effect of his unimpeachable logic but saw only her rigid back. He had no way of knowing that her lips were tightly set and white with rage. She must, he surmised, be completely demolished by the generosity of his offer. Then he boldly vowed, "I would personally challenge any oaf who casts a slur upon your name."

Shanna's arm flung out, and her finger trembled as it indicated the most direct path to the door.

"*Aaaaooout!*" Her voice was a half-strangled shriek.

"Of course, my dear," Sir Gaylord mumbled, never realizing the nearness of his total maiming. "I understand. You are distraught. We can discuss this later."

He took several steps before nearly tripping on his cane, and displaying excellent recall, he suddenly remembered to limp on his bandaged foot; it took the knight a quick step and a hop to avoid the slamming door behind him.

Shanna leaned against the door, and a slow moment dragged out before she could wash the outrage of Sir Gaylord's proposals from her mind. It was a moan from Ruark that emptied the ire from her and sent her flying across the room to his bedside. She saw his face flushed and dark in the dim light. His head rolled from side to side with a loose, disjointed fervor. Anxiously she felt his forehead and found nothing to solace her there. His skin still burned with that hot dryness that put a chill of dread in her.

Silently Shanna cursed the schooling that had given her a fine knowledge of how to curtsy and conduct herself among aristocrats and a skill of composing useless poetry, or sitting for hours before a sampler making neat, precise stitches in a cloth, yet left her helpless and inadequate in most of the skills of everyday living. She was ignorant of balms and medicinal cures and of caring for the sick or injured. The only thing she could rely upon was common sense. When Ruark grew feverish and his brow felt like hot parchment, she bathed him with cool water. When he ranted and raved incoherently, she spoke softly and caressed his brow until he calmed. She had a thin broth brought to the room, and she kept it beside the bed on a warming pan, and when Ruark roused to a half-conscious state, she pressed spoonfuls of the stuff between his dry lips. There was little else to do.

"So damn little!" she groaned to herself in growing frustration. Her vision blurred with tears as an overwhelming sense of despair sank its merciless talons into her, shredding hope and confidence. "Oh, God, please"—her plea was nearly a whimper in the stillness that enveloped them—"don't let him die."

The dark shade of evening crept stealthily across the island, and the moon blossomed on the horizon like an oversized orange flower. It rose high until it faded to a mottled silvery blue and touched all beneath it with the same hues. For Shanna, the hours flowed together, and when Ruark rested in the quieter states of fevered sleep, she curled in a chair beside the bed, sometimes dozing, sometimes just studying him. Listlessly she watched the moon sail lazily above the treetops and listened to the dainty clock ticking the night away. Midnight brooked no refusal of its coming. It approached, it went, and Shanna still kept her vigil.

Ruark began to moan and mumble more violently with a feverish delirium, making Shanna's heart leap within her as he emitted a weird, ragged groan from his parched lips. She feared he might try to get up, and she knew she didn't have the strength to hold him even in his weakened condition. She pressed him back upon the pillow and then half sat on the bed beside him, while she murmured soothingly and tenderly stroked his brow. He lay limp and unresponsive to her soft inquiries. Hoarsely he began to sing a child's ditty—then abruptly he stopped in mid-word, twisting beneath her hands. A fierce grimace contorted his face, and his eyes flew open. He seized her roughly by the shoulders and pulled her close, hurting her with the careless grip of his fingers.

"Dammit! I never saw the girl before!" he snarled. "Why don't you believe—"

With a growl he pushed Shanna away and lay back, staring blankly toward the outflung balcony doors. Sadness sagged the corners of his mouth, and he began in a sing-song voice, "Four walls—ceiling—floor—door. Count the stones, make them more. Count the days, one by one. But how, good lad, since you never see the sun?"

His chant trailed off into an incoherent mumble, and he squeezed his eyes tightly shut. Shanna thought him pained, for he seemed to be caught in a moment of torment. She reached for the cloth in the basin of water but halted as his words became clear again. Sharp and angry they matched in tone the scowl that came swiftly upon his face.

"Then take it all! Take my life! What care I now that the wench is gone! Damn her! Damn her fickle heart! Ah, man, I hate her! Fickle wife! She taunts me, seduces me, cajoles me, flees me, leaves me wanting her all the more. Have I no more will of my own?"

His voice broke, and he sobbed, hiding his face behind an arm flung across it. Shanna's throat tightened, and there was no ease for the ache in her breast. With tears of her own gathering in her eyes she tried to hush him. He heard none of her pleas, but lifted his hands and held them before his eyes, turning them, staring at them as if he had never seen them before.

"But still—I love her. I could take my freedom and fly—but she holds me bound to her." His hands became limp fists which slowly crumpled to his sides as he groaned listlessly. "I cannot stay. I cannot leave." His eyes closed, and swiftly the moment was gone.

Choking on a sob, Shanna bowed her head in abject misery. How carelessly she had woven her web about him. She had not meant to entrap him, no more than she had been willing to see herself ensnared. On that cold, dark night in the London gaol she could not have foreseen this end. It had been a game she played, a challenge to outwit her father, to prove herself as shrewd as any man, a total disregard of other people's feelings and emotions.

Tears fell on hands clenched in her lap as she relented to the sorrow she felt. She was deeply ashamed, contrite in her heart. Of all the men she had wounded with the sharp edge of her tongue, Ruark was the only one she had never really meant to hurt. And now he was near death because of her. And she could do naught but stand aside and watch, while the relentless poisons drained his once exuberant vitality.

"Damn!" she cried in wretched frustration and came to her feet, wringing her hands together. She paced about the room, racking her brain for any tiny bit of knowledge which would aid her. Her mother had caught the fever, and they had bled her. Little help, for Georgiana died, much weakened under their care. And if she relented to the surgeon's arguments and allowed Ruark's leg to be taken, what then? If such a wound as he had now could fester, how much more the raw flesh of a stump? Should the leg be taken, he might die all the more quickly. How, then, would she ever console herself?

No answers came, though Shanna agonized over each fact, each question that presented itself to her. Her mind grew numb with worry and exhaustion until it refused to grasp logic. As if by rote she cared for Ruark, bathing and soothing him, spooning liquid between his parched lips. And still he raved and tossed as if plagued by some unavenged demon.

" 'Twill mean naught to me," he rasped. "Do not press me further. She'll have the gift—"

It became an endless labor. The night wore thin. Finally shafts of light from the dawning sun intruded into the room through the French doors. In her chair Shanna dozed fretfully, her mind skimming the ruffled fringe of sleep, while her head lolled languidly against her shoulder. Dimly she was aware of the door opening and closing behind her. Suddenly a huge, dark shadow stood over her. With a start she came fully awake, a scream half born on her lips, as if she expected to recognize Pellier come to haunt her. To her overwhelming relief, it was Pitney. Her breath sighed heavily from her as she relaxed again in the chair, rubbing a hand across her brow.

"I knew you would trust no one else." His deep, rasping voice touched her gently, but it held a hint of sarcasm in its tone.

Shanna had no defense and stared numbly at Ruark.

"This is useless." Pitney's broad hand swept the room. "You'll soon be no good to him, or yourself. Go to your room and sleep. I will watch."

He would hear none of her protests but dragged her up from the chair and led her to the balcony doors. With a hand on her back he pushed her out and when she faced him with more arguments, waved them off.

"Go!" His tone was stern but eased as he saw her worry. "I will see to your man as well as your secrets."

Shanna could do little but obey. In complete exhaustion she stumbled to her bed, and, still clothed in the gown her father had brought with him on the *Hampstead*, she stretched her weary body across satin sheets and tumbled into the deep vortex of slumber.

It seemed only a moment later that Hergus was shaking her awake. "Come, Shanna," the woman urged. "Have a bite to eat."

Shanna sat up with a start, looking to her clock, and saw that it was nearly three hours into the afternoon. In dismay she snatched a piece of oat cake from the tray and fled out onto the balcony, slipping quickly past the lattice barrier that separated the areas. Pitney had produced a deck of game cards and was playing with them on a small table when Shanna returned. He glanced up and leaned back in his chair, regarding her disheveled appearance.

"Your father dropped in for a moment but left." He gestured to the cards. "He thinks them evil and cannot abide them. But of the two," Pitney nodded toward Ruark who still tossed and mumbled as before, "I thought these less disastrous to his nature."

Shanna found no words to reply and hurried to Ruark. His brow had not cooled even the slightest. Lifting the sheet, she gasped at the sight of the red streaks which had crept almost to his hip and heavily marked the lower leg. Pitney came to stand beside her, and he frowned deeply as he reached out a finger to test the swollen flesh.

"He's likely to lose it," he commented ruefully. He had seen enough—and heard many gory tales—of the barber's surgery. It was a shame to have it practiced on a man. " 'Tis a pity your Mister Ruark is not a horse. We could practice some of his cures on himself. The mare is well healed, with hardly a mark on her."

Shanna wrinkled her nose, remembering the sight and smell of the balm. "A horse remedy," she scoffed. "That stuff would be enough to take his leg off. Rum and herbs which could make a man howl—"

Abruptly she stopped as a memory came flooding back. The leaves Ruark had picked for her heel had also stung when applied to the cut, but the pain soon ebbed, and he had said it would draw the poison.

Her jaw set in grim determination, Shanna faced Pitney. "Fetch Elot. Send him after the leaves Ruark made the balm with. We've strong black rum to add." As Pitney hurried to the portal, she flung over her shoulder. "And tell Hergus to fetch fresh linens and hot water."

The door slammed behind the hulking man, and Shanna bent over Ruark, carefully uncoiling the wrappings from his leg. She was amazed at her calm and clearheaded purpose as she gently washed the area around the ragged flesh. For modesty's sake she draped a cloth over Ruark's hips so Hergus would not be unduly shocked. It was enough to have Berta clucking in disapproval without upsetting Hergus as well.

After an unbearable wait, Pitney returned with Elot's find. New coals were added to the warming pan, and Shanna crushed the leaves into a small amount of water and set it to steam. Soon the chamber filled with a pungent odor. Cloths were steeped in clean, hot water before being placed on the wound to soak away the gore. This brought a renewed thrashing from Ruark, as the pain seeped into his delirium. Pitney laid broad hands on the leg and held it still while Shanna worked, cleaning the oozing holes.

With a silent prayer running through her mind, Shanna mixed the herbs and rum and slapped the warm paste onto the leg. It drew an immediate reaction from Ruark. He cried out with the first touch of it and twisted away in agony as the caustic herb and warmed rum penetrated the torn flesh. Shanna worked all the faster, while Pitney held him down, and Hergus stirred fresh herbs into the kettle. Shanna trickled rum from the bottle over the whole of it and then repeated the process. Over and over again she cleaned away the poultice when it cooled, replacing it with the warm. She did not count the hours she remained at his side doing this. An ache began to grow at the small of her back with her constant bending, and her hands became red from molding the hot poultice around the wound. It was well into night before she paused long enough to realize that Ruark was resting easier. His lips had ceased their endless movement, and he no longer tossed like a man placed upon a rack of torture. Touching his skin, she knew the fever ebbed.

"Fetch my needle and good, strong thread," Shanna bade the maid. "For once in my life, I can see the need of good stitchery."

Hergus was perplexed but hastened away on the errand, returning shortly. The maid stood at the end of the bed watching Shanna painstakingly close the gaping wounds with rum-soaked thread and the needle. It was with some pride at her own fine handiwork that she finished the task and remarked:

" 'Twill hardly be a scar left to even boast about."

Hergus grunted. "As if ye should be fretting about a scar on a man's leg."

"Let the poultice cool on his leg," Pitney offered. "He's through the worst of it."

Agreeing with him, Shanna covered a new batch of the mixture with fresh strips of linen around Ruark's leg and piled towels on either side to hold it all against any movement.

"I'll stay a while longer," Shanna sighed as she sank wearily into the nearest chair.

Hergus shook her head in exasperation. "Canna ye even take a bite and a bath? Why, ye're to skin and bones now with those pirates starving ye. And look at ye! Ye'd scare the mon sure if he came awake now and saw ye."

Self-consciously Shanna ran her fingers through her tangled hair, realizing she had not combed it or seen to her appearance since she last dressed aboard the *Hampstead*. It seemed an eternity ago.

"And yer poor pa downstairs, fretting, wanting to see ye yet saying naught. The bonnie lad there can hold his own now. See to yerself and give yer pa a kind word or two. It nearly laid him low when he learned ye'd been taken by those pirates.

" 'Tis more likely papa flayed the countryside with his rage," Shanna corrected with levity.

Pitney wrinkled his brows together as he remarked gruffly. "Aye, and he vowed to hang Mister Ruark after the bondsmen came back with their tales."

Shanna grimaced gingerly. "What did they tell him?"

"They said he fought for ye and claimed ye as his," Hergus rushed to answer. "Even that he killed a mon to have ye."

"Is that all?" Shanna questioned carefully.

The maid cast a wary glance toward Pitney and, noticeably more reluctant, replied, "Aye, there was more of it."

Pitney was more brusque. "The lot of us were present when the bondsmen agreed that if ye were ravished at all, 'twas Mister Ruark doing it to ye."

He waited effectively as his words sank in, watching her closely as the sea-hued eyes widened in distress. Then he shrugged, taking himself to the door.

"But the bondsmen also admitted there was no way for them to know for sure, since he carted ye off upstairs." Pitney stroked his broad jaw thoughtfully and added for good measure, "Still, if he had no intentions of bedding ye, why would the man fight for ye?"

Shanna groaned despairingly and sank deeper into her chair. "Perhaps I'd best go down"—her smile was weak and pained— "and explain to papa."

Hergus's skirts swished in her haste to follow Pitney out. "I'll see to yer bath."

Entering her own chambers after assuring herself that Ruark was resting peacefully, Shanna was met by a stubborn Hergus who firmly bade her, "Bathe!" and carried the command through by helping her into the tub, scrubbing her back, and seeing her hair washed, towel-dried and combed.

"Yer pa's coming up," the maid informed as she brought the young woman her nightshift and wrapper instead of the chemise and gown Shanna had expected to don. "He didna think ye would be up to giving Sir Gaylord yer best company. And I'll fetch ye a tray, so's ye'll not miss yer dinner. Ye'll be needing the strength to face yer pa."

Shanna glared her gratitude and the woman shrugged, unconcerned.

"Serves ye right, lowering yerself to bed a common bondsman with the lords and all who've begged yer hand and the foin schools and learning ye've taken in. Mind ye, I have na a thing agin Mister Ruark. He canna help being taken wit' ye. And he's a bonnie-faced mon, to be sure. He's given ye his best—but—"

Shanna mumbled under her breath as she belted her wrapper tightly around her slim waist, but the maid either missed or ignored the ungrateful attitude and plunged on, heedless of Shanna's frown.

"What will ye get from him but a fat belly every year and no good name to dub the brood? Ruark?" Hergus wrinkled her nose in distaste. "Sounds Irish, and ye know there's no good in them folk, just mischief and mayhem, abrawling and aloving. If ye had yer wits about ye, ye'd find some Scottish laird with a foin name to equal yer poor dead husband's and settle yerself down."

Shanna sighed in exasperation.

"I do not expect you to understand about Mister Ruark and myself, Hergus, but I am painfully hungry and you promised to fetch me a tray. Would you see me starve while you preach on propriety?"

The maid finally relented and fetched the evening fare, and as Shanna sat at her small table eating, her father knocked lightly and entered. He appeared a little at a loss, and after a terse greeting, he strode about the room, hands folded beneath the tail of his coat. An occasional grunt or two emitted from deep in his throat as he paused beside a curio then stopped to examine a volume of verses. With the tip of his forefinger, he lifted the ornate inlaid top of the music box Ruark had given her and listened for a spell to the tinkling melody before closing it again with care as if he were afraid of breaking the piece.

"Hm! Gadgetry!"

Shanna held her silence, sensing he had something worrisome on his mind. She watched his meanderings while she continued to eat, taking a bite or two of her food and sipping her tea, but scarcely tasting anything.

"You look none the worse for your ordeal, child," he finally remarked. "Indeed, if it be possible, you are more lovely. The sun has agreed with you."

"Thank you, papa," she managed quietly before hiding further comment behind her cup.

Trahern came upon the jerkin folded neatly on the chaise and the dagger and pistol laying on top of it. Taking up the latter, he squinted dubiously over his shoulder at her, and Shanna could only shrug.

"It served its purpose."

Trahern came to stand before her table, and Shanna put down the cup, folded her hands primly in her lap, and lifted her gaze to meet his.

"You did fare well?" he asked with concern.

"Aye, father," she replied, slipping into the more formal address. She braced herself inwardly for the coming interrogation.

"And none of the pirates—touched you?" he questioned gruffly.

"Nay, father. You have heard it that Mister Ruark killed a man for me. 'Twas two, if you're taking count of his deeds. I survived only because of Mister Ruark's cunning and skill with weapons. Had he not been there, I would not be here today."

"And this Mister Ruark—" He let the question hang as he sought for the words to speak of that which nagged him sorely.

Shanna suddenly rose to her feet. She could not face him and moved to the French doors leading onto the balcony and set them wide to catch the night breezes, for suddenly the room was stifling.

"Mister Ruark is a most honorable man. He has brought me no harm, and I am no different from when I left." She faced him with a sweet smile curving her lips and spoke honestly, for truly none of what she had said was a falsehood. "My greatest distress at the moment, papa, is for his welfare and even that seems to be much improved."

For a long expanse of time Trahern stared at her as if considering her words. Abruptly he nodded his head, willing to accept her story.

"Good enough, then."

Satisfied now, he started toward the door, but Shanna's voice halted him.

"Papa?"

Trahern turned and raised his brows questioningly.

"I love you."

With much blustering he stammered out a good night and glanced quickly about as if he had forgotten something. His hands searched his sides, then he snorted.

"Hmph, he's got the damn cane." At the door he paused for one last glance. "Good to have you home, child. Good to have you home."

It was the sound of her name being called that brought Shanna into full wakefulness. For a moment she lay still, wondering if the voice were real or if it had been some spectre from a dream. Then it came again, this time clearly.

"Shanna! Shanna! Don't go!"

It seemed a call of distress, lonely in the silence of night, and she could not mistake the voice. She flew from her bed and out onto the balcony, not pausing for her robe, and entered Ruark's room. He tossed upon the bed and fought against invisible bonds, some imagined restraint. His brow was dappled with sweat, and the nightshirt they had managed to clothe him in was damp with perspiration. Shanna almost laughed in relief as she wiped his face with a towel. His skin was moist and cool. The fever had broken. By the light of the single dim candle, she could now see that his eyes were open and regarding her with some bemusement.

"Are you really there, Shanna? Or does my dream befuddle my sight?" His fingers closed lightly around her wrist and brought it against his lips. Kissing her soft skin, he murmured, "No maiden of my dreams could taste as sweet. Shanna, Shanna," he sighed. "I thought I had lost you."

She bent low to press her trembling mouth upon his. "Oh, Ruark," she breathed against his lips. "I thought I had lost *you*."

He laid an arm about her nape and pulled her down beside him, searching her eyes in the meager glow.

"I'll hurt your leg!" Shanna protested in concern.

"Come here!" he commanded. "I would know if this is a dream or more heady stuff."

His eyes grew lambent, sending her senses reeling, and there was a soft union of tongues and lips as their mouths parted and clung with a leisurely sweetness that held still the very moments of time.

"I do believe the fever's gone," Shanna breathed, nestling against him. "But it must have left you addled in the head. Your kiss speaks much more of passion than of pain." She slipped her hand inside the nightshirt and rubbed his furry chest, reveling in the strength she felt in his lean, muscular ribs.

"Addled indeed!" He smiled at her and sighed. "Must I forever bear the barbs of a disappointed bride?"

Shanna traced a finger in the crisp hair of his chest. "In your madness you said you loved me," she murmured shyly.

His humor fled, and the smile left her lips as she continued, "You said it before, too. When the storm struck, I asked you to love me, and you said you did." Her voice was the barest of whispers.

Ruark's gaze turned away from her, and he rubbed the bandage on his leg before he spoke. "Strange that madness should speak the truth, but truth it is." He met her questioning eyes directly. "Aye, I love you." The pain of longing marked his face with a momentary sadness. "And that is madness, in all truth."

Shanna raised herself from his side and sat on her heels, staring down at him. "Why do you love me?" Her tone was wondrous. "I beset you at every turn. I deny you as a fit mate. I have betrayed you into slavery and worse. There is no sanity in your plea at all. How can you love me?"

"Shanna! Shanna! Shanna!" he sighed, placing his fingers on her hand and gently tracing the lines of her finely boned fingers. "What man would boast the wisdom of his love? How many times has this world heard, 'I don't care, I love.' Do I count your faults and sins to tote them in a book?" He gazed at the timid candle flame. "I am thinking of a mouse-haired girl of plain face, one whose virtue was destroyed before she knew of its existence. Then there is a man of some account who was abused as a slave. Good Gaitlier and his Dora." He looked upon Shanna's face, but she would not meet his eyes. "They stand hand in hand against the taunts of all and tightly close their eyes and shout aloud. 'It makes no difference. We love!' Do men step forth and declaim upon the clever way they chose the object of their devotion? Or if asked, would the young swain more likely shrug and spread his hands with an unminded grin and softly say, 'I love her!' "

Ruark moved his leg onto the pillow and touched the bindings as if he would ease the ache of his wound.

"I dream of unbelievable softness. I remember warmth at my side the likes of which can set my heart afire. I see in the dark before me softly glowing eyes of aqua, once tender in a moment of love, then flashing with defiance and anger, now dark and blue with some stirring I know I have caused, now green and gay with laughter spilling from them. There was a form within my arms that I tenderly held and touched. There is that one who has met my passion with her own and left me gasping."

Ruark caressed Shanna's arm and turned her face to him, making her look into his eyes and willing her to see the truth in them as he spoke.

"My beloved Shanna. I cannot think of betrayal when I think of love. I can count no denials when I hold you close. I only wait for that day when you will say, 'I love.' "

Shanna raised her hands as if to plead her case then let them fall dejectedly on her knees. Tears coursed down her cheeks, and she begged helplessly, "But I do not want to love you." She began to sob. "You are a colonial. You are untitled, a murderer condemned, a rogue, a slave. I want a name for my children. I want so much more of my husband." She rolled her eyes in sudden confusion. "And I do not want to hurt you more."

Ruark sighed and gave up for the moment. He reached out and gently wiped away the tears as they fell. "Shanna, love," he whispered tenderly. "I cannot bear to see you cry. I will not press the matter for a while. I only beg you remember the longest journey is taken a step at a time. My love can wait, but it will neither yield nor change."

His voice took on a lighter note, and his eyes twinkled with golden flecks of mischief.

"You should know by now that I am a willful man. My

mother called me determined, my father called me spoiled."

Shanna sniffed and managed a weak smile. "Aye, I admit that as fact."

He chuckled at the gibe. "But come, my love, worry no more. Lie here beside me and let me feel that warmth and softness. If you cannot declare your love, at least humor a sick man."

Shanna complied and cuddled close to his side, resting her head on his shoulder. She heard laughter deep inside his chest and glanced up in wonder.

"I cannot rest, for I fret sorely on which is worse." She raised on her elbow to frown at him until he explained. "The ache in my leg or the one in my loins."

"You lusty ape," she giggled, dropping her head again into the crook of his arm. "No man is ill who rouses so quickly at the slightest smile."

Ruark held her close for a moment, kissing the softness beneath her ear before searching out her lips. There his mouth stayed long and enjoyed heartily the honey sweet taste. The room grew quiet, and for Shanna it was a most natural place to be, held close within the circle of his arms. Still, many in the house would have raged to find them thus entwined and in one bed.

A morning tray had been delivered by Berta, and Ruark was settling down to eat the first solid nourishment in days, when the door swung open and Pitney entered with a tray loaded with a coffee service. He was followed by Orlan Trahern himself. Soon a steaming cup was placed on his bedside table by the squire.

" 'Tis an early hour but the best time to come and thank you without the interference of my daughter." Trahern jerked his thumb over his shoulder. "She's still asleep, so keep your voice down, or we'll be set upon by more of her fretting."

Ruark chewed on a mouthful of food, not quite sure of his status. He glanced apprehensively toward Pitney, who stood at the foot of the bed, his massive arms folded across his chest. The man returned his stare with a warning frown creasing his brow.

"I have assured Orlan that I know a man who saw ye dragged off onto the pirate ship. He was a bit addled at the time, confused ye might say, and dared say naught of the deed."

Ruark nodded and sipped the coffee to find it heavily laced with brandy. He raised the mug in silent thanks to Trahern and savored the heady aroma that issued from it.

Pitney appeared to have spoken his fill and was satisfied with Ruark's silence. Trahern sat back in the chair beside the bed and folded his hands across his paunch as Pitney drew a straight chair up and straddled it, resting his thick arms on the back. When the room had been quiet for a few moments, the squire spoke.

"Would you tell me the way of it all? I have judgments to make, and I have little enough to go on."

While he ate, Ruark began his narration. He told of the raid and of the voyage to the island. He spoke frankly of his attempted misdirection and its unfortunate results and made a point of the fact that all three of the captured men had wished to return when given the chance. He let it be urged from him of Shanna's time in the pit and his rescue of her. He avoided the details of their days and nights together but let it seem as if they had been caught together by the storm. He mentioned briefly the two men he had killed and his reasons. Included was the episode in which Shanna had slain the one. He related the plan and execution of the escape, with minor details omitted, and made much of Gaitlier's and Dora's part in it. He drew chuckles from both of them over Shanna's valor in the face of adversity.

The two older men seemed well pleased with his tale and grinned in relief when he assured them that no unusual harm had befallen Shanna. The squire let his chin sink to his chest and was lost in thought for a space. Pitney caught Ruark's eye and smiled, nodding ever so slightly his approval. Then abruptly Trahern came erect and slapped his knee in sudden joviality.

"By George," he chuckled, then lowered his voice with a furtive glance toward the balcony. "I see no help for it but to give the three bondsmen a bonus for their service."

Ruark cleared his throat and, as Trahern gave him pause, lent voice to another matter. "Sir, Mister Gaitlier and Mistress Dora risked their lives to no small degree. If the matter of rewards is discussed, surely they must be considered. I fear that they will be cast to dire straits for their effort."

"Rest assured that I have not forgotten and will deal with them handsomely." Trahern coughed and glanced at Pitney. "It has been brought to my attention, though I had already considered the fact, that you have done me a great service in the return of my daughter unharmed. When you are about, I shall give you your papers, paid and clear. You are a free man."

He waited for the expected joyful response, but instead Ruark frowned and pondered first one and then the other of the two men. Ruark noted that Pitney was the more uneasy of the two and well surmised the reason. But Trahern had grown somewhat puzzled by his bondsman's delay in answering.

"Sir, would you have me accept reward for a common decency to another?" Ruark waved away any argument. "I did myself a service in escaping from the band of miscreants, and could not have left other innocents behind. I cannot accept payment for it."

There was double meaning in his words, but Ruark was not about to take any recompense for saving Shanna. Besides, being a bondslave allowed him a good reason to stay on the island with her.

"Bah! You have more than earned your freedom with the two mills," Trahern snorted.

"Those would be yours if I had been hired as a free man to serve you. There is no cost to me there. I but served my employer as best I could."

Orlan Trahern stared at him in bemused amazement, but Pitney avoided looking him in the eye.

"Had I not been forced to purchase expensive clothes," Ruark reminded the squire with a twinkle in his eye, "I would have earned nearly enough to buy my freedom."

Trahern protested as any good, outraged merchant. "I paid far more for your garb than you did!"

Ruark chuckled and then grew serious. He peered askance at Pitney when he spoke and noticed the fine beading of sweat on his brow as Pitney chafed beneath the double edge of his statement.

"I have been known as one who always pays my debts to the hilt." He shifted his gaze and met Trahern's directly. "When I lay the full sum of my indebtedness in your hand, there will be no doubt that my freedom is not another man's gift."

"You are a rare man, John Ruark," Trahern sighed. "I would not see you as a merchant, for you have set aside fair payment."

He heaved himself up from his chair, paused, and studied Ruark closely. "Why is it I feel as if I have been taken to the limits of my purse?"

He shook his head and turned away, moving to the door and letting Pitney precede him out. He looked back again.

"My trader's intuition is outraged. I have been rooked, John Ruark, but I know not how."

☙ Chapter 21 ☙

ORLAN Trahern ate a light, brief breakfast and quickly took himself from the table, thus avoiding any conversation with Sir Gaylord. It had become the custom of the knight to join the family in its morning repast. He was not really as boring as he seemed. It was only that the mention of: money, finances, the sea, England, war, peace, or the prospect of either, ships, water, trade, nations, wind or rain ended in an oration by him on the wisdom of investing in a small shipyard which could supply hundreds of sloops and schooners for the price of a single ship-of-the-line. His topic was noticeably limited, though he seemed remarkably adept at taking any random subject as an entry to it.

Thus it was that Squire Trahern gave a last pitying glance at his daughter, shrugged away her silent appeal, and took his leave with a zeal that belied his age and girth. With a frown of disappointment Shanna watched her father go and managed to bestow a tolerant smile upon Sir Gaylord, who gave his own delicate but effective attention to the well-filled plate before him. His manners did not leave him room to speak with food in his mouth, for which Shanna was immeasurably grateful, but he was not above letting his gaze warm appreciatively as it roamed her trim figure.

The briefest of nods sufficed to excuse her, and on her way to the drawing room she quietly bade Berta bring her fresh tea, now that she would be able to enjoy it in some peace. Alas, it was her undoing. No sooner had she seated herself upon the settee than Gaylord entered, dabbing the last of his meal from his lips and then tucking the napkin into his sleeve. Were it not for the ornate "T" embroidered on it, the cloth might have served as an elaborate kerchief. But then, the man seemed to have a penchant for anything artfully stitched with a letter and a special liking for the "B" which ornately decorated all his clothing. Even his coats had the monogram where it could be worn over his heart. As Berta set out the cups and readied the tea to be poured, he rose and brushed her away.

"Not a manly grace, my dear," he informed Shanna pompously. "But one that must be approached with a skill one rarely finds away from England."

Lifting the teapot with a flourish, he poured into two cups no more than half their fill of the rich brown fluid, topped them off with a like amount of cream and stirred until the cups held a thick pale concoction that on no account resembled tea. He gave no notice to Berta's gasp of horror, but ladled several spoons of sugar into one and then paused over the other, raising a brow toward Shanna.

"One or two, my dear?" he asked solicitously.

"No cream, Sir Gaylord, please. Just the tea and a touch of sweetening."

"Oh!" He responded blankly and paused to sample his own cup. "Delicious, my dear. You really must try it this way. The rage of London."

"I have," Shanna managed without malice and leaning forward poured herself a fresh cup and added a shallow spoon of sugar.

Gaylord folded his frame into a straight-backed chair and crossed his legs before he sipped more of the tea.

"Ah, well, no matter. I trust I shall have a lifetime to teach you the niceties of good British gentlefolk."

Shanna quickly raised her cup and lowered her gaze while Berta paused in her puttering to glare at the knight.

"Shanna, my dear,"—Sir Gaylord leaned back and contemplated her—"you have no idea what simply being near you can do to even a peer of the realm. 'Tis sore upon my heart that we find so little time alone, or I would speak of the wonderful passions that stir my heart."

Shanna gave a small shudder and hastily excused it as she saw he had taken note. "Too much sugar, I'm afraid."

She freshened her cup from the pot and dared not glance at Berta. The housekeeper stood by the doorway leading into the foyer and fingered a heavy figurine, narrowing her eyes in a most uncharacteristic fashion. The old woman seemed to come to a decision and marched forward boldly.

"Ay got tings to do," she informed Shanna, bringing a note of despair to her mistress's face and a shine of new hope in Gaylord's eyes. "You need me, yust call."

Before Shanna could protest, Berta gave a last doubtful glare at Sir Gaylord and left. The room was still for a while as Shanna stared after her, and she almost jumped when the knight cleared his throat and rose from his chair to stand before her again. He fixed her with a limpid stare and set out to pay serious court.

"My dear Shanna, there are so many things we must discuss. 'Tis so rare I can find someone willing to understand the needs of the blooded elite. You are so beautiful and so wealth—uh, desirable. No one else can ease my plight. I am stricken to the quick."

He came a pace nearer, and Shanna was caught in a dilemma. She was equally afraid that he would take her hand or that she would burst into laughter. Some of her struggle must have shown, for he continued apace.

"I pray, do not distress yourself, my dear. Be aware that nothing of what has happened has in any way affected my respect for you," he assured her.

Shanna was nearly frantic. Reason deserted her, and she could summon no rationale for excusal. She felt trapped, but Gaylord read her unease as indecision and grew bolder. His knee had already started to flex as if he would kneel before her when his eyes strayed behind her and he suddenly stiffened.

"Good morning." The voice rang cheerfully from the doorway. "And a fine beautiful day it is."

With a gasp Shanna twisted around on the settee to stare in amazement at Ruark, the last person she had expected to rescue her.

"Mister Ruark! Are you sure you should be up and about?" She forced as much worry and concern into her tone as she could manage so that the burgeoning relief that flooded her might be disguised. "What of your leg? Is it so much improved?"

She knew far better than anyone that three days of rest and well-diluted poultices had done wonders. Only last night the surgeon had changed the dressing and declared the wound pink and healthy. She caught Gaylord's sigh of disappointment as he resigned himself to the obvious fate of further waiting.

Ruark limped in on her father's staff and lowered himself to the sofa beside Shanna. Beneath Gaylord's glower, his smile was brighter and debonair, though a hint of mischief gleamed deep in those amber eyes that so quickly mirrored his changes of mood. Shanna hastened from her seat to fetch a footstool for him and propped his leg comfortably. As she bent low to slip a pillow underneath his calf, she gave no mind to her décolletage or the manner in which it displayed her bosom to Ruark. However, Gaylord chafed as he saw Ruark's gaze roam freely over that which his own gaze craved. He was caught unaware when Ruark's eyes lifted, meeting his, and the bondsman's white teeth flashed in a broad grin of undisguised pleasure.

Covertly admiring Ruark's appearance, Shanna missed the exchange. He had donned a loose white shirt and tan knee breeches over white stockings and, amazingly, brown brass-buckled shoes. She cringed inwardly at the idea of the pain he must have borne to put the left one on. Over the shirt he wore the long leather jerkin he had affected as a pirate captain. Above it, his face appeared darker and leaner, his eyes livelier, his teeth whiter, his hair blacker. She had never seen him more handsome, nor could she hide the soft glow that warmed her eyes as she stared at him.

"Madam Beauchamp!"

Shanna started in surprise, realizing that Gaylord was demanding her attention. "I beg your pardon? I did not hear—"

"Obviously, madam, since I had to repeat the question twice.

I asked if you might care for a stroll in the garden. 'Tis become a bit stuffy in here of a sudden."

"Oh, well, I'll open the doors, then." She rushed to push them wide, ignoring any reply to his inquiry, and stood for a moment enjoying the refreshing touch of the morning breeze.

" 'Tis cool," she informed the room at large, but when she turned, her eyes went to Ruark. "Late September always brings the cooler winds and the evening showers. The clouds gather on the south side of the island all afternoon, and just before dark they slip across the ridge to give us a wetting. This is the time when the cane grows highest."

The glass doors framed her with a master's touch, and the lush greens of the lawns beyond accentuated her loveliness until it was almost painful for Ruark to look at her. She was a vision. Her gown of aqua was just enough different from her eyes to set them asparkle behind the sooty lashes, and Ruark was completely captivated.

Suddenly the three of them were startled by a loud crash which came from the porch, unmistakably the shattering of glass. With a bemused frown Shanna turned and stepped out onto the veranda in time to see Milly skittering around a chair in her haste to leave an overturned planter which had been displaced from its perch near the drawing room doors.

"Milly! What are you doing?" Shanna inquired. She realized with amazement that the girl had to have been eavesdropping to be behind the chair in the first place. But then, she had done that before in the stables, and Shanna could only wonder what she was up to now.

Milly was caught and wheeled about, immediately defensive. "I didn't break it. Ye can't blame it on me!"

"Aye, the breeze is a bit strong today," Shanna quipped with a hint of sarcasm. "But never mind that. What do you want here? Have you brought fish?"

"I—uh—I" Milly glanced past Shanna into the drawing room—then blurted, "I heard Mister Ruark was hurt, and I come to see if 'ere was aught I could do for him."

"You're a trifle late, but come in. He's here."

Shanna led the girl into the room and waved her into a chair beside Ruark, avoiding his questioning glance. Despite his assurance that nothing was between them, Shanna felt a prick of ire at Milly's apparent inability to leave him alone. Sir Gaylord had risen at the entrance of the newcomer, and the girl bobbed a quick curtsy.

"Milly Hawkins I be, gov'na," the young woman boldly introduced herself before wiggling her small fanny into the chair. She eyed Ruark boldly. "Hear ye got it in the crotch, Mister Ruark. Hope 'tweren't nothing serious."

Shanna closed her eyes as if to blot out the sight of Milly while Ruark struggled to contain his mirth. When he regained his poise, he grinned across to Shanna.

"'Twas Madam Beauchamp's attentions that brought me through, Milly, none other's."

"Oooh?" Milly queried, turning wide, dark eyes to Shanna. "Why, she must 'ave sweetened to ye a mite since the last time I seen ye together. She lowered 'at collar on ye pritty good."

Gaylord's interest perked smartly. "Eh? Collar? What do you say?"

"Never mind," Shanna said quickly. "Would anyone care for tea?"

"Berta promised to bring me a tray in here," Ruark rejoined. "I'll have a cup when she comes."

It suddenly occurred to Shanna why the housekeeper had left in such haste. No doubt she had seen Ruark entering the dining room from the foyer.

As it was, Sir Gaylord pondered on much the same topic. Berta barely managed to serve him with civility, yet she catered to the injured bondslave. The hulking Pitney spoke no word to him other than the least required to a knight of the realm, but the fellow seemed to hang on every phrase uttered by this colonial miscreant. Even Orlan Trahern, though certainly no disrespect could be awarded to that fine man, was a trifle reserved, and sought after the advice of this bondsman, who had proven no more than a stone in the porridge of the brave Sir Gaylord.

Berta was once more her cheerful self as she helped Milan serve Ruark his morning fare and Sir Gaylord stood apart from the group and fretted. He felt as if he had just heard a joke whose point had escaped him while others chortled in glee. It was almost more than a proper gentleman could bear, and, to make matters more intolerable, he could not even gracefully question this bondsman's presence in Trahern's parlor.

"Well!" Milly slapped her hands upon her thighs after a long pause of silence and got to her feet. "I didn't mean to stay long. Just to see 'ow ye were doing. Mister Ruark. 'Sides, I can't rightly chitchat with ye when 'ere's so many folk about."

The young woman rolled her hips as she took herself to the door, giving Berta cause to shake her head as her blue eyes followed the gyration. The housekeeper bustled out on the heels of Milan, and Milly turned in the open portal leading into the foyer.

"I'll see meself out the front here," Milly announced to the three remaining. "Daren't go along the porch. Might cut me foot." She wiggled her bare toes as everyone's attentions were drawn there. "I forgot me sandals again."

Leaving them with that, she sauntered out, sending back a coy wave to Ruark and closing the door firmly behind her. Shanna almost breathed an audible sigh of relief but caught herself just in time as Gaylord faced her abruptly, folding his huge hands behind his back and bending slightly forward.

"Now, Madam Beauchamp, about that stroll—"

Shanna brightened. "Of course, Sir Gaylord," and rose to her feet, smoothing her gown of airy lawn over the hooped panniers. "Would you care to join us, Mister Ruark? I think an outing might do you good."

The Englishman's face sagged into a distasteful, pinched frown. "Wouldn't if I were he. Might slip and break his other leg."

Ruark stood up with an ability that amazed Shanna and flashed the dour knight a wicked grin of dazzling whiteness.

"On the contrary, I agree that the exercise would be good for me." He swept his arm before him in a half bow. "After you, madam, of course."

"We'll go through the front," Shanna offered sweetly. " 'Twill be easier for Mister Ruark to go down the steps with the balustrade to aid him."

She glided to the drawing room door and paused demurely for it to be opened. Gaylord was fast of foot and, bowing gallantly, held it wide for her. He was about to take a place at her side when he was interrupted.

"Thank you, Sir Gaylord." Ruark brushed by him and took a place close behind Shanna. "You're most considerate."

Gaylord found himself with no choice but to fall in behind them like some attending lad. Even the sight of Milly still lingering in the hallway did not alter Shanna's sense of relief at having outmaneuvered him.

"Aye, gov'na," Milly's voice echoed in the immensity of the hall as she caught the coin Ralston tossed to her. She immediately tied it safely in her bodice and sauntered to the door, calling back, "I'll be there."

Ralston greeted the three of them soberly and in the presence of Shanna barely managed a brief nod to Ruark. His eyes crossed Gaylord's face, and he hurriedly returned his regard to Shanna.

"I came to fetch some papers from your father's study. If you will excuse me, madam?"

"By all means," Shanna consented coolly. "Shall I send Jason to help you find them?"

"No need, madam," the agent replied stiffly. "Your father instructed me on their whereabouts."

The small group ambled out the door onto the portico while Ralston stood and watched, his face dark with loathing. His fist was knotted about his quirt as if he longed to use it on the questionable Mister Ruark and it was a long moment before he turned and made his way toward the squire's chambers. Taking a place in the squire's chair, he casually began sorting through papers and sketches scattered across the top of the mammoth desk. He studied the drawings of the two mills closely. The construction of the sawmill had taken a hold on Trahern's fancy, and Ralston noted recent markings on the parchment that could only have been made by the bondslave. No doubt the anxious squire had hastened to Mister Ruark's bedside to discuss the project before aught else could delay it. At present Trahern was at the site, taking the place of the architect as much as he could.

Though Ralston carefully followed each line and read each notation, he could understand little of the plan and dismissed the drawings as a weapon to discredit the designer. Arrogantly he leaned back in the chair which seemed to diminish his narrow frame and mused on the success of John Ruark. It grated against his own sense of self-importance that the man had risen to such a state of worth to the squire as to be thought indispensable. Someday, Ralston promised himself, he would have the chance to deal with that bondslave in the manner deserving such a one.

Sir Gaylord also found it difficult to cope with John Ruark and his interference. However crippled the bondsman truly was, he somehow managed to maintain a position between the lady and himself. Gaylord longed only for a private moment to court her and was deeply aggravated to find himself forever speaking around the cocky knave. Finally he begged to be excused.

"Arrogant slaves and servants," Gaylord muttered to himself as he crossed the lawns with his long, gangling gait, "should be horsewhipped, the lot of them." He sneered to himself. "But come the marriage, I'll see them well instructed on the subject of good servitude."

Ruark leaned on the blackthorn staff and watched the man depart. "At least that oaf has the wits to know when he's not wanted."

But as he turned his gaze to Shanna, she was already moving away, strolling among the shrubs, plucking a dead leaf here, pausing to pull withered petals from a blossom, bending to clean a weed from the neatly raked soil. Ruark trailed along behind her, trying to work the stiffness from his leg, setting his weight upon it carefully before taking a step, relying as little as possible upon the cane.

Once they were left alone, Shanna had difficulty maintaining even an outward show of serenity. Her heart hammered in her breast, and she felt like a young girl smitten with her first suitor. Cautiously she kept her gaze averted from his and centered on the flowers and greenery. From the corner of her eye, she saw him stumble and, glancing at his face, caught the quick grimace of pain before he could hide it. Her stilted composure flew from her, and she was at his side in a second.

"Your leg!" It was as if the agony were her own. "It must be hurting you dreadfully."

Ruark raised his eyes to meet hers, and time trembled to a halt. Shanna's hand rested gently on his shoulder, and almost hungrily he searched her face for some sign. They stood motionless, touching, yearning, longing, and those soft, curving lips seemed to draw him closer, closer—

Shanna let out her breath in a rush. Nervously she stepped backward and rubbed her hand as if it still tingled from touching him. She gestured toward his thigh and lamely tried, "We should be getting back. You're not used to this."

"That is truth," Ruark agreed hoarsely. "I am not used to being close to you, and you sorely test my restraint."

Shanna turned away, not wanting to meet his gaze again. She toyed with a large poinciana bloom. Ruark watched her closely for a long moment, somewhat bemused, sensing her uncertainty but seeing no reason for it. He could not know how her pulse raced. He moved to stand close behind her and laid his hand upon her slim waist. Shanna started as if burned and whirled away from his embrace.

"Don't!" She began and struggled in an effort to control herself. "Don't touch me." She attempted to laugh in a gay manner, but it came out half choked and forced. "Must I remind you, sir, that we are unchaperoned? Keep your distance."

The words sounded bare and heavy as she spoke them, not at all light and amusing as she had intended.

"Is it something I've said or done?" Ruark questioned softly.

"No." Shanna tried to smile into those probing eyes, but the effort was a failure. Awkwardly she plucked the blossom, and her fingers whirled it restlessly.

"'Tis been three nights since you—stayed with me," Ruark murmured, his voice low and gentle. "I hear you moving about in your rooms late at night as if you were upset over something. Are you angry with me?"

"No!" The answer came out too sudden, too short, and clipped. Shanna shook her head, her lips tightly clenched.

Ruark leaned forward to caress a lock of her hair where it tumbled over her shoulder. His voice was hoarse, ragged. "May I touch—just for a moment?"

She gave him no answer, but crushed the blossom between hands which sought each other to keep from shaking.

"I want you." His whisper crackled like fire in her ears.

"Oh, Ruark, don't say that!" The words burst out of her in a half sob. "I can't—"

Her hand pressed tightly across her quivering lips, and her eyes squeezed shut as she fought against the flood of emotions that washed apart her every resolve. The flower fluttered unnoticed to the ground.

"Don't touch? Don't say?" Ruark's tone was harsh. "Shanna, are you afraid of me?"

Her eyes flew open and saw the glint of anger in his.

"Yes! Yes! Yes!" Her mind screamed until her skull ached with the pain of it, but her voice was gone, and her hands were clenched at her sides as she stared mutely at him. "Yes," her thoughts raged silently. "I am afraid you will touch me and I will crumble. I am afraid you will say, 'I love you,' and I will melt at your feet. I am afraid that I cannot stand against you anymore. Don't you understand? I am defenseless now. You've known me too closely, and I have known you too dearly. I've tended your hurts and calmed your ravings as you have mine. I have waited in fear for some word of hope from your lips and watched you weak and helpless on the bed. I cannot deny you longer."

But to Ruark she stood with a pained frown marring her beautiful face, twisting her hands together and licking suddenly dry lips.

"I—my father will be home soon." Her voice was shrill, as taut as a bowstring. "I must see to his lunch."

It was the shallowest of excuses, scarcely better than none, but it was enough, and Shanna fled the garden, leaving Ruark to carefully make his way back alone.

Suddenly Ruark's words came back to her, and Shanna halted where she stood, realizing she had again been prowling about her bedchamber. The week had aged, and seven torturous nights had passed since she had gone to him. But her will was crumbling. His eyes haunted her, for she saw in them the mirror of her own passion and desires. Now that he had regained some degree of mobility, he was always near, watching her, waiting. The only relief from his regard was when some of the overseers came from the sawmill to obtain details or clarifications of his sketches, and she would be safe for a time from his unwavering stare.

In the pursuit of the sleep she so sorely wanted, Shanna tried everything: a warm bath, reading, a light snack, poetry, even a glass of warm milk that Hergus had brought to her. Still there was a restlessness in her. The bed seemed overly large and the sheets cold to the touch. Though her clock had chimed the eleventh hour, she felt no yearning for sleep. Indeed, she sensed a new awakening deep within her, so sharp and pungent as to be almost physical. Since her return she had grown more careful of her manners with Hergus and more aware of Berta's gentle, loving nature and of Pitney's sometimes brusque affections, even of her father. She had never been particularly demonstrative of her love with any of them, but like a child had responded with affection when they pleased her and flared in anger when they did not.

Then there was Ruark. His leg was healing with almost magical rapidity, and though Shanna struggled to cool the affair, more and more she found herself comparing all other men with him, no longer using her imagined knight for the contrast. And beside Ruark everyone else seemed lacking. She was afraid to even question the significance of this, fearful she might then have to admit things she refused to let herself think about.

With a slow, thoughtful stride Shanna wandered out onto her balcony. There was just the slightest chill in the cool breeze, and she was glad she had chosen a heavier dressing gown after her bath. Half sitting upon the balustrade, she tugged its soft folds tighter around her naked body and gazed up wistfully at the moonless sky. The stars were brilliant and clear, twinkling against the velvet black of the night. The hazy glow of the Milky Way arched in magnificent display from horizon to horizon.

Shanna began pacing again and found herself standing before the French doors of Ruark's dark chamber. Did he sleep? Was he awake? He had said he often heard her walking about. She felt a driving need to satisfy her curiosity and her slender feet carried her forward against her will. He was there. She could see the shape of him beneath the sheet and the darker expanse of his bare chest. Then she realized his eyes were open and that he watched her in return.

Her hands tugged at her belt, and the robe slid to the floor. Her soft, pale skin glowed briefly in the blackness before she lifted the cover and slipped in beside him. His arms were about her, and his mouth was upon hers, hard, insistent, moving, seeking, finding—stirring fires that had smoldered to an unbearable intensity and were now leaping flames of ecstasy. It was the bliss of homecoming, the thunder of renewed passion, the sweetness of a spring awakening, and the ache of surrender all merged into one and mingled with the mutual rhythmic movements of their bodies as she eagerly took him into her. The blend was explosive, fusing them into oneness, then flinging them aloft on a plunging, soaring flight until it left them breathless and exhausted in its afterglow.

"Ruark?" she whispered against the furry chest.

"Aye, my love?" The answer was soft as his lips touched her brow.

There was a long silence.

"Oh—nothing." She snuggled closer and smiled through the drowsiness that engulfed her before she slept.

And so it was. The last dregs of Shanna's dreams began to break apart under the determined onslaught of Ruark's love. She found her chambers lonely when he was not there with her. When he rode with her father to the mill site, she would watch eagerly for his return as she had in her youth for her father. On a few occasions the overseers came after dinner to air problems of the mill which only Ruark could set right, and on those occasions, to avoid Gaylord's persistent company, Shanna sought the privacy of her chambers. There, waiting for Ruark, the clock's pendulum seemed to stand suspended. More than once, the book of poetry sagged in her hands as sleep overtook her. Then she would awake and smile drowsily as strong arms came around her and a warm, hard body pressed close to hers. A hoarse voice would whisper against her ear, "I love you," and then the moments would speed by, and the sound of the clock would become a chattering she wished she could stop.

The pond so essential to the mill site was above the town but close to where logs could be lifted from the bay below or floated down the small stream from above. The dam had been completed and the flow of the creek dwindled to a trickle; water filled the rock-strewn gully. The mill itself was placed to make it easily accessible for the wagons which would bear the sawn lumber away. A high flume would carry the water and the logs to the mill from the pond wherein they were to be collected. The whole of it was sketched on the design, but many of the details had not been committed to paper. Ruark's hours were well taken between the squire's demand of his attention and the insistent queries of the overseers. The mornings were hectic times, with repeated visits by the taskmasters bringing problems for Ruark to solve. More often than not, the overseers arrived for breakfast and began an immediate discussion of the plans.

On this morning, having ushered the last of the overseers out, Ruark found himself alone in the huge mansion except for the servants. When he sat, Milan or Berta hovered nearby, wishing to please him with some service, however small. When he paced, Jason stayed near the front portal to open it in case the guest of the house should leave also. Ruark began to sense that he intruded upon their routine, which did nothing to ease his agitation. He chafed that Shanna had gone riding with Sir Gaylord. It was a bitter draught to swallow—having to watch others pay homage to his wife while he could not declare his most insignificant rights as her husband. The house became a torture chamber for him, and slipping into the leather jerkin, he left the manor to the servants.

Attila fretted in the stable, unaccustomed to being left behind, and nervously took the sugar lumps from Ruark's hand. Ruark had not ridden since his capture, but he was restless and made the decision to further test his leg.

"Come on, you gourd-head goat." He petted the finely shaped velvet nose. "Let us be about some pleasures of our own."

He held the stallion in close check for a space, proving the strength of his leg. Then finding it sufficient, he shook out the reins and set the steed upon the high road to the cane mill.

The late morning was gusty and warm, but as Ruark crossed the ridge of the island's spine, the breezes whipped fine mist into his face, and before he descended into the small valley which held the mill, his shirt was soaked where the leather jerkin did not cover it. The ride was invigorating. The only thing missing was Shanna to share the elation.

The rollers of the crushing mill were silent, awaiting the new harvest, and only a few supervisors remained. The rest of the men were working on the sawmill, rushing to complete it before Trahern left for the colonies. Ruark entered the cane mill through the cooking room and tossed a cheery greeting to the man who tested and fired the kettles of molasses.

"Why, Mister Ruark, what be ya about here?"

"Just looking things over," Ruark replied. "Any problems?"

The man chortled. "No, sir. Ya built it pretty goot, Mister Ruark. But then, the master can tell ya better about that. He's in testing his rum."

When he entered the distillery wing, Ruark became impressed with the feeling of unhurried activity that pervaded the place. The crackle of the fires beneath the huge boilers mixed with the chuckle of trickling spigots and the hiss of steam through the pipes, filling the place with subtle sounds. The shadow of a man was elongated on the cobbled floor where the sun spilled through the windows at the rear of the room. Calling a question to the master brewer, Ruark began to make his way between the squat kettles which gleamed golden beneath their serpentine coppery coils. The heat was almost unbearable, and steam came from his sodden shirt and breeches. Sweat oozed from every pore, and he wondered vaguely if the man had been cooked alive in the hot, humid air or gone deaf. Then as he was rounding a timber, Ruark's foot slipped on the damp stone floor, and he struggled briefly for balance. The sudden effort on the weakened leg brought a twinge of pain that made him curse sharply. Clutching the timber for support, he leaned against it until the cramp died away.

Suddenly a loud clank of metal rang in the room, and an armsized section of piping swung heavily against the timber where he stood, spewing scalding steam and mash everywhere. Ruark stumbled backward, flinging an arm over his face to shield his eyes. His leg was still too stiff to allow such alacrity, and he sprawled on his back upon the cobblestones but managed to roll away from the spouting geyser of half-brewed rum.

Distant rafters were obscured by the rolling cloud of brownish steam, and Ruark realized that had he taken but another step forward he would have been caught in the midst of the inferno gushing out of the pipe and would have had no chance to escape. Only the brief pause had saved him from agony, even death.

A shout came from behind him, and he glanced around to see a worker crouching low in the doorway, trying to peer through the thick haze. At Ruark's answering call, the man crept forward until he was at his side.

"Are you all right, sir?" The question was shouted over the roaring wheeze of escaping pressure.

Ruark nodded, and the fellow leaned closer.

"There's a valve. I'll try to shut it off." He disappeared into the murky cloud before Ruark could tell him the master brewer was there to do it. After a long moment the hissing bellow began to subside and finally lisped into silence.

"Me lord! What happened here?" The bellow came from the doorway, and Ruark's brows lifted in surprise as he recognized the master brewer's voice. He got to his feet.

"A pipe let go. An accident—"

"No accident, sir." The cooker came forth from amid the haze, "Look at this, will ya." He held up a heavy hammer. "Some bloody idiot hit the joint off wid dis."

"Me kettles! Me rum! Ruined!" The master brewer wrung his hands as he wailed. " 'Twill take me days to clean up the mess." His tone became a shout of rage. "If I catch the bloomin' blighter, I'll hit the joint off his neck!"

"Save a crack or two for me, Timmy," Ruark said tersely, curious as to whose shadow he had soon. "I'd have been cooked proper, but for the timber there."

The master stared at Ruark as if seeing him for the first time and was mutely flabbergasted.

"Aye," the cooker chipped in. "Some toad tried to boil Mister Ruark, 'at 'e did. I check every joining and pipe afore I fire the kettles. This one only started this morn. 'Ere's no way it coulda let loose by itself."

"It could have been that the man meant no harm to me, only to do some mischief. Whatever his intent, we'll let the matter be unless we find a cause." Ruark silenced their objections with an upraised hand. If he meant to do me injury, then I am warned, and I shall be more cautious henceforth."

He dismissed the subject as he spoke to the master. "I came to see if all was well. Do you have any problems?"

"Nay," the man replied with a snort. "Not until this."

" 'Tis my fervent hope you shall have no other trouble the likes of this," Ruark avowed. "I will be gone, then. Rest assured I do not envy you your work." With a last rueful glance upward at the dripping plumbing, he left the room.

Swinging open the small door, Ruark stepped out and leaned against the heavy, planked wall to draw several deep breaths of fresh air as he massaged away the ache that had begun in his thigh. There was no way anybody could have missed his presence in the distillery room, so he could only surmise someone had reason to do him ill.

His eyes roamed the yard for any sign of his assailant, then paused. A short distance away, near the hopper, two men stood, one tall and thin, dressed in somber black. None other than Ralston! The man he spoke with was one of the workmen, a brawny fellow with thick arms. As his eyes met Ruark's, Ralston stiffened. He whirled abruptly and stalked off to his mount, leaving the workman staring after him with jaw aslack.

Ruark frowned heavily. Now that he thought of it, he did remember hearing the clatter of hooves some distance behind him on the trail as he came up the road to the mill. Had the agent followed him with some mischief in mind? Perhaps Ralston was fearful that he could tell Trahern about the purchasing of bond-slaves from the gaol, but then the man must also realize he had to guard the secret himself, as he had more to lose with a hangman's noose around his neck.

Ruark flipped the reins over Attila's head, mounted, and set off down the road. The stallion was in rare form, and Ruark let him stretch his muscles well before he finally turned him toward the creek.

He had stowed the saddle and trappings in their proper place in the stable and was rubbing the sweat from Attila's sides with a handful of coarse sacking when Ruark heard, or sensed, a small movement behind him. He was quick to look lest some other disaster befall him. It was Milly, standing just inside the stable door. For a moment the girl seemed poised to flee, but she plucked up her courage, squared her shoulders, and came toward him swinging her hips in what she hoped was a provocative manner. Ruark continued with his chore, debating whether he should feel relieved or more apprehensive.

The young woman leaned against the post of the stall gate, watching him. "Good marnin', Mister Ruark," she drawled lazily, chewing on a stem of hay. "I seen ye comin' down the high road on that foin piece o' horse there." Attila snorted and nuzzled Milly's shoulder. "I got a way with animals meself, I has." She laughed. "We ain't so far apart."

Ruark grunted noncommittally and spread the rag to dry. He began to comb burrs from the long flowing mane and tail.

"Well, Johnnie, m'deary," Milly's tone became a trifle hard, "ye can ignore me if 'tis yer likin', but 'tis ye, yer ownself, I've come ter see."

Ruark paused and bent her a quizzical eyebrow. "Sure now, lass." He had a fair brogue when he chose. "Meself, 'tis it? And wot foin affair has brought ye to a smelly old stable?"

He threw down a handful of burrs and lifted one of Attila's hooves to check it for pebbles.

" 'Twas the only place I could speak ter ya widout that 'igh Madam Beauchamp 'angin' 'bout yer neck."

Ruark chuckled. "Begorra, now!" he mocked her gently. "And it's soundin' like ye got somethin' dear to be settled."

"Sure I do!" she snapped with surprising rancor. "And what I got is to set that Shanna bitch back on 'er 'eels."

Ruark dropped the last hoof and straightened, looking at the girl over the horse's back. "Now that, lass, I should warn ye 'bout. That woman has a fair ta middlin' temper and might not take kindly to a rash accusation." He came around Attila and rested his arm on a high slat of the stall. "I'd be very cautious of what I bandy about."

Milly braced her feet apart and leaned forward from the hips, her finger pointing to her own chest as she sneered haughtily, "I—got—meself—wid—a—babe."

Each word was accentuated heavily, and all thought of humor fled Ruark. This suddenly became a serious matter. He knew her next words before she spoke them.

"An' you," she jabbed her finger at him, "are goin' ter be its pa."

Ruark's lips became a thin, angry line as his eyes sparked with cold, piercing lights. He flung out a hand. "Milly, do you think I'd let myself be rooked in so easily?"

"Nay." She stood back and leaned again, chewing a straw in supreme confidence. "But I gots me a friend what'll say 'tis so. An' I knows all about ye and Miz High and Haughty. Her pa won't take ter a bondsman sleepin' wid 'is pet. 'At should be worth a foin penny or two from 'er, and I wouldn't be so picky as ta say ye'd not see 'er at all. She might even pay for it, come to think. Could make us an easy livin', dearie."

Ruark stared at her, realizing she meant everything she had spoken, and his scowl grew black as thunder.

"I am not easily coerced, Milly, nor will I be father to some sailor's brat for your comfort." His voice was low but bore a whiplash in it that stung more than the words.

"I'll swear the babe is yours," she challenged.

"You know I've never touched you. You would speak a lie and 'twoud soon be out."

"I'll make ye wed me!"

"I will not!"

"Trahern, 'imself, will see to it."

"I cannot wed you," he growled.

Milly stared at him in wonder.

"I already have a wife." It was the only thing he could say that would stay her. Her mouth sagged open, and she staggered back a step as if he had struck her.

"A wife!" She gave a short, humorless laugh. "A wife! O' course, ye could've 'ad one in England. A wife! An' wee ones, too, I'd wager. Won't Miz High and Haughty be took aback wid 'at." She glanced around wildly and began to laugh, loud and insanely. "A wife!" Half sobbing, half mewling, she fled in distress.

Shanna was riding Jezebel back to the stables and was just about to enter the open door when the mare shied and reared back. Milly, bursting out of the place, almost ran beneath the horse's feet. When she saw the pawing hooves above her, the girl screamed in terror. Jezebel pranced away, and it was all Shanna could do to stay in the saddle. When she had quieted her mount, she turned her attention to Milly who stood staring up at her, a weird half smile twisting her face.

"What the devil are you about now, Milly?" Shanna snapped, angry at the girl's carelessness.

"There she is!" The frightened Milly sobbed as tears flowed unheeded down her cheeks. She skittered sideways in the dust away from the stable and Shanna as if they were both something to be avoided.

"Miz High and Mighty! Miz Shanna Trahern Beauchamp! So ya got yerself a man, do ya? Ye always gets the best, don't ye? and now, ye gots the 'andsomest man crawlin' ter yer bed. Well, I got some news for ya. 'E don't need ya. 'E can't wed ya. 'E's already got a wife.'

Horrified, Shanna attempted to calm the raving girl. "Milly! Milly! You don't know what you say. Be quiet!"

The girl would hear none of it. She spread her hands wide and rolled her head, laughing loudly all the while.

"Oh, wait 'til they hears this!" she wailed. "All them high fallutin' folks who think ye're so lily white and pure. Wait 'til they hears it."

Shanna slid from Jezebel's back. "Milly, don't!" she implored. "You have no idea what this is all about. Milly!"

The girl danced around in a circle, kicking up a small cloud of dust and sending Shanna's mare prancing again.

"Be still, you nag!" Shanna jerked on the reins angrily.

"Oh, lawsy me!" Milly trilled. "Mis Shanna, taken in by a bondsman. An' folks frettin' so for fear them pirates 'ad raped 'er. Oh lawsy, wait'll they hear."

"Milly!" Shanna's voice took on a warning note.

"You, Miz Got-it-all! Never worked for a thing. Never wanted a thing. Got herself a man now. She ain't no better'n me. Honkin' it wid a married man. Betcha she'll have a fat belly, too."

Shanna's face flamed crimson with Milly's last comment. She could bear the insults no longer and flared, "Just who do you think he's married to, anyway?"

No sooner were the words out than Shanna realized what she had blurted. Aghast she clapped a hand over her mouth as if that would bring the words back, but it was too late. The slow dawning was already creeping over Milly's face until she gaped in pained astonishment.

"You!" she barked. "You! Ooooh, nooo!" It became a mournful wail. Now sobbing harshly, Milly whirled and fled down the path toward town.

Lamely Shanna dropped her hand as she stared after the girl, recognizing with sickening dread that she had given over into Milly's possession the secret she had so carefully guarded for these many months. Giving a groan of despair, Shanna stamped her foot in rage at her own foolishness. She turned listlessly and would have taken Jezebel into the stable, but she found herself face to face with an amused Ruark.

"Madame, I fear that you have just told the town crier."

"Oh, Ruark!" Shanna flung herself against him in abject misery. "She'll go straight to my father. He'll be in such a rage he won't stop to listen. He'll send you back to England to hang!"

"Gently, love. Gently." Ruark held her close to him and whispered against her hair. " 'Twill do no good worrying about it. If she tells him, we'll admit it. Your father is a reasonable man. He'll at least allow us to speak our piece."

His calmness and assurance began to affect her, and Shanna took refuge in his strong, encircling arms, heedless of the fact they stood in the open, where any chance glance would find them. Strangely the prospect of having to confess their marriage did not seem as repugnant as it had once.

"At least you won't be bothered by Milly anymore," she sniffed wryly.

Ruark shaded his eyes and peered off across the distant lawns. "And what of Gaylord? Where is the good chap? I know you left with him."

Thinking of the knight's ungainly horsemanship, Shanna chuckled gaily. "The last I saw of him, he was at odds with his mount. That was shortly after we left the stables, and he is even now probably struggling to turn the horse about so he can come home."

"He seems to demand much of your time lately." The words came out sharper than he had meant.

"Why, Ruark," Shanna stood back and rubbed the butt of her quirt along the lapel of his jerkin, smiling up at him coyly. "You cannot seriously be jealous of Sir Gaylord."

Scowling, Ruark half turned from her, and his tan darkened

a shade or two. "I cannot stand his foppish manners, 'tis all." But in more truthfulness he admitted hoarsely, "And I can bear no one fondling or ogling you." The golden flame in his eyes touched her with a warmth full of promise. "That privilege, madam, I claim as mine alone."

"And so you do, sir," she replied, teasing him. A smile curved the corners of her mouth as she leaned forward to murmur confidentially. "And very skillfully."

Giving him a saucy look over her shoulder, Shanna danced quickly past him, leading Jezebel into the stables. With a low growl Ruark swooped his hand around, catching her upon the buttocks, bringing forth a giggling shriek from her, and as his hand lingered to caress her, Shanna skipped away and made a face at him.

"Oafish knave," she flung. "When will you learn to keep your hands to yourself?"

"Never," Ruark assured, leering after her swinging hips. He fell in beside her, taking the mare's reins from her hands. Hooking an arm around Shanna's neck, he brought her close against his side. "For all the times I must look at you and not touch, I vow I shall make up for them when we're alone."

His hand slipped downward over a soft, round breast, and his open, hungering mouth was upon hers, parting her lips, devouring the sweetness. The kiss was heady wine, sapping the strength from their limbs, and sudden, intense passion swept over them like a rampant river.

Ruark's voice was hoarse as he muttered against her trembling lips. "Your father will be gone until late. Come with me to the cottage."

He met no resistance. Willingly Shanna nodded her head, and almost in a daze she felt his arm leaving her. Fused with warmth, she leaned against a heavy timber as he hurriedly attended the horse, glancing Shanna's way often as if his eyes could not get enough of looking at her. Then the gate to the stall was closed behind him, and he was taking her slender hand into his.

It was nearly dusk when Shanna slipped into the manor and quickly ascended the stairs. She had made an effort to recoil her hair into a neat knot, but the gilded tresses had escaped her trembling fingers and she had been only half successful. Her cheeks still bore a rosy blush of passion. The manly scent of him clung to her, and her eyes were like soft, limpid pools of aqua. It was no wonder Hergus, in Shanna's chambers waiting to attend her evening bath, gave a gasp at first sight of her mistress.

"Ye've been with him again!" the servant charged. "And in broad light o' day! 'Tis shameful ye are, awhoring with Mister Ruark beneath yer pa's nose."

Shanna flinched, and her cheeks grew hot with color. "Don't call it that."

"Aye, ye do na want to be reminded o' what ye do." The woman's voice began to burr heavily with a Scottish accent as it always did when her ire was roused. "A foin lady ye were—'till he came along. Now ye canna hold yourself from him. And him! Like an animal he be, sniffing ye out, waiting 'til yer pa's back is turned then tumblin' ye. Aaiiee! I can only see yerself plump-bellied wit' babe an' him smirkin' cause he done it to ye. He must be proud o' what he's got in his breeches to use so often on ye!"

"Hergus! That's enough!"

"Aye, I guess it be," the maid sighed heavily. " 'Ere's no talkin' to ye." But Hergus tried one last appeal. "Lass, ye know I care for ye. But I canna stand this thing ye do to yerself. I've been with ye since ye were a wee babe and I, not much more than a budding woman. Eight-and-ten I were." She drew herself up and gave a sniff. "I see ye now, givin' yerself in a back-door affair to a common bondsman. Me Jamie and me,"—her eyes grew distant for a moment—"we came from a poor highland clan, and we had na long on each other's arms. But ye!" Her attention returned to Shanna, and she said with a vengeance, "Shanna, lass, ye do na care what ye're doin'. Do ye na feel some shame?"

Shanna lifted her chin a notch. Strangely she felt no sense of wrongdoing and wondered why not even the slightest twinge pricked her conscience. What was there when she lay in the comfort of Ruark's arms that made it all seem right? Love? Aye, he loved her. He had avowed as much. But what of herself? Did she love him? How did one recognize love when it came to them? What made her surrender all to Ruark, if not for love?

Passion? Aye, there was that, but there was more, and standing as she was, before Hergus's questioning regard, she could find no answers.

"Nay." She whispered so low the maidservant had to strain to catch the word. Shanna turned her back to the other and began to loosen the bodice of her habit. "I feel no shame. He loves me and I—"

Shanna frowned and shook her head. What crazy thing had she glimpsed in a moment of dawning then seen flit away? She sighed at its loss.

"There is much about Mister Ruark and I that you do not understand, Hergus. I feel 'twill all be out if Milly has her way."

"What does Milly know?"

"Much, I'm afraid," Shanna replied ruefully.

It was one thing for Hergus to criticize her mistress's actions, but an entirely different thing for another to raise voice in anything but praise of her charge. Her loyalty lay firm on that account.

"Then the twit better hold 'er tongue."

Shanna glanced around in wonder, and Hergus shrugged.

"Yer pa is in the parlor with Mr. Ralston, Mister Pitney, and that Sir Billingsham. I canna rightly see even Milly pokin' in on the squire an' his guests. And ye'd best hurry yerself along. He come 'round some time ago and was asking for ye. I'll tell him ye're back, but I wouldna dally were I the one."

Hergus lightly dusted an immaculate curio shelf and flicked her fingers free of imaginary dirt as she turned her gaze to Shanna again.

"I overheard Sir Billingsham asking where ye were off to. He found yer horse in the stable, but ye were gone without tellin' him where. I guess he figures yer pa should be keepin' close watch o'er ye." The woman pondered on. "Maybe yer pa's beginning to wonder about ye up here with Mister Ruark only a few steps away. But then"—Hergus sniffed loudly—"I suppose he feels he can trust ye. Such a pity ye betray him."

Shrugging off the maid's barbs, Shanna began to disrobe. But with her body still flushed and rosy with passion, she could not bring herself to part with her shift. The servant took the hint and left with a last comment flung over her shoulder.

"I'll be back to do yer hair."

Securing the heavy tresses on top of her head, Shanna sank deep into the scented water and began to wash, idly dabbing the soapy sponge along her arm and shoulders. It was a leisurely bath, and her mind was occupied with dreamy thoughts. Leaning back in the ornate tub, she closed her eyes as the heat relaxed her. She was close to drowsing when she heard a gay whistling in the hall outside her sitting room. She smiled softly, knowing it could only be Ruark, and grew giddy with the memory of their afternoon together. The canopy high above his dark face had glowed with an aura of light that pervaded the cottage. With the curtains drawn about the bed, their naked bodies had been suffused with the radiance of daylight shining through the white drapings. His amber eyes had moved over her with a thoroughness that had left her breathless and trembling. Then his hands, with their slow, intoxicating gentleness, had followed, bringing soft sobs of pleasure from her. His kisses had fallen where they would, branding her with their fire. With a low laugh he had caught her to his hardened frame and rolled upon the bed until she lay full length upon him, their limbs entwined, their mouths eagerly blending. His lean fingers had threaded through the shimmering gold of her hair, catching it at the soft nape, and his lips had traced a molten path down her throat.

"Shanna. Lovely Shanna," he murmured huskily. "Your splendor blinds this poor beggar. How beautiful you are, my love."

Tremulously she had brushed a kiss upon his cheek, her feelings too strong for words.

The illusions vanished abruptly as Hergus called through from the sitting room, gave a quick knock on the bedchamber door, and entered. Hastily Shanna rose and snatching a large towel around her, stepped behind the dressing screen to dry herself.

Hergus took umbrage at this and chided, "Ne'er ye mind about the fact I swaddled ye when ye were a babe and helped ye to dress for years. Since ye've taken with yer bondsman, a body would guess ye only trust him to see yer blessed skin. 'Tis not meet that ye should strut about in front of 'im in yer altogether then be so flighty and shy before me whose known ye almost as well as yer own ma."

Shanna gave a worried look toward the French doors, blushing lightly. If Ruark had heard her pacing the floor, then he most certainly overheard this exchange. Donning her shift, she stepped from behind the screen and gave the servant a warning frown as she firmly presented her with a brush.

"If you've come to do my hair, proceed. Otherwise, I'll find a task worthy of your good nature, such as emptying chamber pots in the morning tide."

✖ Chapter 22 ✖

SHANNA'S slippered feet were a blur flitting down the curving stairs, barely seeming to touch the steps. She was like a young girl again, fretful of her tardiness, flushed and breathless and, in her haste, heedless of the display of trim and shapely ankles that flashed beneath her lifted skirts. Hergus had barely contained her curls with a ribbon before the full realization of time struck Shanna. If there was any one thing that consistently roused her father's ire, it was the needless delay of his meal.

Jason stood tall and erect at his post beside the front portal. He seemed to study the far wall, an intense frown pulling his dark face into heavy folds. He gave no notice to Shanna in her immodest haste. As in the days of her youth, Shanna felt his reproof and halting, dropped her skirts and smoothed her teal blue gown, then lifting her head proudly, continued down with a poised aloofness that drew his regard and won a smile of approval from the black man. He bowed stiffly.

"You look mighty fetching this evening, madam."

She gave a gracious nod. "Thank you, Jason."

From the drawing room her father's voice boomed out. "Berta! Go see what's keeping that girl! 'Tis half past the dinner hour."

Shanna eased somewhat as there was still a touch of good humor in his tone. She moved to the door and took a deep breath, feeling much like Daniel before the lion's den. But if Milly had found a chance to tell her father, Shanna reasoned, by now she would have been facing a raging snarl. Summoning an outwardly serene smile, she entered the room and paused as the men rose to their feet. Pitney was already standing beside her father, and they turned together, each with his own choice of libation in his hand.

"Gentlemen, do be seated," Shanna begged softly as her gaze traveled about the room.

Ruark had garbed himself handsomely in his royal blue finery, and his lithe, powerful grace made the long, gangling form of Sir Gaylord seem much like an uncoordinated giraffe as they stepped forward simultaneously. Ralston gave her a brief nod which sufficed for an acknowledgement of her presence.

"I am sorry I'm late, papa," Shanna murmured sweetly. "I didn't realize the time."

Trahern brushed aside his daughter's apology. In the face of her almost girlish radiance, he could do naught but consider that there was, after all, no harm done.

"I am sure the gentlemen will regard the wait well worthwhile, my dear. We were just discussing the voyage to the colonies."

"Is it much like England?" Shanna charmingly presented the question to Ruark. "I suppose 'twill be cold."

"Cold? Aye, madam," Ruark smiled and could not suppress the glow that came into his eyes as he beheld her beauty. "But I think not entirely like England."

"Gracious, no!" Gaylord piped in. He indulged himself with a bit of snuff, taking it from the back of his hand, and delicately applied a monogrammed handkerchief to his pale nostril. His blue-gray eyes watered as he sniffed. "A savage land, hardly fit for a lady. Crude forts, untamed wilderness. Heathens, the lot of them there. I dare say, we shall all be in constant danger."

Ruark arched a dubious brow toward the man. "You seem an authority, sir. Have you ever been there?"

Gaylord bent a cold, withering glare upon the bondsman. "Did I hear you speak?" The inflection in his voice carried a tone of amazement, as if he could not believe he had been addressed by a common slave.

Ruark managed to subdue his mockery and with feigned chagrin replied, "I really don't know what made me do that."

Gaylord tossed his head, missing the twist of sarcasm in Ruark's tone. "Be more mindful of it then. 'Tis odious enough having to share the same table with a bondslave without being interrupted by such." Feeling his power over the man, Gaylord sneered. "And bear it in mind, my good fellow, I think there is much of the knave in you. I do not believe you innocent of the pirate's scheme to spirit away Squire Trahern's treasures, no matter the rumor, and if I were he, I'd keep a wary eye on you while you're in this manor. Mayhap you now seek a more valuable reward." His glance dipped only slightly so as only Ruark noticed it was directed toward Shanna. "A rogue will stop at nothing to gain gold for his purse."

Ruark stiffened at the slur, and his eyes hardened as he met Gaylord's taunting stare. Ralston smirked as he saw the darkening of Ruark's brow and could not ignore the opportunity. He joined the two. His eyes swept the younger man contemptuously as he directed his remark to Gaylord.

" 'Tis most unseemly that a mere bondslave should question an honorable knight's knowledge."

Gaylord drew himself up to his full height and struck an arrogant pose as he realized the truth of Ralston's thinly veiled suggestion.

Over her shoulder, Shanna caught her father's attention and inclined her head toward Ralston with a slight frown. His nod was immediately forthcoming.

"Mister Ralston," Trahern called. "Might I have a word with you?"

Ralston scowled and reluctantly left the two. He had just begun to enjoy himself, and this was a game he loved to play. Still, he could not disobey his employer. As he drew near, Orlan Trahern lowered the glass he sipped from and frowned in mild reproach.

"Mister Ruark is a guest in my household." His voice was low so that only Pitney could hear. "I must see to the peace and tranquility of my home. I insist that you, being only a paid servant yourself, treat my guests with equity."

Ralston reddened and grew rigid with indignation. "Sir? Do you fault me in front of others?"

"Nay, Mister Ralston." Trahern's smile bore little humor. "I only remind you of your station. Mister Ruark has proven his worth. Do not disprove yours."

Ralston suppressed an urge to reply in heat. He had grown accustomed to the rich apartment he maintained in the village and was well aware of the reaches of Trahern's wealth and power but considered the man would hardly miss a few hundred pounds here and there, and, thus, in his years with the squire, Ralston had laid away a goodly sum for himself; his accounts would not bear any close scrutiny. He also knew that Trahern would, with his commoner's petty vengeance, seek punishment if the shortages were found out.

With the fine skill of an experienced diplomat, Shanna had taken it upon herself to allay further confrontation between Ruark and Sir Gaylord. Placing herself between the two men and bestowing a warm smile to Ruark, she presented her back to him and spoke directly to Sir Gaylord.

"Kind sir." Her pitying eyes gave her words the taste of purest honey. " 'Tis indeed a shame we are so far from London and you can find none of your peers to lend good rhetoric to the conversation. It must be a pain to you to hear the common and mundane discourses of earthly things so prevalent out here on the—frontier."

The knight heard only the soft warmth of her voice and was captivated by the distraught beauty of the visage before him. He began to feel as if he had harmed her in some way as she continued.

"I, too, have heard the lofty ideals vividly expressed in the court and know the loneliness you find in your lordly pursuits. You must remember, though, that all, even my father and myself, are of common extraction here and temper your judgments with mercy. Why,"—Shanna laughed as if incredulous at her thought—"you would not ban my good sire and myself from your company, would you?"

Sir Gaylord was equally incredulous. "Of course not, my dear lady. Your father is governor here and you, as his daughter, are most"—he sighed longingly—"attractive."

"Good." Shanna tapped his arm with her fan and leaned close, saying confidentially, "I can say of my own knowledge that Mister Ruark was forcefully taken from this island against his will. I beg you to understand why I must treat him with some deference," she looked aside to Ruark and smiled wickedly.

The knight could only mumble his agreement, though he still struggled with her reasoning.

"You are so kind, sir." She curtsied gracefully and gave her hand to Ruark. "Let us see to our dinner, then."

Shanna looked back over her shoulder toward her father. "Papa, are you ready to eat?"

"Most certainly!"

Trahern chuckled deep in his chest and, realizing he had just witnessed a setdown in the softest feminine way, could almost feel pity for the blundering numbers who had fallen in her wake. With a strange sense of pride, he watched the poised deliberation of his daughter as she walked beside the bondsman. They made a splendid pair, the two of them. And what fine children she would bear him if they—

"Bah! Madness!" Trahern shook his head to shed the thoughts. "I have cast the die too well. She would never deign to wed a bondsman."

Shanna slipped easily into the slow, considered movements which gave her an air of cool aloofness. Her hand rested lightly on Ruark's arm, and she smiled into those gleaming amber eyes. The two of them led the procession into the dining room where Milan had begun to chafe at the delay, seeing only the ruin of delicate flavors as the cook tried to keep the dishes warm. At Shanna's entry the small man's face suddenly beamed, and he clapped his hands together as a signal for the young boys to bring the food. At last dinner was to be served.

"Sit here, Mister Ruark," Shanna directed, indicating the chair near her own which was placed at the end.

Ralston left open the place opposite the bondsman for Sir Gaylord and took a seat across from Pitney, nearer Trahern. If there was trouble to be brewed, he was the master brewer, and he would see this mixture to its best fermentation.

The conversation at the beginning of the meal was somewhat stilted. Gaylord could only gaze at Shanna, and when her attention was diverted, he allowed his eyes to dip appreciatively to her breasts where the stiff bodice pressed the swelling curves into a most tempting display. Annoyed by the knight's lustful perusal, Ruark had to hold tight rein on his own manners. Ralston, unusually verbose, directed his words to the squire.

"I've noted that the *Good Hound* has been brought in to clean her hull. Do you intend, squire, to take the schooner along to the colonies, or do you plan to use her here for trade around the islands?"

Trahern paused in his eating and gestured to Ruark. "Ask the lad there. It belongs to him."

Ralston and Gaylord both turned to stare aghast toward Ruark, who casually stated the situation.

"Gentlemen, it is permissible by English law for a bondsman to own property. I gained the schooner in a fair battle, as Madam Beauchamp will attest."

"This is preposterous!" Gaylord declared. It nettled him sorely that a slave should have a vessel while he, a titled gentleman, was still trying to gain financing for a shipyard.

"However so," Ruark grinned, "the schooner is mine and shall remain mine unless I choose to give it up for my freedom. But then, I think 'twould take me longer to earn the price of a ship than to pay my indebtedness. The *Tempest* will be loaned to the squire for the voyage in return for the price of seeing her made fit. A fair enough exchange as we both see it."

"The *Tempest*?" Ralston queried arrogantly.

"Aye, I've renamed it," Ruark replied leisurely. "Of late I've come to enjoy storms as they seem to bring me naught but good, and I deemed it only fitting."

"My daughter has an aversion to them," Trahern commented absently, missing the spreading color that had risen on Shanna's face with Ruark's statement. "No cause as I could see, but it started when she was a little thing."

"Perhaps I'm outgrowing that, papa," Shanna returned softly, not daring to met her husband's gaze. "After all, it was a storm which enabled us to escape the pirates."

Her father accepted this with a mouthful of lobster then swallowing, muttered, "Good. 'Tis time. You'll be having children of your own someday. Wouldn't do for you to put that fear in them."

"No, papa," Shanna agreed meekly.

"And what of the pirate's treasure on the schooner?" Ralston sneered. "Does that belong to Mister Ruark also?"

"It did," Trahern stated, raising his eyes to his man. "But all that which was not mine he gave to Mister Gaitlier and Mistress Dora for the years they spent in service to the pirates."

The agent's eyebrows raised in surprise. "Generous of the man, considering he could have bought his freedom."

Ruark ignored his tone of derision. "By right it was theirs, and I saw it as fair payment from the pirates."

Gaylord held his silence. He could not understand giving even a small wealth away. Ralston dismissed the subject. He knew such foolish deeds would tend to endear the lady more to the bondsman—and perhaps that was Mister Ruark's ploy, Ralston mused.

"Madam," Ralston addressed Shanna directly. "Are you aware Sir Gaylord's father is a lord and magistrate of the English courts?" He cast a glance awry to Trahern to see if the man was listening and grew piqued that the squire should appear disinterested in the conversation and, instead, savor his favorite dish.

"Indeed?" Shanna presented an inquisitive gaze to the man on her left. "Lord Billingsham? I never heard his name mentioned while I was in London. Has he been a magistrate long?"

Gaylord daintily dabbed the corners of his mouth with a napkin before looking at her earnestly. "I can think of no cause, madam, that might have presented such a fair lady as yourself before him. He judges evil men, murderers, thieves, miscreants of all kinds, and you are far too delicate a flower to be found where those would roam. He has sent many a scoundrel to Tyburn's triple tree, and for the sake of caution he has elected to be known to those rogues only as Lord Harry."

Ralston watched Ruark closely, expecting some reaction from him, as he guessed it may have been more than coincidence. His target only met his gaze for a moment, shrugged casually, and continued with his meal.

Pitney was giving careful attention to his food, and Shanna was as intently studying her own. She remembered too well when Mister Hicks spoke of Lord Harry and his secret handling of Ruark's hanging orders and wondered what game Ralston played.

Only one as familiar with Ruark Beauchamp as Shanna would have noticed his sudden preoccupation with the meal and the gradual hardening of his eyes. His nostrils flared slightly each time the hated name was mentioned, but otherwise he executed well his role of bondsman, and it seemed as if this exchange were simply over his head.

With very great care Shanna questioned, smiling gently at Gaylord, "Lord Harry? 'Twould seem I've heard *that* name before." Her brows drew into a puzzled frown. "But for the life of me I can't remember—"

Pitney's comment was grunted. "I've heard of him. Some called him Hanging Harry. Got that with his liberal use of the triple tree."

Gaylord was offended. "A malicious rumor!"

Shanna seemed bemused. "I've often wondered how a man must feel after he has sentenced another to be hanged for some offense. I'm sure your father sent only the well-deserving to their end, but it crosses my mind what a terrible burden it must have placed upon him. Had you knowledge of his affairs? I suppose he spoke often of them."

"My father's affairs were much beyond me, madam. I gave them no heed."

Shanna brightened. "Oh? What a pity."

They adjourned again to the drawing room after dinner, and there Shanna was beset by Gaylord's close presence on the settee beside her. Over her fan she watched Ruark light his pipe by the French doors and, meeting his eyes, caught the almost imperceptible inclination of his head toward the portico. Fanning herself, she rose and complained demurely.

" 'Tis a bit stuffy in here, papa. If you've no objections, I'll take a stroll along the porch."

Glancing over his shoulder, Trahern nodded his approval, and Ruark was quick to offer.

"Madam, since the pirates' raid 'tis not safe for a lady to go about unescorted. I beg—"

"You're quite right," Gaylord interrupted and, to Shanna's consternation, took her arm. "Please, allow me, madam."

Gaylord had turned the tables deftly, and this time Ruark was left standing while the other man smugly stepped past him with Shanna. As the knight closed the doors behind them, he sneered in the bondsman's face.

Pitney's huge arm halted Ruark before he could lay a hand on the latch, and he was shoved gently backward. Ruark was not in the mood for foolery. The muscles in his lean jaw flexed tensely as he lifted his gaze to find a gentle smile on the older man's face.

"Easy, lad," Pitney rasped in a low tone. "If there comes a need, I will see to it."

His gray eyes flicked toward Trahern in a silent warning, and Ruark glanced behind him to see the squire turn away from the cupboard with a glass of rum and draw out his pocket watch. The man considered it a moment before looking at Pitney.

"Five minutes?" He left the comment hanging, and Pitney drew out his own timepiece.

"Less, I'd say, knowing the eager knight."

"Bitters to an ale?" Trahern wagered.

"Aye," Pitney answered and tucked away the pocket watch as he considered Ruark.

"You have not seen Shanna at her best." He gave a nod toward the French doors. "Better men than he have tried. If you must fret, have a pity for Sir Gay."

The room grew quiet, and only Ruark and Ralston showed emotions. Ruark was uneasy, while Ralston smirked in good satisfaction. Then suddenly from the porch a low enraged shriek came from Shanna. Ruark jumped, and Ralston lowered his glass in wonderment. In a hair's space it was following by a ringing slap, the beginning of a curse growled by Gaylord, followed by a shout—that, too, from the knight—terminated in a loud grunt.

Pitney consulted his watch and said to Trahern, "Ale!"

All of them including Ralston started for the door at once, but before any could touch it, the portal was flung open, and Shanna flounced into the room, holding the torn bodice of her gown shut with one hand while she flexed the other as if it pained her.

Her beautiful face was aflame beneath her wildly mussed tresses.

Trahern halted his daughter with a hand on her arm, and his eyes carefully searched her for some sign of mistreatment. "Is all well with you, Shanna child?"

"Aye, papa," she replied brightly. "Better than you can guess, but I fear our lordly guest has taken to adorning the shrubs with his manly form."

Trahern stepped past her as Ruark doffed his coat and laid it over his wife's shoulders. Shanna gazed at him softly as he took her hand to examine it.

"Shall I avenge you, milady?" he questioned in a low voice without raising his eyes.

"Nay, my Captain Pirate Ruark," she murmured. "Poor fellow, he's had his just reward. Look yonder."

She swept the injured hand toward the doors as her father and Pitney pushed them open. Trahern seemed to choke on something as the dim light spilled onto the porch to illuminate the lanky shape of Sir Gaylord as he struggled to pull himself over the railing that bordered the walkway. Shreds of leaves and broken twigs clung to him, protruding from his rose-colored coat in random array. The knight set his feet on the porch and, unconscious of those who stared, paused to pluck the greenery from himself. He had succeeded only to a slight degree when he raised his head to find three of the four men who watched smiling broadly at him, while the fourth gaped in stunned astonishment. Sir Gaylord was equal to the occasion. Lifting his jowly chin, he stared back at them with a haughty gaze and strode loftily past them as they made way for him, ignoring Shanna completely. Still in all, his bearing lacked something, for his gait had an odd half-step quality caused, no doubt, by his missing shoe.

Tugging the oversize coat about her, Shanna gave a small curtsy. "Good evening, gentlemen," she said and swept out of the room, turning her hand as if it still ached.

Trahern regarded his empty glass for a moment before he sighed almost sadly and went to pour two tall ales, handing one to Pitney. Ralston helped himself to a short brandy and tossed it off before he, half embarrassed, excused himself and left. Trahern poured a third ale and offered it to Ruark.

"Ah, gentlemen," the portly man chuckled after a long pull at his own glass. "I do not know what I shall do for excitement when the lass is gone." His chuckle gave way to rolling mirth, which infected the other two and left him gasping in his chair.

"I think I will retire. I am getting too old for all of this."

He left the room to them and as he went down the hall an occasional chuckle drifted back. Pitney refilled their glasses and nodded his head toward the door.

"A breath of fresh air, Mister Ruark?"

They strolled through the open doors and passed on down the wide veranda and admired the bright full moon, while John Ruark offered his large companion some tobacco from his pouch. To his surprise the man produced a well-browned clay pipe from his pocket and after a first puff of smoke nodded his appreciative thanks.

"Took the habit when I sailed on one of Orlan's ships," he murmured. "Hard to get good tobacco 'way out here. But this is good. Aye, this is good."

They walked on for a space in silence, leaving a fragrant trail of smoke behind them. They had almost returned to the drawing room doors when Pitney paused to knock the dottle from his pipe bowl.

"A pity," the huge man commented as he tapped the pipe against his heel.

Ruark gave him a questioning look.

"A pity your brother, Captain Beauchamp, could not sail with us."

Ruark's face went blank as he sought for some denial.

"My brother?" was all he could manage, for anything more would have been a lie, bold and open.

"Aye," Pitney returned, watching him closely in the meager light. He pointed at Ruark's chest with the stem of his pipe. "And sometimes it tickles me mind that there is even more to Ruark Beauchamp than John Ruark lets on."

Tucking the pipe in his pocket, Pitney went into the house, and when Ruark entered a few moments later, the room was empty.

The hour was late, and the moon was a swollen red ball low on the horizon. It seemed to squat there with ominous deliberation and gave no clue that it would become the pure silver goddess that fled across the sky and lent her name to stricken lovers. The streets were otherwise dark in the village, and Milly Hawkins shuddered as she strolled again by the appointed meeting place to find it still empty. Fretfully she paused and with a worried gaze swept the cobbled street in both directions. The skin on the back of her neck began to crawl, and her spine tingled coldly. She had the distinct feeling she was being watched. She peered into every nook and cranny but saw nothing. Then she gasped in fear as a tall shadow detached itself from a deeper one and came toward her. Her hands trembled to her mouth, and she stared hard for a moment before sagging in relief.

"Oh, 'tis you, gov'na," she giggled. "You gave me quite a start. Aye, 'at ye did. Ye're late."

The man shrugged and offered no explanation. He wore a full black cape which hid his stature, with a high collar pulled up close beneath a tricorn drawn down to hide his features in the darkness. His riding boots were of soft black leather, as were the gloves which covered his hands, and he carried a quirt as if he had just left a horse. As he drew nearer, Milly gave him no pause.

"Well, gov'na, 'ave I got news fer ye. We got to 'ave an understandin' soon. 'At Mister Ruark ain' no good ter me at all like ye said he'd be. 'E's already got him a missus an' ye'd never guess who. Miz Shanna Beauchamp, 'ats who. Only she ain' no widow no more. She's Miz John Ruark, now. An' the fun of it is, the high lady told me 'erself."

Milly paused to savor her news.

"Why, she ain' as good as me, beddin' a bondsman. Ain't got no taste atall. She's kept it a fair secret, though." The girl chewed at a fingernail for a moment, and her eyes took on a gleeful gleam. "Comes ter mind, 'er pa don't know, either. What a foin blow he'll have when I lets 'im in on it. Me ma, too. She's always pointin' out 'at high Miz Shanna and sayin' be like 'er. Well, I's better'n 'er." Milly reached out and caressed the arm of the man, missing the pinched frown he gave her.

"I gots me better'n any bondsman. I best tell ye now, gov'na, ye've got to pay the due. I ain't takin' no seaman what's gone 'alf the time. I wants me a man 'round when I gets me heat up."

The quirt began to slap softly against the top of the man's boot, but Milly did not notice as she bestowed her best smile on him.

"O' course, I ain' one ter tie ye down, and if'n ye roams a bit I ain' goin' ter howl 'bout it. Not so long as ye comes back."

The man slipped his arm around her and began to lead her down the street. Milly reveled in this unusual affection and misread his smile completely. She leaned against him and slipped her hand inside his cloak.

"I know's a quiet spot down by the beach," she murmured, a suggestive look in her eyes. " 'Tis a hidden place with soft moss ter pillow me backside."

In the shadowed street, the echo of her light laughter dwindled.

The next day broke clear and cool, with a sharp edge to it that could almost be felt. At the first hint of dawn Ruark and Shanna awoke, and with a parting kiss, he made his way quietly to his own chamber where he shaved and dressed to await the manor's first stirring. He lounged on the bed, listened to Shanna move about her room then rejected the idea of returning. Hergus scolded her enough without adding more kindling to the woman's fire. It was a nightly occurrence now that they shared a bed even if it was only to lie in the comfort of each other's arms until sleep would descend upon them both.

Making his way to the small dining room, Ruark poured himself a cup of coffee. The pungent, nutty taste of the brew had captured him, and he welcomed the steaming warmth of it on this rare chilly morn.

Milan had set out a platter of meats and small oatcakes, and at the man's invitation Ruark was just seating himself before a liberal plate when Trahern and Shanna entered the room together laughing. The father wondered at the change in his daughter. In the past few weeks she had grown rosy-cheeked and lighthearted and ever since her escapade with the pirates she appeared to have lost much of her starched formality. The frequency of her biting comments had faded until she almost seemed a different person, a warm and gracious woman, whose charm now rivaled her beauty. Trahern chuckled to himself, accepting the good fortune without question. The smell of buttered griddle-cakes filled his nostrils, and he hurried to his chair, leaving the seating of his daughter to Mister Ruark, as it seemed the man's wont, anyway.

A ring of hooves sounded out front, and in a moment Pitney blustered into the house, rubbing his hands and savoring the aroma of the food. He tossed his hat to Jason and joined the others, dragging a chair back from the table for a seat.

He met the amused stares of father and daughter and rumbled, "The floor of me house was much too cold this morn for a man of me age to be stumbling about." He glared about as if daring anyone to question his honesty. "Besides, I finished a table for Mister Dunbar, and he had said he was coming here to see Mister Ruark 'bout that mule of his. Seems the man wants to buy it."

Pitney accepted a plate from Milan and set about easing his appetite. The meal was taken by all with light banter as a side dish and the mood was generally cheerful. But it was not to remain so for long. Milan had renewed Ruark's coffee when a shout was heard, and a banging fist jarred the front door. Jason let in a bondsman from the village who came on bare feet directly back to the dining room. At Trahern's side the man stood nervously turning his hat as he gave fleeting glances at Shanna as if her presence held back his flow of words.

"Mister—uh—yer lordship—Squire Trahern—" The man's tongue stumbled in haste.

"Well, Mister Hanks," Trahern urged impatiently. "Out with it."

The bondsman's face reddened as he looked again at Shanna. "Well, sir, I was out in me boat early, gettin' in a few good fishes for Miz Hawkins. She gives me a threepence or so for 'em. I drew the boat in to fix me lines and bait when I spies a bit o' color up by the bush. The tide was out, so I beached the skiff to see about it." He paused and blushed darkly, lowering his gaze. He crushed the hat between his huge, calloused, square-fingered hands. "H'it were Miz Milly, sir." His voice was choked. "She were dead, beaten bad and tossed in a tide pool."

In the frozen silence he rushed on.

"Miz Hawkins 'as to be told, sir, and I ain't got the right words, it being her only young'un and all. Would ye tell her, sir?"

"Milan!" Trahern bellowed, and the servant almost dropped a

plate at the sound. "Send Maddock to bring my carriage around immediately." He pushed back his chair and all at the table rose with him. "Come and show us where, Mister Hanks."

Numbly Shanna crossed the room, her mind tumbling over itself with the shock of Mister Hanks's announcement. Milly and babe, dead! What hellish being would do such a deed? This would be a terrible tragedy for Mrs. Hawkins to bear, and Shanna felt sick at heart as she wondered why so much trouble had to come to such a good woman.

In the back of Shanna's mind it came to her that her secret was safe once again, but that meant nothing now. She'd have gladly told her father herself if it would have made any difference in this matter of Milly's death. She had not really disliked the girl and certainly never wished any disaster to befall her. Her worrying seemed so trifling now.

Trailing behind Shanna, Ruark was just as stunned. The attempt on his life yesterday and now this murder of Milly—were they somehow related? It was a dark blemish on the happy, serene days he had enjoyed ever since Shanna had lowered all barriers between them.

"Shanna, girl!" Trahern's voice halted them. " 'Tis best you stay here."

"Mister Hanks is right, papa," Shanna returned quietly. "Madam Hawkins must be told. 'Tis fitting a woman be with her. I will go to her."

Both father and husband stared at Shanna, warmly gratified with her wisdom and understanding. Trahern nodded, and the room was emptied in a rush.

Milly lay face down in a shallow depression in the sand. At high tide it would have been a pool, but now the sun had whitened the sand until it seemed the unfortunate girl was but napping on the beach. Her clothes were torn from her until only a few meager shreds remained. Thin weals marked her body and limbs as if she had been thrashed cruelly with a narrow rod or staff. Huge purplish bruises swelled on her arms and upper body where a heavy fist or cudgel had smashed repeatedly into her. An ugly welt marked the side of her face and extended well into the matted hair. One hand still clutched tufts of salt grass, bespeaking her struggle to hold on as the tide ebbed. Her other hand was stretched out and near it was a crude "R" dug into the sand. The short leg of it trailed off and curled under, ending where her fingers had buried themselves in a last desperate convulsive effort.

Ruark stared at her, his mind filled with the sight of another girl who had died in much the same manner. How could this happen so far away with an ocean between? How could it be?

Trahern bent near the girl and peered at the scrawled letter in the sand. " 'Tis an 'R,' " he murmured then straightened to consider his bondsman. "Or it could be a 'P.' But then, I can vouch for Pitney." He pursed his lips thoughtfully. "It could stand for Ruark, but 'tis my inclination to disbelieve that. I am certain I could vouch for you, also, should the occasion arise."

Ruark's throat was dry. The twisted body was all too familiar. He managed a hoarse, "Thank you, sir."

"Or it could stand for Ralston, yet I can hardly envision him with a young girl like this. He much prefers heavier, plumper, older women. More solid and reliable. 'Like England,' he says."

Ruark raised his eyes and scanned the low bluff above the beach. A clump of brush showed broken twigs and higher up a strip of white cloth hung like a banner from a branch.

"There!" He pointed. "She must have fallen from up there." He walked down a ways to a break in the bluff and scrambled up, followed in close order by Trahern and Pitney. Mister Hanks remained below and strolled out toward his boat, wanting no further part of the gruesome affair.

The three found a small glade heavily shaded by trees and hidden by shrubs. Its floor was a thick bed of springy moss, and here was written the rest of the tale. The moss was uprooted in chunks and tossed about, giving a sign of a fierce struggle. Pieces of Milly's clothing were scattered afar, and deep boot marks showed where she had been carried to the brink.

Pitney's voice shook. "The filthy whoreson thought her dead and threw her into the sea. She would have gone out on the tide and disappeared without a trace. The poor lass. 'Twas an evil thing that was done here by an evil man."

His gray eyes caught Ruark's, and for a long moment the two gazes held unwaveringly. When Pitney spoke again, his tone was certain as he directed his statement to the younger man.

"I do not know of such a one who would do this."

Trahern snorted. "Nor do I. 'Tis a beastly thing. Beastly."

"Squire," Ruark began reluctantly, and Trahern faced him with a quizzical stare. "I would have you hear it from me and now." He had to squint almost into the sun to meet the man's gaze, but meet it he did. "Milly claimed she was with babe and needed me to wed her."

"And were you the father?" Trahern inquired slowly.

"Nay, I was not," Ruark avowed. "I never laid a hand on the girl"

After a moment the squire nodded. "I believe you, Mister Ruark." He sighed heavily. "Let's get the girl home. Elot will be along with a wagon any moment now."

The barouche bore the men to the Hawkinses' house where Pitney excused himself and made off for the dramshop. Arrangements had been made for Milly's body to be tended to by a close friend of the fishmonger before the woman could see the abuse her daughter had suffered. Trahern and Ruark stood outside the humble dwelling and braced themselves for meeting the Hawkinses. The yard and exterior were a shambles. A pair of scrawny swine snorted in a corner beneath a haphazard shelter of boards while a dozen or so guinea hens scratched in the path.

With some apprehension the two entered the house. It was neat and clean, though painfully unadorned but for a single wood-carved crucifix hanging on the wall. Mister Hawkins lounged on a lopsided settee and did not even glance at them.

"The old lady's out back," he grunted and sucked long on a bottle of rum, still staring off into the distance.

In back of the house, a roof hung on crooked poles giving shade but little hindrance to rain. Beneath it Mrs. Hawkins stood at a high table, her back to them. With a huge knife she cleaned fish, spilling the offal into a wooden barrel. Shanna sat on a stool to one side and met their eyes with a small shrug, though signs of recent tears still lingered in her own.

"Good day, gentlemen," Mrs. Hawkins spoke over her shoulder without pausing in her task. "Have a seat wherever. I has me work to do." Her voice sounded tired.

Both Trahern and Ruark remained standing and stared at each other awkwardly, wondering what was to be said. The old woman worked on, though she wiped at her eyes with the back of her hand and sniffed loudly once in a while.

"She was an unlucky girl," Mrs. Hawkins's flat voice stated suddenly. She braced her hands on the table and stood with bowed head. She could barely be heard now."I pray she's at peace. She fretted overmuch about things she could not have and was never satisfied with what she got."

The old fishwife turned to face them, her eyes streaming tears of sorrow.

"Milly weren't a bad girl." She smiled and found a clean spot on the apron to wipe her face. "Willful sometimes, aye, that she were. Men gave her trinkets and coins sometimes, and she came to think they would give her whate'er she wanted. She made up stories about some o' them. Oh, I know, Mister Ruark, what she said about you and her, but I'm aware ye never touched 'er. She used to cry in 'er pillow cause ye wouldn't pay no mind to 'er. When I'd wash yer clothes, she'd sit an' moon over ye."

"Mrs. Hawkins," Ruark began gently, "were there any others who were—steady?"

"Many others," the woman sniffed and blew her nose loudly. "But none that lasted. Oh—there was one lately, but I don't know who. She never would say and only met him at night, far away from here."

"Mister Ralston never—" Trahern could not put it to words.

"Nay, not him. He always said she was cheap trash. Even hit at her once with that little whip o' his. The woman laughed briefly. "Milly teased him. Called him old stick bones and sour-face."

The tears began to flow again, and the woman's shoulder shook with suppressed sobs. Shanna rose quickly and went to comfort her. Mrs. Hawkins was half a head taller, but the two of them put their heads together and spoke softly.

When Mrs. Hawkins calmed, she bent and kissed Shanna on the cheek. "Go now, child," she smiled. "Ye've done me good, but we would be alone now for a while."

Orlan Trahern ventured, "If you have a need, madam, do not hesitate." He paused then added. "Milly left a sign in the sand.

An 'R' she traced. Do you know of any—"

Mrs. Hawkins shook her head. "I wouldn't worry meself about Milly's signs, sir. She never took ter writin'."

A long quiet moment passed before Ruark offered, "I'll come by tomorrow to fix the roof."

There was nothing left to be said, and the three departed. The ride back to the manor was overlong and very quiet.

Chapter 23

OCTOBER was middle-aged, and the *Hampstead* was in port for a general replenishing before she would bear Trahern and his extensive entourage to Virginia. While his party visited the Beauchamps, the brigantine and the schooner would play the coastal colonies in trade. Meanwhile, the mill grew like a well-nurtured mushroom. Each day saw its completion nearing, and a crude blade hammered out by the blacksmith was installed until a better one arrived from New York. In fact, several blades for different purposes had been ordered at Ruark's insistence, and it was a grand day when the *Marguerite* arrived with all of them aboard.

The gloom of Milly's death was set aside when Gaitlier and Dora came to the manor house and shyly announced their intentions to marry. After sharing a toast for the occasion, Shanna pressed them into taking a ride about the island with Ruark and herself, only to order the carriage halted before a small building, and there to introduce the prospective bridegroom to the school she had long ago urged her father to build. Gaitlier was ecstatic over the crates of books, slates, and other implements of learning Shanna had shipped home during her own years of instruction. Amid profuse and enthusiastic assurances that he would consent to be the island's schoolmaster, Gaitlier and Dora began to unpack the largess of materials and were left in a welter of happiness.

Amid this activity, Gaylord Billingsham became to all appearances entrenched into the lifestyle of Los Camellos. He did not seem overly affected by Shanna's rebuff and not at all inclined to relieve his host of his presence, however strained Trahern's graciousness was becoming. The knight's manners were polished; his arrogance subdued, if only a trifle; his benevolence almost monkish.

Only two major disruptions disturbed the normal life on the island. One occurred when Gaitlier opened his school for the first day. As acting governor, Trahern had decreed that all children between the ages of seven and twelve should be present and that the only excusals would be made by him. This brought a few objections as some of the older children were well ingrained into the families' economic system. It was not until he personally made an appearance at the homes and kindly pointed out the probability of increased earnings that the goal of having all the children attend school was met. Even then, it was a sad moment when it became known that most of the older children had not the slightest understanding of the rudiments of writing, reading, or ciphering. The older boys had somehow gained the idea that school was a place to have fun, and Gaitlier was soon ensconced as a beast with a hickory stick ever in hand. By the time the first week had passed, however, they were familiar with the proper decorum and began to look upon the small, seemingly meek man with a new respect.

Life on Los Camellos quieted and barely regained its ruts when the day arrived for the marriage of the schoolmaster. Since weddings were rare, this was an occasion seized upon for much revelry and celebrating. There would be dancing and feasting in the streets and with the prospect of various spirits being consumed without heed, Trahern declared the next day a holiday for the safety of all. The townsfolk had raised a small cottage across from the school and furnished it with donations from one and all. Pitney laid his huge hands to wood and built a tester bed the likes of which the island had never seen. Shanna and Hergus together took Dora in hand. The mistress of the manor gifted the young woman with a satin gown of gentle maize, and the Scotswoman washed and curled Dora's hair then painstakingly created a comely coiffure for her. The girl bloomed like a radiant flower under the careful grooming, and when vo ws were spoken, Ruark watched much in awe, for in that moment Dora was truly beautiful.

The night dissolved into a continuous round of merry-making, and as Shanna stood with Pitney and her father on the brightly lit thoroughfare, the tumult of sound, sight, and smell washed over her. Amid the press of village folk, she could feel her own spirits respond to the gaiety and excitement. Garlands and bouquets of flowers were everywhere, filling the eye with a riot of color. Bunches of pungent herbs scented the air, lanterns and torches gave an eerie, shifting, flickering light to the scene, and the roar of laughter and boisterous songs assailed the senses.

Shouting above the din, Ruark appeared beside Shanna and pressed a glass of champagne into her hand. As she sipped, the nose-tickling wine kindled a warmth in her stomach, and Shanna's reserve slipped a notch or two.

The sweet smell of savory foods drifted on the gentle evening breezes and mingled with the tangy spice of newly tapped ale and rum. Bondsman, servant, freeman alike joined the celebration. Pitney strolled with Trahern to the refreshment tables to sample the feast. Shanna found her hand in Ruark's when they were following the newly wedded couple in a rigadoon. Shanna's considered self-control slipped again as a fresh glass of sparkling fluid was thrust upon her by one of the townsmen. Breathlessly she drained it and then gave herself in renewed abandon to the dance. Her happy laughter blended with Ruark's, and her head reeled giddily from the effects of the champagne.

She saw Ruark's dark face before her, white teeth flashing and eyes that burned golden whenever they touched her. Her heart hammered wildly, taking up the intoxicating excitement of the festivities, and the stricture of months of duplicity was stripped away to give her spirit flight and freedom, if only for the moment. Space and time ceased to matter. Gaylord had no chance to intervene, and Shanna gave no heed to the pompous knight angrily directing her father's attention to them or of Hergus's frowning disapproval. Here, in the midst of the crowd, she was alone with Ruark, seeing him, feeling his nearness, and she was ecstatic. Never had she known such carefree bliss. She laughed and danced to her heart's content, and the champagne helped quench her thirst. Its conscience-cooling clarity seemed to lend a vivid buoyancy to her mind, and her head grew as light as her feet.

The squire was enjoying himself as much as his daughter, for his good Welsh blood had a taste for fun and regalement. By damned it did, and the fact had ceased to surprise him that he enjoyed seeing the daughter he had sired in the company of his favorite bondsman. The lad was as adept at the dances as she and the lean, powerful grace of his body complemented her trim womanliness.

Orlan Trahern had often watched his daughter at past affairs such as this, surrounded by posturing dandies and the eager-to-be-rich. He had seen her for her own amusement tease and torment each man, leading him on the chase and then crushing his vanity against her open disdain. These many months since her return from England, it had been obvious that she had held herself in check, as was a widow's proper way, and he could not fault her revelry now. Orlan smiled to himself in retrospect. At least she had overcome her dislike for this Ruark and apparently could accept him as a man if not her peer.

With a worried frown, Gaylord watched the dancing couple from Trahern's side. "What do you intend to do about this, squire?" he demanded. "In England 'twould be a scandalous moment for a bondsman to so handle a lady. This fellow should be reminded of his place. I would not usurp your authority, but were I the governor here, I would see that the man gives proper respect to your daughter as well as to the other ladies present."

Pitney cast a doubtful glance over his shoulder at the knight before exchanging a wondering look with Trahern. Orlan rocked on his heels as he sampled a morsel from a tray of warm breads.

"You may well have noticed, sir, that my daughter demands respect in her own manner." He sipped his wine, considering the knight with an amused smile lightly resting on his lips. "I have learned of late to trust my daughter's judgment in many things, perhaps more so than she does herself. Still, if you are strongly bent to educate the lass, you are welcome to try."

Gaylord straightened his gold satin coat with a jerk and stretched his long neck above the lacy jabot. "Should Madam Beauchamp accept my proposal and become my wife, I would in no way offer her less protection than I do now from such as that one. 'Tis my duty as a knight of the realm."

As he swaggered away Trahern turned to Pitney with a chuckle. "I fear the good fellow learned nothing in the bush. I hope the damage will not be costly."

Ruark's laughter died as a large hand rudely clapped down upon his shoulder, and he was whirled about to face the sneering Sir Gaylord. The bride and groom shared a look of surprise, while Shanna stared in disbelief, amazed at the audacity of the man.

Gaylord's blue-gray eyes ranged coldly over Ruark. " 'Twould seem that I must constantly remind you of your place. It is with the rest of the servants and slaves. I insist that you leave Madam Beauchamp alone. Do you understand me?"

Ruark lazily bent his gaze toward the long fingers crushing the silk of his coat. He was about to comment when Shanna snatched away Gaylord's hand as if it were something distasteful. She faced the knight, her cheeks flushed, her eyes snapping green fire. For the sake of caution, the man stepped back a pace, remembering the firm crack of her slap against his face.

"Sir, you intrude," she charged incredulously. "Have you none?"

The villagers had paused to gape at them. A low, questioning murmur rose from those nearby, and even Sir Gaylord recognized the angry buzz of it. The knight was out of his element, for Ruark had earned his niche in the tiny world of Los Camellos, and Gaylord Billingsham was a foreigner and disliked by most.

Gaylord spoke in a more reserved tone. "Madam, I only seek to insure this man gives proper respect to you. You may feel obligated to him for saving you from the pirates. But 'tis my duty as a gentleman to guard a lady's reputation."

It was ludicrous to Shanna that this clod should feign worry over her honor in the presence of others while in private seek to win her with bungling caresses. She laughed with bright amusement.

"I assure you, sir, I am no proper lady." Looking up into Ruark's amused regard, she giggled. "An improper one, perhaps."

Taking her husband's glass, she passed it with her own to Gaylord. "Will you find a place to set these, sir?" she requested sweetly and slipped her hand into Ruark's, signalling the musicians to begin again. "I should like to dance with my slave."

Ruark grinned leisurely into the reddening face of the knight. "Another time, perhaps."

Tucking Shanna's hand in the crook of his arm, Ruark led her away from the silently raging man. The slim stems of the two goblets snapped, and without a word Gaylord whirled on his heels and stalked away.

The dances livened and grew uproarious as individuals gave their own interpretations of the various steps amid the clamorous approval and the rhythmic clapping of hands until, breathless and exhausted, the couples settled themselves to feasting and drinking to nourish their high spirits. Shanna even found a glass of champagne in her hand, thrust there with hearty and jubilant coaxings to drink up and be jolly. Lightheartedly she sipped, and her laughter sparkled with Ruark's deep chuckles. Finding room at one of the trestle tables, she crowded in beside him on a long bench. The close contact was not unrewarding. In fact, Ruark much enjoyed the arrangement. Her thigh was pressed to his beneath the table, and her shoulder overlapped his. The intimacy provided him with an excuse to place his hand on the bench behind her, and as the lanterns gave off only a meager light here and no one stood at their backs, it was only natural that he indulge himself with a fond caress or two for he found it hard to keep his hands from her.

The dark-haired beauty, Madame Duprey, and her captain husband sat further down the table and were much involved with each other after the Frenchman's long absence from home. Even Shanna was inclined to feel less scornful of the man as he bestowed loving kisses upon the nape of his spouse's neck and along her shoulder.

"How sweet," Shanna smiled aside to Ruark. "I think he actually does love her."

"Ah, lass, not half as much as I love you," Ruark breathed near her ear. "I am near bursting my breeches for the want of you, and you can only sing me praises of another man's devotion. Am I to starve with this feast before me of rosy breasts and silken loins, feigning some indifference to the succulent fruits? I long to taste the apple of your love and would most greedily devour it."

"Shhh," Shanna giggled, leaning against him. "You're drunk. Someone might hear you."

Assured that in the din his words would be unheard by any other than she, Ruark grinned lazily. "Aye, I'm drunk, but only on this nectar that is more heady than any wine I've dared to drink. I have a fever in my blood, a fire only you can quench. I feel it throbbing in my loins. Ride with me, fair damsel. Ride upon this horny dragon, and I shall set to flight any dreams of knights. A kiss, a soft caress, a gentle word, and like a moth I change my scaly armor for the softer coating of man. Ah, love, have care for this great beast. He lumbers in your wake like some poor, plodding soul begging just one glance, some sign of recognition from his adored one. Your gilded locks wave like a gonfalon on an airy breeze, and I think that now the fair damsel will turn and look at me and see me not as a monster, but as the one who would gladly kiss the soles of her feet. Ah, Shanna, my Shanna, be merciful to this besotted beast. Take me to your soft breast and release me from this scaly weight."

Shanna was suffused with a warmth and tenderness she could neither fathom nor explain. It was on the tip of her tongue to deny her dreams as frivolous, a fantasy once held dear by a young girl but outgrown, like porcelain dolls. This was real, the hard feel of Ruark's thigh against her own, her arm against his lean ribs, this cacophony of sight, smell, and noise that surrounded them yet, at the same time, shielded them from prying eyes. He was her lover, whether husband or not, and she gave herself freely to him whenever the moment was ripe. She had stopped denying him. She had ceased calling herself widow. She had come out of mourning, and strangely her spirit thrilled with the awareness of him.

A toast to the newlyweds broke her reverie, and Shanna turned as everyone around them rose to their feet, lifting their glasses high, and quickly followed suit. It was a prelude for the merrymakers to escort the blissful pair to their cottage, a procession which wandered through the streets as a moving celebration. Shanna found herself laughing again, though at times she cringed at the drunken humor of the sailors, which abused the imagination but elicited squealing giggles from the virginal maids.

It was almost a relief when the party began to disperse and Ruark took her back to her father. The carriage was brought, and Shanna was properly seated and left as a search began for Hergus. When the group was formed, complete with Hergus and Gaylord, Shanna was still in her place, her shawl neatly folded and held against her breast, both arms wrapped securely about it. The smile on her face reminded one of a cat well fed at the cost of a flock of canaries. Thus she sat, giving almost no heed as Ruark and Hergus crowded in on either side of her, leaving Sir Gaylord a choice of sharing the footman's bench or a long, lonely walk. Seeing the knight's dilemma, Pitney relented with a smile and sliding tightly against Trahern, causing the squire to give a disgruntled snort, Pitney patted the narrow space beside him in invitation. Gaylord sighed. He was not about to walk or share the seat with a servant and had little choice but to wedge himself in. It was only casually noted by the others that Pitney's huge elbow rested against the knight's ribs, and it was not until the ride commenced that Gaylord, with each bump in the road, was given to sudden abrupt grunts as if he were pained.

Once at the manor, Shanna preceded Hergus up the stairs, and it was not until the door of her chambers was closed behind them that Shanna carefully laid the shawl on the bed and unfolded it to reveal an unopened bottle of champagne. Hergus was taken aback and gaped at her mistress, thinking for sure the lass had taken leave of her senses.

"Now what do ye intend to do with that, miss? I be believing ye've had enough of spirits, seeing how ye were flaunting yer bondsman beneath the noses of every moony-eyed twit who's set their sights on him. And there yer pa was, too! If ye think the squire is an addlepated old man and blind to all yer shenanigans, then ye be lacking the wits I was thinking ye had."

"Oh, I don't think that," Shanna declared with a laugh and went searching for glasses in the sitting room. " 'Tis just that I've come out of mourning, and it seems only fitting to celebrate."

"What do ye mean, mourning?" Hergus called after her in bemusement. "I never knew ye to care overly much for Milly, nor even that the two of ye got along." The maid shrugged and commented much to herself, "Mostly 'cause the little chit, God rest her soul, had it in her mind to be envious of ye. If that Abe Hawkins wouldna taken himself to drinking his life away, she and her ma coulda had a lot more. But then, he hasna ever done an honest day's work."

" 'Tis not for Milly." Shanna came to stand in the doorway with two sherry glasses she had found. She dipped into a low curtsy that made her printed taffeta skirts billow out wide around her. "The widow is no more. I've come out of mourning."

Hergus grunted derisively. "Ye were never married long enough to even consider yerself properly wed. The least Mister Beauchamp coulda done was to live long enough to put a babe in yer belly. Had he done so, I doubt ye'd be fooling 'round now with Mister Ruark." She sighed wearily. "But I suppose if he had lived longer, it woulda been just the luck for himself to be without a fertile seed to give ye."

Abruptly Shanna set aside the glasses, suddenly feeling as if she had, indeed, imbibed too much. She thrust the champagne from her sight, burying it beneath a pillow on her chaise. Observing her, Hergus was inclined to worry that she really had gone daft.

"I'd best get ye ready for bed. I hear Mister Ruark coming up the stairs, and I've had me say without letting him hear me." Hergus shucked the taffeta gown from her mistress, leaving the delicate chemise for modesty as that seemed the girl's wont lately. "Come to the dressing table and I'll brush out yer hair, and then I'll leave ye."

It was a matter soon done. The gilded tresses spread in thick waves of silk over Shanna's bare shoulders before the woman took herself from the chambers. Alone now, Shanna stared at her reflection, that image of soft woman, creamy skin and thinly clad breasts, white shoulders and wistful countenance. Ruark's words of the evening echoed in her brain, and she could almost see herself standing alone on a hill, ignoring the plaintive cry behind her as she searched hard and fast for her knight in armor.

A fickle dream to want something not worth the wanting. She could have Sir Gaylord in a trice, but even now she shuddered in revulsion at the thought of having to submit to his bungling caresses. Much more did she yearn for the vibrant warmth of Ruark's hands upon her, softly titillating, weaving their spell.

The evening breeze stirred the draperies, and in the silence of the house she could hear Ruark moving about his room. Almost as one compelled, she went to the French doors, and like a wraith she was gone, not hearing the door of her sitting room open and close and footsteps coming across the floor.

"Yer pa just said he'll be up shortly—" Hergus blinked in surprise at the now vacant bedchamber and gasped as the realization struck her. "Oh, me lord! She's gone to him again. And there's her pa coming!"

Stripped to the waist, Ruark leaned against the heavy footpost of his bed, his eyes like flaming golden brands as he watched Shanna saunter toward him, moving her hips with an undulating grace beneath the batiste garment. Her ripe breasts pressed wantonly against the gossamer confines, rousing his senses to full awakening. Her bare feet seemed to glide over the carpet, and her lips were bent upward in a totally wicked smile.

"My Pirate Captain Ruark, widow maker, virgin taker. Darkest of all dragons. You weave such a comely thread of words to ensnare an unwary maid. Now say me yea or nay. Was it some scaly beast who laid upon my virgin loins on a stormy winter's night? Nay, I would not think it. 'Twas some dark, handsome wooer who picked the plum but only nibbled the fruit before he vanished in the blackness. Was it some passion's flower he yearned to pluck that brought him to this isle, or some thirst for revenge upon that one who but sought to save herself from that hoary wretch of the dungeons then found, all too late, he was an enchanted lover. What dark dragon do I see before me? What of the raven locks and strong human arms to twine about me? Is it beast's blood flowing in your veins, my gallant cavalier, or the warm blood of man?"

His heated gaze seared her, and he beckoned with his words. "Come, vixen, and I will show you."

Shanna gave a deep, throaty laugh and placed her hands on his hard, flat belly, sliding them upward over his ribs and chest, caressingly, tauntingly, feeling the heavy thud of his heart beneath her palm.

"I perceive you are all too manly, my lord," she purred as his hands came upon her waist. A low growl sounded deep in her, like a she-cat calling her mate. Slowly, deliberately, she leaned against him, first her lips and then the peaks of her thinly clad breasts, rousing his hot blood to boiling as the heat of her touched him.

"Shanna, Shanna," Ruark rasped and folded her in his arms, crushing her to him and bending to cover her soft, reaching mouth with his.

A light gasp made him raise his eyes, and he saw Hergus standing shocked and still in the wide French doors where Shanna had passed but moments before. The woman had a hand over her mouth, and her eyes were wide, though whether from fear, horror, or surprise he could not tell. For Ruark it was like being drenched with icy water.

"We've got company," he muttered and withdrew from the kiss, setting his hands to Shanna's ribs and moving her back a step. As she whirled in bemusement, he turned his back to the maid, since his tight breeches lent him nothing of concealment for his once raging desires. He snatched a robe from the armoire and hastily donned it as Shanna found her tongue with a fury.

"Hergus! Do you spy upon me? What is the meaning of this?"

The maid could only stutter, shamefaced and painfully aware of her mistress's meager garb. It was one thing to be alone with Shanna in the altogether, but another to see her nearly so in the presence of her lover. Hergus was a modest person, and her motherly fondness for Shanna made her embarrassment all the more excruciating.

" 'Tis obvious you have no excuse for spying on me," Shanna snapped, stamping her foot in outrage. Whirling angrily, she flounced to Ruark's bed where she threw back the coverlet and turned down the sheet. The irate, non-widow Beauchamp plumped her round bottom upon the soft feather tick and threw up a hand in disgust.

An amused smile twisted Ruark's lips as he began to fill his pipe. It was his most fervent desire of the moment to join his wife on the bed, but there was yet the Scotswoman to deal with, and she seemed not to have the least intention of leaving.

"Mister Ruark," Hergus groaned, a worried tone in her voice. "There is no time!" She wrung her hands in anguish and hurriedly came to him to whisper, "Squire Trahern said that he would himself come to see her safe abed." The servant moaned in dismay. "And if the squire should find her here— Oh, Mister Ruark, 'twould be dreadful!"

Ruark looked up from lighting his pipe. "How long were you there listening?"

A red flush of color brightened the woman's cheeks, and her eyes fell to her twisting hands. "I didna come to spy, only to warn her that her pa is coming. I only just come. I wouldna lie to ye, Mister Ruark."

"I know that, Hergus."

"I wouldna speak a word of it." Then she added quickly. "Or of anything else, sir. I think ye—"

She halted and stared past him in amazement. Following her gaze Ruark turned to see his wife curled like a child upon his bed, her dark lashes resting against her cheek in deep slumber. He set his pipe down and nodded to Hergus.

"Fold down her bed."

As the maid willingly fled, Ruark crossed softly to the fourposter and carefully lifted Shanna. Feeling his arms close about her, she sighed like a soft kitten and snuggled to him, at once at ease and most content wherein she lay.

Shanna's own sheets were being tucked about her when footsteps sounded in the hall. Ruark quickly took his leave by way of the balcony, pausing outside in the darkness so that his own passage would not be noticed. He heard the door to Shanna's room open and then Hergus's voice, hushed and much relieved.

"She went out like a snuffed candle, sir. I was just putting away her clothes."

Trahern's grunt sounded. "Good enough." A long pause followed, then he said "Hergus, have you seen much of a change in her of late?"

"Ah, n-nay, sir." The maid's words stumbled slightly. "She's grown up a lot, that's for sure."

"Aye, that is sure," Trahern repeated thoughtfully. "I wish her mother were here. My Georgiana was always better with the

child than I. Still, I have learned much these past few months."
His heavy sigh came soft and wistful. "Perhaps between the
two of us we will yet see the best of all of it. Good night, then."

The door closed, and Ruark leaned back against the wall in
relief. Hergus came close to the French doors and, spying him,
marched out to stand before him.

"You're a fool, John Ruark. And you make a traitor of meself.
The good squire trusts me to see what is best for the lass, and
I warn ye now I canna twist me tongue around another lie."

Ruark's frown was hidden in the shadow, but his tone bore
the pain her words inflicted. "Lord willing, I shall not have to
ask you again. There is, indeed, a time to live and a time to die,
but sometimes it seems the time to live is far outweighed by the
other. Have patience, Hergus. I can only swear to you that all
I do and all I intend is for Shanna's good, for you see, Hergus,"
—and his voice became a hoarse whisper—"I love the lass beyond
all else."

Hergus lowered her gaze as she struggled to maintain her
anger and find a scorching answer. Then she realized she was
alone.

Preparations approached the frenzied point as the sailing date
neared, and the mill was readied for its first load of logs. Ruark
was left to see to the final inspections, and this was his labor
just days before the journey to the colonies was to be launched.
With the overseers, he conducted an exacting last check, seeing
that all bearings were well greased and all cogs, wheels, and
walking beams were sturdy and set as directed. The huge water
wheel was checked; it was perfectly balanced and turned with no
more than the gentle pressure of a hand upon it. The new saw
had been laid in place and awaited the first load of logs coming
by wagon from the south plateau.

Ruark was well pleased with all of it. It was an accomplishment he took pride in. He dismissed the overseers, then others,
then walked the flume back to the pond, carefully looking over
the gates and bed as he went. Everything was in readiness.

The seesawing heehaw of a mule higher up the embankment
drew Ruark's attention. The first wagon driver had halted his
load of logs on the road above the mill and made his way down

afoot to be sure where they were to be dumped. The team he had left for the most part dozed in the shade, lazily swishing flies with their tails, except for Old Blue, the rear animal on the far side who brayed discontentedly, laying his ears alongside his head. Old Blue was his cantankerous old self even under Trahern's ownership. The squire had bested Mister Dunbar's offer, and Ruark chuckled as he wondered if Trahern was beginning to question his wisdom in purchasing the beast.

Ruark paused at the pond's edge, gazing out over the mirror-smooth water. All noises were subdued, and there was a tenseness in the air, a sense of expectancy, that in another moment would be crushed beneath the din of activity. The gates were ready to be opened, the logs ready to be dumped. It only awaited his signal.

A splintering, snapping sound intruded upon the quiet, rising quickly in volume and rate. Ruark looked up at the wagon and to his horror saw the side stakes slowly folding beneath the weight of the logs. With a last final crack they gave way, spilling the load down the hillside. They gathered speed as they bounded toward him, thumping and jarring the ground on which he stood. There was no place to flee but the pond.

Ruark leaped high and stretched out. His body cleaved the air in a shallow arc, and he struck the smooth surface almost flat. As the water closed over his head, he bent and dove deep, clawing downward with all the strength he could muster. The butt of a log plunged past him, so close he could see tiny bubbles clinging to its coarse bark. Then its buoyancy checked the descent, and it was gone. Rocks brushed his belly painfully, and he bumped into the slope on the far side. Rolling once, he could see the unsettled, frothy turbulence high above. Another log almost touched the bottom before it shot upward to leap clear into the air like a hooked fish, then fell back to crash and bob upon the surface.

Ruark's lungs burned and were near to bursting. He kicked off the bottom and headed for a clear area above, broaching like the log. Falling back to tread water, he gasped precious air into his lungs. Shouts and angry curses came from the shore where he had stood, and as he struggled to clear his eyes, he saw the foreman and the driver backed by a crowd who anxiously scanned the water for some sign of him. Clinging to a nearby log, Ruark waved his arm and heard the answering shout. He rested a moment and then began to swim slowly back toward them.

"I never meant to inspect the pond quite so thoroughly as that," he gasped as he crawled up on the shore.

"The damned fool left his logs unchained when he came down," the foreman raged.

"Like hell I did!" the driver declared. "Do ya take me fer a bloody boob? I checked 'em good an' they was chained."

"No harm's been done." Ruark took the foremans offered hand and hauled himself to his feet. The sound which had preceded that of the dumping logs did not lend to his peace of mind. "But I've a mind to look at that wagon."

He led the way up the slope. The chains were held in place by a pin through a link and a bracket on the wagon's bed so that the pin could be tapped out and the load dumped. Wooden posts on each side further restrained the logs, but these now lay on the ground with the pins and the small sledgehammer each driver carried. Someone had deliberately knocked the pins out after removing the posts. The partial track of a booted foot was marked into a soft spot of earth, and Ruark could only surmise that Old Blue had had something to bellow about after all. As the men around him wore the flat soles of sandals or work shoes, there was no doubt in his mind that another man had been here. Ruark followed the trail some distance along the road and around a curve protected by thick brush and trees. Here he found another impression of a booted heel along with the marks of a horse's hooves. He frowned in silence, realizing someone had meant to kill him.

Ruark glanced up as Ralston's small carriage came briskly around the bend. The thin man halted beside the workmen who had gathered around Ruark. He climbed down from the high seat with a triumphant sneer on his face.

"Hah! Dawdling again, I see. Squire Trahern may yet be convinced that sterner measures are needed to extract worthwhile labor from slaves."

The man's boots were meticulously clean, or Ruark might have accused him then and there.

"There was a slight mishap," Ruark explained tersely, watching Ralston narrowly. "And it seems 'twas no accident, but intentional."

"Probably the carelessness of one of your precious bondsmen." Ralston gestured with the quirt. "Am I to believe it had something to do with your condition?"

"Aye, ye might say that," the foreman piped in. "Mister Ruark was below when the logs let go. He saved 'imself with a dip in the pond."

"How touching," Ralston smirked and regarded Ruark with a jeer. "You are always in the midst of some foolery, aren't you?" He caressed the end of his quirt and seemed to grow museful. "Yet you turn everything to your betterment. Perhaps you, more than the others, are in need of some discipline."

Ruark stared at him coldly. He did not intend to let the man use that bloody little whip on him. Milly might have cringed and whimpered beneath her merciless beating, but if Ralston had been her assailant then he faced a man now and not some helpless girl.

A clatter of hooves on the road drew the attention of all. Attila came thundering around the bend with Shanna on his back. Seeing the group that had gathered, she hauled the beast to a skidding stop while the more fearful workmen scattered from her path.

"Mister Ruark!" Her eyes went down his sodden attire as she leaned forward to stroke the gray's neck. "Have you taken to swimming in your garments?"

" 'Twas an accident, mum, and he were caught in the middle of it, he were," one of the men volunteered.

"An accident!" Shanna gasped. She disengaged her knee from the saddle horn and found Ruark's hands about her waist, lifting her down. "What happened? Are you hurt?"

The questions came out in a rush, and her worried frown told Ruark she was in no mood for humor. He was about to reassure her when he was roughly shouldered aside by Ralston.

"Keep your distance, fool," the agent raged, waving his whip dangerously close to Ruark. "I shall remind you but once, Mister Ruark, that a bondsman is not permitted to touch a lady of circumstance."

Ralston paused for some reaction from the man he berated, but finding a hard, penetrating stare his answer, he whirled to Shanna.

"Madam, it is not wise to trust these rogues overmuch and most rash to be so familiar with them. They are the scum of civilization and hardly worth your concern."

Shanna was rigid with rage, and her eyes snapped green sparks. "Mister Ralston!" Her voice could have sliced the heart of the staunchest oak. "You abuse the title of man and disregard that of a gentleman! You have thrice stood in my way and sought to chide me for my manners!"

Ralston's face flushed dark crimson at this public chastening, but Shanna gave him no pause. Stepping forward and tapping his chest lightly with the tip of her own quirt, she snapped, "Never, never confront me again! There is much I will have out with you someday, but for the moment get yourself from my sight."

Ralston sputtered, but could only obey. In livid fury he stalked to his buggy but before mounting he glared about. "You men!" he roared. "Get back to work! You have dallied enough. I will see the next laggard flayed where he stands!"

The road was emptied as Ralston got to his seat and whipped his horse into a full run. Ruark watched him go and then gestured for the driver of the wagon to pull on so others could pass.

"Are you hurt?" Shanna asked quietly, her eyes searching him for some sign of injury.

Ruark tossed her a grin. "Nay, love."

"But what happened?"

Ruark shrugged and casually told her of the occurrence, and the evidence of tampering. He related the near disaster at the distillery as well. "It would seem, my love, someone is not pleased with my presence."

Shanna's hand trembled as she placed it on his arm. "Ruark,"—her voice was ragged and tight—"you don't think I—"

She couldn't finish, but Ruark saw her tears as he looked at her in surprise. He smiled gently and shook his head.

"Nay, love. It never entered my mind. I trust you as I would my own mother. Do not fear that."

For a moment Shanna was unable to speak as she struggled to control her shaking, but then she managed. "But what reason would anyone have to harm you?"

Ruark laughed. "Several of the pirates might have cause, but I would doubt their courage to venture here." He tried to ease her worry. "I shall be more wary henceforth."

A workman scrambled up the slope to them, holding a ragged, dripping twist of straw in his hand.

"Yer hat, Mister Ruark." He gave over the mangled mess ruefully. " 'Twould o' been the same fer ya, had ya not been so quick o' wit."

The man did not wait for thanks but turned and slid down the hill again. Ruark contemplated the thing in his hands, trying to see some shape in it, then lifted his gaze to Shanna, and his eyes gleamed with humor.

"I could be a free man now were it not for the cost of new hats," he quipped.

❧ Chapter 24 ❧

THE days began to run together as the *Hampstead* and the *Tempest* took on supplies and goods to barter. Attila and the mare would be taken along, and provision was made for them on the deck of the *Tempest*, this time under Ruark's direction and with padded stalls to protect the beasts. The rush and furor of preparations filled the dwindling days with activity. Hergus scurried in and out of Shanna's chambers like one possessed; once she paused in the hall under Ruark's amused smile, her arms laden with woolen capes and furs.

"Put the winter clothes away. Take the winter clothes out," she said breathlessly. "Seems it'll never stop."

Then the days were gone, and all was aboard the ships which rode an anchor out in the small bay. Amid final shouts and farewells the passengers stepped into the lighters and were rowed out to spend the first night on board to await the first breezes of early dawn.

And the dawn came. The sails creaked aloft to slap and sag until the wind freshened. The anchors were raised as the first sail billowed full and, though motion was difficult to detect, soon a curl of white foam formed beneath the prows, and they were underway. The masts heaved with a loud creaking as the *Hamp-*

stead rose on the first swell clear of the cove. A shot echoed from the island, and Shanna watched the cloud of smoke drift away from signal hill. The *Hampstead* answered the farewell salute with her stern chaser, and a moment later the *Tempest* followed suit.

Los Camellos was only a smudge on the horizon when Shanna finally went below, piqued that Ruark had not seen fit to visit her at the departure. At the morning hour there were only her father and Pitney to greet her at the table with Captain Dundas, a squarish man, much like her father, large and heavy but a bit leaner and more solid from his years on the quarterdeck. Over the meal the conversation was mostly about what raw materials might be found for the mills in England. In fact, Shanna rather gathered from listening to the men that the colonies were full of palisaded forts and crude log cabins. Her imagination failed as she tried to conjure painted, half-naked savages roaming the wilderness. She missed the rich voice of Ruark, and his absence from the table made the morning seem somehow lacking. It puzzled her that her father had not asked him to join them.

Strolling on the main deck moments later, she still saw no sign of him and grew petulant, because she could not go below in search. She felt neglected that he hadn't even taken time to share his company with her. She set herself by the quarterdeck rail where she could survey the entire ship, and it was some time later when she felt a presence by her side and turned hopefully, only to find Pitney regarding her, an expression close to pity in his eyes. Shanna nodded briefly and came to the point.

"I've seen naught of Mister Ruark as yet. What is he about?"

Pitney squinted into the distance. "About two miles, I'd say, give or take a quarter."

Shanna frowned her bemusement, for she could find no sense in his words. Then Pitney inclined his head and pointed. She followed the direction of his arm to where the *Tempest* stood off the starboard beam. It was a long, bewildered moment before the truth sank in. Shanna slowly regained Pitney's gaze, her eyes wide in stunned realization.

"Aye," he answered her unspoken question. "'Twas Ralston's idea that he be near the horses, but Hergus and I agreed." Pitney ignored her outraged gasp. "'Twill avoid much temptation."

Shanna jerked her shawl tighter about her shoulders with an irritated shrug, and her eyes took on a chilling hue as she glared at him. She left, her lips moving with mumbled words that Pitney was relieved not to hear. Angrily she stamped her way below, and a moment later the large man flinched as he heard a cabin door slam.

It was well into the mid-watch of the afternoon when Shanna was seen out of her cabin again. Most of the seamen were old acquaintances, and she exchanged light greetings when she met an old friend. However, when Pitney or Hergus came near, Shanna's eyes took on a decidedly flinty hardness, and her lips stiffened slightly.

The day wore on, and even with so many friends and family about, Shanna was completely beset with loneliness. Her gaze was ever drawn to the small, white-sailed schooner that plunged along beside the *Hampstead*. Night eased her plight, though the bunk was narrow, hard, and cold. Another day followed, and Hergus found herself with nothing to do, for Shanna combed her own hair and would not allow the woman in the cabin. The *Tempest* was sighted at dawn, hull down on the horizon, only her white sail showing, but as the day lagged by she drew nearer to take up her station abeam again.

The next morning dawned gray and cold. The *Tempest* was not sighted until noon. The fourth day out, a light, misting rain raked the decks and only a brief time could be spent in the open before a chill cut to one's bones. The sails were reefed as the wind strengthened and became more easterly. Near evening the course was shifted to a due westerly one. They had sailed northward, taking advantage of the southeasterly winds and passing well east and north of the Bermudas. Now they sailed west to make landfall north of Chesapeake Bay and would let the prevailing northeasterlies blow them down upon it. The schooner would take advantage more of the quartering tail winds and press ahead, making port a good day ahead of the *Hampstead*.

In the ensuing days Shanna grew more restive and short of temper. Her days were empty and long. Once the *Hampstead* turned west, the sun came out, and freshening winds swept her swiftly along toward her goal. Though the weather was warmer, it was still bleak for Shanna, and the poor ship could not travel fast enough to suit her.

It was after the evening meal, and even Sir Gaylord had been unusually gracious. Still it little eased the wintry chill of Shanna's manner, and she finally took to the deck to escape the fruitless attempts at humor her father and Captain Dundas employed to cheer her. She was huddled against the rail, a fur-trimmed cloak drawn snug about her, hiding her nose in a woolen muffler coiled about her neck, when Pitney came to stand beside her. He leaned his elbows on the rail and watched the fickle waves form frothy caps of white. After a long silence in which Shanna ignored him he spoke.

"You seem in poor temper of late, Madam Beauchamp."

Shanna tightened her lips and gave him no answer, but Pitney knew only too well what had soured her happiness.

"Ye're angry and upset because of course ye've been dealt a cruel blow by fate." There was a mocking tone in his voice that lent the words a heavy sarcasm.

"Hardly by fate," Shanna scoffed. "More by trusted friends."

"Ah, ye have a voice," Pitney laughed gently. "Hergus and meself have been wondering about that."

Shanna grew petulant beneath his prodding. "There has been little enough to say to either of you."

"Poor lass," he chided her. " 'Tis a sad thing that ye alone suffer against the outrageous whims of fortune." Pitney paused and rubbed his hands together while he stared at the darkening evening sky. "Shanna child, let me tell ye a story. 'Tis of a young man whose trials might well rival yer own."

Shanna braced herself to hear his platitudes.

"He was not a complicated soul, though he had taken his father's simple smithy and worked it with honesty and sweat into a vast iron trade that hired a round dozen hands. He met a titled lady, the youngest of a wealthy family, alas, all daughters. After a blissful courtship they were discreetly married, and she bore him a son. It gave the family a continuance of heirdom, and they accepted the man into their home.

"The son was coddled by his aunts, and the mother would not tolerate interference by the father who, being common, could not understand the ways of gentlefolk, or so she was convinced to believe by her kinfolk. The father yielded in the matter and let the nanny and tutors rear his son, taking only those rare moments with him when the others did not demand the boy's time.

"The father became an outsider in his wife's home, and her bedchamber was soon moved from his to another wing in the house. He saw her at evening meals but only from across the table and surrounded by a flock of haughty dames who looked upon him like a tolerated leper. Out of pride he left. The son once escaped the manor house and visited his father's shop where the two of them spent joyous hours in comradery before the lad was hunted down by servants headed by the domineering aunt. She wore the bell of the household and warned the father of interfering further with the boy. The man stood upon his rights, but the local magistrate was well impressed with the power of the wife's family, and the poor man found himself barred from the manor house and enjoined from seeing his own son.

"The boy fled again during a winter storm and journeyed through a blizzard in bare feet and sleeping gown to be with his father. The lad was fetched back, and the father was cast into jail for disobedience. But the son was taken with a chill, and the fever soon found him. He died in a barren manor house crying for his father.

"As it served no further purpose, the man was released and wandered the streets drunk and broken of heart. He returned to the manor once more and begged his wife to leave the frigid, lifeless realm of the dowagers and go away with him. Aye, she promised and took him into her bed again."

Pitney paused and stared at his large hands for a long moment.

"The next morning she was found at the bottom of the stairs, broken and dead. The dames all agreed the husband had pushed her, and buried beneath their wealth and influence, he was cast into a dungeon. But with the help of friends he escaped and fled to his sister's house in London. Her husband, a merchant grown wealthy of his own skills, had gained title to a remote island and was soon to take his wife and baby daughter there to live. The condemned man changed his name and garb and went with them where he helped them make their home and found one of his own."

Pitney's gaze raised and rested fondly upon the woman beside him, who smiled back tenderly through her tears.

"I have been with ye since ye were a wee babe, Shanna, lass." His voice was oddly thick. "I rocked ye on me lap and bounced ye on me knee. I've always served yer purpose and do so now as much as it may seem otherwise."

"Uncle Pitney—" Shanna sniffled, wiping away a tear that trickled down her cheek.

"I have seen ye abuse the sensibilities of many men, though most of them deserved it, but this one ye married, this Ruark, has been much afflicted by the world in such ways as few others are. He is a bold man, with a good head on his shoulders, true to what he believes is true. That such a man should be reduced to bondage is odious, but ye, me proud Shanna, have betrayed him at every turn with little care for his honesty or pride. 'Tis of course no fault of yers that ye are a spoiled brat, and me own hand has been lent to that. I have seen little in yer schooling that would have taught ye to have a fondness for simple folk. It may be counted a credit to yer wisdom that ye have been more than fair with most people. Alas, this cannot hold true for those most near and dear to ye. Ye thought all men were foppish fools and when that one came upon ye who was to be valued above all others, ye had no knowledge of how to care for him.

"Ye would have taken him with ye on this ship and in the closeness of it, would only have been a matter of time before one of ye gave the game away. He had to be separated from Sir Gaylord, but ye cannot see that. Ralston is suspicious of ye both, as he is of everyone, and has hounded Mister Ruark's trail for many weeks. I've watched him meself. But ye are oblivious to that. This game ye started has been played out far too long and will bring more harm and hurt, yet I can understand that ye cannot give it up."

Pitney faced his niece and was a trifle bemused at the soft regard she returned to him.

"I would ask two things of ye until the end of it is seen: that ye not hinder the man overly and that ye ask no further favors of me where he is concerned."

Shanna stared into the rolling sea, considering for the first time the full account of what her Uncle Pitney had said.

The deep blue of the open sea gave way to the greener hues

of the shallower water on the tenth day out of Los Camellos, and before the sun had approached its zenith in the sky, the low-lying dunes of a coastline came into view. The lookout gave a shout, and Shanna dragged out her heaviest cloak and despite the chill wind sweeping the decks of the *Hampstead*, joined the men on the quarterdeck. After all, this was Ruark's home, and she was anxious to see for herself what kind of land had borne such a man.

Ralston's spare frame shivered in his woolens and, moaning for the good soft winters of England, he sought the warmth of his cabin. The heartier Sir Gaylord stayed on the deck a whole minute longer, then with a disparaging snort he, too, retired to the shelter of the decks below. Only Pitney and Trahern stayed to watch the green-capped dunes creep nearer. Shanna wedged her way between the two men and huddled there, taking whatever shelter and warmth they could offer. At the captain's order, the ship altered course to parallel the shoreline on a southwesterly heading. Small islands were now seen forming a bastion before the main coast as the brigantine stayed well offshore.

"It seems so barren." Shanna voiced the common opinion in a disappointed tone. " 'Tis naught but sand and shrub. Where are the houses and people?" Dejectedly she watched the bleak coast slide by. She turned to find Captain Dandas standing close behind them. He smiled almost gently. " 'Twill be a good two or three days up the James River before we reach Richmond."

Sometime later they left sight of land again, but in the early afternoon a new coastline was sighted. It was near Hampton that a small lugger headed out to intercept them, and soon Captain Beauchamp's first mate, Edward Bailey, came aboard. "Captain Beauchamp left me here ter see yez safe up the river," he explained before pulling an oilskin packet from his pocket and handing the captain a sheaf of documents from it. "These be me papers and some charts o' the river." He produced a letter from the packet and presented it to Trahern. "A letter from Mister John Ruark 'tis."

Mister Bailey gave them no pause as Trahern opened the missive and began to read it. Smiling broadly the mate turned to Shanna.

"The Beauchamps be anxious to see ye, mum. Everyone named

the captain a liar when he tried ter say how ye looked. Course, he didn't come close ter doin' ye justice."

Shanna was amused at the roundabout compliment and gave the flatterer her best smile.

"I shall have a talk with Captain Beauchamp at the first opportunity," she chuckled. "I will not have my reputation so abused."

"The letter reaffirms that Captain Beauchamp has left transport for us at Richmond. Mister Ruark has gone to see it ready and will meet us there," Trahern stated and gave Shanna a sidelong regard. "I half expected the lad to leave the *Tempest* and seek his freedom." At Shanna's astounded gasp, he shrugged. "*I* would have. I'd have signed over the schooner and taken my leave of bondage." He chuckled in good humor, and his eyes twinkled at her. "I begin to wonder at his wisdom."

Shanna presented her back angrily and refused to be further baited while Mister Bailey's face was a study in blankness. He cast a narrowed eye at the sky and tested the wind.

"Mister Ruark impressed me as a man of rare honor. Why, he could be a Beauchamp and not be found wanting." As Shanna turned her head to look at him over her shoulders, he spoke to Captain Dundas. "Ye can set full sail and steer due westerly. We can make a good distance yet afore dark."

The river became subtly more wild after they passed Williamsburg, and the banks more sparsely settled. Darkness descended, and the ship was anchored for the night. Fog rolled down the river like a smothering blanket of wool, and soon the *Hampstead* was like a small universe suspended in time and space. Shanna could not have vouched that a world existed beyond the heavy grayness that swirled lazily against the sides of the ship. The rhythm of the open sea was gone, and small, erratic movements took place as the *Hampstead* strained against her cables and surged on the errant swirls and currents of the river.

Shanna fought the loneliness of her cabin. A small stove spread some warmth, but the chill of the night soaked in. She missed the nearness of Ruark beside her in bed. Pensively she went to her sea chest and withdrew the music box. He had asked her to bring it along, and it was her closest link with him at the moment. The box was heavy and sturdy, though the exterior gave little hint of it in the wealth of carvings, and it was well weighted to give resonance to the notes.

As she lifted the lid, the tinkling music filled the cabin with Ruark's presence. The song was one she had so often heard him whistling or singing. She hummed softly and closed her eyes as she remembered strong arms about her, golden eyes gazing down into hers, the smile that could taunt, anger, please or soothe, the warmth of him beside her, the rippling strength of his muscles as he labored in the sun or moved softly above her in the dark.

The last echo of the notes died in the stillness of the cabin. Shanna opened her eyes to find that an odd mistiness clouded her sight. A long sigh slipped from her as she put the music box safely away.

There are fires, and then there are fires. Shanna blew out the lantern and snuggled beneath the down comforter and blankets, and the flame that warmed her was not the one in the stove.

"A day or two, my love," she whispered in the darkness. "An eternity, yet as nothing." Her choice of words came to her with full awareness, and tears welled up within her eyes. "Aye, my love! I do love you, Ruark Beauchamp, and you shall never have cause to doubt it again."

The fog hung low on the water until the onshore breezes awoke to set it astirring. Then it drifted up to leave a pathway open beneath it, but still it clung reluctantly about the mast-heads. Mists rose in streamers from the oily surface, and, as the ship began to awaken, Shanna was among the first on deck. Had it not been unseemly of a lady, she would have urged the men to haste as they stumbled up from below and paused to rub sleep from their eyes.

After a light breakfast Shanna returned to the deck with her father, not willing to miss a thing of this new land. Both of them were enchanted with the endless variety of what they saw passing by. Trahern would stare in awe and mutter, "A merchant's dream. An untouched market."

Rich black soil lay bare on the river banks, and small, rounded hills began to thrust upward showing occasional sheer bluffs of stone above the thick forest which came to the water's edge. Houses appeared, some of red brick, large enough to speak of fortunes sheltered within. The river was still more than a mile wide, but the current had stiffened. The morning was not yet gone when the ship rounded a point and the James swept away to the larboard. Henceforth it took a more torturous course, and the crew was worked to their limits. The sails were constantly in need of trimming, letting out, or taking in, and several times it was necessary to tack across the width of the river to make headway.

Shanna was as bright and cheerful as the day was fitful and stormy. She gave herself to waving when persons were sighted along the bank and held her gay spirit even when Gaylord ventured upon the deck in a gloomy mood and bewailed the weather in these climes. But it was much to the relief of all that he shivered in his fox-trimmed cloak and soon took himself back to the nether regions of the ship.

Shanna's day was only dimmed when the night drew nigh and Mister Bailey ordered the anchors cast out, though Richmond was but some twenty-odd miles away. The man was insistent.

" 'Tis not wise to ply the river at night," he asserted. "A stray current could send ye fast aground, and snags cannot be seen. Better to wait the darkness out and be sure of arriving."

The wind keened through the rigging the next morning and drove a stinging spray with it, keeping even Shanna inside. She paced the narrow confines of her cabin, suddenly unsure of her self-control. How could she keep from flinging herself into Ruark's arms in a rush of joy? She would have to reach deep for whatever strength she could muster. A wrong step now could send him to the gallows.

The door burst open, and a gust of wind swept in, bringing Pitney with it. He rubbed his hands and warmed them at the small pot-bellied stove before he spoke.

"We're almost there. Only a mile or two more. The wind is nigh dead abeam, and the current is strong, but another half-hour should see us tying up.' '

Shanna drew a deep breath as the battle raging in her breast blossomed to a din near to bursting. Taking her emotions in a firm grip, she nodded calmly. After Pitney and her father had left for the upper decks, she followed in their wake, outwardly docile.

Crewmen were swarming in the rigging to secure the wind-wild sails as the *Hampstead* was warped closer to the landing. No sooner was the gangway opened and the plank lowered than Ruark came leaping aboard, a dripping cloak whipping about his boot tops. Runnels of rain trickled from his broad-brimmed hat as he thrust his hand toward Trahern and laughed ruefully.

" 'Tis a poor day for a welcome, but there are places where the rain is considered a good omen."

"And I trust 'twill be," Trahern rumbled and broached what had of late become his favorite subject. "By God, Mister Ruark, this land of yours is a veritable warehouse of treasure. I have never seen such untapped riches just waiting"—he chuckled with anticipating relish—"for the touch of a master merchant to bring them alive."

Ruark turned and waved his arm, bringing two carriages and a covered wagon alongside the ship before he gripped Pitney's hand in welcome.

" 'Tis much on my mind, lad," the huge man rumbled, licking his lips, "that a good tankard o' ale would warm me innards. Could it be that your colonials have a dram-shop where a man might ease a terrible thirst?"

"Aye," Ruark laughed and pointed off in the direction of the dock street. "The Ferry Port, that whitewashed building there, has a keg of England's best on tap. Tell the keeper that John Ruark will buy the first."

Pitney left with a haste that gave credence to his plea and made Gaylord step quickly from the plank, else be brushed aside onto the cobbled jetty. The knight glared haughtily at the broad back but Pitney gave no pause or notice. Gaylord continued on his way toward the shipping office to claim the baggage he had sent ahead on the English frigate.

Ralston had also departed the ship, and for a moment Ruark watched as the thin agent stalked across the pier, the hem of his cloak whipping about his knobby calves.

Not so much as a glance had Ruark given Shanna, who waited demurely several paces behind her father. But now he faced her and his eyes told her everything. Her hand trembled as it hid itself in the encompassing warmth of his.

"Shanna—Madam Beauchamp." His voice was only slightly strained and husky. "You have provided the brightest moment in my day." As she started, his lips moved further in soundless vow. "I love you."

The ache in Shanna's throat was almost unbearable as she gave him a casual smile and replied, "Mister John Ruark, I have missed your wit and humor at the table, to say naught of your clever comments and your dancing. Have you been to any festivities of late? Perhaps some colonial lady has caught your eye."

She bent him a cool, questioning gaze, and Ruark laughed lightly.

"You know my heart is committed, and Dame Fortune has decreed that I should find no other as fair."

He watched the slow flush of pleasure spread over her face. He had not released her hand and now tucked it beneath his arm as he cast a wry glance toward the heavens.

"There is an ancient oriental saying about the wisdom of standing in the rain," Ruark mused aloud. "If you will allow me, Madam Beauchamp, I will escort you and your father to a place where you might have a cup of tea while the coaches are loaded."

Trahern looked almost longingly toward Pitney's stalwart back in time to see him disappear through the doorway of the tavern. Heaving a sigh, he gestured with his hand.

"Lead on, Mister Ruark. I suppose a father has some duties toward his offspring that cannot be avoided." He paused in reflection then added ruefully, "Still, there are times when I wish the lass would have been born to a pair of breeches."

Ruark was exceedingly glad she hadn't been, but did not offer any answering comment. Shanna, however, felt the heat of his eyes upon her, and they warmed her more than any verbal reassurance.

Nearly an hour later the driver of the first coach came to tell Ruark that all was ready and that they could be on their way whenever it pleased the squire.

"I'll fetch Pitney," Ruark offered, rising to his feet. He fished in his purse for coin. "I did say I'd buy the first."

The tavern was a noisy place nearly bursting at the seams with seagoing men and common laborers. It was here in the midst of the bedlam that Pitney quietly quaffed his ale, leaning against the bar beside a redhaired man who appeared very emphatic about whatever it was they were discussing. Ruark could not hear above the din, but the man shook his head, hammered the bar with his fist, and jabbed a finger at his companion's chest.

"Nay, I'll not speak me piece now," Ruark overheard, as he inched his way between the brawny chests of several tars who were imbibing close by. "I've got to find the mon meself and know for sure he's the same and only one. Then I'll have it out with ye and the rest who need to know. I'll not be putting a noose about me own neck to save the hide o' a mon I ne'er met."

Ruark grabbed Pitney's arm in a hearty greeting and slapped his coins down on the bar. "Keeper, give this man another to see him through the day and one for his friend besides."

"None fer me," the Scotsman declined, shaking his head. "I've got to get back to me work on the docks."

"Before ye go, Jamie, me friend, I would have ye meet a good man. This is John Ruark," Pitney rasped with a twisted smile. "Or have the two of ye met before?"

Ruark frowned. Now that he looked at the man closely, there was something oddly familiar about him. But Jamie quickly got to his feet and avoided Ruark's gaze.

"Should I know him?" Ruark asked.

"Aye, but as long as I know where to find him, I'll let it go for now." Pitney sipped the ale and lifted the mug in thanks to Ruark. "A good brew. Have one for yerself, laddie. It'll stiffen yer spine for the ride home."

Warily Ruark studied him. "From the way you talk, I would say you've had enough for the two of us."

With a roar of mirth the hefty man clapped Ruark on the back. "Drink up, John Ruark. Ye'll be needing a bracer to keep yer mind off that fine filly ye wed."

When Ruark returned to the coaches, Shanna was already seated in the first one, and as Pitney joined Trahern on the dock, Ruark adjusted Attila's saddle so that he could gaze at the one he most adored.

"Will you be riding, Mister Ruark?" Shanna asked quietly, watching him.

"Aye, madam. With this rain I'll have to check the roads ahead to see if they're fit."

Shanna leaned back against the cushioned seat and drew a thick fur over her lap. A smile of contentment slowly took possession of her face. At least he wouldn't be far.

The interior of the carriage was not richly appointed, but rather gave an air of sturdiness and homey roominess. Piles of fur robes almost filled the seats, and a small iron warming pan was on the floor, giving off a welcome heat against her feet.

Gaylord returned, and it was with some amazement that Ruark watched him assuring the safety of several large trunks into the wagon.

"Sir Gaylord will be traveling with us?" Ruark questioned Trahern.

"Aye," the squire grunted. " 'Tis to our discomfort that he has chosen to present his plans and need to the Beauchamps. And by the amount of baggage he fetched from the warehouse, he'll be their guest for some time."

Pitney chuckled and nudged Trahern with his elbow. "At least the good knight will not be your guest. Someone else will have to feed him."

Ruark snorted and rubbed the back of his hand against his chin. "What makes you dislike these Beauchamps so much?"

Pitney guffawed aloud at the offhanded remark, drawing a chuckle from Trahern.

"If you will take to the carriage, sir," Ruark said, "I shall see that your chests are properly loaded beneath Sir Gaylord's baggage. I've an idea that the Beauchamps should have sent two wagons along. But if all is right, we can be on our way."

Trahern nodded, only too eager to get out of the rain, and Ruark walked back to the last wagon. As he was returning, Ralston paused with one foot on the step of the second carriage and met his gaze with cool contempt; then he gave a shrug and entered. Delaying only long enough to comment derisively on the comfort of Pitney's elbow, Gaylord followed Ralston into the coach.

Ruark tied Jezebel to the rear of Trahern's coach and tossed Shanna's sidesaddle into the covered wagon. When he leaned into the carriage, he saw Orlan examining one of the fur robes, blowing on it as he tested its richness and depth.

"Magnificent!" Orlan murmured. "John Ruark, I could not be more comfortable. Would that I were always served with such foresight. Here I am surrounded by a small fortune, and the Beauchamps use them as lap robes. Remarkable!"

"We're ready, sir. Shall I give the signal?"

At the man's nod, Ruark glanced at Shanna and touched the brim of his hat before he withdrew and closed the door. He stood back and waved his arm. A sharp whistle sounded from the driver as he shook out the reins and cracked his whip over the lead team's head. The coaches moved forward and then lurched as they climbed the lane from the riverside. The drum of the horses' hooves settled into a rhythm as they loped easily through the streets of the small settlement of Richmond.

They traveled for some distance past open fields, before coming to a junction, where they swung off into a narrower track marked by a large tree with three bold cuts upon its trunk.

"Three Chopt Road," Ruark called over the rattle of hooves and the whirl of carriage wheels, and at Trahern's nod, he added, "At the next crossroads we'll stop at the tavern for a bite to eat."

"Good man, that John Ruark," Trahern rumbled in satisfaction as he settled himself back against the seat. "He's seen to our every comfort."

Thick forests took over the land. The way was cleared wide to allow easy passage, but where the trees began, the growth was dense; even a man on foot would have found it nearly impassable. True to Ruark's word, when the caravan came upon another crossing, the drivers swung the carriages from the road and hauled up before a sprawling, many-gabled structure which a weather-beaten sign proclaimed as the Short Pump Tavern. A cheery-faced matron greeted them as the Beauchamp guests, and a table was swept clean and spread with a fresh cloth. No special place was made for Gaylord and with reluctance he joined Trahern, testily dusting the bench with his gloves before sitting. The three drivers casually took places at the far end of the table and gave no more than passing note of the knight's disdainful stare of disapproval. Mugs of warm spiced cider were passed around. Shanna sipped hers with only meager interest as she wondered what delayed Ruark. Her question was answered shortly when he came in carrying an odd musket nearly as tall as he, which he leaned beside the door. Coming to the table, he placed before Pitney the two huge horse pistols which once had threatened him.

"I found these in your sea chest," he explained to the inquiry written on Pitney's broad face.

Doffing a beaver-skin coat which he had taken from the wagon, Ruark spread it to dry in front of the stone hearth, displaying a brace of pistols in his belt. Gaylord found this too much to bear. He shot to his feet in outrage.

"Weapons for a bondsman!" In exasperation he faced Trahern. "Really, squire, I must protest. You treat this bondsman more like a blooded lord."

Sipping his cider, Trahern only shrugged. "If he protects your hide, what difference does it make to you?"

"Protects my hide? The knave'll see it bored through!" Gaylord flung out a finger to Ruark. "You! By what right do you bear arms?"

"By no one's right but my own, of course," Ruark replied calmly. As the knight drew himself up in victorious arrogance, Ruark continued chidingly, as if he lectured a willful child. "There are beasts, large, bold and of a dangerous bent, and highwaymen are not unknown, though rare. Then there are those heathen savages you spoke of." Ruark smiled sardonically. "I saw no one else rushing to the fore to protect the ladies." He grinned into the reddening face of the other. "But rest assured, Sir Gaylord, should you find such a man, I would be much relieved to surrender my arms to him."

Ruark waited while Sir Gaylord sputtered into silence, and when he gave no further suggestions, Ruark took a seat in a space that had strangely opened between Shanna and her father.

The innkeeper set a steaming mug before him and the mistress of the house brought a huge kettle of stew and began filling plates. A young lad fetched a wooden platter piled high with golden loaves of bread and bracketed with dishes of mounded butter. Small crocks of honey and preserves were set out, and soon the meal was well entered with much enthusiasm by the hungry travelers. Shanna found her appetite more than it had been in weeks, and Trahern met each new taste with rich praise until the matron blushed her thanks. When he rose to leave, she pressed into his hands a gift of her own best plum pudding to eat along the way.

As Ruark took up his hat and coat, Ralston approached the door where he lifted the long rifle and ran his hand over the smooth, oiled stock of curly maple that bore an engraved brass plate.

" 'Tis a fine weapon you have here, Mister Ruark," he commented when the younger man came to fetch it. "A costly one. Where did you get it?"

Ruark looked down the barrel toward the two hawkish eyes sighting him, and his own narrowed. Shanna held her breath, for the rifle was pointed straight at Ruark's head, and the thin fingers caressed the trigger as if Ralston wished the gun were cocked.

"I must warn you now if you're not aware of it," Ruark casually gestured to the piece. " 'Tis loaded."

Ralston smiled lazily. "Naturally."

"Mister Ralston!" Orlan Trahern barked. "Put that damn thing down before you blow your own fool head off."

At the command Ralston's smile faded, and reluctantly he relented. Ruark caught the rifle from him and beneath the cold stare of the other man, drew a soft cloth over the stock and shiny plate, carefully wiping away the finger smudges. The insult was small but direct. Whirling on his heels, the thin man stalked out of the tavern, slamming the door behind him.

Three Chopt Road was long, in some places narrow, in others wide. Always the countryside varied. They trailed beneath high granite bluffs and teetered along rock-strewn paths on the brink of cliffs. The road plunged through valleys and jolted over logs laid to cover soft bottoms. In the late afternoon they passed a rare plantation and a few smaller farms with log cabins. A hand-hewn sign appeared by the roadside proclaiming a muddy crossing to be the Middle Valley Post Road. A small community blossomed here and beyond was a large house where a simple shingle swung in front, identifying the place as "Inn."

The road-weary group were mostly silent over the meal of venison. They were content just to sit on a good, sound surface without being jarred or bumped or jostled, and conversation died away almost as soon as it was born.

"We've only three rooms to see you through the night," the

keeper explained. "The men will have to share two and the women the other."

Gaylord glanced up from his plate and pointed to Ruark with his fork. "He can stay out in the stables with the drivers. That should leave Mister Ralston and myself in one and Squire Trahern and Mister Pitney in the other."

Trahern's scowl gathered as the knight spoke, and the innkeeper shrugged apologetically. "I've no more rooms, but there's an old cabin out back that no one uses. Someone might sleep there."

Ruark readily volunteered. Lifting his cup to his lips, he met Shanna's gaze over it. Then he rose, setting down the mug and swinging up his coat. "I'll see to Madam Beauchamp's horses, squire. I would suggest an early bed as we'll see a good day's travel on the morrow, and it will be tiring enough." He clamped the hat on. Turning, he leisurely sauntered across the common room to the door. "Good night."

✠ Chapter 25 ✠

SHANNA chafed beside the snoring Hergus and wondered at the time. No noise of movement or voices came from below or from the rooms down the hall, but she had no way of making sure that everyone was asleep.

"Hergus," she whispered and to her satisfaction received no reply. It was not likely she could test her father or Pitney by the same method. But another half hour, she guessed, might see them all in a good, sound slumber.

Cautiously Shanna rose from the bed and went to the chair where Hergus had laid open her case. A woolen cloak lay atop the one side, and in the dancing firelight she wrapped it around her and then pushed her feet into a snug pair of slippers. Rain still trickled down against the windowpanes, and the wind moaned drearily around the eaves. A cold, wet night, but it would serve her purpose well.

The moments dragged, and Shanna slipped from the room, crept down the stairs, fled across the common room and was out. Free! Her feet splashed through cold puddles as she ran, but her heart had taken flight.

The cabin was a dark shape beneath great overhanging trees, some distance from the inn. Timidly Shanna rapped on the rough wood of the door. Beneath her touch it creaked slowly open. No sound of greeting came from within, and Shanna pushed the door wider. Ruark was nowhere to be seen, though a fire hissed and crackled on the hearth, casting its warm flickering light upon the walls of chinked logs and the sparse and simple, rough-hewn furnishings. As the cabin was the only one behind the tavern, there was no doubt this was the one the keeper had spoken of. The wind and rain pelted Shanna's back and billowed her woolen cloak forward as if to urge her further into the shelter. Its chill breath swept between the folds, penetrating the thin, delicately made batiste nightgown she wore beneath, and with its icy touch made the fire an irresistible lure. Gathering the wrap tighter about her shivering body, Shanna stepped within and turned to shut the door. She gasped as a dark shadow loomed before her. But the fear was short-lived, for the face beneath the dripping brim was the one she sought and welcomed.

"I hoped you would come," Ruark said huskily. He came forward into the light, and his heel caught the door, slamming it shut behind him. The bolt dropped in place of its own, barring them against any intrusion. He tossed a large bundle he carried down before the fire, leaned his rifle beside the door, and sailed his hat off onto the wooden planks of the table.

"Good lord, I missed you," he rasped and took her hard against him, heedless of the icy rain that clung to their garments. His mouth came down like the plummeting attack of a bird of prey and seized hers in a fierce, crushing, impassioned kiss. Shanna clung to him as the only solid thing in her reeling world. Their faces were cold from the wind, but their kiss flamed with the stirring heat of desire. Her cloak slid to her feet, and she was clasped tight against his damp furry coat, but she scarcely felt the chill that soaked through her gown.

"I love you," she whispered against his lips, and tears of gladness sparkled in her eyes as he raised his head to stare down at her. His hands rose to hold her face as he searched its depth for truth. And Shanna repeated the words, with her heart, with her eyes, with all the feeling of a woman in love. "Oh, Ruark, I love you."

Laughing with ebullient joy, he snatched her high, almost upon his shoulders, and spun her about until the sounds of their mirth mingled in a heady swirl. Carrying her closer to the fire, Ruark stood her there, smiling down at her. Very gently he reached out a hand to touch her cheek, and she caressed it with her own, pressing a kiss into his palm. In the dampened gown Shanna shivered, both from the cold and the overwhelming, near-to-bursting sense of contentment that welled up inside her.

"Here, we'll warm you. Wait a moment."

Ruark stood back, and her eyes followed him as if they were fed by the mere sight of him. His clothes were strange to her—buckskin breeches that fit closely to the hard, muscular leanness of his thighs and a coat of beaver fur whereon bejeweled droplets clung; in the twinkling firelight, the droplets gleamed like a thousand rubied eyes. He was more the beast, the lean hunting cat, and she felt both pride and fear. This was his land, and he was free. No man would ever tame him, nor would she in her own mind ever name him slave again. She considered the question her father had started and knew that if Ruark fled to seek his freedom, she would follow wherever he led.

With a tug at the ties, he shrugged the heavy coat from his shoulders and spread it around hers. Shanna snuggled beneath the beaver, still warm from his body, and watched as he added small sticks to the fire until it blazed high. Her gaze roamed the room in wonder, passing in question over the rope and wood frame of a bed that might have once served the occupants of the cottage, but not even a feather tick was in evidence.

Ruark saw where her eyes paused, and his own sparkled. "Have no fear, my love. I have been about this night to see that your comfort is well served."

Shanna laughed and drew the coat close about her as if demure. "Beast! Now that I am trapped in your lair, I fear I shall find myself devoured for a tidbit."

"Devoured?" Ruark pulled the tight, dark linen shirt over his head, and Shanna's breath caught in her throat as his naked torso stretched before her in the shifting light.

"Nay, not devoured, love." He reached out and traced a long tress where it curled over her shoulder. "This is the magic cup filled for lovers at the table of the gods. The more often it is tasted, the richer the nectar. Wealthy kings have beggared themselves trying to draw the limits of this treasure. This is a thing that must be shared, but it can never be devoured in selfish greed."

Shanna touched his arm, her eyes caressing his face in fond possession. "I am nothing but selfish with you, my darling."

Ruark's mouth pressed lightly upon her lips. "And 'tis so with me, lovely Shanna."

Kneeling, he plucked at the ties on the bundle and then straightened, kicking the lot. It spilled wide open, blossoming like some weird, unearthly flower. A pallet formed of rich, luxuriant furs—glossy reds, tawny golds, thick dense roans and blacks, nothing but the choicest of them all.

"Where—"

" 'Tis mine," Ruark said in answer to her unfinished question. He gestured casually. "I fetched it from the wagon."

"But how came you to have them? And those clothes you're wearing. They're yours, aren't they? Made for you—the fit—"

"Aye, 'tis so." He paused to grin up at her, kneeling on one leg and resting his arm across the other thigh. "My family learned I would be passing here, and they sent them, 'tis all."

"Your family?" Shanna moved a space closer.

"Shortly, love," Ruark smiled, "and I will take you to them."

Again he was crouched on the furs, spreading them, smoothing them, setting one aside for cover. In that instant Shanna's vision of a savage formed in her mind and he was it, half-naked, gold and bronze before the fire, hair pulled back to a knot at his nape. Those who thought they could bring this man to heel were fools, whether Gaylord, Ralston, or even her father.

Ruark came to stand before her, a red- and black-hued shape, dark as any savage, and the wild beating of her heart gave evidence of the fact that this new glimpse of Ruark Beauchamp excited her beyond anything she had ever known.

The heavy coat was taken away, and his fingers were at the ties of her gown, slipping it from her shoulders. Shanna closed her eyes in ecstasy as his hands slowly followed its descent, cupping her trembling breasts and stroking her smooth velvet hips. In the warm, wavering glow of the fire, her skin shone with a golden luster, shadowed and highlighted, even lovelier than he could remember. There was a radiance about her he had never noticed before, something different, but he could not name it.

"How lovely you are," he breathed, almost in reverence. "I

could not have believed it, but you have grown even more beautiful. What sorcery has love performed?"

Shanna smiled softly into his eyes. "No sorcery, my love. Your eyes deceive you. You have fasted long and would relish plain porridge for a dainty dish."

"Eh, no plain porridge this," he said thickly and bore her down to the furry pallet. Ruark's hands shook as he set aside his own garments. Then he gathered her close. Her soft breasts were a brand against his chest, a dream fulfilled, a release from the longing torture of the sea voyage. Her silken thighs opened to his questing hand, and his wandering caresses brought soft, breathless cries of trembling joy. His kisses came upon her mouth, warm, devouring, fierce with love and passion, then traced lower to spread their heat over her quivering breasts, which thrust forward eagerly in anticipation. Shanna closed her eyes as the bliss of his greedy mouth swept her every nerve with intense excitement. She felt the bold urgency of him against her, and then he was a flame within her, consuming, searing, setting fire to her until the rippling, molten waves flooded her with almost unbearable pleasure. She heard his harsh breathing in her ear, the hoarse, whispered words of love. His heart beat wildly against her naked breast, and beneath her hands the hard muscles of his back tensed and flexed with manly vigor. Then they were caught together in a shimmering, surging, swelling tide of rapture.

The rain beat upon the oiled skin stretched across the windows, and the wind howled like a banshee in the night, but in the aftermath of their own storm, Shanna and Ruark lay peacefully content. They faced the hearth, her back pressed against the solid bulwark of his chest, his knees tucked behind hers, as they watched rekindled flames eagerly lapping at the flanks of a log. Their voices were hushed and lazy, yet seemed to echo in the silence of the cabin. Their hands raised before the shifting, flickering fire, and they gently entwined slender fingers in a knot of love. Ruark's lips nibbled at the soft flesh of her shoulder and sank warmly against her creamy throat, then paused to taste an ear lobe.

"I'll build you a mansion," he breathed.

Shanna laughed. "This cabin will do—if you are here with me." She wiggled onto her back so she could look up into those soft, begilded eyes and read the gentle love that smiled down upon her. "Stay with me always. Never leave me."

"Nay, love. Never again. I love you."

The corners of her mouth curved softly. "And I you."

Ruark smoothed her tumbled hair across his arm and nuzzled his face into the fragrant curls, breathing in the sweet scent of her.

"I think I've loved you forever," Shanna confessed in wonder. "When the scales of blindness were lifted from my eyes, I saw you not as a dragon, but as the one I would have chosen."

"You did choose me, remember?" Ruark grinned.

Shanna giggled and snuggled closer against him. "Aye, that I did." Then in sudden seriousness she murmured, "You know the way here as if you followed the trail before. Where is your home?"

Ruark stretched lazily, flexing a bronzed arm in the air. "Wherever you are."

Shanna's eyes were soft with love as she gazed at him. "And will our home be like this?"

"A cabin in the wilderness?" He smiled and whispered, "Months on end alone together? Would you fret upon that, my love?"

Like an eager child Shanna shook her head. "Oh, nay, but never leave me."

Beneath his searching hand, she lay soft and pliant, meeting his kisses with gentle ardor.

"Would I leave my own heart, the very breath of my life?" Ruark asked hoarsely.

"And what of children?" she whispered.

"We'll have a dozen," Ruark assured her. "Give or take a score."

Shanna laughed. "Is it enough to begin with one?"

"Oh, one or two." His caresses grew bolder. "Whatever the market bears."

"But of this one—would you be amiss if we had a girl?"

Ruark paused and the silence grew—and grew. Very gently he drew back the cover, revealing her body to the warm light of the fire, touching her taut breasts and the smooth belly.

"That is what is different," he smiled.

"Are you sorry?" she breathed, watching his face.

"Nay!" He grinned wide, covering her with the fur again. "How long?"

"Were I to guess," Shanna drew a breath, "I would say the pirate's isle."

Ruark chuckled suddenly. "More good comes from that with every passing day." He leaned nearer and said soberly, "I need you, Shanna, love." He kissed her softly. "I want you, Shanna, love. I love you, Shanna."

He was caressing, searching, and again their passions bloomed. The fire reddened, the coals grew dark, and the long night passed with a swiftness little noted.

It was still dark when Ruark escorted Shanna back to the inn, but the first rays of the dawning sun were slipping further up on the horizon. All was still within the common room. A hound lazily rose from the cold hearth and sought a softer place on a braided rag rug, giving them no more than a disinterested glance. They eased their way up the stairs and parted at the chamber door with a last, fierce kiss that would have to suffice the day long.

Moments fled, and it was quiet again. Then the door at the end of the hall opened wider, and Ralston strode out of the room he shared with Gaylord, his storklike frame clothed in a long robe. Pausing before Shanna's door, he smirked thoughtfully to himself and tapped his cheek.

"Madam John Ruark it might be, milady," he mused derisively. "But soon you will feel the prick of being a widow again. This I vow."

The rain had cleared, and the sun had made its debut with a frosty nip that stung one's cheeks and nose. Shanna waited with Ruark in the shelter of the doorway as the carriages were hitched and brought about. Her father and Pitney were still inside the tavern, finishing the last of their coffee, while Gaylord stalked in circles a short distance away from the young couple in an effort to drive away the cold. Shanna's hands were clasped deep in her muff, and she huddled in the fur-lined velvet cloak. Though she knew it would be a long day before they arrived at the Beauchamps, she had taken special care with her appearance. The royal blue velvet gown with its frothing of old lace at the throat did her uncommon beauty full credit. Her hair, dressed high beneath the deep hood of the blue cloak, gave her an air of dignity and sereneness, and as Ruark's eyes feasted upon her, he could only wonder at the variety of women he had glimpsed in this small, trim form, from bold, seductive temptress to the quiet, cool, graceful lady she now portrayed.

Sneering, Ralston passed them. He was less than cautious of Shanna this chilly morn as he questioned offhandedly, "Did you sleep well, madam?"

Shanna did not pause. She smiled sweetly. "Indeed I did, sir. And you?"

He tapped his whip against his boot. "Restless most of the night."

Without further comment Ralston walked away to where Gaylord chafed and grumbled, leaving the two to stare after him in bemusement.

"What do you suppose he meant by that?" Shanna asked, looking up at Ruark.

"That, my love, only he knows for sure," Ruark replied, staring at the man from under his brows.

After Trahern seated himself in the coach, Pitney climbed in and took a place beside the portly squire, drawing a raised eyebrow from Trahern, who realized that the girth of the two could have been more evenly distributed. Orlan tapped the knee of his stalwart companion and spoke his piece.

"Watch your flapping wings, my good man. I can well imagine the bruises you put upon Sir Gaylord's ribs, and I'll have none of the same."

The seating arrangement left Shanna to be handed in by Ruark. Gaylord, seeing the lass alone on the seat, made bold to join her, brushing the bondsman aside and setting his foot on the step to climb in, but Trahern's staff suddenly barred the way.

"Would you mind riding in the other coach?" the squire requested, "I would like a word with my bondsman."

The knight straightened himself arrogantly. "If you insist, sir."

Trahern nodded once and gave a small smile. "I do."

Once upon the road, the conversation was mostly about the lands they passed and the wealth of the countryside. The relentless motion combined with the brevity of sleep in the night past made Shanna drowsy. Her eyelids sagged, and with a stifled yawn she yielded to slumber, bracing herself back against the cushion, but it was a natural place in sleep to rest her head on her husband's shoulder, and soon she was snuggled close, her arm flung across his hips. Ruark welcomed her nestling weight, but under that more burdensome one of Trahern's stare, he shifted uncomfortably.

"Did you say you had something to discuss with me, sir?" he questioned, clearing his throat.

Trahern pursed his lips thoughtfully, regarding the sleeping face of his daughter. "In actuality little enough, but there was much I would rather not have discussed with Gaylord." He paused as Ruark nodded and then inquired, "You seem distressed, Mister Ruark. Is she heavy?"

"No, sir," Ruark replied slowly. A smile twisted his lips. " 'Tis just that I have never held a woman with her father across from me before."

"Relax, Mister Ruark," Trahern chuckled. "As long as it goes no further, I will deem it your kindness to be my daughter's pillow."

Pitney lowered his tricorn upon his brow and peered at the younger man from beneath it, which lent considerably to Ruark's unease. He began to sense the huge fellow knew more about them than either he or Shanna had ever offered.

At the noon hour they stopped alongside the road and feasted upon a box lunch packed at the tavern. Soon after, they resumed the journey. The teams labored up a long incline from the valley floor and the rolling foothills and green forest were left behind. Here the trees bore little hint of green but rather were garbed in a splendorous riot of color and only an occasional sheltered oak still raised its arms in summer color, or a rare tall pine or spruce.

Finally all the coaches stood in Rockfish Gap. A magnificent panorama spread out beneath them in all directions. The mountains ranged north and south, their brilliant autumn colors dimmed by the bluish haze that clung to the peaks. The sheer beauty of the view took one's breath away. Shanna stared in awe of the countryside, which was gilded with dark coppery hues and where the late afternoon sun touched, bright golds and brass. Even the memory of soft, misty evenings in Paris or the lush, tended fields of England dimmed in contrast with this wild untamed kaleidoscope of color before her. She respected the soft pride that rode in Ruark's voice as he drew their attention here or there. When she would turn, she would find him watching her closely, almost expectantly, as if he waited for some reaction from her. Then, at her wondering look, he would just smile while his eyes glowed with intimate warmth.

"The rains may have washed out or softened some of the roads," he explained as Trahern climbed into the coach again. "I'll ride on ahead and leave sign for the drivers. They know the way and from here 'tis mostly downhill. I'll either join you again or be waiting."

Tipping his hat, he strode away without pausing for a reply. A quick thud of hooves rang out, and he was gone.

The drivers shook out their reins, clucked to the teams, and the coaches began to move again. A quick series of sharp bends, and they left the ridge to ease out across a low shoulder, then traveled southward as the way straightened out in a slow curve around the hip of a mountain. They crossed a narrow trail where a small tavern and a trading post squatted beside the road. Further on, a wider road crossed, and here the coaches slowed to make the turn, now heading northward along the mountains. The horses galloped loose in the traces as if the coach were only a light weight behind them. The brake shoes whined as the coachmen rode with one foot on the long brake lever and slowed the headlong plunge as the hard-packed road dipped ever lower into the valley.

Wide fields began to show on the left where the valley fell away. Shanna's heart rose in her throat as the carriage dipped and careened downward almost on the horses' heels, and now the fields stretched out on either side. Still the valley floor rolled with hills and vales, a copse of woodland here and a broad field there.

Suddenly a horse was dashing alongside them, and Shanna recognized the gray of Attila. The coachman talked and sang to his team, slowing the carriage to a halt. As Trahern leaned out the window, Ruark reined Attila close.

"We're almost to the Beauchamps', sir. Only a short distance further. I was wondering if Madam Beauchamp would care to ride the rest of the way on horseback."

Trahern turned to ask his daughter, but Shanna was already pulling on her gloves. She leaned forward from the door, and Ruark swept her from it, onto Jezebel's back. Soon the caravan was rushing on. The two riders led the way, and, as Pitney could see from his window, they drew ever further ahead.

"The vigor of youth," Trahern sighed and leaned back, bracing his feet upon the opposite seat.

Pitney raised his jug of ale in silent salute. "Best arrive soon," he mumbled. "There's only a wee drop left."

The way was open and the sun warm. The pair left sight of the coaches and were on their own. Where the trail was smooth, they ran far apace, but as the way roughened, they had to slow their mounts to an easy trot. Surreptitiously, Shanna gazed at Ruark's profile. He seemed absorbed in the countryside and studied it as they passed. He rode easily and looked both the part of a gentleman and a woodsman in the soft buckskin breeches and fitted waistcoat, his white linen shirt and tied stock. He was handsome, and her eyes glowed with love and pride as she watched him.

The Beauchamps' red brick mansion rose immense and tall between oak trees whose trunks would have taken three men to girdle. Shanna stared in amazement, for it was one of the largest homes they had seen since landing. There were wings jutting out on either side, and the main portion had a roof steep and dormered, bracketed with tall chimneys. As they neared the house, excited cries came from within, and in a moment the front door burst open, and a young woman hurried out onto the small portico.

"Mamma! Here they come!"

A flood of people swarmed out at the urging, and as Ruark lifted Shanna down from Jezebel's back, Nathanial descended the steps and came forward to take Shanna's hand and lead her away from Ruark.

An older couple had come to stand on the lawn and beside them stood a tall, dark-haired woman and a younger boy whose grin nearly split his face.

"My father and mother," Nathanial announced as he brought Shanna before the elders. "George and Amelia Beauchamp."

Shanna sank into a respectful curtsy, and as she straightened, the older man smiled down at her, looking her over carefully through wire-rimmed spectacles. A handsome man he was, tall, lean, black of hair, and broad of shoulders, ready with a quick smile.

"So this is Shanna." There was a note of firmness in the gentle drawl of his deep voice. He nodded in approval. "A pretty lass she is. Aye, we'll claim her as a Beauchamp."

The older woman, with brown eyes and gray-streaked auburn hair, was more reserved and considered Shanna for a long, uncertain moment before she gave a quick, worried glance at her eldest son. As if with decision, she sighed and took the girl's hand in both her own.

"Shanna. What a beautiful name." She searched the sea-green eyes and finally managed a smile. "We've much to talk about, my dear."

Shanna puzzled at the woman's manner, but she had little time to muse upon it, for Nathanial drew the tall, dark-haired woman to his side.

"My wife, Charlotte, the vixen!" he grinned, slipping an arm about her narrow waist to hug her close. "You'll meet our brood of children later."

Charlotte laughed and extended her slender hands toward Shanna. "I fear the name Madam Beauchamp will draw too much attention here—or none as the case may be. May we call you Shanna?"

"Of course." Shanna was completely taken with the easy friendliness of the woman and accepted the feeling as mutual as the slender fingers squeezed her own.

"Jeremiah Beauchamp." Nathanial gestured to the grinning lad. "My youngest brother. At seven-and-ten, he's only just now appreciating the fairer gender, so don't mind if he gawks a bit. You're the prettiest thing he's seen in a long while."

A dark blush stained the youth's face but still the grin remained. Like his father, he was tall and reedy but bore the auburn hair and brown eyes of his mother.

" 'Tis a pleasure, Jeremiah," Shanna murmured sweetly, offering her hand.

"And this is my sister, Gabrielle." Nathanial gently chucked the chin of the girl who had rushed out, and she bobbed vivaciously. "You'll meet her twin, Garland, later."

"I think you're just too beautiful for words," Gabrielle exclaimed. "Have you really been to Paris? Garland said it must be an evil place. How do you manage to make your hair stay like that? Mine would be down around my shoulders by mid-morning."

Shanna responded with gay laughter and spread her hands at the rush of questions.

"Gabrielle!" Amelia placed an affectionate arm about the girl. "Let Shanna at least catch her breath."

"Our son has been remiss in his duties," George said. "He should have brought you to us long ago." His face took on a sparkle of humor. "Welcome to The Oaks, Shanna."

Just then, the two mud-splattered and begrimed coaches careened into the lane and skidded to a stop before the manor. The steeds, sensing an end to the journey and smelling the pastures of home, had outdistanced the heavier wagon, which was nowhere in sight. Ruark threw down the steps of the first and opened the door. Trahern heaved himself from his seat and laboriously climbed down, as Nathanial came forward to greet him. Pitney had also descended and renewed his acquaintance when Sir Gaylord joined the group.

"Gaylord Billingsham," he named himself and almost daintily extended his hand. "Knight of the realm and gentleman of the court. I sent you a letter some months ago when I learned Squire Trahern would be traveling here."

"Aye, I remember," Nathanial responded. "But 'tis no time to speak of business. Let us see to the amenities."

Guiding the gentlemen to his parents, Nathanial began the introductions. It was not felt by anyone but the knight when he was presented last, or at least nearly so, for Ralston was the only one who followed him.

The sun had touched the hilltop to the west, and the day was growing darker. It was the senior Madam Beauchamp who put an end to the conversations that were beginning on the lawn.

"Good sire and ladies," she chided. "'Tis unseemly that we should take a chill when a fine, warm house is close at hand. Come." She took her husband's arm and caught Shanna's with her other. "We shall have a table set after a while. The gentlemen would no doubt enjoy a libation before we eat, and I, for one, am cold."

Amelia led them all within, and soon the men were enjoying well-aged brandy. A light sherry sparkled in Shanna's glass, but she took care only to sip a tiny bit, for since Gaitlier's wedding her stomach had formed a slight aversion to intoxicants. Her eyes smiled at Ruark, who had trailed along and stood watching from just inside the door.

Gabrielle sidled close to Nathanial and nudged him with her elbow then inclined her head toward Ruark. "Who's that?"

"Oh, of course." Nathanial seemed embarrassed for a moment. "This is—ah—John Ruark, another associate of Squire Trahern."

"Oh, the bondslave!" Gabrielle spoke over her shoulder with childlike innocence. "Mama? Should he be in the house?"

Shanna held her breath in shock. Would the Beauchamps take offense? She had not even considered it.

Gaylord did not miss the exchange. "A bright young lass, quick to grasp the nuances of class. She would go far at court." He caught Shanna's cold glare but smirked at his own cleverness.

"Hush, Gabrielle," Amelia Beauchamp sternly commanded.

The young woman stared boldly at Ruark, who returned her regard with a frown that hinted of violent thoughts. Gabrielle's voice came just loud enough to be heard as she spoke aside to Nathanial.

"How could anyone be so witless as to let themselves be sold for money?"

Gaylord was, as usual, ready with an explanation. "A lower class of people, young lady, unable to handle the simplest affairs of life."

Tense silence greeted his observation before the eldest Madam Beauchamp reproached her offspring.

"Gabrielle! Hush your prattle! Mister Ruark cannot help what he is."

Gabrielle wrinkled her nose in distaste. "Well, anyway, I wouldn't want a bondsman for *my* husband."

"Gabby!" George Beauchamp spoke softly but with such a tone as to brook no disobedience. "Mind your mother. 'Tis not Christian to bait the less fortunate."

"Yes, father," Gabrielle meekly complied.

Shanna caught a glimpse of Pitney laughing into his cup and mused in sudden rancor, "For an uncle he's not too bright. He has sipped himself into a stupor with his jug of ale and guffaws like a mindless idiot while they poke fun at Ruark."

But when she glanced at her husband, Shanna grew puzzled, for he seemed relaxed and not at all angry as his gaze followed the young woman, Gabby. Indeed, there was something akin to pleasure in his face until Gabrielle turned and, catching his attention on her, flashed him a smile of pure innocence. His eyes narrowed threateningly.

Setting her glass aside, Shanna found Gabrielle's deep brown eyes upon her and wondered at the sudden worried frown that marked the young woman's brow.

"Squire Trahern was kind enough to the man," Gaylord continued imperiously. "Took Mister Ruark into his own house and treated him like a member of the family. Too good for him, I say. The slaves' quarters will do for him. No need to trouble you good people further with the likes of him."

"'Tis no room there," Amelia snapped. As her husband dropped an arm about her shoulders, she continued in a softer tone, "He can stay in the house."

"As I've said before, the chap is fond of horses." Leisurely the knight took a pinch of snuff. "Let him make his bed with them."

"I'll not—" Amelia began in a burst of heated ire, but Ruark interrupted.

"I beg your pardon, madam, but I'd just as soon sleep there, if you have no objection." He leaned back against the door frame and folded his arms as Gaylord glared at him.

Suddenly Shanna felt a strong desire to confront them all with the truth. It nearly burst from her lips as she rose trembling from her chair. She ached to defend her love and her marriage to this bondsman. The only thing that stilled her words was the fear that Gaylord would rush to his magistrate father to bear the news that a man he had condemned to hang was alive. She placed an unsteady hand to her brow.

"Madam Beauchamp, could I lie down for a moment before dinner? I fear the ride exhausted me more than I realized."

Trahern lowered his glasses, concern obviously written in his countenance. Like a vivacious child, Shanna had always seemed to possess inexhaustible energies. Here, as well, he'd have to readjust his thinking.

Ruark shared his worry and stepped toward Shanna anxiously but abruptly found himself facing Charlotte's back as she moved into his path. Amelia Beauchamp went to Shanna's side and took her arm.

"Of course, child," she soothed. "It has been a long, tiring trip for you. Perhaps you would like to freshen up as well."

As she passed the bondslave, Amelia paused. "Mister Ruark, would you carry the lady's cases upstairs? I believe the wagon has arrived."

"Yes, ma'am," he replied respectfully and took his leave.

The stairs led straight up against the wall of the entrance hall, and as Mrs. Beauchamp escorted Shanna up, her dark taffeta gown swishing with her every movement, Ruark came into the house again, carrying a small sea chest on his shoulder and another case beneath his arm. Without a word he mounted the steps behind them and followed on into the bedchamber at the back corner of the house. A fire danced brightly on the hearth like spirited red and gold elves frolicking on a log. There was a warm cheeriness and mannish comfort about the room. A soft, dark Oriental carpet cushioned the feet, and chairs of leather and wood sat about the room. A massive four-poster was spread with a heavy velvet coverlet of a rust hue, and the same material draped the windows.

"This is my son's room when he's home," Mrs. Beauchamp explained, lighting the tapers in a candelabrum. "I didn't think you would mind using this, as all the other guest rooms will be taken. It does lack something of a woman's touch, I suppose."

"It's fine," Shanna murmured. Her eyes met Ruark's inquiring gaze as he set her cases down. She flushed and folded her hands in embarrassment as she realized the woman had turned and stood watching them.

"My large trunk. Did you see it, Mister Ruark?" she managed.

"Aye, I'll go down and get it now."

"Have David help you bring it up, Mister Ruark," Amelia suggested.

The door closed behind him, and the elder woman bent to fold down the bedcovers.

"I sent your girl Hergus to bed with a tray. Poor woman, she seemed to have suffered greatly from the ride."

No doubt, with Gaylord and Ralston sharing the coach, Shanna mused. Aloud she voiced, "She's never taken well to traveling."

Idly Shanna thumbed through a leather-bound book on the writing desk which stood beside the back window and then raised a questioning gaze to Mrs. Beauchamp, realizing there was not a single word in it that she could understand.

"Greek. 'Tis my son's," the woman replied, fluffing a pillow. "He was always reading and doing, even as a young lad."

There was a soft rap on the door, and it was opened to admit Ruark and the tall, rather elderly man in spotless servant's attire who had let them into the house. Between the two of them, they managed to get Shanna's huge trunk to the foot of the bed. Even Ruark was panting as he straightened, and he paused to catch his breath, his eyes sparkling at Shanna with silent jest, before he followed David out the door.

Amelia directed her attention back to Shanna, who still stared at the closed portal. "I'll help you with your gown, child. Would you like a tray to be sent up?"

"Oh, no. I'll only rest for a while."

Shanna presented her back to Amelia and stood quietly as the woman unlaced her gown. Stepping out of it, Shanna waited almost timidly in her light chemise as the woman put away the velvet dress.

"Can I fetch a nightgown for you?" the older woman offered kindly. At Shanna's negative shake of the head, Amelia smiled and walked to the door. "I'll leave you, then. Have a good rest."

She opened the door then paused, gazing back over her shoulder at the young and beautiful woman.

"I think if a man can win your father's approval as Mister Ruark has apparently done, then he's a man to handle himself whatever's given to him. I wouldn't worry, child."

When she left, Shanna slowly sank onto the edge of the bed where she stayed for a very long time. She hadn't realized her emotions were so apparent that they could be read without flaw. And if they were readily visible to Mrs. Beauchamp, then Orlan Trahern might soon recognize that his daughter was in love with his bondsman.

The sound of a door slamming somewhere in the house brought Shanna wide awake. She lay across the bed, still in her shift, but now a fluffy comforter was spread over her. A small clock on the mantel indicated it was half-past eight.

Shanna sat up with a start. She had only meant to rest for a few moments, but hours had gone past instead. They could not have waited dinner for her this late, and she was suddenly aware that she was intensely hungry. Nearly ten hours had passed since she had eaten and no sight of a tray. But then, she had told Mrs. Beauchamp she would be down.

Finding a heavy velvet dressing robe in her case, she slipped into it, fastening it high at her throat. Even if she had to go to the stables to fetch Ruark to help her, she was going to find something to eat. Never in her life had she known such a plaguing hunger.

"It must be because of the babe." She smiled in wonder, realizing the change in her body, and her spirits soared. Suddenly she was impatient to hold a wee nestling form close in her arms. Lass or lad, it mattered naught. It seemed in that moment she could have loved every baby in the world. What a difference a year had made in her thoughts, for then she had worried for fear she was with child by Ruark. An innocent she had been to believe there was even a chance. He was a bold man to have taken her virginity in the coach. But then, it had taken a bold man to win her respect—and her love.

Restraining her lighthearted step, Shanna went carefully down the stairs. All was quiet within the dining room and parlor. Only a dim lantern burned there. But voices came from the back of the house. Servants, perhaps? Would they fetch her food? It was a chance worth taking.

Down the hall, through a smaller dining room, she went

quietly, following the sound of voices. Then the aroma of food hit her, and she forgot everything else. She set her hand to push open the door. This had to be the kitchen, and the fact that it was attached to the house seemed not unusual in this frigid clime. A burst of laughter greeted her as she swung open the door, and she saw Nathanial guffawing beside his father, who wore a wry smile.

"Shanna!" Charlotte's voice came from beside her, and Shanna turned to see the woman standing with Amelia and Jeremiah. At the table Gabrielle rose to her feet in some surprise, and the men's humor fled as they stared, too.

"I'm sorry," Shanna murmured, half embarrassed, realizing there was only family here. "I didn't mean to intrude."

She started to leave when Amelia raised her hand.

"Wait, child. Come in," she beckoned and turned to her daughter. "Gabrielle, fetch her the plate."

"But, mama—"

"Never mind. Do as I say. Hurry with you. Can't you see the poor girl is hungry?"

"I'm not dressed," Shanna smiled lamely. "I'd better go back."

"Nonsense. We kept a plate warm for you. Come sit yourself down," Charlotte urged, sliding back a chair.

A whistling came from outside the house, and the back door burst open to admit Ruark with a load of wood in his arms. Seeing Shanna, he stopped then glanced around at the expectant faces.

"Well, set the wood down, boy," George directed after a tense moment of silence. He gestured to the wood box. "You did say you were hungry, didn't you?"

"Aye, sir," came the reply, and Ruark deposited his load, catching Shanna's confused glance. " 'Twas the least I could do to repay these good people for supper."

"Hmph!" Amelia raised her eyebrow sharply, and Jeremiah hastened forward, rubbing his hands nervously on his breeches.

"Mister Ruark, how would you like to go hunting along the ridge tomorrow? I saw some big tracks up there. Early in the morning, if you can manage it."

"I'll have to ask the squire," Ruark replied, tossing a couple of logs onto the fire and giving Shanna a glance askance.

More worried about her own intrusion, Shanna took the seat

Charlotte had offered and folded her hands self-consciously. Gabrielle rushed to set a heaping plate before her and hurried back to the hearth to slip another one from the brick oven.

"Mister Ruark, sit down please," she said, placing the platter.

Two large glasses of cold milk were poured by Charlotte and placed beside their plates as Ruark slipped into the chair next to his wife. As they ate, the conversation warmed again until Shanna found herself laughing with the rest of them. Ruark's easy wit joined theirs, and, to Jeremiah's delight, he was soon relating the riotous tale of a Scottish hunt. It was a pleasant time, and, strangely, Shanna felt a part of the family. She wondered yet if it could not be true. Perhaps Ruark was some distant cousin, some kin? Captain Beauchamp had denied the fact. Or had he? It was something to think on.

Well after the hour of eleven, when the family began to drift away to their rooms, Shanna rose from the table and said good night to the father and Nathanial, who remained standing near the hearth. Ruark started to get to his feet, but George rested his hand on his shoulder and pressed him back into the chair.

"You were telling me of this stallion, and there is much I would ask. Stay a while."

Ruark's gaze followed Shanna out; then the door swung closed behind her. The way was dark for Shanna, lit only by a candle burning on the sideboard in the dining room, and in the hall, the only radiance came from the lantern from the drawing room. There, in the shadows of the foyer, Shanna stood before the small square panes of crystal that composed the larger window, attracted by the sight of the full moon. Its pale light streamed through the half-naked branches of the giant oaks on the front lawn.

The creaking of the kitchen door interrupted her reverie, and Shanna half turned as Nathanial came striding down the hall. The man caught her movement, paused a moment, then came toward her.

"Shanna," he smiled in the meager light. "I thought you would be in bed by now."

"I was admiring the view," she murmured somewhat apologetically.

He peered out the window over the top of her head at the

breathtaking scene. "You see with the eye of an artist," he remarked.

Shanna gave a soft chuckle. "Aye, I've wanted to be that, too."

"Would you care to talk?" he invited.

Shanna leaned against the window frame to further contemplate the wintry night. "About what, sir?"

The answer was slow in coming. "Anything." He shrugged his broad shoulders. "Whatever would please you."

"And what do you think would please me?"

"Mister Ruark," he said softly.

She searched for some hint of displeasure or contempt in his shadowed face, but only a gentle smile met her inquiring eyes.

"I cannot deny it," she whispered and stared out the window again, twisting the gold band on her finger. "You saw us before. You may not approve, but I love him—and I carry his child."

"Then why this farce, Shanna?" His voice was low and gentle as he questioned. "Would the truth be so pitiful?"

"We are trapped in it," she sighed dejectedly. "He cannot claim me for other reasons, and I've yet to find a way to set aside my father's wrath." She shook her head and stared down at her hands. "I cannot ask your word or vow, for that would make you party to my deceit. I can only depend upon your discretion. The day rapidly approaches when it will all be out."

A long pause ensued before Nathanial spoke again. "You may rely upon my discretion, Shanna, but there is this that I would say." He drew a deep breath. "I think the both of you do all of us a grave discredit. Do you see your father as some cruel ogre? Would he punish you for your love? Do you see about you a host of enemies, or would you find naught but friends and allies waiting to help you? 'Tis a sad report that I and mine would leave a lady in distress and not raise our voices, yea our arms, in her defense. I dare say your father would rise to your defense if you declared your love. Do you think him so doddering with age that he has forgotten the fires of youth? I find Orlan Trahern to be most reasonable, yet he has a spirit of fire of his own."

Nathanial took several steps toward the stairs and turned back to her again.

"Aye, I think you both do us ill. But I shall await your revelation as you have said, in your own good time." He held out a hand to her. "Come, Shanna, let me see you to your room. The hour is late."

He laughed softly, and Shanna felt his good humor infecting her. "I wonder how long either of you can hold your secrets."

✦ Chapter 26 ✦

PALE sunlight streamed in through filmy underdrapes and warmed the room with its midmorning brightness. In half-awakened pleasure Shanna stirred in the wide bed and lazily opened her eyes. A bit of color beside her on the pillow caught her eye, and she lifted her head to see a single dark red rose on her pillow. She raised the flower and tested its fragrance as she lay back and admired the fragile beauty of it. The thorns had been carefully removed from the long stem.

"Oh, Ruark," she breathed, smiling.

The impression on the pillow beside her own gave her to know that he had been there beside her in the night. With a low, happy laugh Shanna snuggled the pillow to her breast. But she tossed it wide as a soft rap abruptly sounded on the door. At her call Hergus came in.

"Good morn'n, lass," the maid greeted cheerfully. "Did ye sleep well?"

Shanna bounced from the bed and stretched like a contented feline. "Aye, very. But I am starving."

Hergus looked at her suspiciously. "That, lass, is an awesome sign."

Shanna shrugged innocently. "Whatever do you mean?"

Hergus busied herself laying out garments from the trunk. "I think ye know. The way ye've taken pains to avoid me seeing ye in the altogether, I think ye ought to be telling Mister Ruark he's going to be a father."

"He knows," Shanna replied quietly and met the woman's astonished stare. "You guessed rightly. I'm going to have his child."

"Ooooh, naaaay," the servant groaned. "What are ye going to do?"

"The only thing that can be done. Tell my father." Even now, the thought of doing that brought a chill of dread to Shanna's heart. "I hope he will not be too angry."

"Huh," Hergus grunted. "Ye can bet he'll see yer Mister Ruark gelded good and proper."

Shanna whirled and faced the woman with green lights of rage in her eyes. "Say no more to me of what's good and proper. What's good and proper is me loving Ruark, having his child." She stamped her foot to emphasize her words. "I will not stand for another slur against my Ruark, from anyone!"

Hergus knew when she had reached the limits of Shanna's patience and carefully changed the subject. As she helped her mistress dress, conversation seemed appropriate and she found it hard to keep her silence.

"The men have eaten breakfast and gone, all except Sir Gaylord. He seems much attracted to Miss Gabrielle."

Shanna scoffed. "The greedy fop. He'll find himself a rich wife yet. I must warn Gabrielle."

"No need," Hergus giggled behind her hand. "She set him back on his heels. She told him that she wouldn't have his hands on her and to mind where he put them in the future."

"Then I suppose he'll be after me again," Shanna heaved a disheartened sigh. "Perhaps we can find him some doddering old widow with a heavy stick to keep him in line."

Hergus raised her shoulders in a shrug. "He doesna seem to like the older ones. But a fine eye he has for the bonnie lasses. Why, passing through Richmond he nearly broke his neck craning it out the coach to watch a pretty young thing skittering across the road." She sniffed loudly and lifted her nose primly in the air. "I wouldna have him."

Shanna's lovely brows drew into a thoughtful frown. "I wonder if he's convinced the Beauchamps to put money in his shipyard. They might agree just to get rid of him."

"Not likely," Hergus chuckled. "I passed the knight in the hall this very morn talking with that fine Captain Beauchamp. The captain didna seem to be too taken with the idea."

"Good," Shanna smiled. "Perhaps he'll soon leave, then." It would be better if he weren't around when she spoke to her father.

When Shanna descended the stairs Amelia called to her from the drawing room door. "Come join us, Shanna. I'll have a tray fetched for you here and a pot of tea."

Charlotte and Gabrielle played a last tinkling melody on the harpsichord before they rose and came to sit in the chairs beside the settee where Shanna took a place.

"The men left early this morning to show your father around, and it's been so quiet in the house with them all gone," Amelia laughed. "I think I could hear a feather drop."

A loud crash seemed to punctuate her words, and the ladies turned to stare in amazement at the cause. A serving girl, standing at the door of the drawing room, gaped down in horror at the spilled tray at her feet. Beside her, Gaylord testily dusted his satin coat and lacy jabot.

"Addlepated twit! Be more careful next time," he snapped. "Rushing about like that you could have ruined my coat."

Helplessly the girl looked at Mrs. Beauchamp and twisted her thin hands in distress, her small chin beginning to quiver and her huge eyes brimming with a rush of tears.

"No need to fret, Rachel," Amelia soothed kindly and went to help the tiny maid pick up the shattered pieces of the china teapot and plate. Handing her the last piece, Amelia dusted her hands on her handkerchief and watched the servant make her way very carefully across the hall toward the small dining room. Then the mistress of the manor turned with a deliberateness that bespoke of her authority.

"Sir Gaylord, while you are in this house you must remember not to display your criticism of the less fortunate. I will not stand for it. Rachel was indentured before she came to work for us and abused. She has not been with us long, but she is a good girl and as her services are valuable to me, I wouldn't want her to leave because a guest of ours was needlessly harsh to her."

"Madam, are you taking me to task for my manner?" Gaylord inquired in astonishment. "Madam, I come from one of the finest families in England, and I know how to deal with hirelings." He looked down his nose at her. "The magistrate, Lord Gaylord, you might know of him. He is my father."

"Indeed?" Amelia smiled tolerantly. "Perhaps, then, you know the Marquess, my husband's brother?"

Gaylord's jaw dropped sufficiently, and much satisfied with his reaction, Amelia swept around with a swish of silk and moved to take her place again among the three smiling ladies.

"The Marquess!" Gaylord stammered and came a step nearer. "The Marquess de Beauchamp of London?"

Amelia raised her eyebrow lazily and regarded him. "Is there any other? I wasn't aware of it." She motioned Rachel in; the girl cautiously made a wide path around Sir Gaylord. "Now, ladies, where were we?"

"You were marvelous, mama," Gabrielle cried with delicious enthusiasm when the man had retired from the room.

"It was a wicked thing I did," Amelia confessed. She shrugged girlishly, and her laughter sparkled in the room. "But just the same, it felt good. The way Gaylord ordered Mister Ruark away from our table last night, a body would think he's made himself squire here."

"Nathanial said he heard that Sir Gaylord's father was in Williamsburg visiting," Charlotte announced, taking a cup from Amelia. "I wonder if he's a boor like his son."

Then her dark eyes turned, almost worried-looking, to Shanna, who had suddenly stopped stirring her tea. Beneath the woman's stare Shanna quickly bent her attention to her plate, afraid her distress might be noted. She could only consider how she might escape the house to warn Ruark that Hanging Harry was close enough to be dangerous.

"My goodness, Shanna, that was rude of me," Charlotte apologized. "I should allow that you might like the man. Gaylord did say this morning at the table that you and he were close to being betrothed."

Shanna choked on a buttered muffin. "Me?" She swallowed

some tea to help the crumbs go down and shook her head in a definite manner. "I assure you 'tis his own wishing. I gave him my answer,"—she rubbed her wrist with the memory—"and it was most certainly a refusal."

"Then why should he continue to press you, Shanna?" Gabrielle asked. "He hasn't even cast a glance toward me since this morning, which truly relieves me, but for a few moments today one might have sworn he was ardently in love with me. If you have told him nay, then why does he speak of your betrothal?"

Shanna could only shrug. Then Charlotte broke out into amused laughter.

"Perhaps Shanna was a little more delicate with her refusal, Gabby dear. 'Tis rather deflating to any gentleman to be told by a young lady that he's old enough to be her father and to be reminded of his paunch besides."

Shanna giggled in her cup. "And I thought my answer was brutal. If his cheek doesn't smart, my hand still does."

"Oh, gracious," Gaby beamed. "Did you really? Good for you, Shanna. But why does he still pester you? You would think he'd give up."

"I suppose Mister Ralston informed him that my father wanted me to marry a man of title," Shanna replied. "No doubt Gaylord still hopes I will be influenced by his knighthood."

"But the squire doesn't seem to care for the man, either," Amelia responded. "In fact, he became quite angry when Gaylord told Mister Ruark to leave and eat with the servants. You missed something of a row, my dear, with your father declaring he'd take his dinner with his bondsman, and George telling everyone he'd be master in his own house and invite whomever he would to our table, and there was poor Nathanial trying to soothe everyone's temper and not accomplishing much at that. 'Twas a full quarter-turn of the hand before any of us realized Mister Ruark had gone. But George and the squire haven't given Gaylord a civil word since."

"Then, perhaps, 'tis best I left when I did," Shanna remarked wryly.

It was a short time later when Shanna found herself alone with the eldest Beauchamp woman and wondered at the excuses the two others had given as they hurried from the room. Through the front windows Shanna could see Gaylord stalking across the yard, his hands folded behind his back, his head down, as if he pondered some deep subject.

"I suppose, Shanna, that you've heard many tales that impress you with the idea that Virginia is a savage land." Amelia chuckled at her nod. "Aye, 'tis savage, but I've never regretted coming here to build our home. We lived in a log cabin until we could clear the land and build this house. We only had Nathanial then, and we were but children ourselves. My parents were fearful. They wanted me to stay behind in England until George could make a home for us. They thought he would give up and come back. And he has often said that he might have if I hadn't come with him."

"You have a lovely home, Madam Beauchamp, and a lovely family."

"Oh, we've had many hardships that we might not have faced in England," Amelia continued. "But I think we're better people because of the troubles we've shared—and stronger, perhaps. I could not abide a foppish son like Gaylord. My own, perhaps, would be out of place at court, but I can vouch for the fact that they are men and do not depend on another's riches to give them a soft bed. And because I love them, I desire their happiness. 'Tis only natural for a mother to want the best for her children. So far, they've been blessed in finding that one they have needed in this world. God willing, Gabrielle and Jeremiah will do the same."

Absently Shanna sipped her tea, wondering if Ruark's mother would accept her with the same warmth and graciousness Amelia displayed toward Charlotte. Charlotte could almost be envied, but then the woman who had raised Ruark had to be someone special, too.

"Are you comfortable in my son's room?" Amelia inquired softly.

"I feel very much at home there," Shanna stated truthfully. "And I suppose that in the summer the room is quite cool with that huge tree right out the back to give it shade. Where *is* your other son?"

'Would you care for more tea, my dear?"

"Only a half cup, please. Thank you."

"He's here off and on."

"I'd like to meet him sometime."

Amelia glanced at her young guest. "I believe you will, my dear. I believe you will."

A short time later, Shanna came down the stairs dressed in a deep green velvet riding habit that lent to her eyes a darkness of hue very close to emerald. Gabrielle was just coming in the front door.

"Is there a path where I might ride and not get lost?" Shanna asked.

The woman responded by leading her toward the back of the house. There, they could gaze out from the windows upon the rolling hills that rose beyond their place.

"There's a trail that leads up to the high valley by that big oak." Being a little taller, Gabrielle gazed down at Shanna and added casually with a half shrug, "You'll probably see Mister Ruark up there with Jeremiah."

Shanna relaxed into the rhythm of Jezebel's gait and felt the exhilarating breeze as the tawny grass raced by beneath the horse's hooves. The wind whipped at the curved plume of her velvet riding cap, and in the sheer joy of the moment Shanna shook out the reins. The mount responded to her urging and stretched out, seeming almost to take flight. It was familiar ground Jezebel roamed, and she raced on. Shanna let her run until they had passed the large oak and entered the forest on an overgrown wagon trail. Here, she reined down to a saner pace.

The air was cool, but the sun was high, and there was a feeling of chaste virginity in this wilderness. Shanna caught a glimpse of a doe passing in the dark, mottled shadows. Then the trail began to climb. High hills rose on either side, and the track skirted a low bluff. On rounding it Shanna gave a gasp of amazement and halted the mare.

A wide valley spread out before her, fertile and rich like a precious gem. Down the center of the vale, a chain of small ponds shone bright blue beneath the brilliant sky, fed by a tumbling waterfall that spilled down a cliff through glistening rainbows round about its feet. Beyond the ponds, beneath the high branches of a stand of pines, stood a small hut of simple and crude construction, and from its chimney a thin wreath of smoke curled into the air.

Shanna noted the tracks of several horses, and she urged Jezebel on faster, past a bunch of willows, to splash across a small, clear stream and then onto the ground that rose to the cabin. The door stood ajar, and an ax lay amid a pile of new chips. Beyond the cabin a rail fence surrounded a pasture in which grazed a sizable herd of horses that rivaled in grace and beauty the one that she rode. Restlessly Jezebel pawed at the thick matting of grass beneath her hooves as Shanna held the reins tight in her gloved hand, gazing out across the beauty of the peaceful valley.

A small sound came from behind her, and Shanna turned the mare to find Ruark leaning his long rifle against a stump. Grinning, he came to lift her from the back of the horse.

"How did you know where I was?"

She smiled up into his eyes as he stood her on the ground. "Gabrielle told me."

His hands caressed the velvet along her ribs. "I'm glad."

He bent, and his mouth covered hers in a long, searing kiss of welcome. Shanna sighed contentedly, nestling against his leather jerkin as his arms folded about her. But then she remembered her business there.

"Hanging Harry is in Williamsburg," she murmured, slipping her own arms around him and leaning back to meet his gaze.

"The bastard," Ruark grunted.

"What shall we do?" Shanna asked, worry in her voice.

Ruark caressed her cheek with his lean knuckles. "Do not fret, love. We'll see our way clear of this yet."

Kissing her lips again, he stepped back and, lifting his head, gave a soft, cooing call. A movement in the brush behind the cabin caught Shanna's attention, and a moment later Jeremiah came into view. He, too, bore a long musket and was garbed much as Ruark, in soft buckskin breeches, waistcoat, and linen shirt.

"Mister Ruark," Jeremiah called, his voice strangely heavy with laughter. "I think I'd better go fix that break in the fence before the mares find it. It'll take me a while."

With that he hefted the ax and set off with a strange shuffling trot across the field. Shanna could have sworn she heard a chuckle drifting in the air behind him as he left.

Ruark watched him go, a twinkle in his eyes. "Bright lad, that one. Always ready to do more than his share."

Shanna frowned slightly, feeling as if something had passed between them that she had completely missed. But what did it matter as long as she and Ruark could be alone?

He gathered the back of her habit in his hand and lifted the hem from the damp grass. "You'll need a pair of breeches to wear if you're going to wander around up here. Let me put Jezebel away before she strays. Then I'll show you around."

Holding her skirts high, Shanna followed along. At the corral Ruark removed the bridle from the mare, looped it over the saddle, then loosened the girth. The mare followed him like a trained dog as he led her to the gate and let her through.

Happily Shanna ran ahead into a dark bower of shadows beneath a tall pine. She danced and kicked at the thick carpet of pine needles. Then returning to Ruark, she came into his arms like a young girl freshly in love. Her laughter rippled through the glade. Raising her arms, she stretched them high above her head, arching her body in sheer rapture before throwing them about his neck and leaning forward to let their lips meet as one.

"Do you want to see the cabin?" he asked huskily against her mouth.

Shanna nodded eagerly and slipped her hand into his, letting him lead her back to the clearing. In front of the cabin Ruark swung her up into his arms and carried her through the low door of the place. It was simple within, dimly lit by the fire that blazed in the hearth. Setting Shanna to her feet, Ruark let her look about as he bent, lifted a glowing brand from the fireplace, and puffed his pipe alight. Intrigued with the sturdy comfort of the interior, Shanna rubbed her hand across the surface of a hand-hewn table and peered inquisitively into a great iron pot that swung away from the fire. She bounced playfully on the huge down tick spread over the bed, felt the rich fur robe that covered it, then turned about in the middle of the room.

"Oh, Ruark, wouldn't it be wonderful if we could have something like this?" she exclaimed enthusiastically.

He looked at her dubiously through the wreath of smoke that curled from his pipe and smiled. "Now, Shanna, would you really be satisfied here?"

She pouted winsomely. "Do you doubt that I could be? I am of sturdy stuff, Mister Beauchamp, and given a challenge I will make the best of it. I will learn to cook. Perhaps not as well as the cooks in papa's kitchen, but then I don't like fat husbands." She patted his lean belly then smoothed the velvet over her own. "Will you still love me when I've grown fat-bellied with child?"

"Oh, Shanna," Ruark chuckled, folding her in his embrace. "I will love you on my dying day."

She clung to him and answered his warming kisses. "How long will Jeremiah be gone?"

Ruark reached behind him to latch the door. "Until I call him."

The stark branches of the oak tree scratched forlornly at the panes in the bedroom window as Shanna gazed out into the star-glazed night. Her afternoon with Ruark in the cabin had made her intensely aware of the fact that she wanted a life with him, whatever hardships or happiness it might contain. Her mind was already set on its course, but she felt lonely beyond belief. It was as if she stood alone in the world and all the weight of her folly rested on her shoulders. What she was about to do might well leave her with no one—Ruark, her father, no one. Would the Beauchamps really receive her in all her shame, as Nathanial had said?

Shanna rested a hand on her belly and was vividly awake to the life that blossomed there. Suddenly she knew she would never be alone.

Orlan Trahern sat in a leather chair in the guest chamber and pored over a sheaf of charts and ledgers. The produce of this land was rich enough to tweak his merchant's heart. In fact, he had begun to see the advantages of obtaining property here himself, perhaps on the James River where his fleet of ships could come and go.

A light tapping on his chamber door interrupted his musings, and Shanna's voice called softly, "Papa, are you awake?"

He dropped the papers on the desk and urged, "Come in, Shanna, come in."

The door opened, and Shanna slipped in, closing it behind her. She came across the room to press a kiss upon his brow and saw his amused smile.

"Is something wrong, papa?" she asked wonderingly.

"Nay, child. I was just remembering." He gazed at her with fondness. She seemed tiny within the loose, flowing velvet folds of her dressing gown. "You sounded frightened, just as you did when you were a child and the storms came. You would tap on our door and call and then come and snuggle between your mother and me."

Shanna cringed inwardly and sought a chair to ease her shaking. She could only sit and look at her trembling hands, though she knew his eyes were on her and that he waited.

"Papa, I—" Her voice was low and thin, almost tremulous. She drew a breath and blurted it all out in one rush. "Papa, I'm with child, and the father is John Ruark."

A moment of dead silence followed, and Shanna could not lift her eyes to see the shocked anger on her father's face.

"*Good lord, woman!*"

Shanna jumped as his voice roared out. Orlan shot out of his chair and in a step was standing in front of her. Shanna braced herself again, but his voice came lower, even though it still sounded coarse and loud in the quiet room.

"Do you know what you have done?"

Her eyes were squeezed tightly shut, and tears hung on the thick lashes, threatening to fall as she hunted for a way to express her feelings. Then his words fell on her ears and filled her mind.

"You have solved for me, dear child, a problem which has soured my stomach every day these weeks past. How could I, with all my prattling of blood and titles, ask my daughter to wed a bondsman?" He bent and took her hands from her lap and lifted her chin until he could look into her face. "If you would have given it to me to choose, I would have begged you take the man, Ruark. But as I vowed, 'twas your choice to make, and I would interfere no more." He searched her face. "Do you love him?"

"Oh yes, papa." She rose and, throwing her arms about his neck, hid her face against his shoulder. "Oh yes, I love him." Her whisper was soft and happy.

"Does he love you? Will he see you properly wed?" He gave no pause. "By damn, he will!" His voice began to raise in anger. "He will, or I will see him—"

Shanna's fingers went across his lips, hushing him. It was in her mind to blurt out the whole story, but the truth of her deception might well cause harsher feelings to stir. A little at a time was better than pressing good fortune.

"Papa, there is a difficulty. I will tell you all in good time, but there is a reason we cannot bring it to light for a while." She saw his frown and begged him. "Trust me, papa. It will come out for the good. Trust me?"

"I suppose you have good cause," he yielded reluctantly. "But it must not be too long. I would spread the word of my offspring."

"Thank you, papa." She kissed him and fled the room, returning to her own. There she closed the door behind her and strolled deep in thought toward the bed, smiling and tearful at the same time. A shadow rose from the chair across the room, and she gasped before she recognized Ruark. She flew into his arms and laughed against his chest, holding him tightly.

"I told him, Ruark. I told papa about us."

"I guessed as much." His lips touched her hair. "I heard his bellow of pain."

"Oh, nay!" She leaned back and looked up at him. "He approves, Ruark. He was happy with it."

Ruark's brows lifted in surprise.

"Oh, I didn't tell him we were married, only that we had made a baby together."

Ruark threw up his hands and groaned. "Thanks a lot, madam. Now I am a molester of widows."

"Cad!" Shanna danced away from him, and gazed back coyly over her shoulder. "Were I in truth a widow, that might be true. Of course,"—she faced him with an angry pout well feigned—"there is that hennaed widow. Is that the one you refer to?"

"Nay, madam. Rather a young, tawny wisp of a woman who tempts my ardor overmuch."

Coming to a conclusion of his own, Ruark grew serious. "Shanna, love, since the night seems one to bring out the truth, I, too, have something to confess."

"Ruark, I have no fear of your former loves," Shanna laughed. "Ply me with no secrets now. My nerves are still aquiver." She went to the door and turned the lock. She glanced about the room, somewhat puzzled. "How did you come here? David was about below. I saw him from the stairs. Have you grown wings of late?"

"Nay, my love." Ruark gestured to the window. "The oak that grows beside the kitchen makes a good enough ladder. I thought you might have need of company." He set his hands upon her narrow waist and drew her to him. "But, Shanna, there is a thing I would tell you. This is my—"

Shanna silenced him with her lips and pressed herself tightly against him.

"Come, tell me of your love, Sir Dragon," she murmured. "And afterwards let me see some proof of it."

"I love you," Ruark whispered as his arms slipped around her beneath her robe. He felt the heat of her soft body under the thin silk of her gown, and all other thoughts fled his mind. "I love you as the earth must love the moon which climbs like a silver goddess in the night and brings light to the tiny creatures of the dark."

Pulling him to the bed, Shanna purred against his chest and caressed its hard, bare firmness.

"I love you like the flowers love the rain and spread their petals to bear their tender hearts before its gentle touch." His mouth sought hers. "I love you, Shanna, love, beyond all else."

Shanna came awake with a start and then lay still, wondering what had intruded into her sleep to shatter it so completely. The clock on the mantel delicately chimed the third hour as she listened. She felt Ruark's naked body snuggled against her back, his arm thrown across the cover over her hip. Then she realized that he, too, lay tense and rigid, his breathing subdued. She rolled her head on the pillow and in the dim glow from the fire could see that he was propped on an elbow, staring across the dark room toward the door. Then Shanna heard it, the rattle of the doorknob as it was twisted and slowly eased back in place; the locked portal gave no entry. Her eyes turned questioningly to her husband.

Ruark placed a finger across his lips, signaling her to silence. Slipping carefully from the bed, he reached for his breeches and pulled them on. With a quick, noiseless stride he crossed the room as Shanna snatched her gown over her head. If he was going to confront anyone beyond that door, she was not going to be be caught naked.

Very gently Ruark turned the key until a soft click freed the bar from the jamb. Then with a swift movement that made Shanna start, he stepped back and flung the portal wide.

No one was there. Nor in the passageway outside her chamber. The hall was dark with deep shadows and, though Ruark wandered noiselessly along it, peering into the shadows, he could find no one. Frowning, he returned to the bedchamber and closed the door, locking it again.

"Who could it have been?" Shanna whispered as he sat beside her on the bed.

"I'm beginning to have my suspicions," Ruark replied. After a few moments he rose and shucked his breeches, climbing beneath the covers again.

"You're cold," Shanna shivered, snuggling to him.

Abruptly Ruark sat up, leaving Shanna staring at him in surprise.

"What the hell is that?" He canted his head to listen better. In the silence of the room the faint but angry whinny of a horse could be heard.

"Attila," Shanna whispered, sitting up beside Ruark. "Something is disturbing him."

Ruark threw back the covers and snatched up his breeches again, jerking them on. "I'll see." He tugged his shirt over his head and spoke through it. "Lock the door behind me. If anyone tries to get in, scream. Someone should hear you."

Shanna was suddenly fearful. It seemed too much of a coincidence to be awakened from a sound slumber and then to hear Attila. Had they been asleep they wouldn't have heard him at all with the windows closed and the stable a goodly distance from the house.

"Ruark, don't go," she pleaded, "I don't know what, but I sense something is wrong here."

"I'll be careful." He kissed her lips quickly. "Keep my side warm. I'll be cold when I come back."

Shanna frowned with worry and followed him to the door. "Please be careful."

The portal was locked behind him, and Shanna began to pace the room uneasily, chewing on a long fingernail. Only the red glow of embers gave her light, and with the chill of the room she shivered in her nightgown. Kneeling before the fireplace, she stirred the hot coals until a tiny flame appeared and then placed upon it two heavy chunks of oak from the woodbox. Afterwards she could not have said how long she sat watching the fire blaze up again and enjoying its warmth. But cold dread was brought sharply to her heart as a scream pierced the night, and she heard Charlotte shriek from a bedroom down the hall.

"The stable! The stable is burning! Nathanial, wake up. The stable's on fire!"

Shanna came to her feet with a cry. A brief, fearful glance to the window showed her a light flickering on the drapes.

"Ruark!" With a strangled scream she was at the door, clawing at it, shaking fingers fumbling at the key. "Oh, no! Please, no! Ruark!"

Heedless of her bare feet and nightgown, Shanna flung the door wide and ran into the hall, nearly colliding with Nathanial, who had barely managed to don a pair of breeches. Charlotte was behind him, carrying a lantern and hugging a quilt about her shoulders for a wrap. Beyond them in the wide hall, doors had already begun to fly open.

"Ruark!" Shanna sobbed almost in hysteria. "He's in the stable!"

"Oh, my God!" Charlotte clapped a hand over her mouth, her dark eyes wide with fear.

Nathanial had no time to comment, but now fully awake he tore down the stairs as if a demon were at his heels. Shanna flew after him and barely recognized that Charlotte threw a blanket about her. They ran through the house to the back, flinging doors wide as they went, and did not pause as they crossed the lawn.

Flames were licking like hungry tongues up the walls of the stable, and they found the doors closed, the broad ones barred and the small one with a heavy post braced against it. The snorts and screams of the animals within rent the night, and the crackle of flames grew into a roar.

Shanna caught Nathanial's bare arm, her long nails digging into his flesh. "Ruark!" she screamed above the din. "He came to see about the horses!"

They drew near the small door, and Nathanial snatched buckets of water from the trough to splash onto the flames that threatened the sills as Shanna struggled against the dead weight of the heavy post. He brushed her aside, and with a single heave sent the post tumbling. Sobbing, Shanna snatched at the latch. The hot metal burned her fingers, and she wrapped her hand in the end of the quilt and managed to lift the post.

Heavy billows of smoke rolled out as the door swung free, choking Shanna and forcing her back, gasping for air. Nathanial snatched the quilt from her back and doused it in the trough then, flinging it over his head and shoulders, crouched beneath the roiling, strangling black clouds, and entered the inferno.

Attila's scream of terror shredded the air, and Shanna pressed shaking hands over her ears, sobbing against her own fear. Men were running all over now. Lines were formed to pass buckets of water and throw them on the towering mass of flames. A shower of sparks fell within, and Shanna's breath froze in her throat. Sickening horror congealed in her chest as her imagination did its worst with her, flashing before her mind's eye a vision of Ruark writhing in flaming agony. Panic would have brought her screaming into the barn like a frenzied banshee, but then she saw a form struggling toward her through the smoke. Drawing a deep breath, Shanna plunged forward into the eye-searing smoke. Nathanial staggered against her with Ruark flung across his shoulders, the blanket draped over them both. Snatching his arm, Shanna led him out, her own lungs near to bursting.

They cleared the stables as other men ran past to free the horses, Orlan Trahern in a wine velvet dressing robe stepping lightly for his girth and Pitney charging across the lawn, the tails of his long nightshirt flapping loose over his britches. Nathanial fell to his knees, choking, gasping for breath, and Ruark sprawled limply from his shoulders, tangled in the wet quilt. Charlotte was at her husband's side, bending over him, while

Shanna frantically tore the sodden cover from Ruark. He groaned as she lifted his head to her breast.

"Oh, my darling. My darling." She wept in relief as his eyes blinked open. "Are you all right? Are you hurt?"

"My head." He winced as her fingers touched his scalp. Shanna stared in amazement—the sleeve of her nightgown was smeared with blood.

"You're bleeding!" she gasped.

Charlotte came around to kneel on the other side of him, bending over his head. Her slim fingers carefully parted his hair away from a small gash and gently probed at the swelling knot, drawing a grimace from Ruark.

"There's a cut here," Charlotte announced. "Did you hit your head?"

"Some damn bastard hit me from behind," Ruark growled low. He sat up beside Shanna, gingerly touching the back of his head.

"He was on the floor by the stalls, and the stable doors were barred from the outside," Nathanial panted. "Whoever set the fire intended him to roast in it."

Pitney ran by, leading the mare, Jezebel, and other men hurried out of the burning stable, bringing more horses to safety. Amelia had come to stand above Ruark, her tall, slender frame hidden in the folds of her husband's robe. In the bright firelight her face appeared pinched and drawn as she questioned in a strained voice:

"Are you all right?"

"Aye," Ruark assured her with an effort. He rolled over and attempted to come to his feet but fell back to his knees and grasped his head as if to hold it in place. Worried, Shanna watched him closely and, as Gabrielle wrapped a patchwork quilt around her shoulders, reached out with a corner of it to wipe his soot-grimed face.

Clad only in a nightshirt, George paused to ask, "What the hell happened?"

An enraged scream, not of an animal, forestalled any reply, and they all turned to the fiery stable. Attila came dashing out, half bucking and fighting against the dark form that clung to his side. Ruark gave a piercing whistle, and the steed swung toward them, coming to a halt by Shanna. The horse stood trembling and snorting as he pawed the grass, and the dark form resolved itself into a bedraggled Orlan Trahern.

"Thank God!" Orlan wheezed. "I was afraid he was headed for the woods."

He held his loose robe gathered in one hand, and it could now be seen that one end of the robe's belt was wrapped about the stallion's neck and the other end was twisted firmly in Trahern's other hand.

The elderly Trahern was a mess. His hair was singed about the ends and stood away from his head in a silvered corona. His face was smudged and streaked with soot, and his best dressing robe was mottled with black-ringed holes where myriad sparks had touched it. One slipper was missing and his foot and leg were smeared with a brownish stuff, while his other slipper had an oddly crushed look about it.

Shanna gaped. "Papa! What on earth—"

"The beast was tied in his stall," Trahern puffed, sagging against the horse's shoulder, his hand still locked in the twisted belt. "When I loosed him, the nag trod upon my foot and would not let me take the lead."

Gingerly he tested his foot and growled with pain as it touched the turf. "Ungrateful beast!" Trahern moaned. "You have injured me sorely. I should see you fed to the dogs."

The stallion snorted, nudging the squire's side with his head.

"Eh, what's this?" Trahern caught the rope halter and held the steed's head. "He's all bloody."

Ruark forgot the pain in his head and came to his feet to examine Attila's nose and face where long, bloody welts showed in the firelight, crisscrossing the velvet snout.

"He's been beaten. And you say he was tied?"

"Aye!" Trahern untwisted his hand and flexed it as if he were somewhat doubtful he could still use it. "And with his head low, close against the boards."

George stepped near to peer through his spectacles and mused aloud, " 'Twould appear it was done to get someone into the stable."

He gazed thoughtfully at Ruark and then at Shanna who had risen to take her husband's arm. The fact that Ruark had stated he would sleep in the stables was not questioned as George concluded. "With each moment that passes, I think this deed has more the taste of murder. But in heaven's name, why?"

"I can't say why," Ruark growled and turned to the other men. "Are the horses safe?"

"Aye!" Pitney answered gruffly. "But look here what I stumbled over." He held up a buckshot-weighted quirt which had blood gleaming on its black surface and short gray hair clinging to the sticky red.

Ruark's lips tightened as he reflected on the brutal mind that would so cruelly beat an animal. "Damn the bastard!" he vowed vehemently. "If I ever get my hands on the bloody bitch's son who did this, I may well throttle him."

"Well, whatever you do to him, you'll have to use your hands," Nathanial drawled wryly. "I believe I saw your pistols and musket in the stable before supper. They're probably part of what's warming your backside now."

The stable blazed into a soaring inferno, defying the best efforts to douse the flames. Some of the men had chopped a hole in the tack room's outer wall, and most of the harnesses and saddles had been saved. Dawn began to glow above the hilltop before the last charred frames of the place collapsed in a heap upon the burning rubble.

It was a tired, black-faced group who returned to the house. The women had been forced to retreat sooner from the cold. Amelia, still in her husband's robe, met the men in the house and quickly served glasses with a rich amber brew twinkling in the bottom of each, the only exception being a tall, brimming mug of chilled ale for Pitney. Recognizing that it could have been a worse disaster, the group wearily raised their drinks in a grateful salute to their health. Amelia watched with growing amusement as they sampled the stuff, and her husband glanced up in question.

" 'Tis a fine lot you are," she chuckled.

George examined his broken eyeglasses with a rueful smile. "Aye, warriors from the field." He heaved a sigh and matched her smile. "Now I can have the stable on the oak hill where I've always wanted it."

"Good fortune, then," Amelia returned gently. "Except, of

course, for the squire's foot, Mister Ruark's head, and your spectacles. Whatever happened?"

"Your youngest son, madam, mistook me for thin air. In the fray he tried to run right through me."

His dry humor brought responsive laughter from the tired men and a much reddened hue to Jeremiah's face.

"Mister Ruark," Amelia said over her shoulder as she left the room. "You may use Nathanial's old room. 'Tis next to Shanna's. I think you can find it." She gave the smallest of laughs. "That poor old tree is stunted enough being so close to the kitchen."

A bustle of activity pervaded throughout the house as the servants rushed to prepare baths for the Beauchamps and their guests. Ralston's bed had not been slept in, and he was nowhere to be found. Gaylord snoozed peacefully, his snores echoing loudly from his chambers.

It was a late hour when the rest of the household took their morning meal. Orlan hobbled into the dining room on a bandaged foot. Despite Shanna's pleas Ruark had refused a bandage for his head and quietly took a place beside her at the table. No one questioned his right to sit there, and in the absence of both Gaylord and Ralston the dining was a warm and hearty affair. As the tale was retold, Shanna was amazed at how quick the Beauchamps were to laugh at themselves, as if the loss had not affected them in any manner. With rich enthusiasm they began to plan the new stable, and the ease with which Ruark offered his advice almost made Shanna wonder.

Gaylord appeared, and his bland, bluish-gray eyes surveyed the group around the table before he consulted his watch in some bemusement. "Hmm," he minced genteelly, tucking the timepiece away. "Is it some local holiday I have missed?"

"You slept the whole night through?" Shanna asked, her own amazement showing.

"Of course," he sighed. "I read from a volume of sonnets until a late hour, but from then on—" He paused and scratched his cheek thoughtfully with an immaculate forefinger. "It seems there was some disturbance, but after a while the house quieted, and I much assumed I had dreamt the whole of it."

He seated himself in a chair and began to fill a plate. For a man of much leisure, his appetite never seemed to flag.

"Why do you ask?" he questioned. "Is aught amiss?"

"You rest exceedingly soundly, sir," Ruark observed, only mildly satirical.

"Mm, yes," Gaylord smiled as he spooned a liberal serving of fruit perserves on a slice of hot bread. "A trait of the breeding, I assure you. An honest mind is a peaceful one."

He fixed Ruark with a jaundiced stare, taking note of his proximity to Shanna.

"I believe you have forgotten yourself again, bondsman. No doubt these good people are too polite to remind you of your place."

Ruark snorted derisively. "But you will, of course."

Beneath the table Shanna's hand lightly squeezed her husband's thigh, cautioning him to be careful. It was best to avoid any confrontation with the man that might somehow bring Lord Harry's notice to Ruark. Soon Gaylord would be gone, and the truth could be revealed to her father. Then, perhaps, they could set about clearing Ruark's name. Ruark's thin, brown fingers slipped over Shanna's beneath the tablecloth, tightening briefly to quietly assure her, and remained to hold them.

George had lowered his teacup and now spoke firmly. "Mister Ruark is welcome at my table sir."

Gaylord shrugged. " 'Tis your home, of course."

They were leaving the table when the knight asked of his host, "I say, would you have a servant fetch a gentle steed for me from the stables? I've a yen to see this country you boast of so much, to try, if possible, to find some merit in it."

Casting him a dubious glance, Ruark inquired with a hint of sarcasm. "Can you find your way alone, or do you need a guide?"

Pitney hid a smile of amusement as the knight glared his contempt at the bondsman.

"Whatever, I shall not need you to fetch me," Gaylord sneered.

"The stable burned to the ground this morning," Amelia interrupted the two men, eyeing each and appearing somewhat worried.

Gaylord's eyebrows lifted. "The stable, you say? And the horses as well?"

Pitney rasped gruffly. "We saved them all. As it appears, someone set the fire off after locking Mister Ruark inside. But of course ye were asleep and wouldn't be knowing 'bout that."

The knight snorted. "No doubt that's the bondsman's story after he carelessly touched it off himself. A good ruse, I would say."

"That can hardly be the way of it," Nathanial interceded, "since the doors were bolted from without."

"Perhaps the slave has made some enemies." Gaylord shrugged. "But that is of no importance to me. I only asked for a steed, not a full accounting of everyone's misfortune."

"One will be fetched," George announced brusquely.

It was to the relief of all that Sir Gaylord did manage to mount a horse and, his loosely jointed frame bouncing in the saddle, galloped off from view. Family and guests congregated in the drawing room, for it was decided the day would be spent much in relaxing. George's vision was somewhat impaired with broken eyeglasses, and Orlan's crippled state did not lend to a great deal of mobility. He was carefully ensconced in a massive chair, his heavily wrapped foot propped on a footstool. A determination had been made that no bones were broken, but the foot was badly bruised and swollen to a point of discomfort.

It was a short time later that the sound of a carriage coming up the lane drew the attention of all. Gabrielle went to the window, brushing aside the silken panel to look out. Past her shoulder, Shanna caught a glimpse of a young woman with a baby in her arms descending the steps of a landau with the aid of her driver. Dropping the drapery, Gabrielle whirled to face her mother, eyes wide.

" 'Tis Garland! Didn't you tell her to stay away?"

Amelia gasped and dropped her needlework. She came to her feet but appeared undecided as to which way to move. "Oh dear! Garland!" she fretted. "Good heavens!" She turned in supplication to her husband. "George?"

Ruark, as well, seemed suddenly disturbed. Shaking his head as if pained, he moved away from Shanna's side and went to lean against the mantel, folding his arms across his chest and frowning with what was apparently genuine disgust. Quite bemused by his actions, Shanna turned to stare at him wonderingly.

Garland's entry was like a whirlwind coming in the door, a fresh, airy breeze sweeping through the house. She did not pause as she came into the drawing room, but went straight to her mother to place the child in her arms. Glancing away from Ruark, Shanna saw only Garland's slim, velvet-clad back and a wide-brimmed hat that completely hid her face. Without a glance toward anyone else, the new arrival went boldly across the room to Ruark. He smiled tolerantly as she stood on tiptoes to place a kiss on his mouth.

"Welcome home, Ruark," she said in a voice soft and warm.

Garland turned, sweeping off her hat and came directly to Shanna, who could only stare agog at the raven hair, golden eyes, and the dazzling smile and looks. There was no doubt in Shanna's mind that here was Ruark's sister. But then, Garland was Gabrielle's sister—and Nathanial's—and Jeremiah's! Brothers and sisters all and to—Ruark Deverell Beauchamp!

"And of course you would be Shanna," Garland beamed. "Nathanial did not do you justice with his words."

"Oh!" The gasp escaped Shanna as she roused from shock. Her eyes flew to Ruark, who could only smile lamely as he shrugged. "You!" No other word would come, and Shanna stared at the girl again. "You're—oh!"

Her face flaming with her own foolishness, Shanna whirled and fled the room, up the stairs, and into the bedchamber that she had been using. Locking the door behind her, she faced a surprised Hergus who had been tidying the room. It was as if Shanna saw her surroundings for the first time and the realization came this was Ruark's room. It was his desk, his book of Greek, his bed, his armoire. Oh, how he had tricked her!

Orlan Trahern's voice rang loud in the suddenly subdued drawing room. "Will someone tell me what's going on?"

A chuckle escaped Pitney as Ruark stepped before Trahern and with a click of his heels, gave a slight bow.

"Ruark Beauchamp at your service, sir."

"*Ruark Beauchamp!*" Orlan bellowed.

His bondsman did not wait to explain, but hastened after Shanna. Trahern rose and started to follow but was painfully reminded of his injured foot. He snatched the staff and hop-skipped to the bottom of the stairs and roared upward:

"*How in the hell can she be a widow if you're Ruark Beauchamp?*"

Ruark replied over his shoulder. "She never was a widow. I cheated."

"*Damnation. Are you married or not?*"

"Married." Ruark was halfway up the stairs.

Orlan bellowed louder. "*Are you sure?*"

"*Aye, sir!*"

Ruark disappeared down the hall, and Trahern hobbled back into the drawing room, his head bowed in thought, his brow furrowed in a frown. He looked accusingly at Pitney, who only shrugged and lit his pipe. Glancing around, Orlan saw the worried frowns of all the Beauchamps, the deepest on the face of the girl, Garland, who seemed not at all sure now that she had done the right thing. Trahern's belly began to shake, a chuckle burst forth and became rolling laughter. A few hesitant smiles appeared. Limping forward to George, Orlan stretched forth a large hand.

"Whatever else, sir, I am sure we shall not suffer from boredom."

Ruark tried the knob and found the way barred. "Shanna?" he called. "I would explain."

"Go away!" her shriek answered him. "You made a fool of me in front of everyone!"

"Shanna?" he rattled the knob again. "Open up."

"Get away!"

"Shanna?" Ruark's own anger rose, and he leaned a shoulder against the portal to find it as solid as he remembered.

"Leave me be, you mewling jackanape!" Shanna gritted out. "Go play your puns on some other fool!"

"Dammit, Shanna, I can explain."

"Damn what? Damn me for a fool?" she hurled. "Get thee gone, you many-named goat!"

"*Open this door!*"

"*Nay!*"

Ruark stood back and kicked with all his might. The panel was solid oak, but the latch and jamb were not meant to take such abuse. With a splintering crash, the door flew wide, and a shower of plaster and wood fell from the side of the adjoining wall. Down below, Amelia laid a worried hand on her husband's arm, but he patted it reassuringly.

Ruark stepped through the door, glancing in momentary wonder at the wreckage he had wrought, but where he had expected to see Shanna, there stood a horrified Hergus. Her hands were clenched to her mouth, and her eyes were wide as moons.

"M-M-Mister Ruark!" she stuttered and then found her tongue. "Get ye gone from this room, Mister Ruark," she stammered. "I'll not see ye doing yer dirt here with these nice people."

Ruark ignored her and stepped toward Shanna, who had her back to him. But the Scotswoman scurried to block his path.

"Get out of my way," Ruark growled. He was not in a mood to allow interference.

The maid was firm. "Mister Ruark, ye will not do this here!"

"Woman, you stand between me and *my wife*!" He almost matched Trahern's tone and moved forward menacingly. "*Get out*."

Hergus gaped at him, her jaw sagging. Very meekly she moved aside and left the room, shaking her head and mumbling to herself.

"Shanna!" Ruark began angrily, but he realized full well the hurt she had suffered. "Shanna?" His voice was softer, then softer still. "Shanna, I love you."

"Beauchamp! Beauchamp!" She stamped her foot with each word. "I should have known."

"I tried to tell you last night, but you would not listen."

Shanna faced him, and her eyes brimmed with tears. "Then I am Madam Beauchamp of the Virginia Beauchamps. I am no widow, nor have I been. I shall be the mother of a Beauchamp, and my father shall have all he wished for."

"To hell with your father's wishes." Ruark took her in his arms, "You shall have all you wish."

"You played me the fool from the first," she accused, resisting his embrace. She kept her arms folded between them as she stared up at him. "You could have told me and spared me much."

"Remember, my love, on Mare's Head when you told me you could accept me if I were rich and came from a family well-named?" he questioned softly and then stated without waiting for her answer, "I wanted you to love me, Shanna, whether bondsman or Beauchamp. Had I told you, I would never have been sure."

" 'Tis all yours, isn't it? This room? The high valley? The cabin there and the bed where we made love? The horses? Even Jezebel was your gift to me, wasn't she?"

"Whatever I have I gladly yield to you," Ruark murmured.

Shanna's brows drew together as a new thought struck her. "How did you come to know so much about mills?"

His hands slipped up her back as he tried again to bring her closer, but still she refused him. He answered quietly, "I have built three of my own on the James and a big one at Well's Landing above Richmond."

"And ships?" She raised her gaze and contemplated him suspiciously. "It always puzzled me about the schooner, how you handled her. You seem to have a talent for sailing ships as well as all your other accomplishments."

The pins escaped her hair beneath his fingers, and the tresses tumbled free of the sedate coil.

"My family has six that ply the coast." Ruark's eyes softly caressed her face. "I own two, three now with the schooner."

Shanna groaned in despair. "You're as rich as my father."

He gave a low chuckle. "I doubt that heartily, but I can afford whatever gowns you wish."

A hot blush stained Shanna's cheeks as she was reminded of their quarrel and her own denials of him. "You laughed at me all the while," she moaned disconcertedly. "How you must have ached, being unable to lay hold upon some of your wealth so you could free yourself and flee Los Camellos."

"I told you once, money was not my problem." He stepped to the music box and much to Shanna's amazement slid open a concealed door at the end of it, revealing a chamber that ran the length of the base. From it, Ruark removed several wadded pieces of oiled buckskin and then two small leather bags. A very solid "clink" sounded as he hefted them in his hand. "I've had this ever since Nathanial came to Los Camellos. He even sent me the box to put it in. There's more than enough here to pay my bondage and my fare to Virginia. If I hadn't wanted to be with you, I could have left."

He returned to her, and his hands smoothed her hair before

they moved to cup her face, lifting it up so their eyes met.

"I love you, Shanna. I want you to share my life and that which belongs to me. I want to build you a mansion, as your father did for your mother, as my parents did here. I want to give you children, with dark hair and light, and watch them grow, bathed in our love. I have properties on the James. The land is good, and 'twill nourish our offsprings. It only waits your word to say where the house will be."

Shanna sniffed. "I rather entertained the idea of living in a cabin with you." Ruark's embrace tightened about her, and she murmured against his chest, "I should have your scalp, you know that."

"Will not my baby do as well, madam?" he asked tenderly.

"Captain—pirate—John—Ruark—Deverell—Beauchamp. How shall I call you?" Shanna brushed at her tears.

"Lover! Husband! Father to your children! Love of your life. You will know me by whatever name."

"Father Beauchamp?" Shanna shook her head in distaste. "Husband Beauchamp?" She wrinkled her nose. "Ruark? Lover?" Her arms slipped about his neck, and her mouth raised to meet his. The kiss blended their lips in joyous love.

It was a long moment before they parted and were brought to full awareness again by a polite clearing of the throat which came from the doorway. This time they turned with no fear of discovery and met Nathanial's grin.

"I always seem to be intruding," he chuckled.

Shanna giggled as she snuggled happily within Ruark's embrace. "I shall not ask for your discretion, sir. Tell whom you may."

Ruark beckoned his brother in. "What is on your mind?"

Nathanial scratched his cheek thoughtfully, and his brown eyes were warm with humor. "I was afraid Shanna might think me a liar for not claiming you as my brother, and I just wanted to set the record straight now that the secret is out."

Impulsively Shanna pressed a kiss upon Nathanial's cheek. "I forgive you. No doubt Ruark swore you to silence."

"Aye, that he did," Nathanial responded. "When we put into port at Los Camellos, Ruark sought me out. I gave him money to pay for his bondage, but he refused to leave or have the story out. I thought him mad or beguiled by a witch." The captain gave a humorous laugh. "Then I met you, and I could understand at least a part of his reasoning. With all due respects, madam,"—he bowed slightly in apology—"I had indeed accounted for all my brothers when I talked with you. 'Twas no lie I gave you."

"But how came you to be there?" Shanna questioned. "Surely it was not coincidence."

"When I put into port in London, I made inquiry as to the whereabouts of Ruark. I learned he had been accused of murder and hanged for the deed. The Newgate records reflected that his body had been delivered to the servant of one Madam Beauchamp. At the docks I was informed that that same lady and her retinue had sailed to an island called Los Camellos. My curiosity was stirred, so I made it a stop on my return voyage. I should also tell you another thing that may ease your mind somewhat. I hired barristers in London, and they promised me a most serious investigation into the matter of the girl's death, although as yet I have received no encouraging word."

"But surely it will come," Shanna said. "It must! Ruark didn't kill the girl. And we don't want to spend the rest of our lives hiding from the world. There will be more children after this one. They'll need a home and a name."

Ruark moved close behind his wife and folded his arms about her. "Aye, there'll be many more," he agreed. "Beauchamps all for the world to know."

"Have you told your father yet about the baby?" Nathanial peered at Shanna.

She leaned back against the long form at her back and caressed the lean, brown hands resting at her waist. "Aye, last night."

Nathanial nodded in satisfaction. "Then that, too, has ceased to be a secret."

"Forgive me, my love," Ruark spoke. "I bore the news to my family before I brought you to them. I came down to greet them from the trail."

"And I thought Gabrielle a little twit for taunting you," Shanna laughed.

"They were all reluctant to play the game, but Gaylord's presence convinced them of its importance. Mother would have had it out right away but for him," Ruark explained. "She doesn't tolerate deceit in anyone."

"It was terrible of you," Shanna pouted, but her eyes danced as they turned askance to meet his. "I could have left, you know. I was that angry."

"I would have followed you," Ruark assured with a flash of white teeth. "You have my heart and my baby. You would not have escaped."

"Aye," Nathanial chuckled. "And you can believe that, Shanna. He was determined to win your love, and I would guess he's gotten that."

"Oh yes, truly," Shanna responded radiantly.

"Then I will leave you two alone." At the doorway Nathanial glanced back with a grin, indicating the damaged portal. "Though I suppose there's no cause now with so little privacy."

Chapter 27

THE families below, now joined into one, were congratu-
lating each other and truly had not long to wait before
Shanna and Ruark came down. As Nathanial had surmised, when one's bedroom door is permanently ajar, not even
a very amorous couple has much to do. Ruark went to Trahern,
took the squire's hand, and placed within it a long, slim bag.

"They're fifty-pound gold pieces, sir," he announced. "You'll
find thirty of them in it. The price of my bondage. Fifteen hundred pounds." Ruark waited a moment while Trahern hefted the
bag with a merchant's skillful hand. "If you would be so kind as
to sign my papers and mark them paid in full."

Trahern reached into an inner pocket of his velvet coat and
withdrew a packet which he gave to Ruark without opening it.
"They've been signed since you brought back my daughter."

"A poor judgment, squire," Ruark smiled. "Now I take her
from you again."

"Damn!" Trahern fussed in mock fury. " 'Tis unjust that I
should lose my daughter and my most valued bondsman at the
same time."

"You've lost nothing, squire," Ruark assured him. "You will
never be rid of either of us." He caught Shanna gently against

616

his side and gazed down warmly into her smiling eyes. "And God willing, we shall lay a host of smaller troubles at your door, sir."

George sighed in audible relief and removed his broken spectacles. "I was warned not to take these off lest you discover the resemblance between my son and me, and I'm glad the secret is out so I can view the world clearly once again." His golden eyes twinkled as he smiled at Shanna and took her hands into his. "My son has made a fine choice. You do the family proud, Shanna."

Garland came forward rather hesitantly, holding her sleeping daughter in her arms. "I am sorry for the disturbance I caused, and I hope you will forgive me for bursting in like that."

"At the time I was tempted to take you across my knee" Ruark grinned. "But having the matter out in the open is a great burden removed, so I suppose I should thank you."

"You are Gabrielle's twin?" Shanna inquired uncertainly and glanced back and forth between her husband and his sister, wondering if there might be more surprises yet to come. The close resemblance was startling.

Garland laughed gaily. "Of course, but Ruark and I have always looked more alike than the others. And that has really confused people when they know I'm Gabrielle's twin. Ruark and I resemble father, while the rest favor mama."

The baby stirred in Garland's arms, and Shanna watched in fascination as the infant yawned and stretched her tiny limbs.

"I wonder if I might hold her?" Shanna asked softly.

"Oh, yes, indeed. Here." Garland beamed with pride and placed her daughter into the waiting arms. Almost fearfully Shanna accepted the bundle which was light as a feather and soft as thistledown. The cherubic face looked up with curious wonder at this stranger's visage, and Shanna, who had never even been close to a small baby before, was just as awed. Ruark's arms came around Shanna as he silently admired his niece.

"She's so tiny," Shanna said in amazement.

"Oh, but they all are at the beginning." Garland assured her. "You'll see."

Orlan Trahern sat back with a smug smile of satisfaction. There were many things that had to be explained yet, but he was confident that that would come in all due time. What mattered most was that his daughter had far exceeded his expectations in finding herself a husband and, to top it all, had gotten herself with babe. He was a happy man, and even the pain in his foot could little dim his joy.

So it occurred that in the aftermath of disaster, a great happiness was found. Ruark had taken his bride on his arm and presented her to the world, daring any to dispute his claim or to disparage her in any way, though none present would have. They were an impressive pair, he as handsome and proud as a man could be, and she as beautiful, loving and content as a woman ever. Both sides of the parentage looked upon the couple and had no doubts that this was a fine mating.

It was a joyous time for everyone. Even the maid, Hergus, suffering for so long under the weight of her secret, smiled from the doorway as she watched Shanna and witnessed her joy. Pitney, too, was proud of his sometimes questionable role in the marriage. Still, he knew a nagging uncertainty, for not all the questions had been answered and many remained to be asked. All too soon, his unease was extended to the others.

Ralston returned, and almost immediately an oppressive air settled over the formerly happy group. The thin man handed his long cloak to the doorman and came into the drawing room. With a puzzled frown on his face, his eyes roved over the normal-appearing assemblage as if he searched for some clue and then settled on Trahern with his singed hair and bandaged foot.

"I—" He began hesitantly, staring at the squire's foot. "I would have taken my mount to the stable, but I could see no trace of the place from the road."

Trahern gave a low chuckle. "To find the stable, one must look low on the ground." As Ralston gave only blank wonder to his statement, he explained. "It went up in smoke early this morning, and only ashes remain." Orlan paused and considered his agent for a long moment. "Now that I think on it, I saw no sign of you. Where have you been?"

"Your pardon, squire," Ralston hastened to reply. "I had news of an acquaintance who lives in Mill Place, and I took myself hence to seek him out. But you say the stable burned?"

"Aye," Pitney answered gruffly. " 'Twould appear you missed the whole of it." He let his statement hang so it was almost a question.

Ralston shrugged. "By the time I found my man, it was too late to come back, and he pressed me to stay the night. I did not think it to be unusual. Did you have need of me, squire?"

Trahern waved away the man's apprehensive inquiry. "No harm done. I did not know you had friends among the colonials, 'tis all."

Ralston sniffed. "A friend of the family, nothing more. A reckless chap, given to unwise speculations. Hardly one to appreciate the finer points of good English manners."

Ruark's brows lifted dubiously. He could well imagine the gaiety of an evening with Ralston.

"You seem to have misplaced your riding crop, Mister Ralston," Pitney commented casually.

"Misplaced! Huh!" Ralston sneered a trifle angrily. "I put it down while my mount was being saddled yesterday, and, when I was ready to leave, I could find neither hide nor hair of it. I had no time to question the stableboy as I was in a hurry, but rest assured I shall see that he returns it or suffers for his thievery."

George Beauchamp's brows drew together at the suggestion that his man was responsible, but Amelia rested her hand on his arm and caught his attention with a small, almost imperceptible, shake of her head.

Trahern diverted Ralston away from further accusations. "Enough! There has been too much ado about the fire and that mangy Hun who has the gait of a plow horse and as little care whereon he plants his hoof." He prodded his bandaged foot with the butt end of his staff and winced. "Should I ever touch that mule again 'twill be with the heavy end of my cane."

"Come now, papa," Shanna chided in defense of Attila. " 'Tis well said that he who would contredanse with a horse must be exceptionally light of foot."

The round of chuckles was a bit subdued and died out quickly. Ralston gave no smile, but checked his timepiece against the mantel clock. Conversation became stilted, and the drawing room knew long periods of uneasy silence. Ralston's presence brought a decided dearth of merriment.

It was in the hush of one of the long, quiet times that Trahern sat restlessly drumming his fingers on the arm of the chair. He stopped and slowly raised his hand to stare at it. The drumming continued, and all eyes in the room came to rest upon him. The sound resolved into hoofbeats drawing near, and Charlotte went to the window as a stentorian voice bawled out a series of unintelligible orders, and the thundering of hooves ceased.

"Redcoats," Charlotte informed from the window. "A dozen or so."

In the excitement of the arrival, it was only Pitney who noted that Ralston wore a smile of satisfaction and glared with open hostility at Ruark. A knock came upon the door, and shortly the doorman ushered an English officer into the drawing room. Ruark had been standing with his backside to the hearth, but at the man's entry he immediately presented his back to the room, bracing a hand against the mantel as he stared down into the flickering flames. Two soldiers with muskets followed the officer in and took up stations on either side of the door.

"Major Edward Carter, Virginia Detachment of His Majesty's Ninth Royal Fusiliers," the officer announced.

"Squire George Beauchamp." George stepped forward and offered his hand, which was taken briefly by the other. "Master of this house and lands by royal grant."

Major Carter nodded but remained stiff and formal. "I am about His Majesty's business," he informed George. "I respectfully request that my men be allowed to water and stable their mounts. Since we will remain the night, I also request shelter for my men."

The eldest Beauchamp smiled ruefully at the man. "We seem to be short one stable, major. But there are other barns, and as for your men I am sure some arrangements can be made."

"Whatever you can spare, sir." The major relaxed a bit. "I would not inconvenience you in any way." He cleared his throat. "Now, as to my business here. I have been informed that an escaped murderer is here. According to an unsigned letter I received from Richmond, the man goes under the name of Ruark. John Ruark."

Silence fell like a shroud over the room. A feather falling to the carpet would have raised a din by comparison. Only Ralston did not give way to absolute surprise. Shanna dared not move, though her eyes went discreetly to Ruark. With a sigh of resignation, Ruark turned from the fireplace and met the major's eyes boldly, a laconic smile on his lips.

"I surrender myself to you, Major Carter. I shall make no effort to escape." Ruark nodded toward the soldiers. "No need for violence here."

The major's eyes slowly roamed the room and the tense, waiting faces of the others present. "I believe I shall accept your promise. You realize, of course, you are under arrest?"

Ruark nodded, and the officer dismissed the two men by the door. He returned his gaze to Ruark, and a smile began to play about his lips.

"Beauchamp! I should have guessed." The major repeated Shanna's words unwittingly and rubbed his jaw in reflective memory. "Ruark Deverell Beauchamp, as I recall."

Now Ralston showed the surprise that had been absent earlier. His mouth sagged open, and he stumbled a step toward the officer. "Wha—" His tongue was no lighter than his feet. "Him? Beauchamp?" His finger stabbed at Ruark repeatedly. "Him? But—"

His dark eyes moved to George and then to Amelia, Gabrielle, Shanna, Jeremiah, and Nathanial. His longest stare of all was at Garland, who smiled sweetly back at him.

"Oh!" He swallowed. He toyed with the glove on his left hand and finally pulled it off as he retired to the fireplace and took his turn at regarding the coals.

"You were a captain the last time we met." Ruark gestured to the officer's rank.

"Aye!" The major rubbed his chin again. "I remember very well, Mister Beauchamp, and I am much relieved that I have brought more men this time."

"I'm sorry about that, major," Ruark replied and did seem genuinely apologetic. "I can only suggest that it was being so roughly aroused without explanation that stirred my ire somewhat."

Major Carter chuckled. " 'Tis my earnest desire that I never be present when your ire is fully roused. I beg you, however, not to worry overmuch about the broken jaw. These times of peace make promotions come very hard. It was the injury which brought my name to the fore and assured the rank to me, preventing at the same time my being cashiered. Good luck it was, albeit rather harsh." He surveyed the room. "You seem to be a member of the household."

"My son." Amelia's voice was sharp and tight as she took her husband's arm. "This has all been a terrible mistake. I am certain Ruark is not guilty of that hideous thing. And we intend to lend our full efforts to proving it."

"Of course, madam," Major Carter returned gently. "You may rest assured that a full investigation will be conducted into this matter. We have much to look into here." He peered at George. "Sir, it has been a long ride from Williamsburg, and I believe it nearly tea time. I see you have some brewing. I wonder if I might beg a cup."

"My hospitality has slipped," George responded. "Would you prefer something stronger? I have some excellent brandy."

"Sir, you are overkind to a poor servant of the crown." The major grinned as a snifter was pressed into his hand and closed his eyes almost in ecstasy as he rolled the first sip over his tongue. " 'Tis a boon to the weary." He took another sip and enjoyed it no less than the first.

"Good heavens!" the major suddenly exclaimed. "I'll be forgetting my boots next." He fumbled in the inner pocket of his coat before drawing forth a packet of envelopes. "Is a Captain Nathanial Beauchamp present?"

Nathanial came forward and identified himself.

"They seek to make the best use of an officer's time these days," the major said ruefully. "These be dispatches from London bound to you through the postmaster at Williamsburg and myself. At least one of them bears the royal seal."

Taking the letters, Nathanial withdrew to the window where the light was better.

Shanna came to Ruark and slipped her arm through his, hugging it close. Having witnessed her graceful movement across the room, Major Carter stared at them somewhat uncertainly. He had taken note of the beauty soon after his entry and heaved a sigh of disappointment as Ruark gave the introduction.

"My wife, sir. Shanna Beauchamp."

The major bowed before her. "You are most beautiful, madam! A light in the wilderness as it be. I am indeed pleasured. He straightened and regarded her carefully. "The name? Shanna? Would you perhaps be—or rather were you—Mistress Shanna Trahern?"

"Aye," Shanna replied graciously. "And this is my father, Orlan Trahern." She swept her hand to the seated one.

"Lord Trahern!" The major was obviously impressed and hurried to Trahern's side. "I have heard much about you, sir."

"Humph!" Trahern refused the extended hand. "Mostly bad I'd wager, but my temper will be greatly improved when this foolishness about young Ruark is done with. You may inform your superiors, major, that my influence and moneys will also be lent to his cause."

The officer was ill at ease. If there were two names and two fortunes that could more upset the peace of the crown, he was not aware of them.

Nathanial left off his reading by the window and rejoined them. "I believe no moneys need be expended today." He extended an official-looking document, replete with seals, toward the major. "This is to be delivered to the nearest officer of the crown, sir. Will you accept it?"

Heaving a reluctant sigh, the major took the letter from Nathanial's hand. He began to read, his lips moving with his eyes. He glanced at Ruark, set down his glass, and read further. He began to speak the words aloud.

". . . Thus in view of new evidences and in light of a petition made by the Marquess de Beauchamp, all proceedings in the case of Ruark Deverell Beauchamp are herein set aside until such time as further investigation has determined the facts in this matter."

Major Carter lowered the paper and spoke to the room at large. "It bears the seals of both the Marquess and the Court of Peers." He looked to Ruark and Shanna, a much-relieved smile spreading slowly across his face. "It seems that you are free, Mister Beauchamp."

With a happy cry, Shanna flung her arms about Ruark's neck and nearly strangled him in her excitement. Relieved sighs were released about the room.

"Do you mean to say"—Ralston's strident voice cut through the immediate gaiety, and everyone turned as a body to stare at him—"that an escaped murderer can be set free by a"—he stalked forward and flicked the corner of the document before the major could move it beyond his reach—"by a piece of paper? 'Tis injustice, I say! A gross miscarriage!"

The major drew himself to his full height. "This letter explains it all, sir. The woman had a husband and was seeing other men besides. There had been complaints before from men she had robbed. They claimed that after visiting her, none could remember anything but waking up to find themselves dumped a goodly distance from the inn. Further, several gentlemen in Scotland acknowledged Mister Beauchamp's arrival from the colonies. He could not have fathered her babe as she was well along, and they now suspect the husband of killing her in a jealous rage."

"A good English girl was brutally slain and she with child, and now her assailant is to go free?" Ralston had grasped only what he thought pertinent to his case.

"Mister Ralston!" Trahern bellowed.

Major Carter casually rested a hand upon his sword. "Do you challenge an order of the Court of Peers, sir?"

The disapproval of these two men of authority was enough to quiet the agitated Ralston. However, it was the flare of anger in Shanna's eyes as she came toward him, that made him retreat.

He stammered, "I only— Nay! Of course not!" He swallowed, his Adam's apple bobbing convulsively, and stared down at the woman who in untamed rage almost trod upon his long, narrow toes.

"Part your lips with my husband's name again, and I will tear them from your face." Though Shanna's voice was a bare whisper, Ralston understood her as well as if she had shouted. He nodded eagerly.

"Aye! Aye! I mean—Never! Anything!"

Ralston stood very still until she withdrew. He carefully eased his foot from the hearth and brushed the hot ashes from the sole of his boot. He followed Shanna with his gaze until she was safe on her husband's arm again. The agent had just begun to recover his poise but lost it when Pitney touched his arm.

"Mister Ralston, I found this. I believe it yours." The huge man held out the quirt he had shown Ruark earlier and watched the other closely.

"Oh! Why, thank you." Ralston was most relieved and accepted the whip. "Aye, 'tis mine. Most difficult you know to ride with only a willow switch." He paused and, giving a disgusted grimace, turned the thing over in his hand. "What is this all over it?"

"Blood," Pitney grunted. "And hair. Attila's. It was used to beat the horse until he whinnied and brought Ruark to the stables. But, of course, you would know nothing about that. You were gone the whole night. What did you say your friend's name was?"

"Blakely. Jules Blakely," Ralston answered absently.

"Blakely. I know the man." George added the comment from across the room. "He has a cottage just outside Mill Place. I have heard him speak of a relative in England, but 'twas, let me think," —he rubbed his chin thoughtfully then eyed Ralston—" 'twas his wife's brother."

Ralston would meet no one's gaze and stared at the floor. His voice was hoarse, and almost a whisper when he finally spoke.

"My sister—when I was but a lad, was falsely accused of thievery and sold into bondage. She—married the man, a colonial." The shame of this last admission seemed almost more than he could bear.

Major Carter had been standing by Trahern, taking in all that transpired. He pursed his lips from time to time and finally reached down into the large pocket of his coat to withdraw a rather thick manual with a plain cover. Leafing quickly through it, he paused to read intently upon a page and began to pace, his head down, deep in concentration. After several circuits of Trahern's chair, he stopped and launched a musing oratory.

"I have been a line officer most of my career, except for that tour in London." Smiling slightly, he nodded to Ruark. "And hence I am well schooled in the art of battle. Thus, being an officer of the crown in times of peace is another matter. However, the best wigs of the court have put together a manual which is supposed to take the place of experience and is also suggestive and not directive in nature." He held up the book and waved it a bit for their notice. "It leaves one with a choice of following it to the letter, or of ignoring it and chancing a court-martial. It does say, right here, that when an officer finds in the civil field a matter which seems uncommonly confused and/or suspicious, he must take it upon his own authority to investigate and obtain the facts." He tapped the page with his finger. "As presumptuous as it may sound, I could not have found better words to describe this situation."

He met all the stares he had attracted, turned, and faced Pitney.

"This matter of the stable. Did you mean to say the fire was deliberate?"

"No doubt of it," Nathanial interjected emphatically. "The entrance was secured with a log against it, and my brother had been struck on the head."

Under the major's urging, the tale was told, and at its end the officer flung up his hands in complete bemusement.

"Gentlemen, please. I am trying to understand this, and 'tis most confusing. Perhaps 'twould be best if we started from the beginning." He turned slowly and surveyed them all, halting as he faced Ruark again. "Mister Beauchamp." He smiled quickly and his eyes went back to the other two Beauchamp men. "Mister Ruark Beauchamp," he corrected. "It has much upset me that your name appeared on the hanging orders, yet you stand here apparently little the worse for the event. How can that be?"

Ruark spread his hands. "I only know that I was taken from my cell, placed in another with other men, then later transferred to a ship which sailed to Los Camellos." He nodded over the major's shoulder. "Perhaps Mister Ralston there can better explain. 'Twas he who arranged the whole of it."

"What?" Trahern sat up in his chair and twisted around to stare at Ralston. "You bought him from Newgate?"

"Brought is hardly the term for it, papa," Shanna replied for the man. "The gaol keeper, Mister Hicks, had fine regard for shiny coin as I can well attest." She regarded Ralston closely. "What did Mister Hicks charge for his trouble? One hundred, two hundred pounds?"

Ralston spluttered and could not meet the major's eyes. Then he looked at Shanna as if a new thought dawned. "You have threatened me and accused me on several occasions, madam, but how is it that you wed one Ruark Beauchamp when that same man was lodged in the cellar of Newgate?"

Trahern turned slowly in his chair to face Shanna with a questioning brow arched. "Hmmm," he nodded. "That *would* be most interesting to hear, Shanna, child." He waited.

Shanna closely examined the brooch she wore, scuffed at the carpet with a daintily slippered toe, smiled ruefully at Ruark, then drew a deep breath, and met her father's gaze directly. "It was there I went to seek out a name to please you and fulfill the terms of your wishes. I found one that could not be questioned and whose bearer, I thought, would not burden me overlong. We struck a bargain, we two." She smiled over her shoulder at Ruark and reached out a hand to him. He took it and stood beside her, slipping an arm protectively about her waist. She spoke again to her father. "The lie was bitter as I gave it, and it turned against me, for when I found out that I was not in truth a widow, I could not admit it." She leaned comfortably against Ruark. "I am sorry for the deceit, papa, but if I could be certain that the end would be the same, I would do it all again."

Trahern laughed merrily to himself and was still chuckling when he looked up at her again. "I was wondering how long you would take that ultimatum. For a while I was sure you had yielded, but now I see you have more than an even share of Trahern blood."

Shanna eyed the major hesitantly. "Another man was buried in the coffin I thought was Ruark's. Perhaps an unnamed corpse bound for potter's field. Beyond that, I have no knowledge."

Pitney stepped forward and took up the tale. "I received the coffin from Mister Hicks at Newgate. In it was an old man, withered and dried, dead of hunger or disease, I could not tell. Whoever the fellow was, he lies well beneath fine stone with a high name upon it. There is little else to tell, only that I found a man who claims to be the husband of the murdered wench in London." And as the major opened his mouth to speak, Pitney held up a hand to give him pause. "I know now that the man is suspect. At this moment he is in Richmond. The man was well in his cups in London and only told me then that Ruark could not have done it."

Pitney saw Shanna's accusing stare and hastened to add, "When I found that Ruark had escaped the hangman, I saw no reason to make a further stir over it. 'Twas only in Richmond that the girl's husband said he'd soon be able to prove Ruark innocent, so I left him to do what he was intending. It might have been a ruse to see himself clear." Pitney shrugged. " I trusted the man."

"There was a girl murdered on our island," Trahern mused aloud. "And she traced an 'R' in the sand."

Pitney turned his gaze to Ralston and rested it there until that one began to chafe beneath the weight of it.

"You accuse me?" Ralston barked. "I abhorred the little twit, but I had no reason to kill her. She was nothing to me."

Shanna frowned at him. "Milly was with child, and you gave her coins. Ruark and I both saw you with her in the hall at the manor house."

Ralston waved his narrow hand. "She was to bring me fish. 'Twas all."

"Why did you follow Ruark about the island?" Pitney questioned. "I saw you on many occasions doing so."

The thin man's jaw flexed angrily. "You would like to accuse me of trying to murder him, wouldn't you? You and she"—he gestured to Shanna—"connived in London behind my back to arrange the marriage," Ralston sneered. "Well, I didn't know he was wed to her when I saw them together near the mill. Mister Ruark was free enough with his hands to make me realize there was something between them. As I was responsible for him being on the island, I knew if he were accused of tampering with the squire's daughter, questions would be aroused, and I would have to answer more than a few of them myself. I only learned that they were married on the sea voyage here, and as soon as we landed I sent a letter to the authorities. I understood Mister Ruark a murderer, don't you understand? Mister Hicks said as much."

Shanna and Ruark exchanged glances that communicated the fact that they had both caught the significance of what Ralston had said. Besides Pitney, only Milly had known of their marriage.

"Mister Ralston," Pitney rasped out. "You are an amazingly innocent man."

"Major!" Ralston called for the attention of the officer. "I am a citizen of England, due the protection of the law." He worried at the glove he still wore on his right hand, snatched it off, and flung the both of them to a table. "If anyone is to accuse me, let him do it in a court. Then I will answer. But this mockery is unbearable. I demand the protection of a king's officer."

Amelia had moved to Ruark's side as the man finished his tirade, and now her elbow began to dig at his ribs. He glanced down at her, and she cast her eyes at Ralston. Bemused, Ruark frowned and with a sigh Amelia pointed to Ralston's right hand. Ruark looked at the man's hand and frowned at his mother again. Amelia's brows drew together, and she gestured again. This time Ruark looked closely and suddenly saw her reason for such insistence.

"Mister Ralston?" Ruark asked gently. "Where did you get that ring?"

Ralston raised his hand to stare at the ring and answered sharply. " 'Twas payment for a debt. What of it?"

Ruark shrugged and mildly stated. "It has been in my family for several generations. I believe it was stolen from me."

"Stolen? Nonsense! I lent a man some money, and he had no means to pay. He gave me this instead."

Ruark half faced the major and spoke as much to him as to Ralston and the others. "My mother gave me the ring to present to my wife when I chose one. I wore it on a chain about my neck, and there it was when I went to the wench's chambers in England. That was the night she was murdered. Whoever took it had to have been in the room that night."

Ralston's jaw sagged as he realized the full implication of what

Ruark had said. The major's hand came to rest upon his pistol, and a horrified expression crept over Ralston's features as once more he became the center of attention.

"Nay! 'Twas not me! I did not kill her!" He began to sweat. "You cannot lay this to me. Here, take your damned token." He twisted the ring from his finger and flung it across the room. His eyes grew wild as he stared back at them all. "I tell you—I did not kill her!"

His voice grew pleading as he turned to Ruark. "How can you accuse me? I never did anything to hurt you. Good lord, man. I paid the money to save you from the hangman. Is that worth nothing?"

Suddenly Ralston remembered the chains on the man, the threats he had heaped upon him. No mercy would be found here. He faced Pitney to present his plea.

"We traveled together." But Ralston recalled the bloody quirt and knew the hulking man suspected him. No help from this quarter. He stared at Trahern and saw the angry gaze in return and heard the words gritted out.

"You brought me men from the gaol and pocketed the balance?"

Panic! Fear! Ralston's world was collapsing around his ears. He fought to still his trembling hands and a quaking in his knees. Then Ruark spoke calmly.

"Who gave you the ring, Mister Ralston? Sir Gaylord, perhaps?"

The agent stopped and gawked. Then he laughed in sudden, overwhelming relief. "Of course. He repaid me for some moneys I had lent him."

"And where did Sir Gaylord say he had gotten it?" Ruark questioned above the murmurs of surprise.

"Why, from a Scotsman, he said. For a debt the man owed him."

"Jamie is a Scotsman," Pitney offered, frowning. "He could have taken the ring from Ruark."

"Where is Sir Gaylord?" Ruark asked, his voice flat. "Riding still?"

"No one has seen him," Amelia replied.

"We'll get to the bottom of this when he returns," the major stated.

"How much *did* you pay for Ruark?" Trahern broke in to question his agent.

Ralston's relief turned abruptly to distress, and he gulped out the answer. "Two hundred pounds."

"Fifteen hundred you told me. I can only assume you cheated me before." Trahern hefted the bag of money before he tossed it back to Ruark. "There was never any fair debt of bondage against you, and your services have more than repaid my investment in you." Without turning, he added, "Mister Ralston's accounts on Los Camellos shall go as repayment for what he's cheated me of."

Ralston stammered in outrage. "That's everything I have in the world!"

"You'd best have enough to live on here in the colonies for a time," Trahern said, fixing Ralston with a cold stare, "for you are no longer in my employ." Then the squire continued almost jovially. "Perhaps Mister Blakely will accept your bondage. Whoever your next master is, I urge you not to cheat him."

The thin man's shoulders sagged. He had lost more here than he had ever gained through trickery. It was a cruel blow, indeed, if he should have to live out the rest of his days in the colonies. If Gaylord couldn't repay him, then he was truly in dire straits. The room grew still as Ralston slumped into a nearby chair.

With much of the excitement passed, Shanna felt a sudden weariness sweep over her. It had been a long morning beginning with the stable fire. And then there had been the fear of Ruark being taken by the redcoats. As all the tensions ebbed from her, she realized she was nearly exhausted. Murmuring a word to Ruark, she let him make the excusal. He escorted her up the stairs and closed the draperies over the windows. She smothered a yawn and sagged on the edge of the bed. He smiled as he came around to lean a shoulder against the massive post at the end, and his eyes spoke above the silence as he gazed at her.

"The door won't close," she reminded him impishly and laughed as she flung herself back across the bed. "Do you realize that we won't have to sneak around anymore?"

Ruark went to the armoire and opened it to draw out a fresh shirt. "Now that I can claim my room, I'm going to claim everything else in it."

He leered at her, drawing a playful giggle from her.

"Not with that door open. Cool your lusts, sir, until it's repaired."

"I'll see it done posthaste, madam."

Shanna watched him remove the leather jerkin and draw the shirt over his head, and her eyes were soft with love. "There is that which bothers me still, Ruark," she said quietly. "Who tried to kill you?"

"I have strong suspicions," he replied and spoke through the linen shirt as he pulled it over his head. "And I intend to find out for certain."

Stuffing the shirttail into his breeches, he came back to the bed. He bent down, bracing his arms on either side of her, and his mouth found hers, then savored its eager response.

"I love you," Shanna whispered, looping her arms around his neck.

Smiling into her eyes, Ruark repeated the words as his hand slipped downward along her body in a soft caress. Abruptly his wandering fingers halted just below her knee, and he frowned his bemusement.

"Have you grown lumps of a sudden, madam?"

Shanna giggled and raised her skirts and chemise to show him the sheathed dagger stuck in her garter. "After this morning I decided you needed protection."

Ruark was more intrigued with the display of shapely limbs and continued his fondling along her naked skin. His kisses grew bold, and hot blood surged within his loins. Breathlessly Shanna whispered against his parted lips.

"The door. Someone might see us."

"We seem to have a problem with privacy," Ruark returned huskily and dropped a kiss upon her velvet-smooth belly before pulling down her billowing skirts. "I'll go see what I can get to fix the door. Don't go away."

"I won't, she assured him.

As she listened to the sound of his footsteps hurrying down

the hall, Shanna smiled to herself and snuggled against the pillow. He had not bothered to silence his steps. It was a long moment, and her eyelids sagged as her bliss gently sailed her into peaceful slumber.

❧ Chapter 28 ❧

SHANNA came slowly into full awareness. A small, furtive sound had disturbed her sleep, yet it was not one that aroused apprehension or fear. She lay still, gathering her wits and teetering on the precipice of slumber. The light scraping noise came again. It was the branch of the oak tree brushing against the windowpane. Shanna rolled her head on the pillow and in the muted light of the room made out the figure of a man just stepping into the chamber from the windowsill.

"Ruark?" she murmured sleepily. "What game are you playing now?"

The dark form straightened and turned. Shanna gasped and sat upright on the bed, a scream hovering at the base of her tongue. The man came toward her, a smirk etched across his lips.

"Gaylord!" Shanna was surprised, but her trepidation waned. Surely this foppish knight was harmless. She snapped angrily. "What are you about, sneaking into my chamber?"

"Why, my dear Shanna," the knight sneered. "I was imitating what I've watched your gallant husband do. Am I not at least as handsome as he is?"

"Certainly not!" she stated bluntly. She shook her head

lightly. Her mind was still heavy with sleep. But—he had not been present when Garland arrived. Indeed, he had been absent for the entire furor. How could he have known of their marriage? There was something in this that gnawed at her and stirred both her suspicion and her curiosity.

"Before I call the servants and have you cast out, I ask again, Sir Gaylord. What is your purpose here?"

"Rest easy, my lady." He leaned a long-barreled musket against the back of a chair and took a seat, propping his muddy boots on another. "I have been about business of my own and only sought to have a word with you in private."

Shanna rose and smoothed her velvet gown and sleep-mussed hair, conscious of his roving eyes upon her. She tucked her feet into her shoes and glanced at the clock on the mantel. The hour was shortly past noon. She had only slept a few brief moments after all, and Ruark would be returning soon to repair the door.

"I cannot imagine what topic we have in common, Sir Gaylord," Shanna declared haughtily as she folded the quilt and laid it neatly at the foot of the bed. If the boorish dolt was bent on renewing his courtship, she would put short shrift to it. She had no intention of staying to listen to his panted endearments.

"Ah, my lovely Lady Shanna." Billingsham leaned back in the chair and pressed his fingertips together, forming a steeple over his belly. "The ice queen! The untouchable one! The perfect woman!" There was an evil echo in his soft, wheezing laughter. "But not so perfect. My dear, you have practiced deceit and now the debt falls due. The time has come to pay."

Shanna frowned at the knight. "What are you saying?"

"Your marriage to John Ruark, of course. You don't want anybody to know about it, do you?"

So, he did *not* know that the secret was out. But he knew about the marriage. She led him on.

"Sir? Do you mean to extract money from me?"

"Oh, nay, my lady," he averred, his eyes following her with undisguised hunger as she moved a bit away from him.

Gaylord came to his feet and, with a seemingly casual stride, positioned himself between Shanna and the door. He faced her abruptly and struck that inane pose with his cocked knee as he fixed her with a glowering gaze.

"Nothing at all so devious," the good man smirked. " 'Tis only that I need your assistance and you have something to yield in return. If you will convince your father and the Beauchamps to invest a goodly sum in my family's shipyard, I shall say nothing of your marriage to this Ruark chap, nor will I inform the authorities that your husband is, in fact, an escaped murderer."

Shanna's face was carefully blank. "And how do you know that?"

He snorted. "The fool, Ralston, told me on the *Hampstead* of his dreaded secret, that he had bought a murderer from the gaol and that that same one was John Ruark. I had followed my father's writings very carefully on your husband's trial. Of course, he was Ruark Beauchamp then. What bemused me most was how you came to be married to the rogue. I understood that he had been hanged, and when you portrayed yourself his widow, I was surprised, for I had thought the man unmarried, or so my father's documents stated. I had never seen Ruark Beauchamp, so I couldn't name John Ruark as the same until Ralston informed me of his misdeed, and I could only surmise that John Ruark and Ruark Beauchamp were one and the same. You did marry him in the gaol, didn't you?"

Shanna gave a slow nod. "Aye. And what will you do should I submit to your demand?"

"Why, I am off to London, of course," he replied with an offhanded gesture, "to see to my affairs there."

"Back to London, you say." The faintest glimmering of a notion began to tickle at the back of Shanna's mind. She had thought to ridicule the man with the truth, but she decided now to further satisfy her curiosity. She kept her voice in the same half-angry tone she had used but asked a different question. "It occurs to me, Sir Gaylord, that you have been much in need of coin. You plead your poverty but comport in a most splendorous fashion. You were friends with Mister Ralston. You might have borrowed a few pounds from him—"

"And what if I did, madam?" He was at once nervous and almost angry. "Is it any affair of yours?"

"Of course not." Shanna smiled to allay his fears and continued more casually. " 'Tis only that he had a ring of much value, and he insisted it was payment for a debt." She urged him to reply. "A cameo one? Of some age?"

"Oh, that!" the knight seemed relieved. "Most of my jewelry and some coin were in the baggage sent to Richmond. I borrowed a bit from him until I could reach the port and repay him."

"And the ring? How did you come by it?"

He looked at her narrowly. "I paid out some coins to a Scotsman, and I took that piece for his debt."

" 'Twould seem there are many debts in this world."

"Aye, but why this interest in the ring, madam?" His voice betrayed an aroused suspicion. The idiot Ralston had taken on that one piece and insisted upon it for payment.

"There is another thing I would ask." Shanna tried to shift the topic to one less sensitive. "How is it that you came to know that John Ruark was my husband? You were obviously the one who told Ralston." She tipped her head and mused aloud as he gave no sign of an inclination to answer. "Many people knew parts of the secret, but few knew of the marriage between John Ruark and myself. I cannot guess who—"

A coldness coursed in Shanna's veins, and she went to the window to draw aside the heavy drape, blinking as the bright sunlight invaded the room again.

"There was only Pitney—and Milly. As I trust Pitney, it had to be Milly. Poor Milly, she was with child . . ." Shanna's voice slowed, and she stared openly at Gaylord. "Ruark could not wed her, and she must have gone to—" Her jaw sagged as it all came together.

"You!" Shanna choked out in horror. "And Milly! You killed her, too!"

Shanna began to realize her own danger as Gaylord's eyes narrowed and his face set. She knew she must flee and darted suddenly toward the door. Gaylord caught her easily, his long, bony fingers locking firmly around her arm. With a snarl he flung her backwards, and she sprawled upon the bed. His tall form towered over her, looming ominously as if he would throw himself down upon her. Her mind screamed for Ruark to hasten back.

"Aye, Milly!" the knight sneered. "And do not fancy yourself above a like fate, so hold your tongue, my lady."

He withdrew a heavy quirt from beneath his coat and slapped the butt suggestively against his palm. Shanna recalled the long welts on Milly's body and remembered Attila's nose and could find no desire to sample the same for herself. Obligingly she held her tongue.

Gaylord began to pace the floor restlessly, never leaving Shanna a clear path to the door, and carefully staying within a pace or two of her. He raved as he walked.

"That common bitch! Daughter of a fishmonger! Ha! She got herself with babe and saw me as a fine catch." He whirled on his heels and waved the riding crop. "But she changed her mind. Aye, that she did! She whimpered for mercy and vowed she would say nothing. I made sure of it."

Shanna was nauseated with the vision of Milly trying to dissuade the knight, pleading for her life beneath the cruel blows. She sat on the edge of the bed and tried to quell the sickening fear that gripped her. The man was insane. He would kill on a whim. No doubt he had murdered the girl in London as well because she had proven a hindrance to him. And the thought came to Shanna that should he become convinced she was also a threat—

She could not let herself dwell on that. She must say something to distract him.

"My father will—" she began haltingly.

"Your father!" Gaylord's nostrils flared as he glared at her, and his face became a twisted mask of rage. "*Lord* Trahern!" he mimed angrily. "A commoner! Son of a thief! How I hated to beg for his money. Him! A merchant cheating the gentler breed of its rightful wealth, taking their homes and lands because they could no longer meet his outrageous demands. Worthy lords and peers reduced to groveling at his feet for a tuppence. Good men with plans that might sway the fate of all of England coming to a common merchant to beg for funds."

Shanna's ire rose in defense of her father. She would not allow a murderer to slander him. "My father cheated no one! 'Twas their own lack of good sense that brought them to grief."

"My uncle would argue the point." Gaylord took haughty offense. "He was ordered by the court to surrender the family estate for his debts. I believe your father now calls it his country house. But you defend him, my dear Shanna, when you have woes of your own. You know far too much for me to allow your freedom."

He paused thoughtfully for a moment and scratched his chin with the end of the quirt.

"What am I to do? I need your father's money, but I cannot let you free to spread your tales." He came to stand near her. "Then there is your curiosity about the ring. Tell me why it was so quickly noticed?"

He put his foot on the bed and rested an elbow on his knee, bending low to stare into Shanna's face. She shrugged and answered as innocently as she could.

" 'Twas only that it seemed richer than his means would allow."

Gaylord sucked on his teeth and sighed, "Madam, I have little time for pleasant banter and even less patience."

As Shanna opened her mouth to reply, his hand lashed out in a savage swipe. The force of the blow hurled her back on the bed, and Shanna's head reeled as she struggled up to an elbow and touched her numbed cheek.

"The next time I ask you a question, try to give me a better answer, my dear." His tone was hard. "Now, why the ring?"

"It belonged to Ruark." Shanna spat between angry white lips.

"Much better, my dear." He studied her intensely. "Then your Ruark already suspects me of the bitch's murder in London? He didn't believe I had gotten it from the Scotsman?" Gaylord held up a hand. "No need to lie again. You did say I had killed Milly, too. And he has, of course, talked to your father?" He nodded as Shanna's eyes flared in renewed contempt. "Ah, yes, I see. Then my masquerade is done!" He straightened away from her. "Well enough! I weary of playing the foolish fop for your good humor."

Shanna realized her face betrayed her again.

"What's this? You are surprised, my dear?" he jeered arrogantly, the lisping accent gone from his words. "I was well aware that your common minds would find amusement with a clumsy, bumbling fop. Still, I am injured, madam, that you, of all, believed it so readily."

Shanna glared her utter hatred for the errant knight.

"I see, my dear Shanna,"—Gaylord chuckled and scratched at his collar—"that you could not give even pity to an afflicted knight of the realm, but you reserve your adoration for a colonial bumpkin. I wonder if he really faced the pirates as boldly as is told and if you survived as pure and untouched as you would have us believe."

Gaylord began to pace again, his head bowed in thought, but his wary eyes ever touched her.

"Pirates!" He chortled, halting and shaking his quirt at her. "By the devil, that's the way! A ransom!"

He went back to the chair and quickly returned with the long rifle. Shanna's eyes widened. She recognized it as Ruark's, the one he had left in the stable before it was set on fire.

"Aye, my lady," Gaylord leered, seeing where her eyes wandered. "Your husband's. I took his weapons from the stable after I hit him. I should have finished the task then and there, before I set fire to the place. I lured him from your side when I knew the house was asleep. Clever of me, I must say, using Attila to draw him out. Had I planned better for the other two attempts, I would have seen him gone sooner, but I just happened by and saw that the opportunity was ripe. Then, I didn't know he was your husband. I was in the loft with Milly while you two were playing beneath. I realized, then, that I had to do away with him, because you were obviously in love with the rogue. Your infatuation hindered my marriage plans, and, you see, I really needed your father's wealth. Why," he laughed, "I couldn't have avoided my creditors this long had it not been for the treasure I found in the girl's room in London. She tried to pry a few coins from me, you know, but I had naught to keep her quiet. She deserved to die."

Snatching a long scarf from the armoire, Gaylord came back to haul Shanna roughly to her feet. His fingers bit in calculated cruelty into her arm.

"No sound, my dear," he warned close to her ear. " 'Tis your continued fortune that I have found a use for you."

He pulled her arms behind her and bound them tightly with the scarf as he leered over her shoulder at her taut bodice.

"Be docile, my dear." He lightly caressed her bosom and the

full length of her body. Bound or not, Shanna could not tolerate his mauling. She opened her mouth for an enraged shriek but found it stuffed with a handkerchief. She tried to spit out the dry linen, but he wrapped another scarf over her mouth, drawing it tight. Sir Gaylord rifled through her trunk until he found a heavy cape and draped it over Shanna's shoulders. The knight then slipped the strap of the rifle over his left arm and drew a pistol from his belt with his other hand. He held the latter beneath his cloak, reached out, and twisted his hand in Shanna's hair until she winced with pain.

"So that you will not leave me on a whim, my dear," he laughed.

Sir Gaylord paused, and his eyes gleamed as they swept the room. "But how shall they know?" he spoke as if to himself. The small writing desk sat in the corner and there his gaze stopped. "Of course! A note for them. Come, my dear."

He dragged her across the room and, laying the pistol on top the desk, flipped the shelf down. He snatched a sheet of paper and plunged the quill into the well. He wrote boldly:

From the Beauchamps and Lord Trahern, I demand fifty thousand pounds each. Instructions later.

For the signature he scrawled an ornate "B" ending the letter at the bottom with a flourished scroll. With a snorted laugh, he sailed the paper to the bed, retrieved the pistol, then led Shanna into the hallway.

They had approached the top of the stairs when suddenly he thrust Shanna against the wall and pressed the pistol against her throat to ensure her silence. He peered around the corner to watch as the front door was pushed open by a wiry, red-haired man who stepped aside to let Ruark enter. The latter's hands were filled with tools and odds and ends of wood. The man followed Ruark in and, after closing the door, helped him place his load in the corner.

"Jamie Conners is the name. I be looking for a Mister Pitney."

Shanna could see Gaylord's frame stiffen as the stranger introduced himself.

"Mister Pitney is right in here." Ruark led the man into the drawing room.

Once the hallway was clear, Billingsham took Shanna to the bottom of the stairs, forcing her in front of him as if to shield himself and pressing against the wall, waving the pistol as if a host of enemies threatened him. He dragged her to a halt. Voices could be heard from within the room. Shanna considered pulling loose and flinging herself away from her captor, but even as the thought came, Gaylord's hand caught a fresh hold in her hair and twisted her head painfully to one side as if to warn her to silence.

"Nah, I had no reason to kill me girl, but I know 'oo did," the Scotsman's voice came to them. " 'Tain't this one here. The one I'm after was bigger and heavier."

Ruark watched the man flex his arms to indicate greater strength.

"But he's here, the damn blighter is. Begging yer pardons, ma'ams." The man snatched his hat from his head and crushed it in his hands. "He come when I weren't about the dock and took his baggage what I followed clear from London. Off to the Beauchamps' place they said he was." The small man studied each face before him carefully. "Ye ain't got no others? About so tall?" He held his hand a full head higher than his own. " 'Bout as tall as Mister Pitney here. Sort of a dandy one he were, with lordly garb and a big feathered hat. Aye, a knight of the realm he were."

"Sir Gaylord Billingsham!" Ruark snorted.

"Aye, that's the name!" the Scotsman chortled. "Sir Gaylord Billingsham!"

Shanna twisted in Gaylord's grasp, but he turned a silent snarl to her face and raised the pistol as if he would strike her. Pushing her ahead of him, he rounded the stairs and headed for the back of the house. The servants had gathered in the kitchen to prepare the midday meal, and it was an easy matter for Gaylord to push Shanna through the back door without being seen. In a moment they had gained the shelter of a line of shrubs that led near the former stable. He swung her easily over the rail fence and was soon urging her toward a stand of forest.

By the time they entered the copse, Shanna was breathless

beneath the stricture of the gag. There, Jezebel and a saddled horse of the Beauchamps waited. The mare wore only a blanket tied on with a rope. Two bags of provisions had been thrown across her back. Without pause, Gaylord lifted Shanna astraddle and tied her feet with a length of rawhide wrapped beneath the horse's belly. Standing back, he surveyed his labors then laughed with a chilling lack of humor.

"Not the usual comfort, perhaps, but adequate. As you can see, I was going to use the mare as a pack horse but she will serve to carry you instead, my dear."

He reached out and freed her hands, prodding her with the muzzle of the rifle.

"In front if you don't mind, my lady." He bound her hands together and, giving a dour chuckle, laid a hank of the mare's mane across her fingers. "Be sure to hang on, my dear. 'Twould hurt me no end should you fall, not to mention yourself, of course."

He snickered at his own humor and stepped into the saddle of the other mount, displaying a skill at horsemanship that had not been evident on his other attempts. Jezebel had no bridle, only a rope halter, and now Gaylord looped the loose end of the lead rope about his arm and set his heels to the flanks of his steed. Helplessly Shanna looked back over her shoulder, and ragged fear assailed the courage she tried to muster. There was no sign of an alarm being raised as yet from the manor, and her hopes of escaping this madman dwindled rapidly. Whether bent on murder or rape, he'd have his way, just as he had with Milly and the other girl.

There was little she could do to delay the flight, but whatever there was she would seize upon and work to its limit.

They crossed the open pasture at a fierce pace, heading straight for the tall oak on the far side. Shanna kneed the mare to one side and the other, trying to hinder the retreat as much as possible. The horse snorted and lunged at this misuse, and, if not succeeding in delaying, Shanna at least had the satisfaction of seeing Gaylord's arm stretched to its limit.

They entered the forest, and the path was one Shanna knew. It led to Ruark's cabin in the high valley. Of course Sir Gaylord could not know that the place where he thought to take his refuge was the least safe of all.

They were well into the woods and had begun to climb when Gaylord slowed and, dropping back beside her, loosened the gag and snatched it away. Shanna spat to rid her mouth of the taste of sweaty linen.

"Scream if it suits you, my dear. As loud and as long as you wish." Gaylord chortled. "There is no one to hear you now. Moreover, I would not hide your beauty any longer than necessary."

"Enjoy yourself, my lord." Shanna gave him a calm, almost gentle smile. "Your end is approaching apace. I carry Ruark's child, and he will hunt you down. He has killed before, men such as yourself who tried to take me from him."

Gaylord stared at her in surprise, then laughed with a wheezing snort. "So you bear his child. Do you think that matters aught to me? Believe what you will, madam, but be careful. I have felt the sting of your arrogance oft enough. Turn your mind to the consideration of my temper, and you may yet see this through without undue pain. There is no one behind us. They cannot know which way we've come."

"Ruark will come." Shanna still managed the same assured smile.

"Ruark!" Gaylord snorted.

He urged his horse ahead and tried to drag the mare at a faster pace. Shanna sat back and with her knees commanded Jezebel to halt. It was a struggle as they passed along the trail, but it diverted Shanna's mind from her own thoughts and fears.

The major rose to his feet and asked almost angrily, "And how do you know it was Sir Gaylord who killed your wife?"

Jamie Conners suddenly became nervous. "Well, I—"

Clamping his mouth shut, the Scotsman would speak no more, only shuffled his feet and twisted his hat as the major pressed him for an answer. Through the whole of it, Jamie cast quick, apprehensive glances toward Ruark, until Ruark realized that he himself was the reason the man would not speak. "Speak freely, man," Ruark urged. "We have waited long enough already. I will make no charge against you, and I think the major will agree that what you have to say will set to rest a greater crime, one which you, as well, would see justice meet."

"Well," Jamie began slowly. "The wife and I, we had this little thing. She made bold with the men and got them to the room then slipped a potion in the drink she gave them. Whilst the men were asleeping, we—ah—helped ourselves. Just a little purse, a bit of a bauble." He hastened to assert, "We never hurt no one. We—"

"But how do you know it was Sir Gaylord?" the major questioned sternly.

"I'm coming to that. Ye see, we got this bloke here," he nodded to Ruark, "and he passes out on her bed. I took his purse and she a few other things to put in her safe box. Saving up a bit to go back to Scotland, we was, and we almost had it. Now the whole lot of it is gone. 'Tweren't enough he beat her to death, but he took our hard-earned savings, too." The Scotsman seemed blissfully naïve as to propriety.

Ruark drew out the ring and showed it to him. "Do you remember this?"

Jamie stared at him and finally answered reluctantly. "Aye, she took it from ye. On a little chain thing round yer neck, it were. And she thought it pretty. She had nothing like that of her own. Good lass, she was. Sturdy and loyal." He sniffed loudly and rubbed his nose on the back of his hand. "Miss the girl, I do. Ain't never found another like her."

"About Sir Gaylord?" the major reminded him roughly.

"I'm gettin' to that!" the man chafed. "It's comin'! Be a little patient. Well, this bloke is on the bed, and we gots his things, and we put them away. Then there comes a knocking on the door. Now I can't be seen there, 'cause she's got this other thing where she's pressing a couple of fine gentlemen for some money, saying the babe was theirs and threatening to go to their families. Sir Gaylord was one of them. He raised a bit of a tiff when me girl said she'd tell his pa, and that high lord. Well, Sir Gaylord was there at the door, wantin' to talk to her. I slid down the gutter spout and sneaked around the front to take an ale or two in the common room while I waits on them. Then he comes out, pulling his big, floppy hat down, like he don't want none to see him. I waits a wee bit. Then I goes and slips back to me girl's room. And there was she, all bloody and dead, and there was Mister Ruark, still cold as a cod on the bed. Ain't moved a muscle since I left, and she'd thrown a blanket over him, so the good Sir Gaylord wouldn't know he was there. But that knight, he found the safe box, he did. I don't think she had put it away. A small fortune, there was, and all I got was Mister Ruark's purse."

Ruark laughed but without much amusement. "Aye, and a small fortune that was, too."

The man bobbed his head in apology. "I spent it following his bloody lordship, or at least tagging after his baggage and that frigate he sailed on from London."

George took the major's arm and now interrupted. "Major Carter, I, for one, have heard enough. I would ask that you post some men around the house. Sir Gaylord will no doubt be back. If he does not return we can begin searching for him."

Ruark went to the door. "I shall see to some temporary repairs upstairs if you gentlemen will excuse me!"

He gathered his tools and wood. Nathanial's gentle chuckle followed him as he made his way up the stairs. Ruark entered his bedchamber, stepping carefully around the door where it leaned askew. He lowered the tools on a tabletop and glanced toward the bed.

Empty?

His gaze quickly searched the room then returned to the four-poster. He had seen the open desk and now espied the note. He went nearer, and a moment later his bellow of rage trembled the house. He leapt down the stairs, taking them three at a time and dashed into the drawing room where he flung the crumpled sheet of paper in Trahern's lap.

"He's taken her!" he choked through the red haze of his wrath. "The bastard's got Shanna!"

It was Amelia's voice, firm and commanding, that finally broke into his mind. "Ruark! Control yourself. You will do her no good this way."

Ruark shook his head as if to clear his mind and realized it was Nathanial who held his arm and his father who took from his now unprotesting hands the rifle he had unthinkingly snatched up. He returned to reality, and though the heat of his rage was gone, the cold fire still burned in the pit of his belly.

As Pitney watched Ruark he was reminded of a venging beast and was at the same time deeply relieved that this time the savage fury was not turned upon himself, for there were no restraining chains. The foolish one who had roused this beast of prey would do well to never rest his feet.

Trahern frowned at the note in his lap. The initial scrawled on the bottom ran over and over in his mind as a multitude of emotions washed through him. The sum would only tweak the shallowest depth of his wealth, and there was enough to cover the total sum in a strongbox on the *Hampstead*. But 'twas the anger in his mind that hurt him most. For all his skill in judging men, he had let this serpent nest in his own household.

Ralston sat meekly in his chair, not daring to interfere. He had known nothing of Gaylord's vices and had only hoped to gain a part of the dowry.

George paced the floor, wanting to fling himself into some activity, but having no direction for it. Nathanial stood with the women, who silently gripped hands in their fear for Shanna. Jeremiah was close by, clutching his rifle with white-knuckled determination. Whatever happened, he would take part in it. No childish excuses anymore.

Pitney rose and worked his hands convulsively as he read over Trahern's shoulder. His voice was the first to break the tense quietness. "I've seen that thing at the bottom before."

"Of course you have," Trahern snapped with unusual rancor. " 'Tis marked on every one of his kerchiefs, his shirts and anywhere else he can put it. It's a "B" for bastard."

"Nay! Nay!" Pitney ranted. "I mean somewhere else. Something not so—aye, that's it. Milly's 'R'! 'Twas no 'R.' The lass could not read or write and only gave us what she saw. A 'B' with a little curlique at the bottom, for Billingsham."

Trahern lifted the paper and shook it at the major. " 'Twas that knight of yours who killed Milly!"

"With all respects, sir," the major replied calmly. "He is not my knight."

Pitney snorted. "I heard the tale from a young lieutenant in the dramshop on Los Camellos. It seems a horse stepped on Sir Gay's foot, and he fell against a Marshal as a mortar burst nearby. The Marshal gave him credit for saving his life and lauded the brave deed until Gaylord was awarded the badge of knighthood."

The major raised his brows and half apologized. "Such things happen in battle."

"You'll see! You'll see!" the Scotsman raved, nearly beside himself. "He'll do your little girlie the same as he did mine, with his bloody little whip and his bloody big fist!"

The Scotsman felt a strange chill creep up his back. Raising his eyes from the paper, he met Ruark's stare and shuddered. The man's face was blank and his eyes cold and flat, shining with a light that seemed to come from somewhere in the depth of them. He gave no word, but there was death in every inch of him. The Scotsman had heard a story once of a mythical lizard who could stare into your eyes and draw the life from you. He looked away quickly, nervously, because that was the same cold feeling he caught from the other man, that same one who had been hung and yet stood here. . . . Jamie shuddered again and reconsidered his religion most fervently.

Suddenly George stopped his pacing and came to them. "If a man's to go far with a captive, he would have to have horses, and the only ones about are down at the barn."

He reached for his rifle as did Pitney, but as the other men were stirring into action, the front door was already swinging shut behind Ruark. They all seized weapons and raced after him, leaving the women to console themselves, Ralston standing undecidedly, and Orlan Trahern fuming in his chair. Finally the squire heaved himself up and braced on his staff.

"Aarrgh," he snarled. "If you think I'll sit here with the womenfolk, you're daft!" He took a step with his crutch and another, and then, hurling the blackthorn staff flat upon the floor, he went after the rest, ignoring his bandaged foot.

George Beauchamp arrived at the barn in time to hear his son tersely questioning the sergeant.

"Horses, man! Who has taken horses today?"

"Only Sir Gaylord, sir," the sergeant answered, bewildered. "He came down shortly before midday and ordered a horse to be saddled. He'd been out all morning and wanted a fresh mount. Saddled it meself, I did. Then he took the little roan mare, too, the one with the scars on her legs. Said he might need to tote some stuff." The sergeant paused then added a bit defensively, "Said he had the master's permission."

"It's all right, sergeant," George assured the worried man

It was the sudden sharp whinny and thud of hooves behind them that made the men turn. Attila pawed at the boards of a stall with his hooves then whirled and stamped and snorted.

George jerked his thumb at the beast and asked of the sergeant, "What's the matter with him?"

"Can't rightly say," the sergeant shrugged. "He started fretting when Sir Gaylord came and got hotter when the man took the mare out."

George raised a brow at Ruark, and their eyes locked in silent exchange for a moment. Ruark nodded and ran to push the barn doors wide, while his father went to the stall and motioned the rest of the men aside, out of the way. George loosed the latch and swung the gate wide. Attila snorted and came out, his hooves ringing on the bare stone floor. He tossed his head, saw the open doors, and turned toward them instantly. Before he could gather speed, Ruark seized a handful of the thick gray mane and swung himself up onto the broad back. Attila skidded to a halt and started to prance angrily until Ruark clamped down with his knees and gave a sharp whistle. The horse then knew his rider and, sensing they were about the same mission, leaped for the doors. Behind them, Nathanial and the major began shouting orders.

Attila rounded the manor house and in an easy bound, cleared the gate beside the burned stable. Ruark let him have his head and only clung to his back, giving no guidance. They entered the copse of trees, and the gray skidded to a halt in the clearing. He paused but a moment, tossing his head, sampling the air, then was off again in a rush of hooves. They crashed through the brush and were out in the pasture, running like the wind The smell of Gaylord was hot in Attila's nostrils, but more than that, the scent of the mare. They were both somewhere ahead. The air was cool and bracing. The stallion settled into an easy run, not straining but stretching out with each stride until his hooves barely seemed to touch the sod. The tall oaks flew by in a brownish blur, and now they were on the trail. As Ruark saw the way, he began to guide the beast, and the two of them were as one, bent on a single purpose.

Gaylord chafed as he glanced back toward Shanna. Her sureness and composure were disquieting. He had a need to see her subdued, if only by fear. He dropped back beside her again, and the horses' pace slowed to a walk.

"Even a fool knows when he has met his master," he began.

"And you, sir,"—her reply came with that same calm smile— "have at last met yours." Shanna felt the weight of the small dagger against her leg. She dared not try to get it now. There would come a time, she assured herself silently. Forcing herself to relax, she stared straight ahead, afraid that some of her self-control might crumble.

Gaylord tried to reason with her. "I am not a cruel man, madam, and you are most beautiful. A small amount of grace upon your part might prompt me to find mercy in my heart. I but wish to share a moment of pleasure with you."

"My pleasure, sir," her soft voice mocked, "would be to never set eyes on you again."

The bitch! How could she deny him so?

"You are helpless!" he shouted and raised in the stirrups to his full height. "You are in my power, and I will do what I want with you!"

Shanna hid the shudder that went through her and laughed scornfully. "Sir? In a damp forest? You'll muss your clothes."

"There is no one to rescue you!" he bellowed.

And the reply came as soft as ever. "Ruark is coming!"

Gaylord shook the rifle at her in rage. "If he is, then I will kill him!"

Her fear was almost overwhelming, and she spoke to keep her lips from trembling. "Have I told you, sir, that he spent some time with the savages and learned their ways? He even won their respect. All of this when he was but a lad. Have I told you, sir, that he can pass through the forest like a shadow without stirring a leaf? Have I told you, sir, that he is a marksman? And when angered, he fights like a savage. Indeed, is a savage." She gave a short laugh. "The pirates could well attest to that. They feared him, you know."

From the corner of her eye, Shanna saw Gaylord glance back over his shoulder, and he scanned the trail ahead with a care unusual for one so bold.

"Have you ever thought, sir, how one man against so many could bring all of us out unscathed from the pirate's isle?"

They passed a high spot where the trail dipped down into the valley, and Gaylord halted his abbreviated column to scan the path behind them again. Shanna cocked her head to one side as if listening carefully, and suddenly the assurance she had given tongue to was oddly heavy within her. Sir Gaylord was watching her with angry suspicion on his face. She straightened and met his gaze squarely, nodding ever so lightly.

"Aye, Ruark is coming."

Her words were little more than a whisper, but they seemed to enrage the knight. With a snarl he jerked the rope, making the mare prance. Shanna fought to keep her seat and frantically clutched the handful of mane, just as they charged full tilt down into the valley. They rounded the last bend, leaving black slashes where the racing hooves tore the soft moss to shreds. Gaylord hauled the mounts to a skidding halt before the cabin, gritting his teeth in pain as the mare half stumbled. He calmed the steeds and stepped down from his own, tying the mare to the hitching rail and flexing his shoulder as if he knew a persistent ache in it. He took the bags from behind Shanna, and unlatching the cabin door, threw them within. He returned, stretching his muscles, and walked about a bit, seeking his own ease before seeing to Shanna's. When it finally met his whim, he came to her. He untied one of her feet then went between the horses to loosen her other. He took some time with this task, and his long fingers unduly caressed her slim ankles and were wont to venture needlessly up her leg. Shanna held her breath, fearing he might discover the dagger.

Suddenly a rattle of hooves at the mouth of the valley drew their attention. For a moment the gray flank of the horse and the dark brown of its rider were visible through the trees. Shanna's spirit thrilled with the sight, and briefly her eyes blurred with joyful tears, but she sobered as Gaylord snatched up the rifle. Chuckling to himself, he pulled back the heavy hammer and steadied the piece across the saddle of his mount, drawing a careful bead where the trail made its final curve.

It was another of his many mistakes that Gaylord turned his back on Shanna. As the hooves thundered near the curve, she raised her foot and struck the mare's outward side with all her strength. With a sharp whinny Jezebel leapt away from the blow, and her movement caught Gaylord between the mounts, crushing the breath from him. The rifle shot upward like a misdirected arrow and sailed in a neat arc into the brush just as Ruark came racing around the bend on Attila's back.

The mare caught a blow with a sharp elbow in the ribs and pranced away, leaving Gaylord to stumble out from between the two horses, gasping for breath. He looked up to see a huge gray stallion, eyes red, nostrils flared, ears laid back upon his head, charging straight for him, and a man crouching on the heaving shoulders like an avenging spirit.

Gaylord forgot the rifle as a chill went up his spine. Snatching Shanna roughly from the mare's back, he dragged her to the cabin and shoved her through the door. With arms still bound, she stumbled across the dirt floor and sprawled upon the bed. Stepping in, Gaylord slammed the door and was reaching for the heavy bar when the whole of it, hinges, hasp, and all, was torn loose and crashed in upon him.

Ruark had launched himself from the gray's back feet first, all the speed of the charge behind him. His legs were half numbed by the blow, but he rolled on a shoulder and came to his feet ready to fight.

"Come on, bastard," he growled. "If you want my wife, you'll have to kill me with your bare hands! No burning stable this time."

Gaylord was no small man, and now the heat of the battle was upon him. He flung the stout door off himself and lunged to his feet, pawing for the pistols which were no longer in his belt but lay, instead, outside, beneath the horse's hooves. The knight had only time enough to realize his loss before Ruark attacked. A howl of rage broke from Gaylord's lips to answer the snarl of Ruark. At last, Billingsham could openly battle this bondsman who had plagued him from the first. With a thud, the two men met chest to chest, and their arms locked in a test of sheer strength.

Even through his righteous wrath, Ruark was amazed at the power of his antagonist. Their breath whistled through clenched teeth, and the tendons of both strained with their efforts. Gaylord's feet slipped on the dirt floor as he was slowly straightened and bent backward. He had no choice but to give way or be flung on his back. He tried to dive to one side, but Ruark held on. They crashed as one to the floor in a cloud of loose dirt, and to Shanna's eyes, became a thrashing welter of twisting arms and legs.

Shaking with her own emotions and her anxiety for Ruark, she lifted her skirts and clawed for the hilt of her dagger. Her bound hands were almost numb, but she managed to loosen the knife and tuck the hilt between her knees. Frantically she began to saw the ropes against the blade.

The two men rose on their knees. Ruark thrust his head beneath Gaylord's chin and clasped his arms about the narrow ribs of the knight, hugging him like a bear until the other's spine was bent to the breaking point. Gaylord moaned beneath the pressure then suddenly twisted aside. The hold was broken. They teetered and fell and again were obscured in a cloud of dust.

The knight's flailing hand touched a smooth, hard length of wood, and he snatched its weighty length up. A small, cured pelt of an animal clung to one end, but he had no time to shake it off. Laughter wheezed from his laboring lungs as he rolled above Ruark and brought the stick across the bondsman's neck, leaning all his weight on it. Ruark caught the wood, and the tendons stood out in his neck and arms like taut cordage as he strained to hold the piece from choking him. The staff moved upward ever so slightly and Gaylord shrieked his dismay. Ruark's knee worked beneath the knight's belly and lifted some of the weight away. His foot slid beneath the knight's hip, and he heaved, hurling Gaylord over his head and away from him, releasing the staff as Gaylord sailed over him. The fur pelt came free. Then the realization dawned on Ruark with sudden clarity that the end of the smooth stick bore a wide double-bladed head. It was the ax he had left in the cabin.

Shanna gasped, and Gaylord chortled in high glee, shifting the double-bladed weapon in his hands as Ruark scrambled to his feet. Ruark seized a length of firewood to defend himself as the knight moved forward. Ruark could only move back as the keen-edged blade threatened him in the narrow confines of the cabin.

The edge of the table caught Ruark on the back of the thighs, and he could retreat no further. With a shout of triumph, Gaylord swung a two-handed blow downward as Shanna cringed and smothered a scream. Ruark dove to one side, and the table, with a rending, splintering crack, fell in halves as the ax cut it clean through. As Gaylord struggled to pull the blade from the shreds, Ruark threw the firewood low at the shins of the man and snatched another piece. The ax swung in a short swipe at Ruark's belly, and the blow was barely parried with the short stick of wood. The ax swung again. Ruark leapt back to avoid the blade then crashed to the floor as his feet tangled in the wreckage of the table.

Gaylord's bellow of victory ended in a shriek of pain. He had caught the bright flash and jerked away, but he had still caught the point of the tiny dagger on his cheek and felt the red hot shock of it slash downward along his neck, laying open flesh as it went.

In his lust for blood, he had forgotten the lady, Shanna, again. Indeed, no lady! She had freed herself and joined the fray with the silvered thorn, as fiercely protective of her husband's life as he of hers. Snarling, Gaylord flung wide his arms, and she was thrust away, the small dagger flying into a corner. But as Gaylord grasped the ax again, she returned to rake his lightly shirted shoulder with her claws. She finally gained his attention. His bony fist struck hard, and Shanna stumbled back as it caught her along the jaw. Dazed and reeling, she sprawled again upon the furry bed, her world suddenly gone black and void.

Now, it was the other beast Gaylord had ignored too long. A half-voiced, bellowing snarl sounded in his ear, and the ax was snatched from his grasp as if from a child's. He recoiled and thought to see it flash, ending his life. And flash it did, but straight upward with such force the blade was half buried high in a timber of the roof, its handle quivering well out of reach. Gaylord's relief was short-lived, however, for he was seized in a vise that slowly crushed the breath from him. He was in the grip of a maddened beast who gave no quarter but slowly lifted him from the floor in arms of steel. Hurled halfway across the room, he rebounded from the wall and was immediately beset by punishing blows that took him from every side. He saw bared white teeth beneath dark-rimmed golden eyes in a snarling face that promised only death. Blows rained upon him, taking away his strength. He began to fear defeat and, worse than that, death. He raised an arm and weakly struck out but was attacked with such renewed savagery he stumbled back across the room and could only shelter his head beneath his arms. He fell to his knees and reeled as a hard fist struck him on the face. His hand was suddenly full of soft velvet and dimly he saw a woman's face above him.

"Stop him! Stop him!" he sobbed. "He'll kill me!"

Shanna struggled against the grayness that engulfed her, and through the buzzing in her ears, she heard a distant cursing mingled with a whimpering cry. She shook her head to free herself from the daze, and some vision returned. She saw Sir Gaylord at her feet on the floor, clutching the hem of her gown, begging for his life. Suddenly her mind was clear. What he had not given to others would be granted to him. Mercy. She stepped over the sprawling knight and caught Ruark's arm to her breast.

"Ruark," she pleaded. "Let him have his day with the hangman." She slipped a hand behind Ruark's head and, with the other, pushed his rigid body back. Stepping before him, she pulled his face close to hers and kissed his lips until his sanity began to return and she felt the stiffness of rage leave him. She knew she had won when he took her in his arms and lifted her against him in a fierce, crushing embrace.

Shanna was sitting on the stump, holding still while Ruark applied a cool wet cloth to her bruised cheek, when Nathanial and the major halted their mounts before the cabin. Gaylord sat nearby on a rough-hewn bench, well wrapped in a length of rope.

The latecomers surveyed the scene that greeted them as George and the others joined them. Considering the unhinged portal, George chuckled down at Ruark.

"My son, you truly have a way with doors."

Gaylord was put on a horse, and Shanna was lifted to Attila's back, where she perched in the arms of her husband. She would have traded no part of her world away. The door of the cabin was roped in place, and the party was preparing for the return journey when suddenly a shout rang out from the trail and a rattle of hooves drifted down to them. They waited in wonderment until an ancient mare with stiff legs and a spine-jolting gait came trotting around the bend. It could not be said which wheezed the harder, the gallant mare or her courageous rider. A string of jolted curses drifted ahead of them as the mare neared. Nathanial stepped down from his mount and mercifully assisted Trahern to the firm turf. Stripping the saddle from Trahern's mount, he laid it on the back of Jezebel, that mare of gentler gait, while George led the aging mare to the pasture and turned her out to graze in peace.

Dusk was gathering over the land as the mostly jovial party neared the manor house, and no one noted that Attila with his double load chose to lag far behind the rest. Indeed, it was questionable whether any hand guided him, since both his riders seemed much occupied with each other.

The returning party went directly to the barn where George pointed out a heavily planked stall intended to contain the occasionally errant stud or bull. It was little used. A small table and a stool were placed within, along with a pile of fresh straw and several blankets. The ropes were stripped from Sir Gaylord, and he was thrust into his stall-cell. Glaring about him, he rubbed his wrists then sneered at his captors.

"You may abuse me like this if you will, but as a knight of the realm I can be tried before no less than the high tribunal of His Majesty's court in London."

"Perhaps," Major Carter replied musingly, "that will be up to the magistrate in Williamsburg."

"I will have none of your bumbling colonial justice!" Gaylord snarled. "My father will see that I am cared for."

"The same, of course." The major rubbed a finger along his chin. "Lord Billingsham has come to the colonies to—uh—improve the crude system, I believe he said. He has taken the bench in Williamsburg and will be the first to hear your case."

Gaylord's mouth gaped open, and his eyes grew dim and distant. He seated himself on the stool and stared at the blank wall, seeming not to hear any further comments. His lips moved briefly, and the whisper was barely heard.

"Old Hanging Harry." His shoulders sagged, and his air of arrogance deserted him.

A moment later George entered the manor and stalked through the room directly to the brandy decanter. Close on his heels came Nathanial and Jeremiah, their broad grins warning of good news, while Pitney and the major assisted a ruffled, bone-weary Trahern to his chair. He plumped down and stared at the muddled, grass-stained wrappings of his injured foot, once more propped on its hassock. Bringing up the rear, Shanna and Ruark strolled in with their arms entwined and happy smiles on their faces as if the day had borne nothing but blissful togetherness.

The uproar of relieved laughter and shouts filled the house until it fair danced on its foundation. The tale was told, then retold, and each added his own part until it was complete. Backs were pounded, hands clasped, toasts proposed and properly completed, and in the darker corners the heroes were welcomed home in a much quieter fashion. Only Orlan Trahern sat in his chair in a dour mood and sipped from a rum and bitters Pitney had managed to prepare. It was into this riot of congratulations that Hergus bore a tray of tidbits to whet the appetites of the starving men. Her shriek of recognition was ear-splitting.

"Jamie! Jamie Conners!"

The Scotsman turned and stared at the woman who called his name, as did everyone else in the room.

"Hergus?" he said slowly, his eyes widening in amazement. "My Gawd! Hergus! Me own true love!" He burned beneath the slow regard the surprised woman bent on him.

"Humph, a score of years ye been gone and not a word! Ever!"

Hergus presented her tray and a warm smile to Pitney and her stiff back to Jamie, as she recalled in a rush the multitude of wiles she had watched Shanna use on various suitors. Her love had strayed and ere there would be a reconciliation, his price would be dear.

"I—I—" the poor man stammered, "I found no trace of ye when they finally let me go."

No answer came as Hergus calmly served the others from the tray. But as Shanna caught her eye, she could well read the slow smile and lowering of eyelids. At the moment Shanna almost felt sorry for Jamie, but she saw something new in Hergus, both soft and firm at the same time, and guessed that with proper retribution the Scotsman might regain what he had lost.

Shanna stepped to her father's side and gazed down at him for a moment. At the glowering frown she gently asked, "Does your foot pain you, papa?"

" 'Tis not my foot that aches as much as another part," he snorted. "It took a dire threat to put me atop a horse, but should the very earth crumble beneath my feet, I will not straddle another. Now I cannot find comfort either standing or sitting. I would hie myself to my bed to find aught of ease."

Shanna began to chuckle and could not stop, though his scowl grew deeper as he glared up at her.

"Oh, papa, 'tis the worst of it that you should have done it for me." She bent and kissed his brow.

"Bah!" Trahern shifted in his chair as if to ease some ache and spoke to Ruark who had come to stand beside Shanna. "I hurt in every bone, and she chortles like some half-wit. Beware, my son, ere she drive you harried and haunted to your grave."

"If I knew that as fact," Ruark laughed, "I would change no small whit of it."

Shanna took her husband's hand and squeezed it lovingly, then sat on the arm of her father's chair and rested her own arm about his shoulders.

"I am beset with beasts in the two of you." She smiled softly to belie her words. "A dragon on my left and a hoary bear on my right. Am I ever to fear your fangs?"

"Keep her with child, lad!" Trahern chuckled, his mood easing. " 'Tis the only way. Keep her with child!"

"Much my own thoughts, sir." Ruark met Shanna's eyes, and their love glowed in unspoken communication.

Ruark was at the window, watching the gray streaks of dawn spread across the sky. Lying in bed, Shanna, too, was wide awake. He came back and slid beneath the covers.

"You're cold," Shanna told him.

"Warm me." They snuggled close together.

"It's been almost a year," she murmured.

"Aye, and with each dawning," he whispered in her ear, "the sun has come to part us. But no more."

A moment of silence passed as they nestled in each other's arms. Ruark traced a curl where it fell across her arm.

"Have I slain your dragon, my love?"

"Slain my dragon? Nay, and I will hear no more such talk." Shanna slipped her arms about his neck. "Let the devil take the shiny knights. Come, Dragon Ruark, breathe your fire and warm me. The day is just beginning for us."

Epilogue

ORLAN Trahern sat in the small church on the island of Los Camellos and listened to the minister's voice droning on from the pulpit. His mind was not on the sermon but drifted to other topics.

The island seemed lonely of late. There was something missing. Life here moved on as usual, slowing in the heat of the day, hastening when the harvests of cane and timber called. It accommodated the rush of the mills, and the new wealth was liberally disbursed to be enjoyed by all. It was what he had always dreamed of, but now the edge was gone from the achievement.

He thought of his daughter and her husband. The babe would be born by now, but weeks would pass before he received word of it. He glanced toward the small oil painting of his wife, Georgiana, which hung near his church box and knew she would have thrilled at the prospect. Indeed, she would have insisted they go to be with Shanna at her labor. He could almost see his wife smiling back at him with her ever-tolerant, knowing gaze.

He had of yesteryear considered his blood to be aged and thin, but now it quickened with the fervor of youth as he imagined the wealth of new markets that waited a knowing hand in the colonies. More and more he longed to be put out in the marketplace with a wad of credit slips in his purse and a shipload of merchandise at the dock. He yearned to elbow his way through a throng and hear the jargon of barter, the rhythmic song of an auctioneer, and to feel the lift of that moment when a good bargain is struck. He wanted to whet his mind against the sly half truths of the seller and hone his appetite with a taste of the same on a wary buyer.

Even Pitney had grown restless of late and spoke often of leaving the island to seek out a fortune in the new land. Trahern guessed that the man had fallen in love with the vast spaces and found life here now narrow and restrictive. A ship had been sighted as they were on their way to church, and Pitney had gone down to the docks to meet it, a fire of adventure beginning to glow in his eyes.

"By God, it is a tempting thing," Orlan Trahern thought. "And in my journeys up and down the colonies, I could stop often to see my grandchild." His eyes went again to the painting. "I'd come back here, too, Georgiana, often, and I would ever cherish the memories we set to seed here."

The minister had finished his sermon and was calling the congregation to its feet for a song when he paused and stared speechless toward the rear of the church. Before Trahern could turn, a huge hand gripped his shoulder, and he glanced up to see Pitney grinning down at him.

Trahern frowned and began to rise. Then a small, blankered bundle was thust gently into his arms. He had barely time to see the dark hair before another one was placed in his other arm. He looked back and forth between the two, seeing the black hair and a glint of green in the baby blue of their eyes.

The squire's jaw dropped. He raised his gaze in wonder to meet Shanna's brightly beaming visage. "A boy and a girl, papa."

"This was news no letter could bear," Ruark smiled. "We were overdue a visit, anyway."

Orlan Trahern was speechless. He stared down at the twins again and could not for the life of him bring forth words to express his joy. He looked up at the painting on the wall, and his voice was choked and broken as he whispered:

"More than we ever dreamed, Georgiana. More than we ever dreamed."